DISNEY · SQUARE ENIX

KINGDOM HEARTS

FINAL MIX

SHIRO AMANO

ORIGINAL CONCEPT: TETSUYA NOMURA

2

KINGDOM HEARTS
FINAL MIX 2

SHIRO AMANO
ORIGINAL CONCEPT:
TETSUYA NOMURA

Translation: Alethea and Athena Nibley
Lettering: Terri Delgado, Alyssa Blakeslee

Yen Press
Hachette Book Group
1290 Avenue of the Americas, New York, NY 10104

www.HachetteBookGroup.com
www.YenPress.com

Yen Press is an imprint of Hachette Book Group, Inc. The Yen Press name and logo are trademarks of Hachette Book Group, Inc.

First Yen Press Edition: May 2013

ISBN: 978-0-316-25421-2

10 9 8 7 6 5 4

BVG

Printed in the United States of America

Disney SQUARE ENIX

KINGDOM HEARTS FINAL MIX

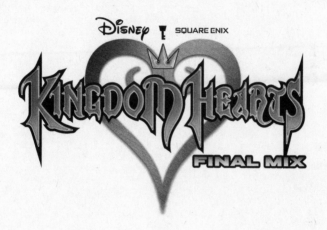

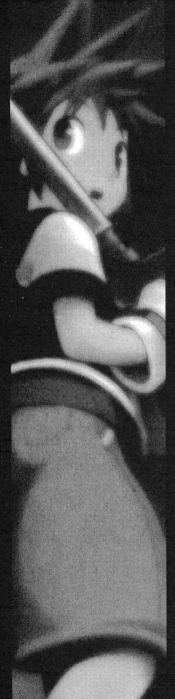

KINGDOM HEARTS
FINAL MIX
VOLUME 2

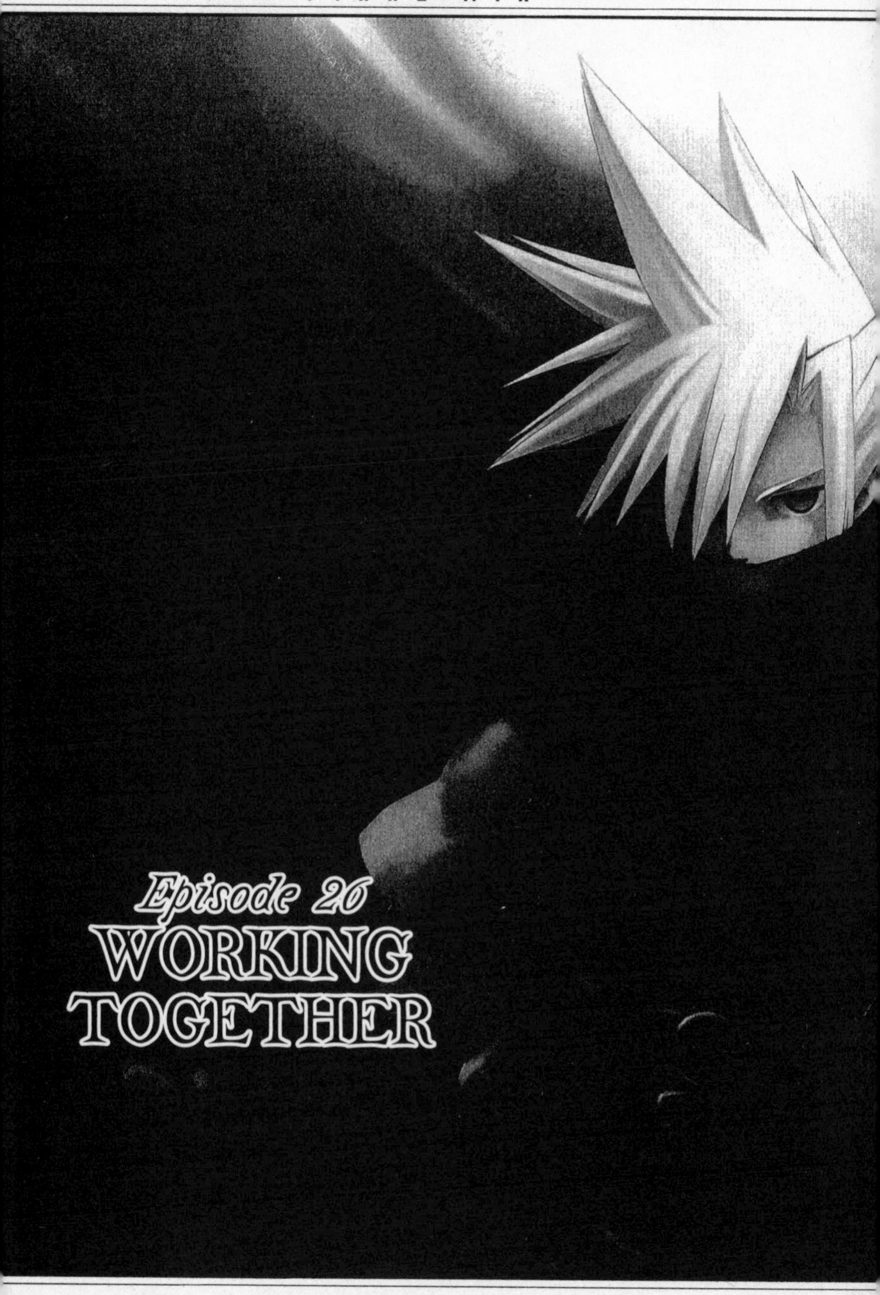
Episode 26
WORKING
TOGETHER

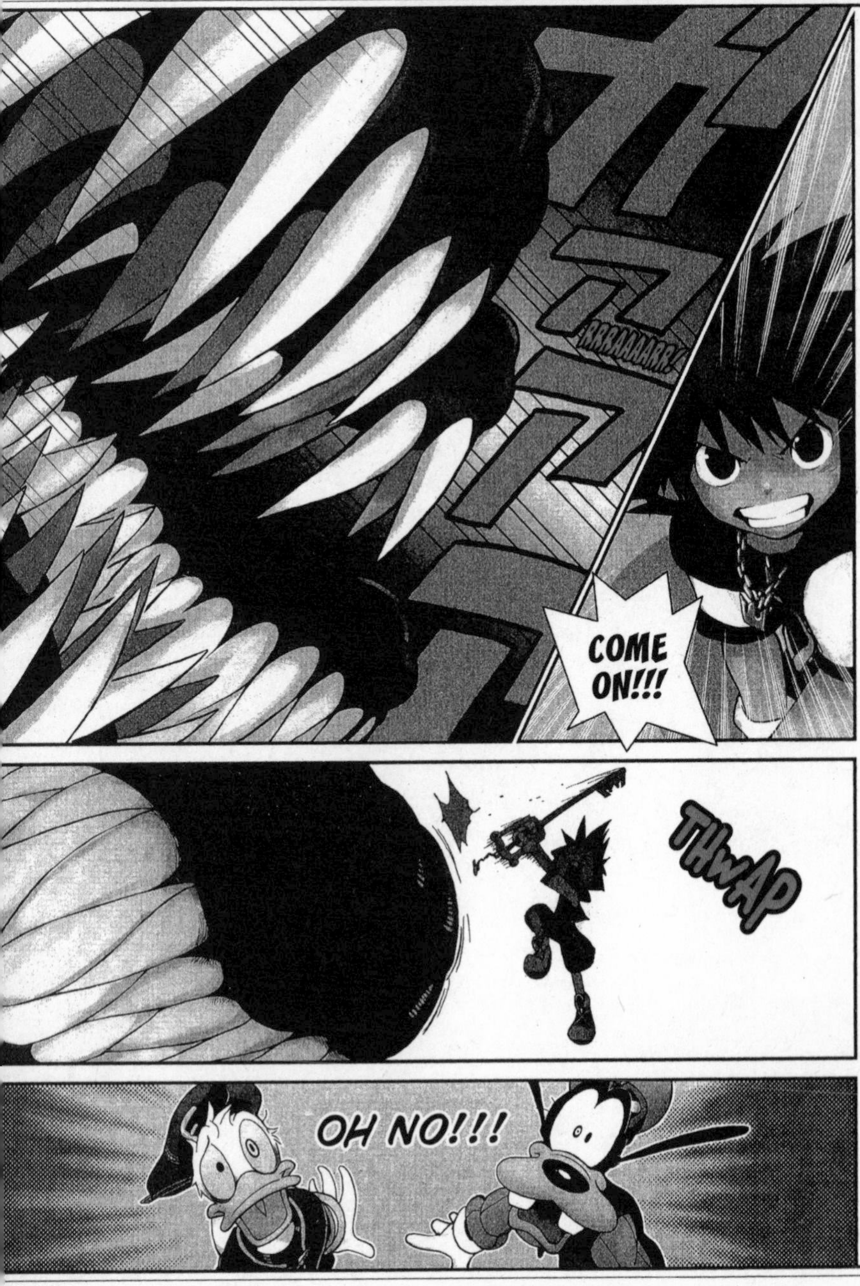
RRRAAAARR!
COME ON!!!
THWAP
OH NO!!!

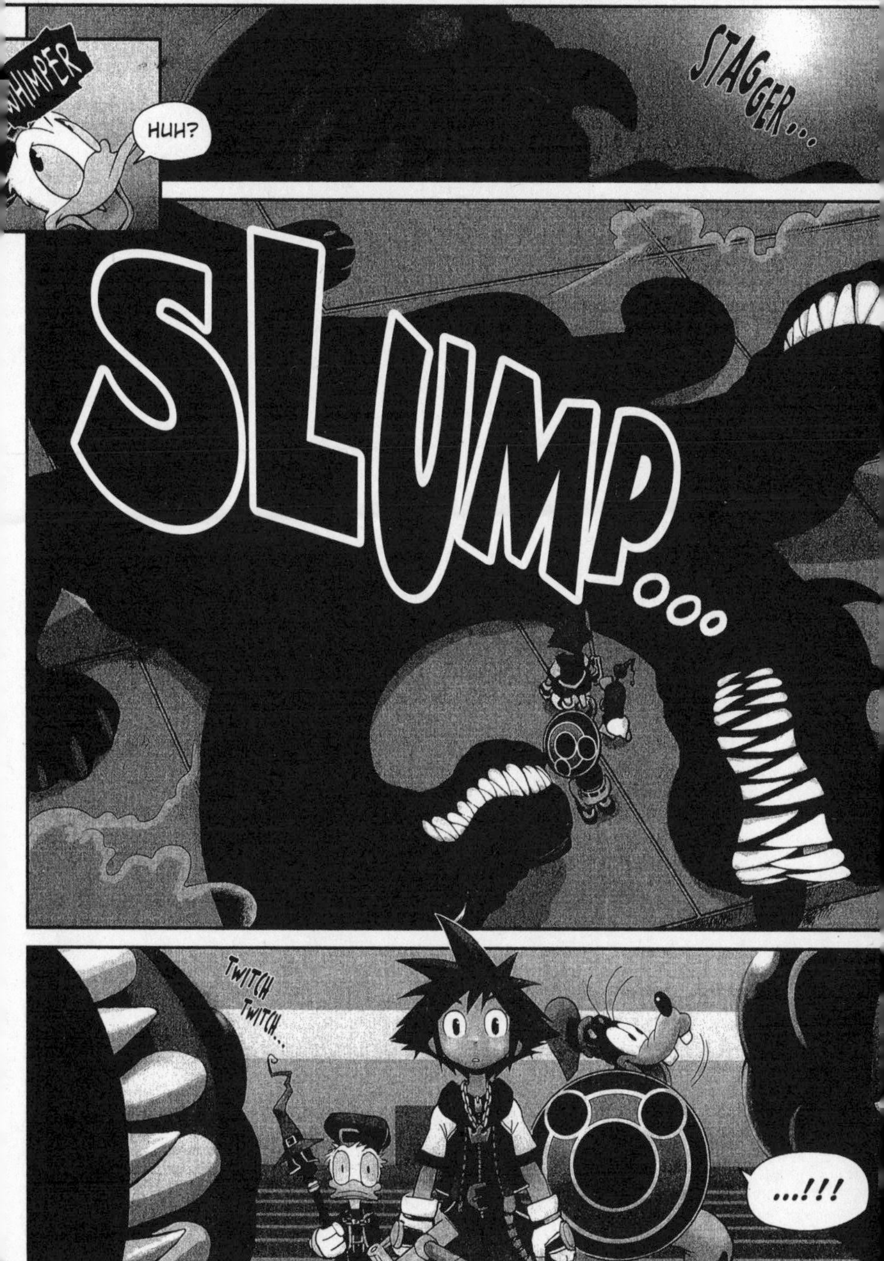
WHIMPER
HUH?
STAGGER...
SLUMP...
TWITCH
TWITCH...
...!!!

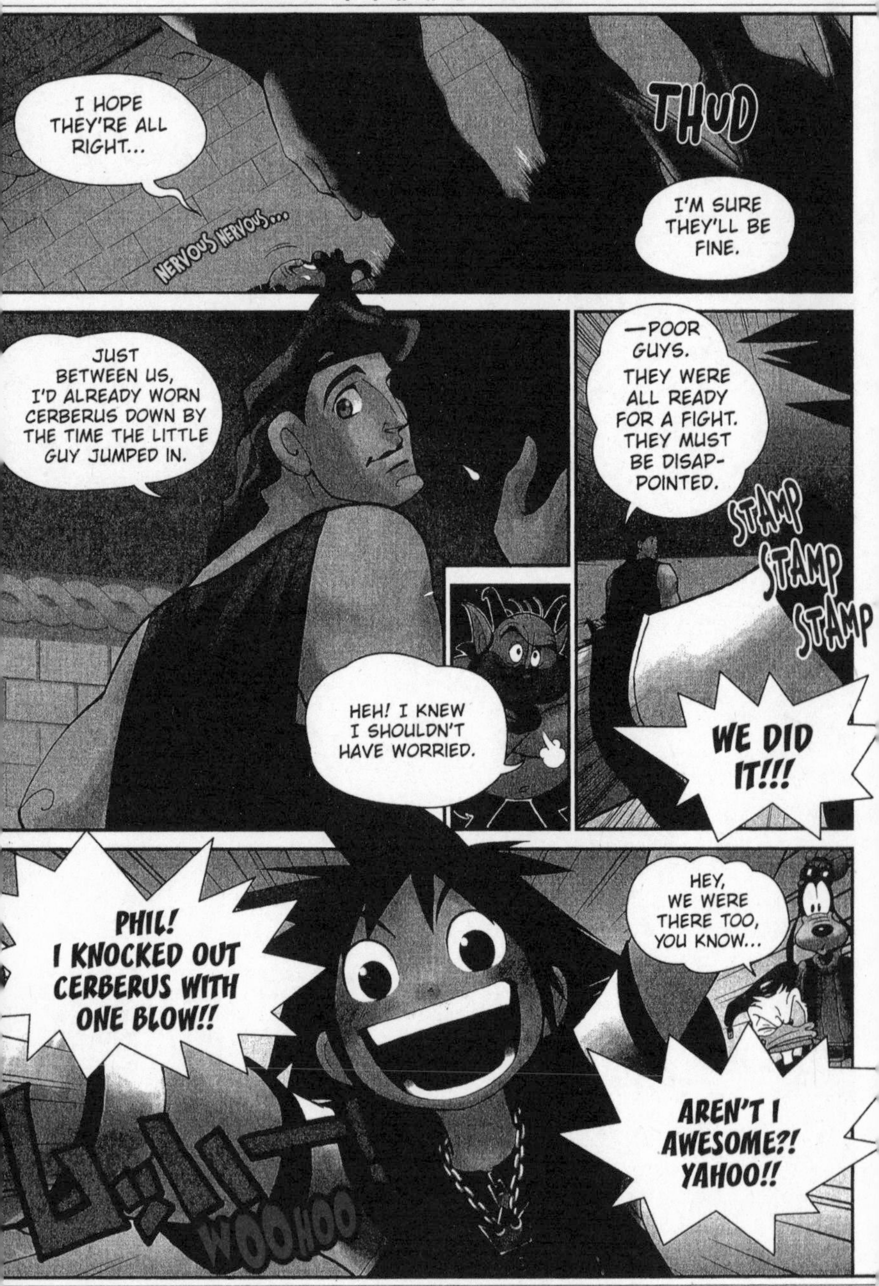
I HOPE THEY'RE ALL RIGHT...
NERVOUS NERVOUS...
THUD
I'M SURE THEY'LL BE FINE.
JUST BETWEEN US, I'D ALREADY WORN CERBERUS DOWN BY THE TIME THE LITTLE GUY JUMPED IN.
HEH! I KNEW I SHOULDN'T HAVE WORRIED.
—POOR GUYS. THEY WERE ALL READY FOR A FIGHT. THEY MUST BE DISAP-POINTED.
STAMP STAMP STAMP
WE DID IT!!!
PHIL! I KNOCKED OUT CERBERUS WITH ONE BLOW!!
WOOHOO
HEY, WE WERE THERE TOO, YOU KNOW...
AREN'T I AWESOME?! YAHOO!!

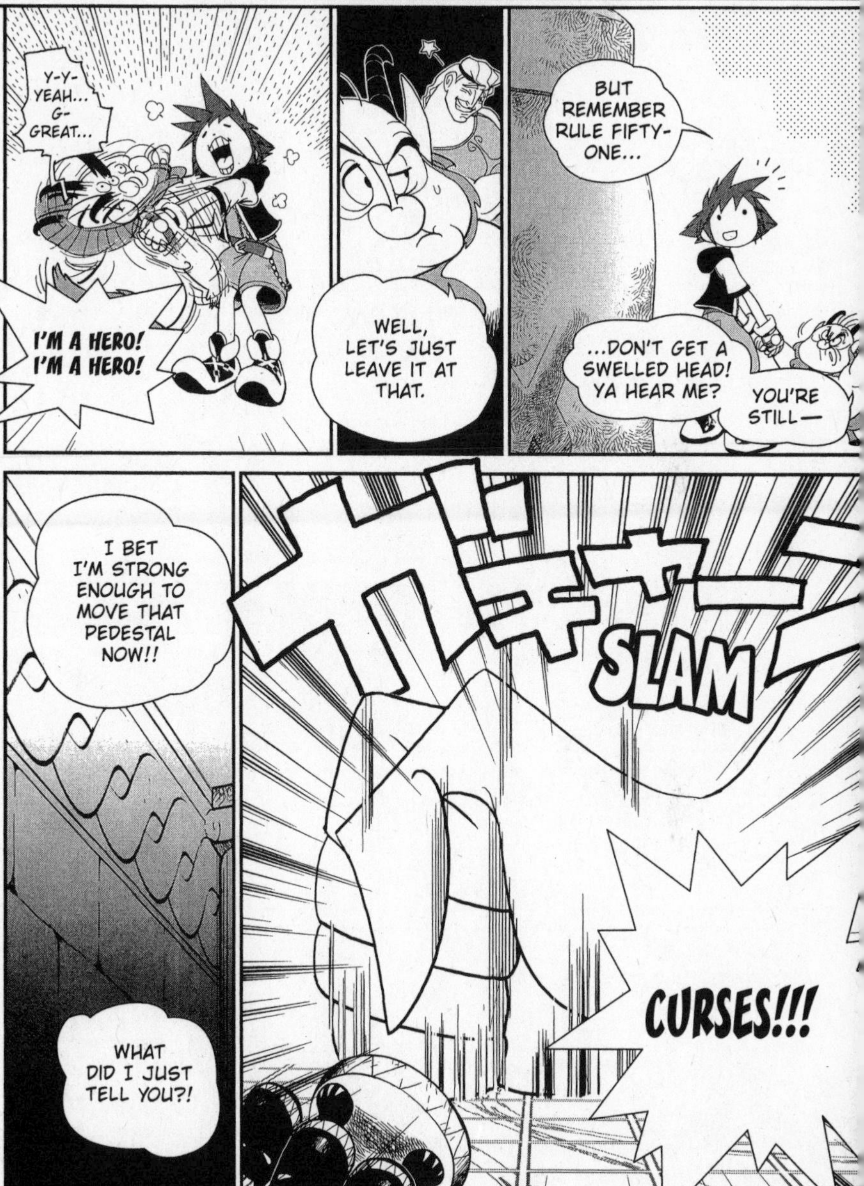
Y-Y-YEAH... G-GREAT...
I'M A HERO! I'M A HERO!
WELL, LET'S JUST LEAVE IT AT THAT.
BUT REMEMBER RULE FIFTY-ONE...
...DON'T GET A SWELLED HEAD! YA HEAR ME?
YOU'RE STILL—
I BET I'M STRONG ENOUGH TO MOVE THAT PEDESTAL NOW!!
WHAT DID I JUST TELL YOU?!
SLAM
CURSES!!!

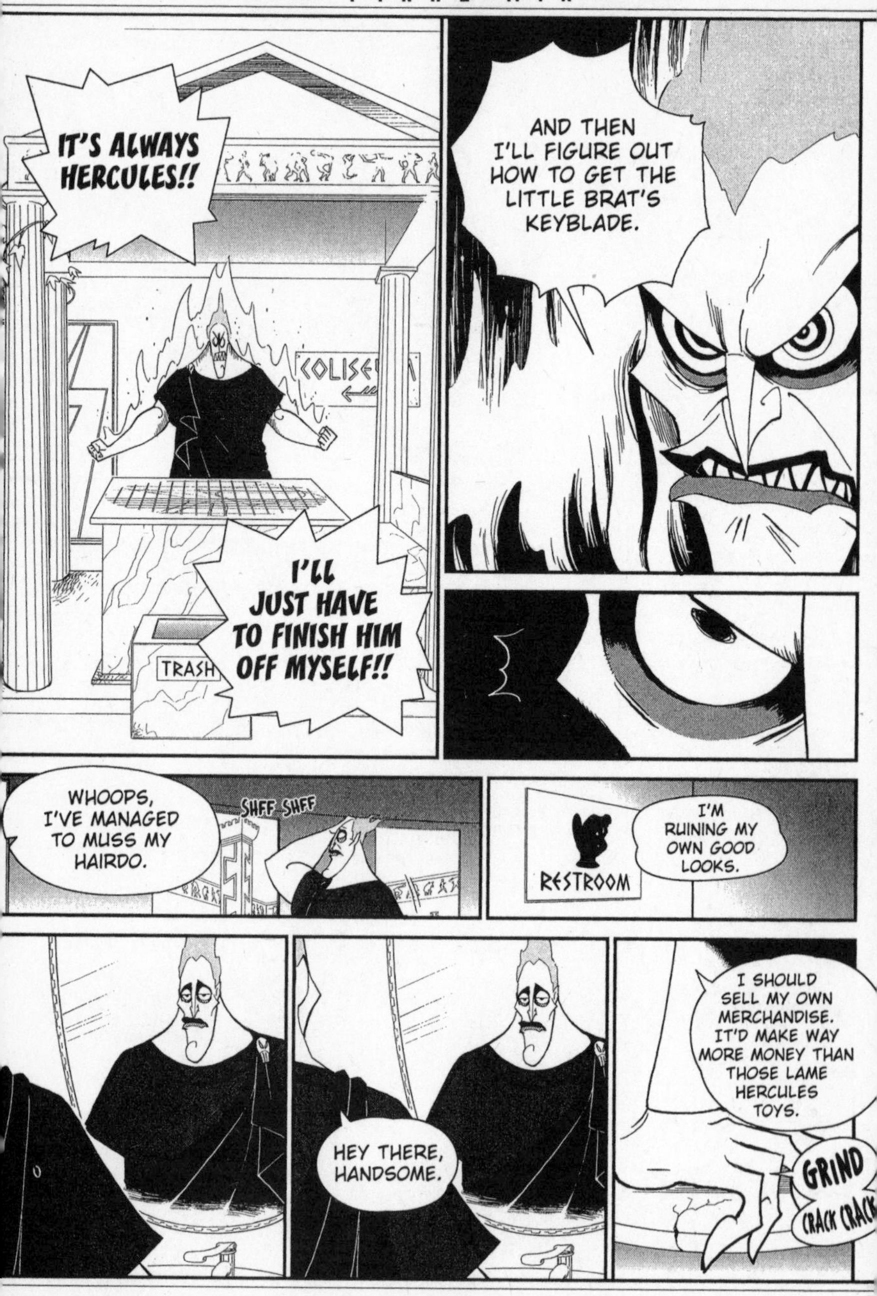
IT'S ALWAYS HERCULES!!
TRASH
I'LL JUST HAVE TO FINISH HIM OFF MYSELF!!
AND THEN I'LL FIGURE OUT HOW TO GET THE LITTLE BRAT'S KEYBLADE.
WHOOPS, I'VE MANAGED TO MUSS MY HAIRDO.
SHFF SHFF
RESTROOM
I'M RUINING MY OWN GOOD LOOKS.
HEY THERE, HANDSOME.
I SHOULD SELL MY OWN MERCHANDISE. IT'D MAKE WAY MORE MONEY THAN THOSE LAME HERCULES TOYS.
GRIND
CRACK CRACK

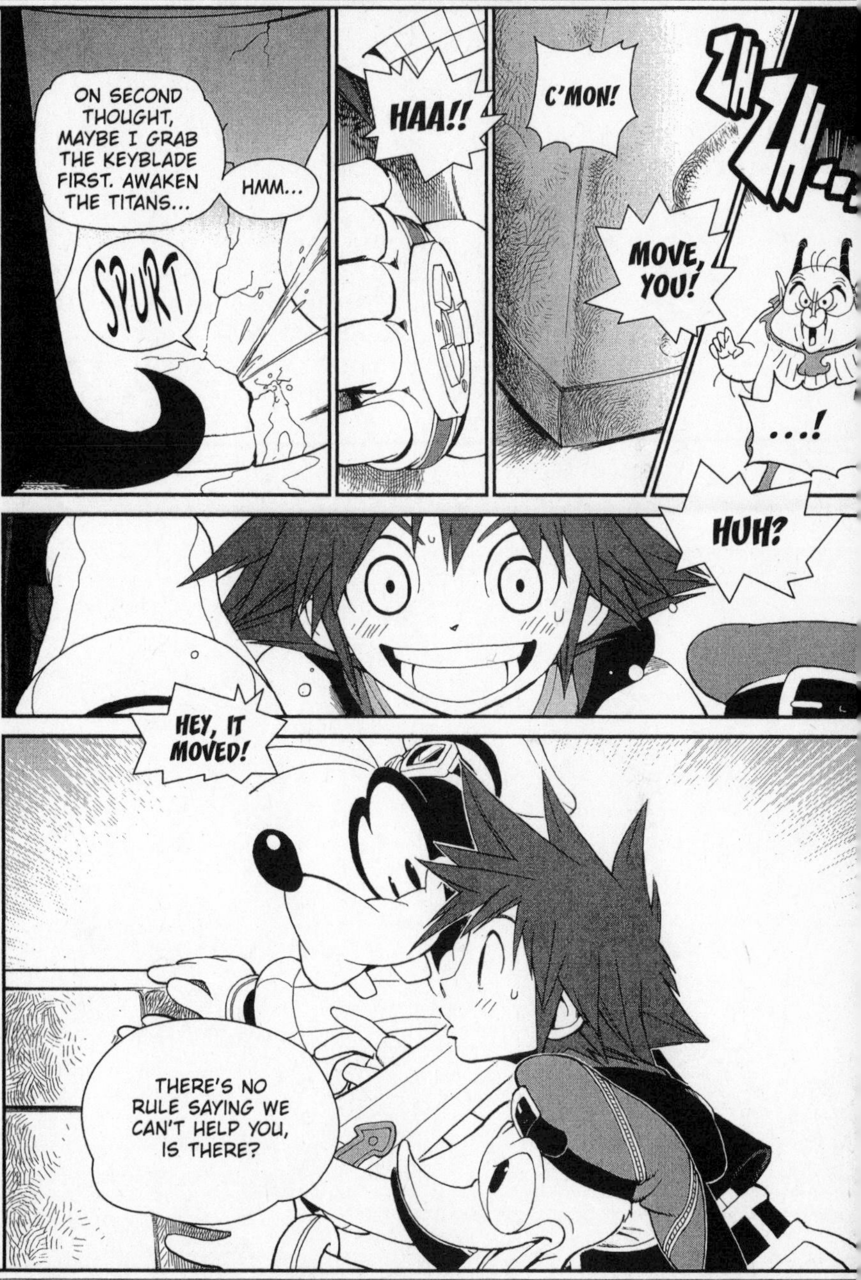
ON SECOND THOUGHT, MAYBE I GRAB THE KEYBLADE FIRST. AWAKEN THE TITANS...
HMM...
SPURT
HAA!!
C'MON!
ZH ZH...
MOVE, YOU!
...!
HUH?
HEY, IT MOVED!
THERE'S NO RULE SAYING WE CAN'T HELP YOU, IS THERE?

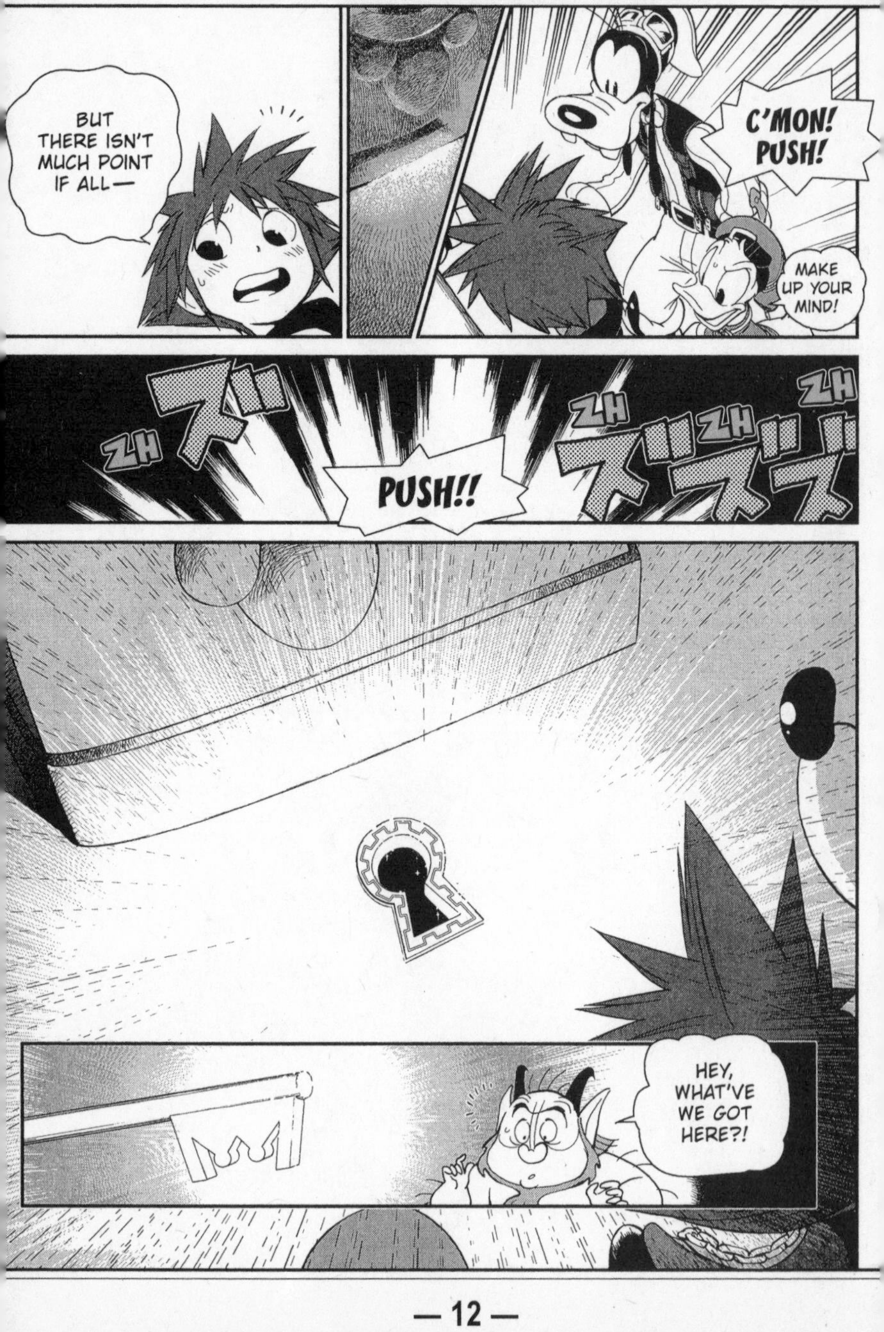
BUT THERE ISN'T MUCH POINT IF ALL—
C'MON! PUSH!
MAKE UP YOUR MIND!
ZH
ズ
PUSH!!
ZH
ZH
ZH
ズズズ
HEY, WHAT'VE WE GOT HERE?!

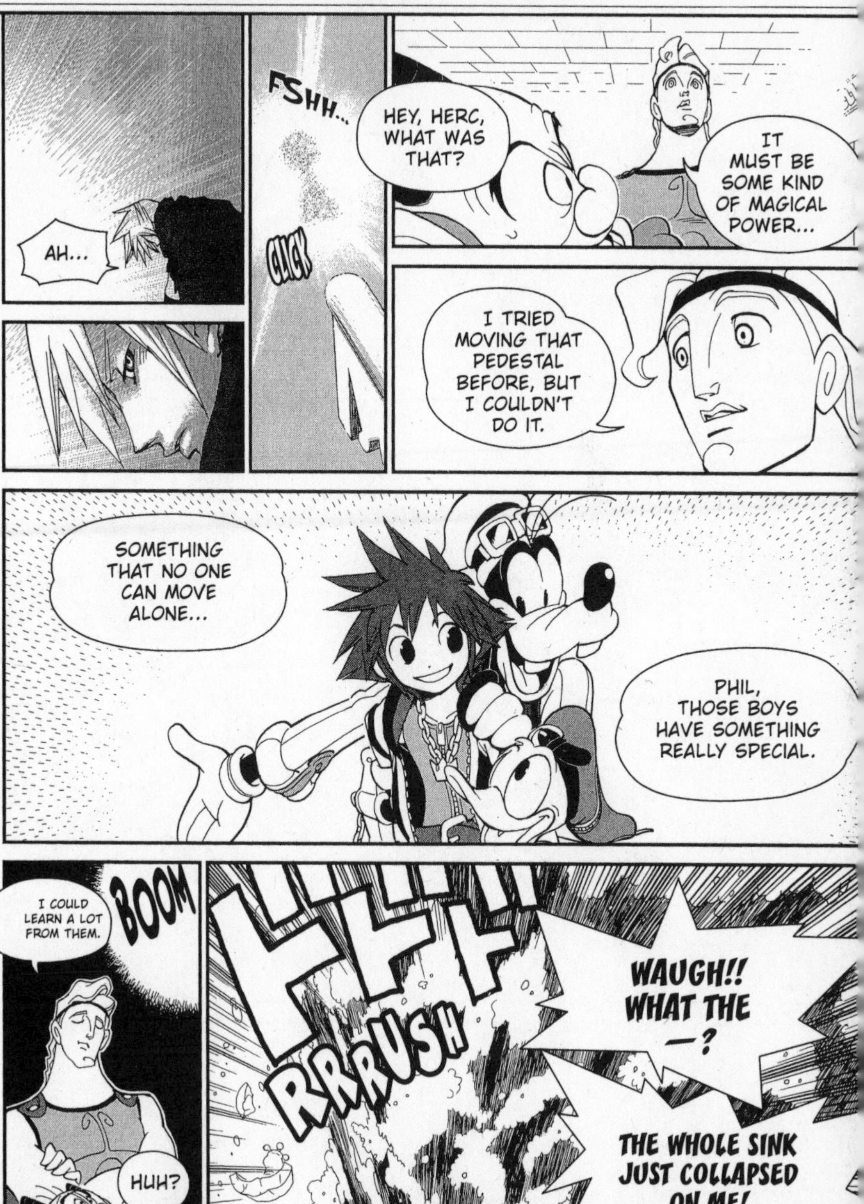
AH...
FSHH...
CLICK
HEY, HERC, WHAT WAS THAT?
IT MUST BE SOME KIND OF MAGICAL POWER...
I TRIED MOVING THAT PEDESTAL BEFORE, BUT I COULDN'T DO IT.
SOMETHING THAT NO ONE CAN MOVE ALONE...
PHIL, THOSE BOYS HAVE SOMETHING REALLY SPECIAL.
I COULD LEARN A LOT FROM THEM.
BOOM
HUH?
RRRUSH
WAUGH!! WHAT THE —?
THE WHOLE SINK JUST COLLAPSED ON ME!

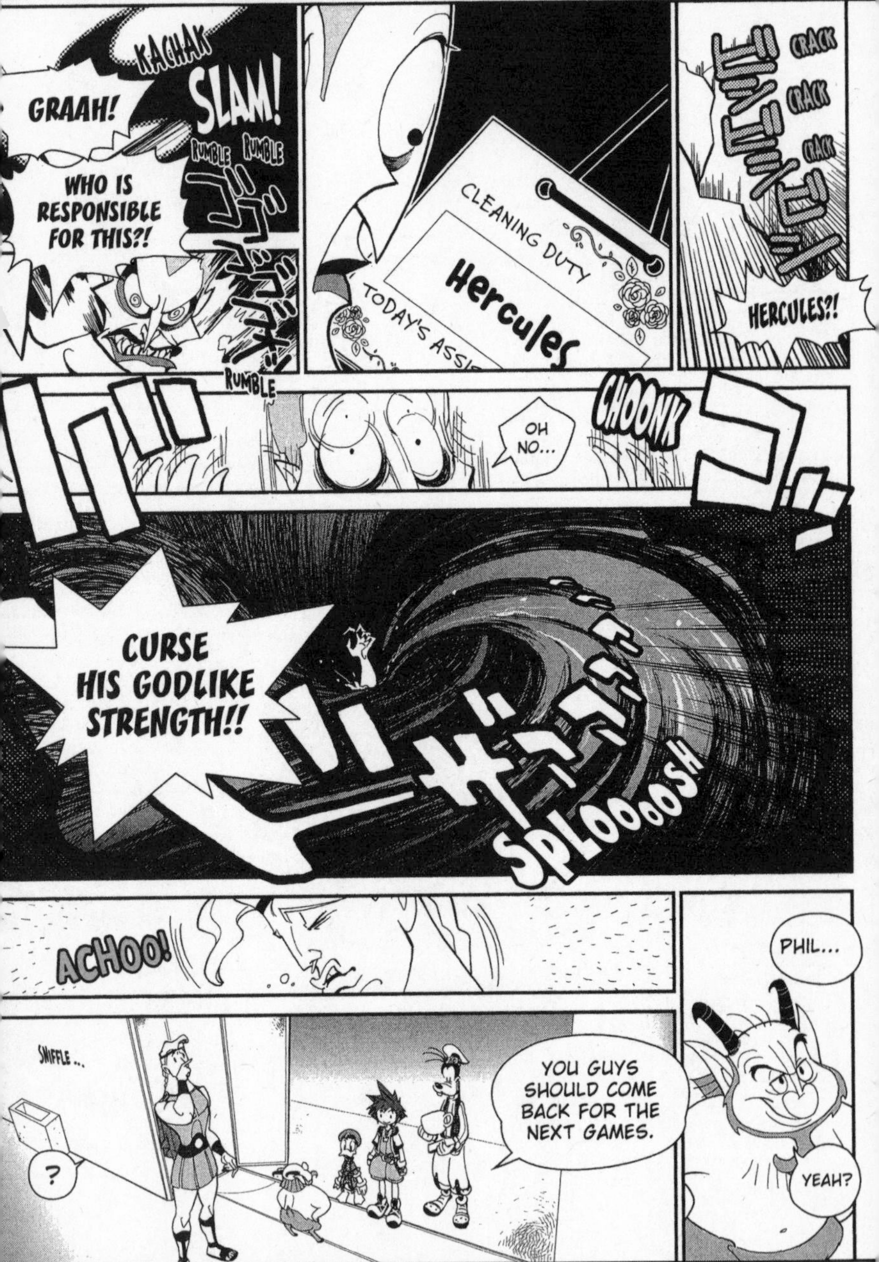
GRAAH!
KACHAK
SLAM!
RUMBLE RUMBLE
WHO IS RESPONSIBLE FOR THIS?!
RUMBLE
CLEANING DUTY
TODAY'S ASSI
Hercules
CRACK
CRACK
CRACK
HERCULES?!
OH NO...
CHOONK
CURSE HIS GODLIKE STRENGTH!!
SPLOOoOOSH
ACHOO!
PHIL...
SNIFFLE...
?
YOU GUYS SHOULD COME BACK FOR THE NEXT GAMES.
YEAH?

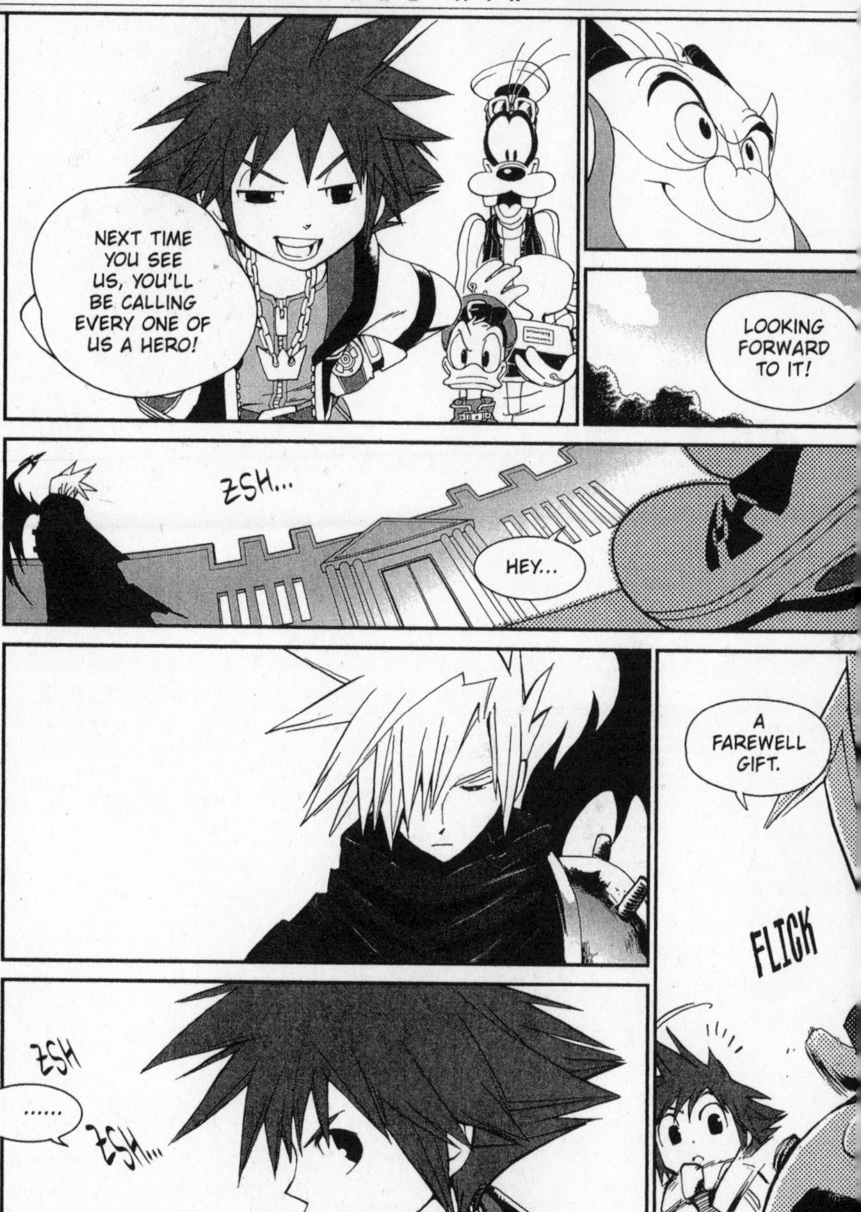
NEXT TIME YOU SEE US, YOU'LL BE CALLING EVERY ONE OF US A HERO!
LOOKING FORWARD TO IT!
ZSH...
HEY...
ZSH
......
ZSH...
A FAREWELL GIFT.
FLICK

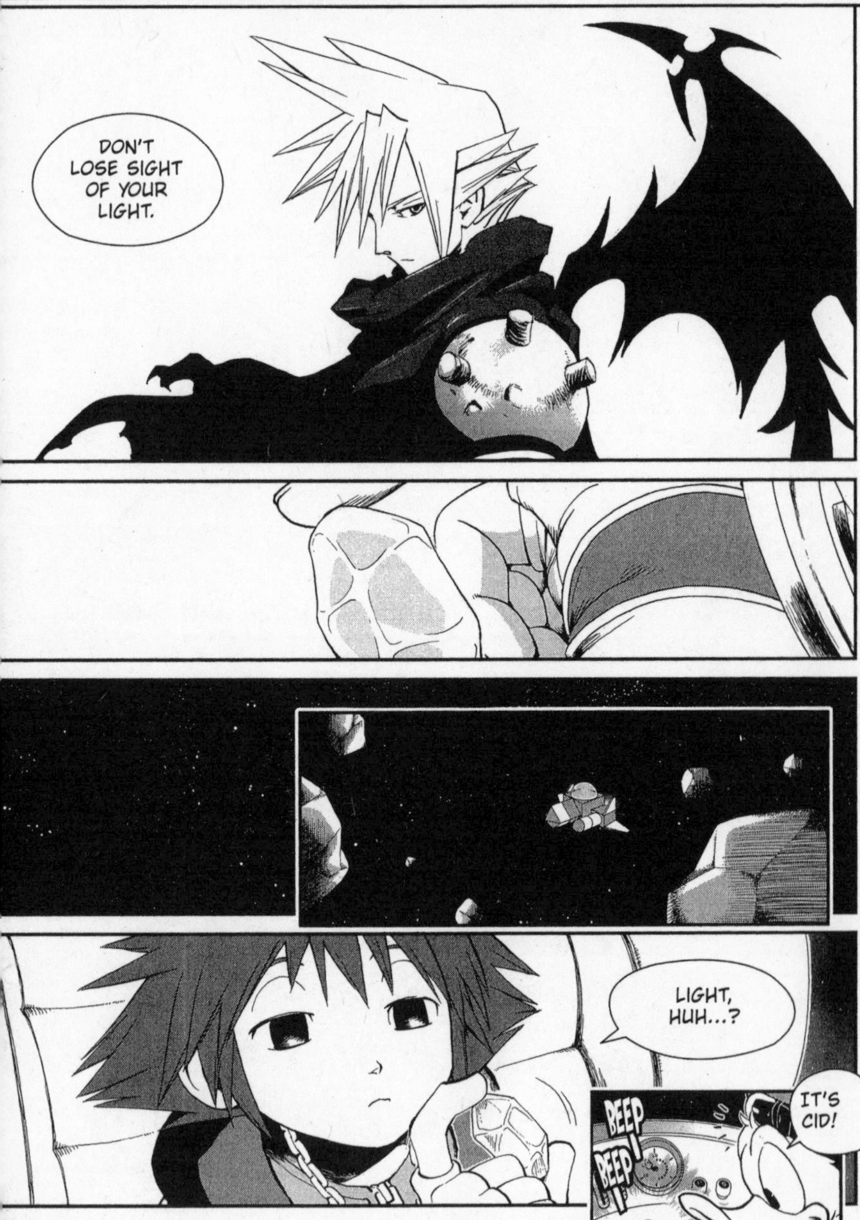
DON'T LOSE SIGHT OF YOUR LIGHT.
LIGHT, HUH...?
BEEP
BEEP
PUSH ME!
IT'S CID!

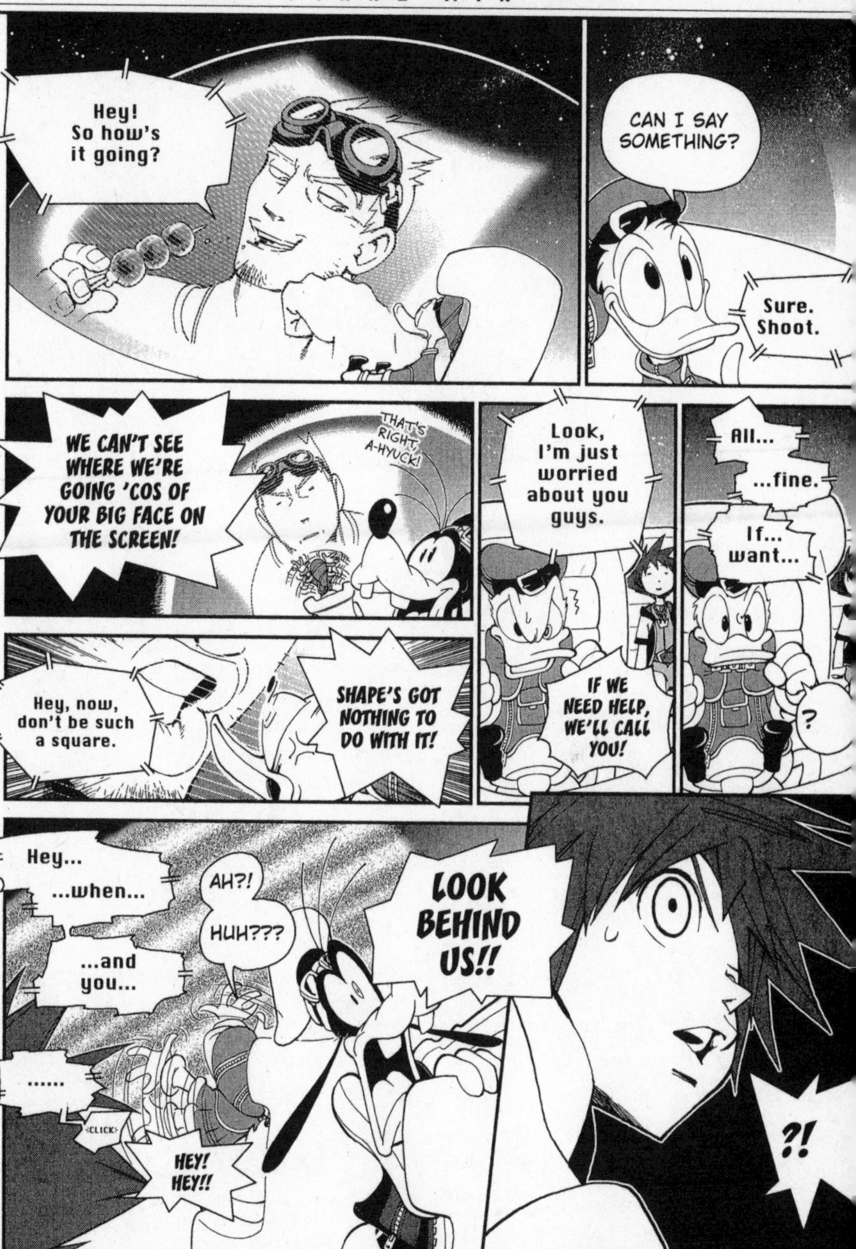
Hey!
So how's it going?
CAN I SAY SOMETHING?
Sure. Shoot.
WE CAN'T SEE WHERE WE'RE GOING 'COS OF YOUR BIG FACE ON THE SCREEN!
THAT'S RIGHT, A-HYUCK!
Look, I'm just worried about you guys.
All...
...fine.
If...
want...
Hey, now, don't be such a square.
SHAPE'S GOT NOTHING TO DO WITH IT!
IF WE NEED HELP, WE'LL CALL YOU!
?
Hey...
...when...
...and you...
......
CLICK
AH?!
HUH???
HEY! HEY!!
LOOK BEHIND US!!
?!

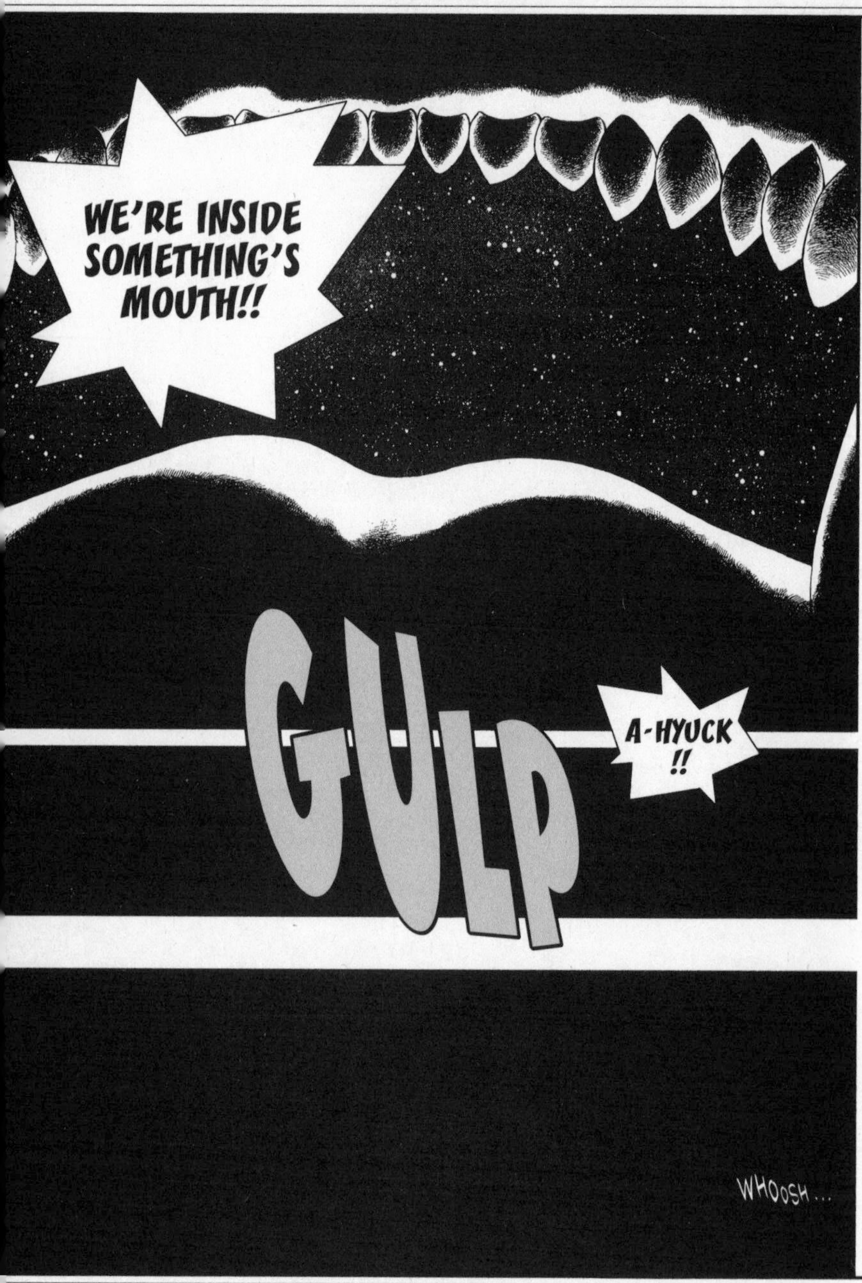
WE'RE INSIDE SOMETHING'S MOUTH!!
GULP
A-HYUCK !!
WHOOSH...

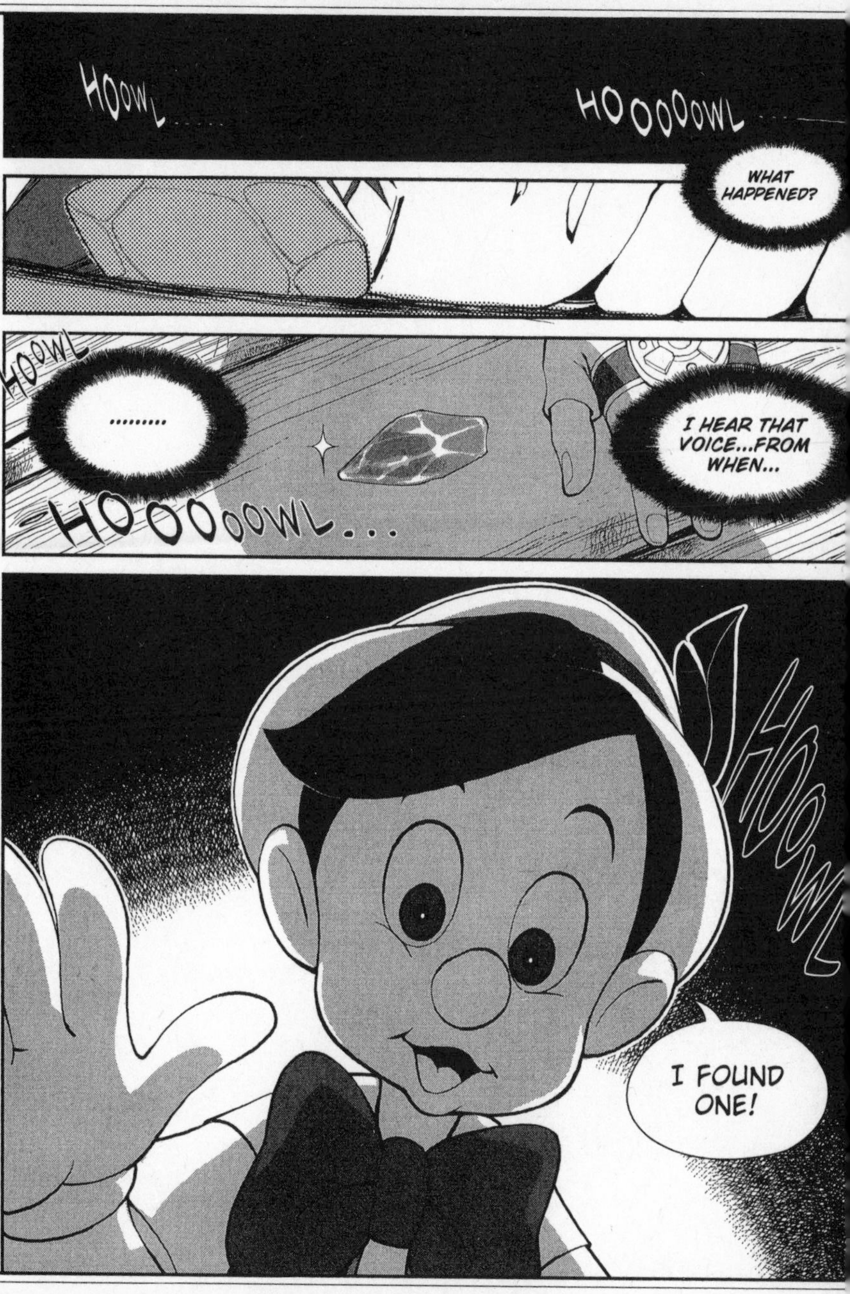
HOOWL......
HOOOOOWL
WHAT HAPPENED?
HOOWL
....
I HEAR THAT VOICE...FROM WHEN...
HOOOOOWL...
HOOWL
I FOUND ONE!

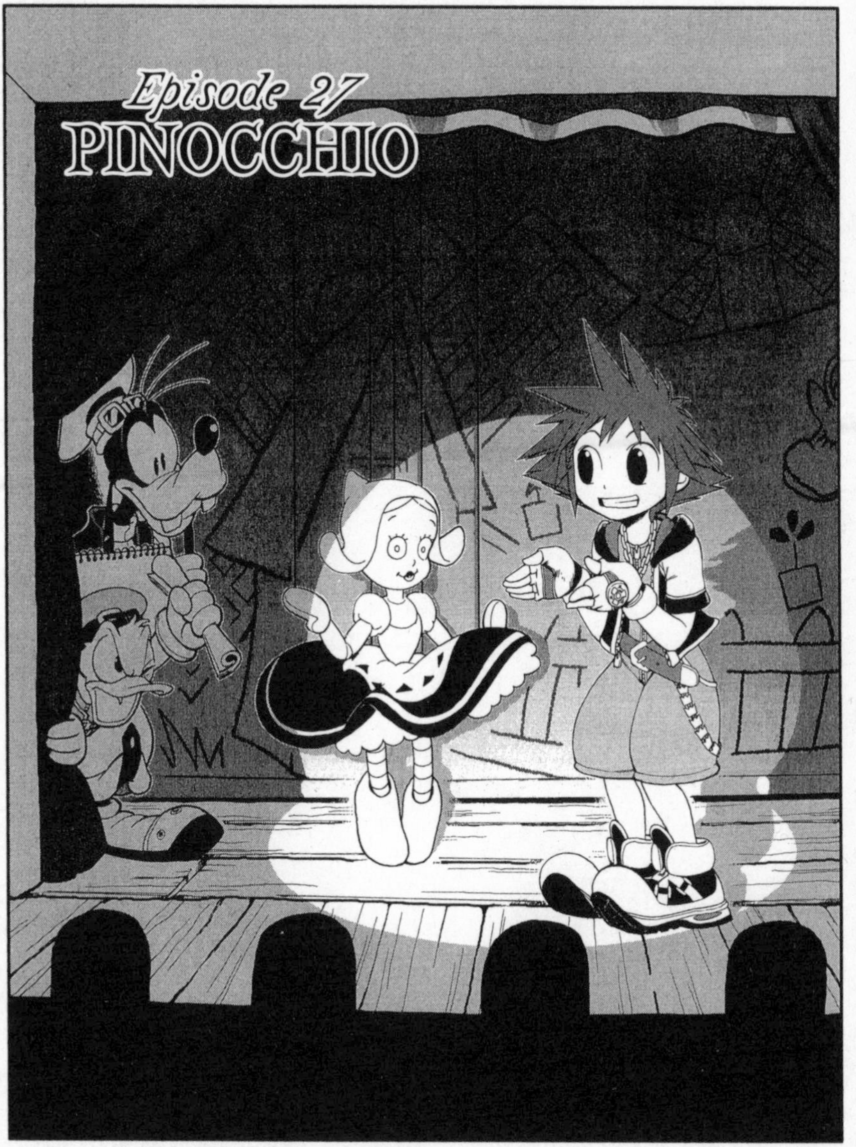
Episode 27
PINOCCHIO

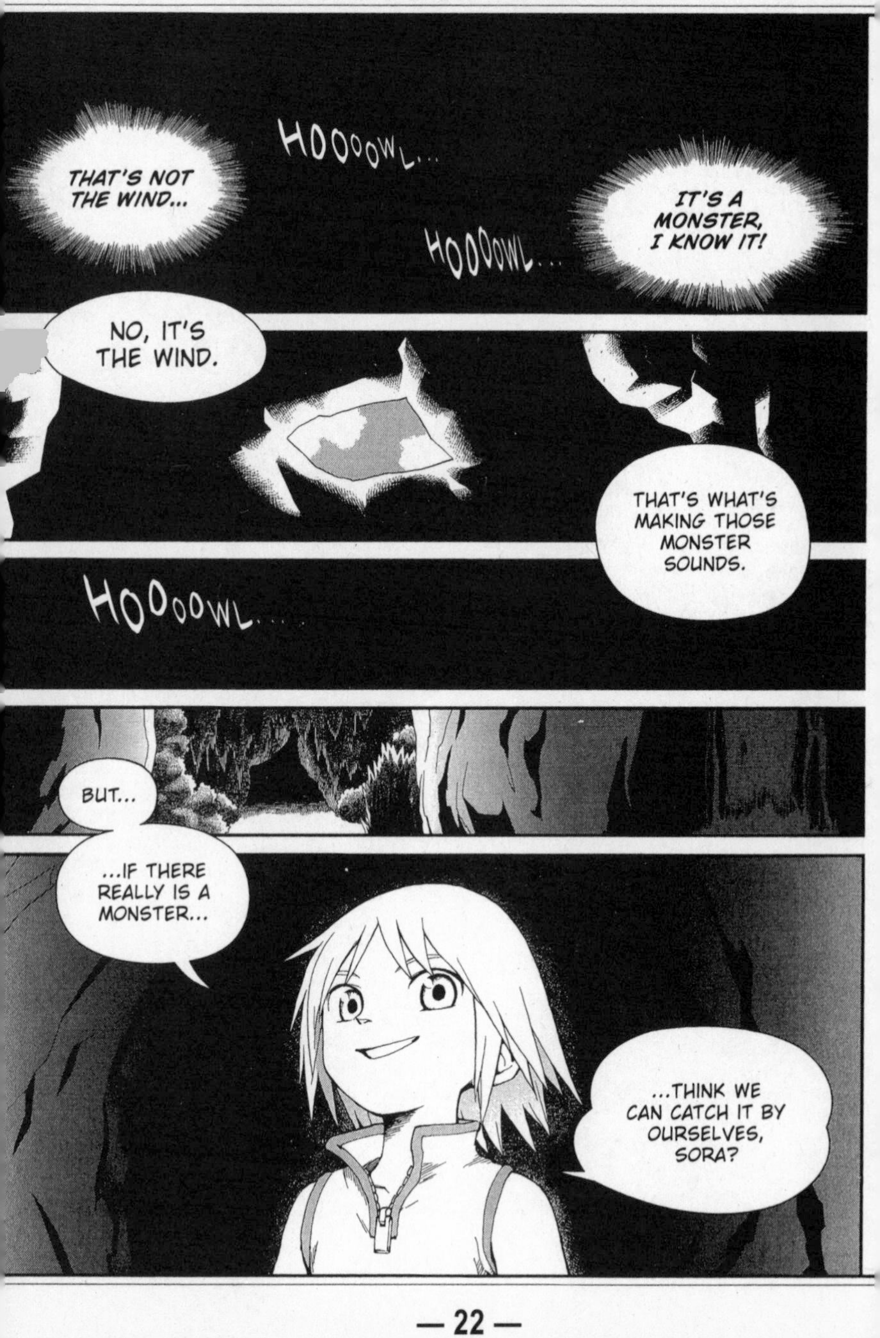
THAT'S NOT THE WIND...
HOOOOWL...
HOOOOWL...
IT'S A MONSTER, I KNOW IT!
NO, IT'S THE WIND.
THAT'S WHAT'S MAKING THOSE MONSTER SOUNDS.
HOOOOWL......
BUT...
...IF THERE REALLY IS A MONSTER...
...THINK WE CAN CATCH IT BY OURSELVES, SORA?

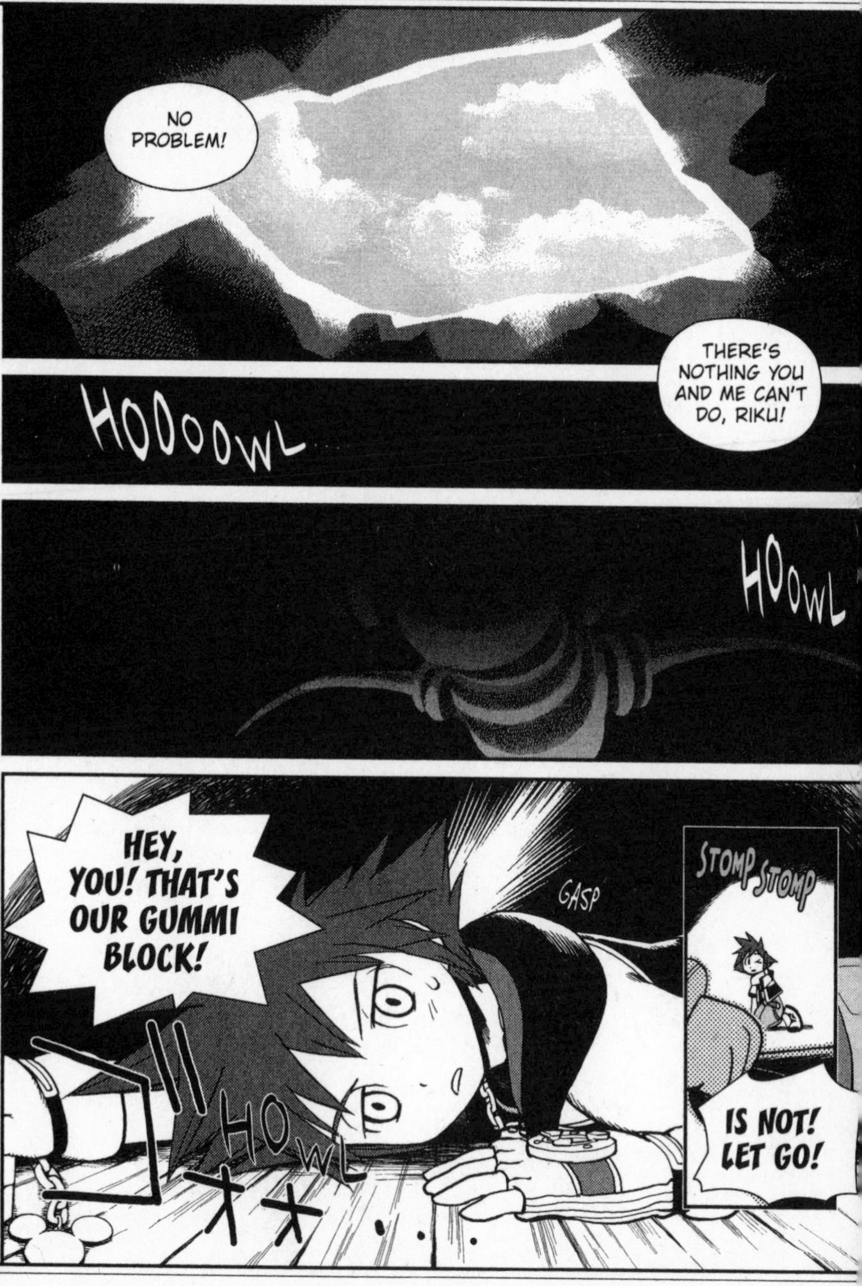
NO PROBLEM!
THERE'S NOTHING YOU AND ME CAN'T DO, RIKU!
HOOOOWL
HOOWL
HEY, YOU! THAT'S OUR GUMMI BLOCK!
GASP
HOWL
STOMP STOMP
IS NOT! LET GO!

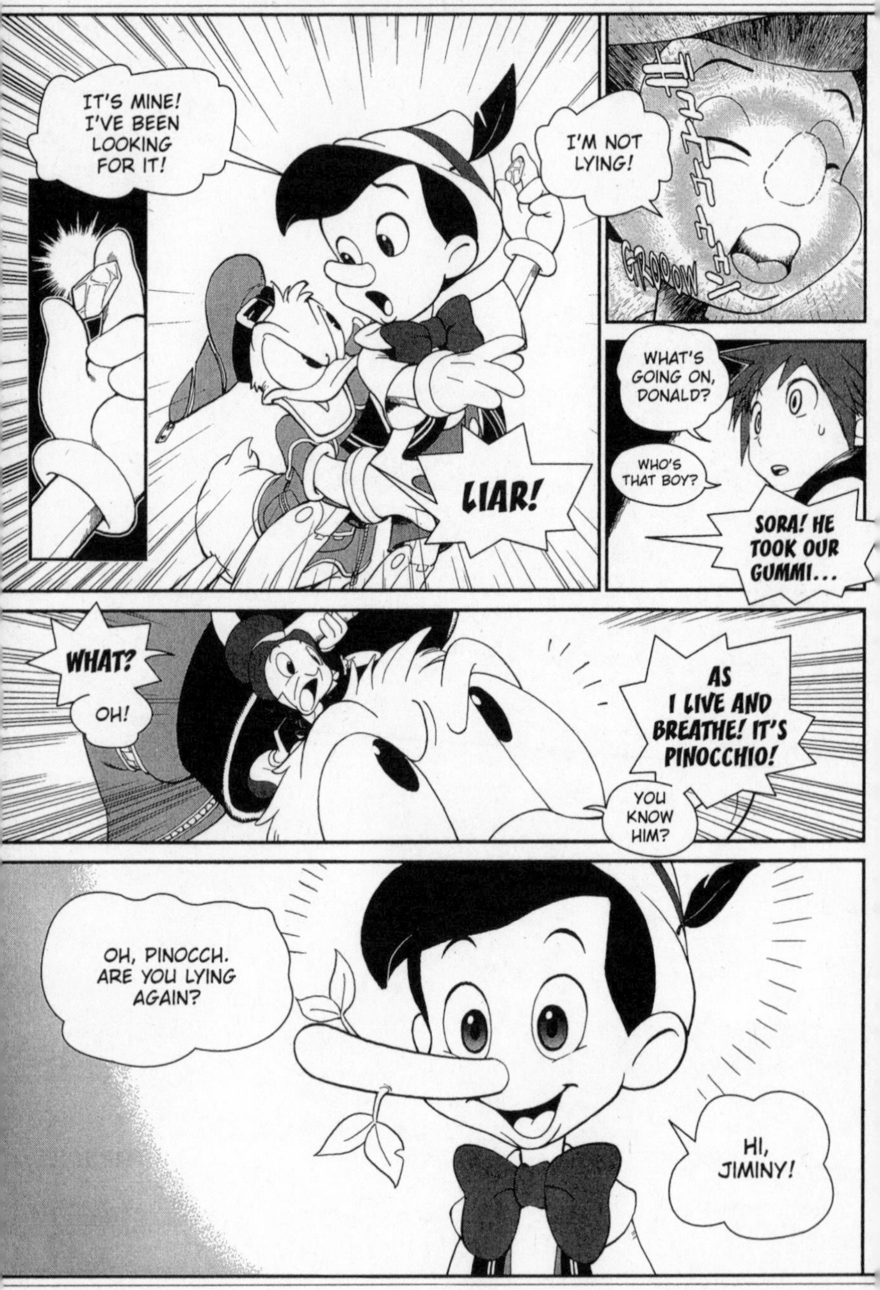
IT'S MINE! I'VE BEEN LOOKING FOR IT!
I'M NOT LYING!
LIAR!
WHAT'S GOING ON, DONALD?
WHO'S THAT BOY?
SORA! HE TOOK OUR GUMMI...
WHAT?
OH!
AS I LIVE AND BREATHE! IT'S PINOCCHIO!
YOU KNOW HIM?
OH, PINOCCH. ARE YOU LYING AGAIN?
HI, JIMINY!

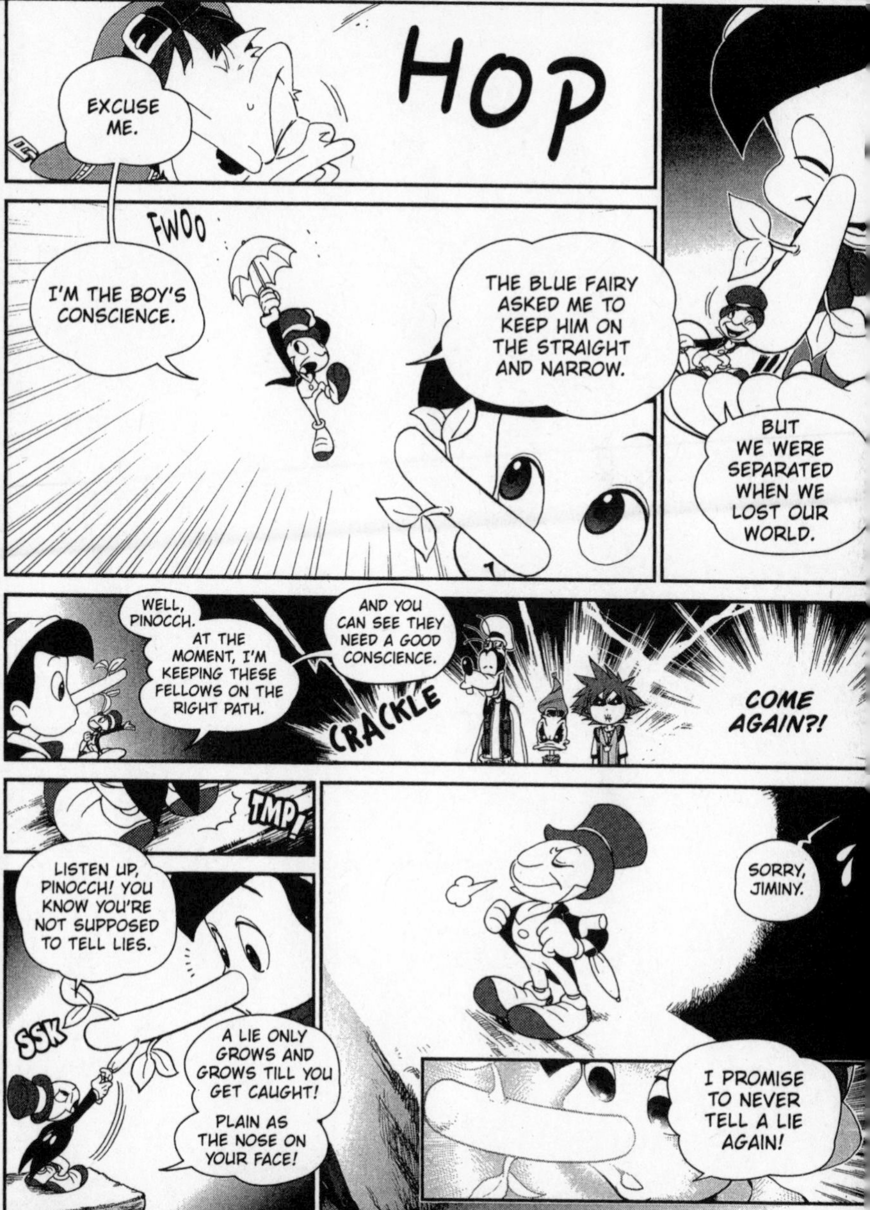
EXCUSE ME.
HOP
FWOO
I'M THE BOY'S CONSCIENCE.
THE BLUE FAIRY ASKED ME TO KEEP HIM ON THE STRAIGHT AND NARROW.
BUT WE WERE SEPARATED WHEN WE LOST OUR WORLD.
WELL, PINOCCH.
AT THE MOMENT, I'M KEEPING THESE FELLOWS ON THE RIGHT PATH.
AND YOU CAN SEE THEY NEED A GOOD CONSCIENCE.
CRACKLE
COME AGAIN?!
TMP!
LISTEN UP, PINOCCH! YOU KNOW YOU'RE NOT SUPPOSED TO TELL LIES.
SSK
A LIE ONLY GROWS AND GROWS TILL YOU GET CAUGHT!
PLAIN AS THE NOSE ON YOUR FACE!
SORRY, JIMINY.
I PROMISE TO NEVER TELL A LIE AGAIN!

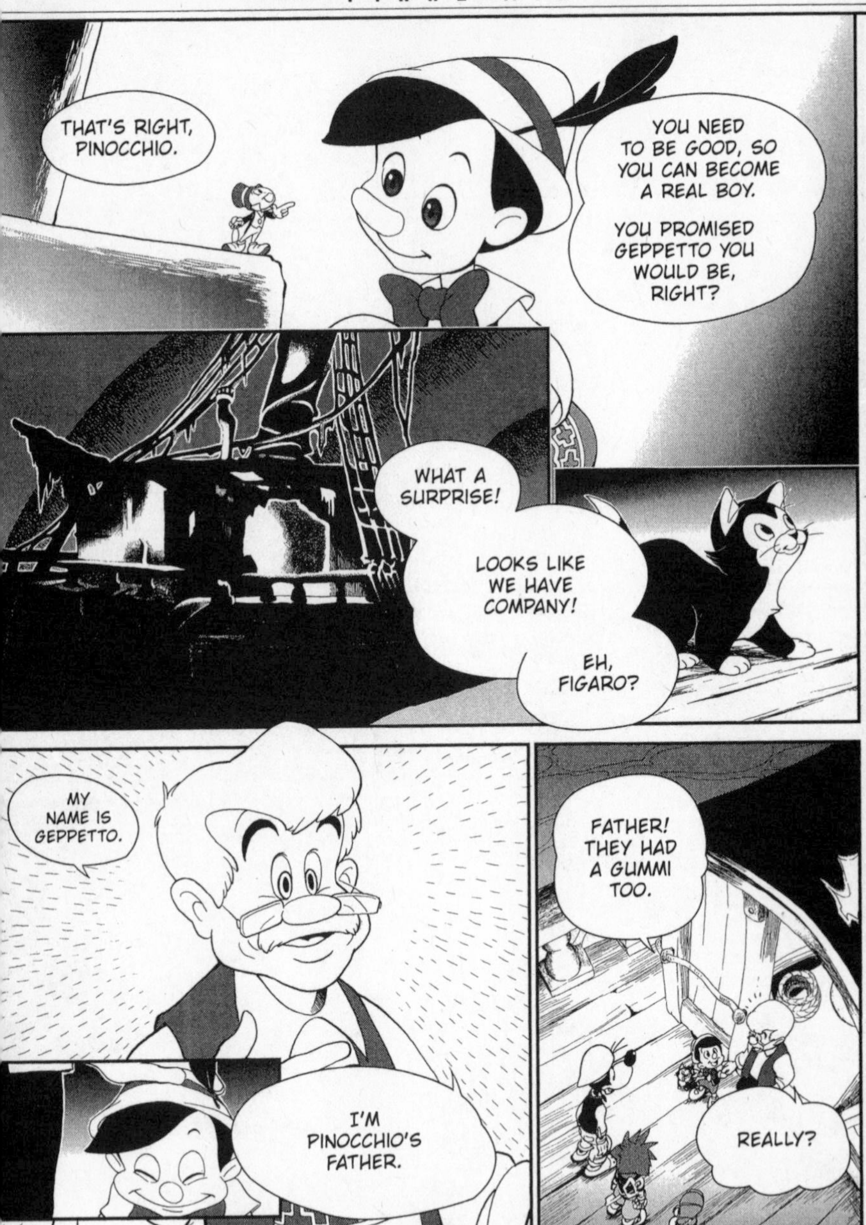
THAT'S RIGHT, PINOCCHIO.
YOU NEED TO BE GOOD, SO YOU CAN BECOME A REAL BOY.
YOU PROMISED GEPPETTO YOU WOULD BE, RIGHT?
WHAT A SURPRISE!
LOOKS LIKE WE HAVE COMPANY!
EH, FIGARO?
MY NAME IS GEPPETTO.
I'M PINOCCHIO'S FATHER.
FATHER! THEY HAD A GUMMI TOO.
REALLY?

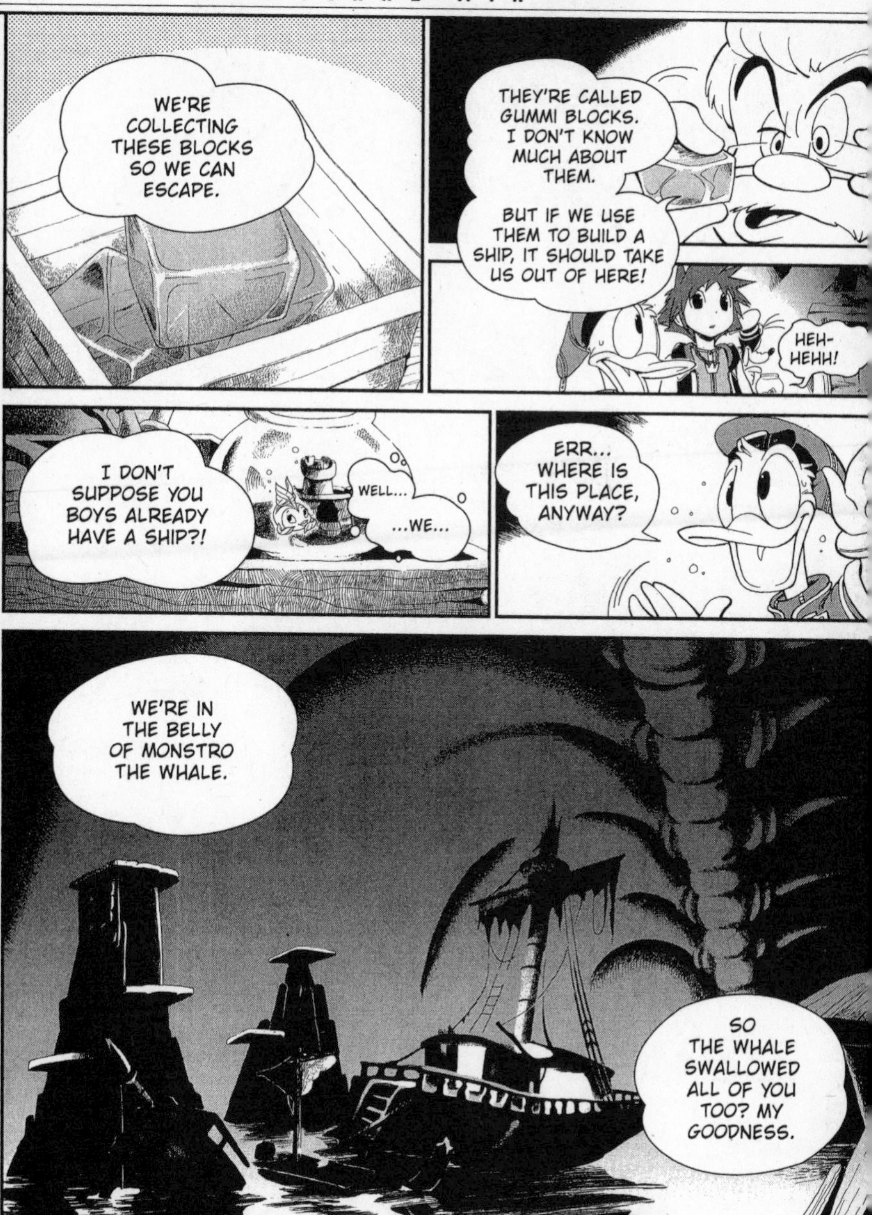
WE'RE COLLECTING THESE BLOCKS SO WE CAN ESCAPE.
THEY'RE CALLED GUMMI BLOCKS. I DON'T KNOW MUCH ABOUT THEM.
BUT IF WE USE THEM TO BUILD A SHIP, IT SHOULD TAKE US OUT OF HERE!
HEH-HEHH!
I DON'T SUPPOSE YOU BOYS ALREADY HAVE A SHIP?!
WELL...
...WE...
ERR... WHERE IS THIS PLACE, ANYWAY?
WE'RE IN THE BELLY OF MONSTRO THE WHALE.
SO THE WHALE SWALLOWED ALL OF YOU TOO? MY GOODNESS.

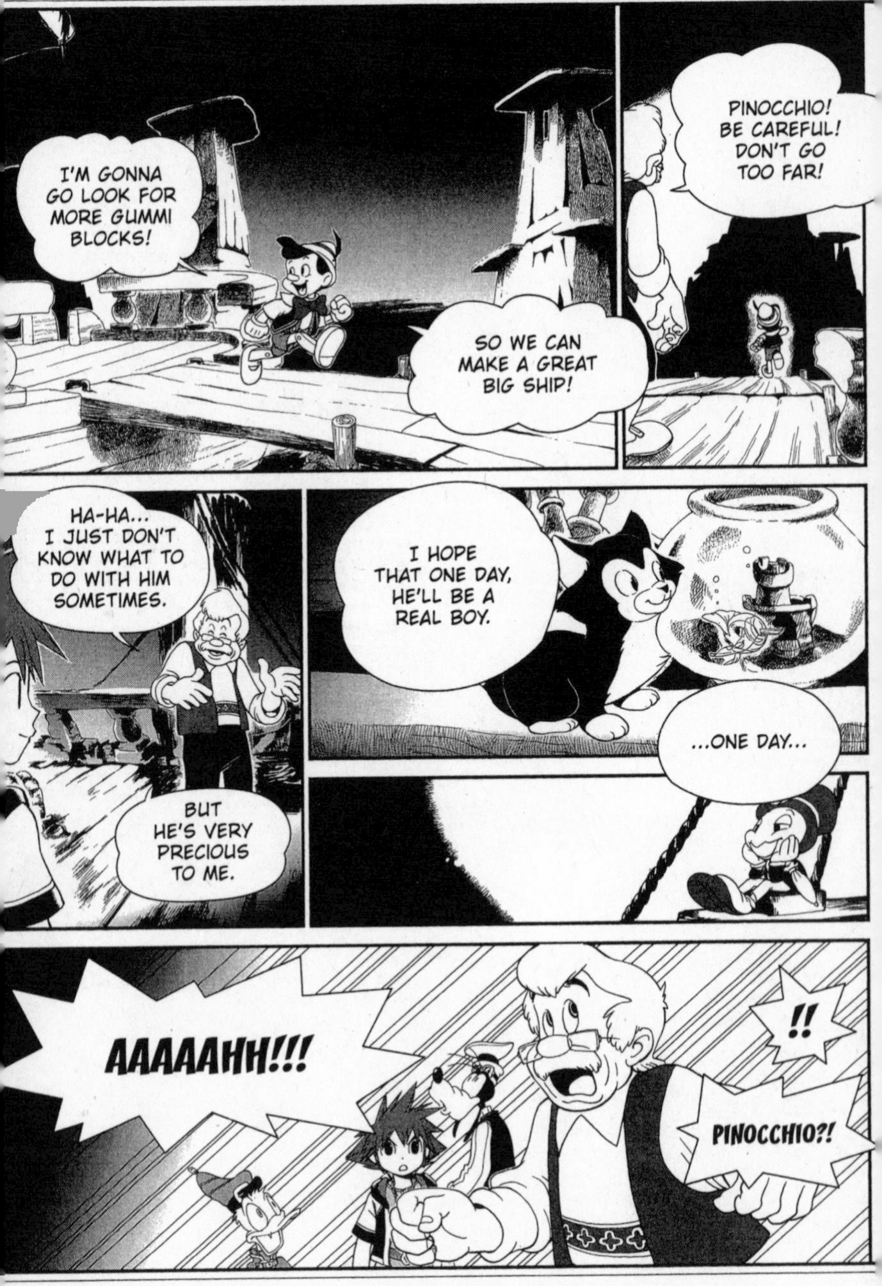
I'M GONNA GO LOOK FOR MORE GUMMI BLOCKS!
SO WE CAN MAKE A GREAT BIG SHIP!
PINOCCHIO! BE CAREFUL! DON'T GO TOO FAR!
HA-HA... I JUST DON'T KNOW WHAT TO DO WITH HIM SOMETIMES.
BUT HE'S VERY PRECIOUS TO ME.
I HOPE THAT ONE DAY, HE'LL BE A REAL BOY.
...ONE DAY...
AAAAAHH!!!
!!
PINOCCHIO?!

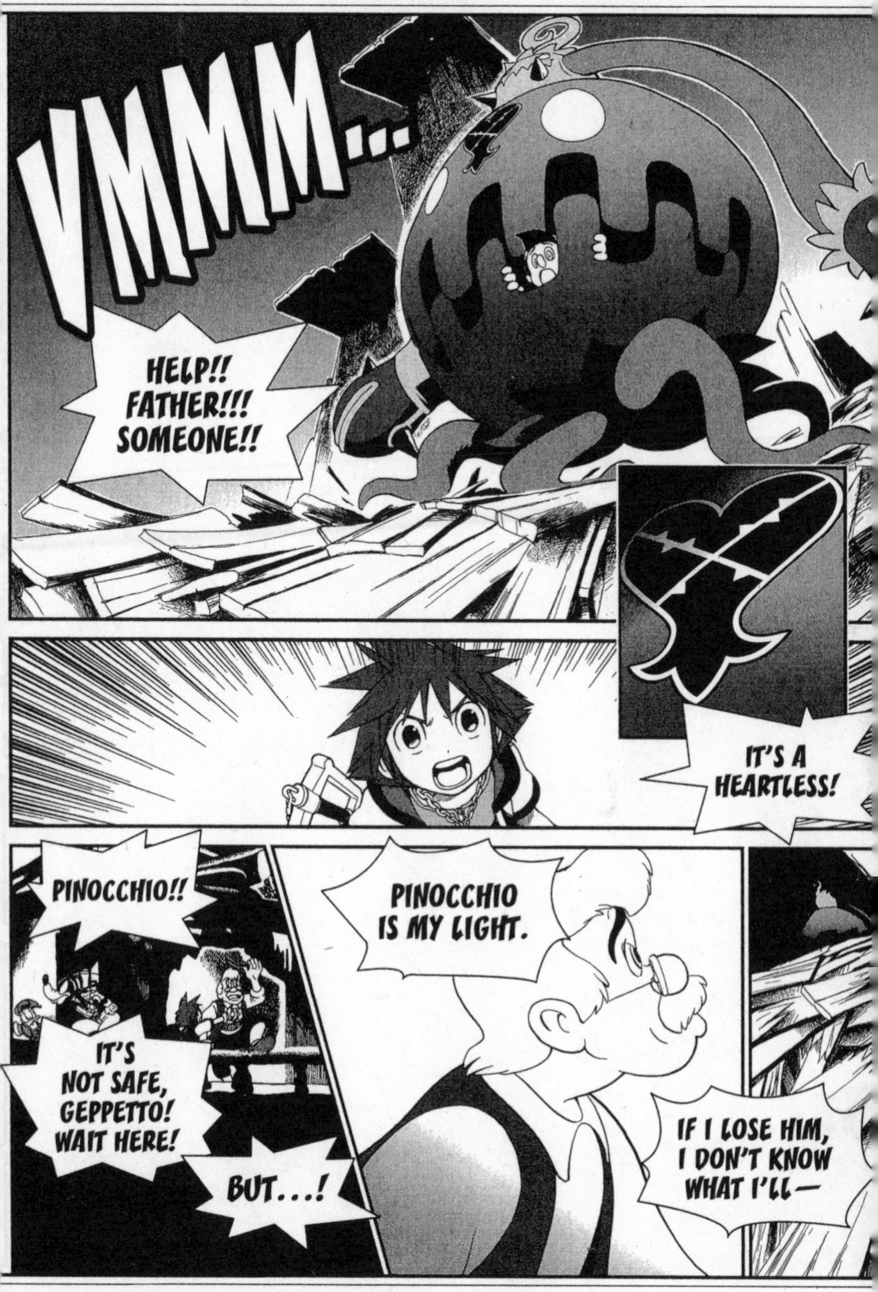
VMMM...
HELP!! FATHER!!! SOMEONE!!
IT'S A HEARTLESS!
PINOCCHIO!!
IT'S NOT SAFE, GEPPETTO! WAIT HERE!
BUT...!
PINOCCHIO IS MY LIGHT.
IF I LOSE HIM, I DON'T KNOW WHAT I'LL—

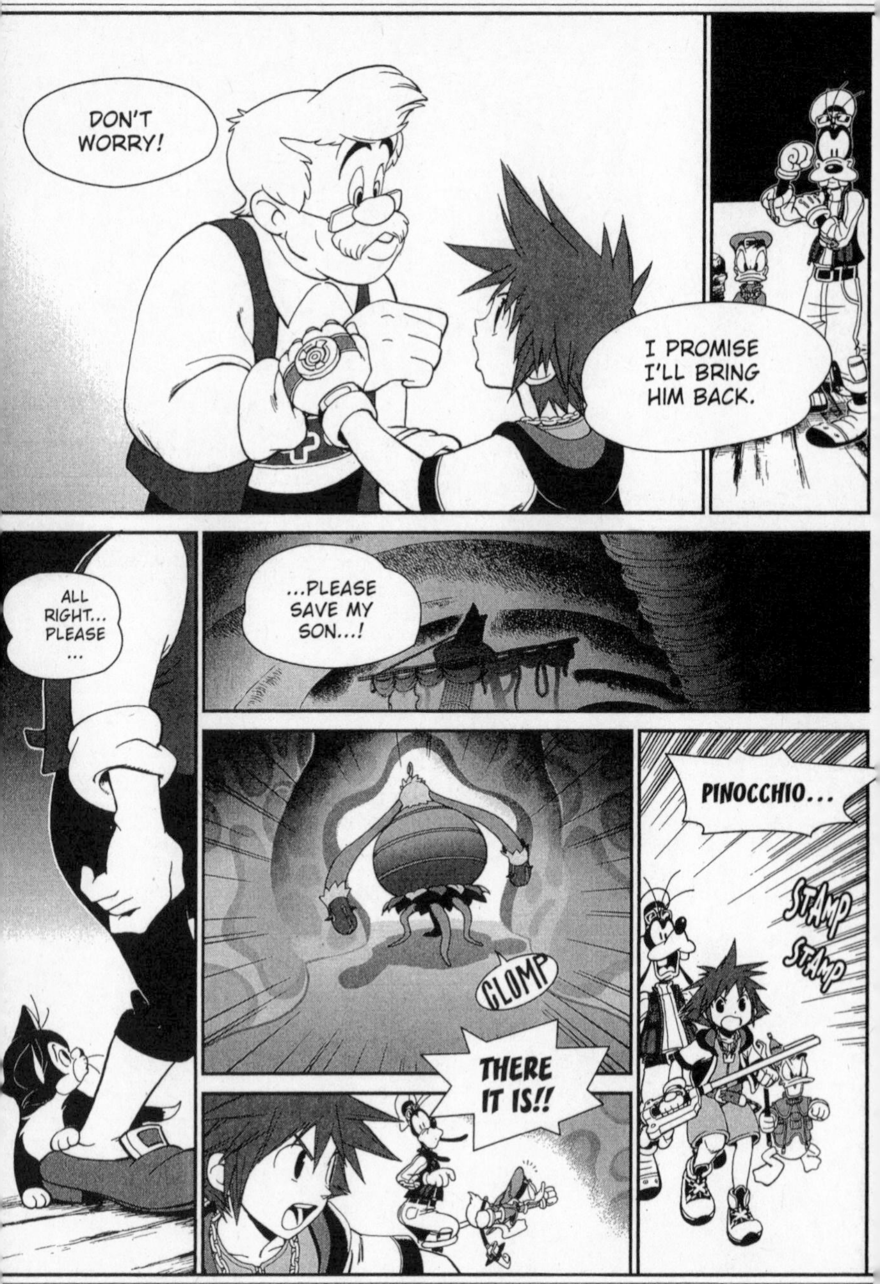
DON'T WORRY!
I PROMISE I'LL BRING HIM BACK.
ALL RIGHT... PLEASE ...
...PLEASE SAVE MY SON...!
CLOMP
THERE IT IS!!
PINOCCHIO...
STAMP
STAMP

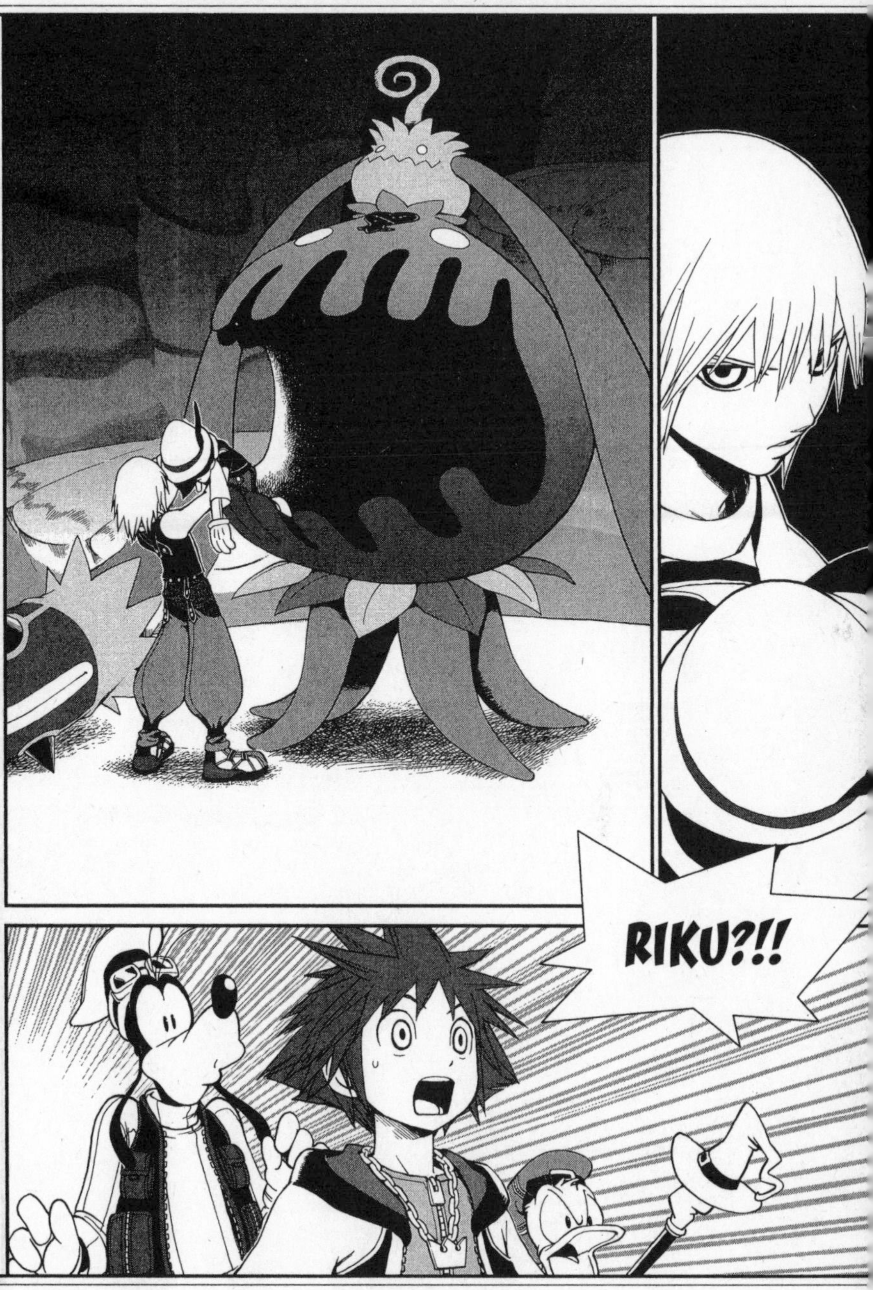
RIKU?!!

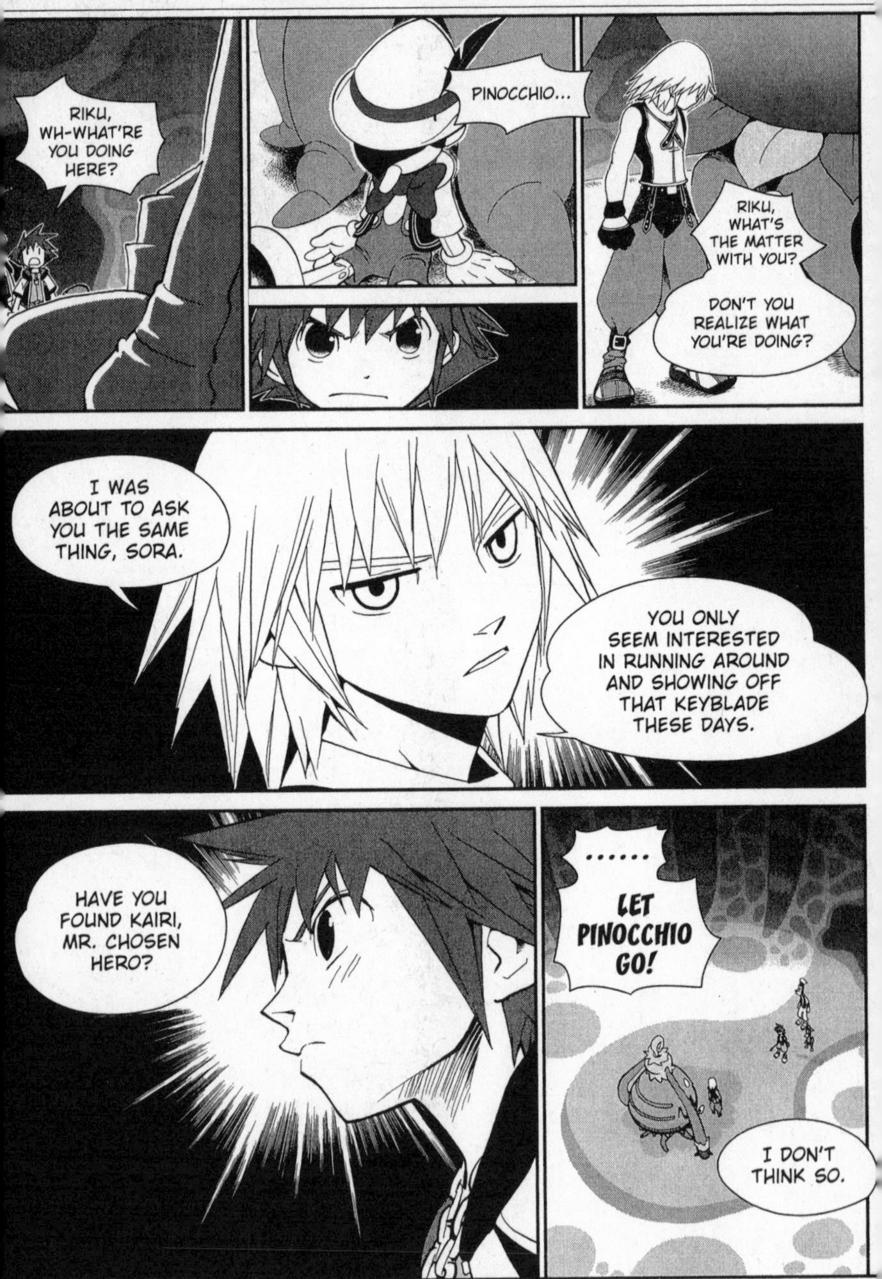
RIKU, WH-WHAT'RE YOU DOING HERE?
PINOCCHIO...
RIKU, WHAT'S THE MATTER WITH YOU?
DON'T YOU REALIZE WHAT YOU'RE DOING?
I WAS ABOUT TO ASK YOU THE SAME THING, SORA.
YOU ONLY SEEM INTERESTED IN RUNNING AROUND AND SHOWING OFF THAT KEYBLADE THESE DAYS.
HAVE YOU FOUND KAIRI, MR. CHOSEN HERO?
......
LET PINOCCHIO GO!
I DON'T THINK SO.

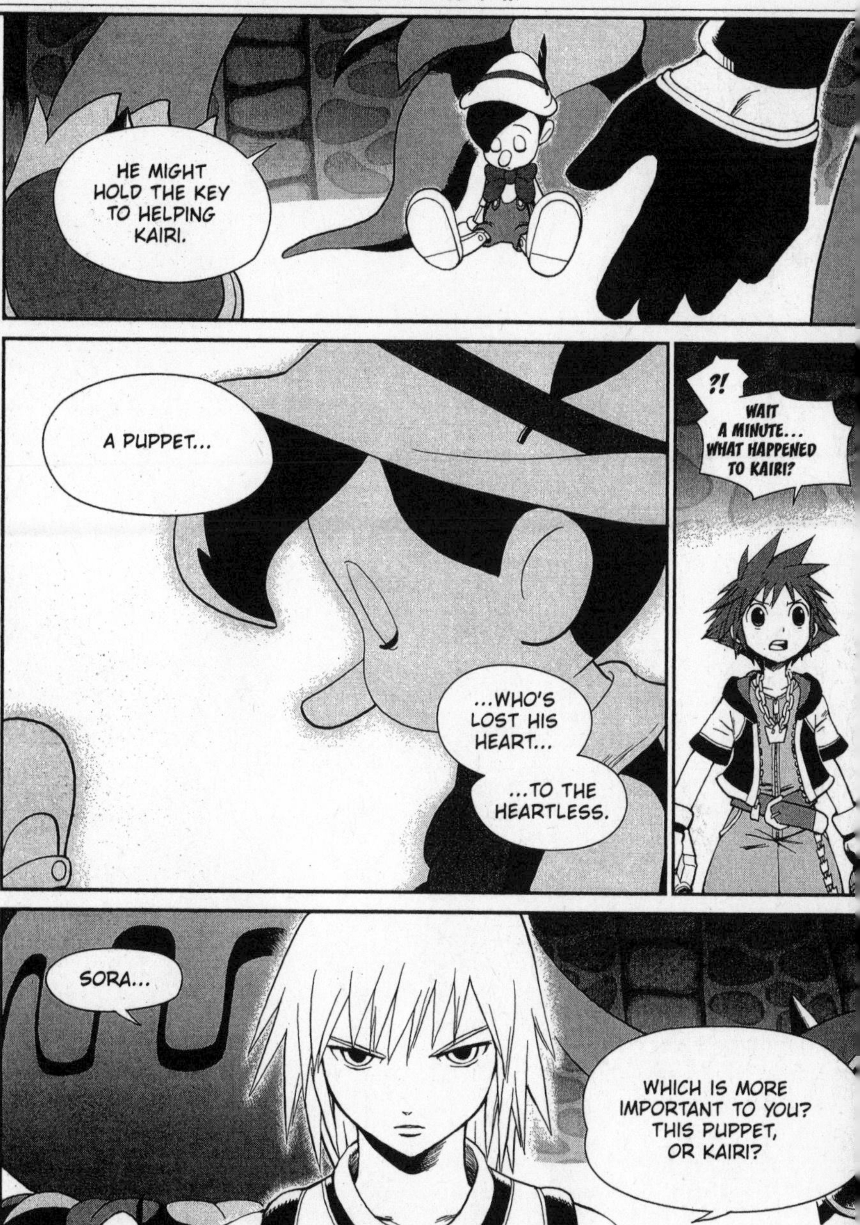
HE MIGHT HOLD THE KEY TO HELPING KAIRI.
A PUPPET...
...WHO'S LOST HIS HEART...
...TO THE HEARTLESS.
?!
WAIT A MINUTE... WHAT HAPPENED TO KAIRI?
SORA...
WHICH IS MORE IMPORTANT TO YOU? THIS PUPPET, OR KAIRI?

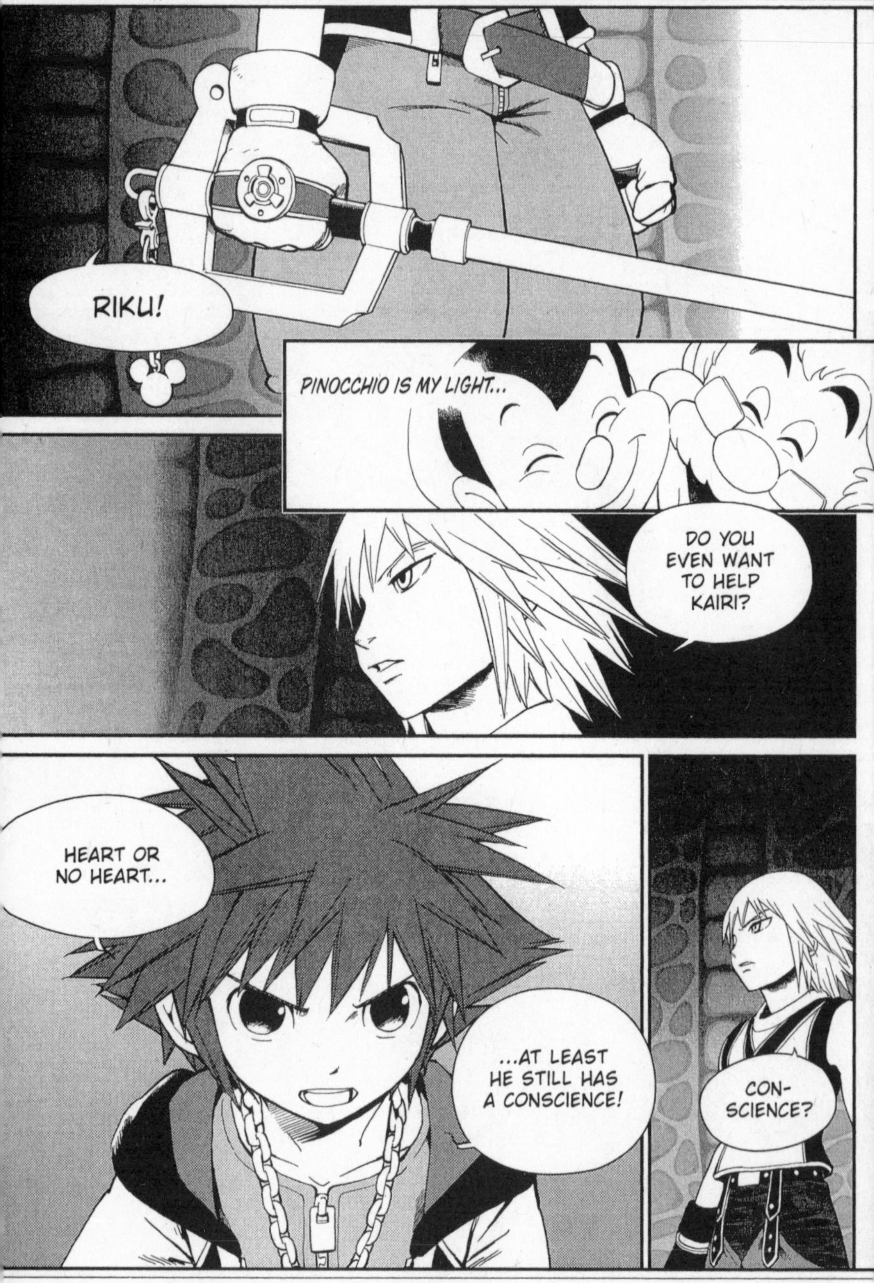
RIKU!
PINOCCHIO IS MY LIGHT...
DO YOU EVEN WANT TO HELP KAIRI?
HEART OR NO HEART...
...AT LEAST HE STILL HAS A CONSCIENCE!
CON-SCIENCE?

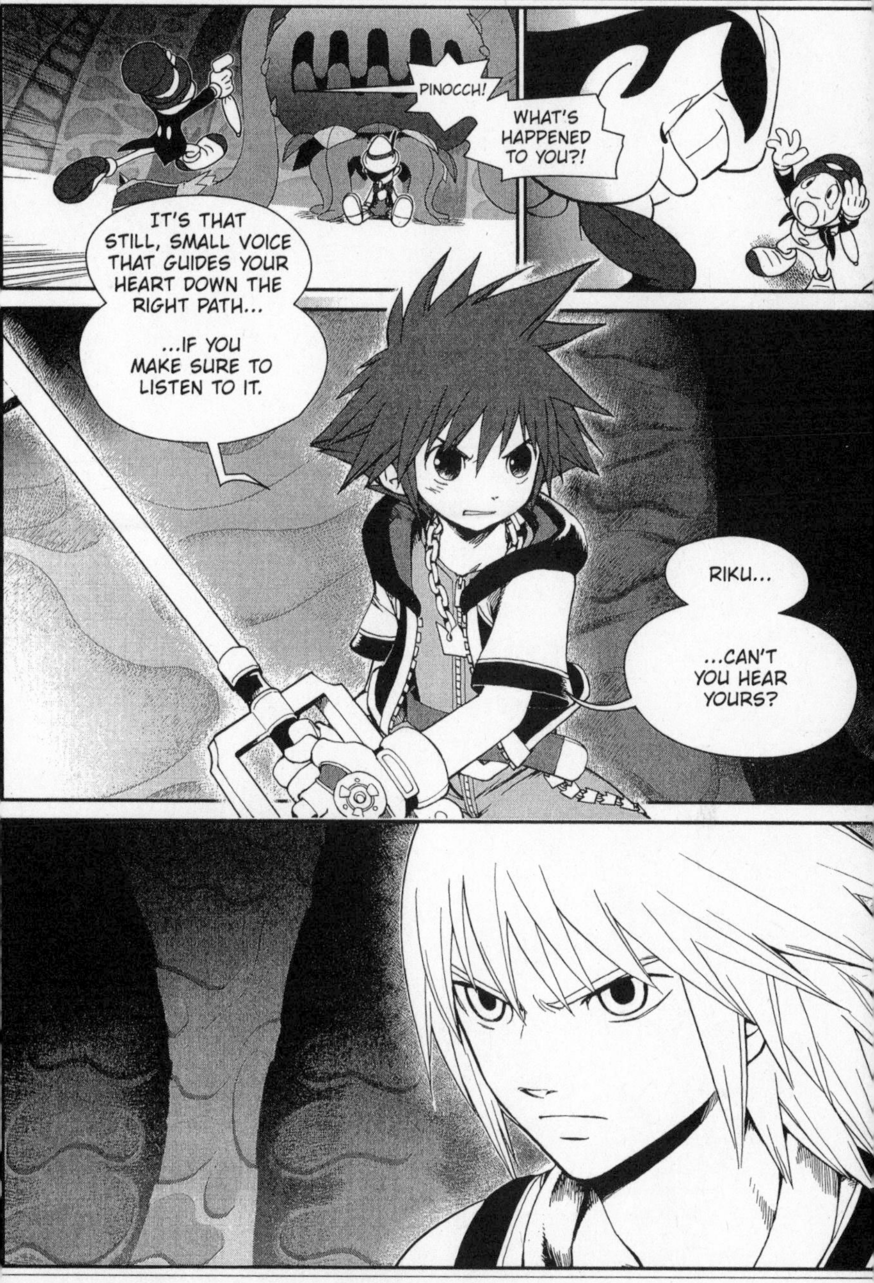
PINOCCH!
WHAT'S HAPPENED TO YOU?!
IT'S THAT STILL, SMALL VOICE THAT GUIDES YOUR HEART DOWN THE RIGHT PATH...
...IF YOU MAKE SURE TO LISTEN TO IT.
RIKU...
...CAN'T YOU HEAR YOURS?

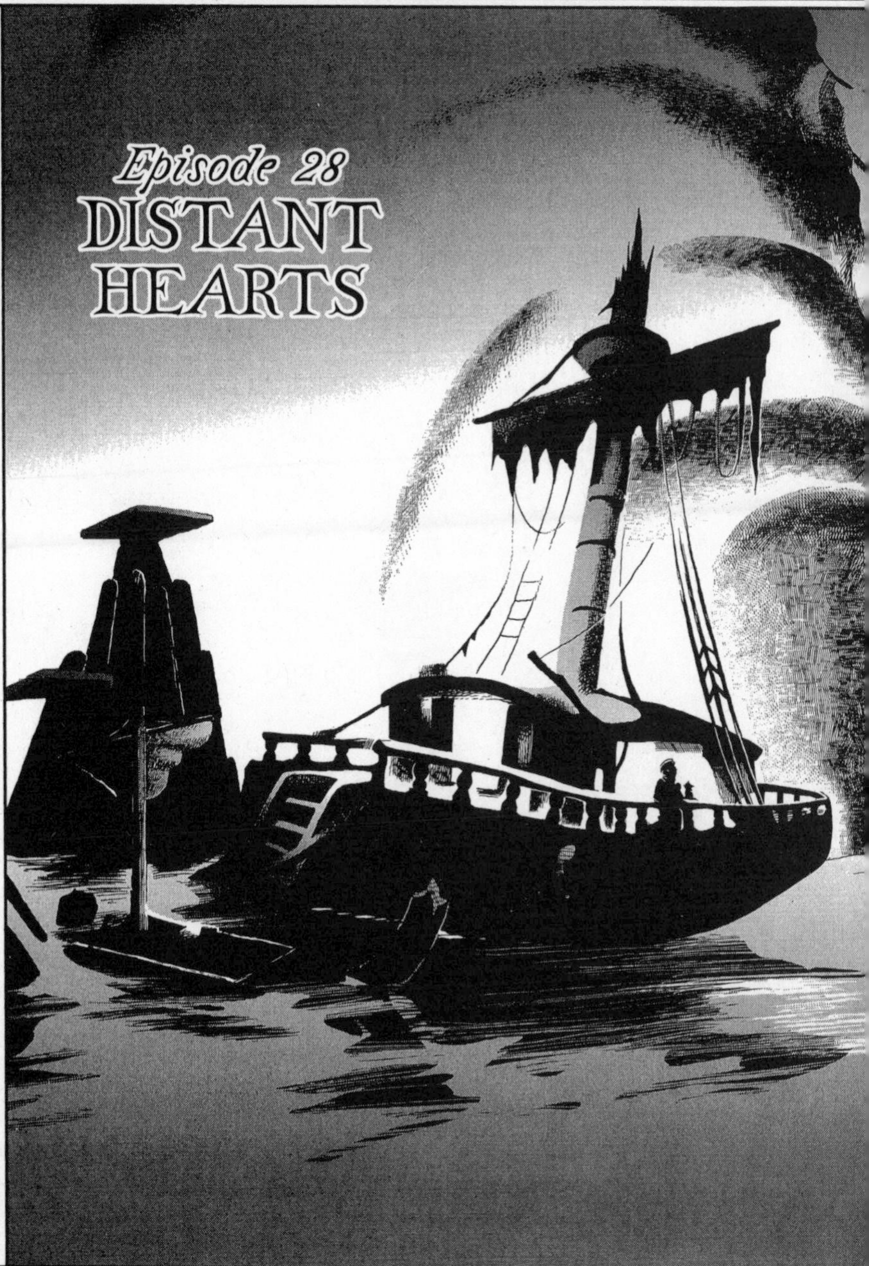
Episode 28
DISTANT
HEARTS

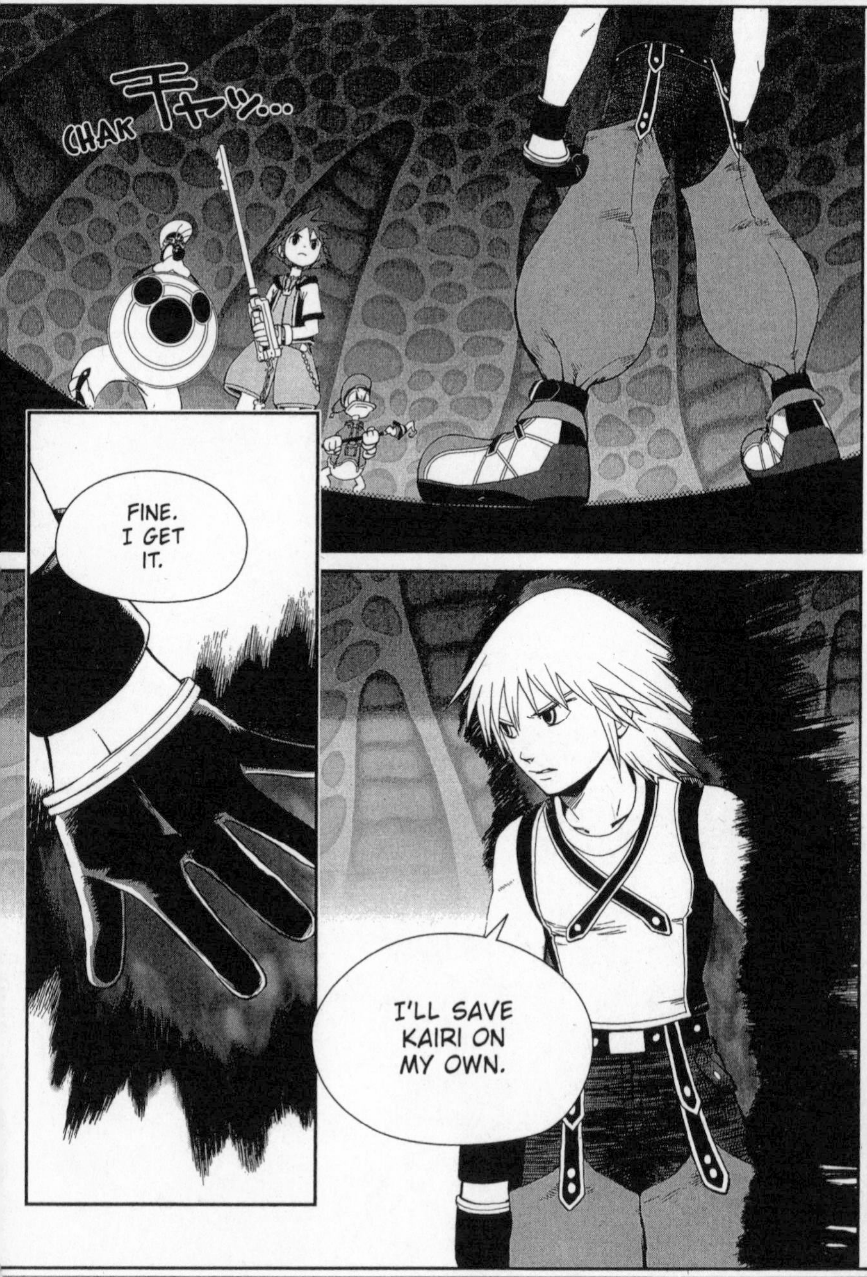
CHAK チャッ...
FINE. I GET IT.
I'LL SAVE KAIRI ON MY OWN.

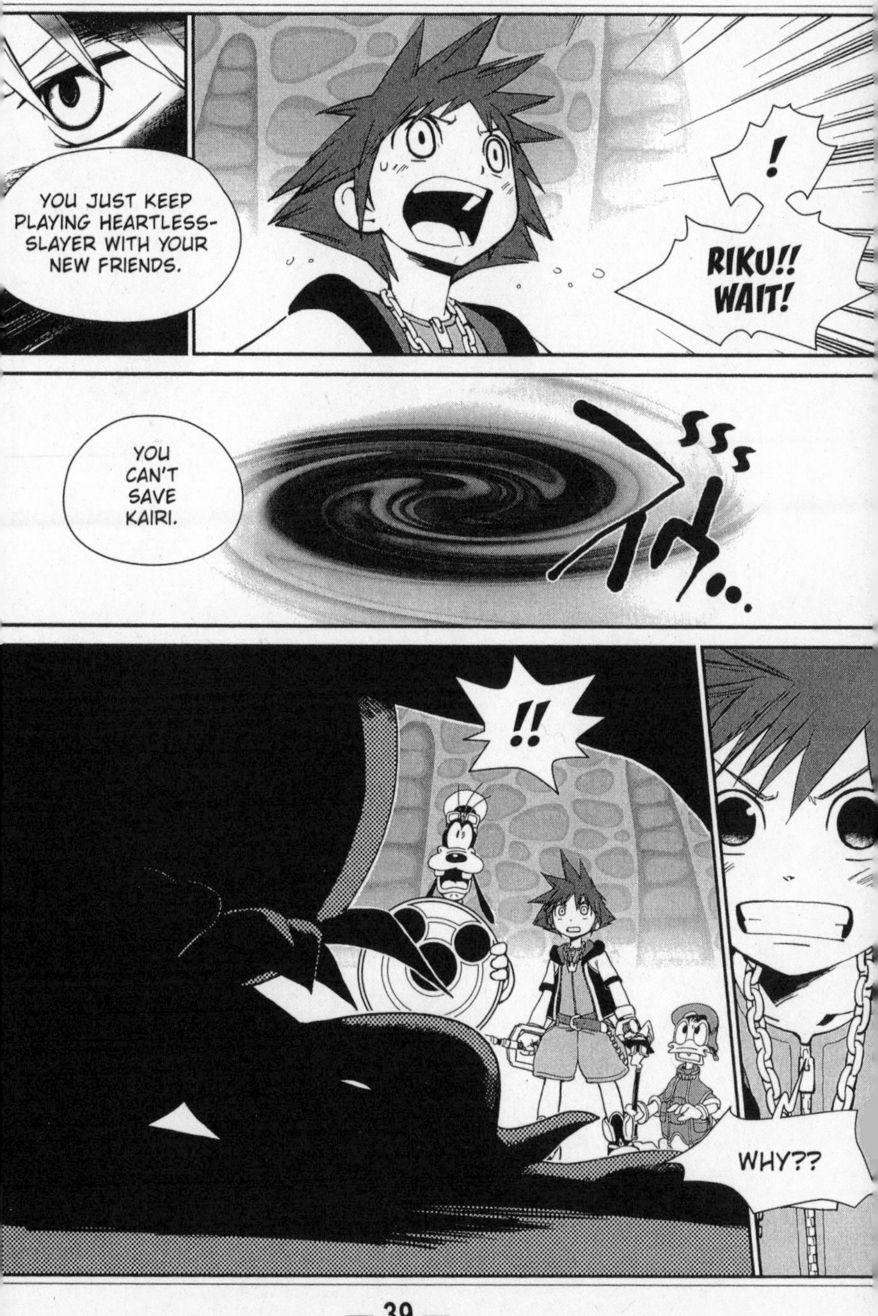
YOU JUST KEEP PLAYING HEARTLESS-SLAYER WITH YOUR NEW FRIENDS.
!
RIKU!! WAIT!
YOU CAN'T SAVE KAIRI.
!!
WHY??

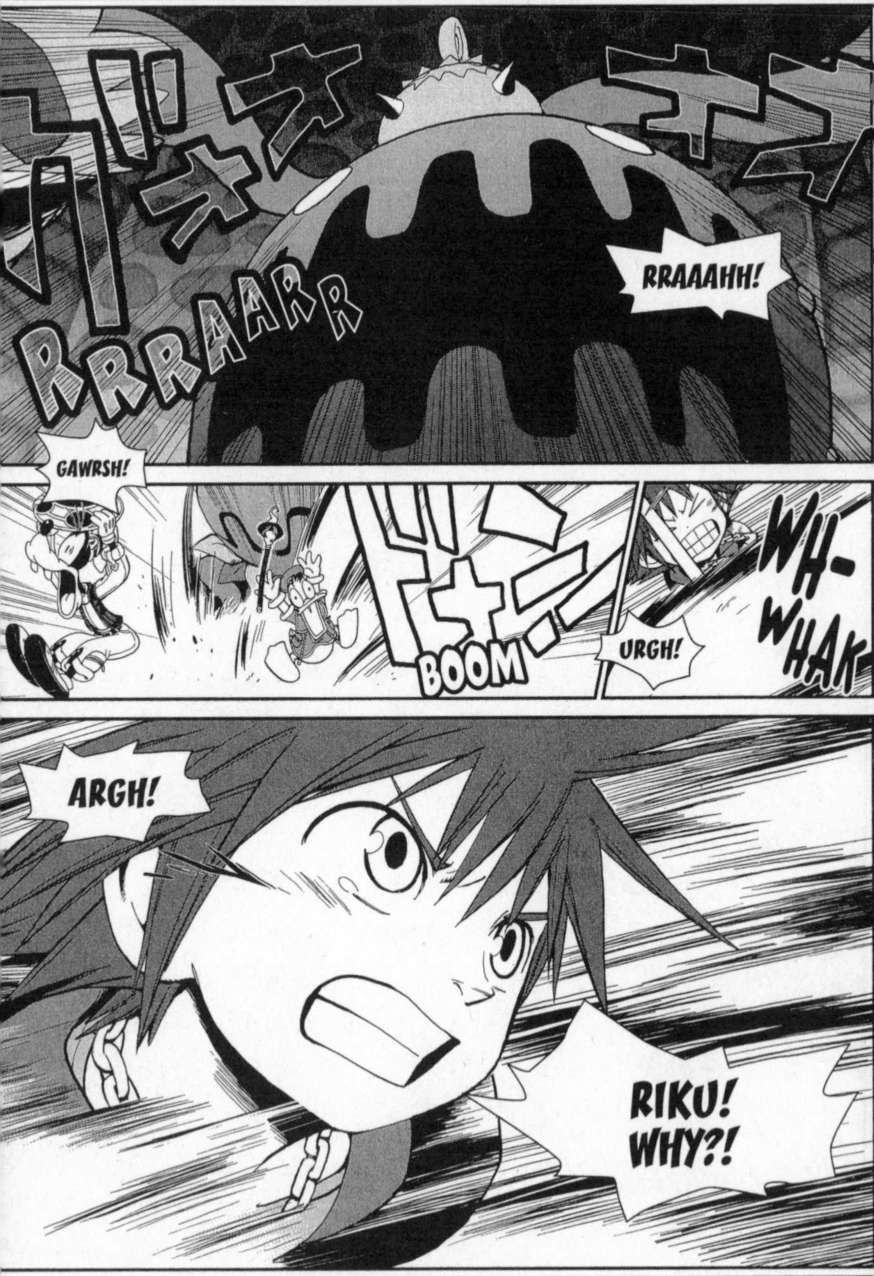
RRRAARR
RRAAAHH!
GAWRSH!
BOOM
URGH!
WH-WHAK
ARGH!
RIKU! WHY?!

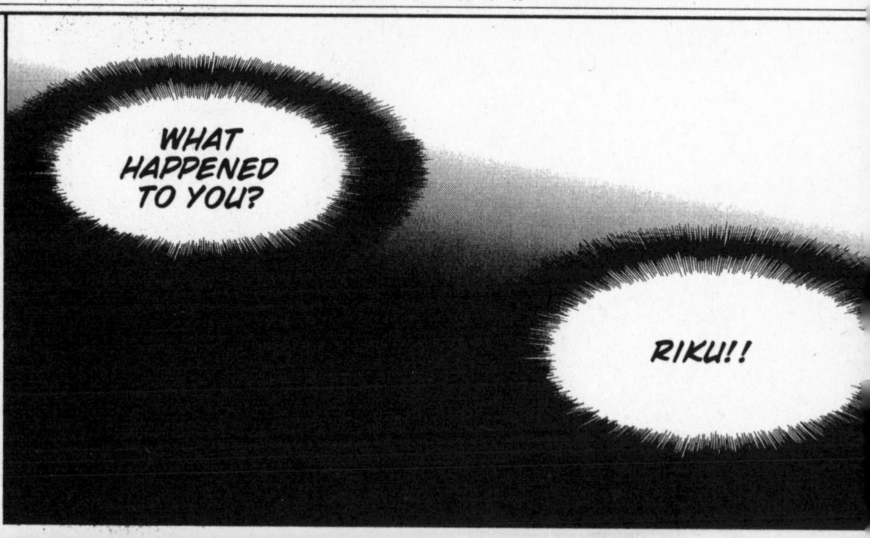
WHAT HAPPENED TO YOU?
RIKU!!

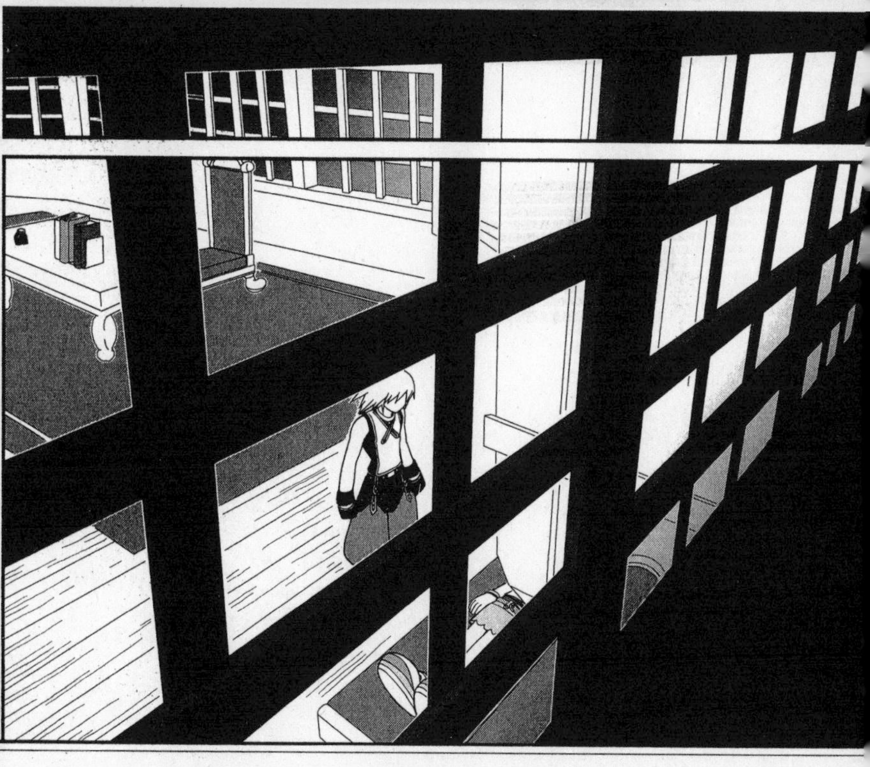

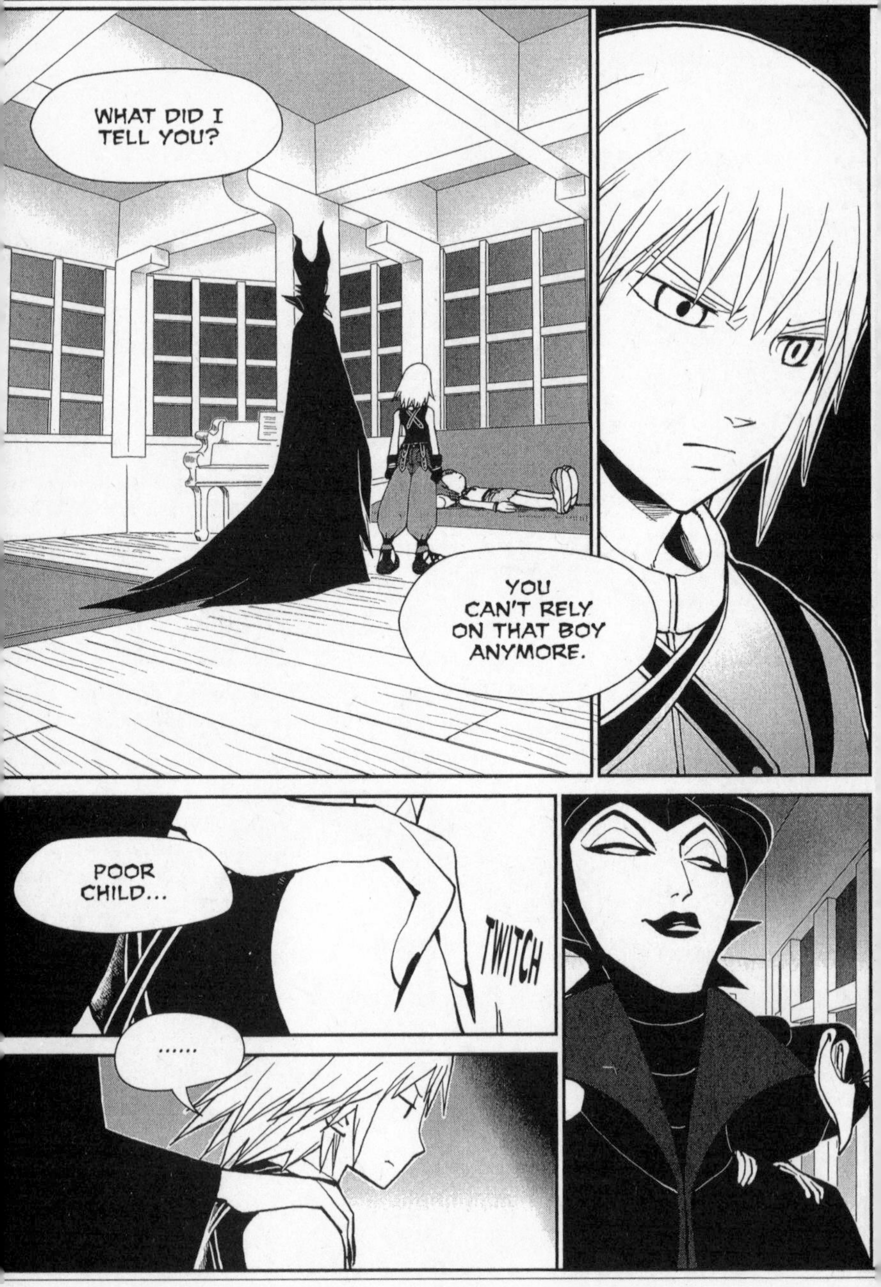
WHAT DID I TELL YOU?
YOU CAN'T RELY ON THAT BOY ANYMORE.
POOR CHILD...
TWITCH
......

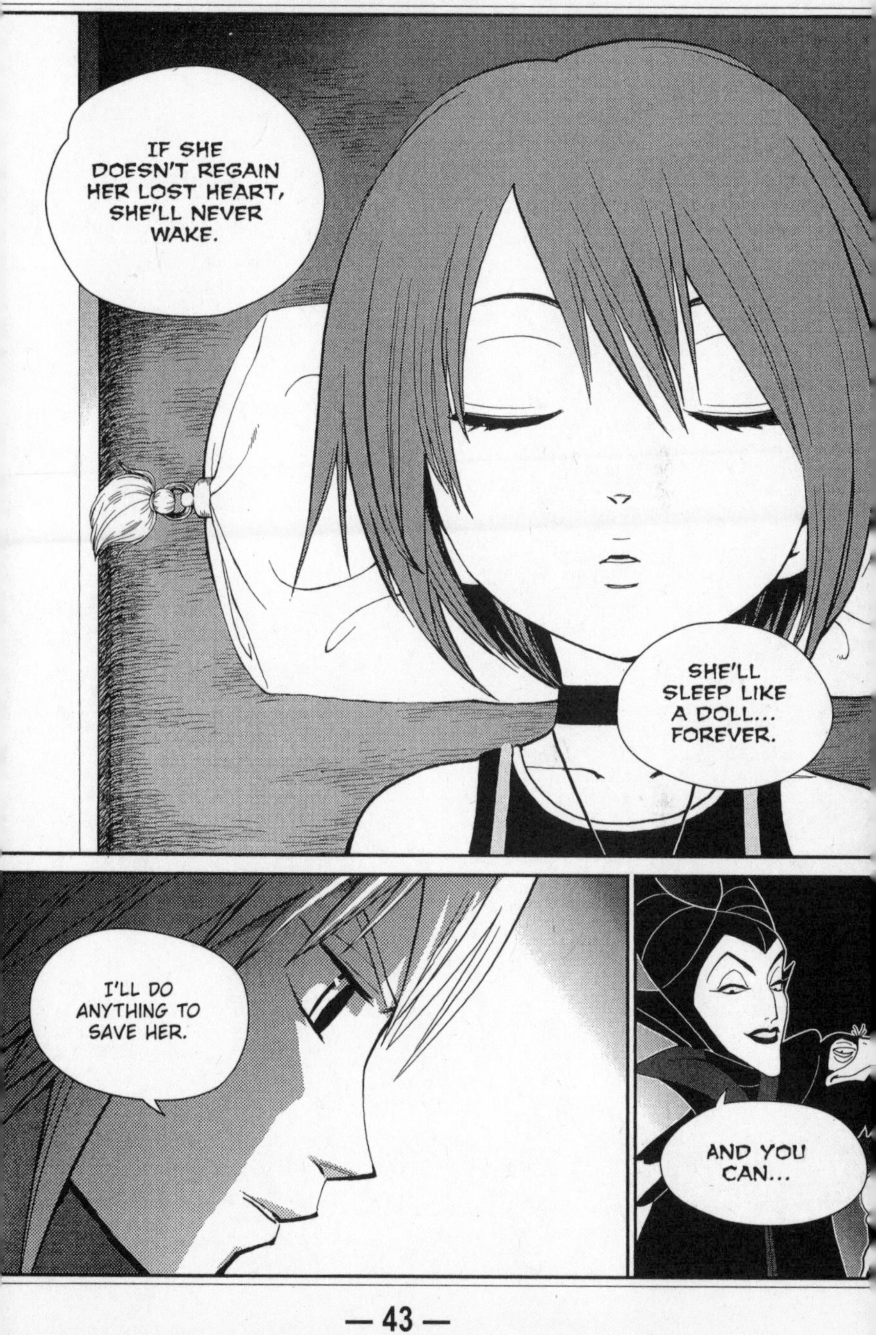
IF SHE DOESN'T REGAIN HER LOST HEART, SHE'LL NEVER WAKE.
SHE'LL SLEEP LIKE A DOLL... FOREVER.
I'LL DO ANYTHING TO SAVE HER.
AND YOU CAN...

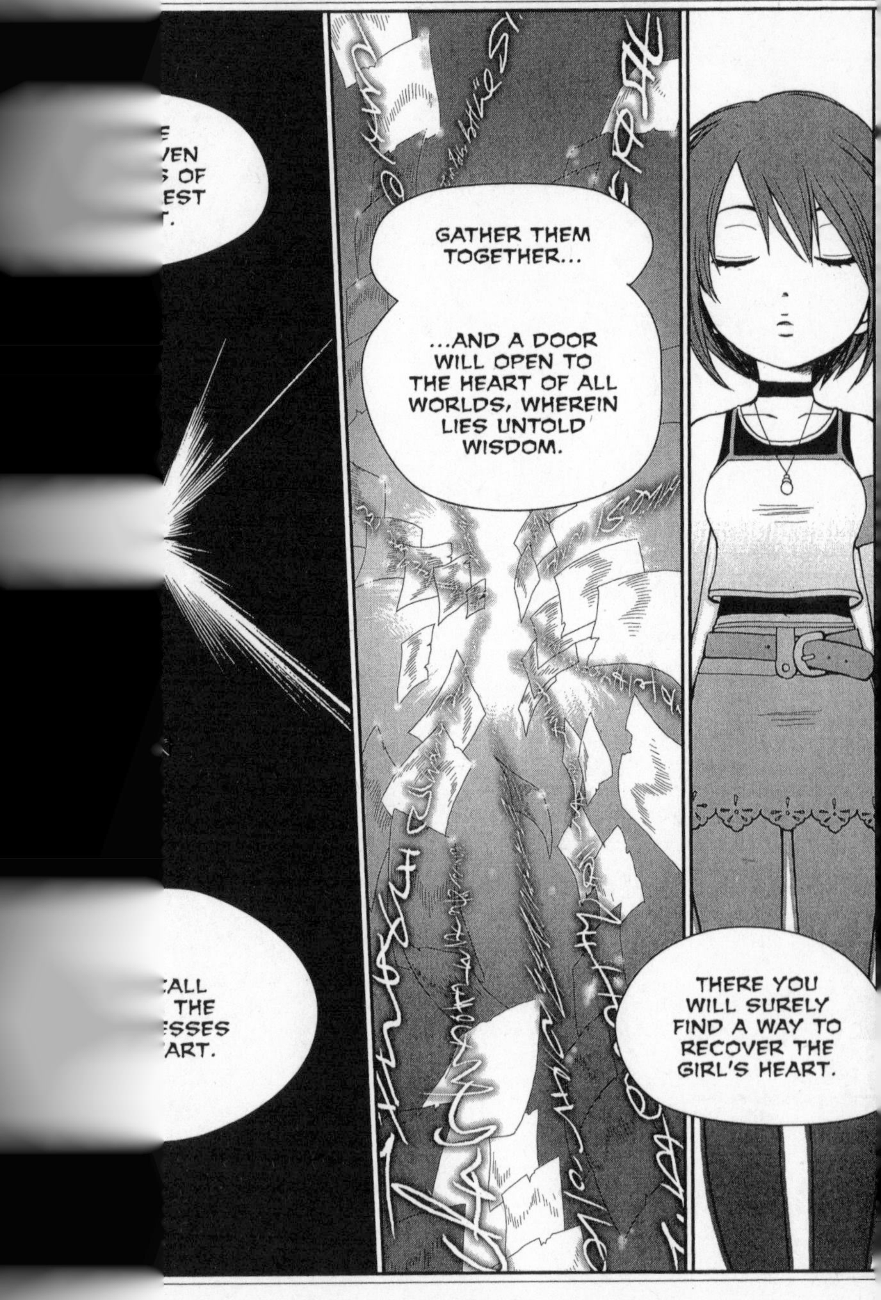
E VEN S OF EST T.
GATHER THEM TOGETHER...
...AND A DOOR WILL OPEN TO THE HEART OF ALL WORLDS, WHEREIN LIES UNTOLD WISDOM.
ALL THE ESSES ART.
THERE YOU WILL SURELY FIND A WAY TO RECOVER THE GIRL'S HEART.

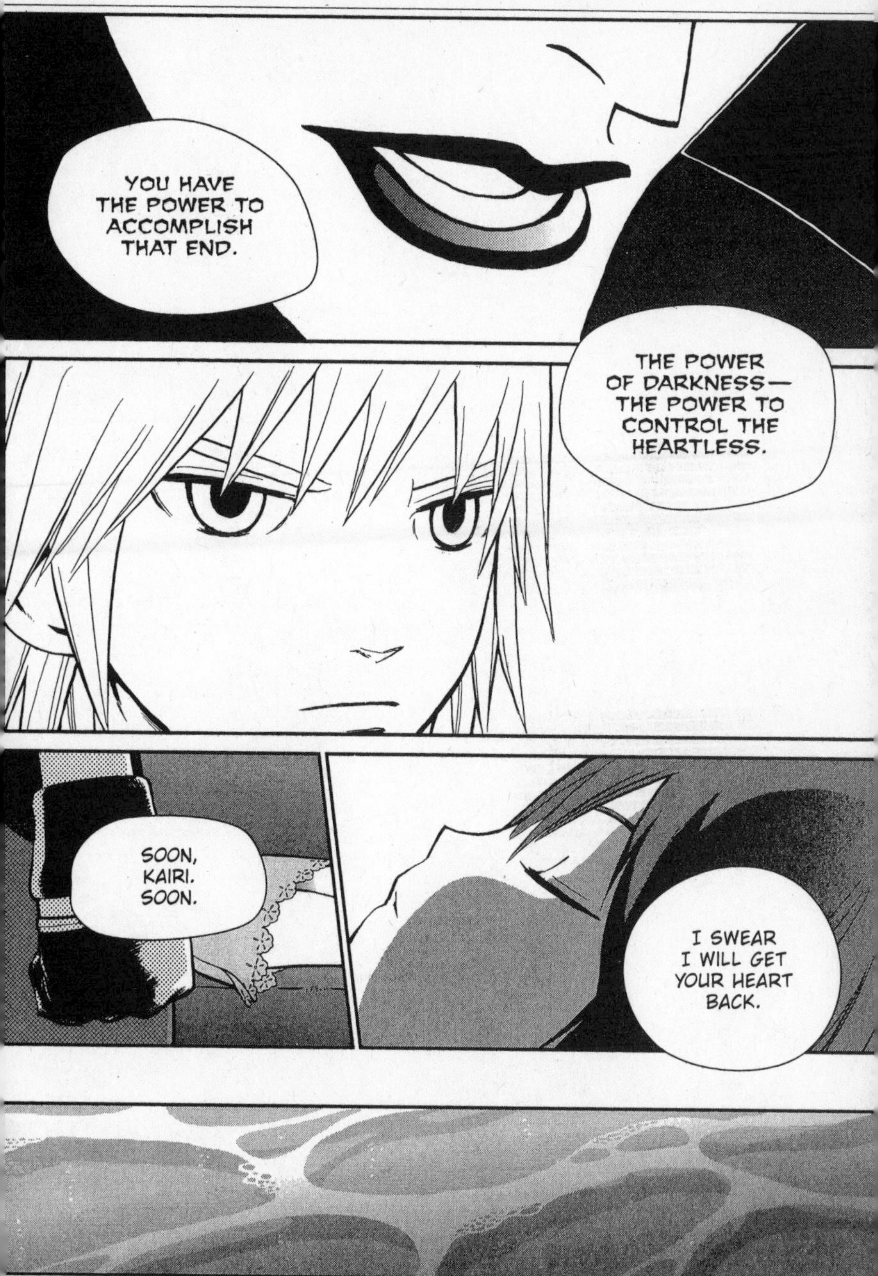
YOU HAVE THE POWER TO ACCOMPLISH THAT END.
THE POWER OF DARKNESS—THE POWER TO CONTROL THE HEARTLESS.
SOON, KAIRI. SOON.
I SWEAR I WILL GET YOUR HEART BACK.

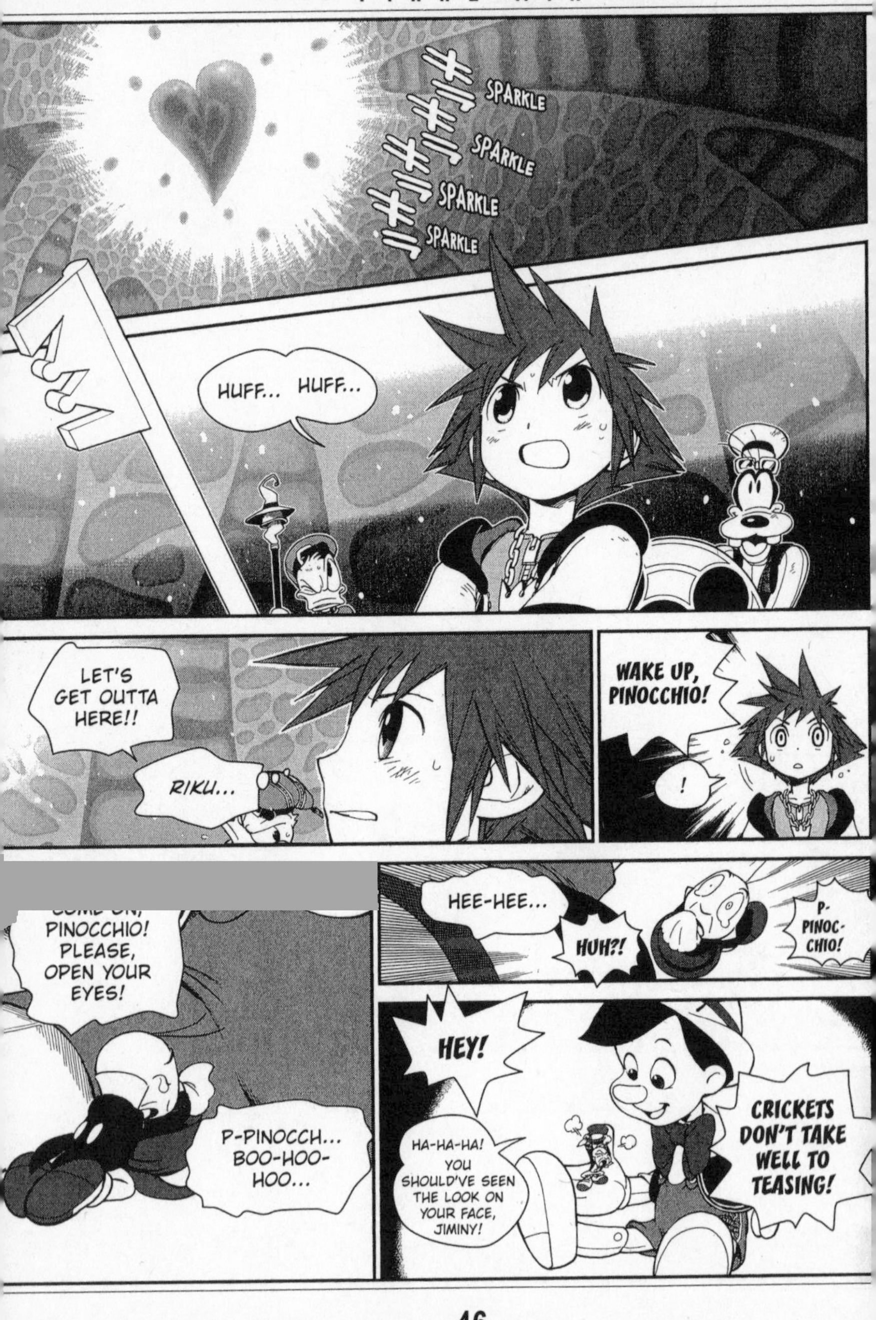
SPARKLE
SPARKLE
SPARKLE
SPARKLE
HUFF... HUFF...
LET'S GET OUTTA HERE!!
RIKU...
WAKE UP, PINOCCHIO!
!
PINOCCHIO! PLEASE, OPEN YOUR EYES!
P-PINOCCH... BOO-HOO-HOO...
HEE-HEE...
HUH?!
P-PINOC-CHIO!
HEY!
HA-HA-HA! YOU SHOULD'VE SEEN THE LOOK ON YOUR FACE, JIMINY!
CRICKETS DON'T TAKE WELL TO TEASING!

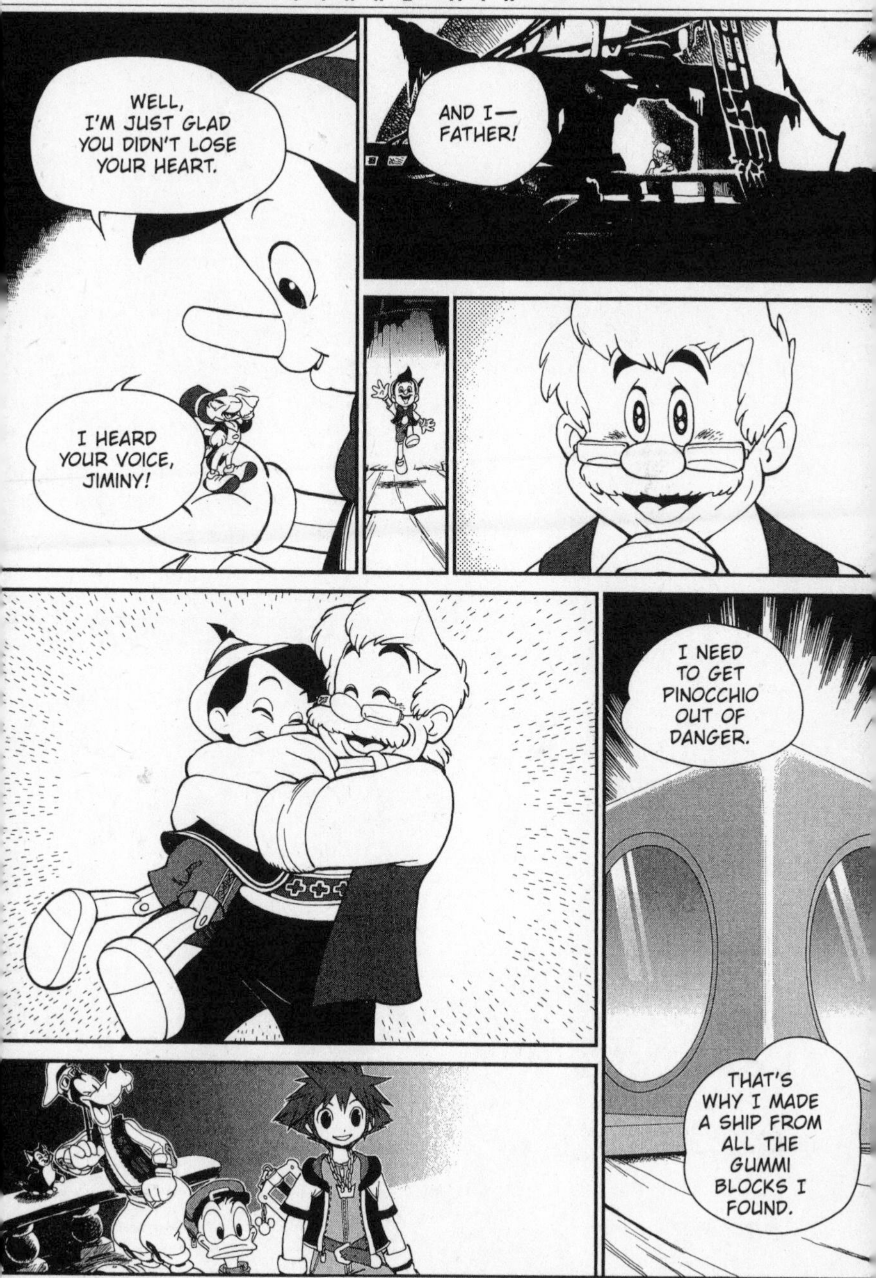
WELL, I'M JUST GLAD YOU DIDN'T LOSE YOUR HEART.
I HEARD YOUR VOICE, JIMINY!
AND I— FATHER!
I NEED TO GET PINOCCHIO OUT OF DANGER.
THAT'S WHY I MADE A SHIP FROM ALL THE GUMMI BLOCKS I FOUND.

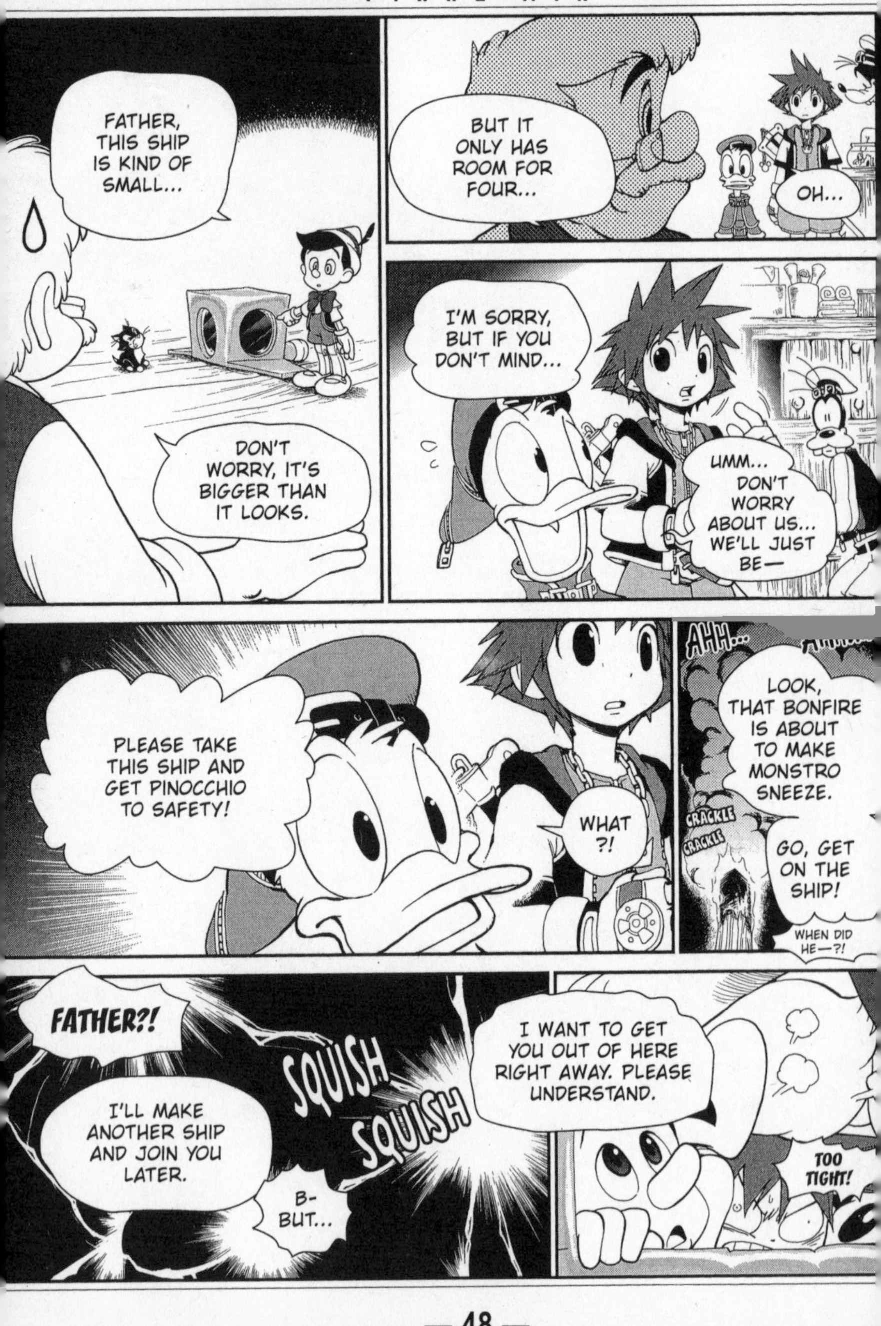
FATHER, THIS SHIP IS KIND OF SMALL...
DON'T WORRY, IT'S BIGGER THAN IT LOOKS.
BUT IT ONLY HAS ROOM FOR FOUR...
OH...
I'M SORRY, BUT IF YOU DON'T MIND...
UMM... DON'T WORRY ABOUT US... WE'LL JUST BE—
PLEASE TAKE THIS SHIP AND GET PINOCCHIO TO SAFETY!
WHAT ?!
AHH...
LOOK, THAT BONFIRE IS ABOUT TO MAKE MONSTRO SNEEZE.
CRACKLE
CRACKLE
GO, GET ON THE SHIP!
WHEN DID HE—?!
FATHER?!
I'LL MAKE ANOTHER SHIP AND JOIN YOU LATER.
B- BUT...
SQUISH
SQUISH
I WANT TO GET YOU OUT OF HERE RIGHT AWAY. PLEASE UNDERSTAND.
TOO TIGHT!

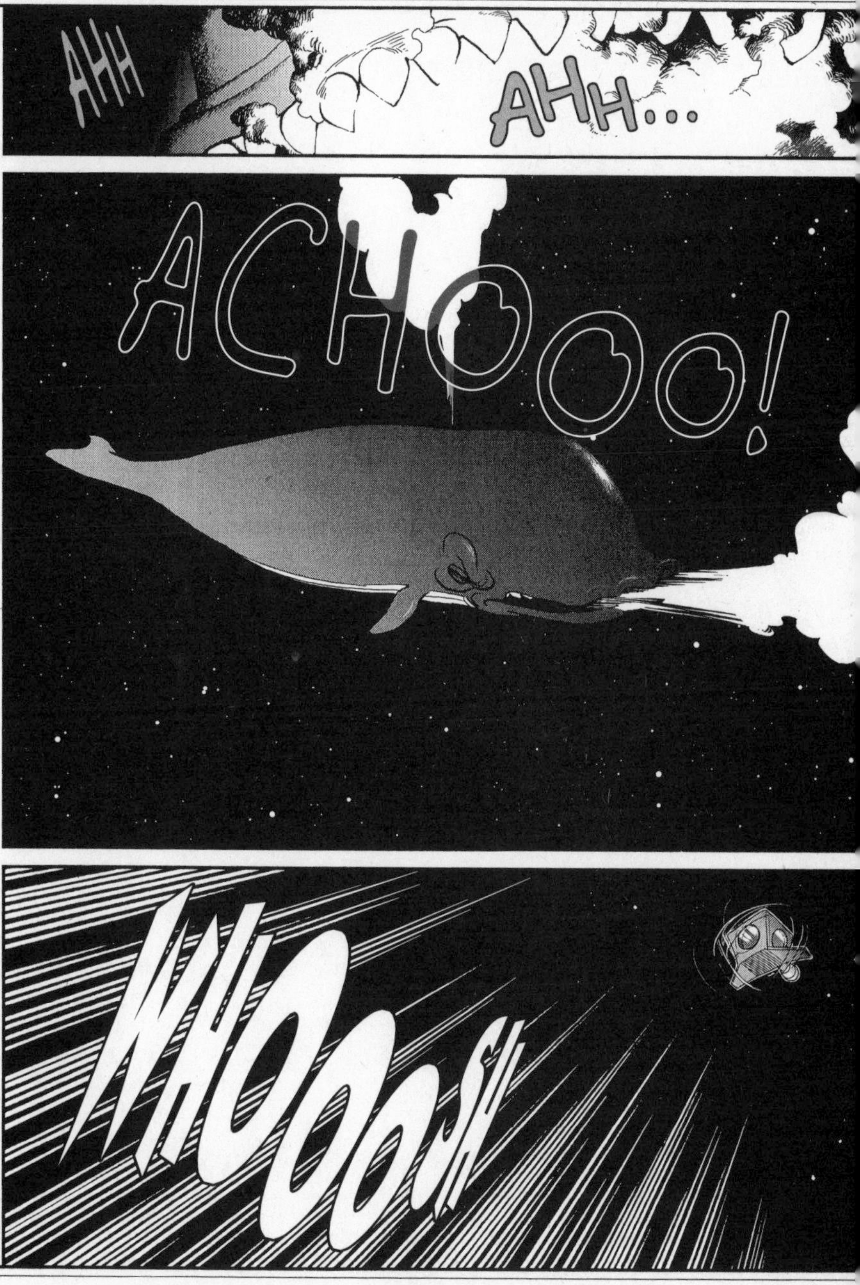
AHH
AHH...
ACHOOO!
WHOOOSH

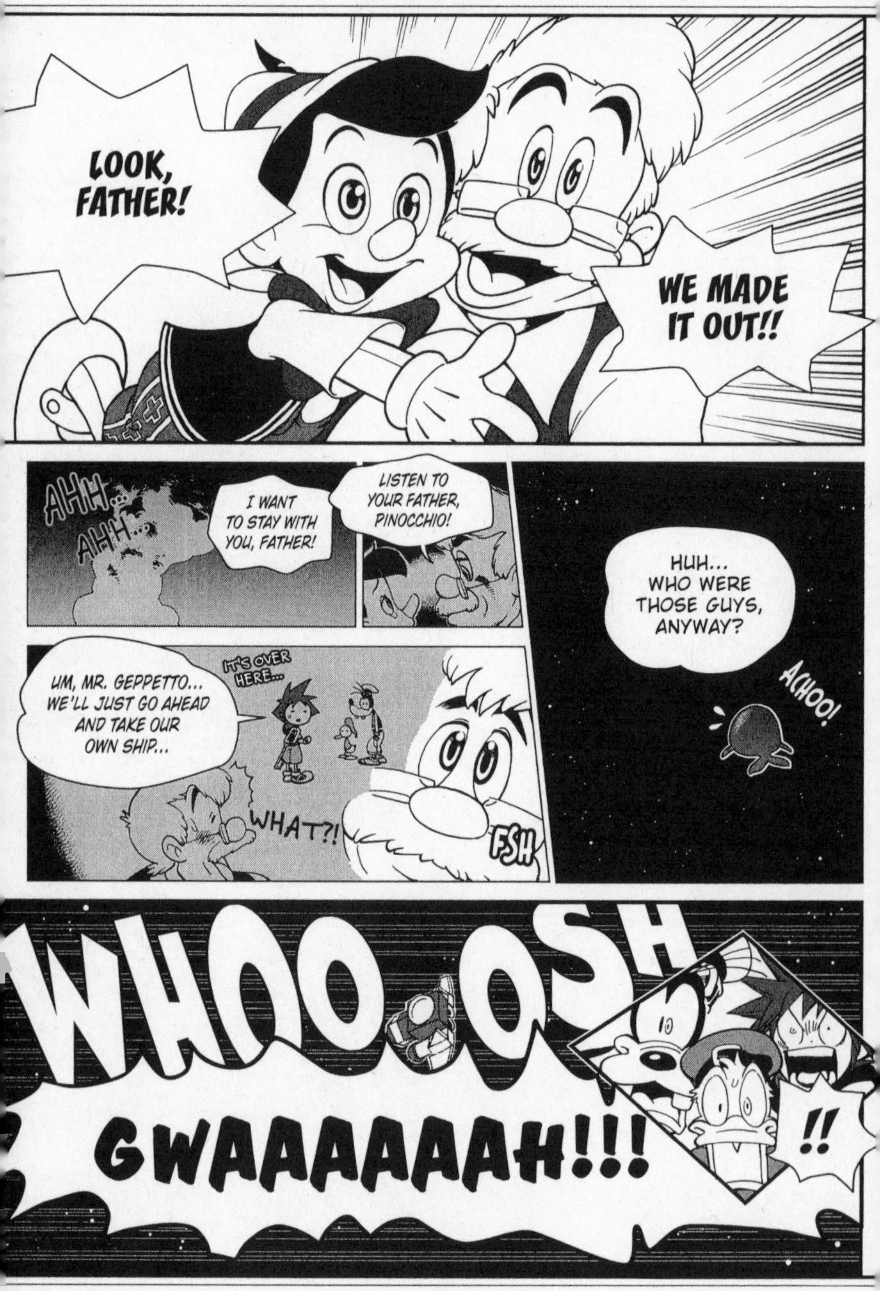
LOOK, FATHER!
WE MADE IT OUT!!
AHH...
AHH...
I WANT TO STAY WITH YOU, FATHER!
LISTEN TO YOUR FATHER, PINOCCHIO!
HUH... WHO WERE THOSE GUYS, ANYWAY?
UM, MR. GEPPETTO... WE'LL JUST GO AHEAD AND TAKE OUR OWN SHIP...
IT'S OVER HERE...
WHAT?!
FSH
ACHOO!
WHOOOSH
GWAAAAAAAH!!!
!!

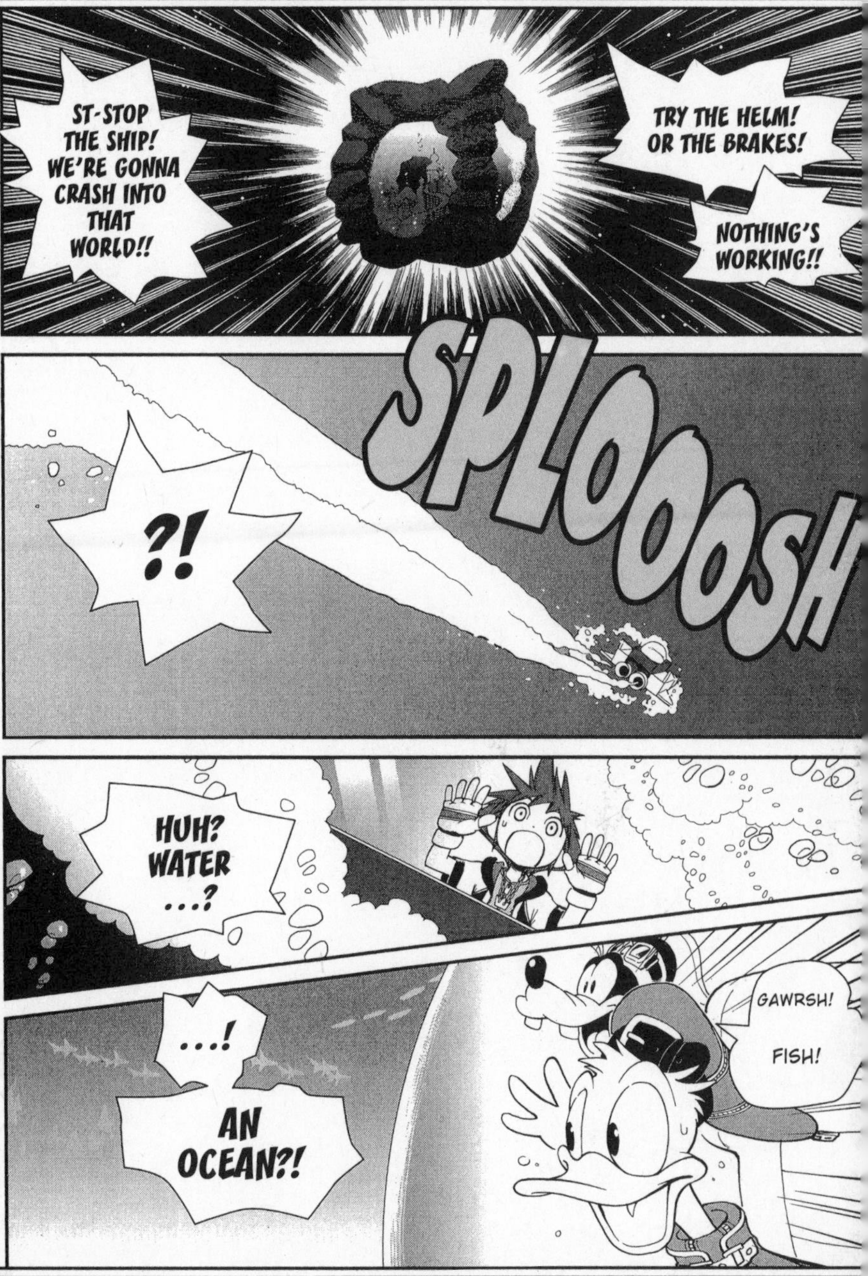
ST-STOP THE SHIP! WE'RE GONNA CRASH INTO THAT WORLD!!
TRY THE HELM! OR THE BRAKES!
NOTHING'S WORKING!!
?!
SPLOOOOSH
HUH? WATER ...?
...!
AN OCEAN?!
GAWRSH!
FISH!

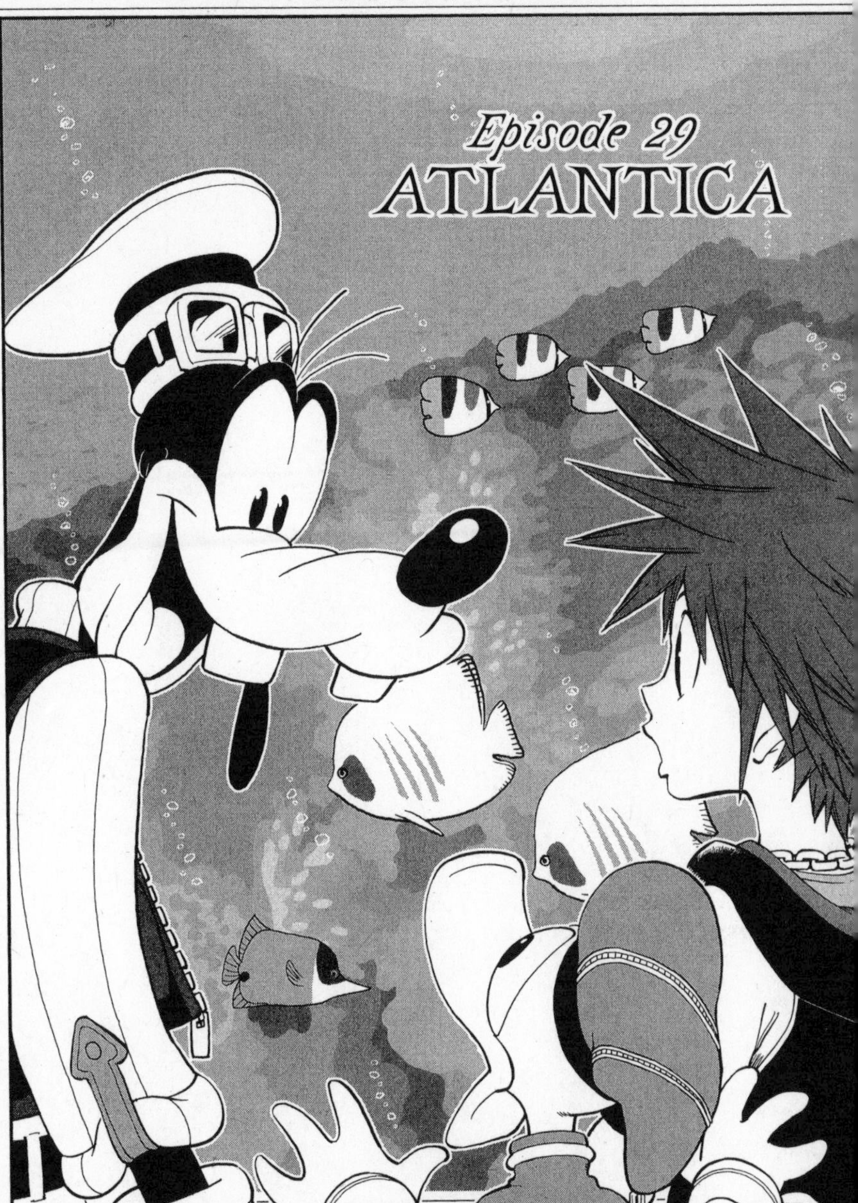
Episode 29
ATLANTICA

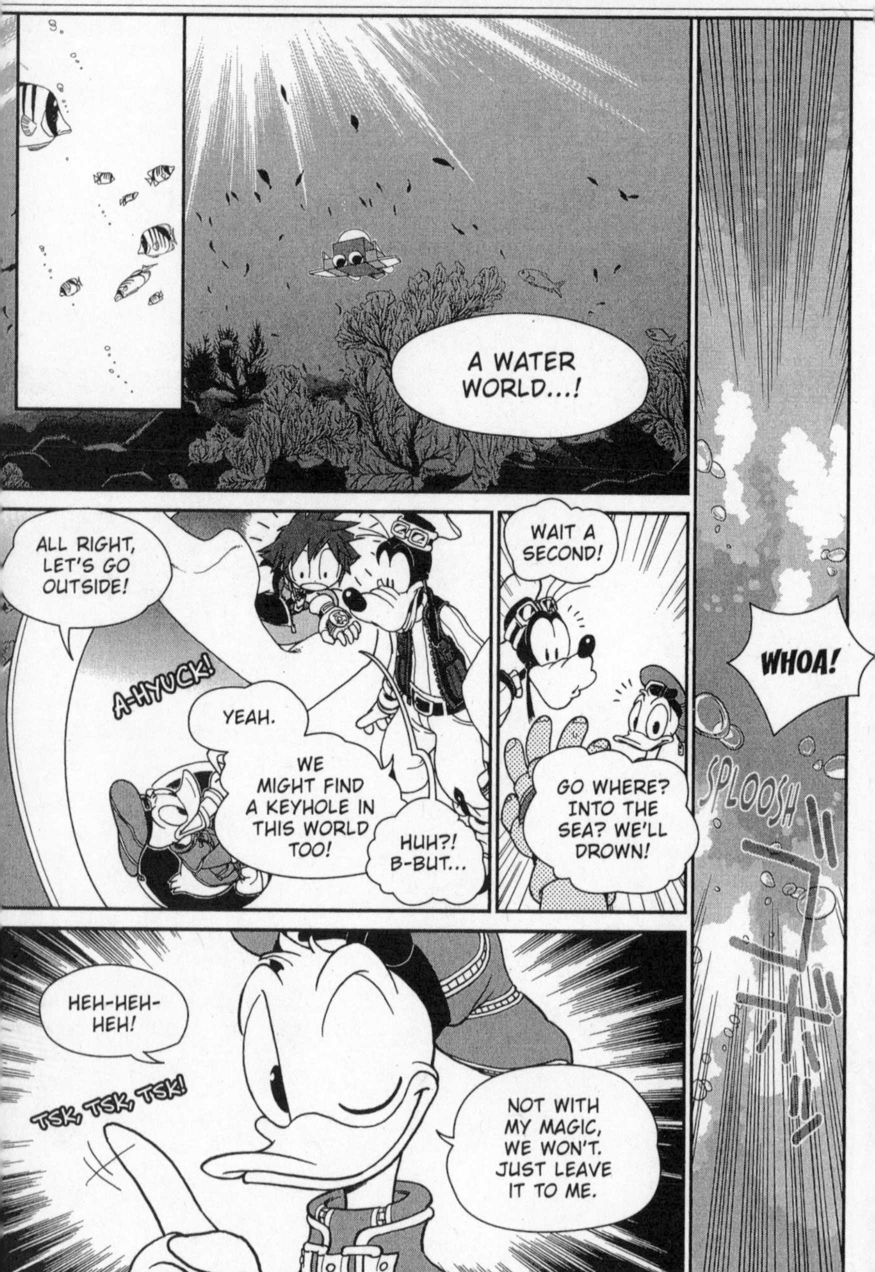
A WATER WORLD...!
ALL RIGHT, LET'S GO OUTSIDE!
A-HYUCK!
YEAH.
WE MIGHT FIND A KEYHOLE IN THIS WORLD TOO!
HUH?! B-BUT...
WAIT A SECOND!
GO WHERE? INTO THE SEA? WE'LL DROWN!
HEH-HEH-HEH!
TSK, TSK, TSK!
NOT WITH MY MAGIC, WE WON'T. JUST LEAVE IT TO ME.
WHOA!
SPLOOSH

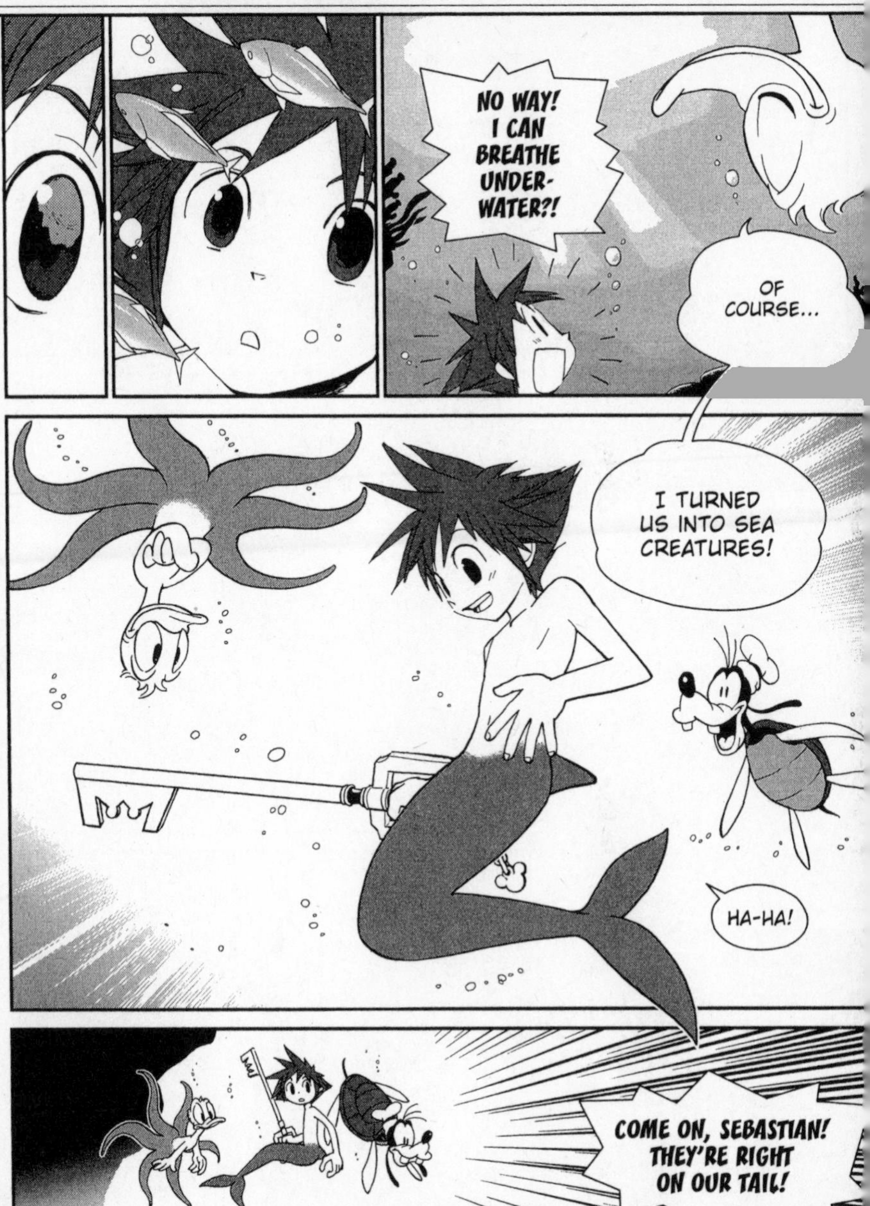
NO WAY! I CAN BREATHE UNDER-WATER?!
OF COURSE...
I TURNED US INTO SEA CREATURES!
HA-HA!
COME ON, SEBASTIAN! THEY'RE RIGHT ON OUR TAIL!

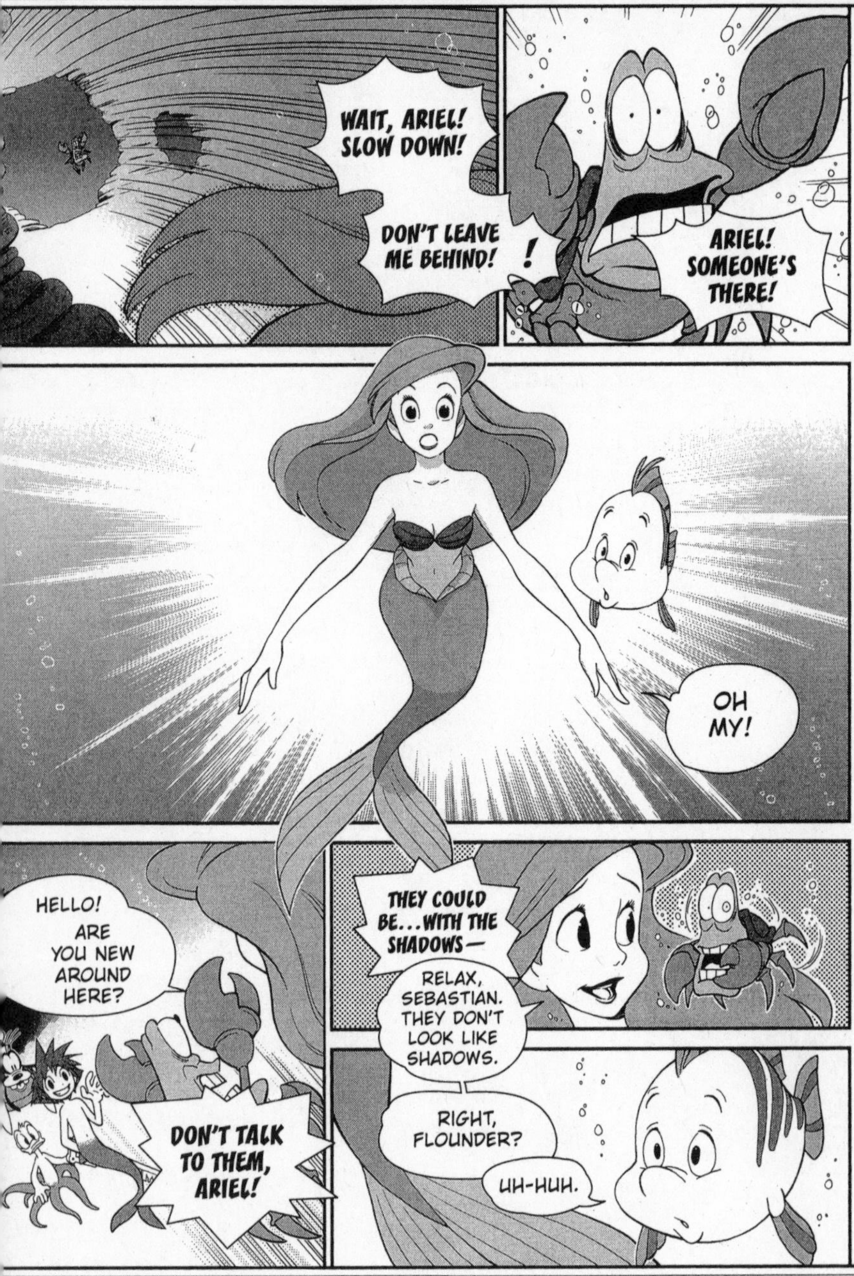
WAIT, ARIEL! SLOW DOWN!
DON'T LEAVE ME BEHIND!
!
ARIEL! SOMEONE'S THERE!
OH MY!
HELLO! ARE YOU NEW AROUND HERE?
DON'T TALK TO THEM, ARIEL!
THEY COULD BE...WITH THE SHADOWS—
RELAX, SEBASTIAN. THEY DON'T LOOK LIKE SHADOWS.
RIGHT, FLOUNDER?
UH-HUH.

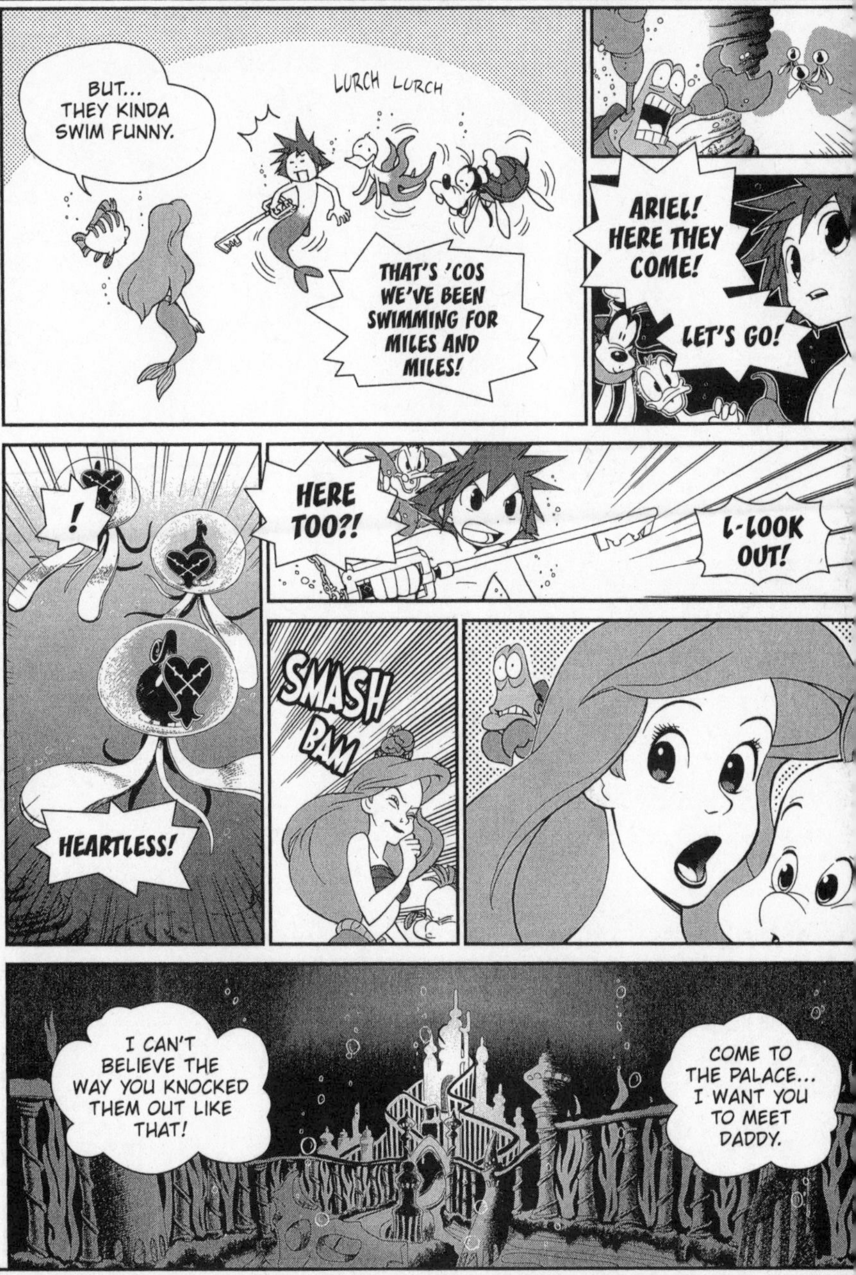
BUT... THEY KINDA SWIM FUNNY.
LURCH LURCH
THAT'S 'COS WE'VE BEEN SWIMMING FOR MILES AND MILES!
ARIEL! HERE THEY COME!
LET'S GO!
!
HEARTLESS!
HERE TOO?!
L-LOOK OUT!
SMASH
BAM
I CAN'T BELIEVE THE WAY YOU KNOCKED THEM OUT LIKE THAT!
COME TO THE PALACE... I WANT YOU TO MEET DADDY.

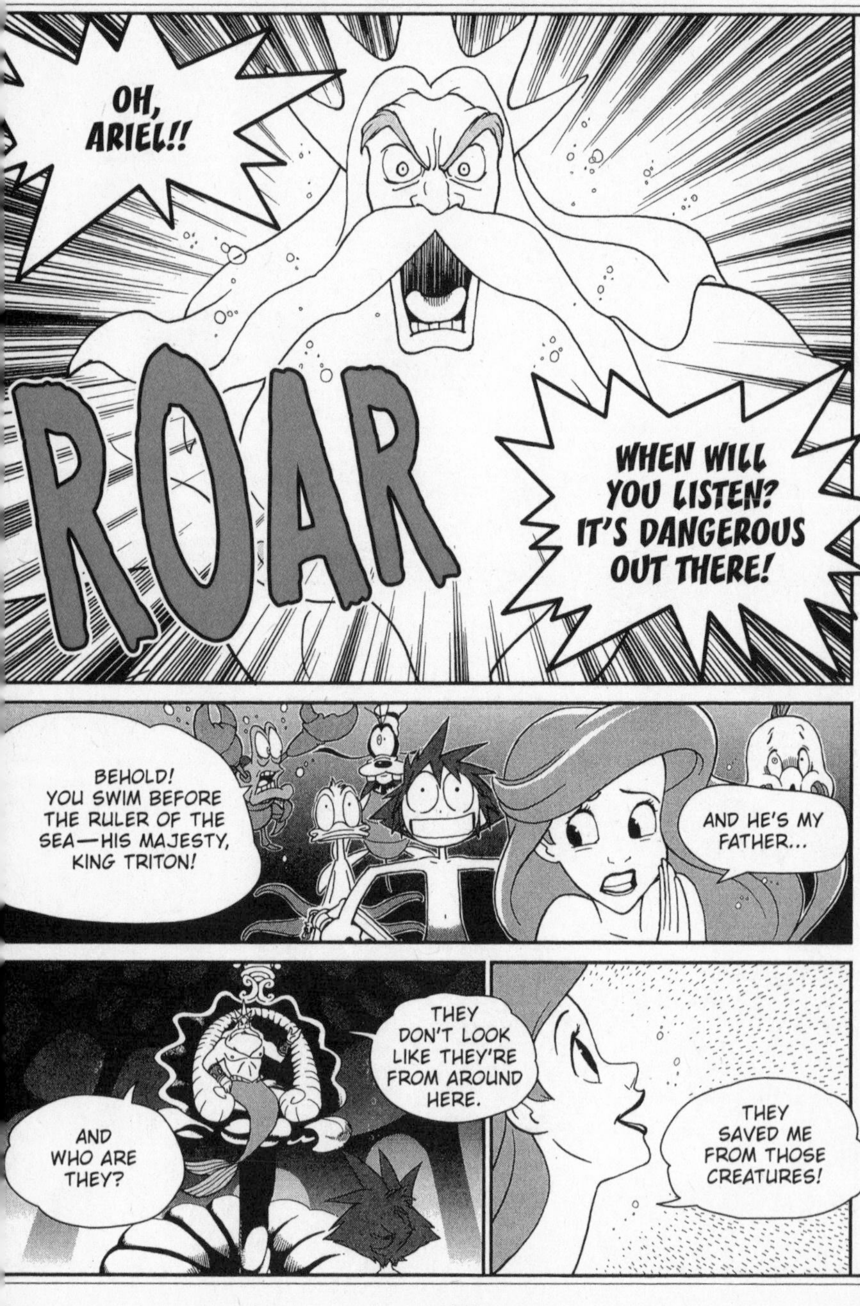
OH, ARIEL!!
ROAR
WHEN WILL YOU LISTEN? IT'S DANGEROUS OUT THERE!
BEHOLD! YOU SWIM BEFORE THE RULER OF THE SEA—HIS MAJESTY, KING TRITON!
AND HE'S MY FATHER...
AND WHO ARE THEY?
THEY DON'T LOOK LIKE THEY'RE FROM AROUND HERE.
THEY SAVED ME FROM THOSE CREATURES!

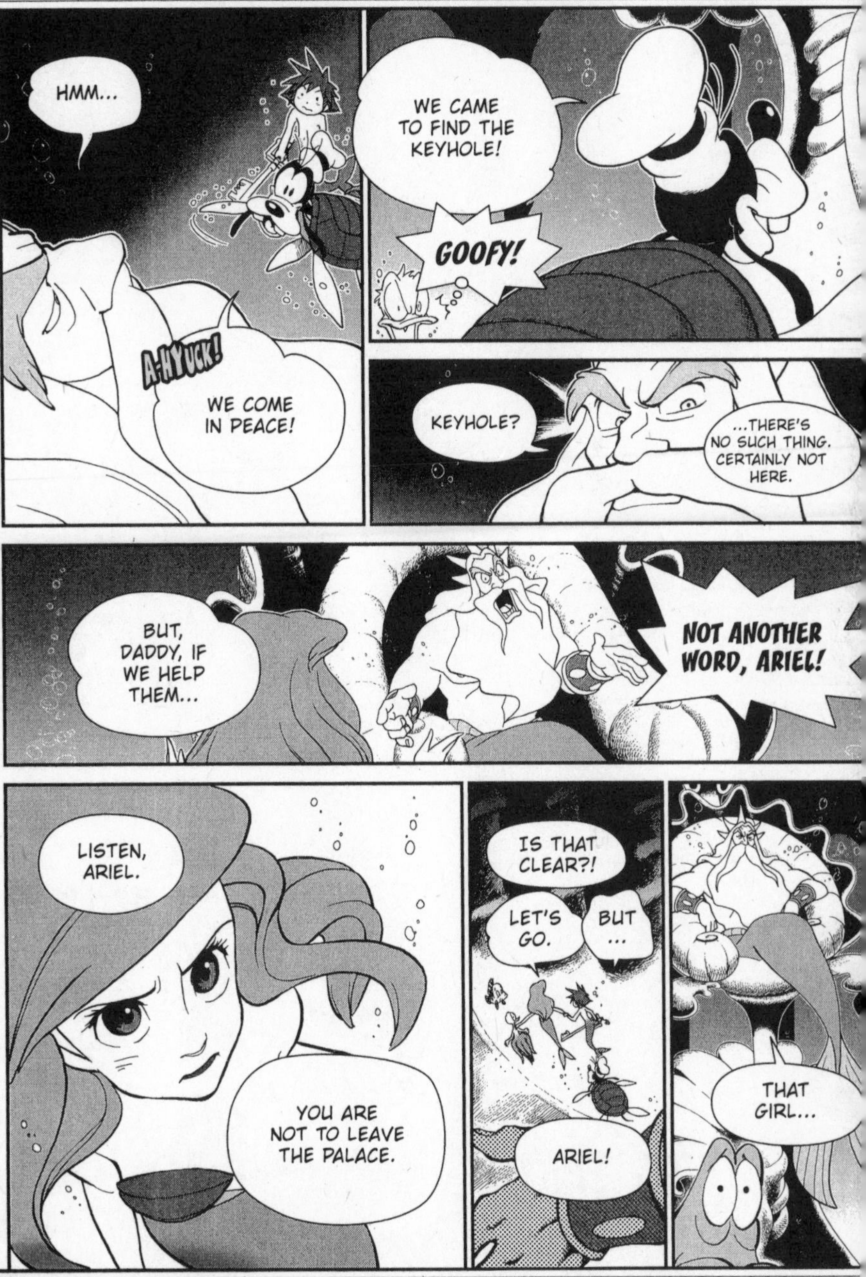
HMM...
A-HYUCK!
WE COME IN PEACE!
WE CAME TO FIND THE KEYHOLE!
GOOFY!
KEYHOLE?
...THERE'S NO SUCH THING. CERTAINLY NOT HERE.
BUT, DADDY, IF WE HELP THEM...
NOT ANOTHER WORD, ARIEL!
LISTEN, ARIEL.
YOU ARE NOT TO LEAVE THE PALACE.
IS THAT CLEAR?!
LET'S GO.
BUT ...
ARIEL!
THAT GIRL...

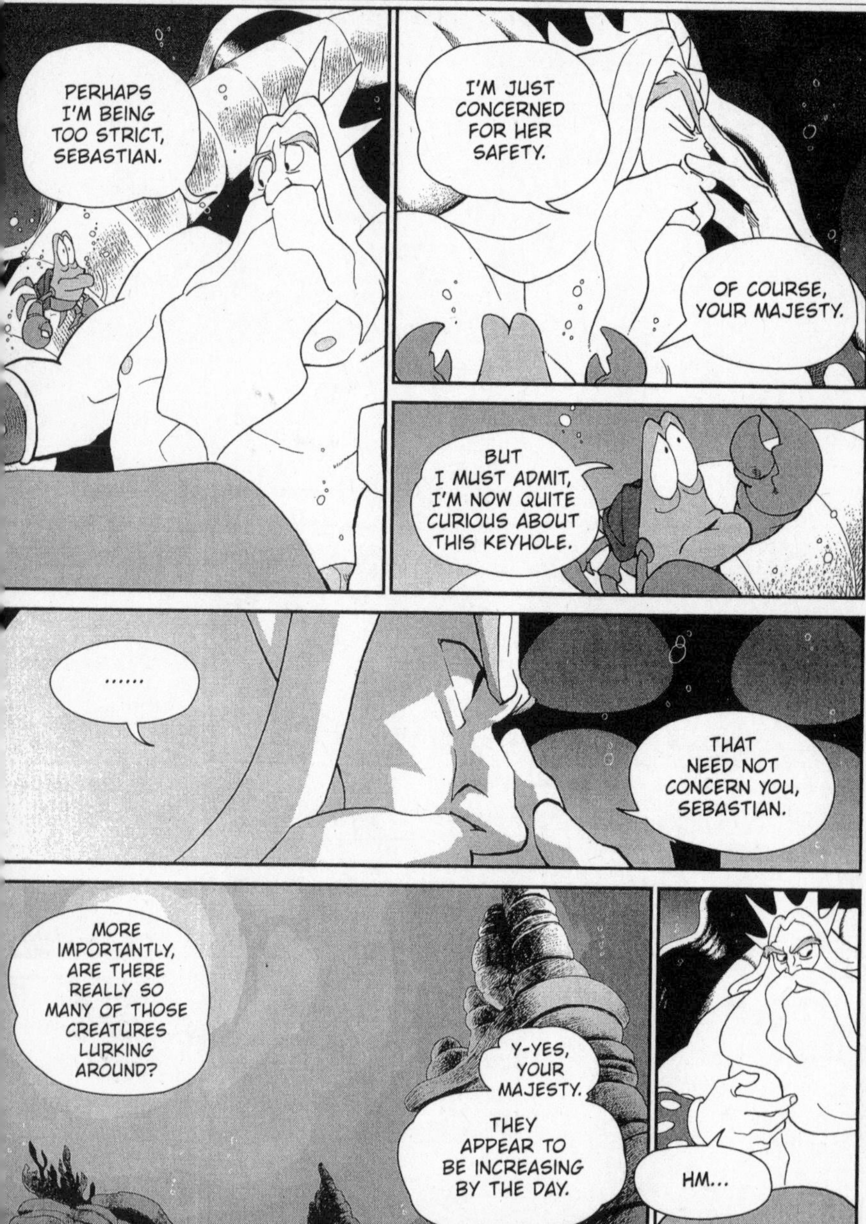
PERHAPS I'M BEING TOO STRICT, SEBASTIAN.
I'M JUST CONCERNED FOR HER SAFETY.
OF COURSE, YOUR MAJESTY.
BUT I MUST ADMIT, I'M NOW QUITE CURIOUS ABOUT THIS KEYHOLE.
......
THAT NEED NOT CONCERN YOU, SEBASTIAN.
MORE IMPORTANTLY, ARE THERE REALLY SO MANY OF THOSE CREATURES LURKING AROUND?
Y-YES, YOUR MAJESTY.
THEY APPEAR TO BE INCREASING BY THE DAY.
HM...

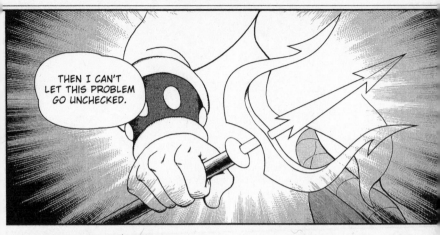

THEN I CAN'T LET THIS PROBLEM GO UNCHECKED.

MY FATHER IS SO STUBBORN!

HEY, WHY DON'T WE TRY LOOKING FOR THAT KEYHOLE YOU WERE TALKING ABOUT?

BUT YOUR FATHER SAID—

IT DOESN'T MATTER!

SOMEDAY, I'M GOING TO SEE WHAT'S OUT THERE. I WANT TO SEE MORE OF THE WORLD.

MY FATHER JUST... JUST DOESN'T UNDERSTAND.

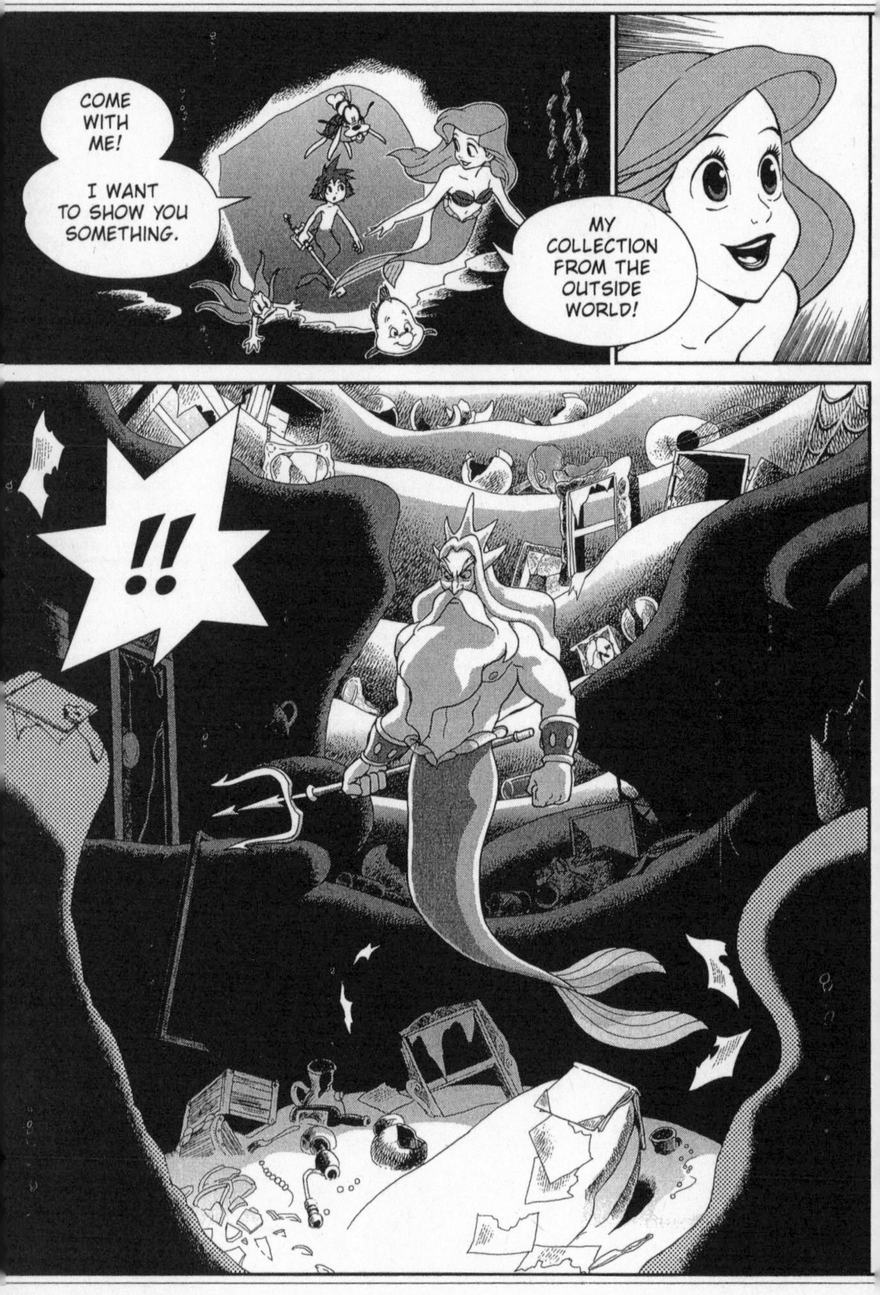
COME WITH ME!
I WANT TO SHOW YOU SOMETHING.
MY COLLECTION FROM THE OUTSIDE WORLD!
!!

......

DADDY?

ARIEL...

....!

I TOLD YOU NOT TO LEAVE THE PALACE!

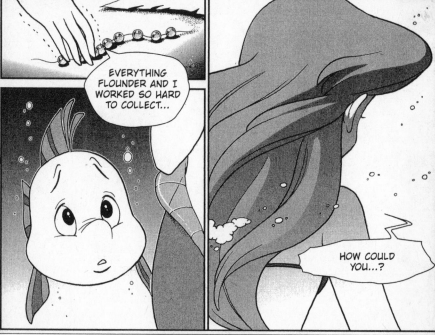

EVERYTHING FLOUNDER AND I WORKED SO HARD TO COLLECT...

HOW COULD YOU...?

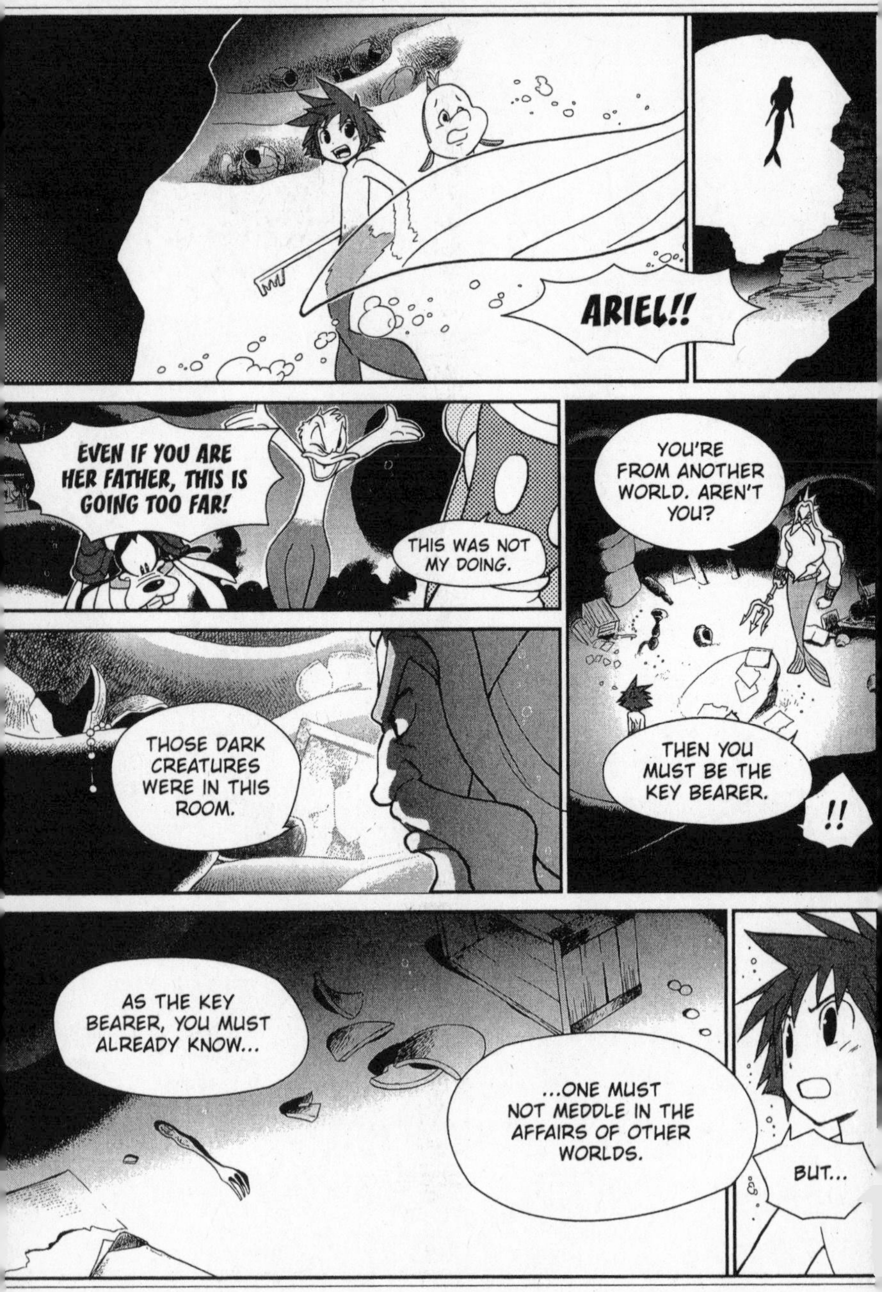
ARIEL!!
EVEN IF YOU ARE HER FATHER, THIS IS GOING TOO FAR!
THIS WAS NOT MY DOING.
YOU'RE FROM ANOTHER WORLD. AREN'T YOU?
THOSE DARK CREATURES WERE IN THIS ROOM.
THEN YOU MUST BE THE KEY BEARER.
!!
AS THE KEY BEARER, YOU MUST ALREADY KNOW...
...ONE MUST NOT MEDDLE IN THE AFFAIRS OF OTHER WORLDS.
BUT...

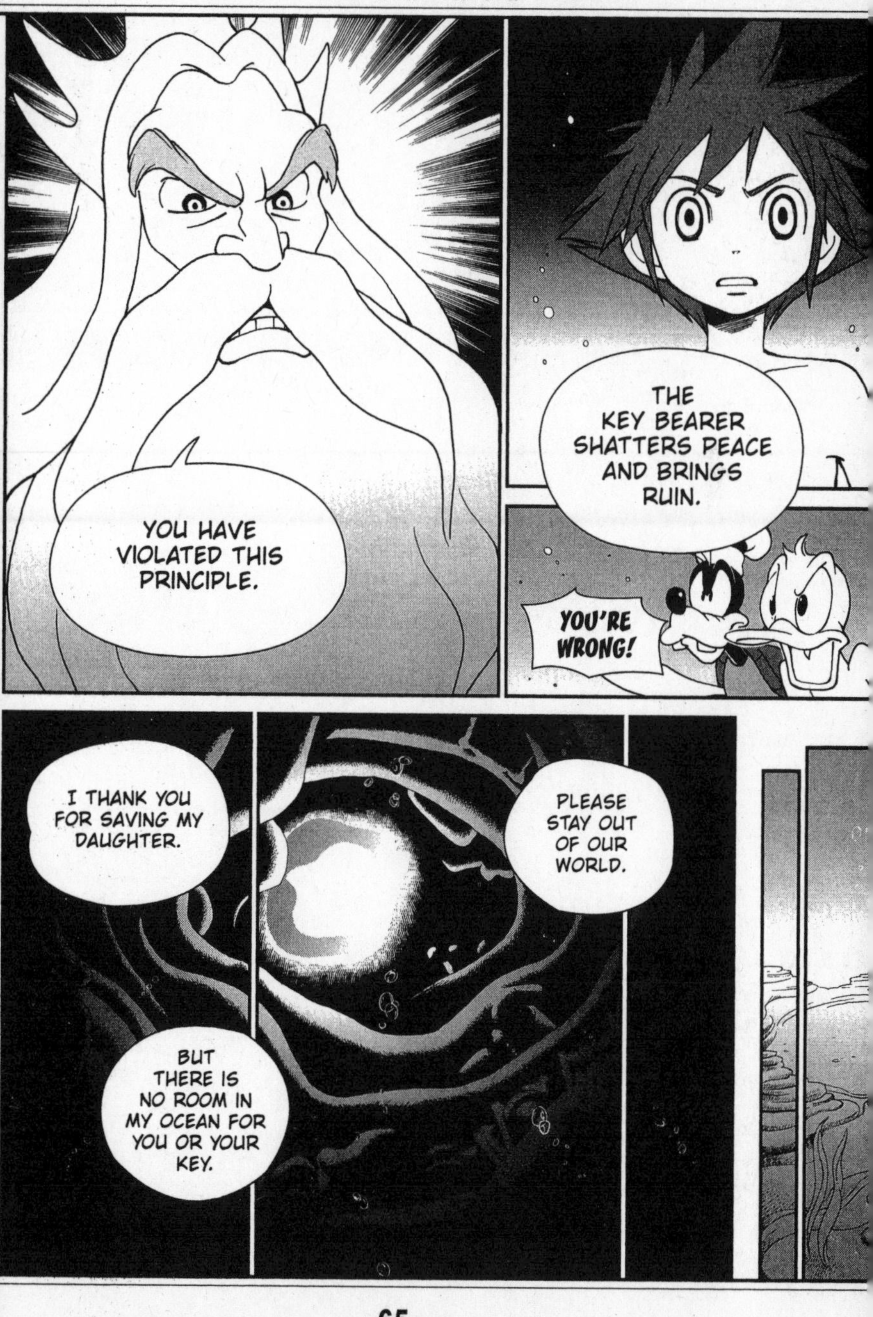
YOU HAVE VIOLATED THIS PRINCIPLE.
THE KEY BEARER SHATTERS PEACE AND BRINGS RUIN.
YOU'RE WRONG!
I THANK YOU FOR SAVING MY DAUGHTER.
BUT THERE IS NO ROOM IN MY OCEAN FOR YOU OR YOUR KEY.
PLEASE STAY OUT OF OUR WORLD.

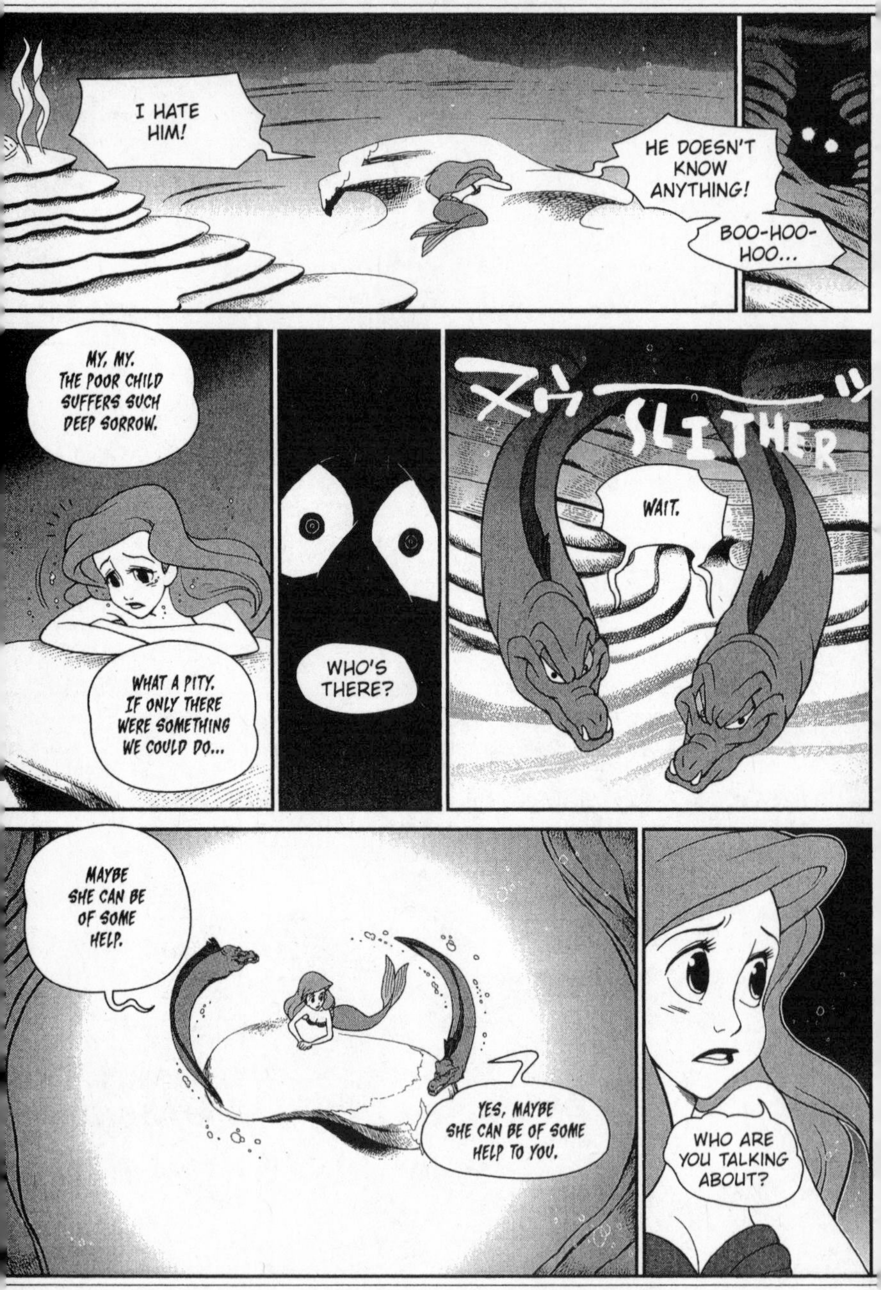
I HATE HIM!
HE DOESN'T KNOW ANYTHING!
BOO-HOO-HOO...
MY, MY. THE POOR CHILD SUFFERS SUCH DEEP SORROW.
WHAT A PITY. IF ONLY THERE WERE SOMETHING WE COULD DO...
WHO'S THERE?
SLITHER
WAIT.
MAYBE SHE CAN BE OF SOME HELP.
YES, MAYBE SHE CAN BE OF SOME HELP TO YOU.
WHO ARE YOU TALKING ABOUT?

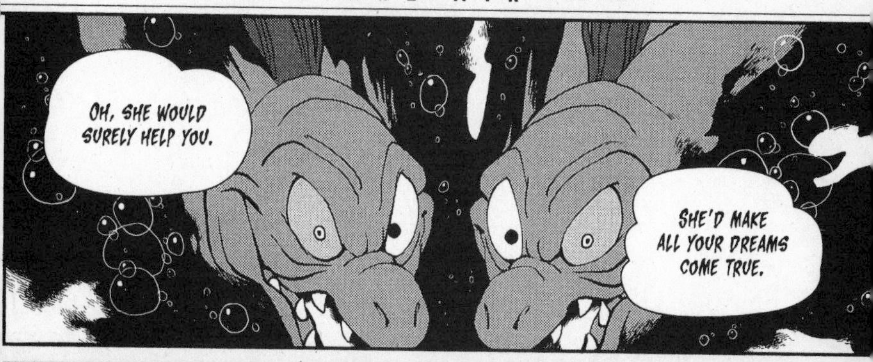
OH, SHE WOULD SURELY HELP YOU.
SHE'D MAKE ALL YOUR DREAMS COME TRUE.

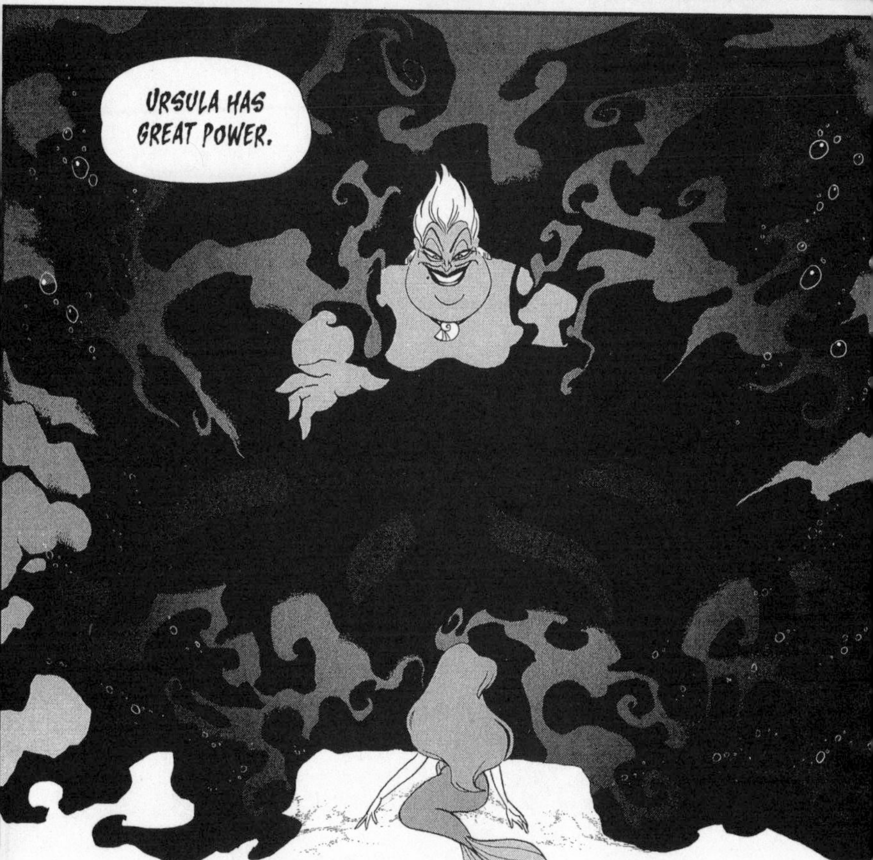
URSULA HAS GREAT POWER.

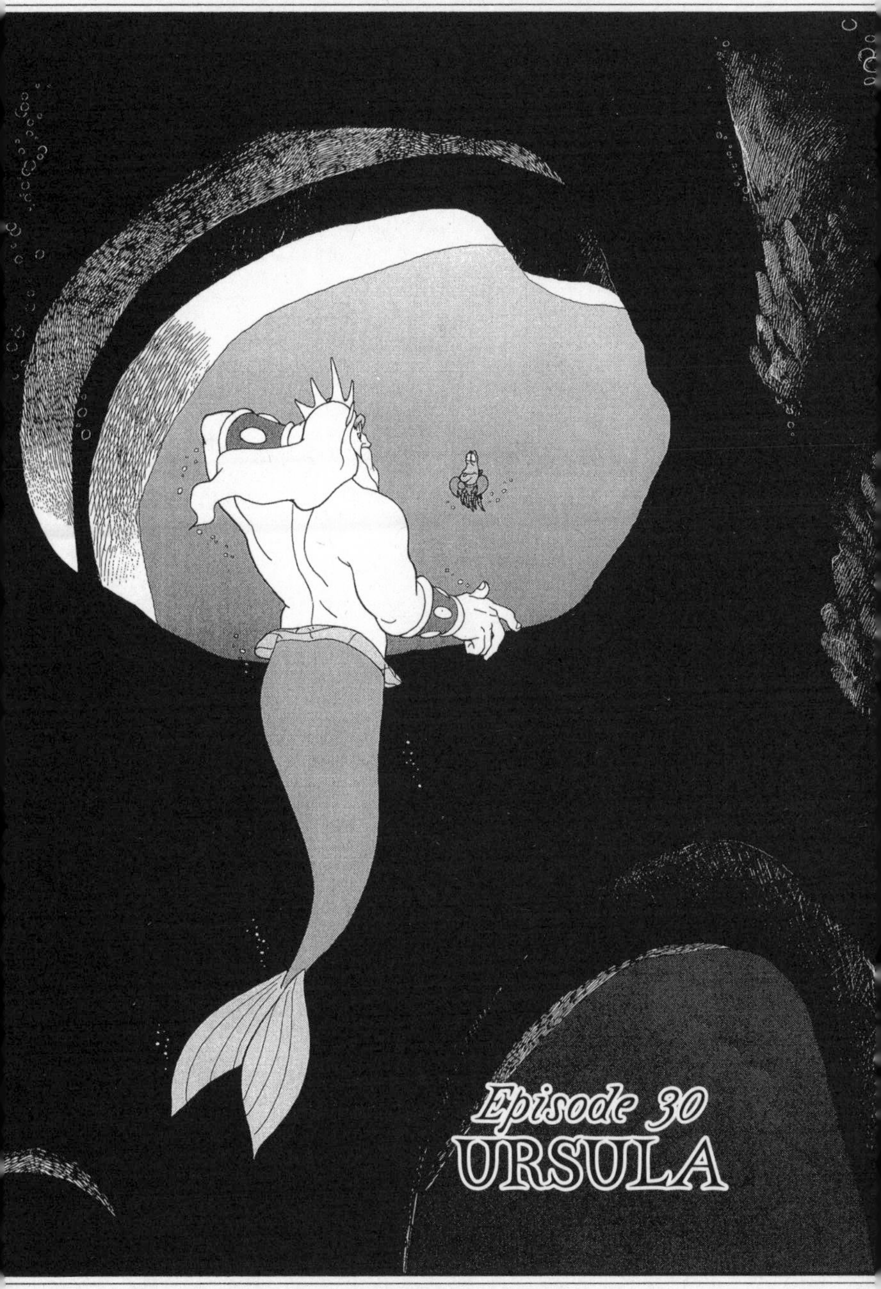
Episode 30
URSULA

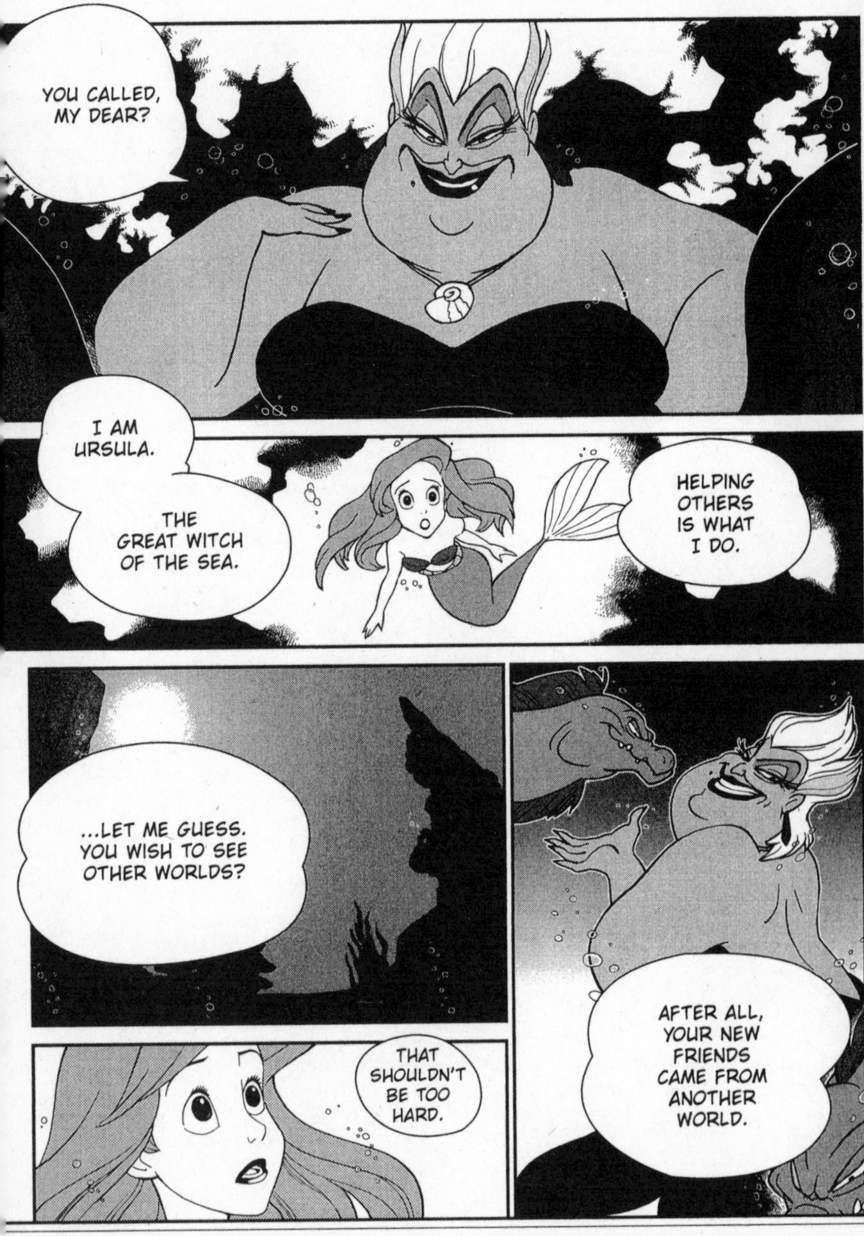
YOU CALLED, MY DEAR?
I AM URSULA.
THE GREAT WITCH OF THE SEA.
HELPING OTHERS IS WHAT I DO.
...LET ME GUESS. YOU WISH TO SEE OTHER WORLDS?
THAT SHOULDN'T BE TOO HARD.
AFTER ALL, YOUR NEW FRIENDS CAME FROM ANOTHER WORLD.

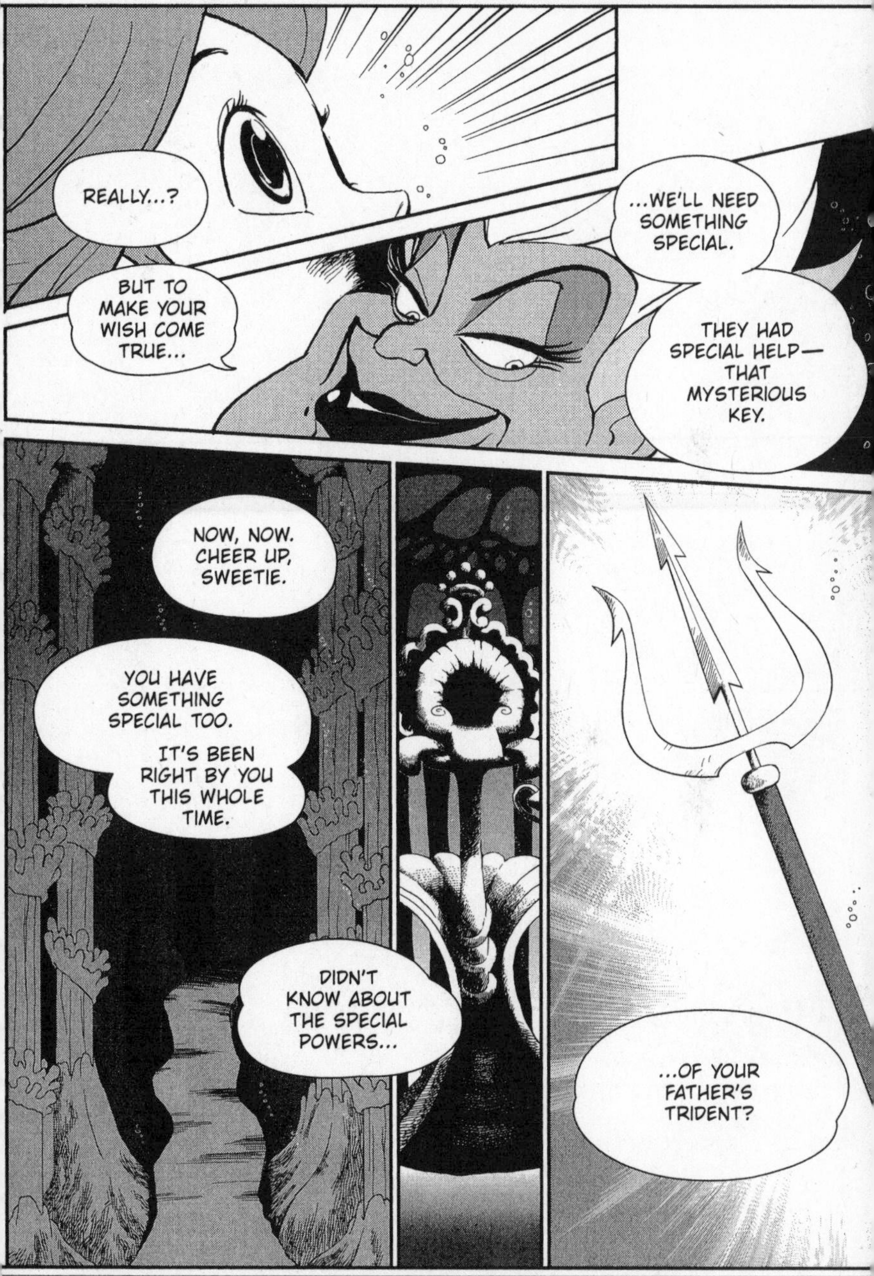
REALLY...?
BUT TO MAKE YOUR WISH COME TRUE...
...WE'LL NEED SOMETHING SPECIAL.
THEY HAD SPECIAL HELP—THAT MYSTERIOUS KEY.
NOW, NOW. CHEER UP, SWEETIE.
YOU HAVE SOMETHING SPECIAL TOO.
IT'S BEEN RIGHT BY YOU THIS WHOLE TIME.
DIDN'T KNOW ABOUT THE SPECIAL POWERS...
...OF YOUR FATHER'S TRIDENT?

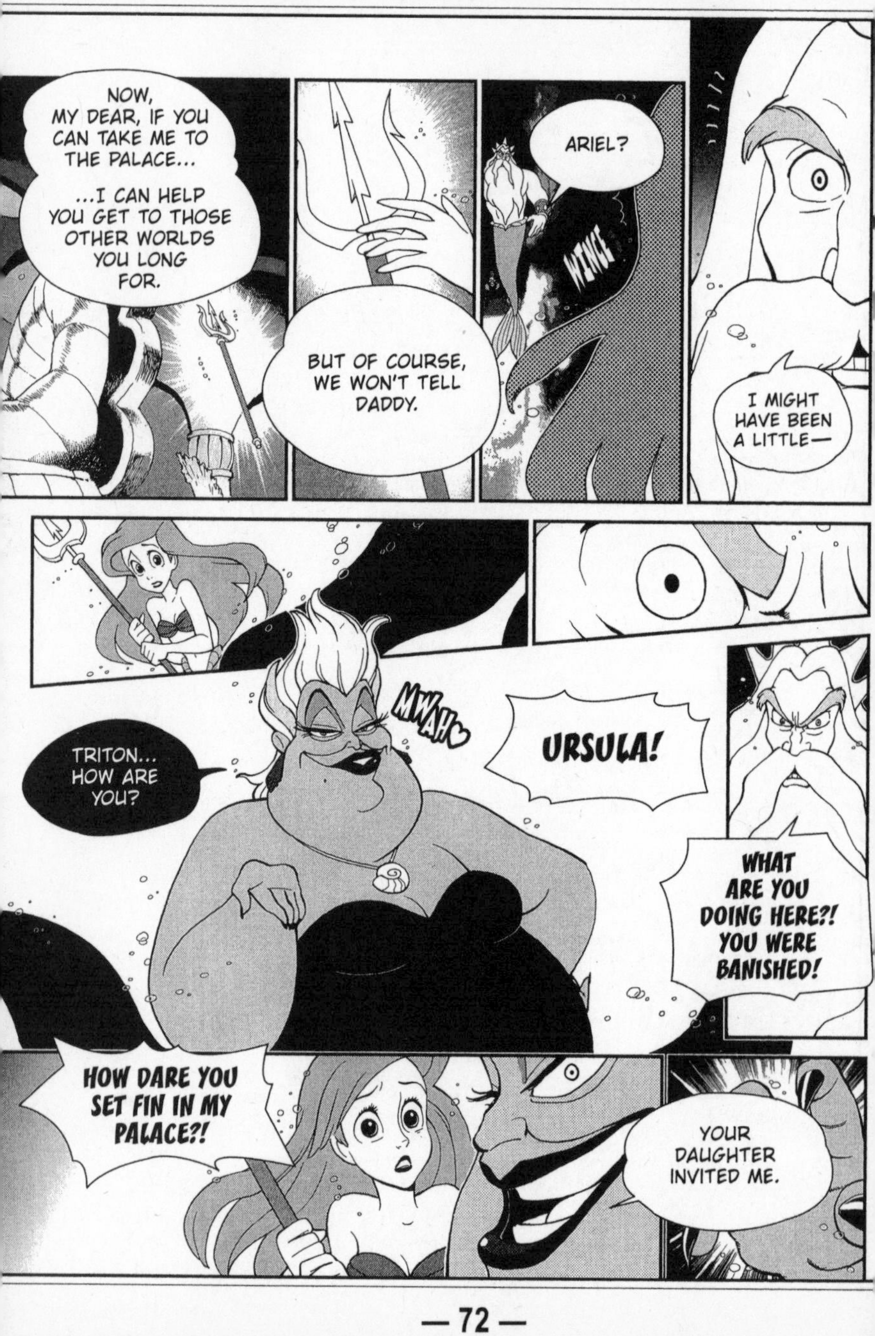
NOW, MY DEAR, IF YOU CAN TAKE ME TO THE PALACE...
...I CAN HELP YOU GET TO THOSE OTHER WORLDS YOU LONG FOR.
BUT OF COURSE, WE WON'T TELL DADDY.
ARIEL?
WINCE
I MIGHT HAVE BEEN A LITTLE—
TRITON... HOW ARE YOU?
MWAH♥
URSULA!
WHAT ARE YOU DOING HERE?! YOU WERE BANISHED!
HOW DARE YOU SET FIN IN MY PALACE?!
YOUR DAUGHTER INVITED ME.

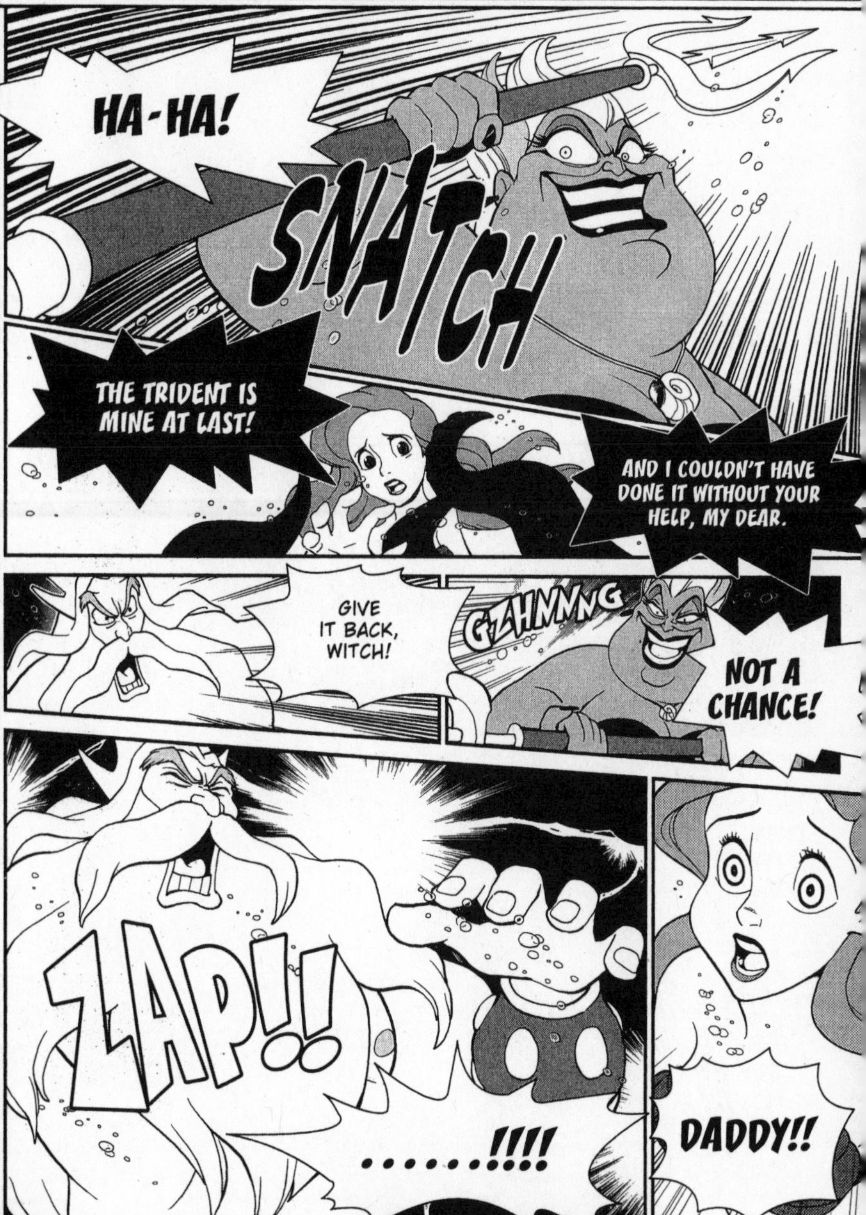
HA-HA!
SNATCH
THE TRIDENT IS MINE AT LAST!
AND I COULDN'T HAVE DONE IT WITHOUT YOUR HELP, MY DEAR.
GIVE IT BACK, WITCH!
GZHNNNG
NOT A CHANCE!
ZAP!!
.......!!!!
DADDY!!

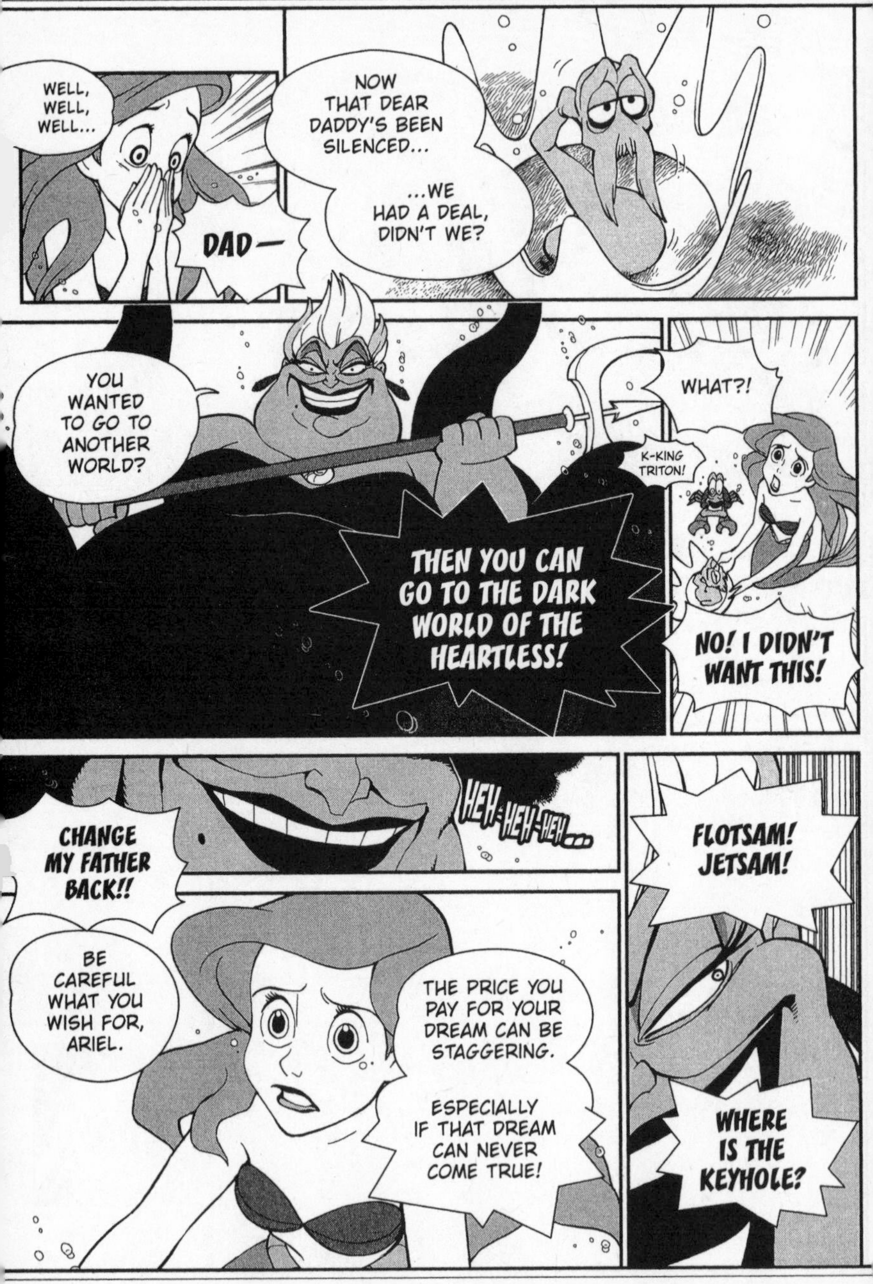
WELL, WELL, WELL...
DAD—
NOW THAT DEAR DADDY'S BEEN SILENCED...
...WE HAD A DEAL, DIDN'T WE?
YOU WANTED TO GO TO ANOTHER WORLD?
THEN YOU CAN GO TO THE DARK WORLD OF THE HEARTLESS!
WHAT?!
K-KING TRITON!
NO! I DIDN'T WANT THIS!
HEH-HEH-HEH...
CHANGE MY FATHER BACK!!
BE CAREFUL WHAT YOU WISH FOR, ARIEL.
THE PRICE YOU PAY FOR YOUR DREAM CAN BE STAGGERING.
ESPECIALLY IF THAT DREAM CAN NEVER COME TRUE!
FLOTSAM! JETSAM!
WHERE IS THE KEYHOLE?

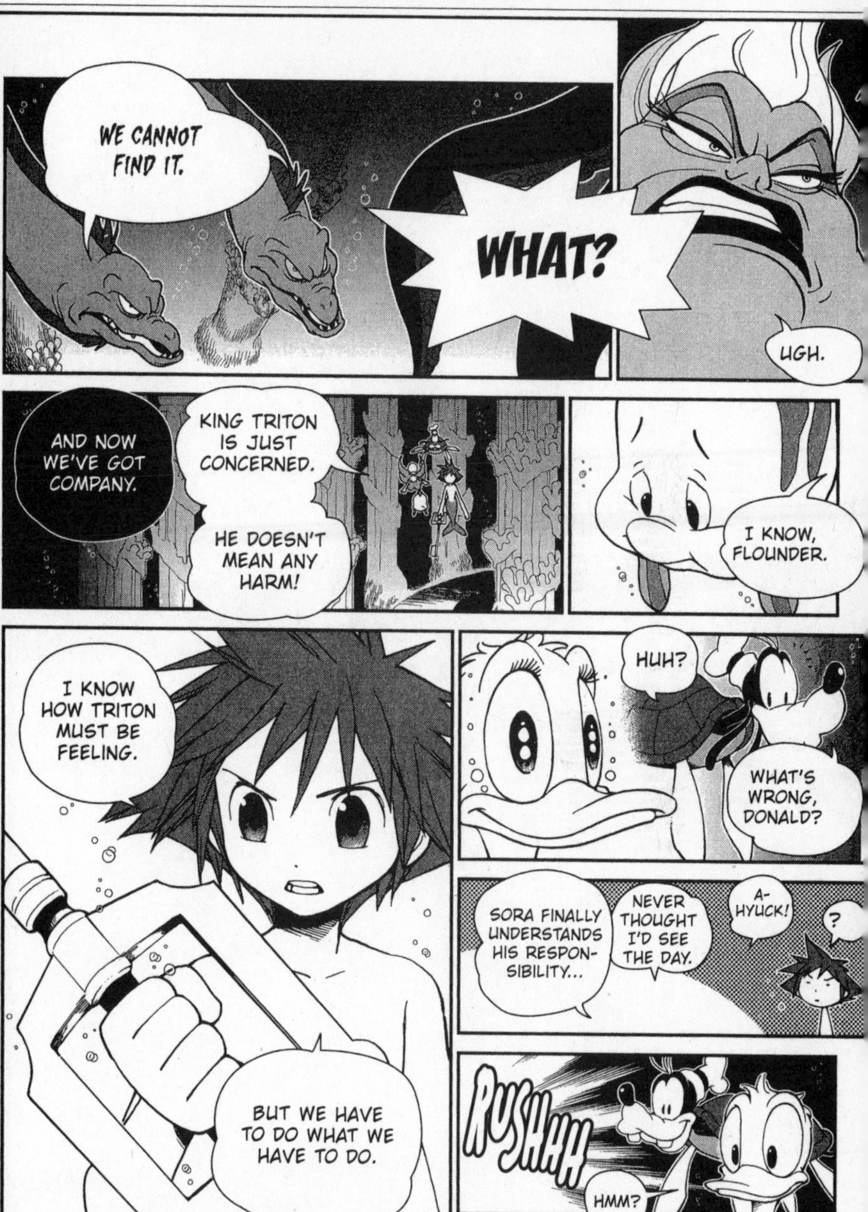
WE CANNOT FIND IT.
WHAT?
UGH.
AND NOW WE'VE GOT COMPANY.
KING TRITON IS JUST CONCERNED.
HE DOESN'T MEAN ANY HARM!
I KNOW, FLOUNDER.
I KNOW HOW TRITON MUST BE FEELING.
BUT WE HAVE TO DO WHAT WE HAVE TO DO.
HUH?
WHAT'S WRONG, DONALD?
SORA FINALLY UNDERSTANDS HIS RESPON-SIBILITY...
NEVER THOUGHT I'D SEE THE DAY.
A-HYUCK!
?
RUSHHH
HMM?

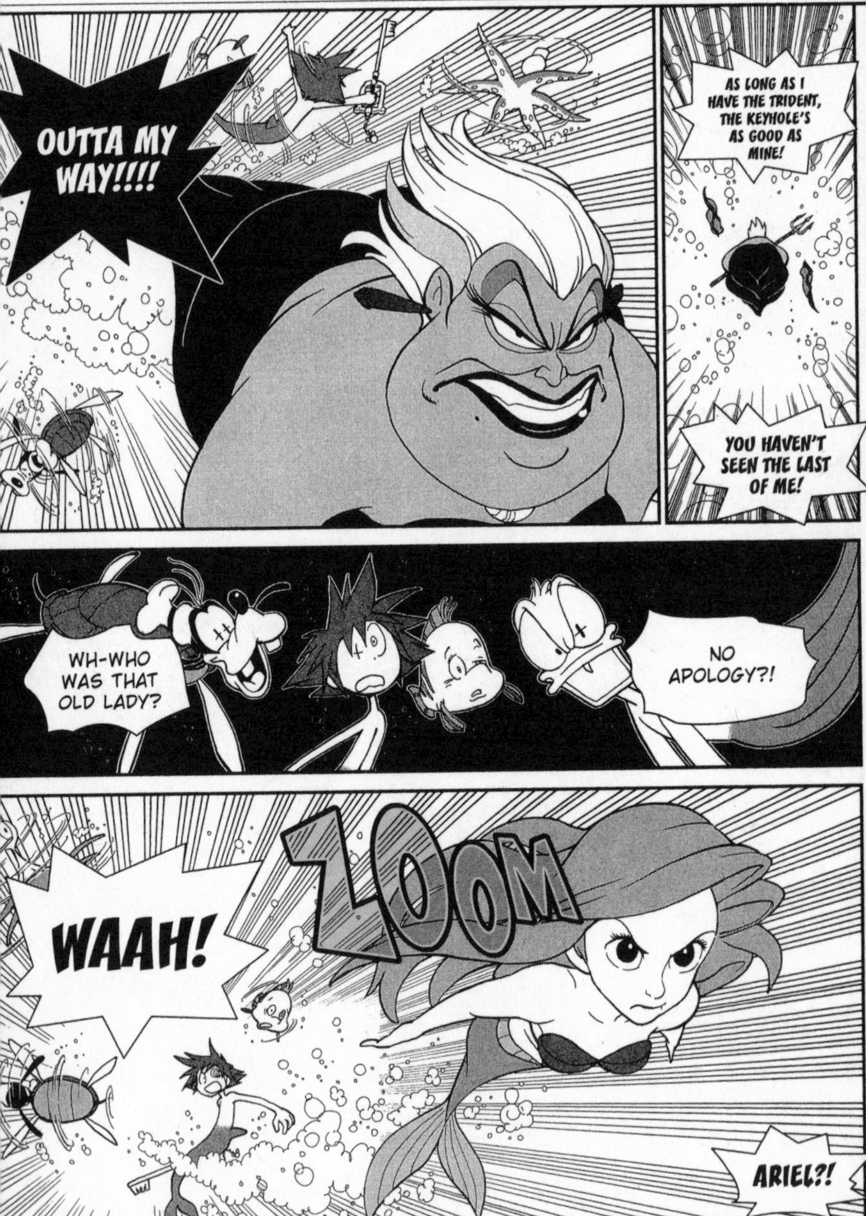
OUTTA MY WAY!!!!
AS LONG AS I HAVE THE TRIDENT, THE KEYHOLE'S AS GOOD AS MINE!
YOU HAVEN'T SEEN THE LAST OF ME!
WH-WHO WAS THAT OLD LADY?
NO APOLOGY?!
WAAH!
ZOOM
ARIEL?!

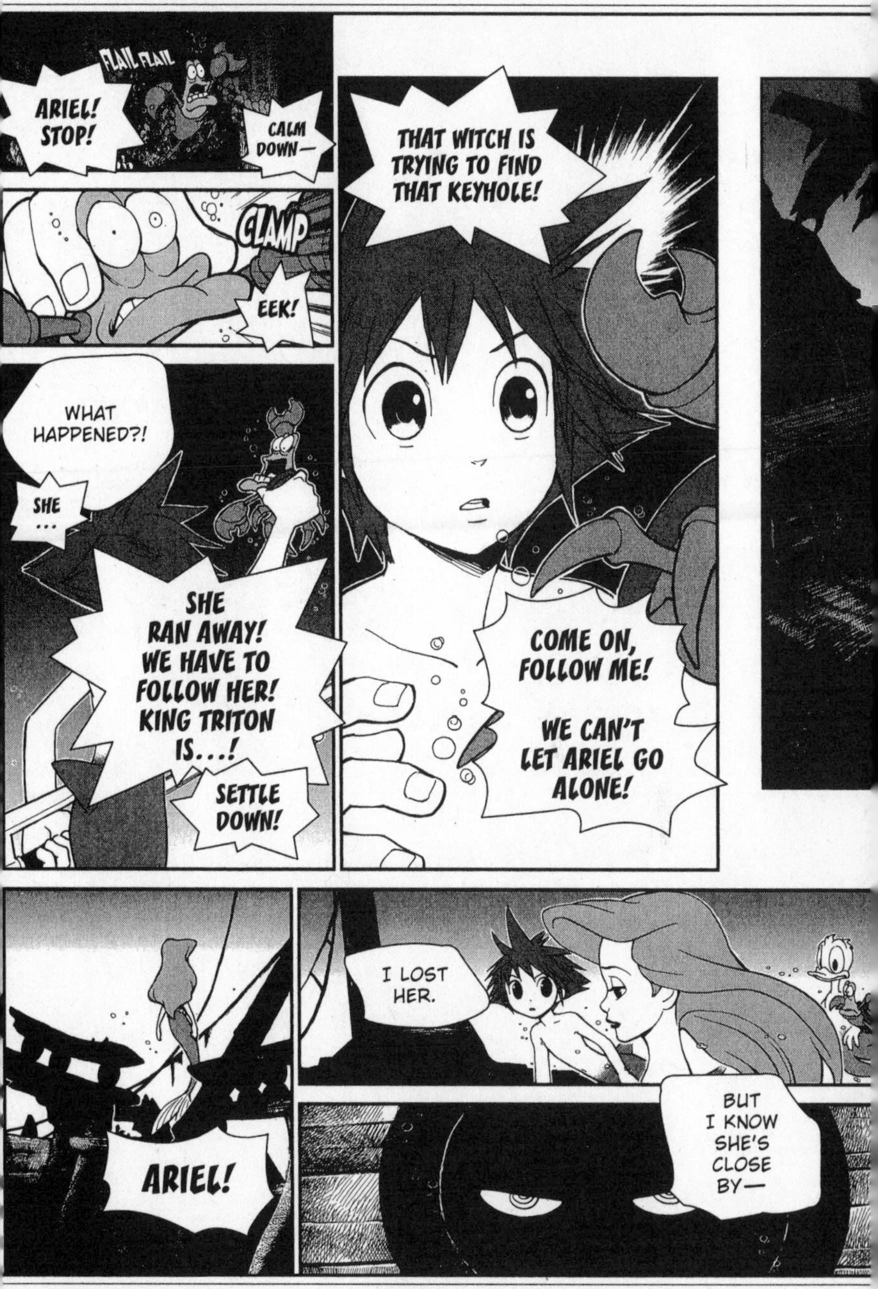
ARIEL! STOP!
FLAIL FLAIL
CALM DOWN—
CLAMP
EEK!
WHAT HAPPENED?!
SHE...
SHE RAN AWAY! WE HAVE TO FOLLOW HER! KING TRITON IS...!
SETTLE DOWN!
THAT WITCH IS TRYING TO FIND THAT KEYHOLE!
COME ON, FOLLOW ME!
WE CAN'T LET ARIEL GO ALONE!
ARIEL!
I LOST HER.
BUT I KNOW SHE'S CLOSE BY—

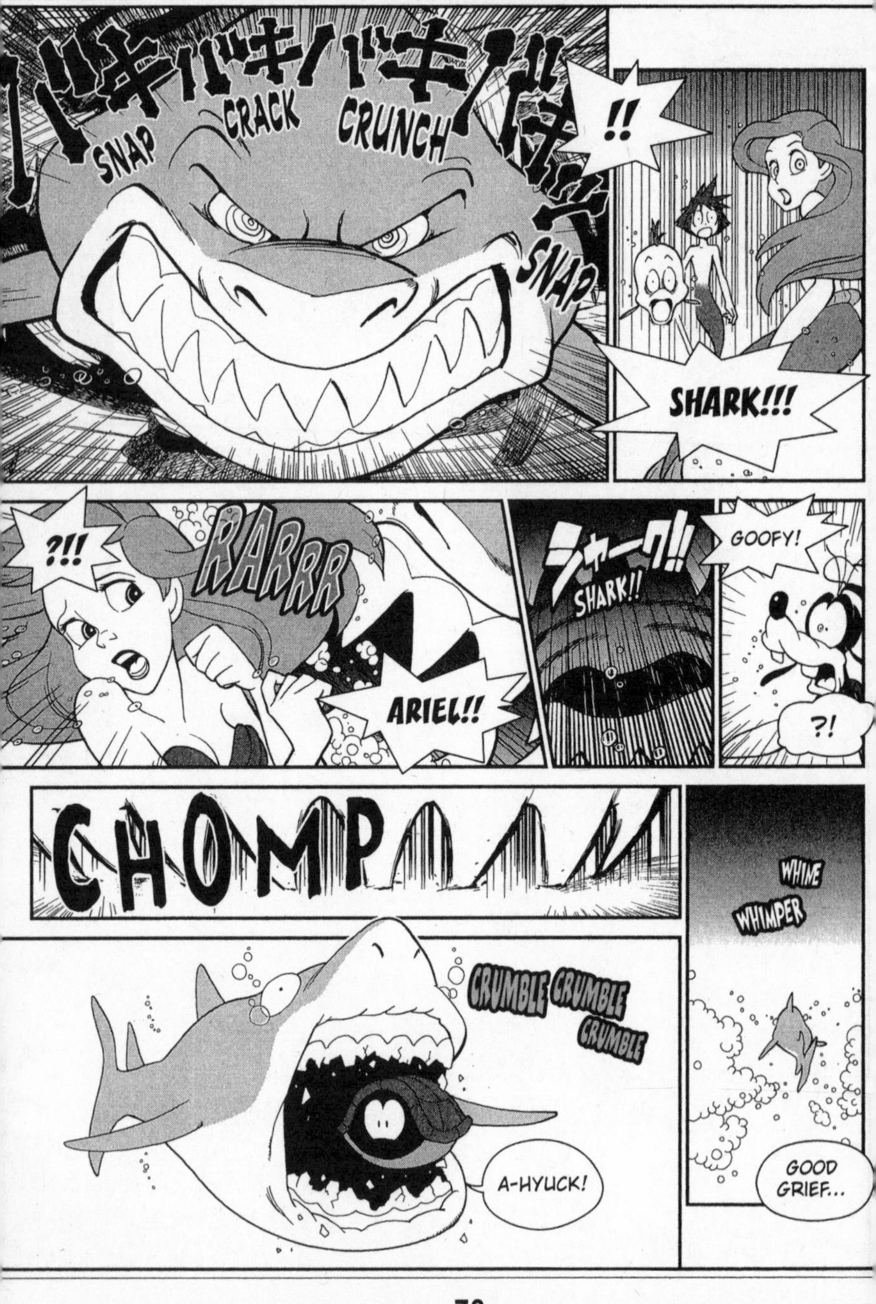
SNAP
CRACK
CRUNCH
SNAP
!!
SHARK!!!
?!!
RARRR
ARIEL!!
シャーク!!
SHARK!!
GOOFY!
?!
CHOMP
CRUMBLE CRUMBLE
CRUMBLE
A-HYUCK!
WHINE
WHIMPER
GOOD GRIEF...

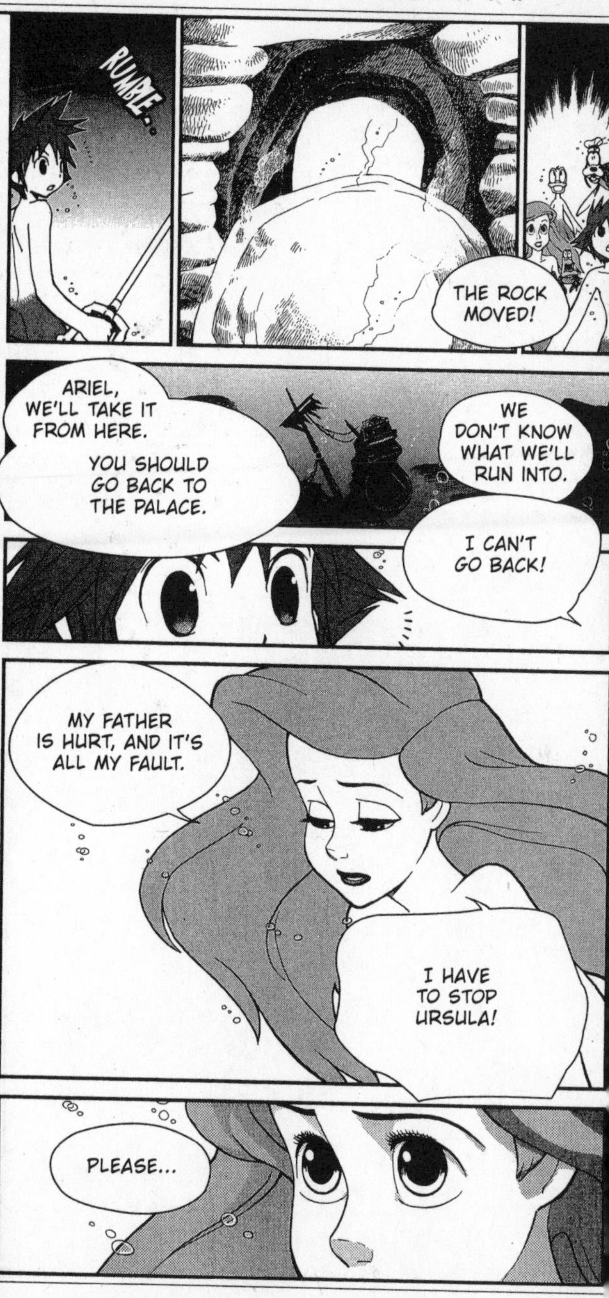
RUMBLE...
THE ROCK MOVED!
ARIEL, WE'LL TAKE IT FROM HERE.
YOU SHOULD GO BACK TO THE PALACE.
WE DON'T KNOW WHAT WE'LL RUN INTO.
I CAN'T GO BACK!
MY FATHER IS HURT, AND IT'S ALL MY FAULT.
I HAVE TO STOP URSULA!
PLEASE...

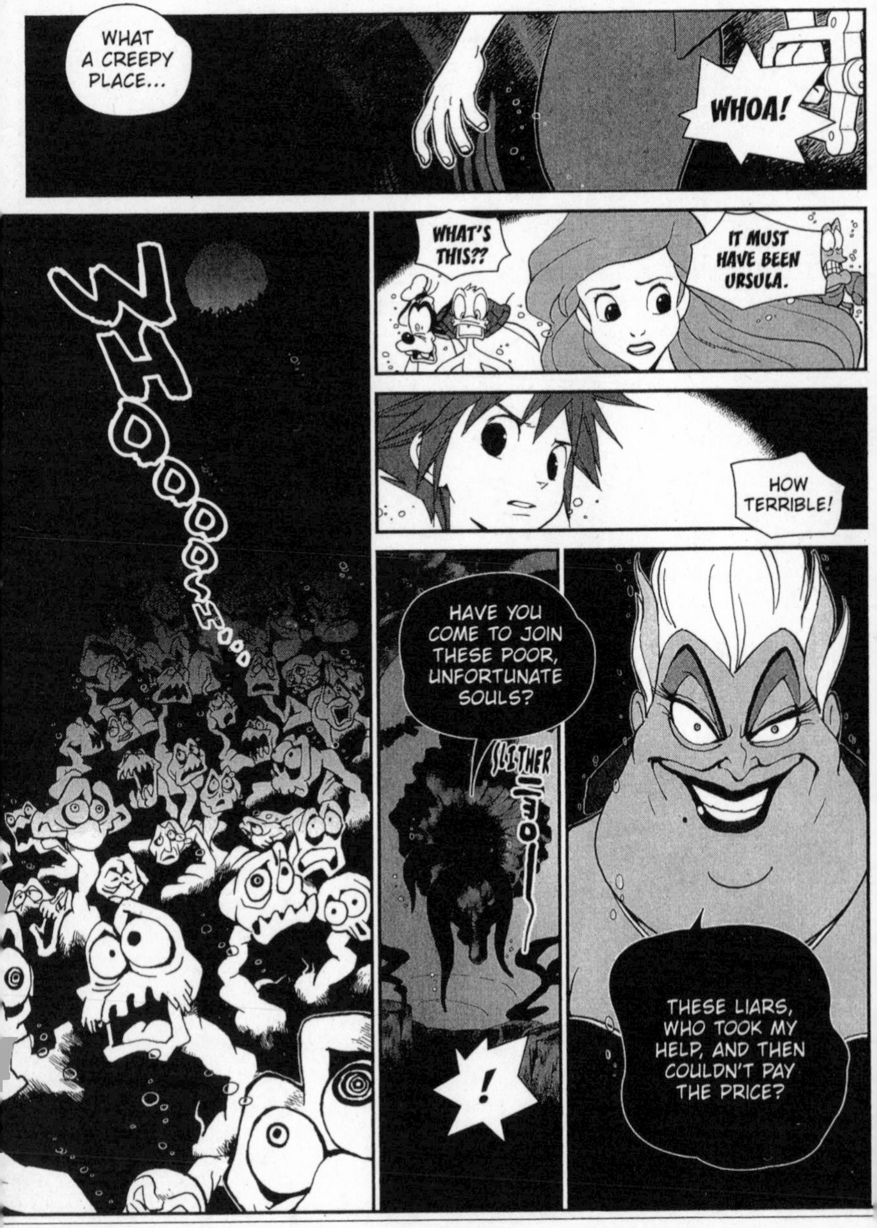
WHAT A CREEPY PLACE...
WHOA!
WHOOOOOO
WHAT'S THIS??
IT MUST HAVE BEEN URSULA.
HOW TERRIBLE!
HAVE YOU COME TO JOIN THESE POOR, UNFORTUNATE SOULS?
SLITHER
!
THESE LIARS, WHO TOOK MY HELP, AND THEN COULDN'T PAY THE PRICE?

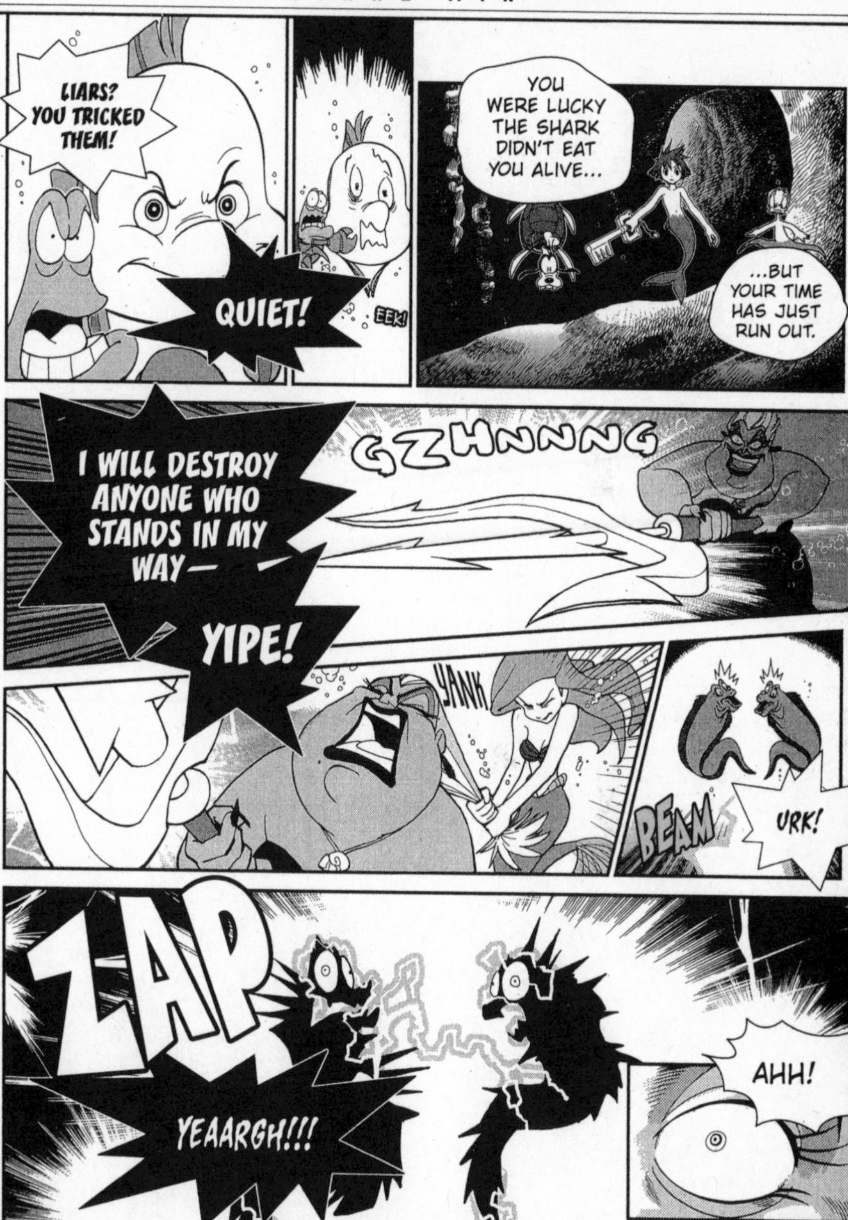
LIARS? YOU TRICKED THEM!
QUIET!
EEK!
YOU WERE LUCKY THE SHARK DIDN'T EAT YOU ALIVE...
...BUT YOUR TIME HAS JUST RUN OUT.
I WILL DESTROY ANYONE WHO STANDS IN MY WAY—
GZHNNNG
YIPE!
YANK
BEAM
URK!
ZAP
YEAARGH!!!
AHH!

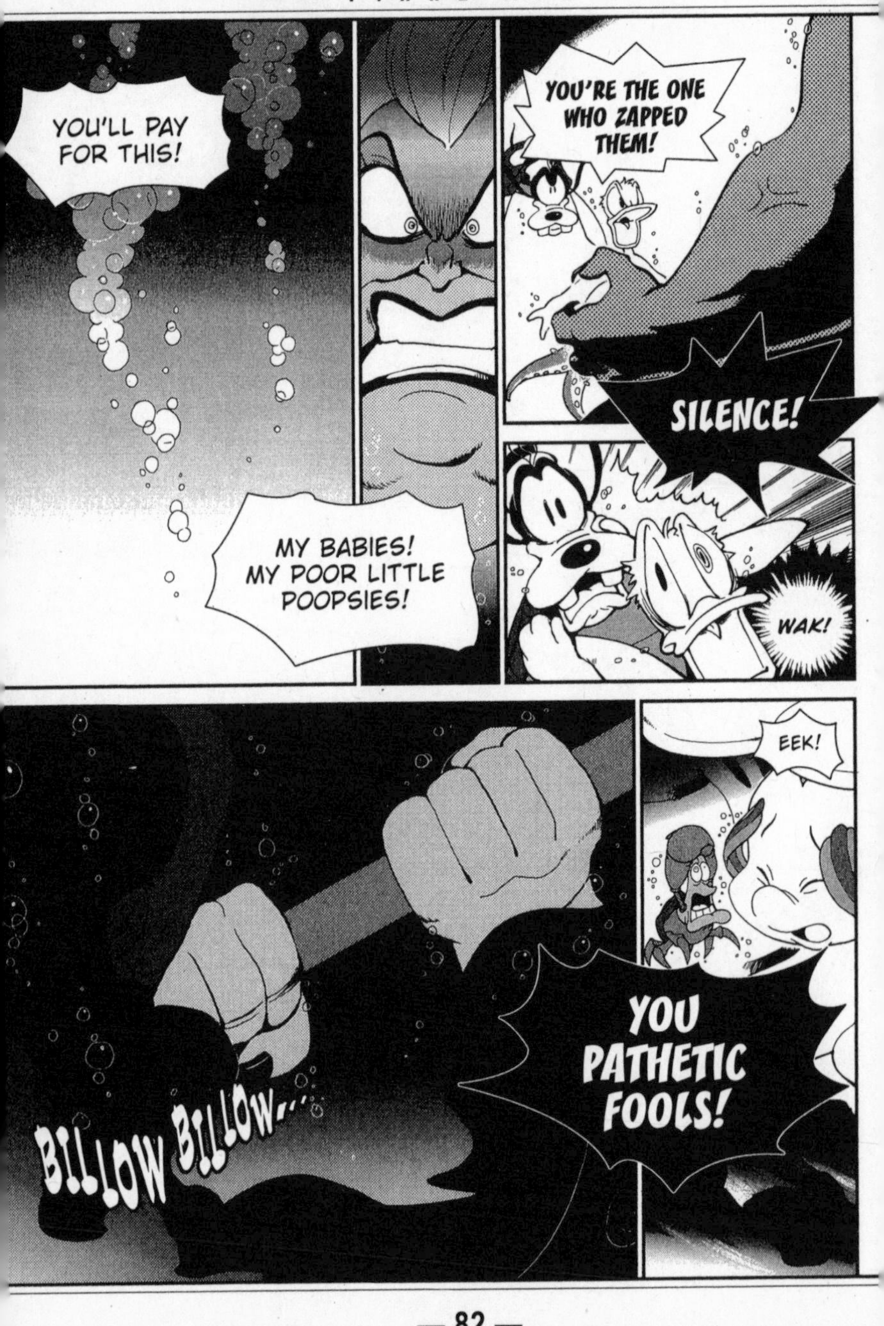
YOU'LL PAY FOR THIS!
MY BABIES! MY POOR LITTLE POOPSIES!
YOU'RE THE ONE WHO ZAPPED THEM!
SILENCE!
WAK!
BILLOW BILLOW...
EEK!
YOU PATHETIC FOOLS!

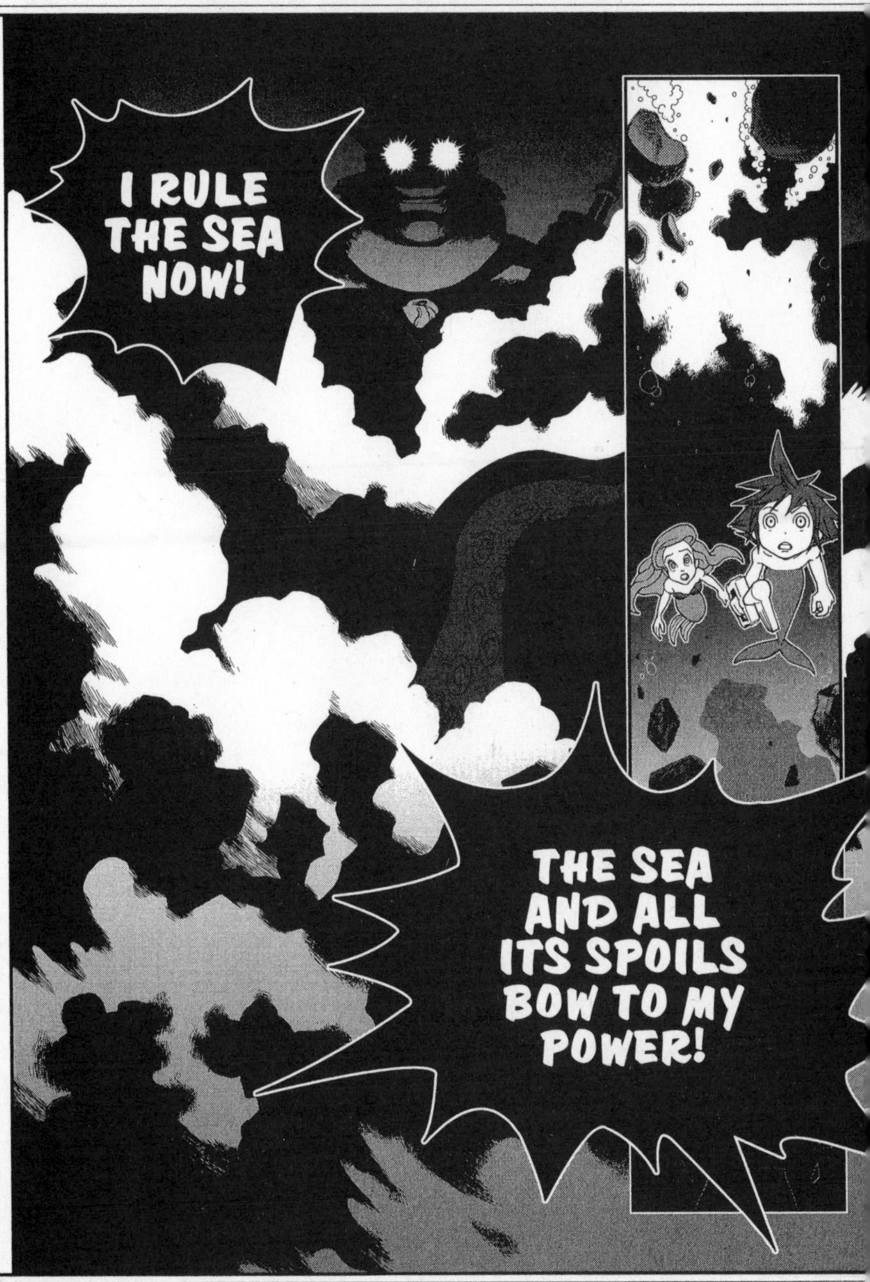
I RULE THE SEA NOW!
THE SEA AND ALL ITS SPOILS BOW TO MY POWER!

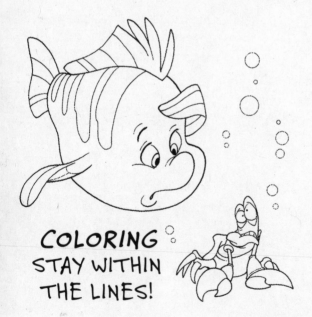

COLORING
STAY WITHIN
THE LINES!

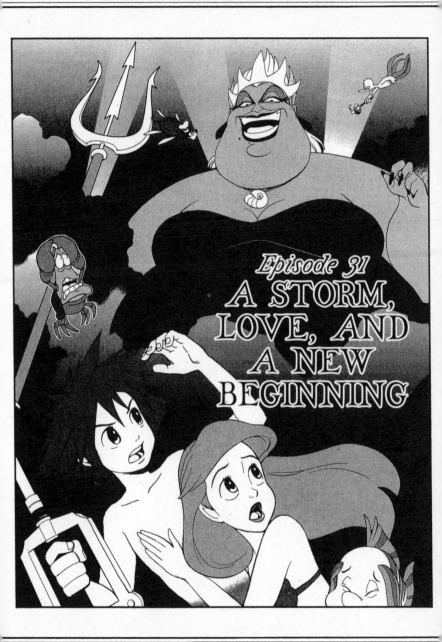

Episode 31
A STORM,
LOVE, AND
A NEW
BEGINNING

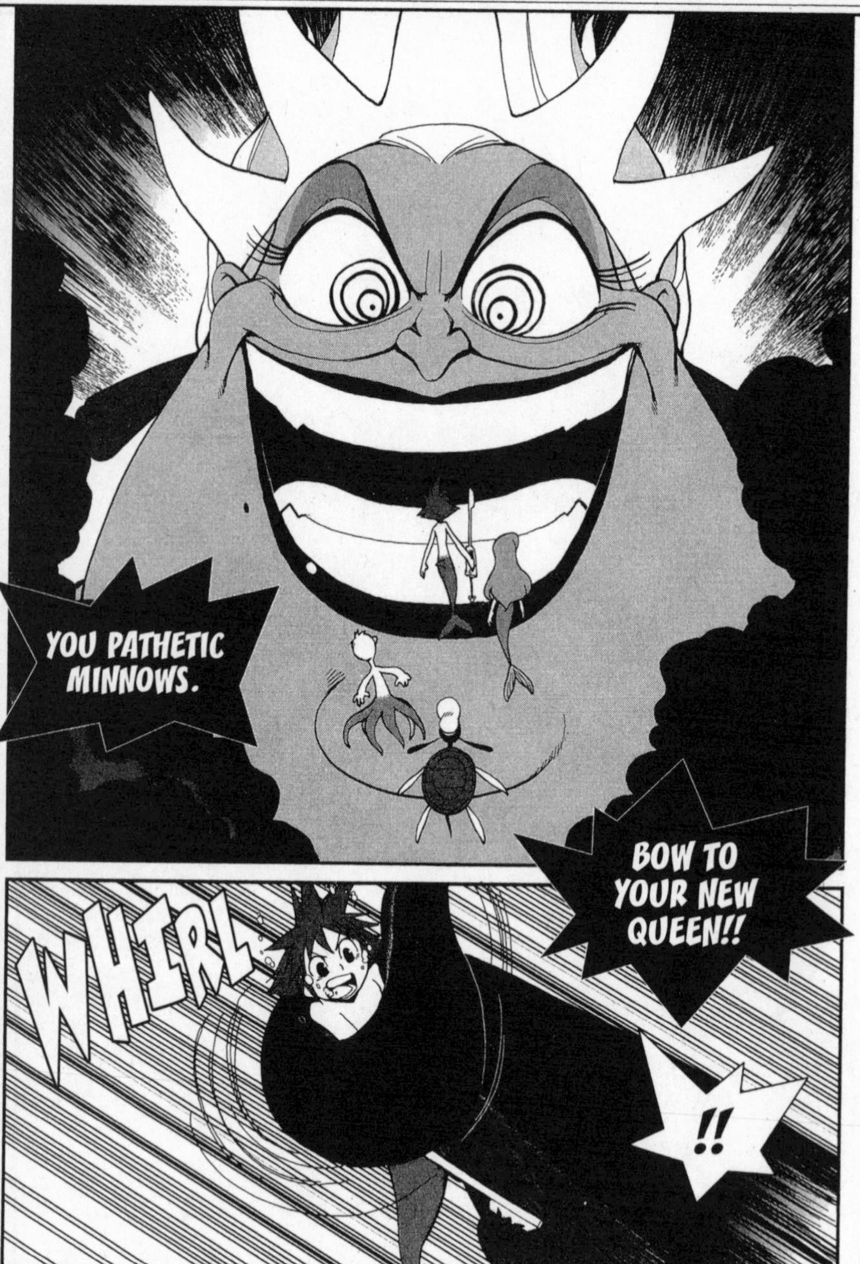
YOU PATHETIC MINNOWS.
BOW TO YOUR NEW QUEEN!!
WHIRL
!!

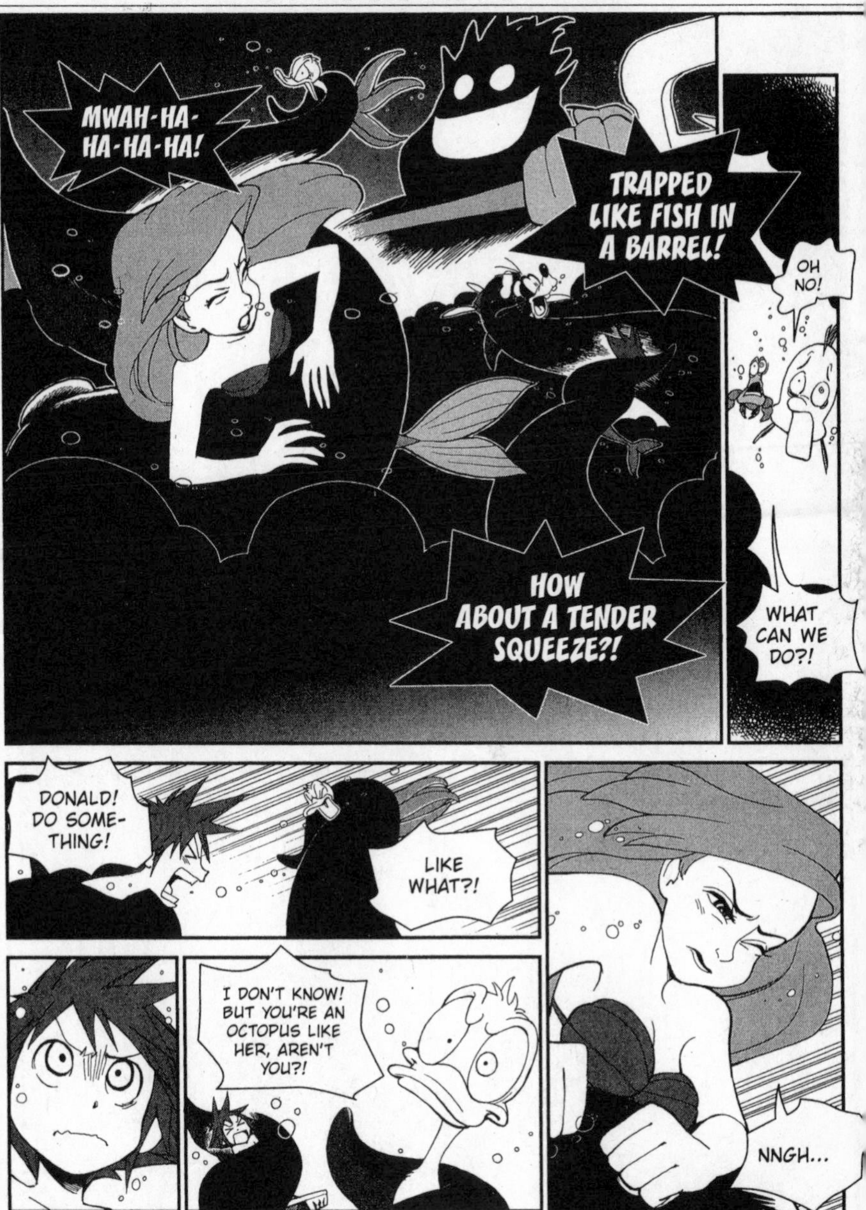
MWAH-HA-HA-HA-HA!
TRAPPED LIKE FISH IN A BARREL!
HOW ABOUT A TENDER SQUEEZE?!
OH NO!
WHAT CAN WE DO?!
DONALD! DO SOME-THING!
LIKE WHAT?!
I DON'T KNOW! BUT YOU'RE AN OCTOPUS LIKE HER, AREN'T YOU?!
NNGH...

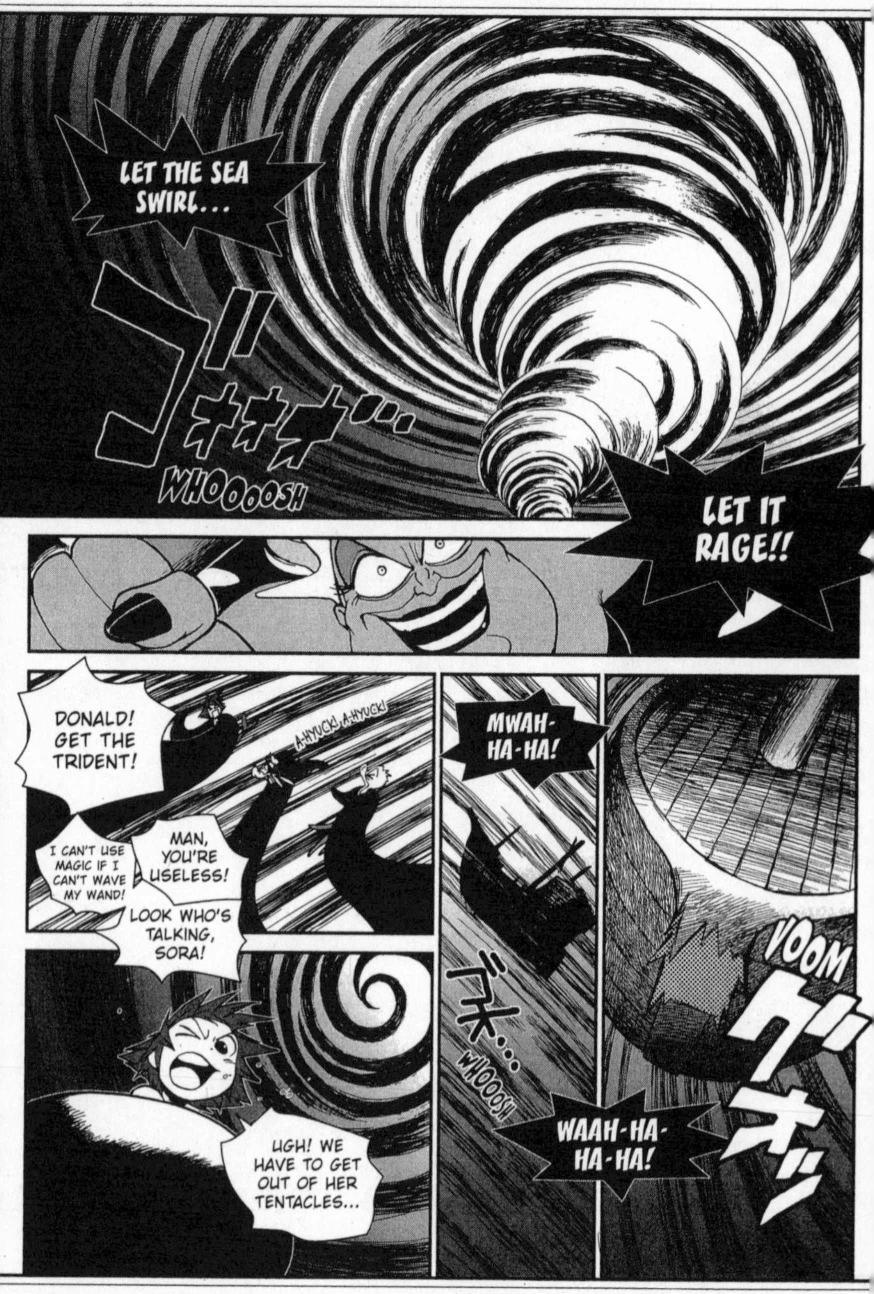
LET THE SEA SWIRL...
ゴォォォ
WHOOOOOSH
LET IT RAGE!!
DONALD! GET THE TRIDENT!
A-HYUCK! A-HYUCK!
I CAN'T USE MAGIC IF I CAN'T WAVE MY WAND!
MAN, YOU'RE USELESS!
LOOK WHO'S TALKING, SORA!
UGH! WE HAVE TO GET OUT OF HER TENTACLES...
MWAH-HA-HA!
ゴォ...
WHOOOSH
WAAH-HA-HA-HA!
VOOM
グォッ

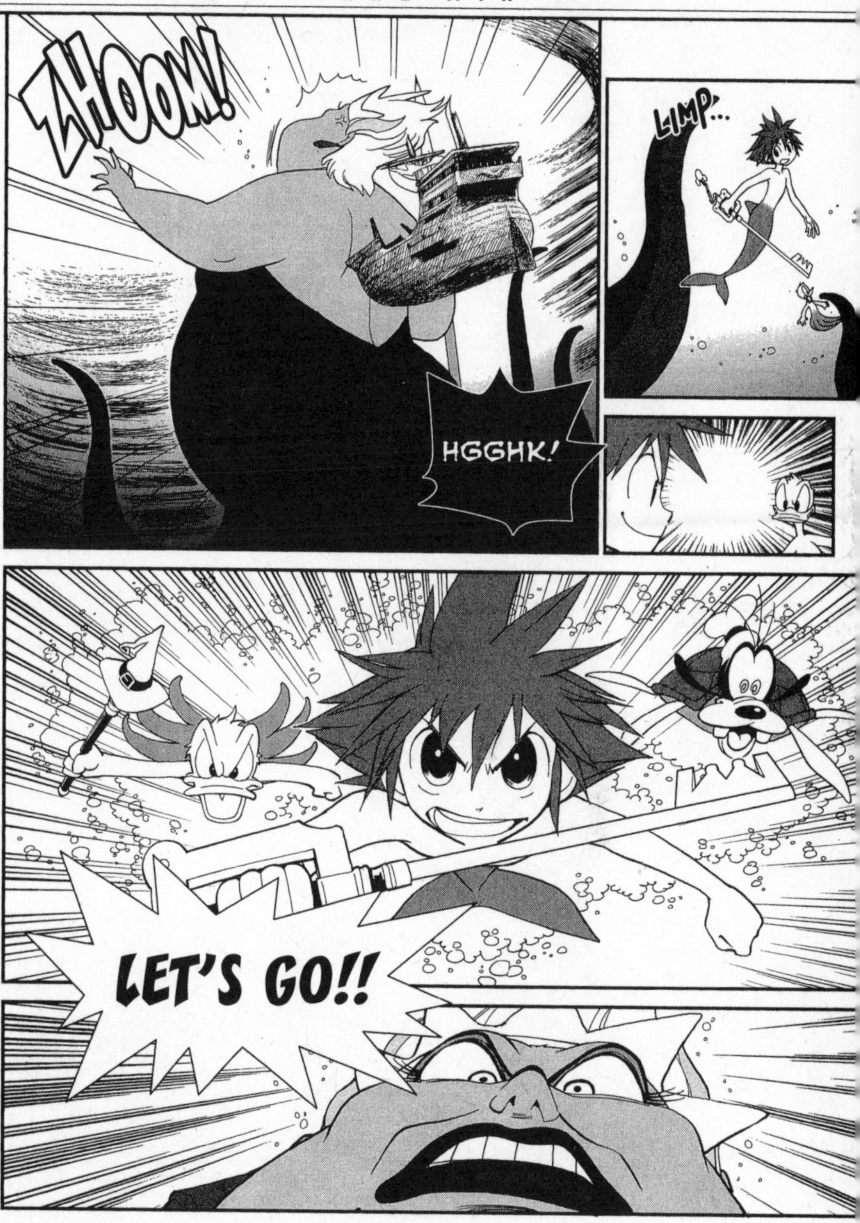
ZHOOM!
HGGHK!
LIMP...
LET'S GO!!

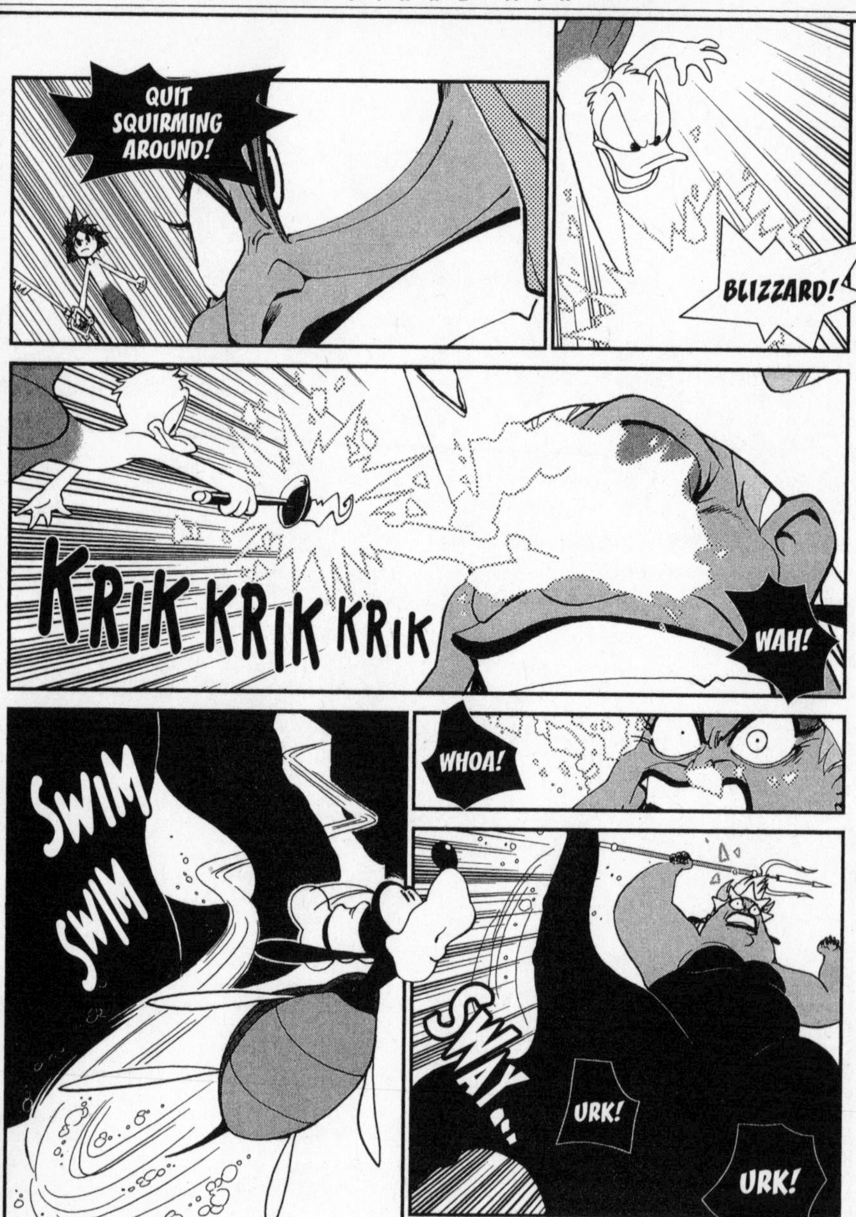
QUIT SQUIRMING AROUND!
BLIZZARD!
KRIK KRIK KRIK
WAH!
SWIM SWIM
WHOA!
SWAY...
URK!
URK!

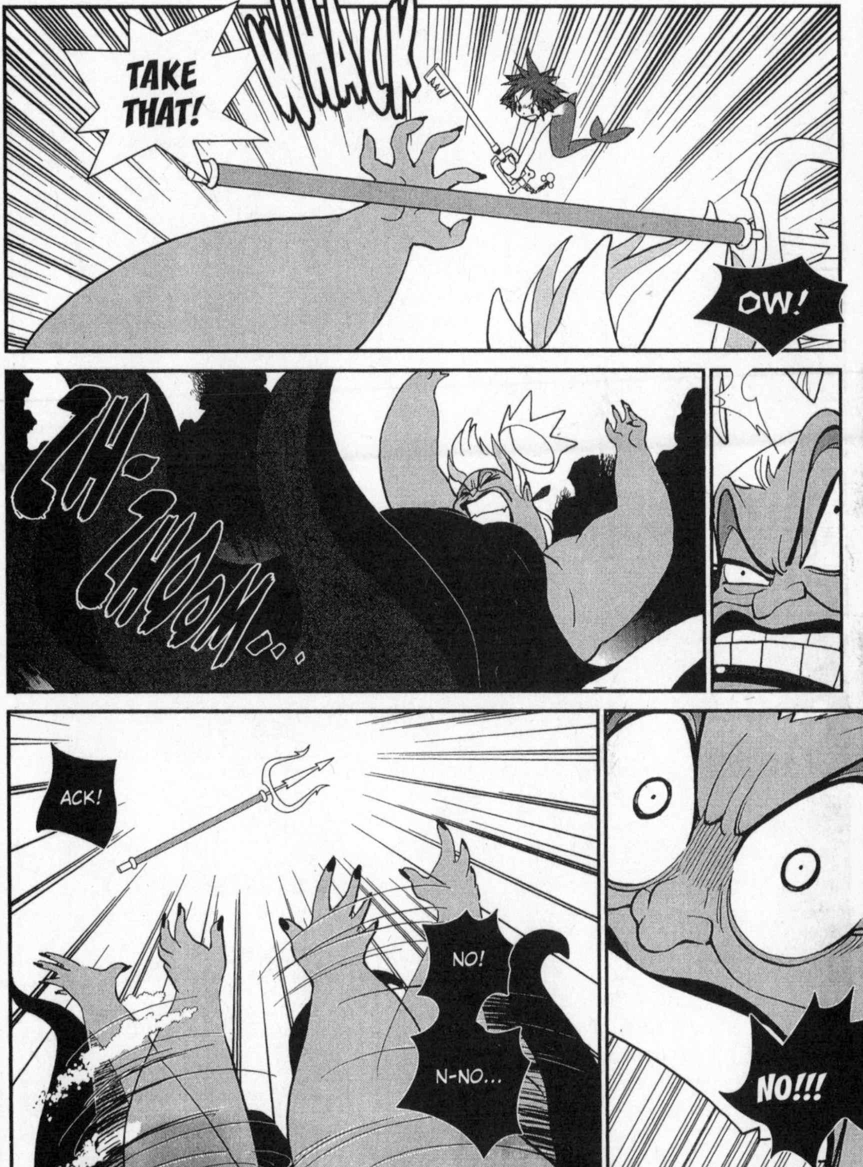
TAKE THAT!
WHACK
OW!
ZH-ZHOOM..
ACK!
NO!
N-NO...
NO!!!

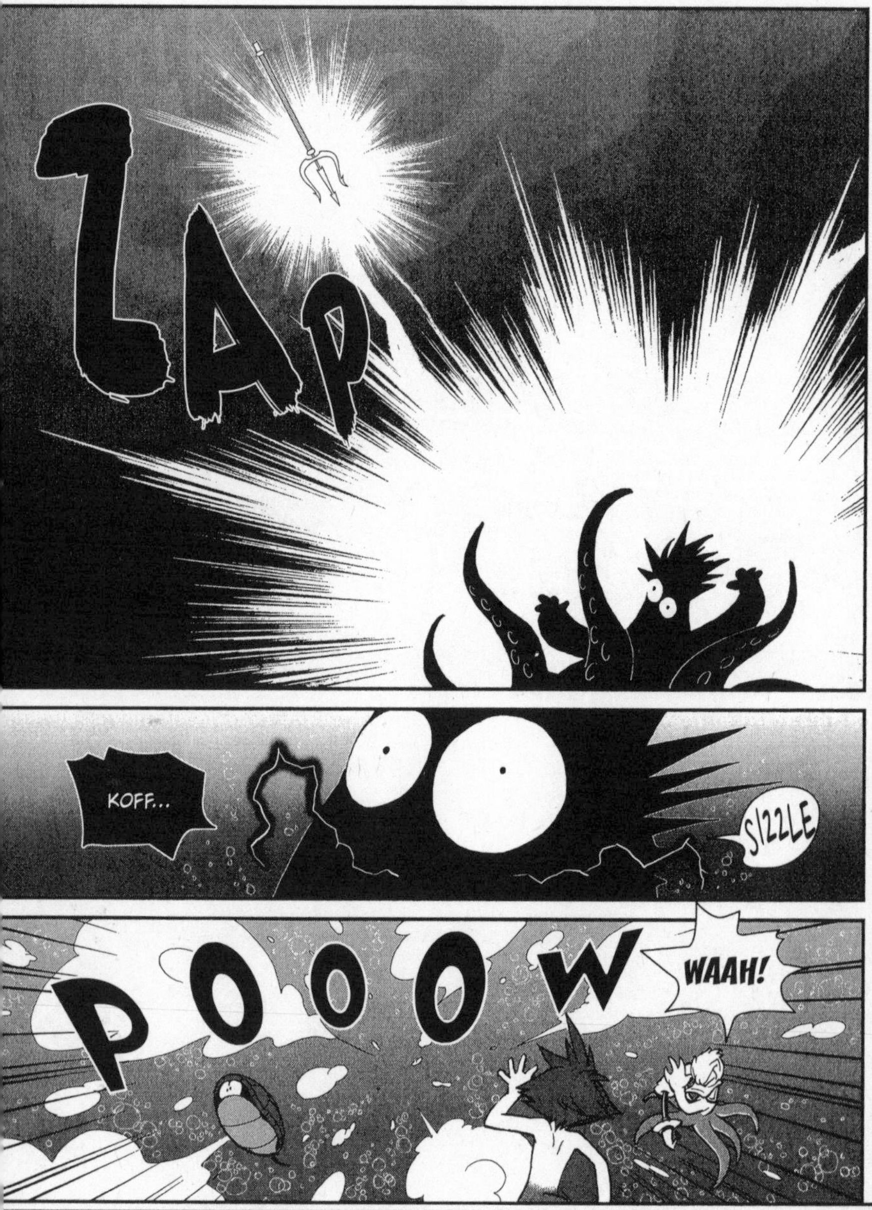
ZAP
KOFF...
SIZZLE
POOOW
WAAH!

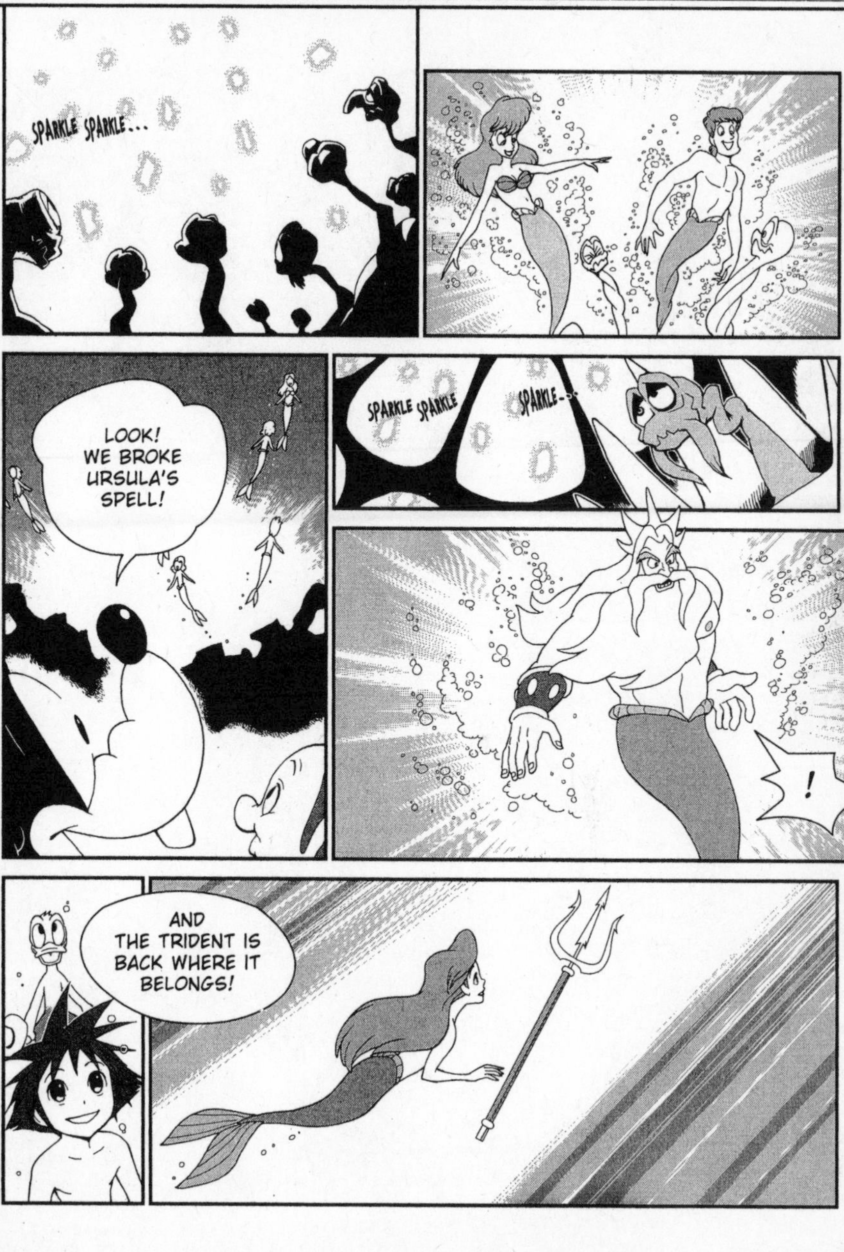
SPARKLE SPARKLE...
LOOK! WE BROKE URSULA'S SPELL!
SPARKLE SPARKLE SPARKLE...
!
AND THE TRIDENT IS BACK WHERE IT BELONGS!

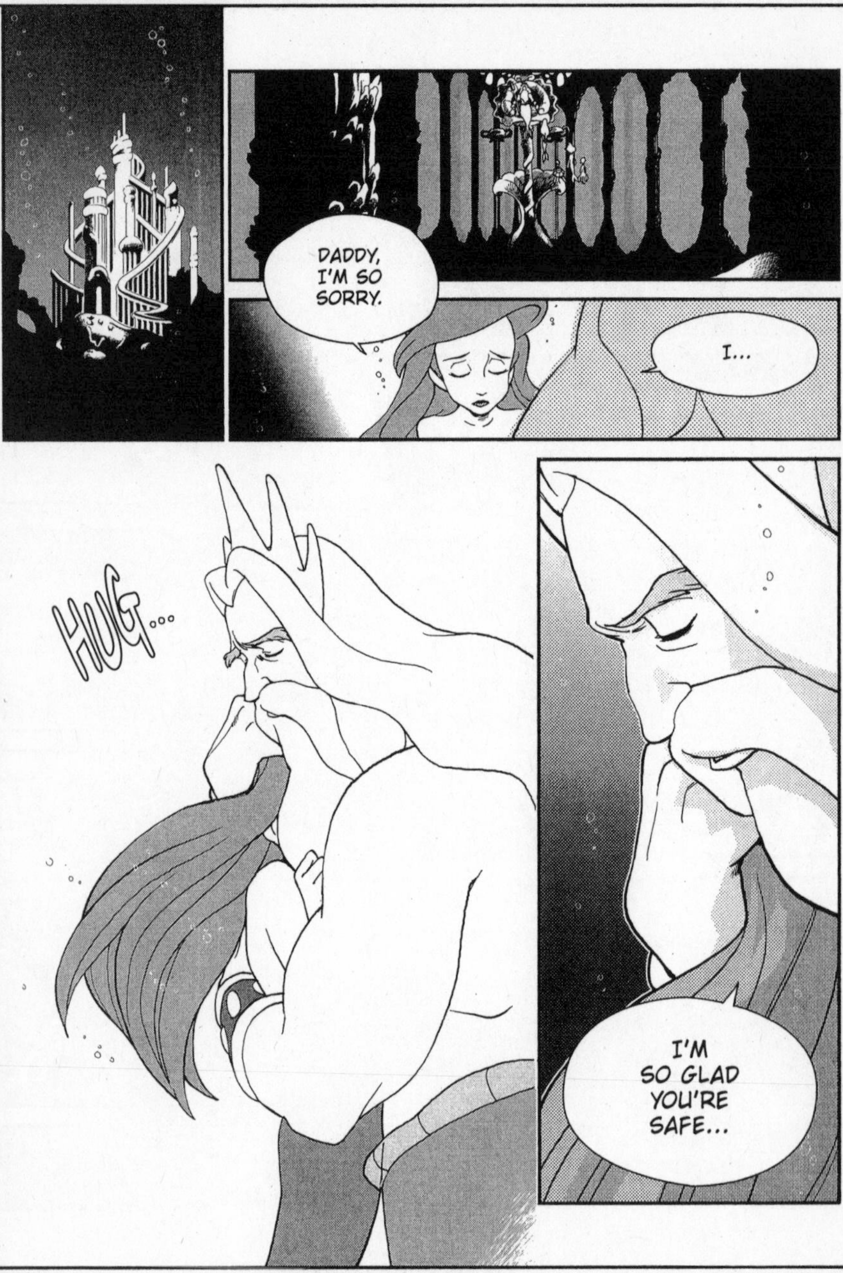
DADDY, I'M SO SORRY.
I...
HUG...
I'M SO GLAD YOU'RE SAFE...

I WANTED TO KEEP YOU SAFE FROM HARM.

BUT I WASN'T LETTING YOU FOLLOW YOUR HEART.

PLEASE FORGIVE ME.

DADDY...

I WAS UNFAIR TO YOU THREE AS WELL. FOR THAT, I APOLOGIZE.

KEYBLADE MASTER...

...I HAVE ONE REQUEST.

SEAL THE KEYHOLE.

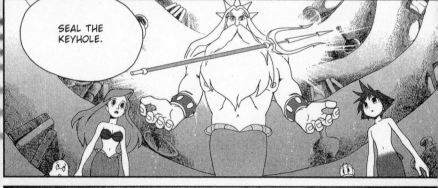

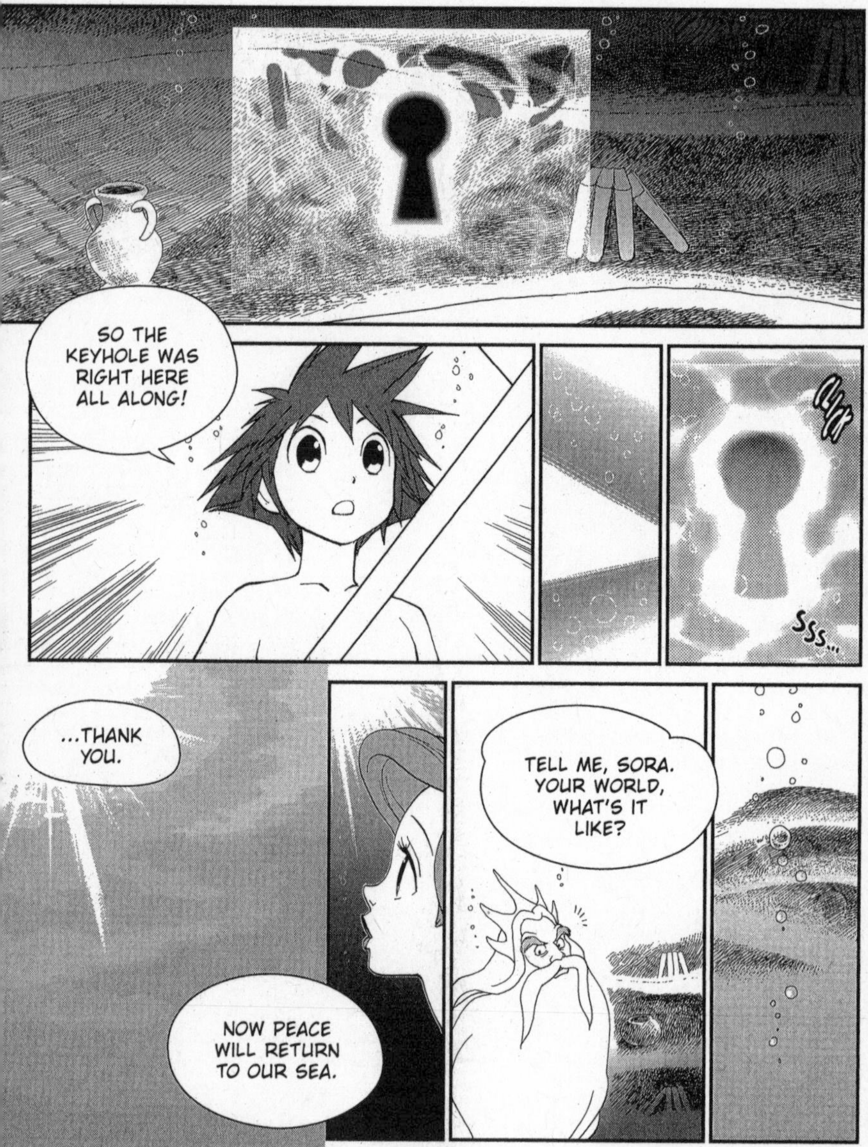
SO THE KEYHOLE WAS RIGHT HERE ALL ALONG!
SSS...
...THANK YOU.
NOW PEACE WILL RETURN TO OUR SEA.
TELL ME, SORA. YOUR WORLD, WHAT'S IT LIKE?

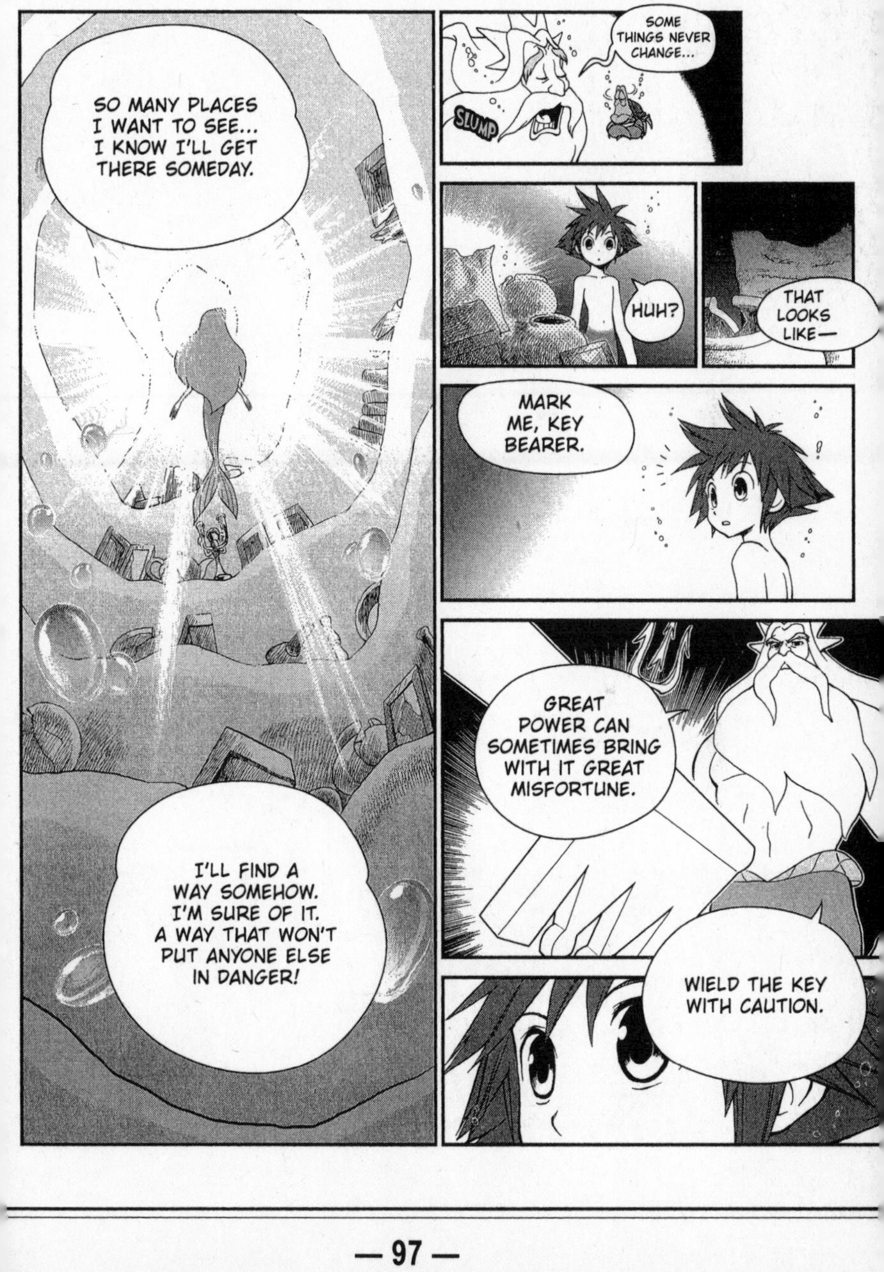
SO MANY PLACES I WANT TO SEE... I KNOW I'LL GET THERE SOMEDAY.
I'LL FIND A WAY SOMEHOW. I'M SURE OF IT. A WAY THAT WON'T PUT ANYONE ELSE IN DANGER!
SOME THINGS NEVER CHANGE...
SLUMP
HUH?
THAT LOOKS LIKE—
MARK ME, KEY BEARER.
GREAT POWER CAN SOMETIMES BRING WITH IT GREAT MISFORTUNE.
WIELD THE KEY WITH CAUTION.

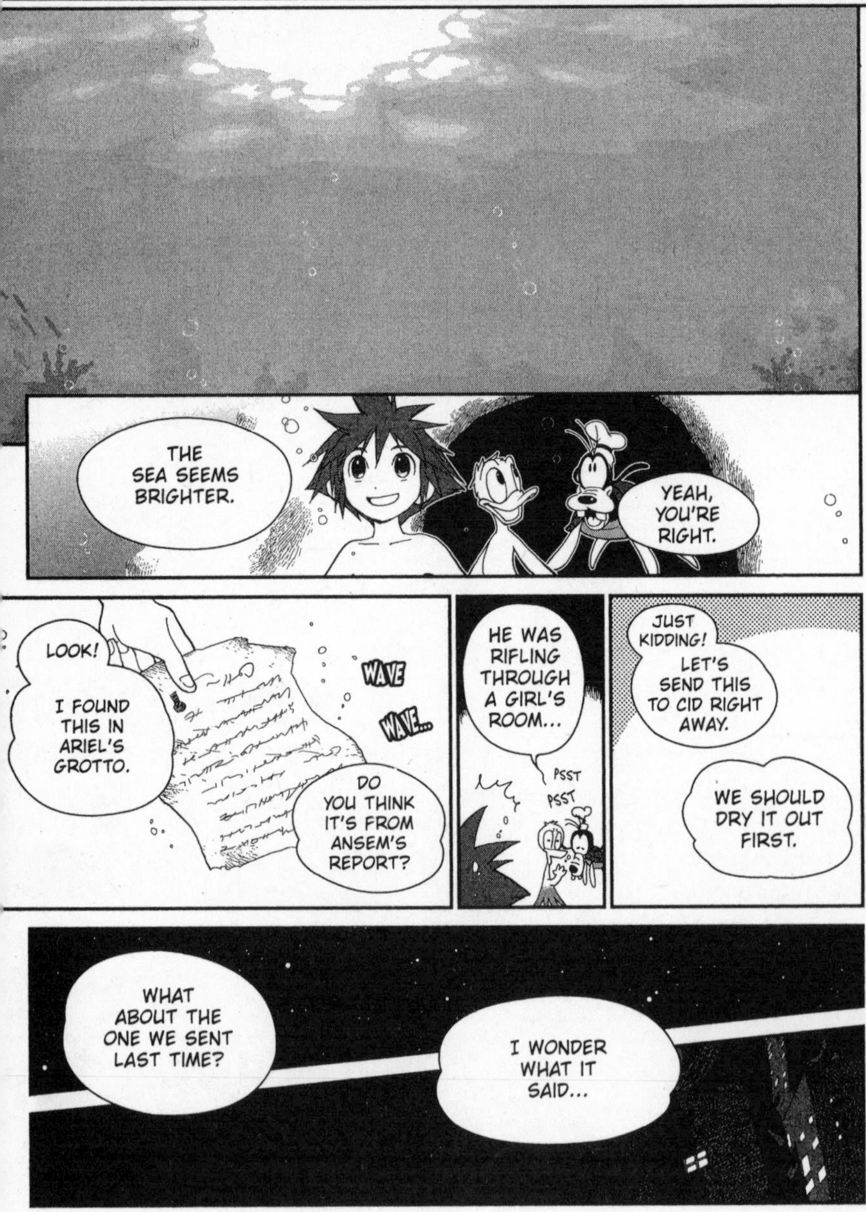
THE SEA SEEMS BRIGHTER.
YEAH, YOU'RE RIGHT.
LOOK!
I FOUND THIS IN ARIEL'S GROTTO.
WAVE
WAVE...
DO YOU THINK IT'S FROM ANSEM'S REPORT?
HE WAS RIFLING THROUGH A GIRL'S ROOM...
PSST
PSST
JUST KIDDING!
LET'S SEND THIS TO CID RIGHT AWAY.
WE SHOULD DRY IT OUT FIRST.
WHAT ABOUT THE ONE WE SENT LAST TIME?
I WONDER WHAT IT SAID...

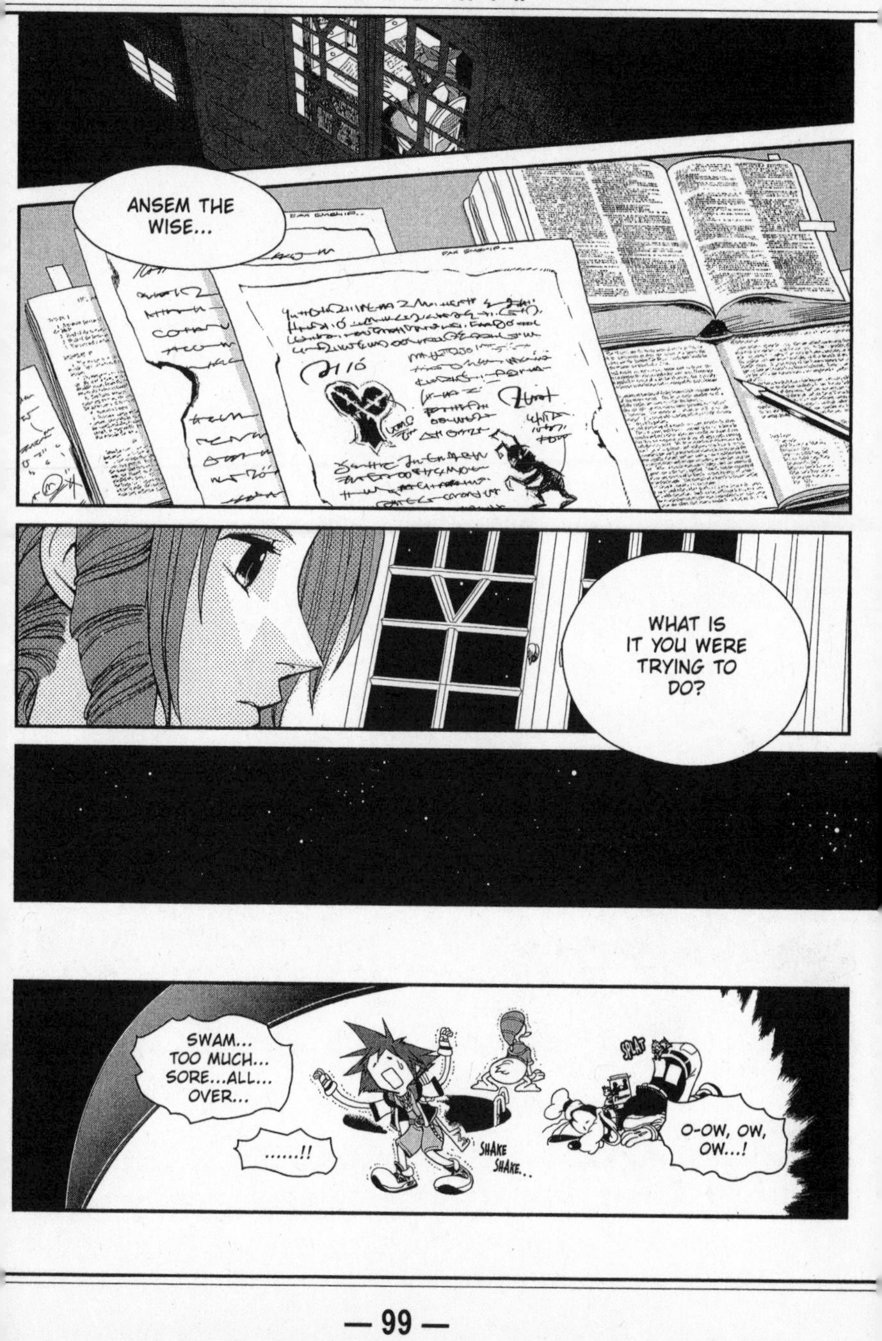
ANSEM THE WISE...
WHAT IS IT YOU WERE TRYING TO DO?
SWAM... TOO MUCH... SORE...ALL... OVER...
......!!
SHAKE SHAKE...
SPLAT
O-OW, OW, OW...!

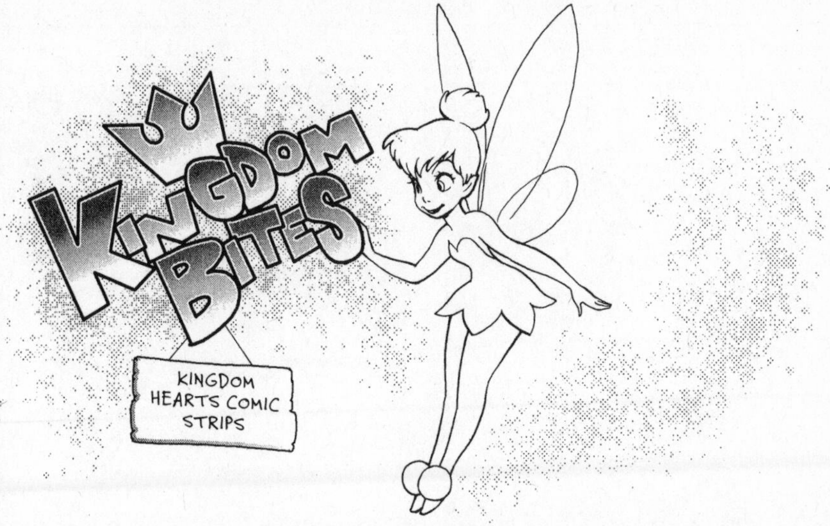
KINGDOM BITES
KINGDOM HEARTS COMIC STRIPS

A DAY IN THE LIFE OF CAPTAIN HOOK

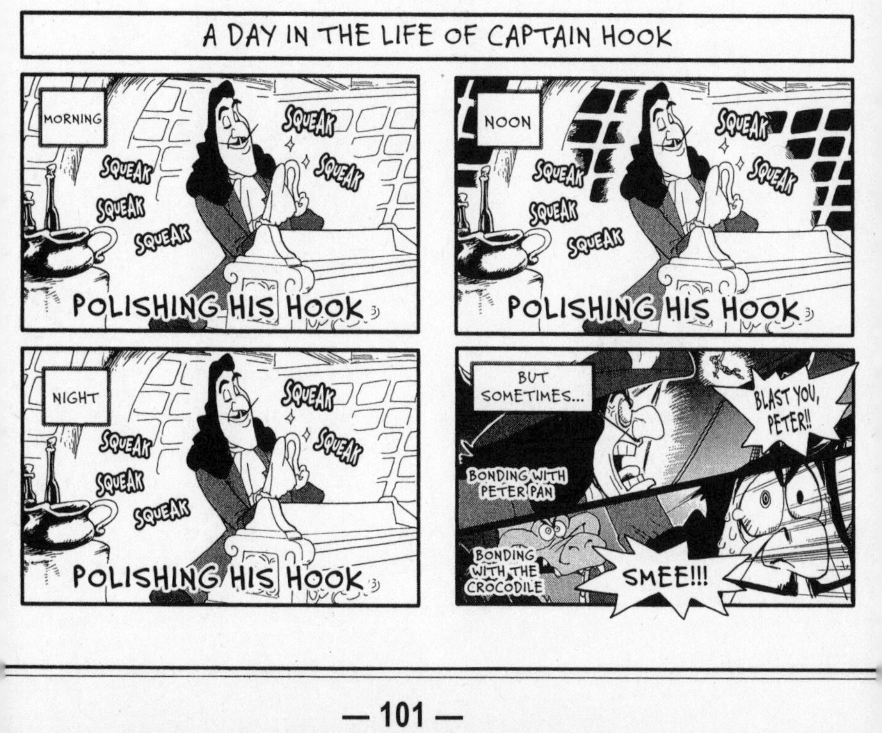
MORNING
SQUEAK
SQUEAK
SQUEAK
SQUEAK
SQUEAK
POLISHING HIS HOOK
NOON
SQUEAK
SQUEAK
SQUEAK
SQUEAK
SQUEAK
POLISHING HIS HOOK
NIGHT
SQUEAK
SQUEAK
SQUEAK
SQUEAK
SQUEAK
POLISHING HIS HOOK
BUT SOMETIMES...
BLAST YOU, PETER!!
BONDING WITH PETER PAN
BONDING WITH THE CROCODILE
SMEE!!!

FAREWELL GIFT

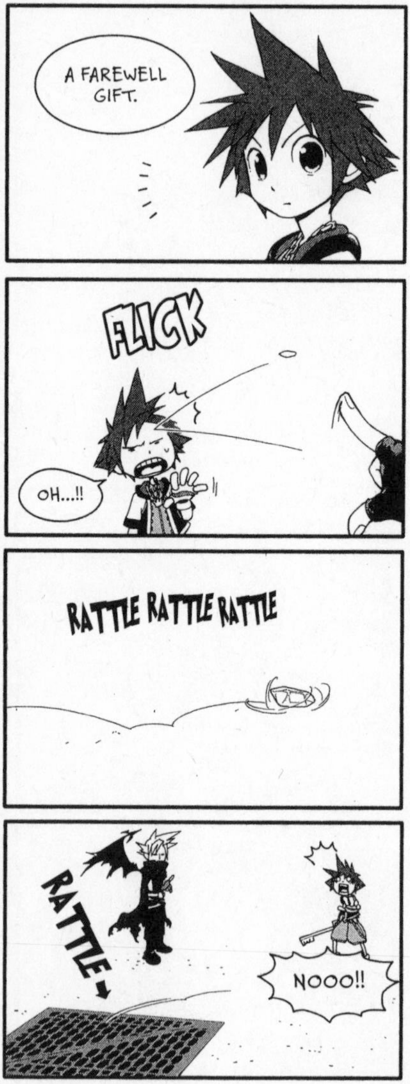
A FAREWELL GIFT.
FLICK
OH...!!
RATTLE RATTLE RATTLE
RATTLE
NOOO!!

DINNER

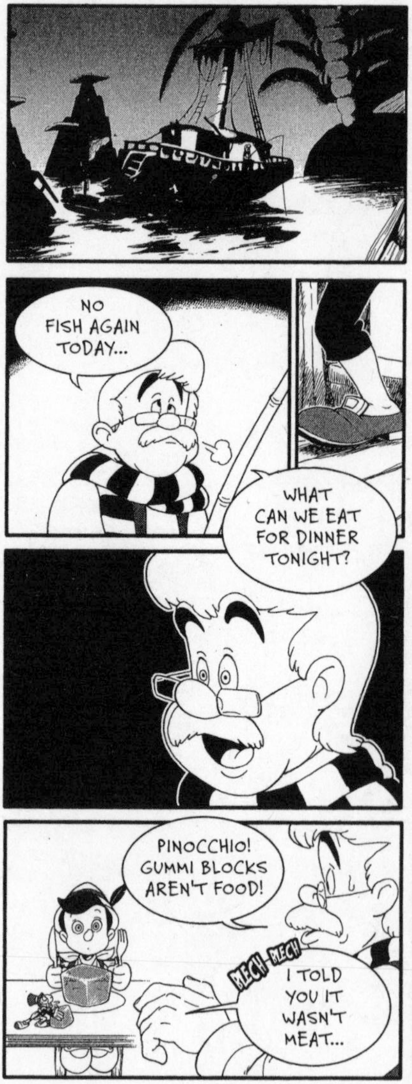
NO FISH AGAIN TODAY...
WHAT CAN WE EAT FOR DINNER TONIGHT?
PINOCCHIO! GUMMI BLOCKS AREN'T FOOD!
BLECH BLECH
I TOLD YOU IT WASN'T MEAT...

PRESENT

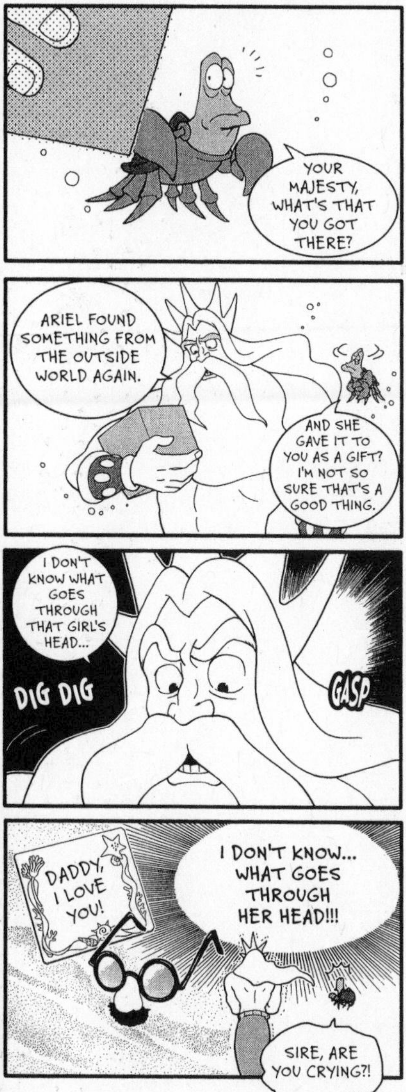
YOUR MAJESTY, WHAT'S THAT YOU GOT THERE?
ARIEL FOUND SOMETHING FROM THE OUTSIDE WORLD AGAIN.
AND SHE GAVE IT TO YOU AS A GIFT? I'M NOT SO SURE THAT'S A GOOD THING.
I DON'T KNOW WHAT GOES THROUGH THAT GIRL'S HEAD...
DIG DIG
GASP
DADDY, I LOVE YOU!
I DON'T KNOW... WHAT GOES THROUGH HER HEAD!!!
SIRE, ARE YOU CRYING?!

ANSEM'S MEMO

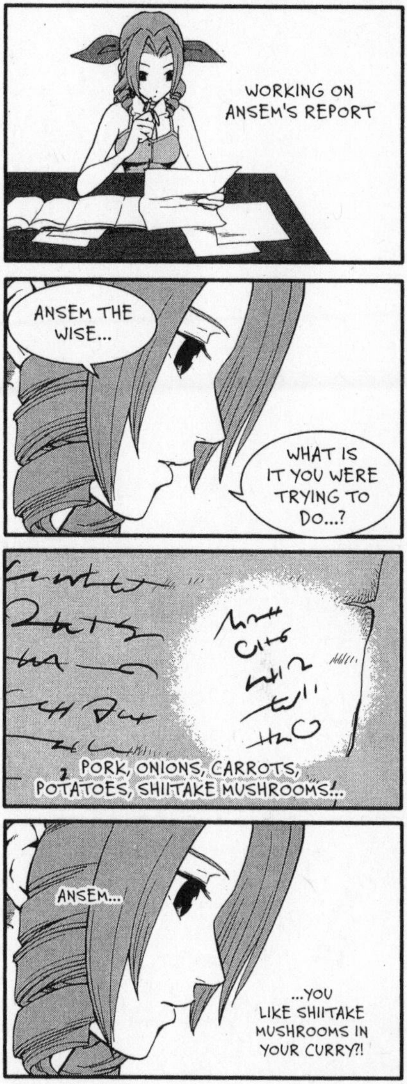
WORKING ON ANSEM'S REPORT
ANSEM THE WISE...
WHAT IS IT YOU WERE TRYING TO DO...?
PORK, ONIONS, CARROTS, POTATOES, SHIITAKE MUSHROOMS...
ANSEM...
...YOU LIKE SHIITAKE MUSHROOMS IN YOUR CURRY?!

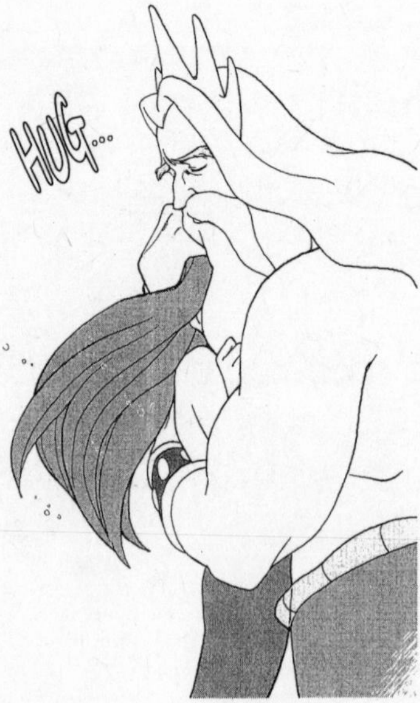
HUG...

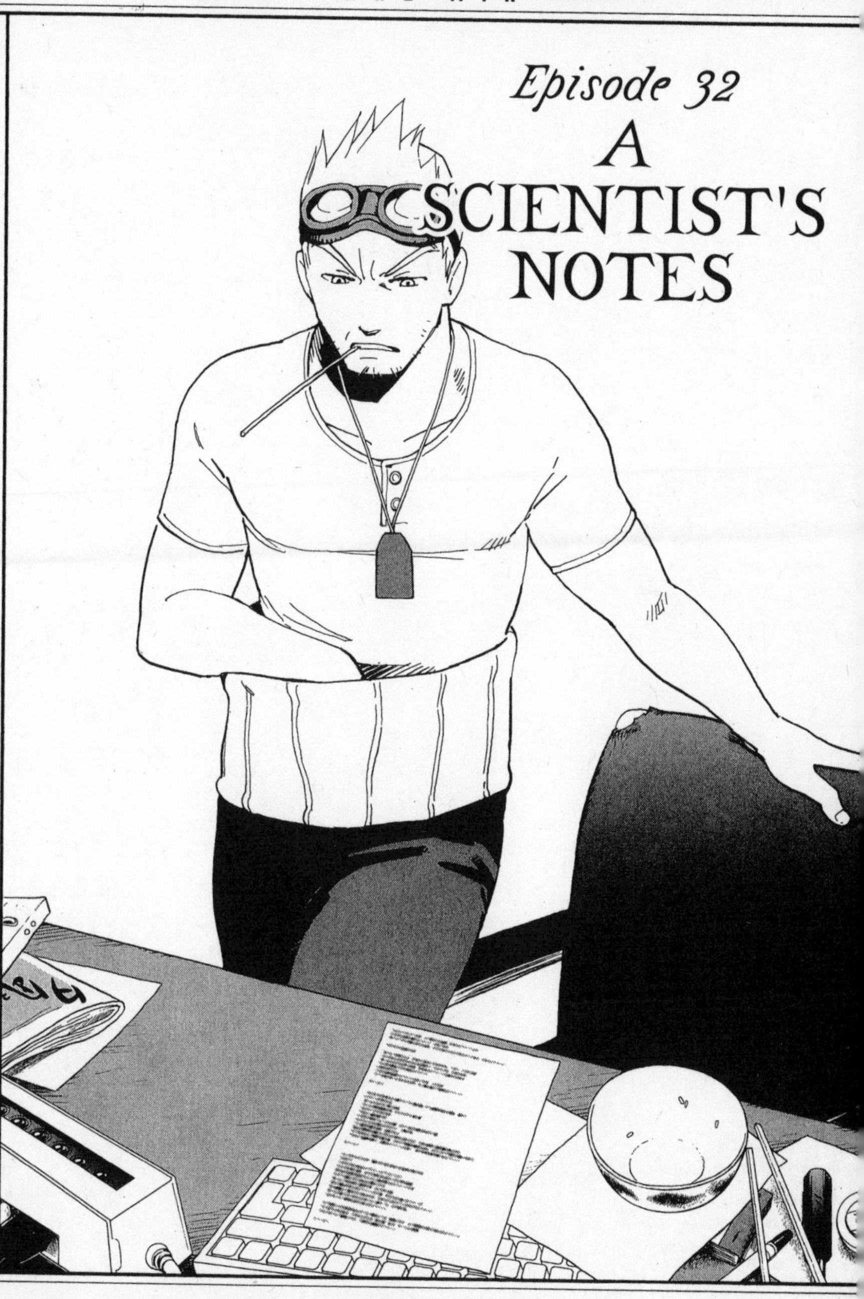
Episode 32
A SCIENTIST'S NOTES

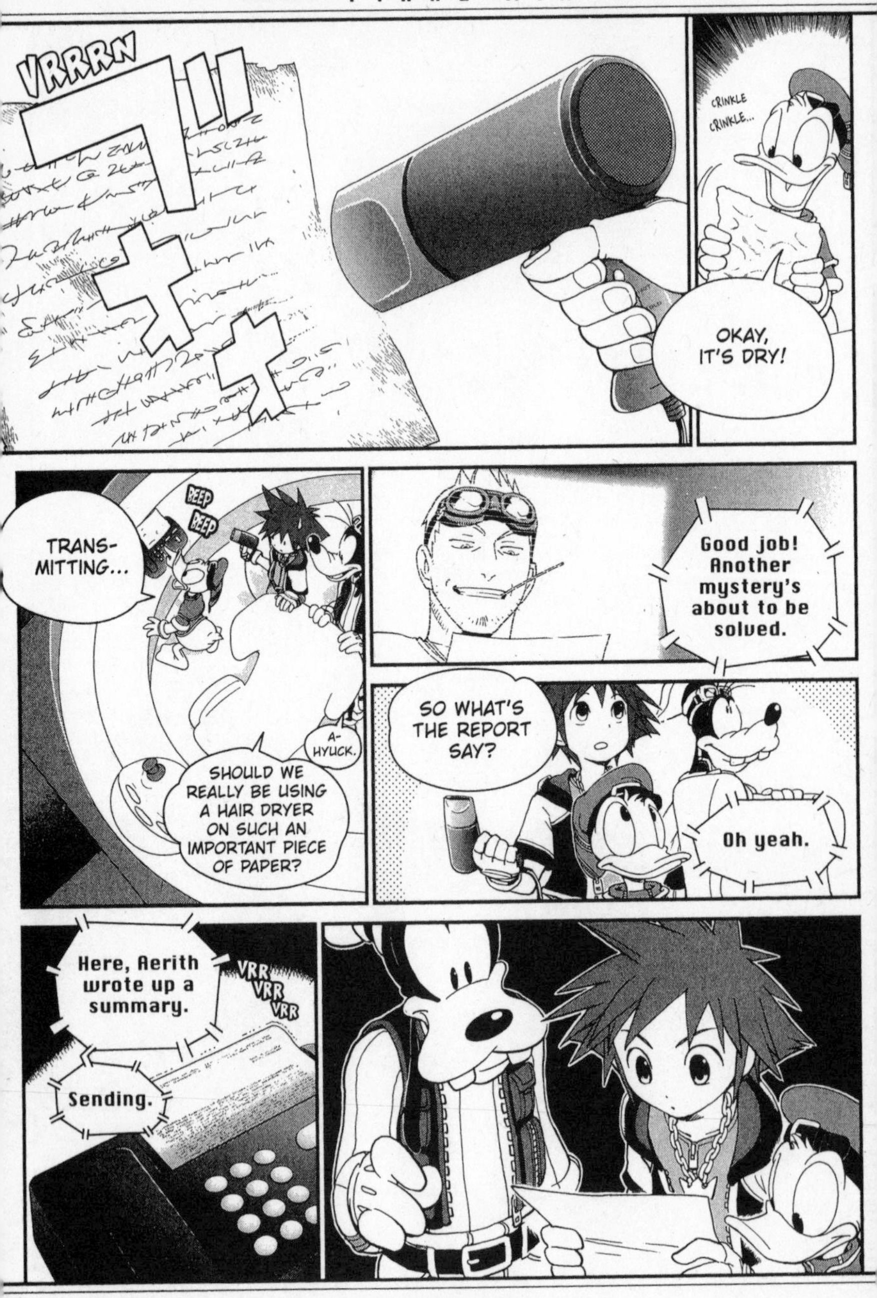
VRRRN
CRINKLE CRINKLE...
OKAY, IT'S DRY!
BEEP BEEP
TRANS-MITTING...
A-HYUCK.
SHOULD WE REALLY BE USING A HAIR DRYER ON SUCH AN IMPORTANT PIECE OF PAPER?
Good job! Another mystery's about to be solved.
SO WHAT'S THE REPORT SAY?
Oh yeah.
Here, Aerith wrote up a summary.
VRR VRR VRR
Sending.

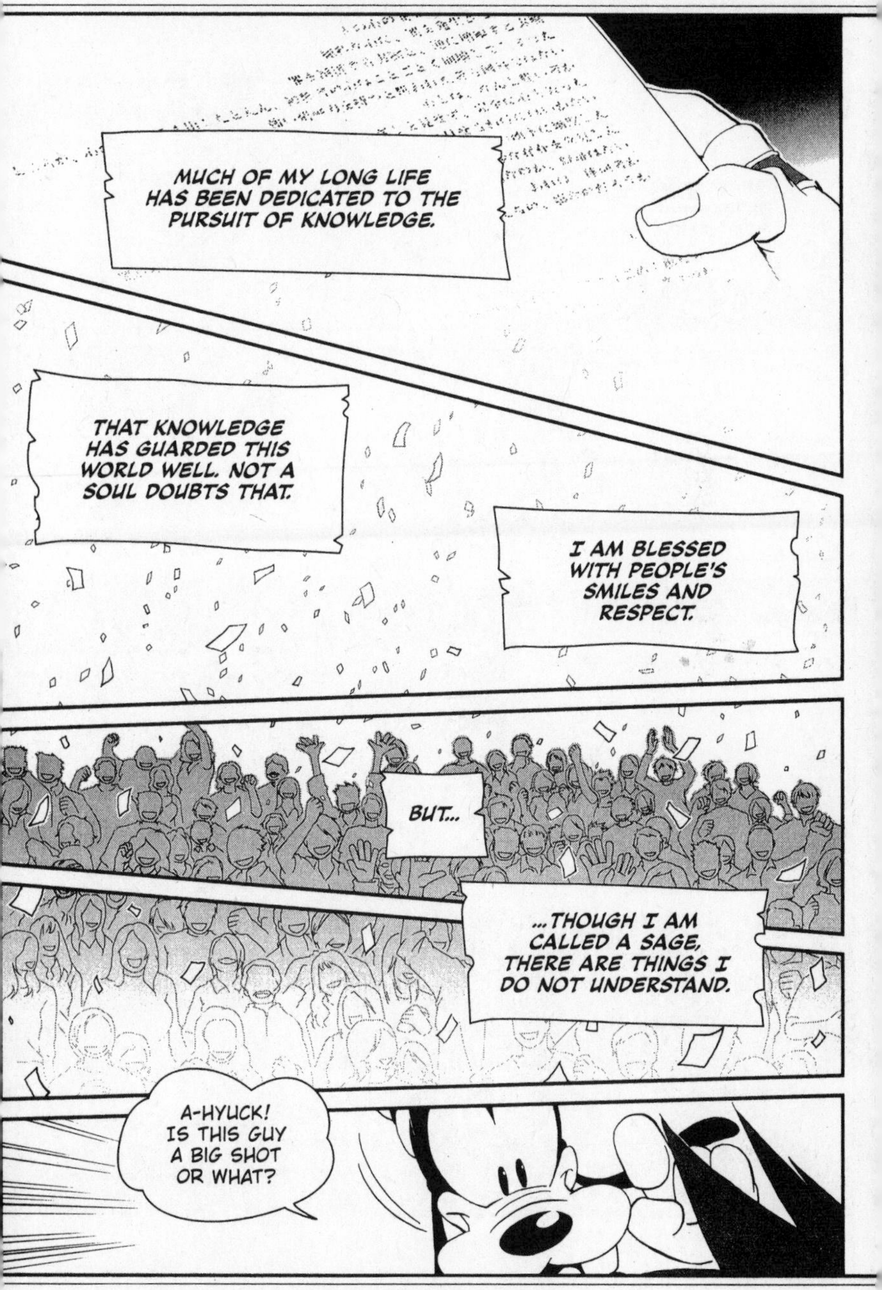
MUCH OF MY LONG LIFE HAS BEEN DEDICATED TO THE PURSUIT OF KNOWLEDGE.
THAT KNOWLEDGE HAS GUARDED THIS WORLD WELL. NOT A SOUL DOUBTS THAT.
I AM BLESSED WITH PEOPLE'S SMILES AND RESPECT.
BUT...
...THOUGH I AM CALLED A SAGE, THERE ARE THINGS I DO NOT UNDERSTAND.
A-HYUCK! IS THIS GUY A BIG SHOT OR WHAT?

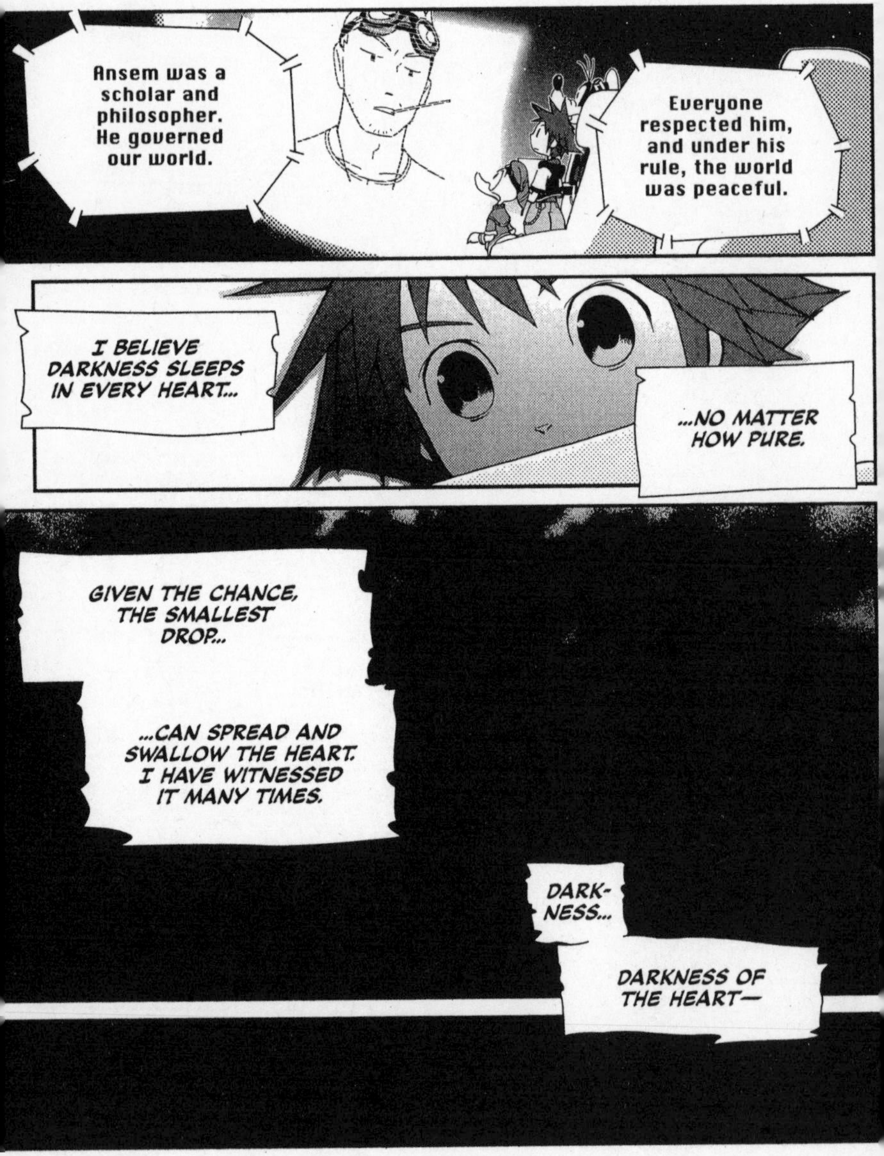
Ansem was a scholar and philosopher. He governed our world.
Everyone respected him, and under his rule, the world was peaceful.
I BELIEVE DARKNESS SLEEPS IN EVERY HEART...
...NO MATTER HOW PURE.
GIVEN THE CHANCE, THE SMALLEST DROP...
...CAN SPREAD AND SWALLOW THE HEART. I HAVE WITNESSED IT MANY TIMES.
DARK-NESS...
DARKNESS OF THE HEART—

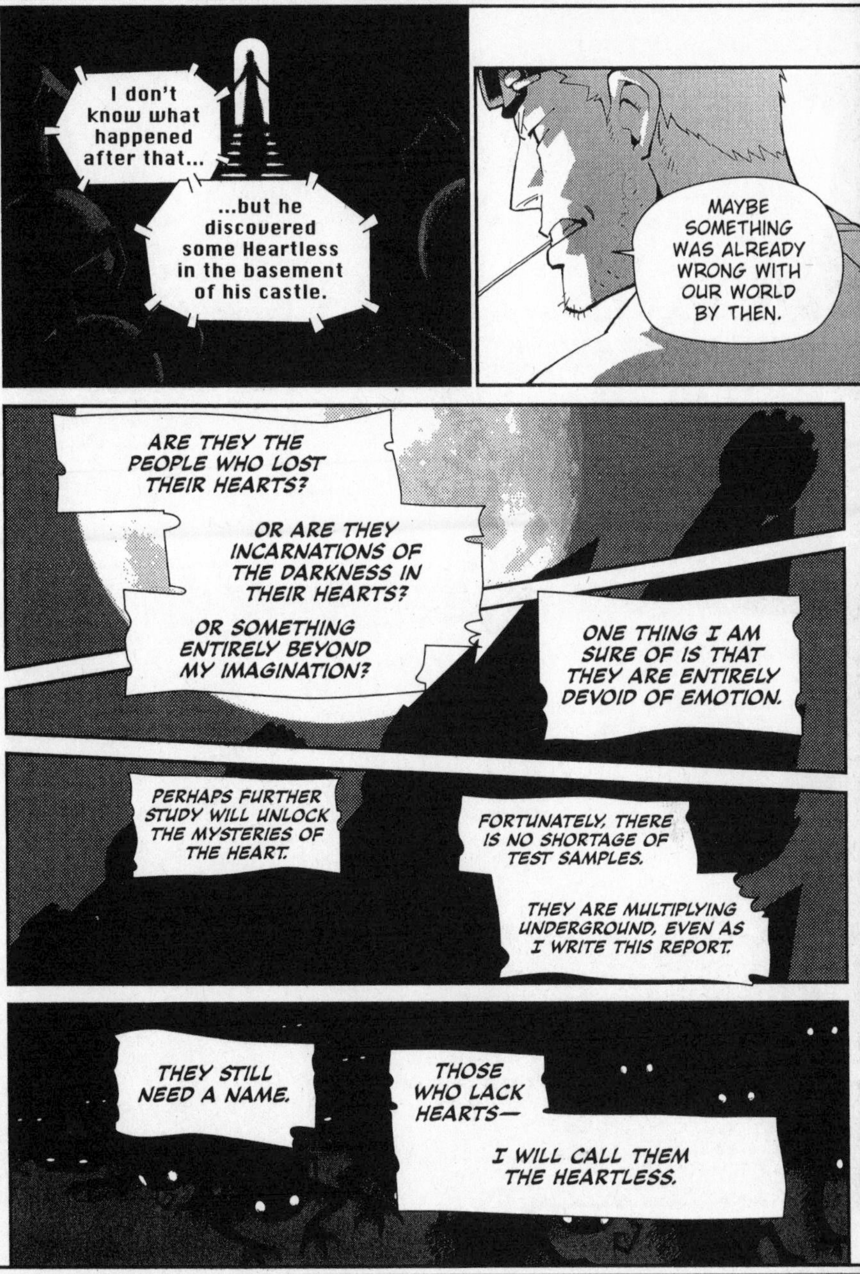
I don't know what happened after that...
...but he discovered some Heartless in the basement of his castle.
MAYBE SOMETHING WAS ALREADY WRONG WITH OUR WORLD BY THEN.
ARE THEY THE PEOPLE WHO LOST THEIR HEARTS?
OR ARE THEY INCARNATIONS OF THE DARKNESS IN THEIR HEARTS?
OR SOMETHING ENTIRELY BEYOND MY IMAGINATION?
ONE THING I AM SURE OF IS THAT THEY ARE ENTIRELY DEVOID OF EMOTION.
PERHAPS FURTHER STUDY WILL UNLOCK THE MYSTERIES OF THE HEART.
FORTUNATELY, THERE IS NO SHORTAGE OF TEST SAMPLES.
THEY ARE MULTIPLYING UNDERGROUND, EVEN AS I WRITE THIS REPORT.
THEY STILL NEED A NAME.
THOSE WHO LACK HEARTS—
I WILL CALL THEM THE HEARTLESS.

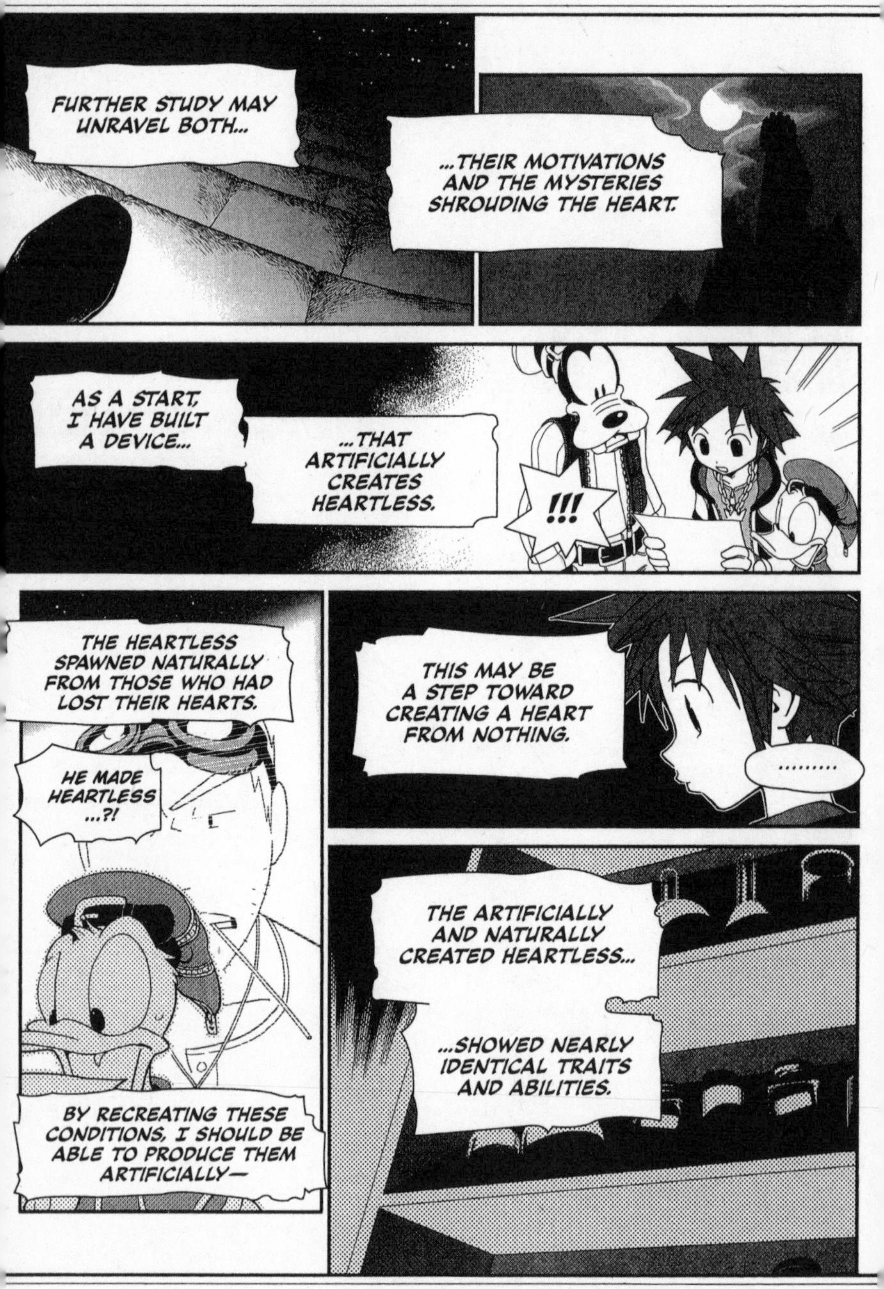
FURTHER STUDY MAY UNRAVEL BOTH...
...THEIR MOTIVATIONS AND THE MYSTERIES SHROUDING THE HEART.
AS A START, I HAVE BUILT A DEVICE...
...THAT ARTIFICIALLY CREATES HEARTLESS.
!!!
THE HEARTLESS SPAWNED NATURALLY FROM THOSE WHO HAD LOST THEIR HEARTS.
HE MADE HEARTLESS ...?!
BY RECREATING THESE CONDITIONS, I SHOULD BE ABLE TO PRODUCE THEM ARTIFICIALLY—
THIS MAY BE A STEP TOWARD CREATING A HEART FROM NOTHING.
....
THE ARTIFICIALLY AND NATURALLY CREATED HEARTLESS...
...SHOWED NEARLY IDENTICAL TRAITS AND ABILITIES.

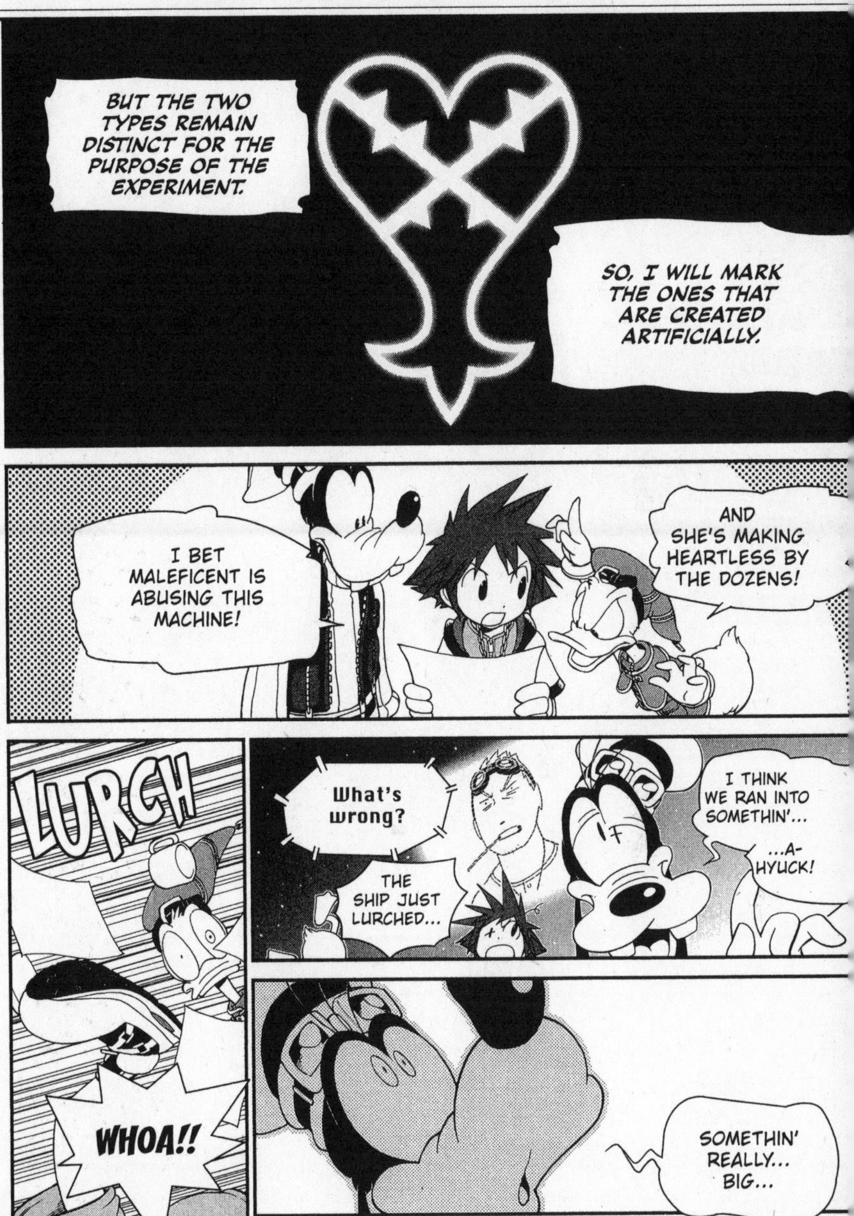
BUT THE TWO TYPES REMAIN DISTINCT FOR THE PURPOSE OF THE EXPERIMENT.
SO, I WILL MARK THE ONES THAT ARE CREATED ARTIFICIALLY.
I BET MALEFICENT IS ABUSING THIS MACHINE!
AND SHE'S MAKING HEARTLESS BY THE DOZENS!
LURCH
WHOA!!
What's wrong?
THE SHIP JUST LURCHED...
I THINK WE RAN INTO SOMETHIN'...
...A-HYUCK!
SOMETHIN' REALLY... BIG...

IT'S A PIRATE SHIP!!

HEY!

WAIT!

BOOP

OH NO! WHAT'S HAPPENED TO—

FWEEE

OH! THE HOT WATER'S READY!

RAMEN

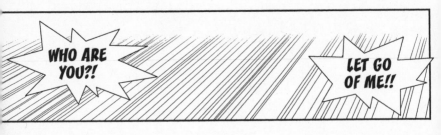

WHO ARE YOU?!

LET GO OF ME!!

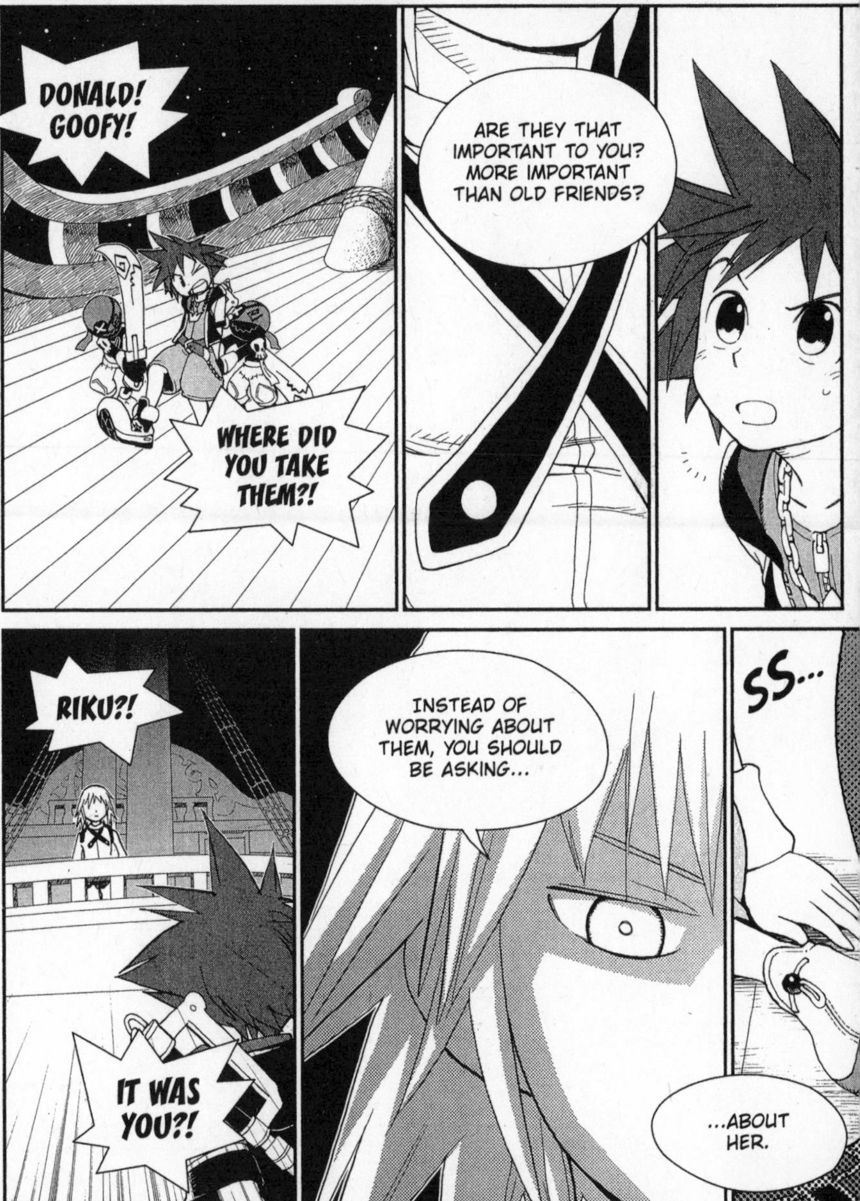
DONALD! GOOFY!
WHERE DID YOU TAKE THEM?!
ARE THEY THAT IMPORTANT TO YOU? MORE IMPORTANT THAN OLD FRIENDS?
RIKU?!
IT WAS YOU?!
INSTEAD OF WORRYING ABOUT THEM, YOU SHOULD BE ASKING...
SS...
...ABOUT HER.

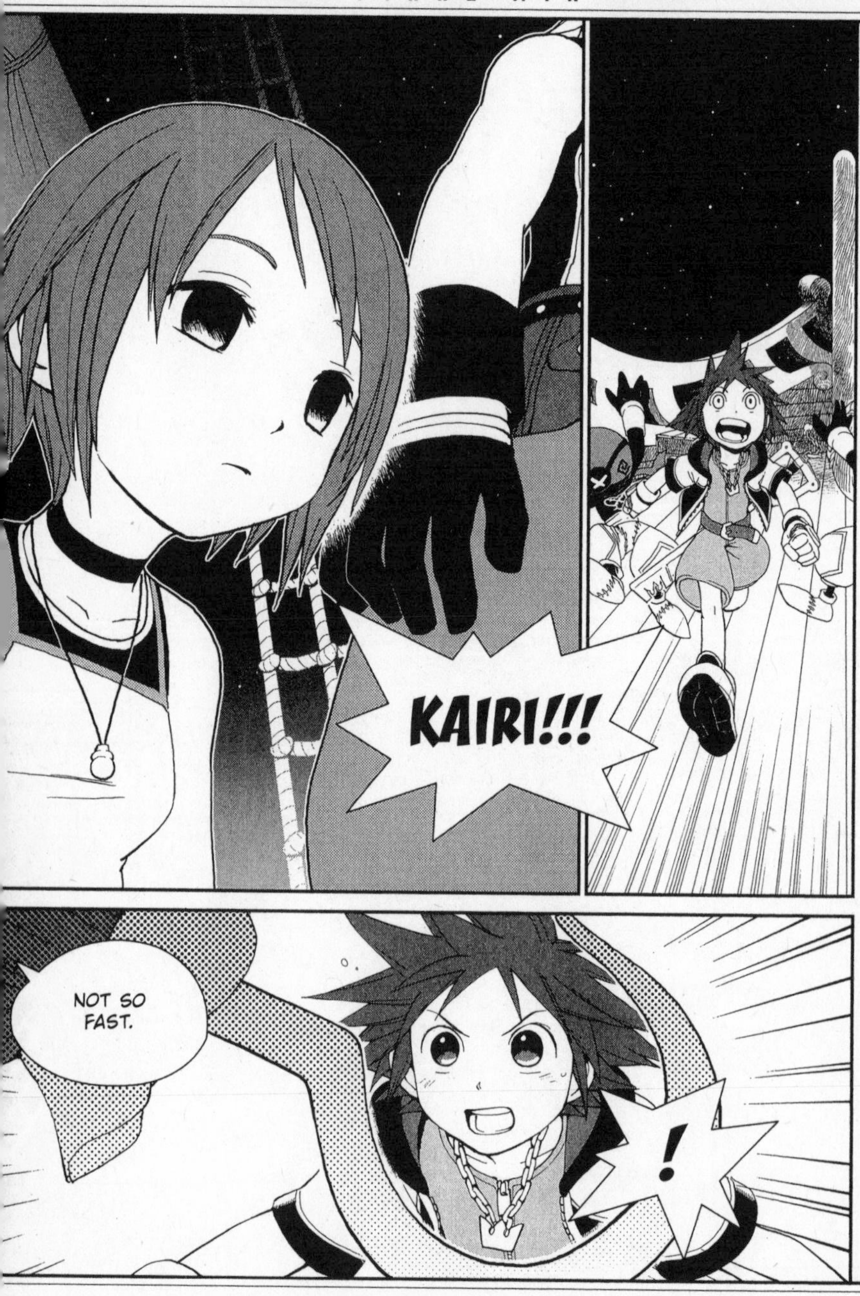
KAIRI!!!
NOT SO FAST.
!

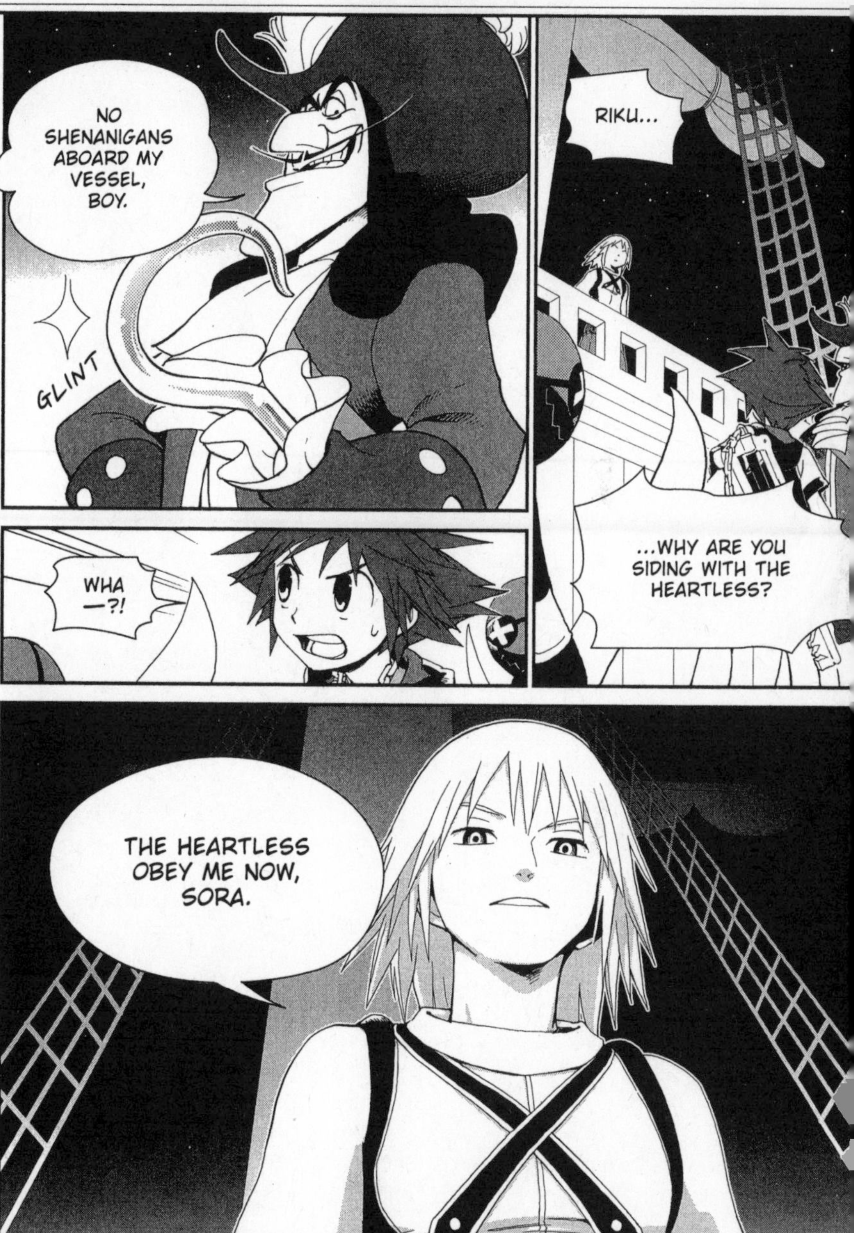
NO SHENANIGANS ABOARD MY VESSEL, BOY.
GLINT
WHA —?!
RIKU...
...WHY ARE YOU SIDING WITH THE HEARTLESS?
THE HEARTLESS OBEY ME NOW, SORA.

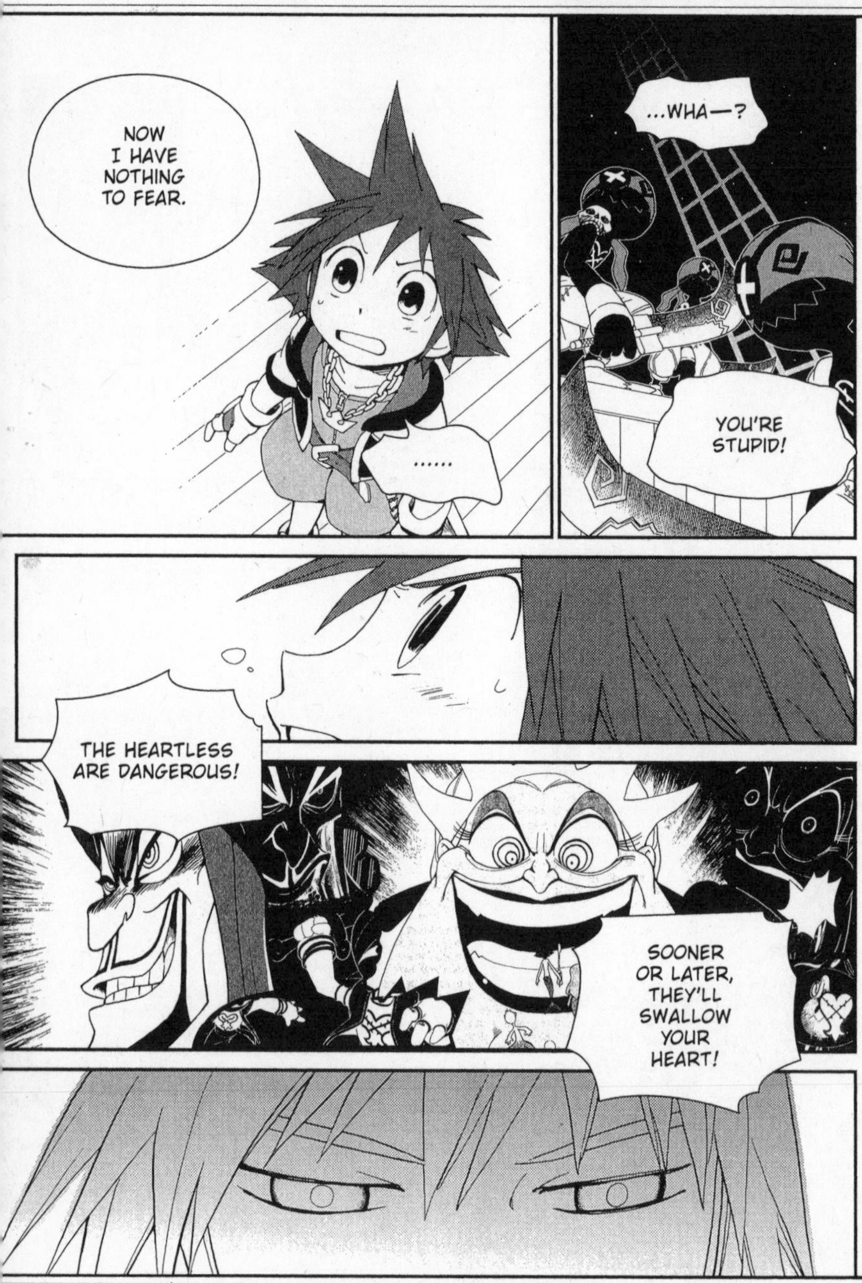
NOW I HAVE NOTHING TO FEAR.
......
...WHA—?
YOU'RE STUPID!
THE HEARTLESS ARE DANGEROUS!
SOONER OR LATER, THEY'LL SWALLOW YOUR HEART!

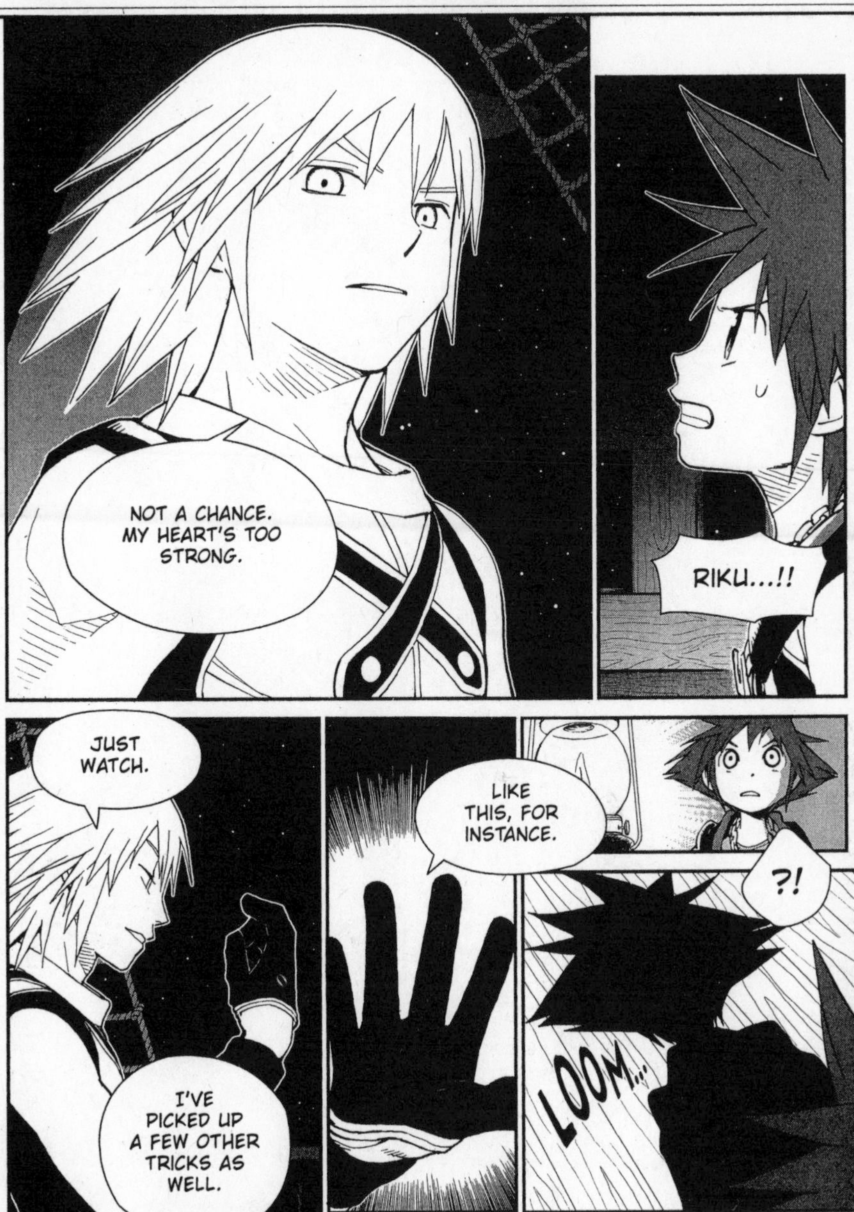
NOT A CHANCE. MY HEART'S TOO STRONG.
RIKU...!!
JUST WATCH.
I'VE PICKED UP A FEW OTHER TRICKS AS WELL.
LIKE THIS, FOR INSTANCE.
?!
LOOM...

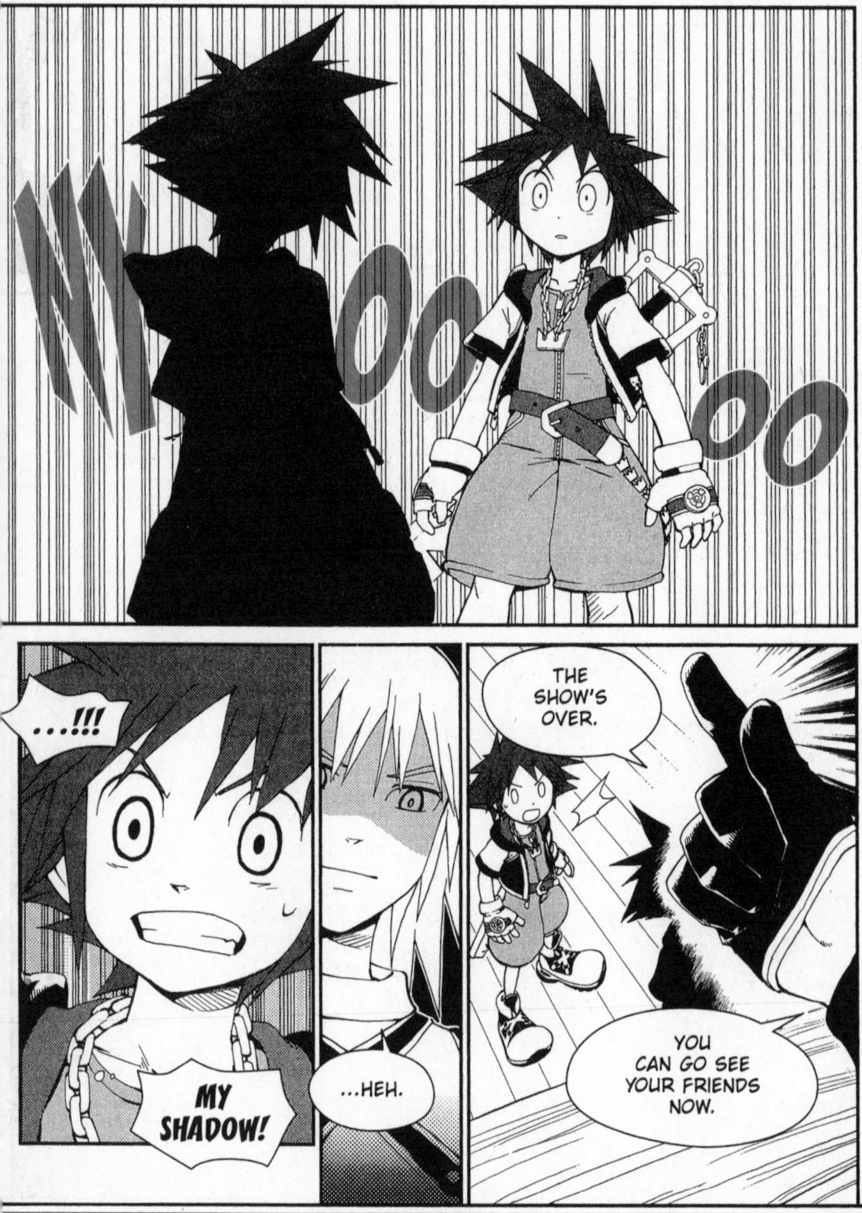
NYOOOO
...!!!
MY SHADOW!
...HEH.
THE SHOW'S OVER.
YOU CAN GO SEE YOUR FRIENDS NOW.

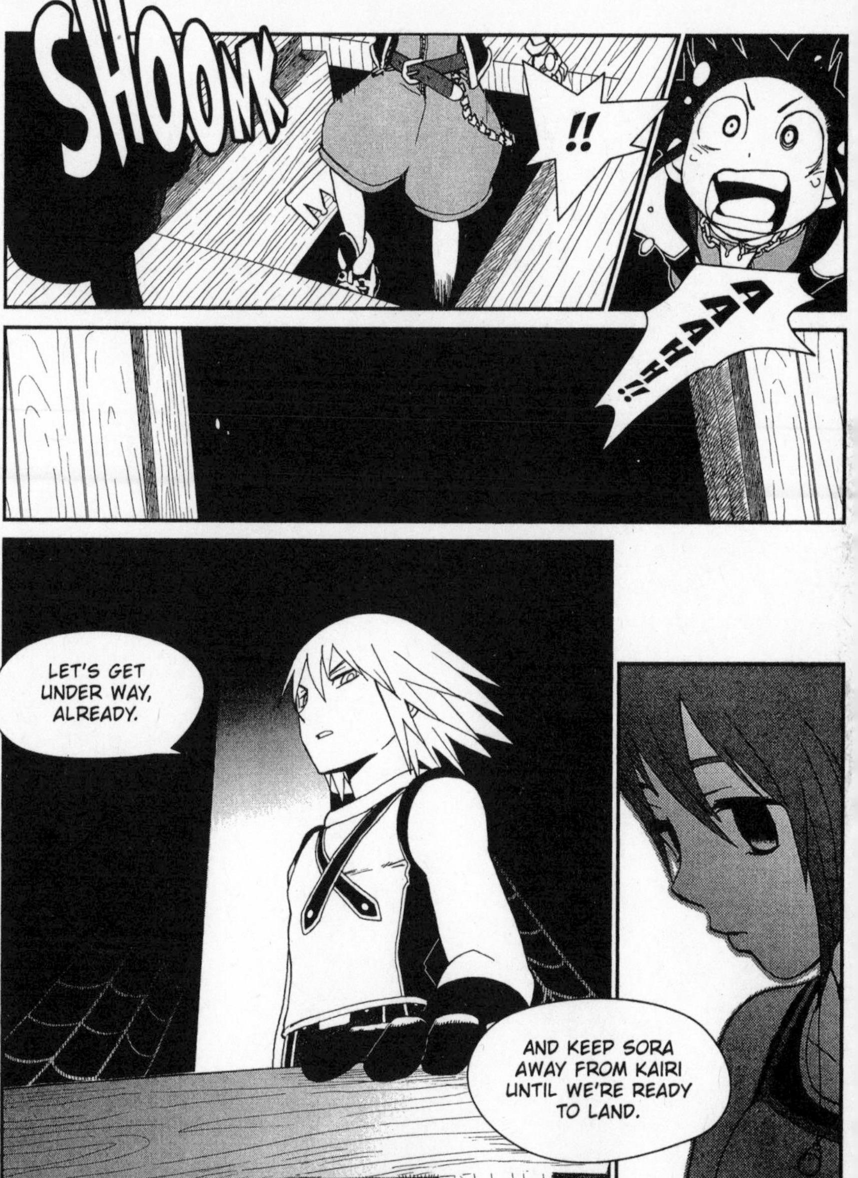
SHOOM
!!
AAAHH!!
LET'S GET UNDER WAY, ALREADY.
AND KEEP SORA AWAY FROM KAIRI UNTIL WE'RE READY TO LAND.

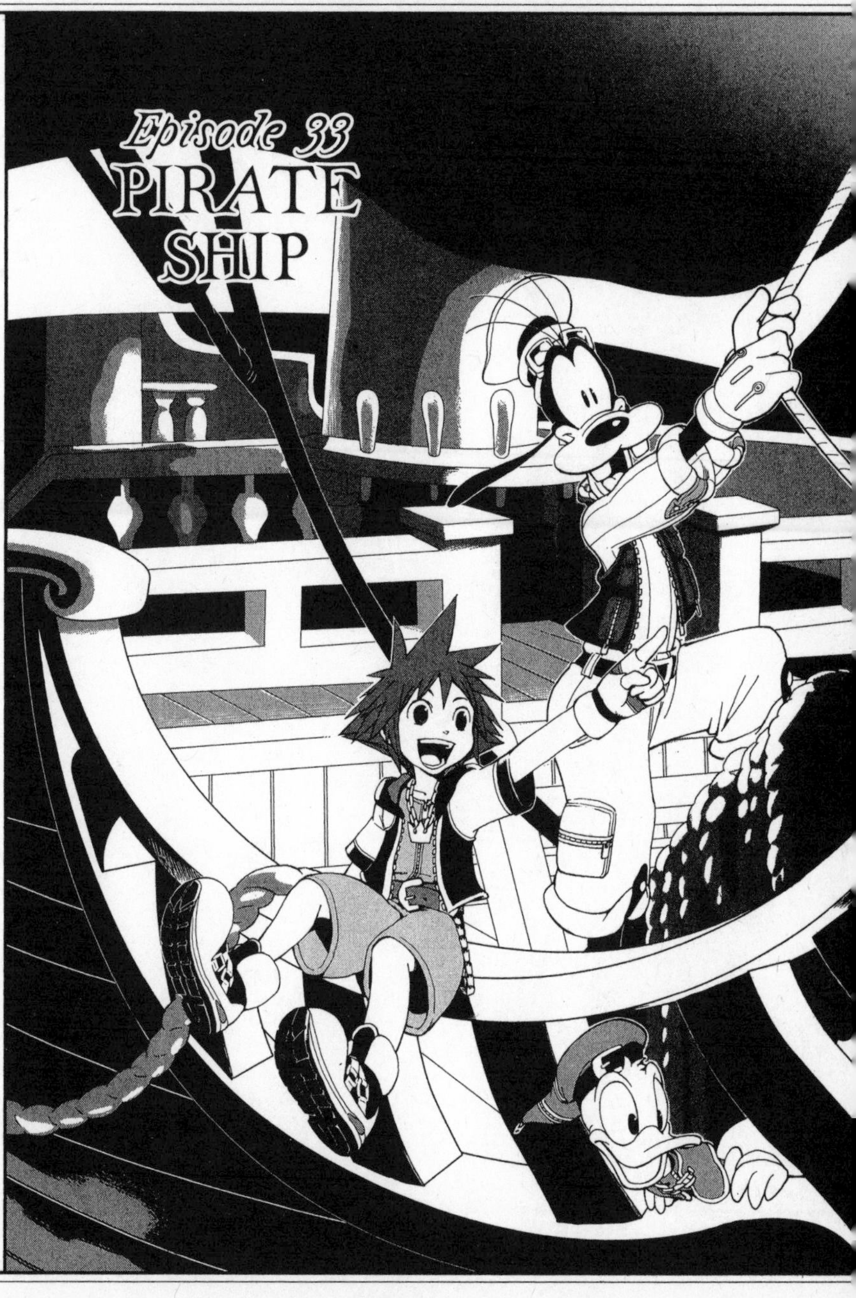
Episode 33
PIRATE SHIP

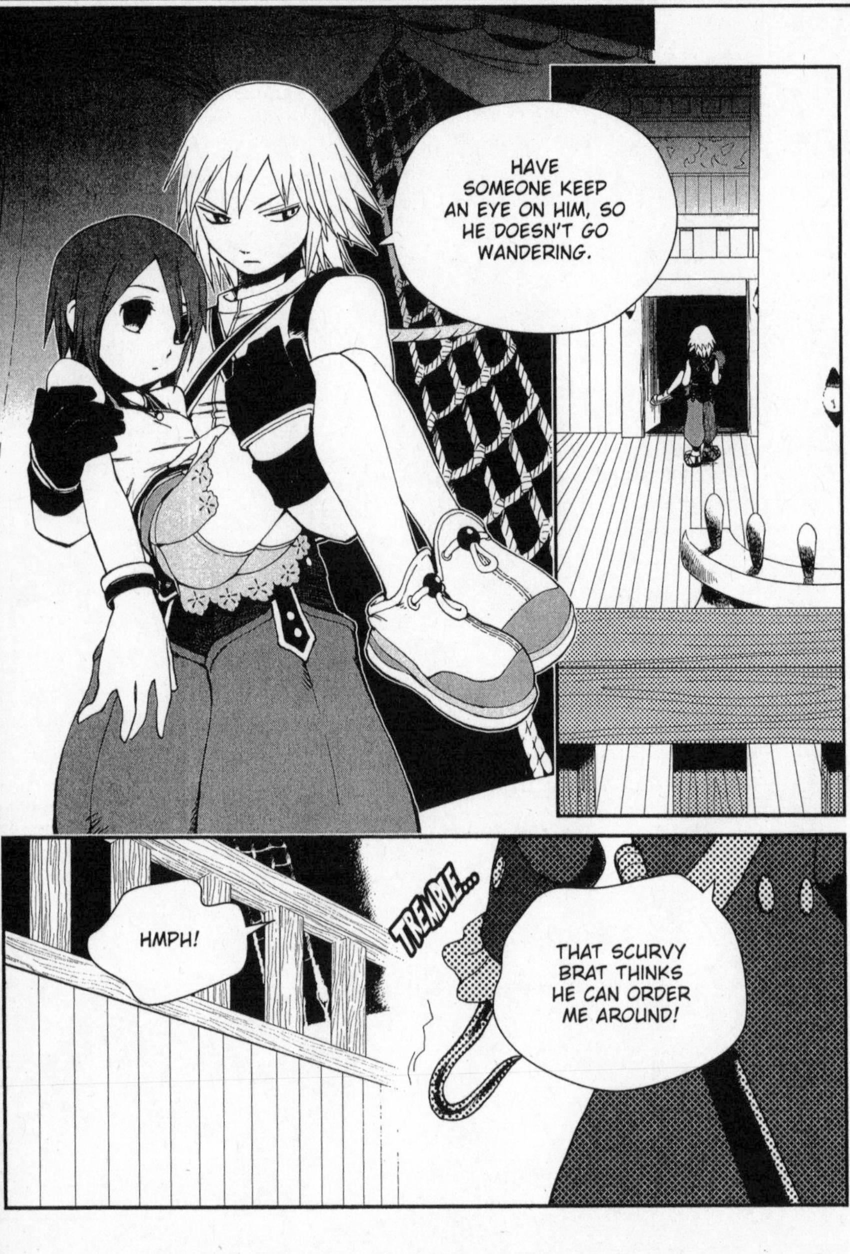
HAVE SOMEONE KEEP AN EYE ON HIM, SO HE DOESN'T GO WANDERING.
HMPH!
TREMBLE...
THAT SCURVY BRAT THINKS HE CAN ORDER ME AROUND!

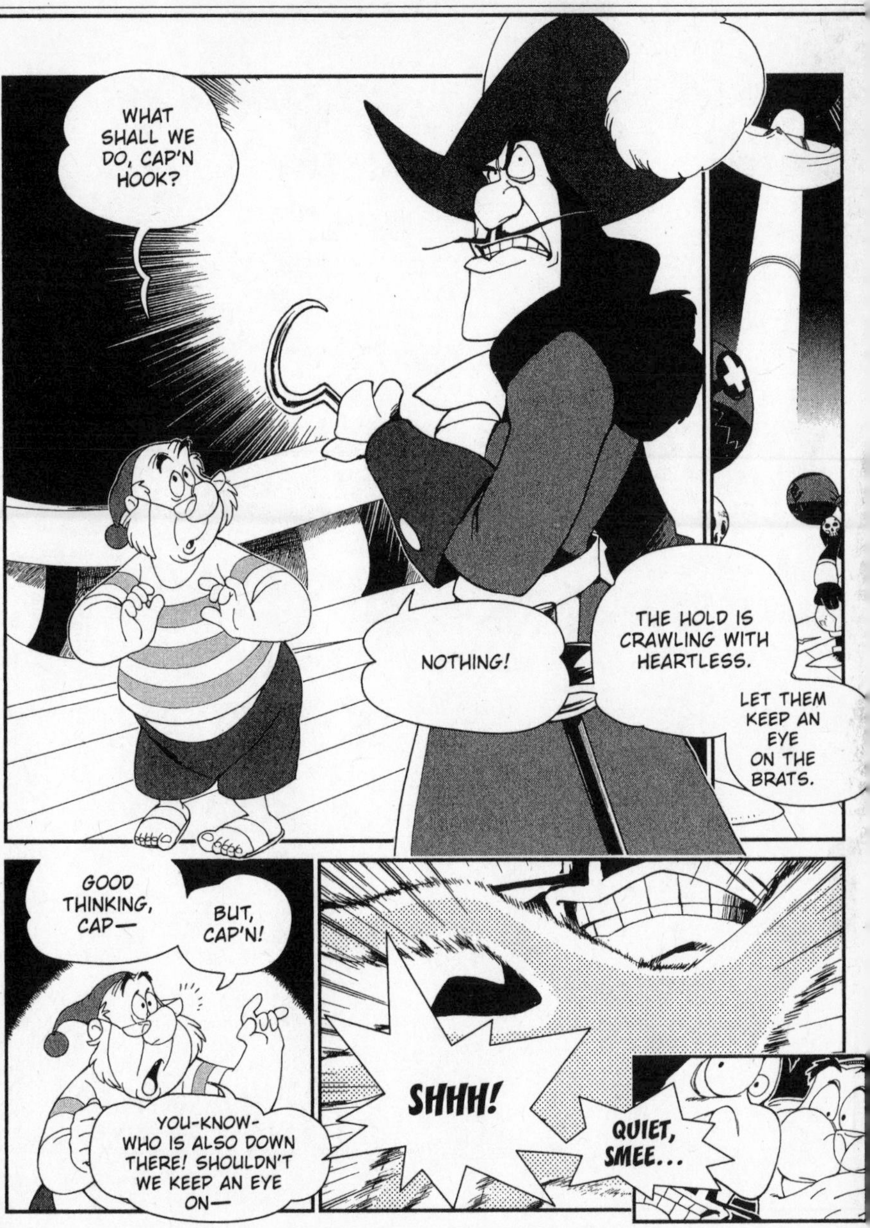
WHAT SHALL WE DO, CAP'N HOOK?
NOTHING!
THE HOLD IS CRAWLING WITH HEARTLESS.
LET THEM KEEP AN EYE ON THE BRATS.
GOOD THINKING, CAP—
BUT, CAP'N!
YOU-KNOW-WHO IS ALSO DOWN THERE! SHOULDN'T WE KEEP AN EYE ON—
SHHH!
QUIET, SMEE...

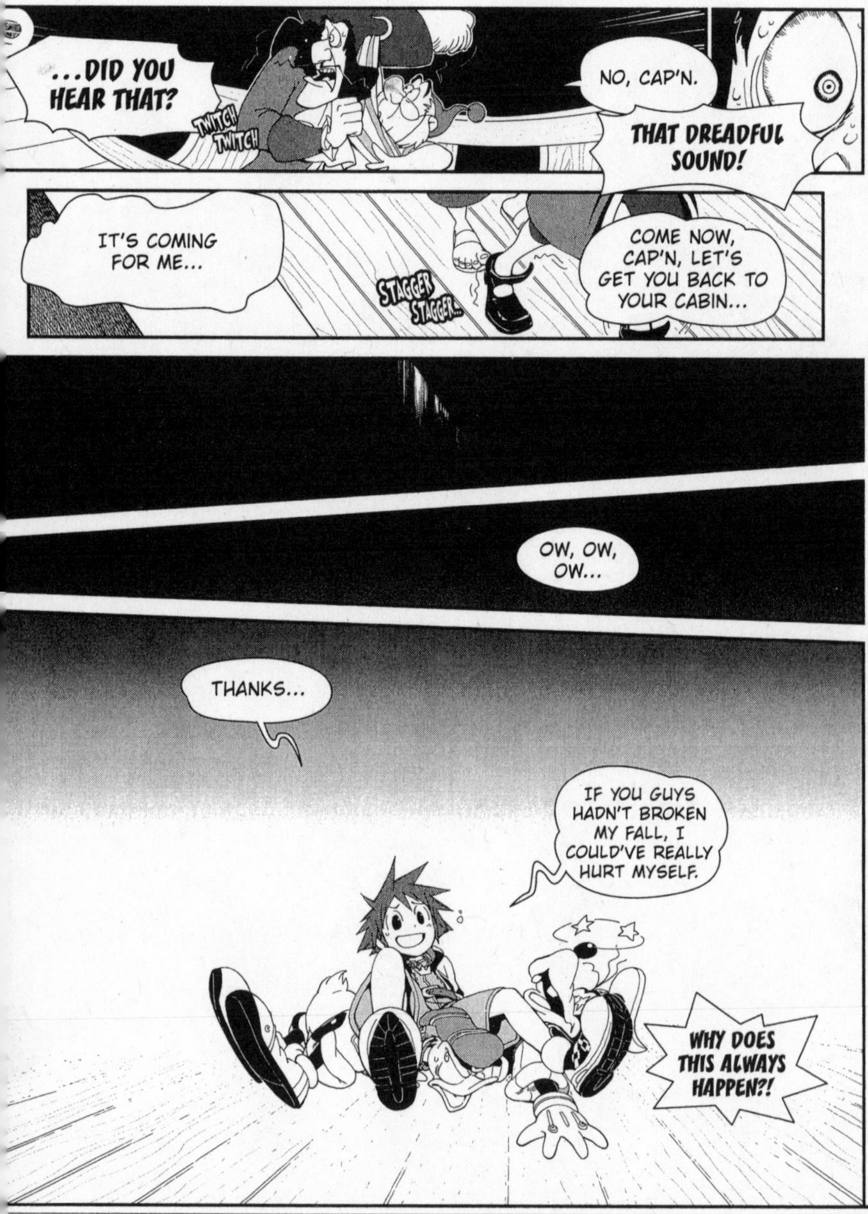
...DID YOU HEAR THAT?
TWITCH TWITCH
NO, CAP'N.
THAT DREADFUL SOUND!
IT'S COMING FOR ME...
STAGGER STAGGER...
COME NOW, CAP'N, LET'S GET YOU BACK TO YOUR CABIN...
OW, OW, OW...
THANKS...
IF YOU GUYS HADN'T BROKEN MY FALL, I COULD'VE REALLY HURT MYSELF.
WHY DOES THIS ALWAYS HAPPEN?!

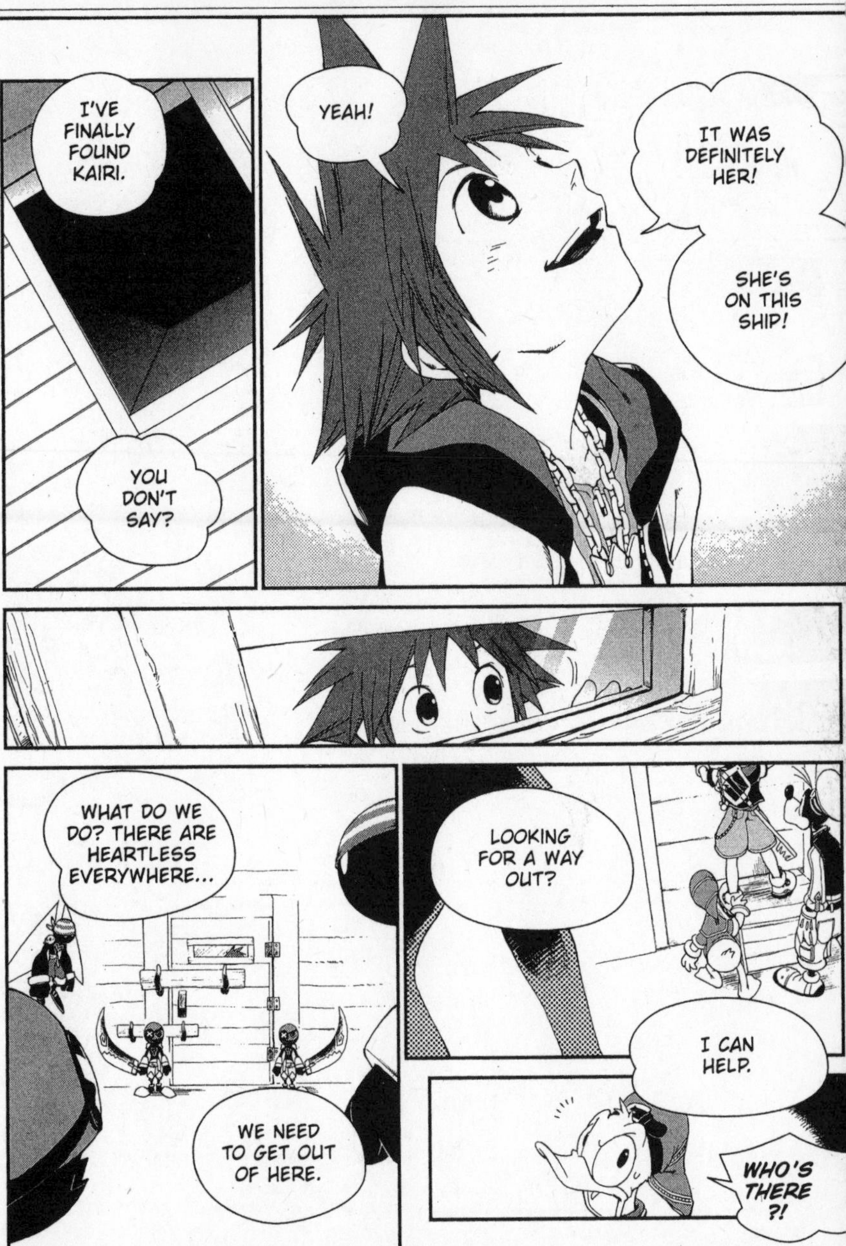
I'VE FINALLY FOUND KAIRI.
YOU DON'T SAY?
YEAH!
IT WAS DEFINITELY HER!
SHE'S ON THIS SHIP!
WHAT DO WE DO? THERE ARE HEARTLESS EVERYWHERE...
WE NEED TO GET OUT OF HERE.
LOOKING FOR A WAY OUT?
I CAN HELP.
WHO'S THERE ?!

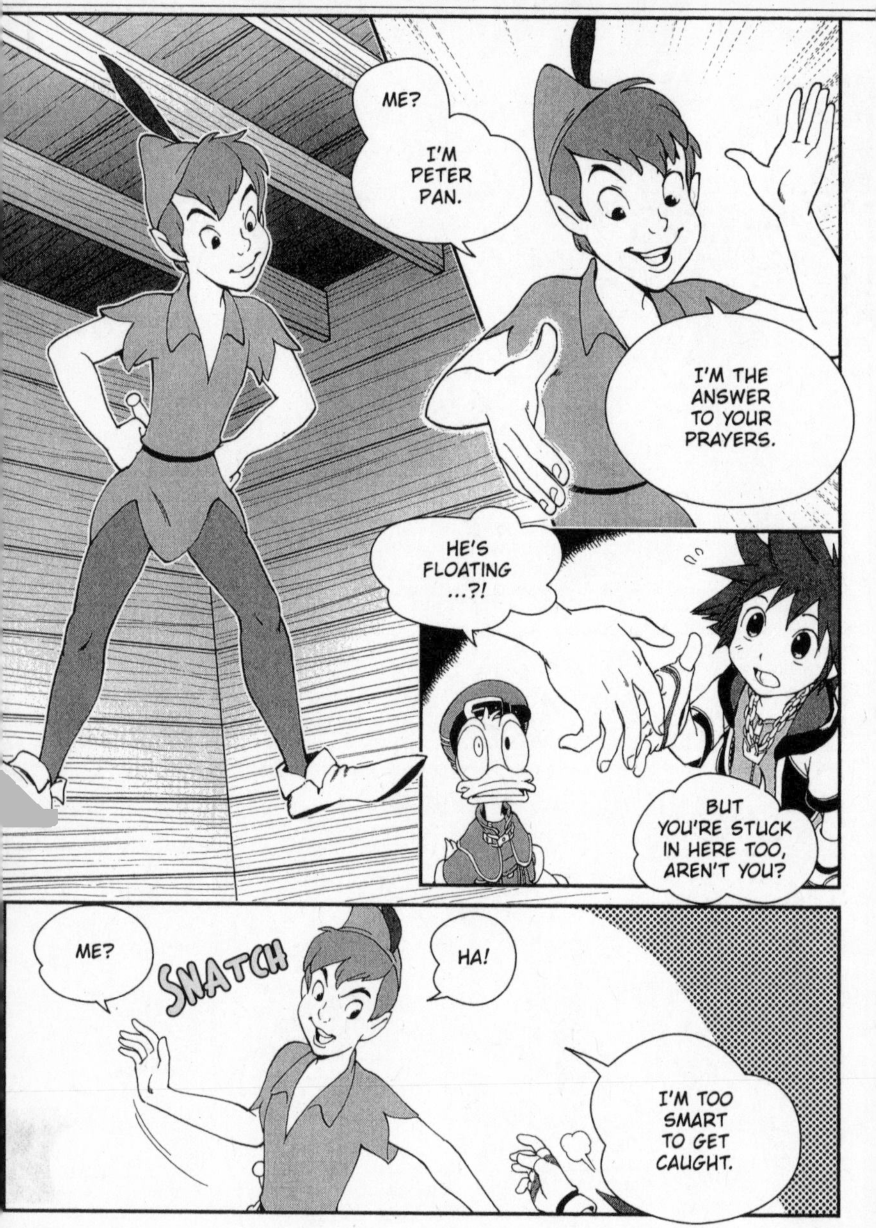
ME?
I'M PETER PAN.
I'M THE ANSWER TO YOUR PRAYERS.
HE'S FLOATING ...?!
BUT YOU'RE STUCK IN HERE TOO, AREN'T YOU?
ME?
SNATCH
HA!
I'M TOO SMART TO GET CAUGHT.

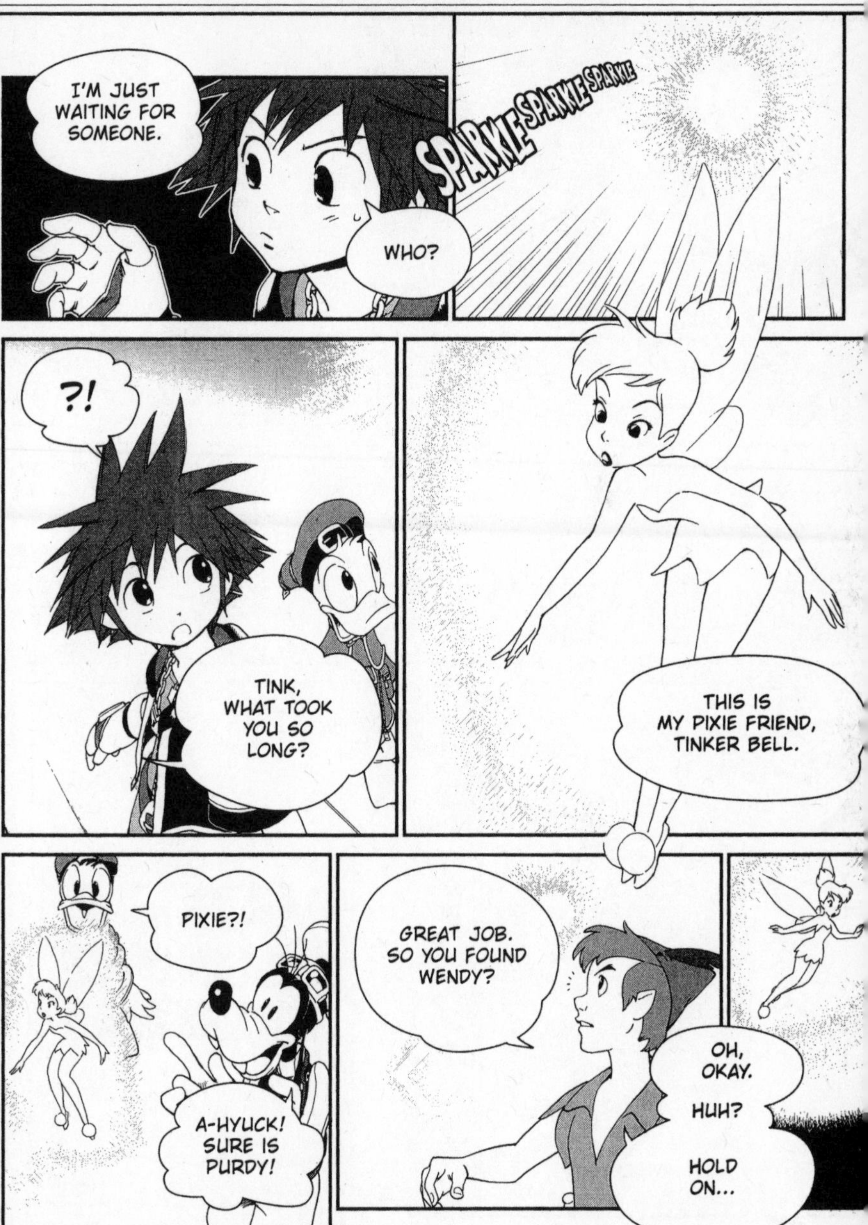
I'M JUST WAITING FOR SOMEONE.
WHO?
SPARKLE SPARKLE SPARKLE
?!
TINK, WHAT TOOK YOU SO LONG?
THIS IS MY PIXIE FRIEND, TINKER BELL.
PIXIE?!
A-HYUCK! SURE IS PURDY!
GREAT JOB. SO YOU FOUND WENDY?
OH, OKAY.
HUH?
HOLD ON...

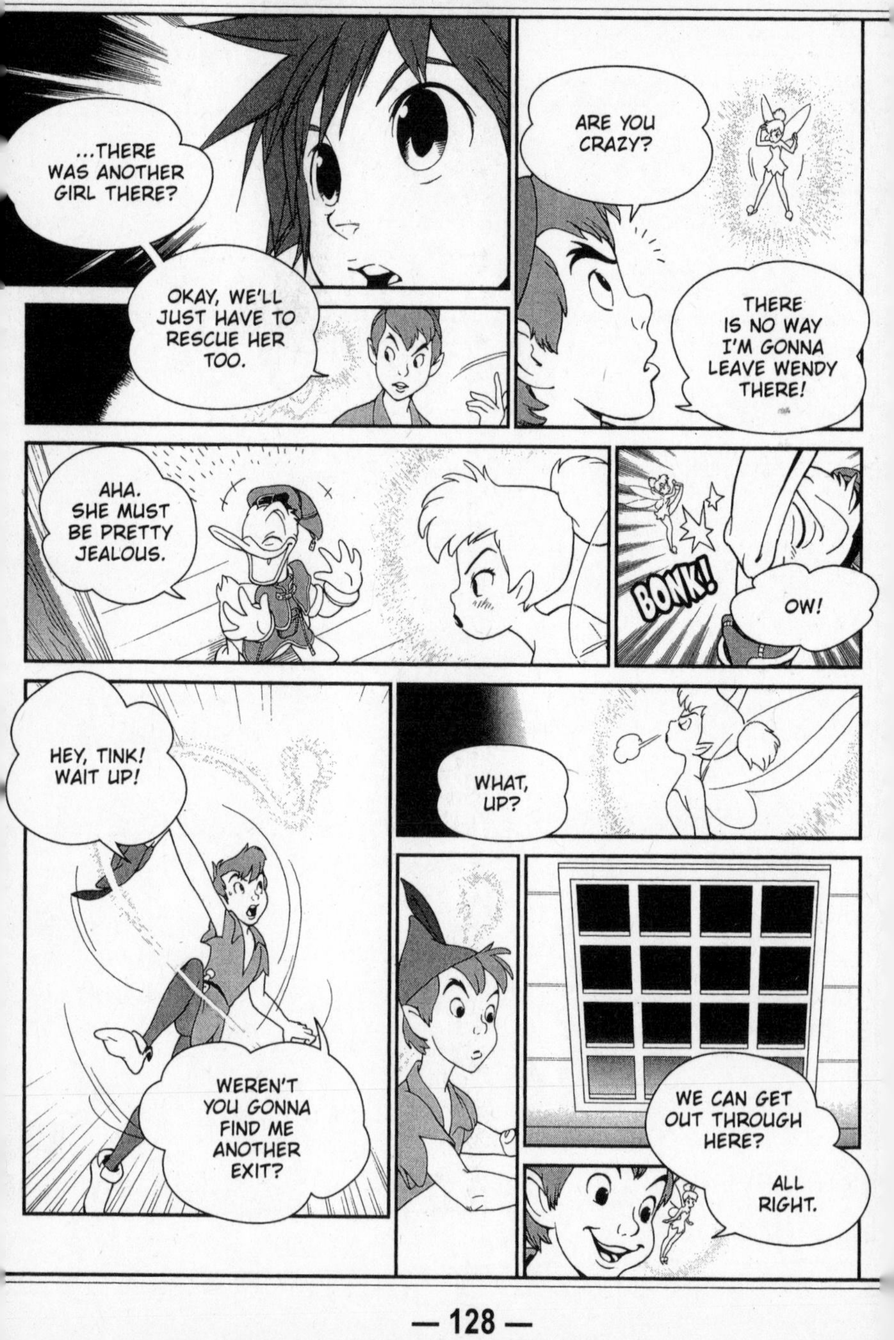
...THERE WAS ANOTHER GIRL THERE?
OKAY, WE'LL JUST HAVE TO RESCUE HER TOO.
ARE YOU CRAZY?
THERE IS NO WAY I'M GONNA LEAVE WENDY THERE!
AHA. SHE MUST BE PRETTY JEALOUS.
BONK!
OW!
HEY, TINK! WAIT UP!
WEREN'T YOU GONNA FIND ME ANOTHER EXIT?
WHAT, UP?
WE CAN GET OUT THROUGH HERE?
ALL RIGHT.

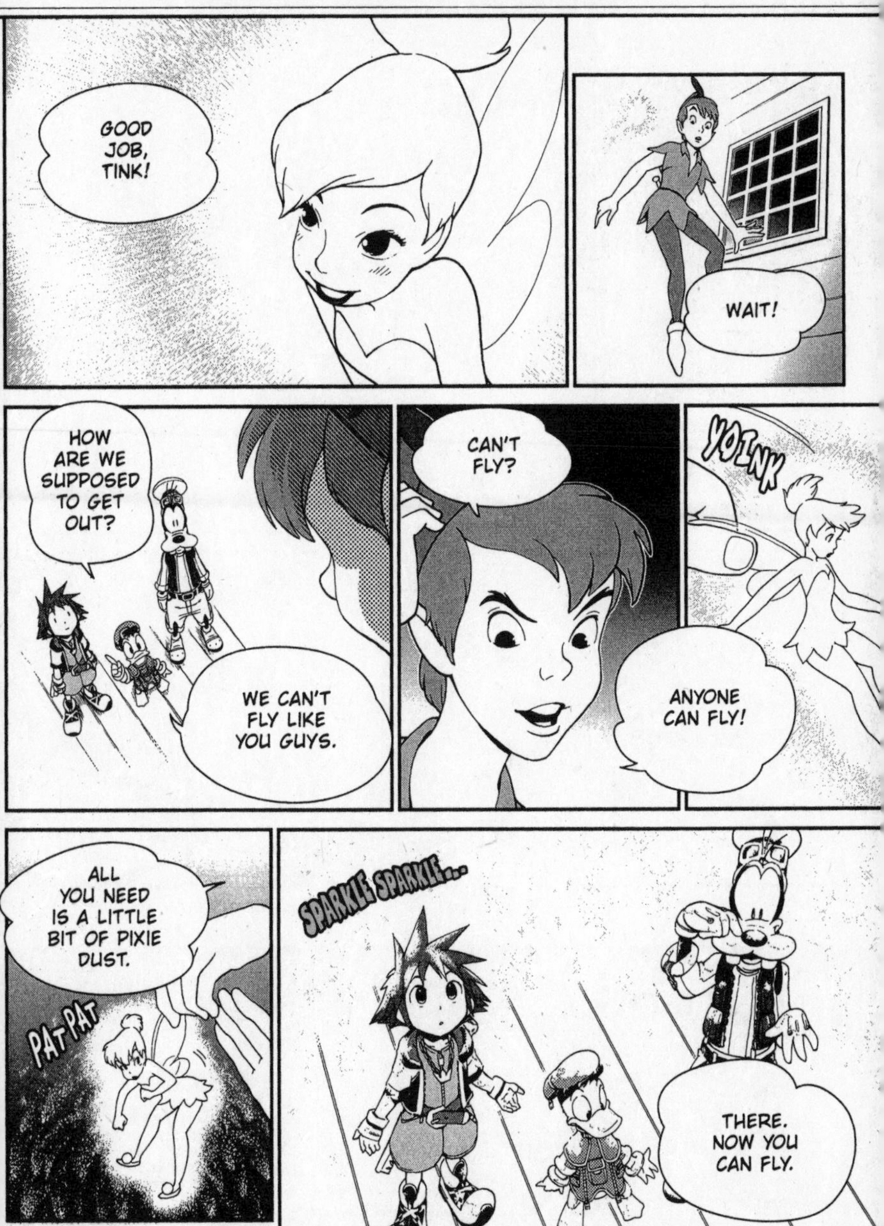
GOOD JOB, TINK!
WAIT!
HOW ARE WE SUPPOSED TO GET OUT?
WE CAN'T FLY LIKE YOU GUYS.
CAN'T FLY?
ANYONE CAN FLY!
YOINK
ALL YOU NEED IS A LITTLE BIT OF PIXIE DUST.
PAT PAT
SPARKLE SPARKLE...
THERE. NOW YOU CAN FLY.

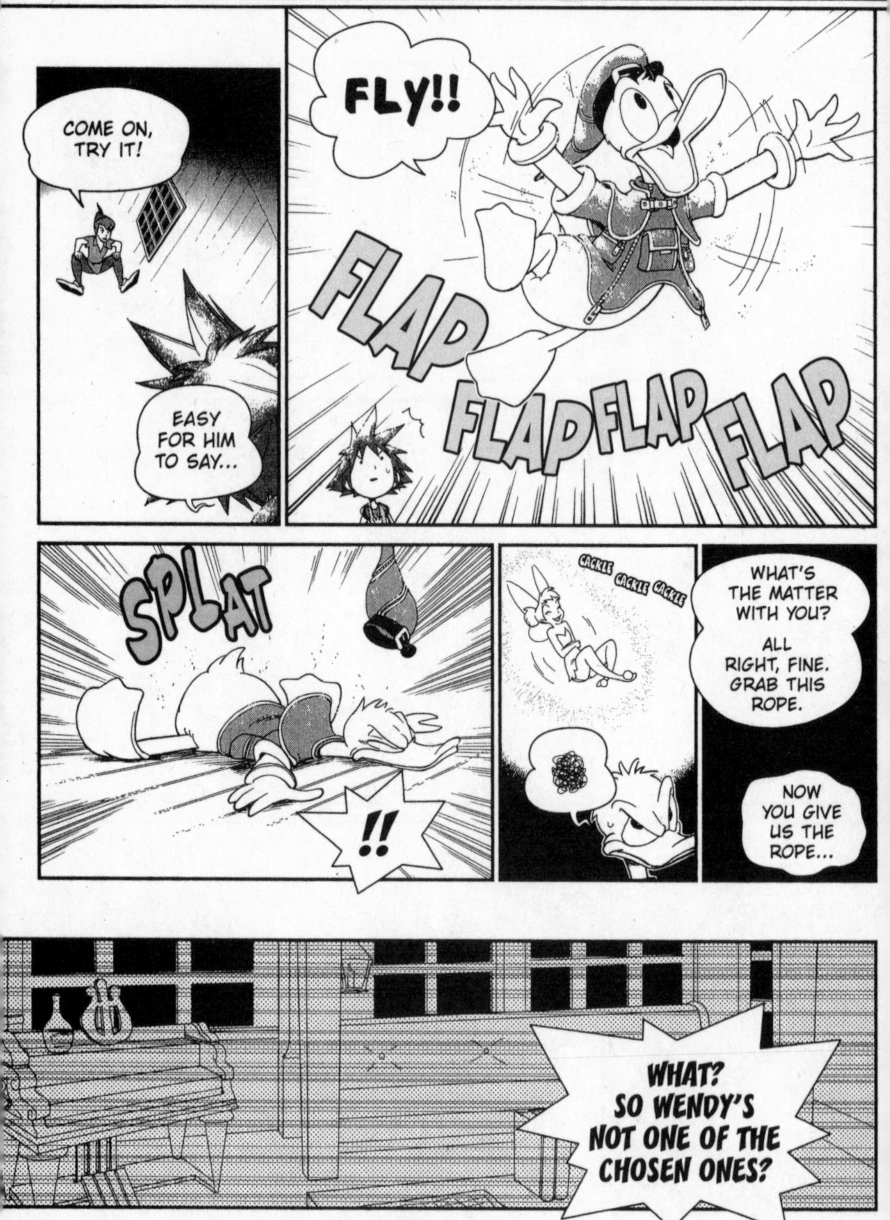
COME ON, TRY IT!
EASY FOR HIM TO SAY...
FLY!!
FLAP
FLAP FLAP FLAP
SPLAT
!!
CACKLE CACKLE CACKLE
WHAT'S THE MATTER WITH YOU?
ALL RIGHT, FINE. GRAB THIS ROPE.
NOW YOU GIVE US THE ROPE...
WHAT? SO WENDY'S NOT ONE OF THE CHOSEN ONES?

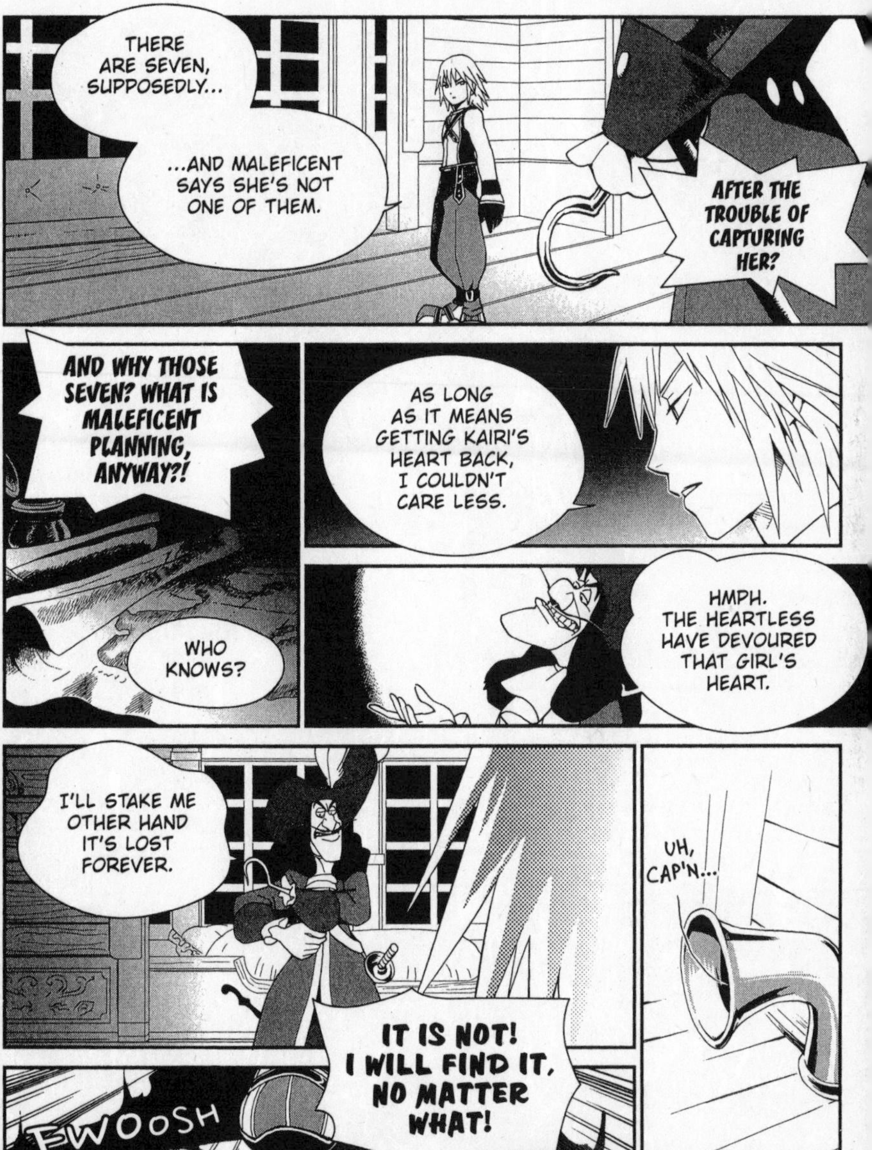
THERE ARE SEVEN, SUPPOSEDLY...
...AND MALEFICENT SAYS SHE'S NOT ONE OF THEM.
AFTER THE TROUBLE OF CAPTURING HER?
AND WHY THOSE SEVEN? WHAT IS MALEFICENT PLANNING, ANYWAY?!
WHO KNOWS?
AS LONG AS IT MEANS GETTING KAIRI'S HEART BACK, I COULDN'T CARE LESS.
HMPH. THE HEARTLESS HAVE DEVOURED THAT GIRL'S HEART.
I'LL STAKE ME OTHER HAND IT'S LOST FOREVER.
FWOOSH
IT IS NOT! I WILL FIND IT, NO MATTER WHAT!
UH, CAP'N...

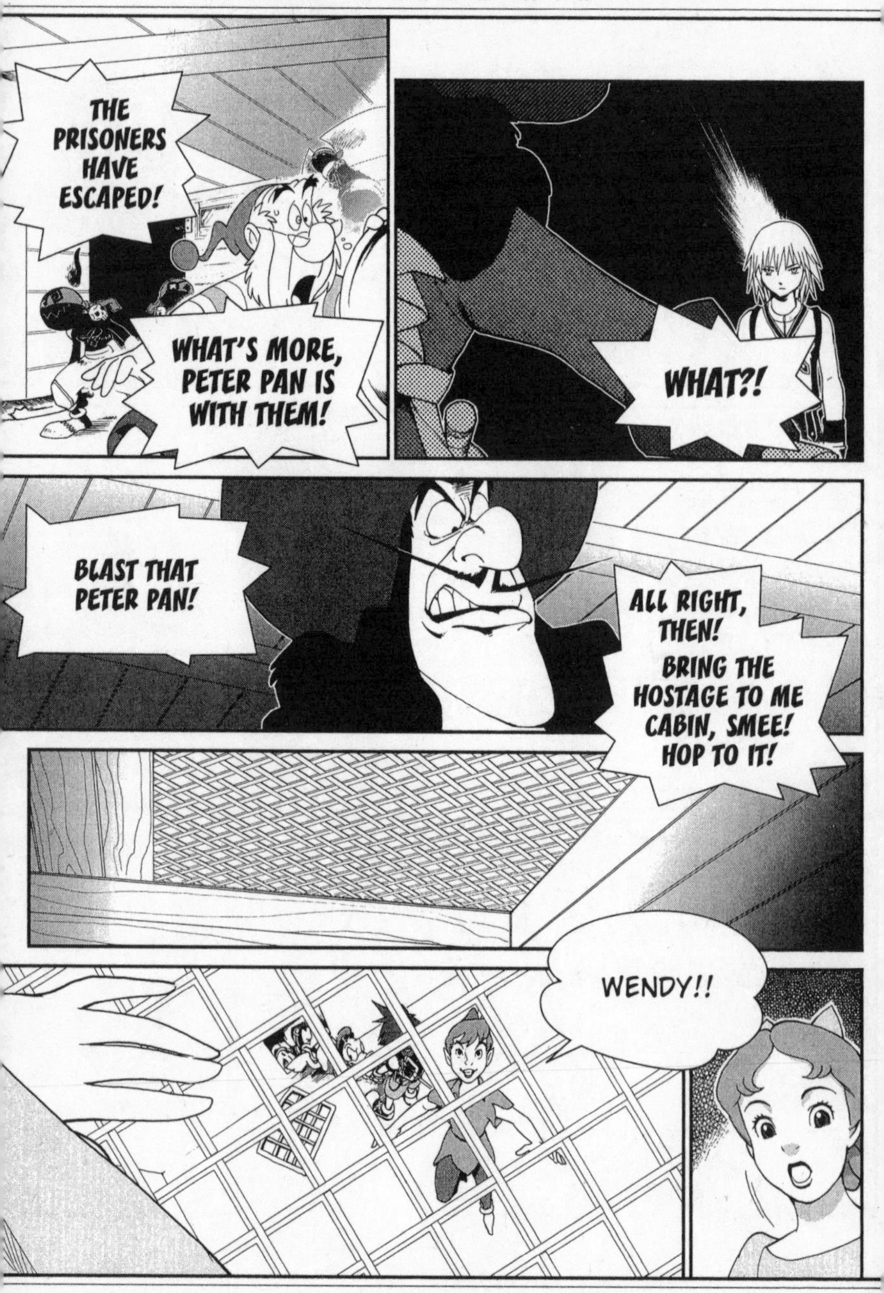
THE PRISONERS HAVE ESCAPED!
WHAT'S MORE, PETER PAN IS WITH THEM!
WHAT?!
BLAST THAT PETER PAN!
ALL RIGHT, THEN!
BRING THE HOSTAGE TO ME CABIN, SMEE! HOP TO IT!
WENDY!!

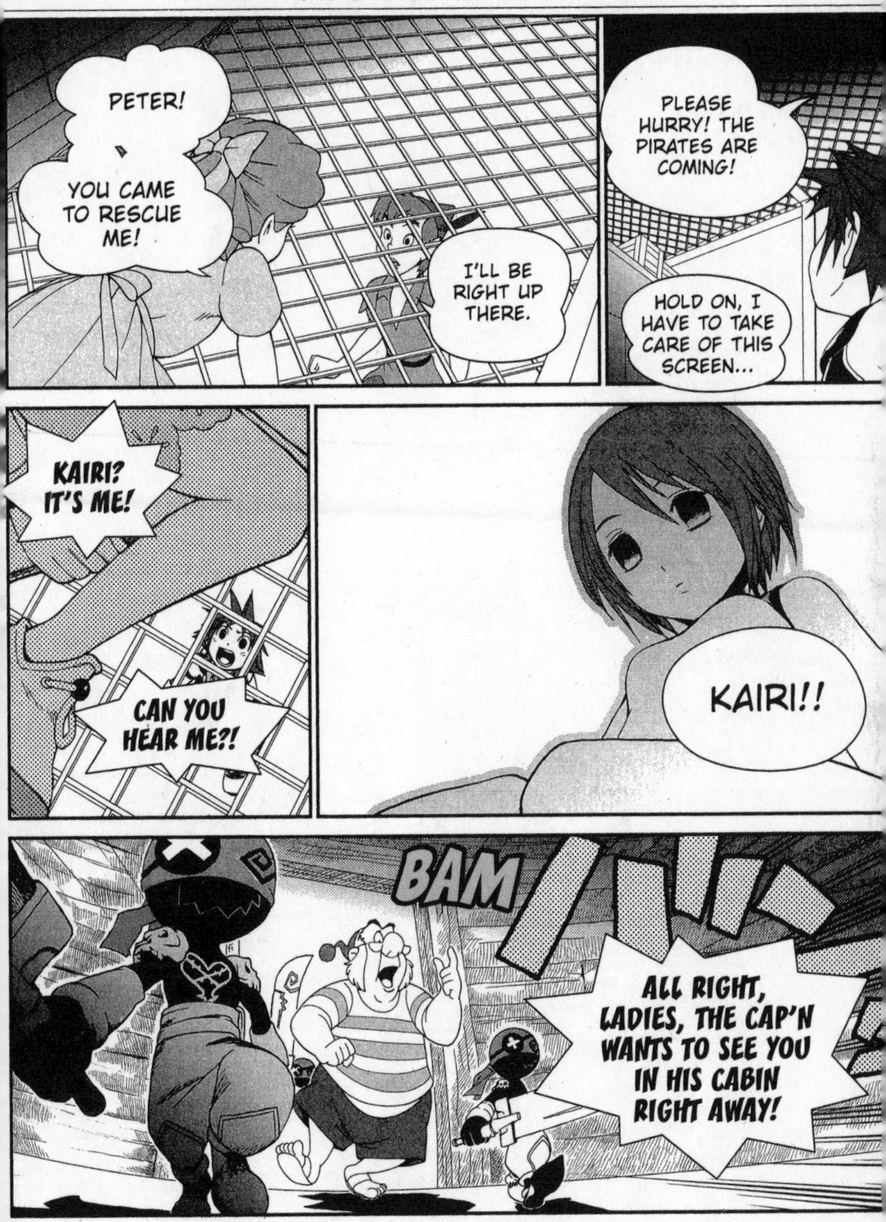
PETER!
YOU CAME TO RESCUE ME!
I'LL BE RIGHT UP THERE.
PLEASE HURRY! THE PIRATES ARE COMING!
HOLD ON, I HAVE TO TAKE CARE OF THIS SCREEN...
KAIRI? IT'S ME!
CAN YOU HEAR ME?!
KAIRI!!
BAM
ALL RIGHT, LADIES, THE CAP'N WANTS TO SEE YOU IN HIS CABIN RIGHT AWAY!

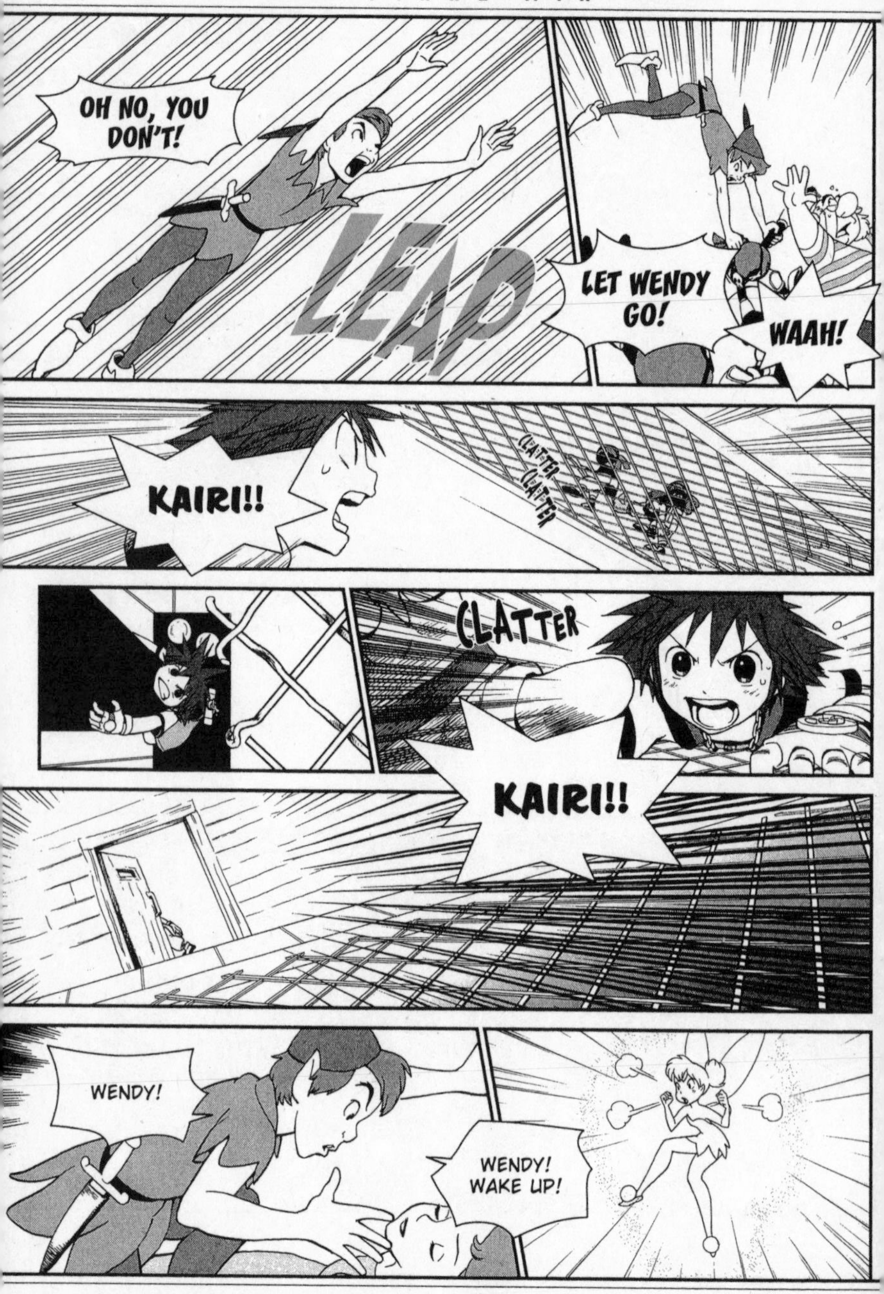
OH NO, YOU DON'T!
LEAP
LET WENDY GO!
WAAH!
KAIRI!!
CLATTER CLATTER
CLATTER
KAIRI!!
WENDY!
WENDY! WAKE UP!

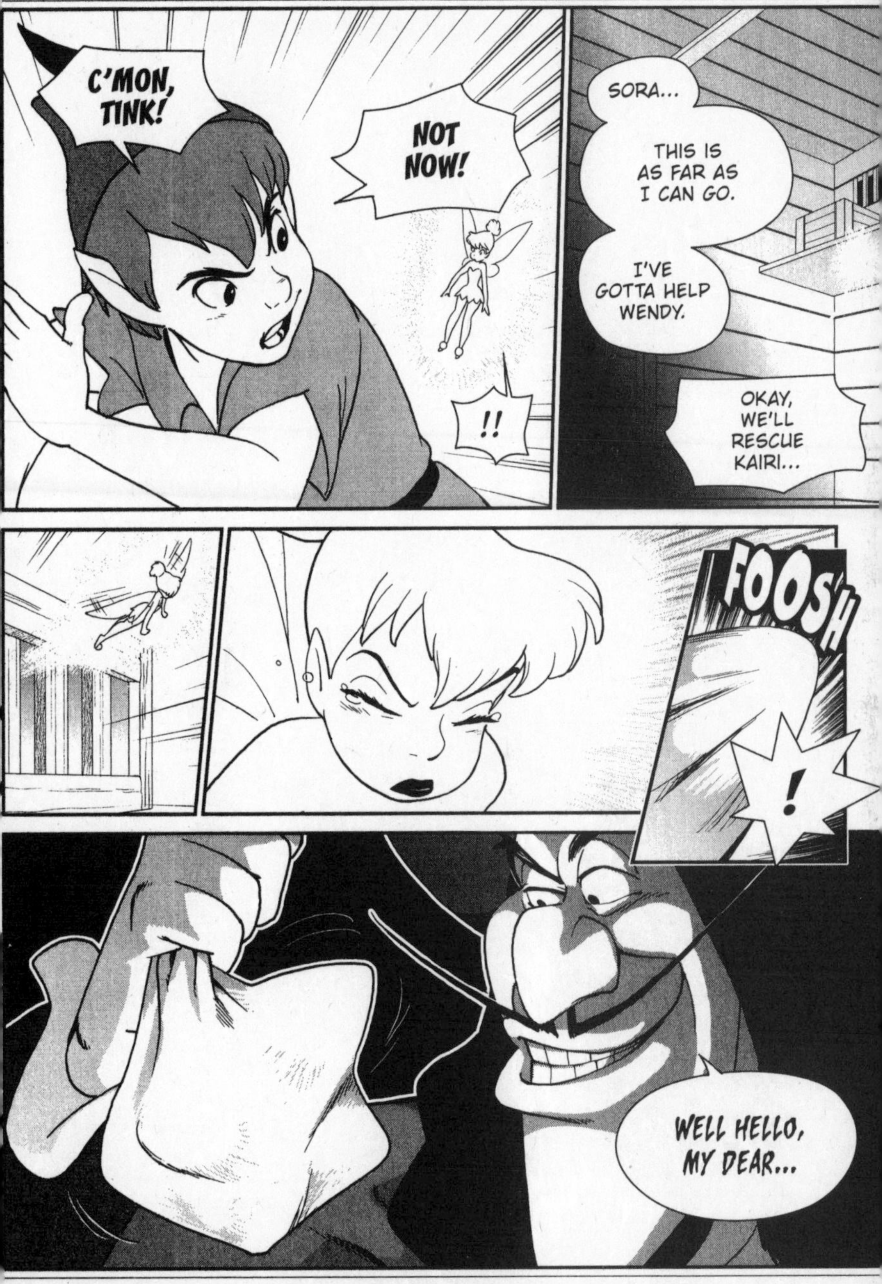
C'MON, TINK!
NOT NOW!
!!
SORA...
THIS IS AS FAR AS I CAN GO.
I'VE GOTTA HELP WENDY.
OKAY, WE'LL RESCUE KAIRI...
FOOSH
!
WELL HELLO, MY DEAR...

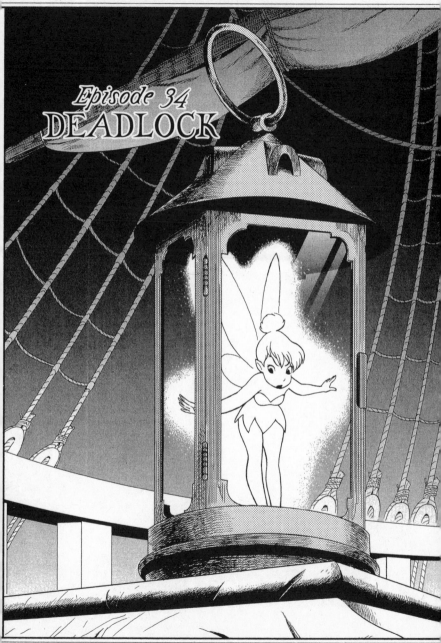

Episode 34
DEADLOCK

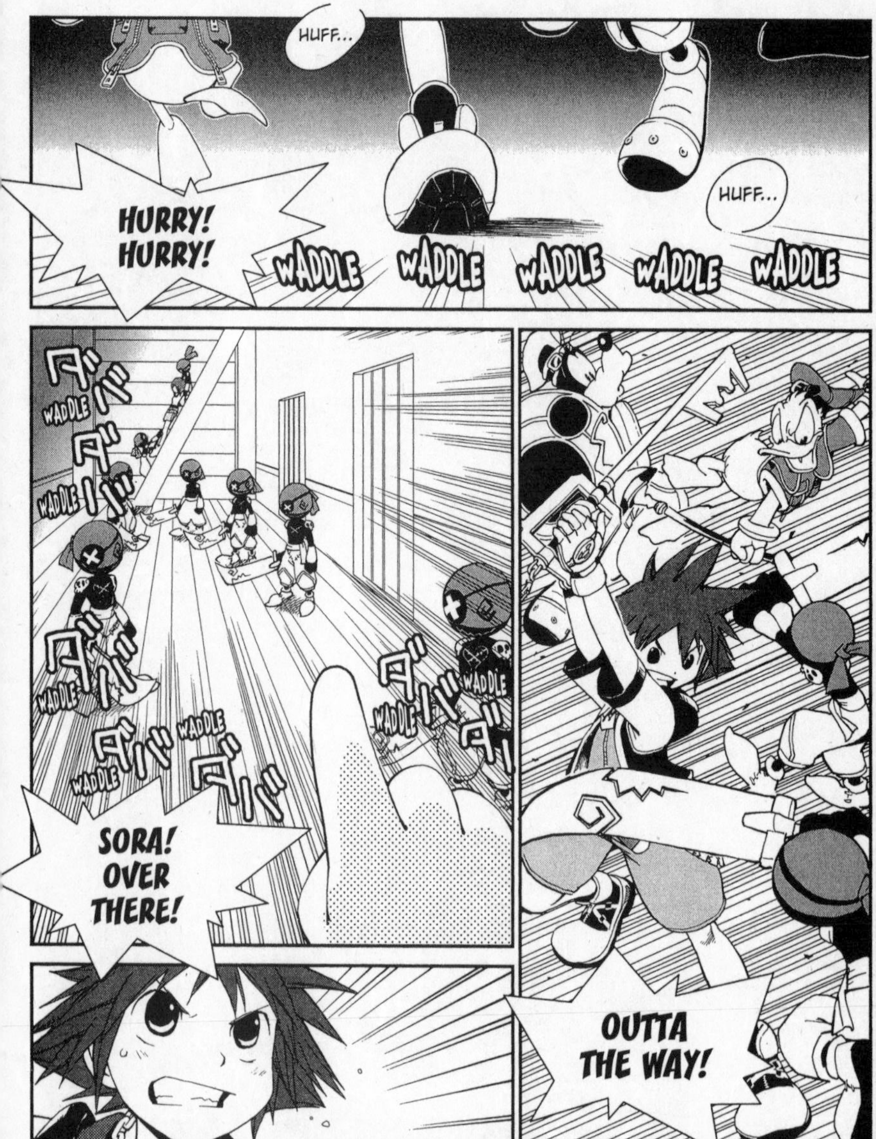
HUFF...
HURRY! HURRY!
HUFF...
WADDLE WADDLE WADDLE WADDLE WADDLE
WADDLE
WADDLE
WADDLE
WADDLE
WADDLE
WADDLE
WADDLE
SORA! OVER THERE!
OUTTA THE WAY!

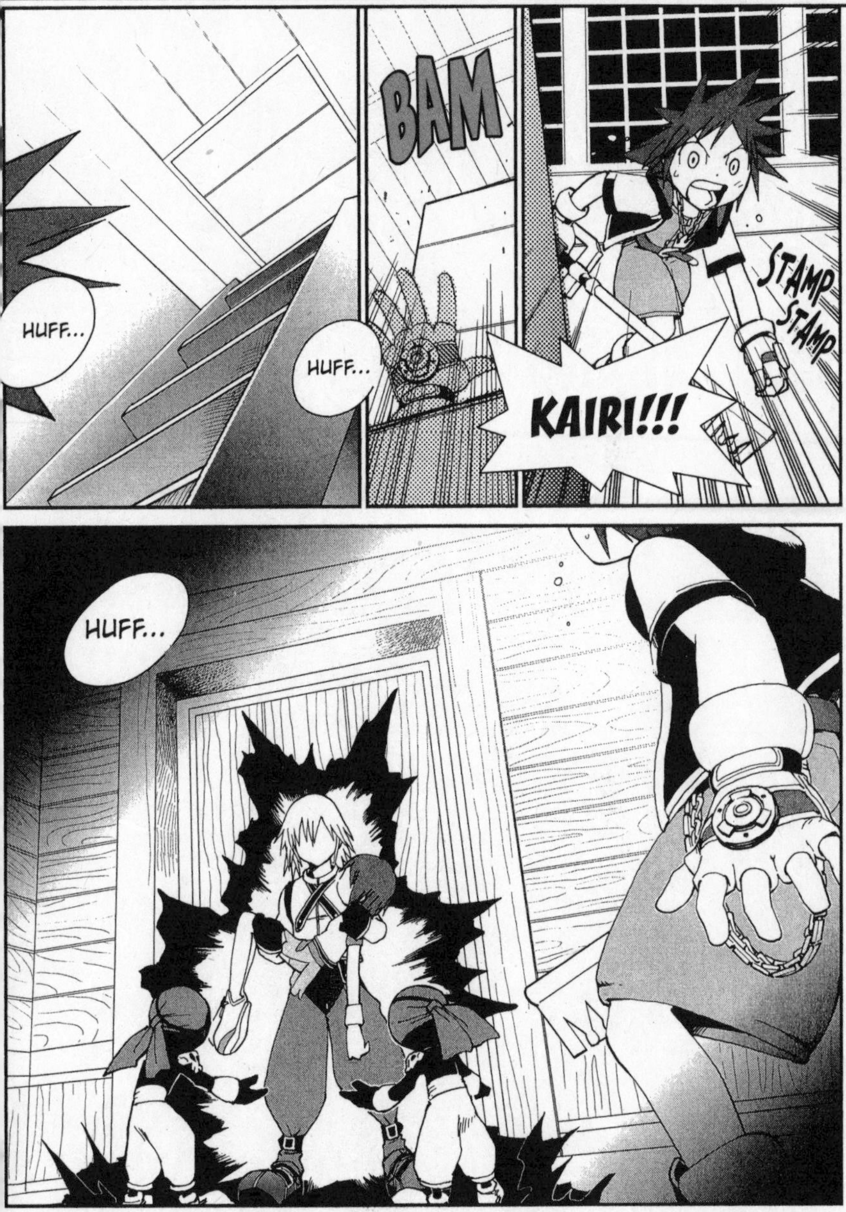
HUFF...
BAM
HUFF...
STAMP STAMP
KAIRI!!!
HUFF...

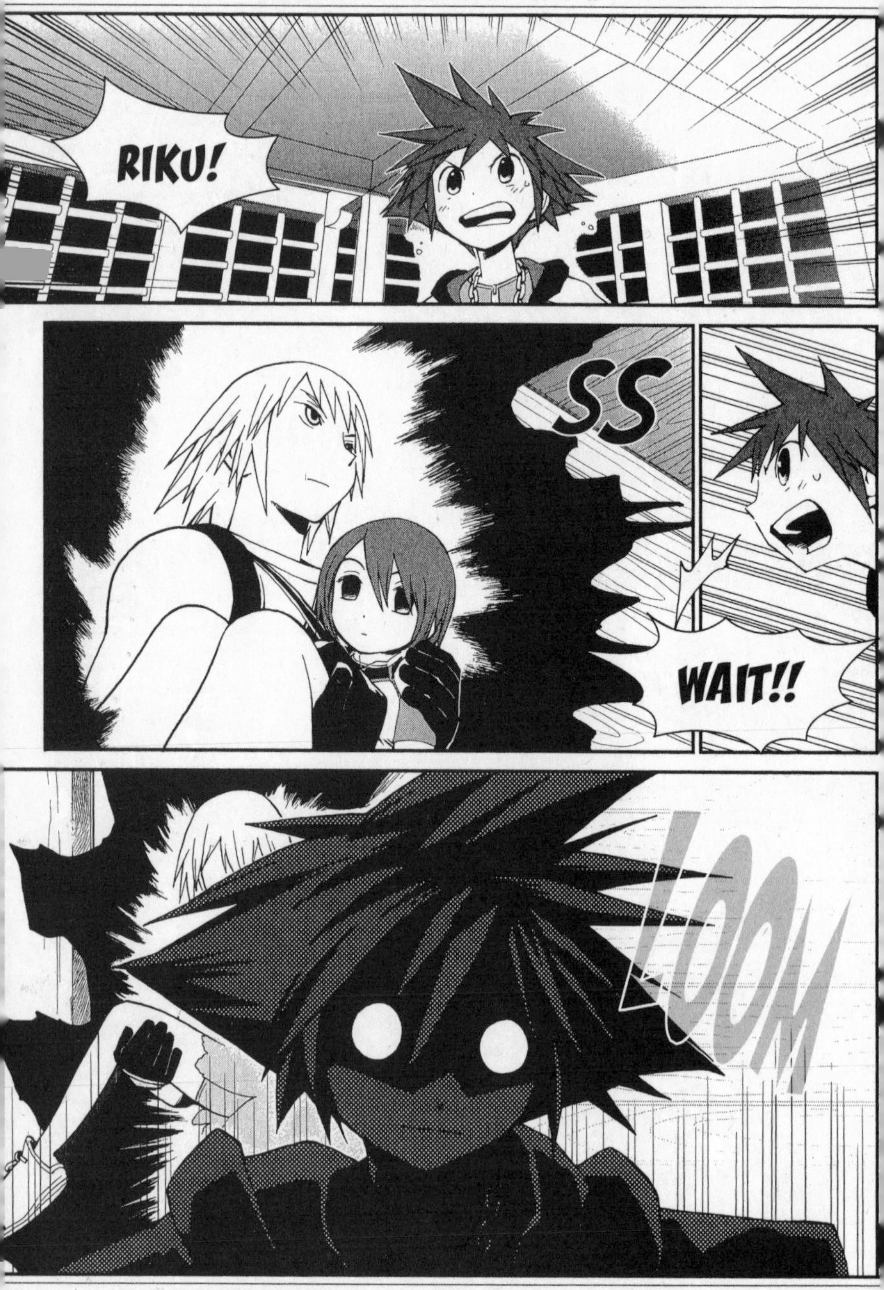
RIKU!
SS
WAIT!!

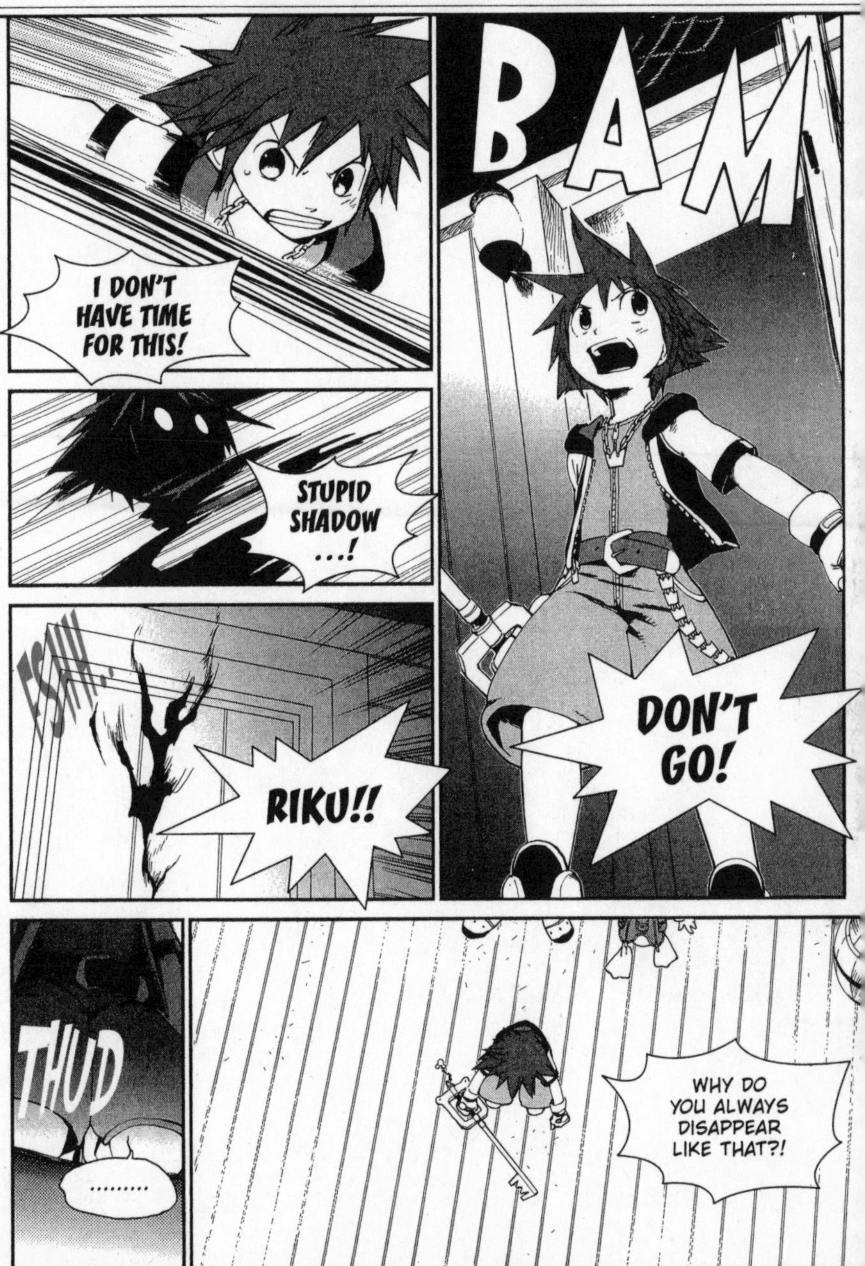
I DON'T HAVE TIME FOR THIS!
BAM
DON'T GO!
STUPID SHADOW ...!
FSHH...
RIKU!!
THUD
....
WHY DO YOU ALWAYS DISAPPEAR LIKE THAT?!

NOT MUCH OF A FRIEND, THAT RIKU...

...RUNNING OFF WITH THAT GIRL WITHOUT EVEN SAYING GOOD-BYE.

......

RUN OFF WHERE? TELL ME, WHERE DID HE GO?!

CLACK

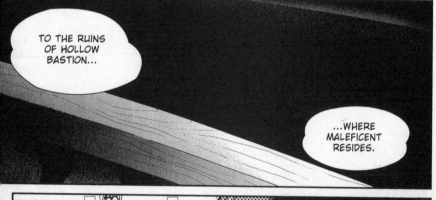

TO THE RUINS OF HOLLOW BASTION...

...WHERE MALEFICENT RESIDES.

MALEFICENT?!

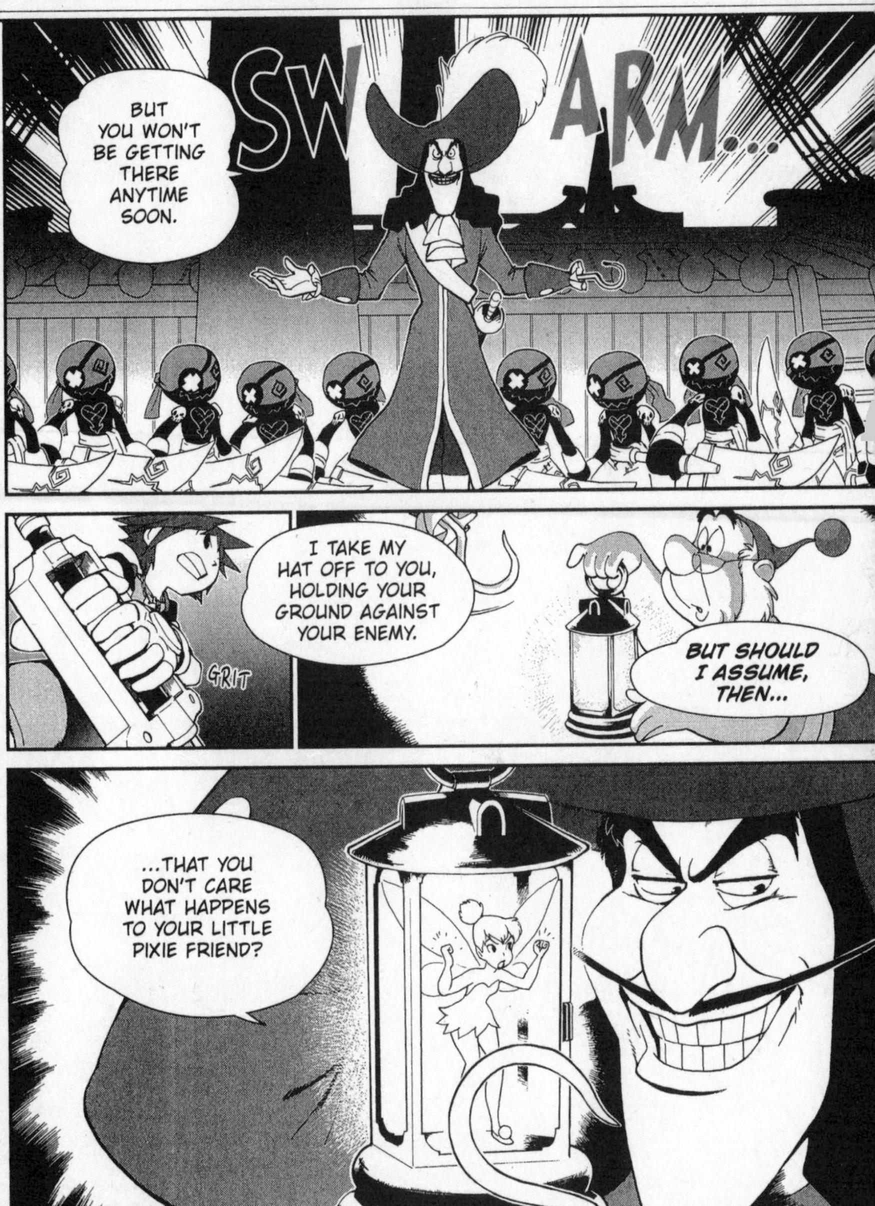
SWARM...
BUT YOU WON'T BE GETTING THERE ANYTIME SOON.
GRIT
I TAKE MY HAT OFF TO YOU, HOLDING YOUR GROUND AGAINST YOUR ENEMY.
BUT SHOULD I ASSUME, THEN...
...THAT YOU DON'T CARE WHAT HAPPENS TO YOUR LITTLE PIXIE FRIEND?

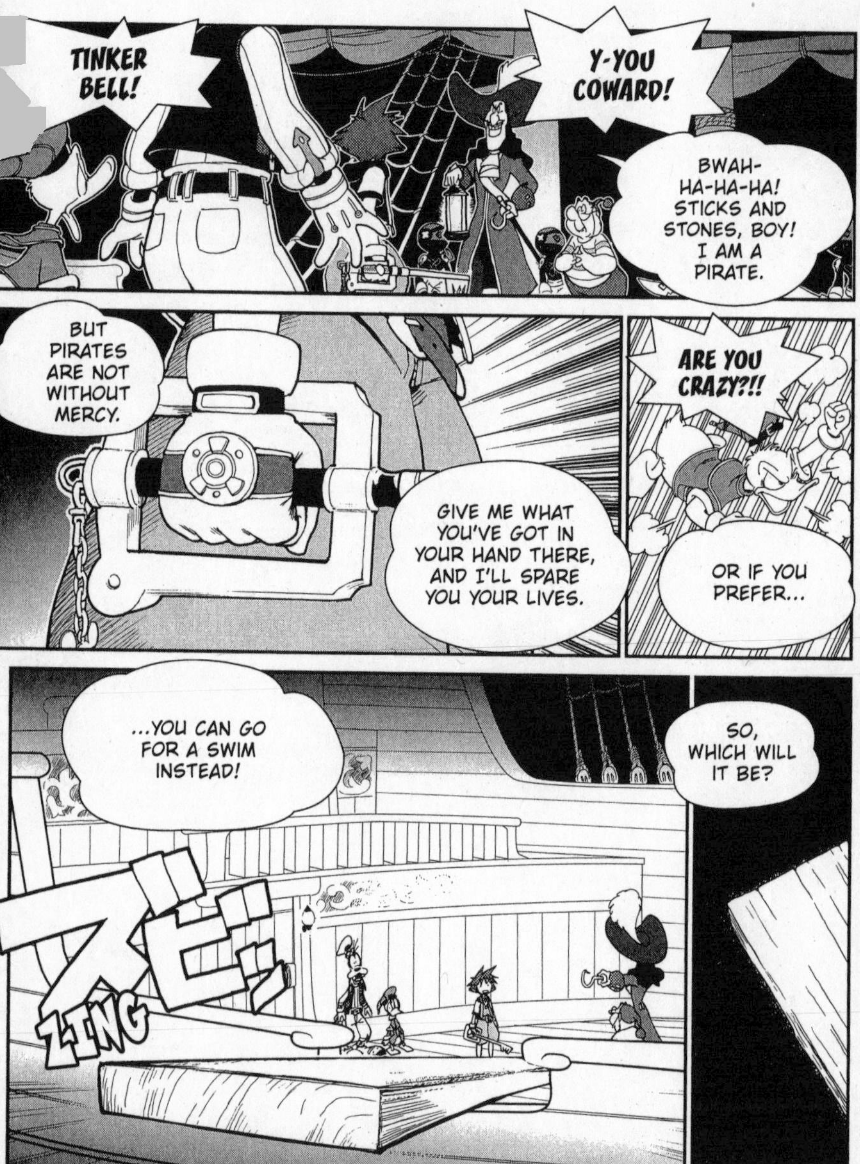
TINKER BELL!
Y-YOU COWARD!
BWAH-HA-HA-HA! STICKS AND STONES, BOY! I AM A PIRATE.
BUT PIRATES ARE NOT WITHOUT MERCY.
GIVE ME WHAT YOU'VE GOT IN YOUR HAND THERE, AND I'LL SPARE YOU YOUR LIVES.
ARE YOU CRAZY?!!
OR IF YOU PREFER...
...YOU CAN GO FOR A SWIM INSTEAD!
ズビ
ZING
SO, WHICH WILL IT BE?

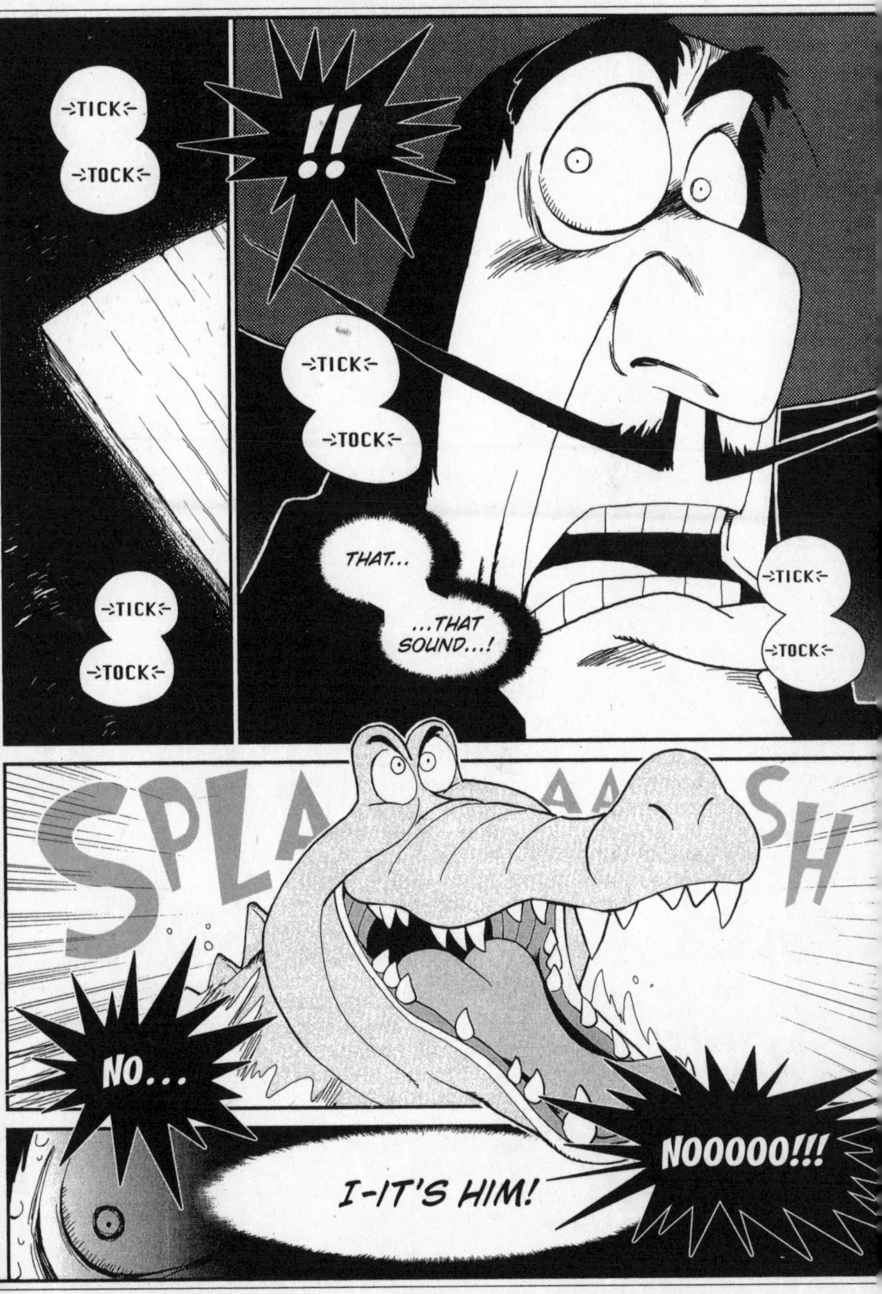
TICK
TOCK
TICK
TOCK
!!
TICK
TOCK
THAT...
...THAT SOUND...!
TICK
TOCK
SPLAAAASH
NO...
I-IT'S HIM!
NOOOOO!!!

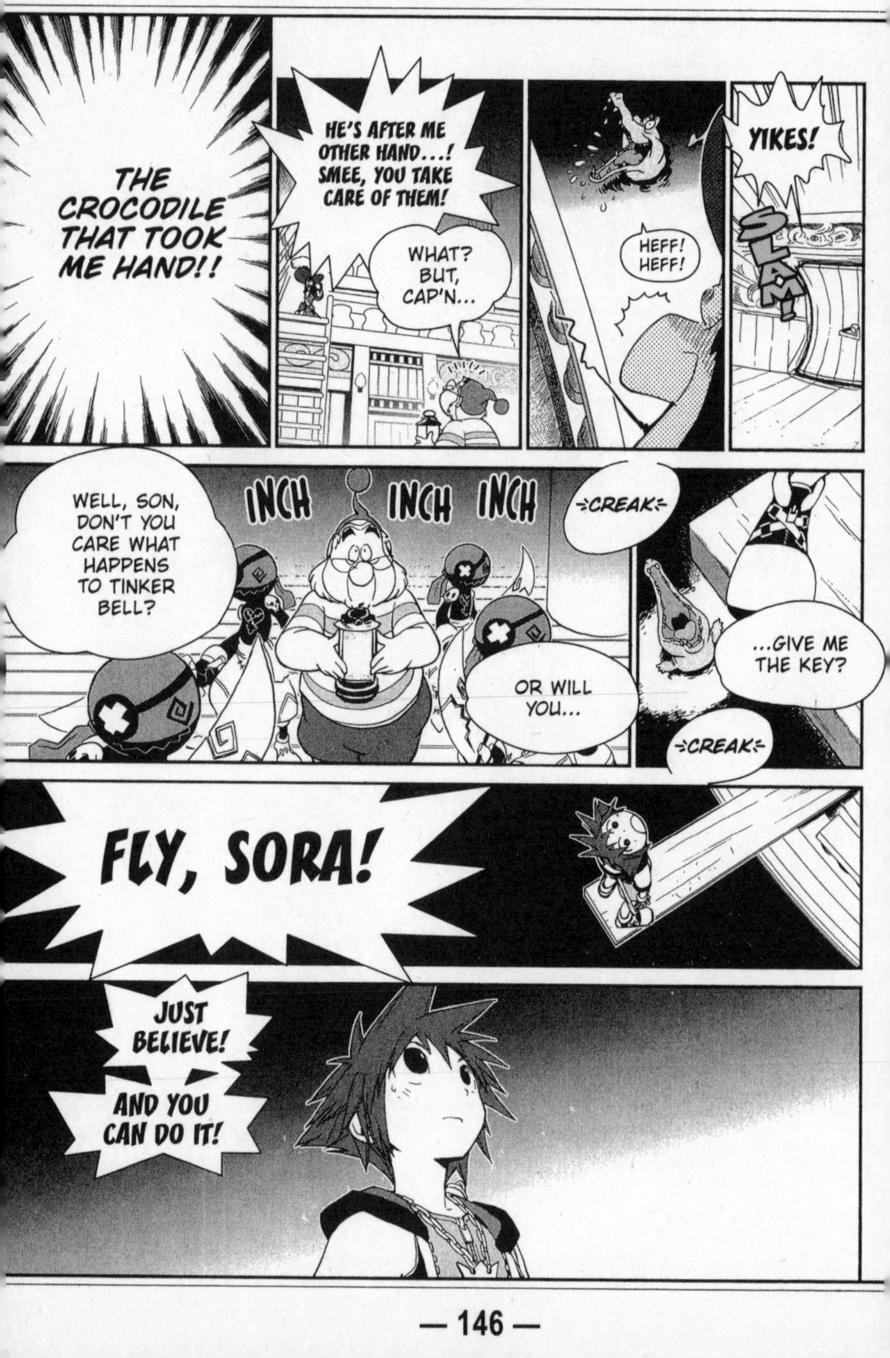
THE CROCODILE THAT TOOK ME HAND!!
HE'S AFTER ME OTHER HAND...! SMEE, YOU TAKE CARE OF THEM!
WHAT? BUT, CAP'N...
HEFF! HEFF!
YIKES!
SLAM
WELL, SON, DON'T YOU CARE WHAT HAPPENS TO TINKER BELL?
INCH
INCH
INCH
OR WILL YOU...
CREAK
...GIVE ME THE KEY?
CREAK
FLY, SORA!
JUST BELIEVE!
AND YOU CAN DO IT!

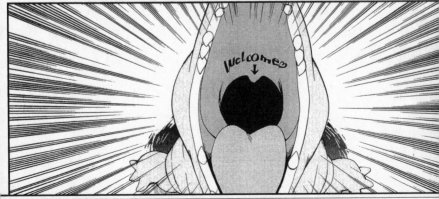

Welcome

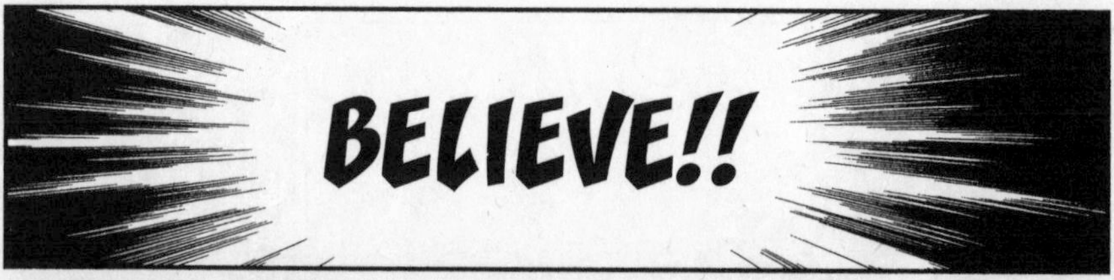
BELIEVE!!

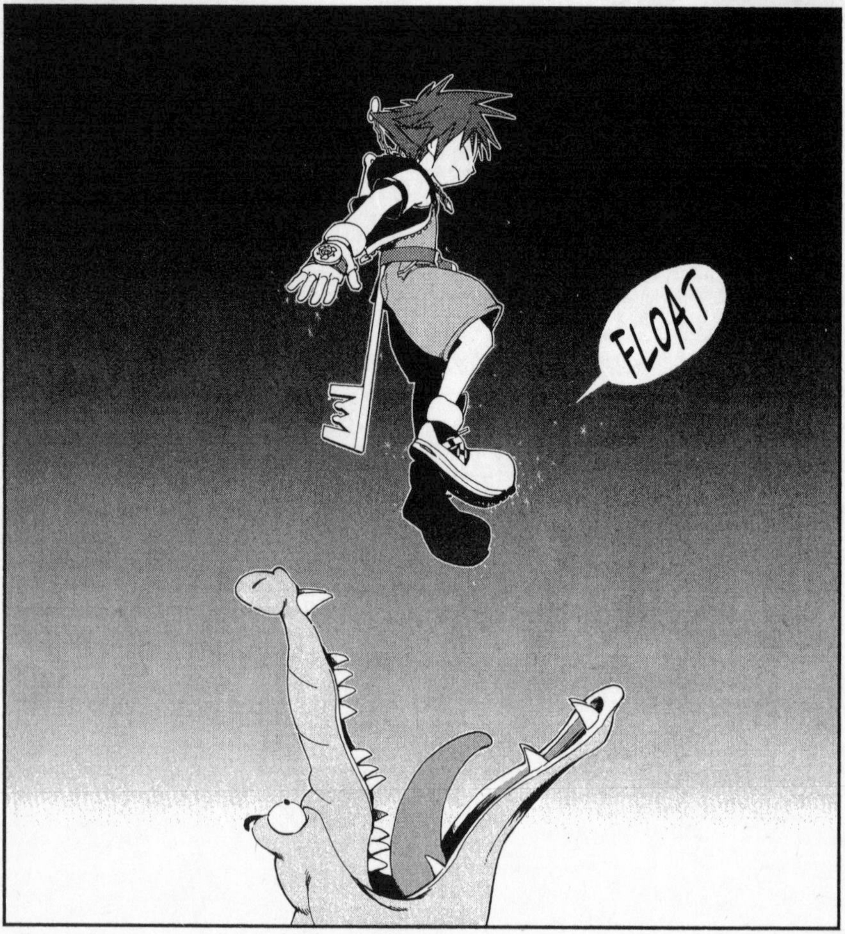
FLOAT

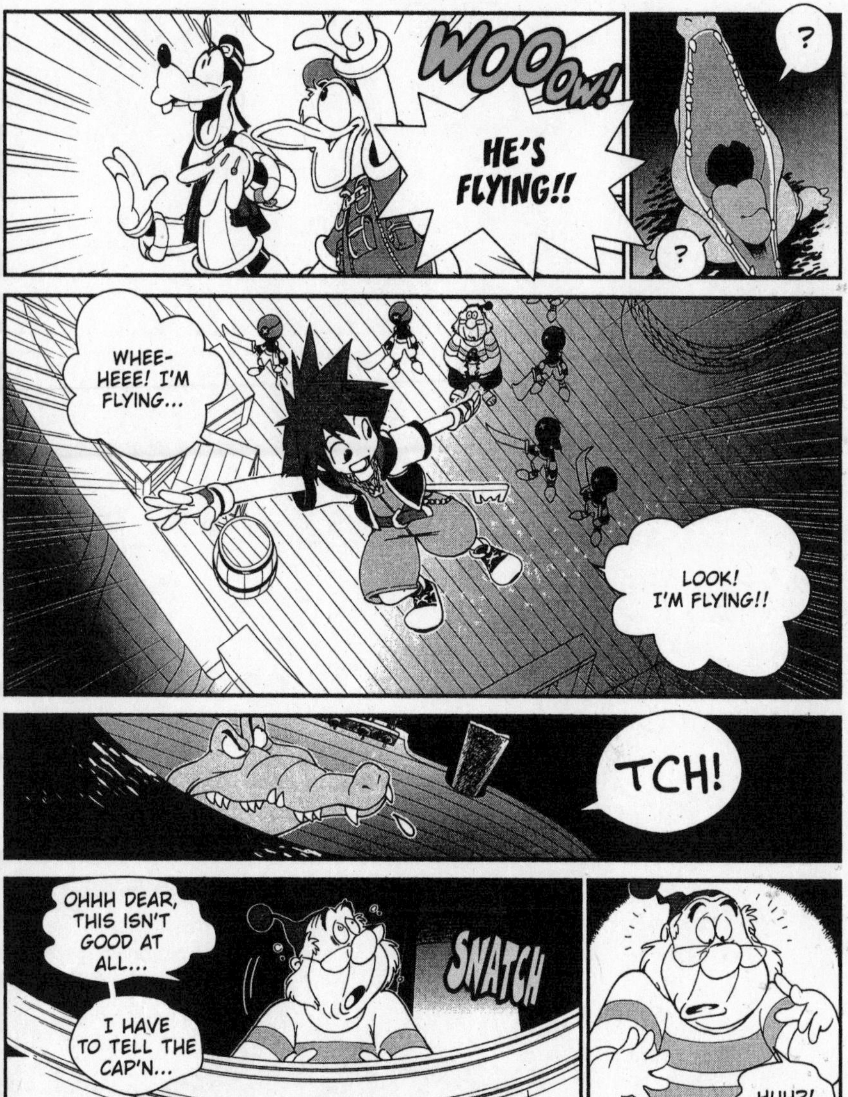
WOOOOW!
HE'S FLYING!!
?
?
WHEE-HEEE! I'M FLYING...
LOOK! I'M FLYING!!
TCH!
OHHH DEAR, THIS ISN'T GOOD AT ALL...
I HAVE TO TELL THE CAP'N...
SNATCH
HUH?!

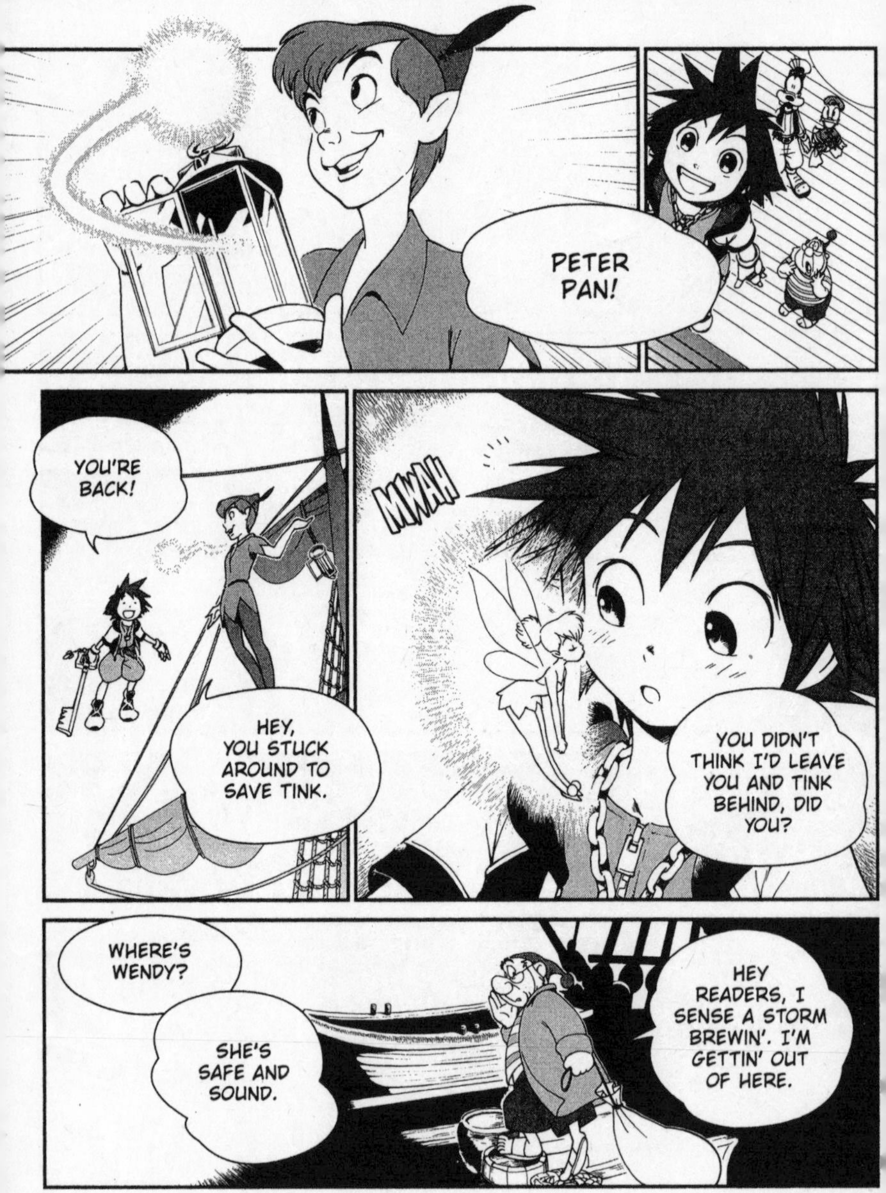
PETER PAN!
YOU'RE BACK!
HEY, YOU STUCK AROUND TO SAVE TINK.
MWAH
YOU DIDN'T THINK I'D LEAVE YOU AND TINK BEHIND, DID YOU?
WHERE'S WENDY?
SHE'S SAFE AND SOUND.
HEY READERS, I SENSE A STORM BREWIN'. I'M GETTIN' OUT OF HERE.

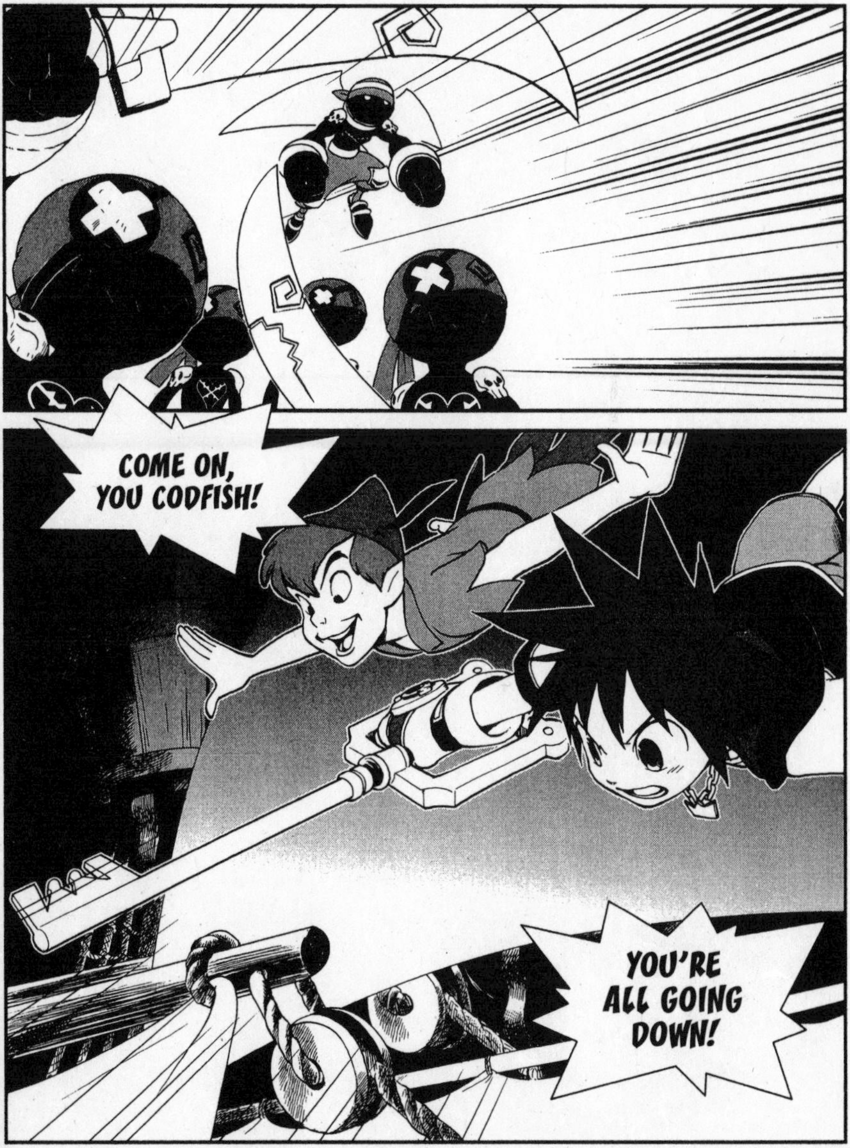
COME ON, YOU CODFISH!
YOU'RE ALL GOING DOWN!

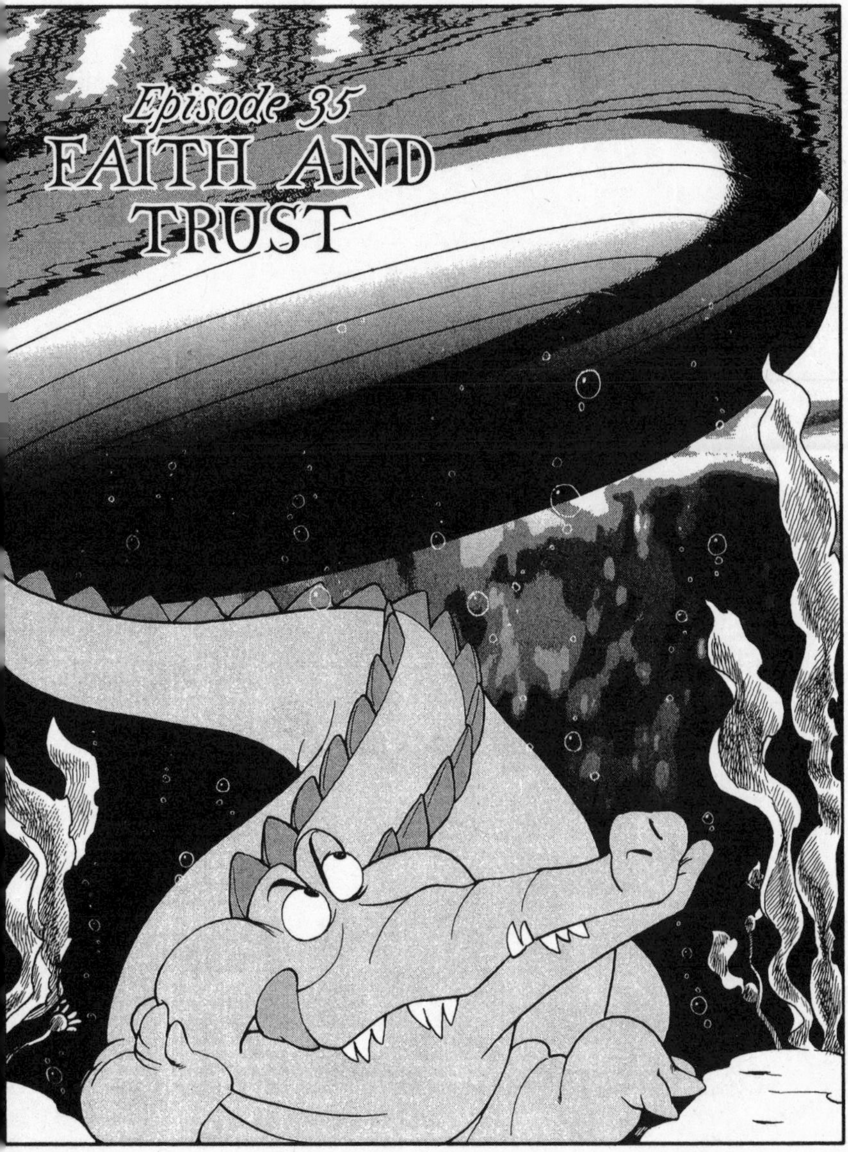
Episode 35
FAITH AND TRUST

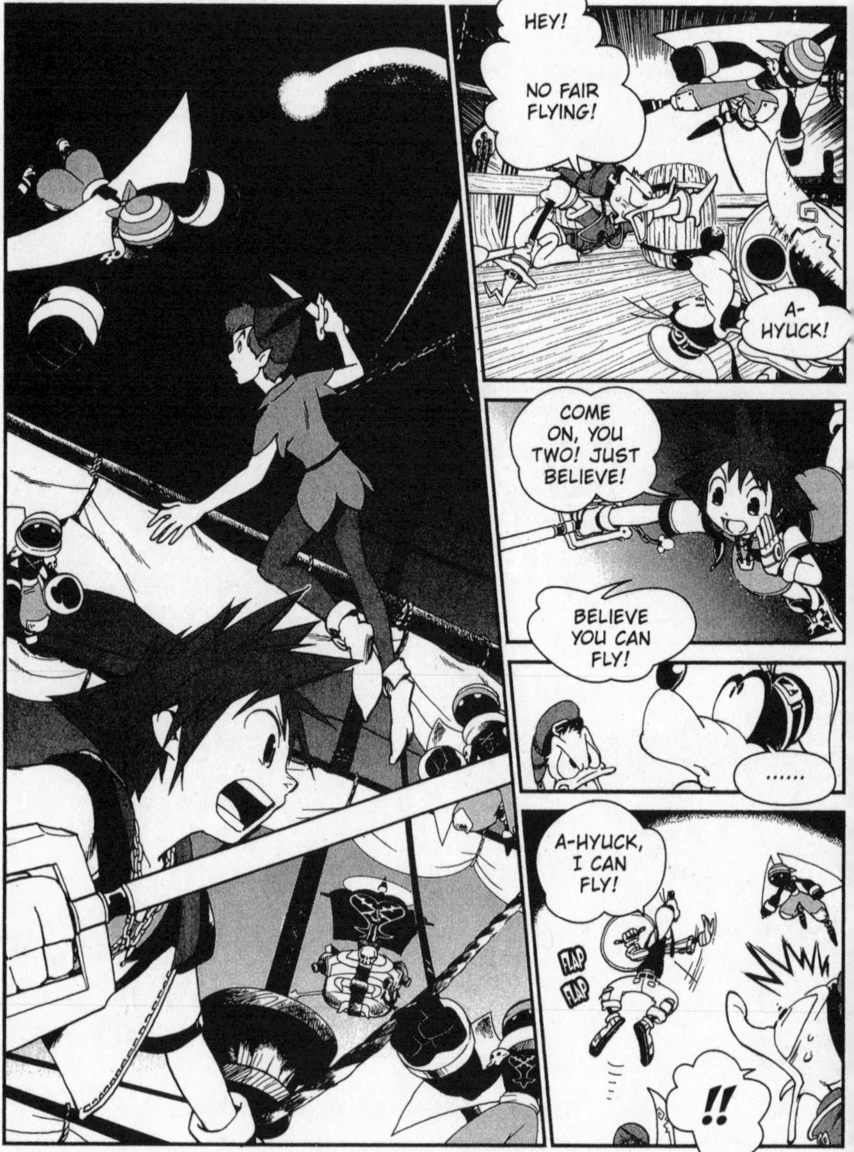
HEY!
NO FAIR FLYING!
A-HYUCK!
COME ON, YOU TWO! JUST BELIEVE!
BELIEVE YOU CAN FLY!
......
A-HYUCK, I CAN FLY!
FLAP
FLAP
!!

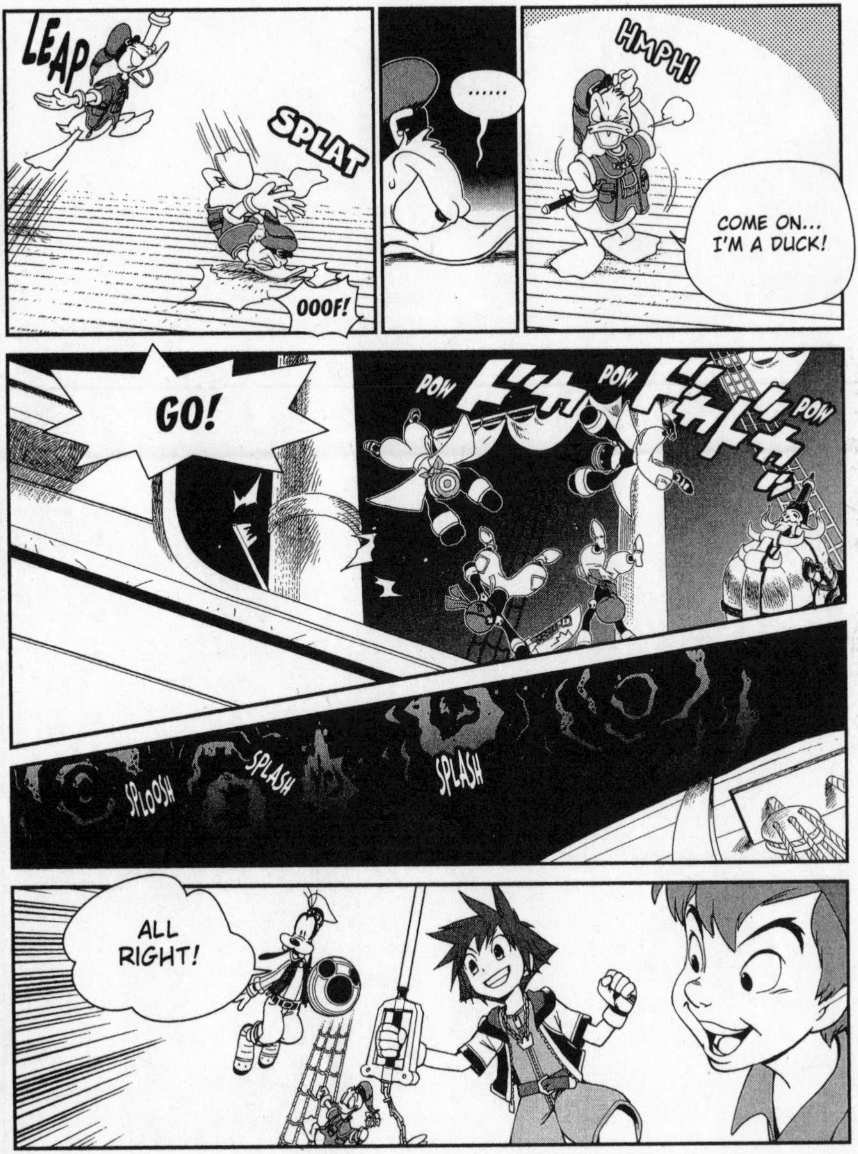
LEAP
SPLAT
OOOF!
......
HMPH!
COME ON... I'M A DUCK!
GO!
POW
ドカ
POW
ドガッ
POW
ドカッ
SPLOOSH
SPLASH
SPLASH
ALL RIGHT!

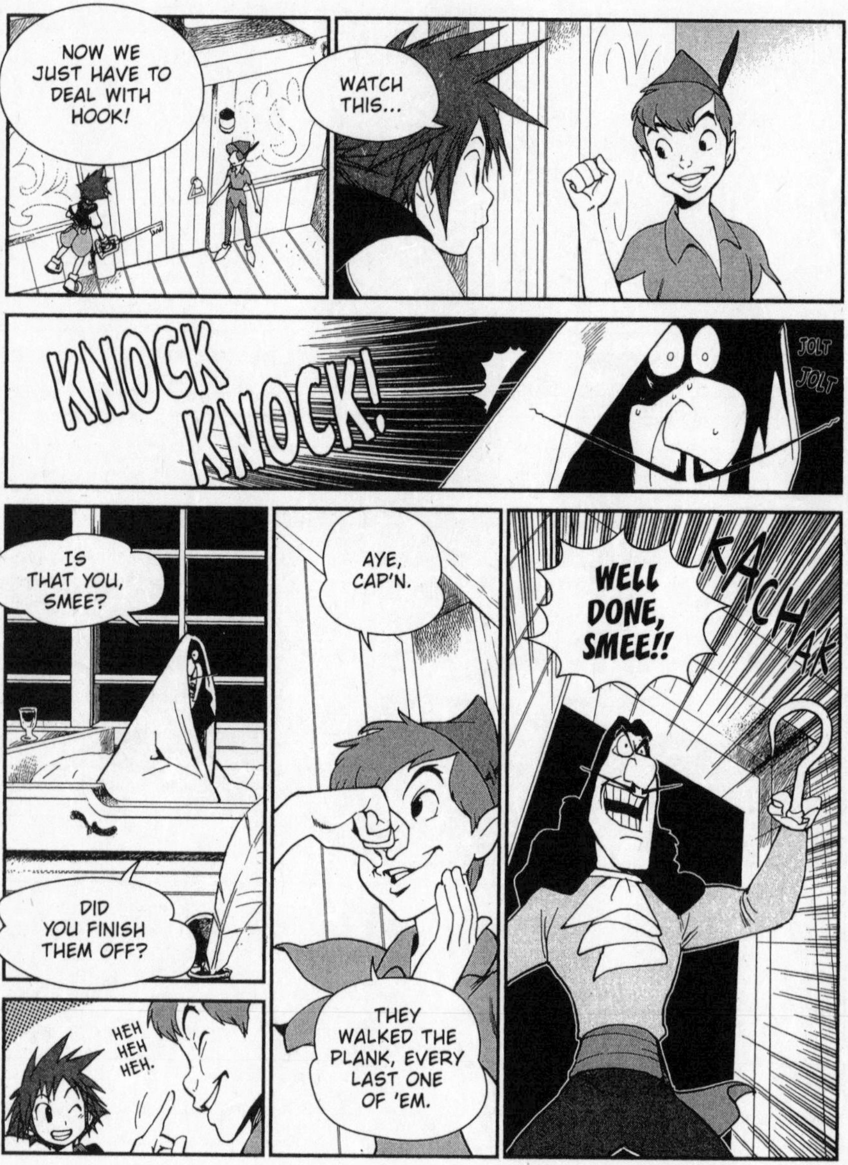
NOW WE JUST HAVE TO DEAL WITH HOOK!
WATCH THIS...
KNOCK KNOCK!
JOLT JOLT
IS THAT YOU, SMEE?
DID YOU FINISH THEM OFF?
HEH HEH HEH.
AYE, CAP'N.
THEY WALKED THE PLANK, EVERY LAST ONE OF 'EM.
WELL DONE, SMEE!!
KACHAK

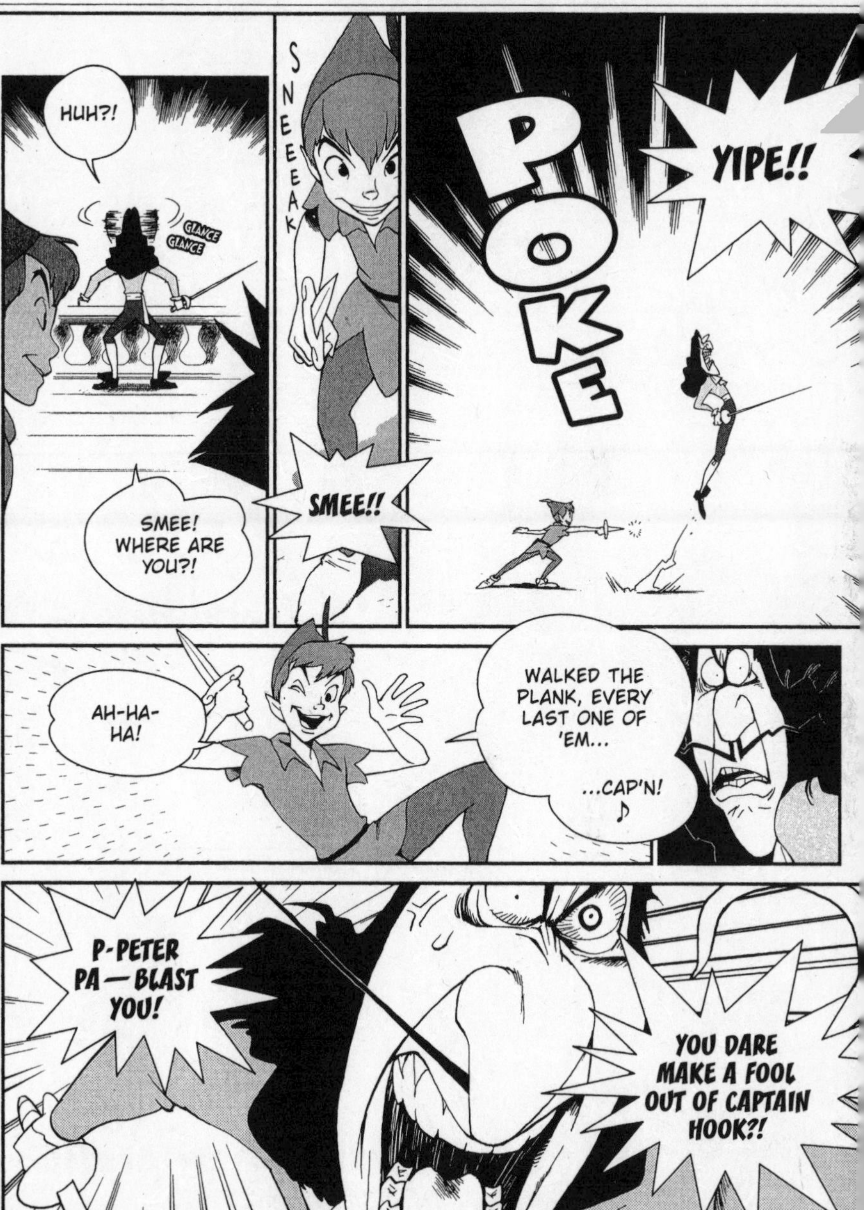
HUH?!
GLANCE GLANCE
SMEE! WHERE ARE YOU?!
SNEEEAK
SMEE!!
POKE
YIPE!!
AH-HA-HA!
WALKED THE PLANK, EVERY LAST ONE OF 'EM...
...CAP'N! ♪
P-PETER PA—BLAST YOU!
YOU DARE MAKE A FOOL OUT OF CAPTAIN HOOK?!

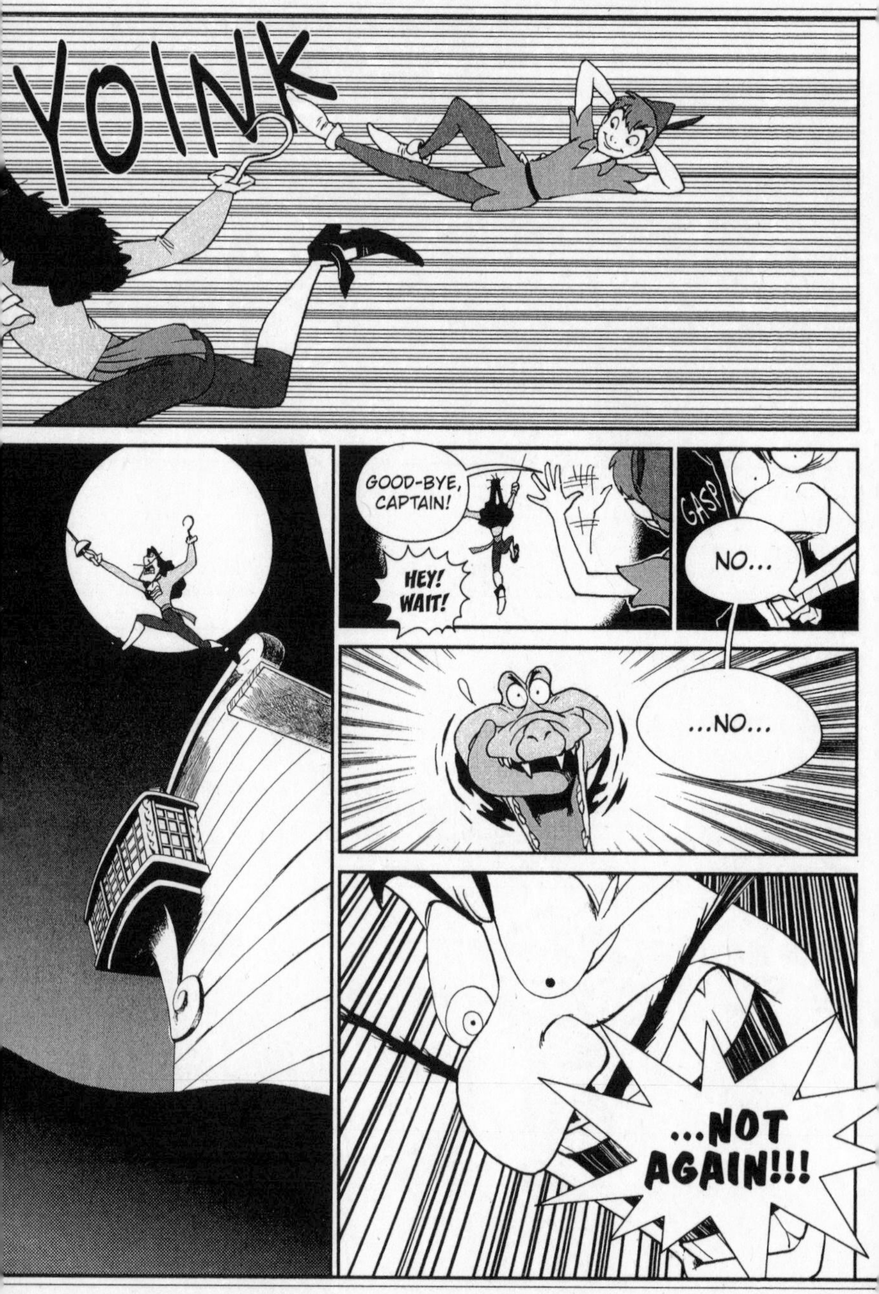
YOINK
GOOD-BYE, CAPTAIN!
HEY! WAIT!
GASP
NO...
...NO...
...NOT AGAIN!!!

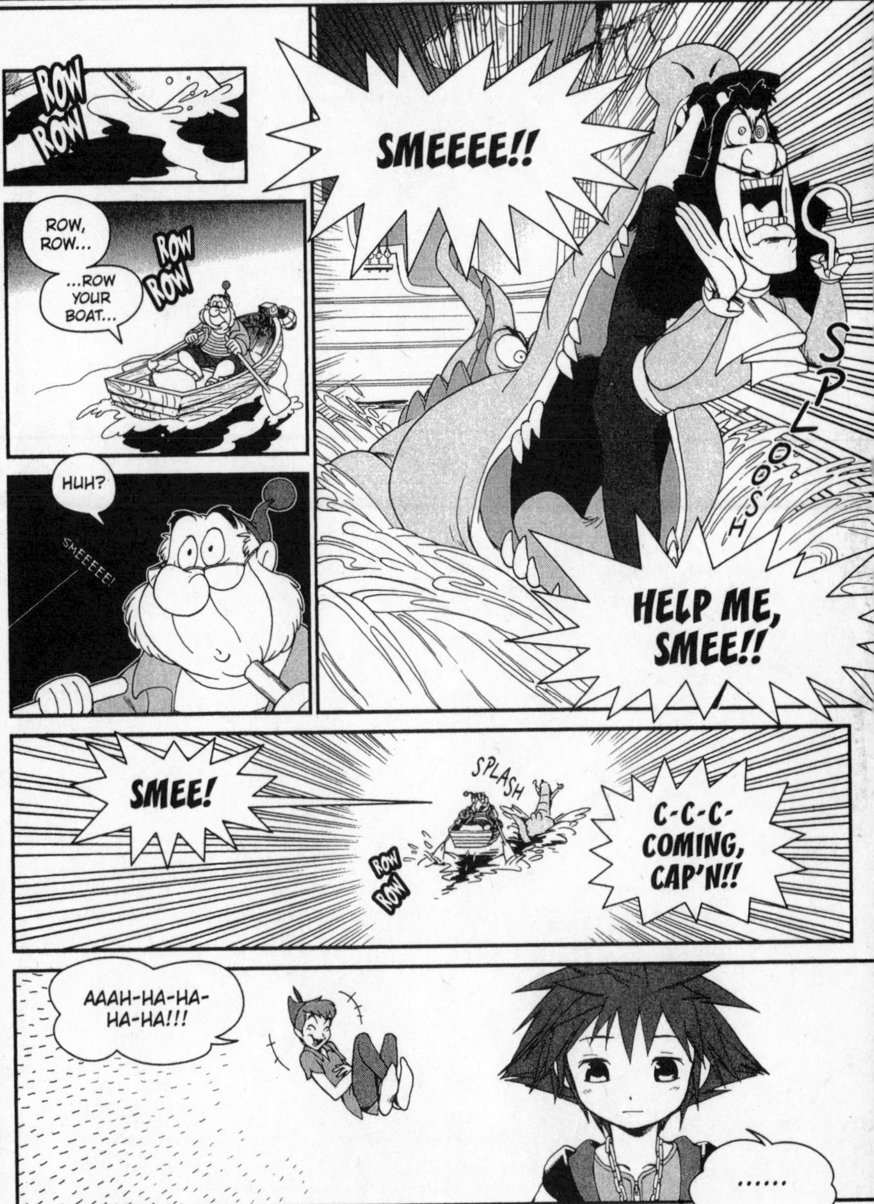
ROW ROW
ROW, ROW...
...ROW YOUR BOAT...
ROW ROW
HUH?
SMEEEEE!
SMEEEE!!
SPLOOSH
HELP ME, SMEE!!
SMEE!
SPLASH
ROW ROW
C-C-C-COMING, CAP'N!!
AAAH-HA-HA-HA-HA!!!
......

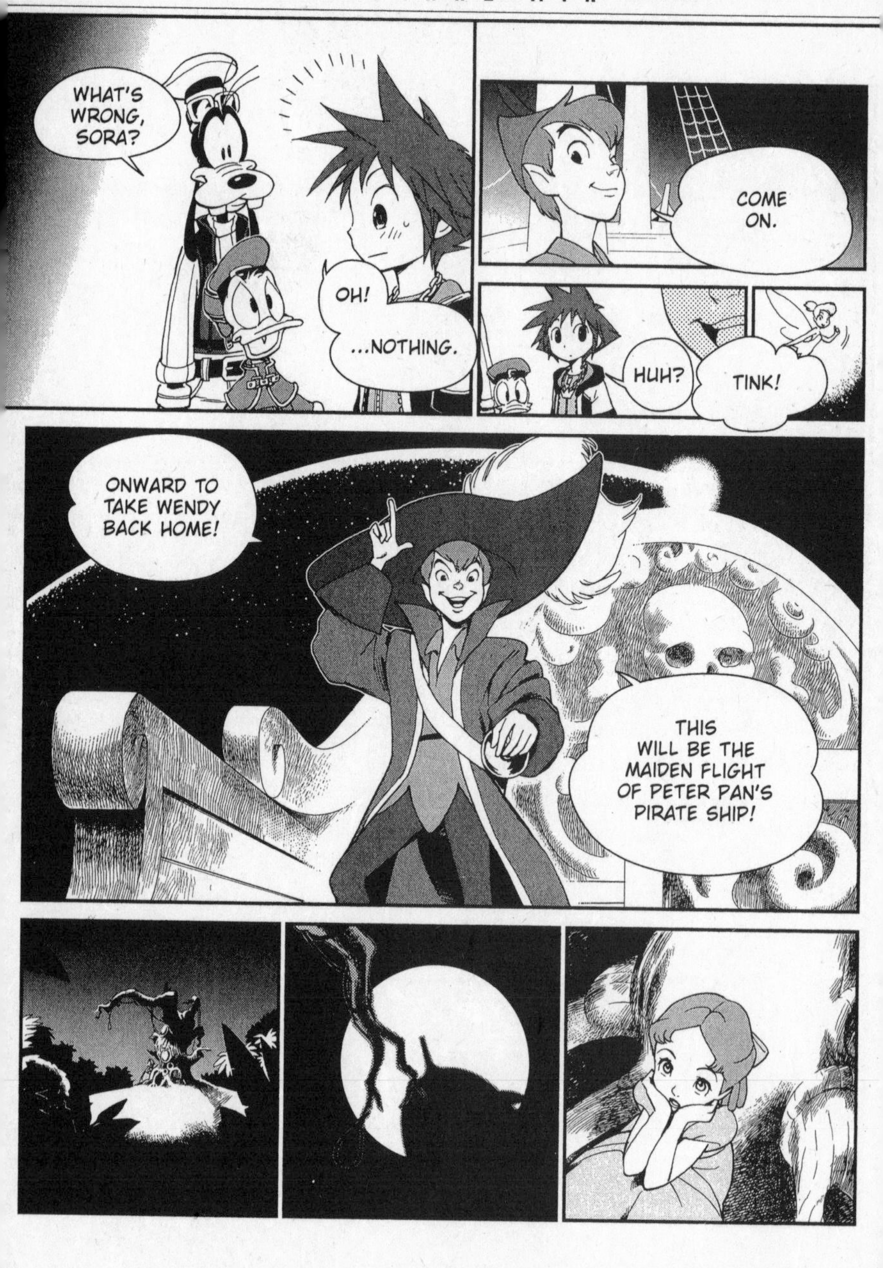
WHAT'S WRONG, SORA?
OH!
...NOTHING.
COME ON.
HUH?
TINK!
ONWARD TO TAKE WENDY BACK HOME!
THIS WILL BE THE MAIDEN FLIGHT OF PETER PAN'S PIRATE SHIP!

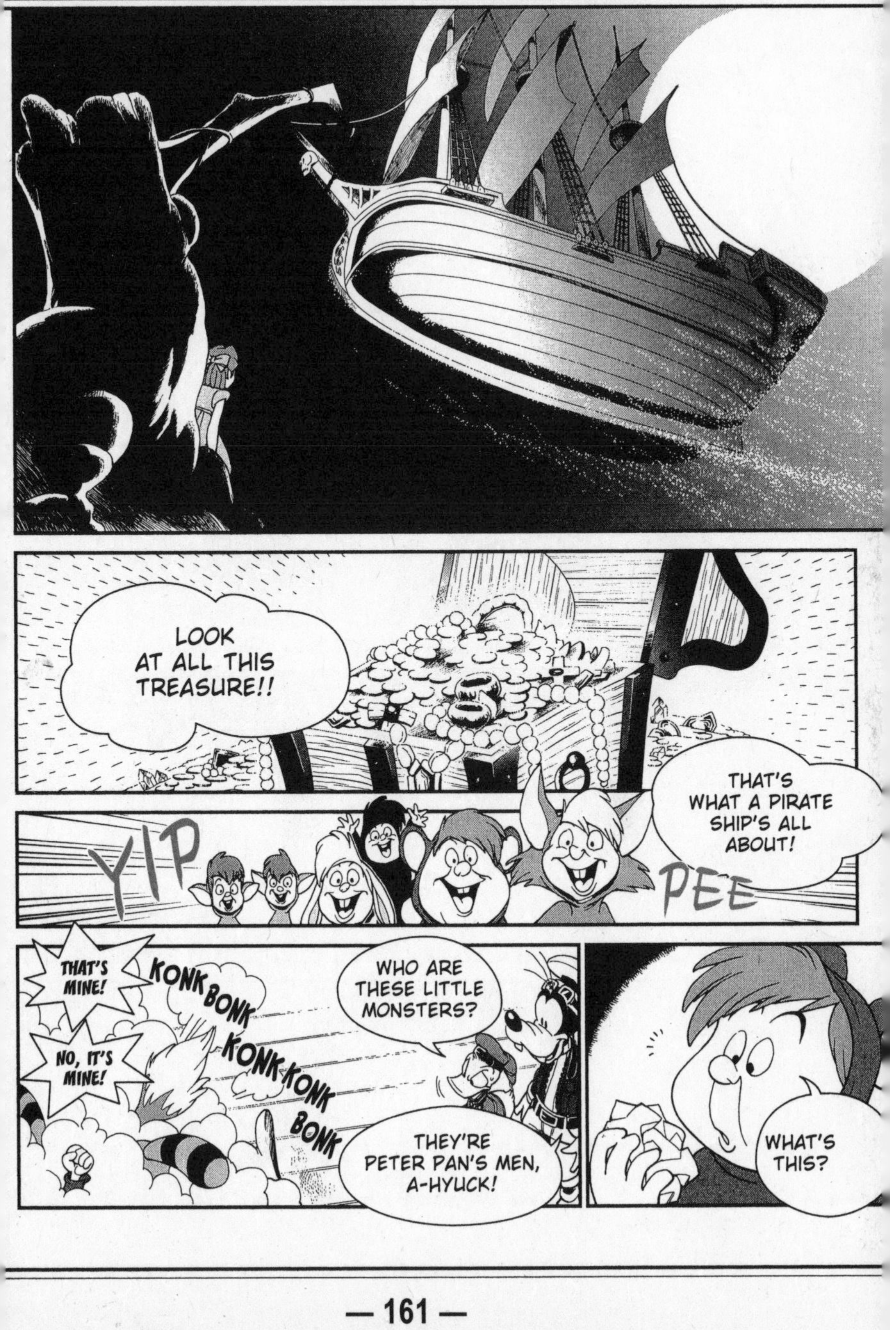
LOOK AT ALL THIS TREASURE!!
YIP
THAT'S WHAT A PIRATE SHIP'S ALL ABOUT!
PEE
THAT'S MINE!
NO, IT'S MINE!
KONK BONK
KONK KONK
BONK
WHO ARE THESE LITTLE MONSTERS?
THEY'RE PETER PAN'S MEN, A-HYUCK!
WHAT'S THIS?

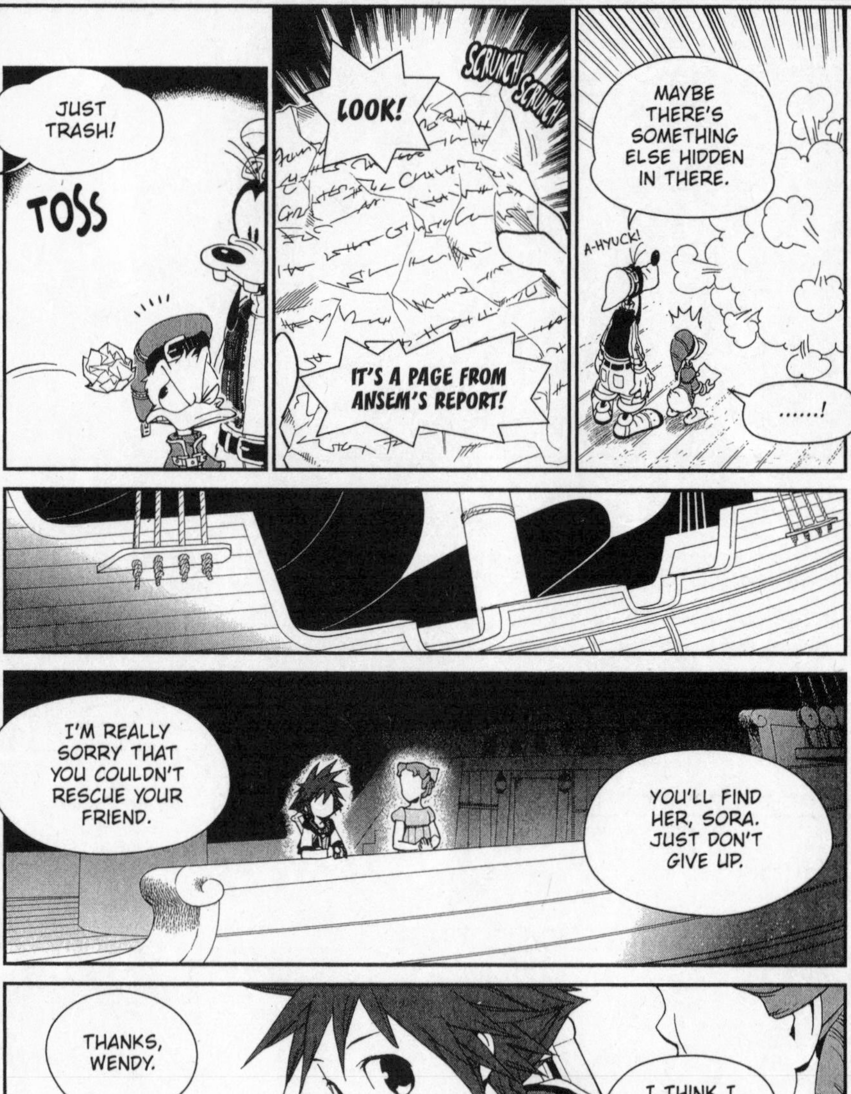
JUST TRASH!
TOSS
LOOK!
SCRUNCH SCRUNCH
IT'S A PAGE FROM ANSEM'S REPORT!
MAYBE THERE'S SOMETHING ELSE HIDDEN IN THERE.
A-HYUCK!
......!
I'M REALLY SORRY THAT YOU COULDN'T RESCUE YOUR FRIEND.
YOU'LL FIND HER, SORA. JUST DON'T GIVE UP.
THANKS, WENDY.
I THINK I UNDERSTAND NOW.

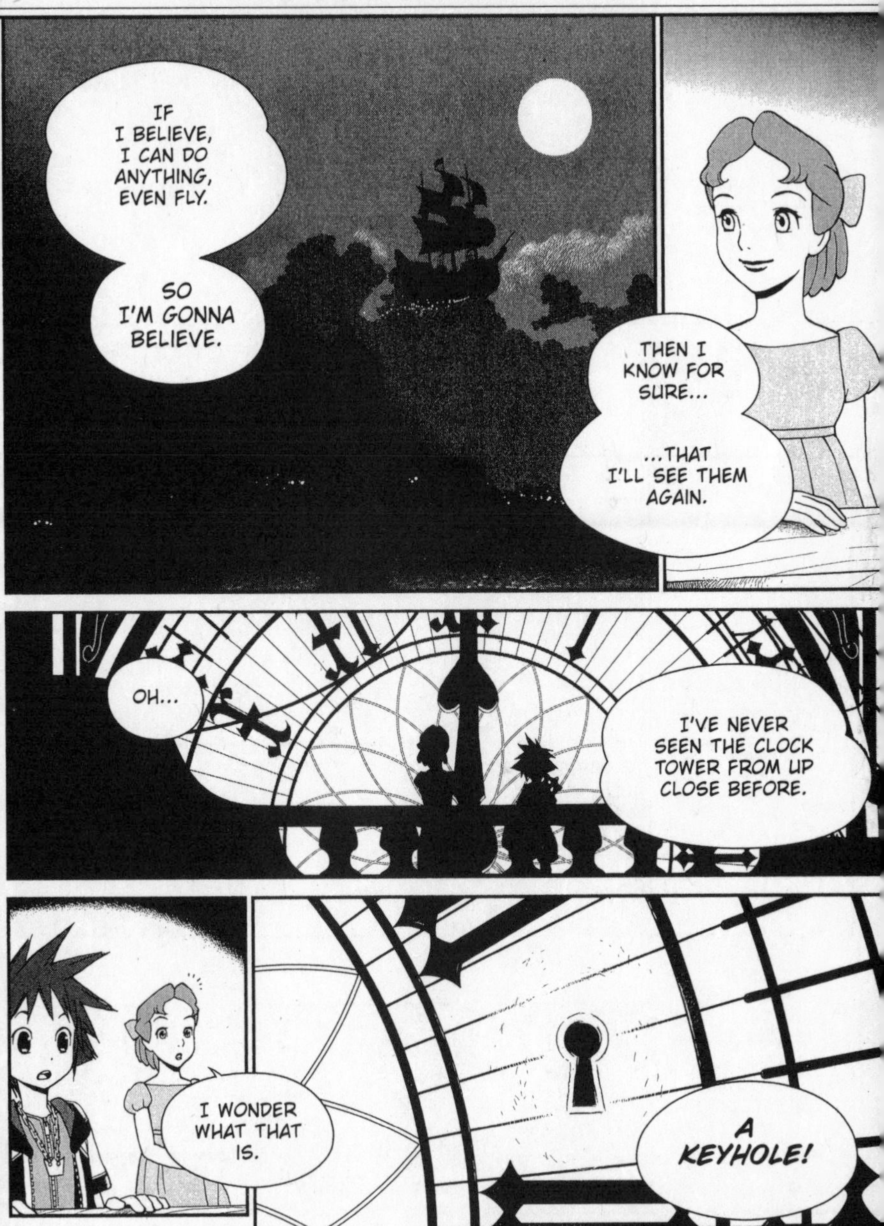
IF I BELIEVE, I CAN DO ANYTHING, EVEN FLY.
SO I'M GONNA BELIEVE.
THEN I KNOW FOR SURE...
...THAT I'LL SEE THEM AGAIN.
OH...
I'VE NEVER SEEN THE CLOCK TOWER FROM UP CLOSE BEFORE.
I WONDER WHAT THAT IS.
A KEYHOLE!

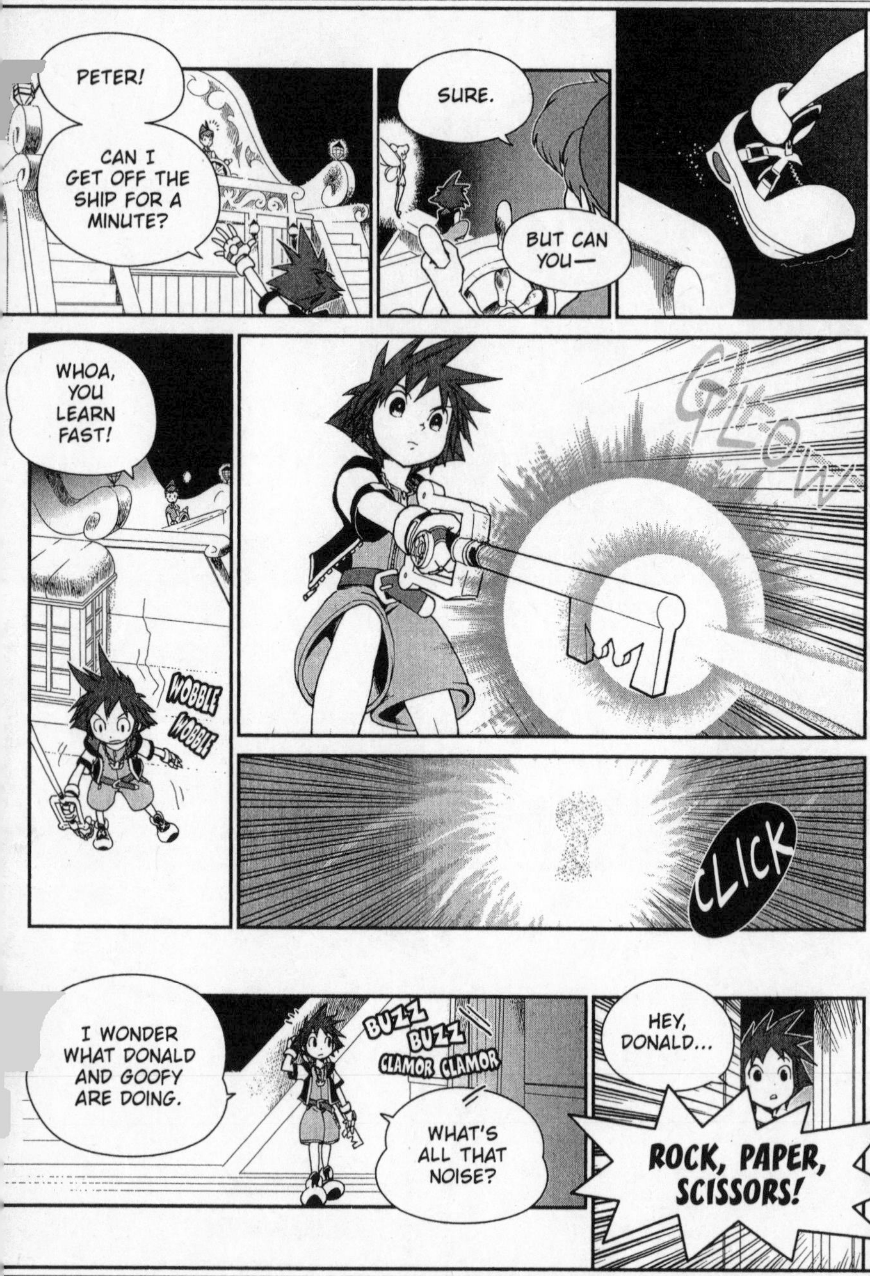
PETER!
CAN I GET OFF THE SHIP FOR A MINUTE?
SURE.
BUT CAN YOU—
WHOA, YOU LEARN FAST!
WOBBLE WOBBLE
GLOW
CLICK
I WONDER WHAT DONALD AND GOOFY ARE DOING.
BUZZ BUZZ
CLAMOR CLAMOR
WHAT'S ALL THAT NOISE?
HEY, DONALD...
ROCK, PAPER, SCISSORS!

I WIN!

THIS IS MINE! GOT IT?

WHAT'S THAT DUCK'S PROBLEM?

WHAT A BEAUTIFUL VIEW...

I CAN SEE THE ENTIRE CITY FROM HERE.

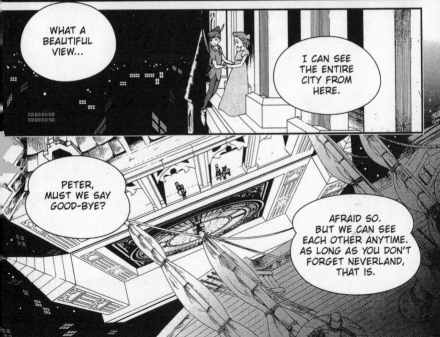

PETER, MUST WE SAY GOOD-BYE?

AFRAID SO. BUT WE CAN SEE EACH OTHER ANYTIME. AS LONG AS YOU DON'T FORGET NEVERLAND, THAT IS.

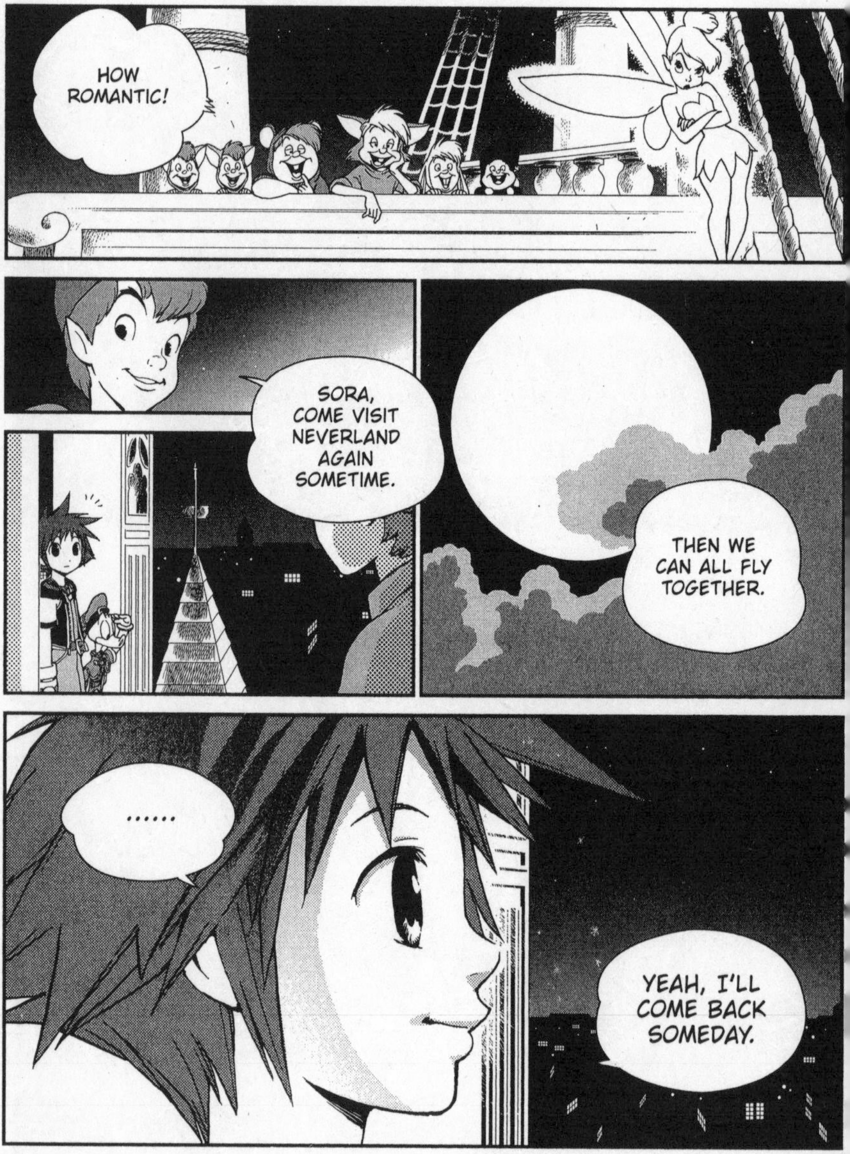
HOW ROMANTIC!
SORA, COME VISIT NEVERLAND AGAIN SOMETIME.
THEN WE CAN ALL FLY TOGETHER.
......
YEAH, I'LL COME BACK SOMEDAY.

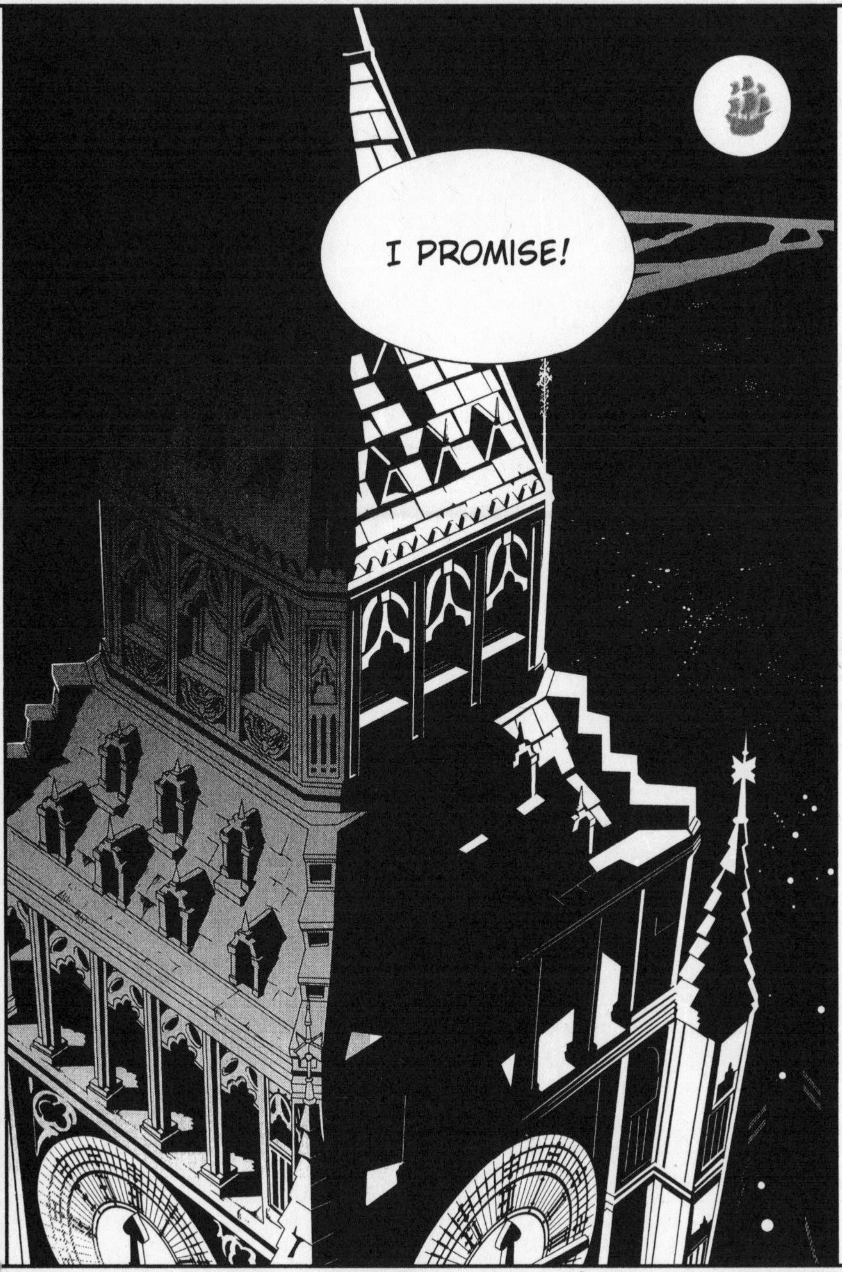
I PROMISE!

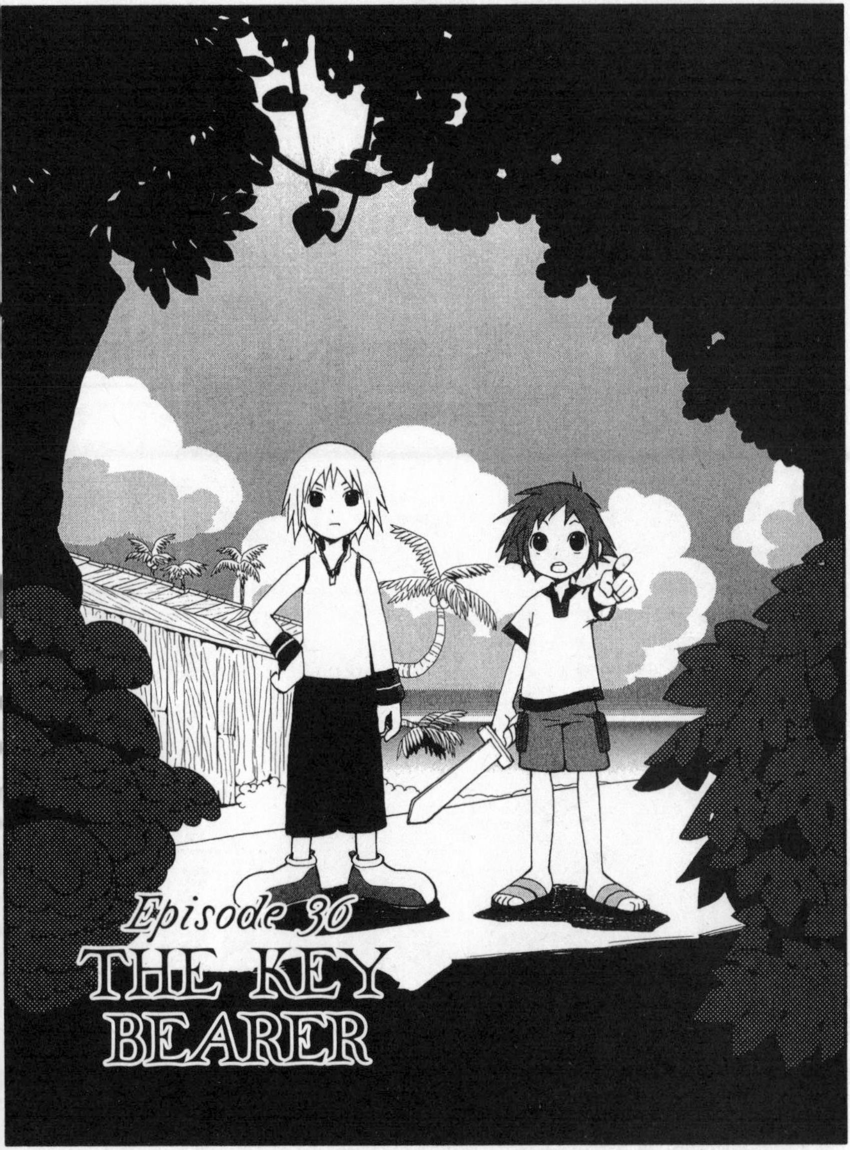
Episode 36
THE KEY BEARER

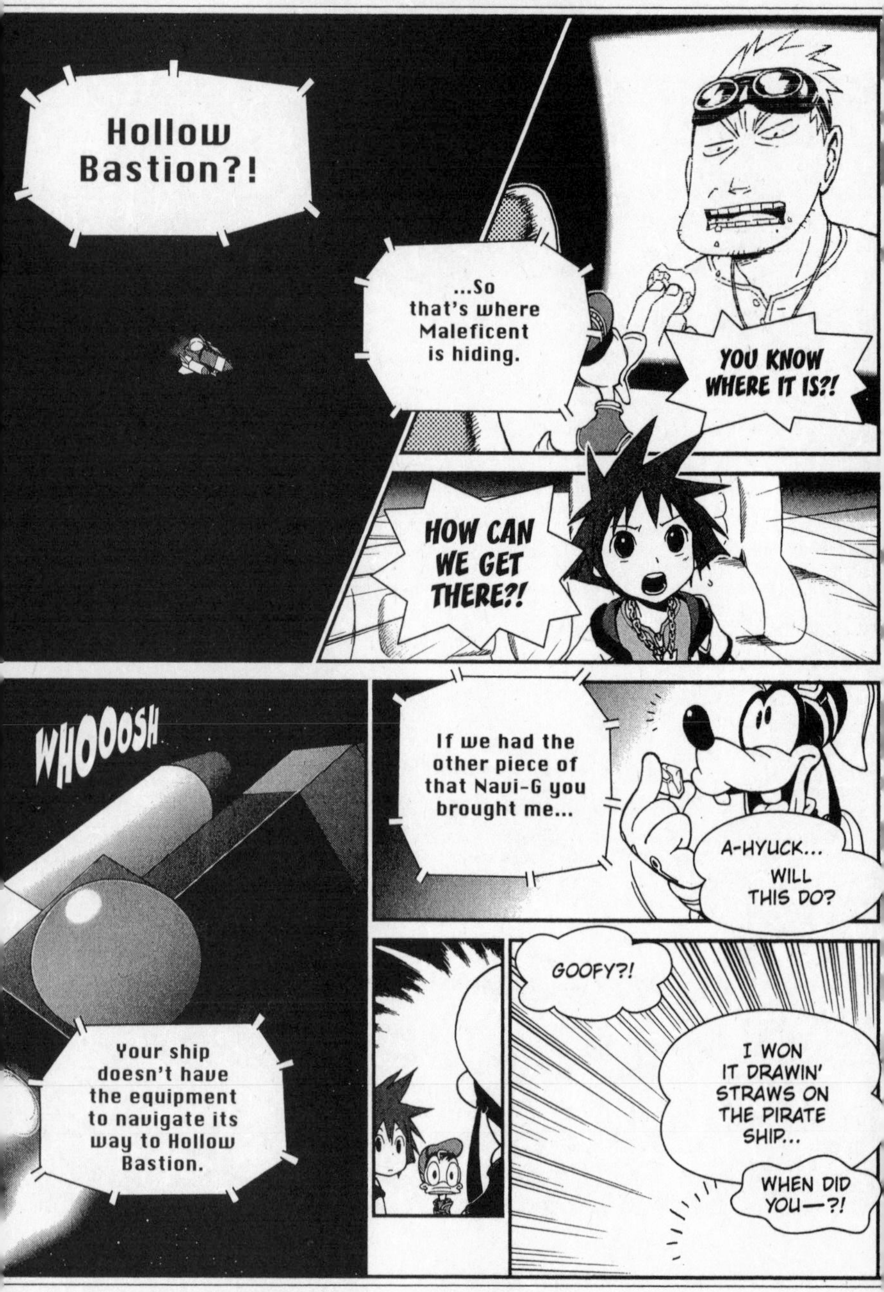
Hollow Bastion?!
...So that's where Maleficent is hiding.
YOU KNOW WHERE IT IS?!
HOW CAN WE GET THERE?!
WHOOOSH
Your ship doesn't have the equipment to navigate its way to Hollow Bastion.
If we had the other piece of that Navi-G you brought me...
A-HYUCK... WILL THIS DO?
GOOFY?!
I WON IT DRAWIN' STRAWS ON THE PIRATE SHIP...
WHEN DID YOU—?!

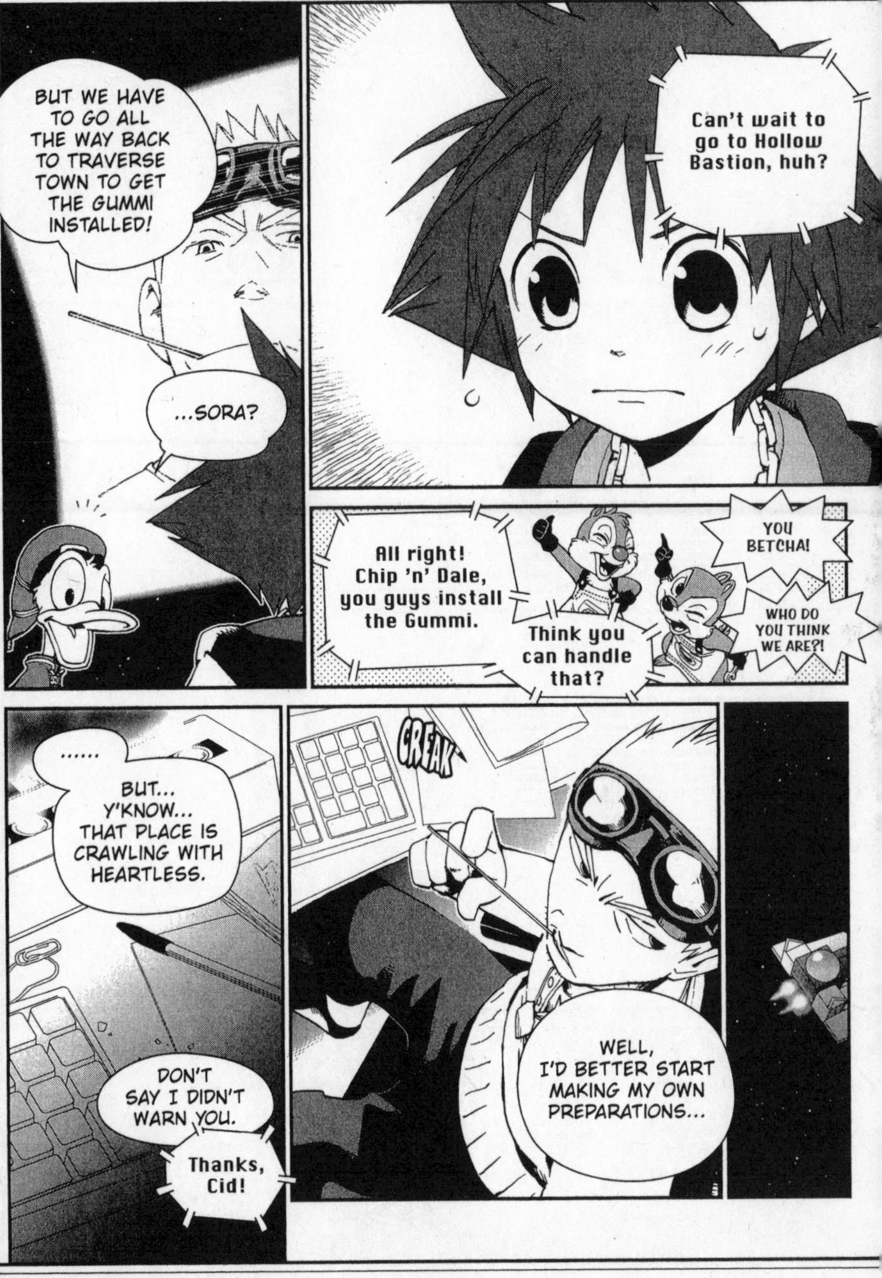
BUT WE HAVE TO GO ALL THE WAY BACK TO TRAVERSE TOWN TO GET THE GUMMI INSTALLED!
...SORA?
Can't wait to go to Hollow Bastion, huh?
All right! Chip 'n' Dale, you guys install the Gummi.
Think you can handle that?
YOU BETCHA!
WHO DO YOU THINK WE ARE?!
......
BUT... Y'KNOW... THAT PLACE IS CRAWLING WITH HEARTLESS.
DON'T SAY I DIDN'T WARN YOU.
Thanks, Cid!
CREAK
WELL, I'D BETTER START MAKING MY OWN PREPARATIONS...

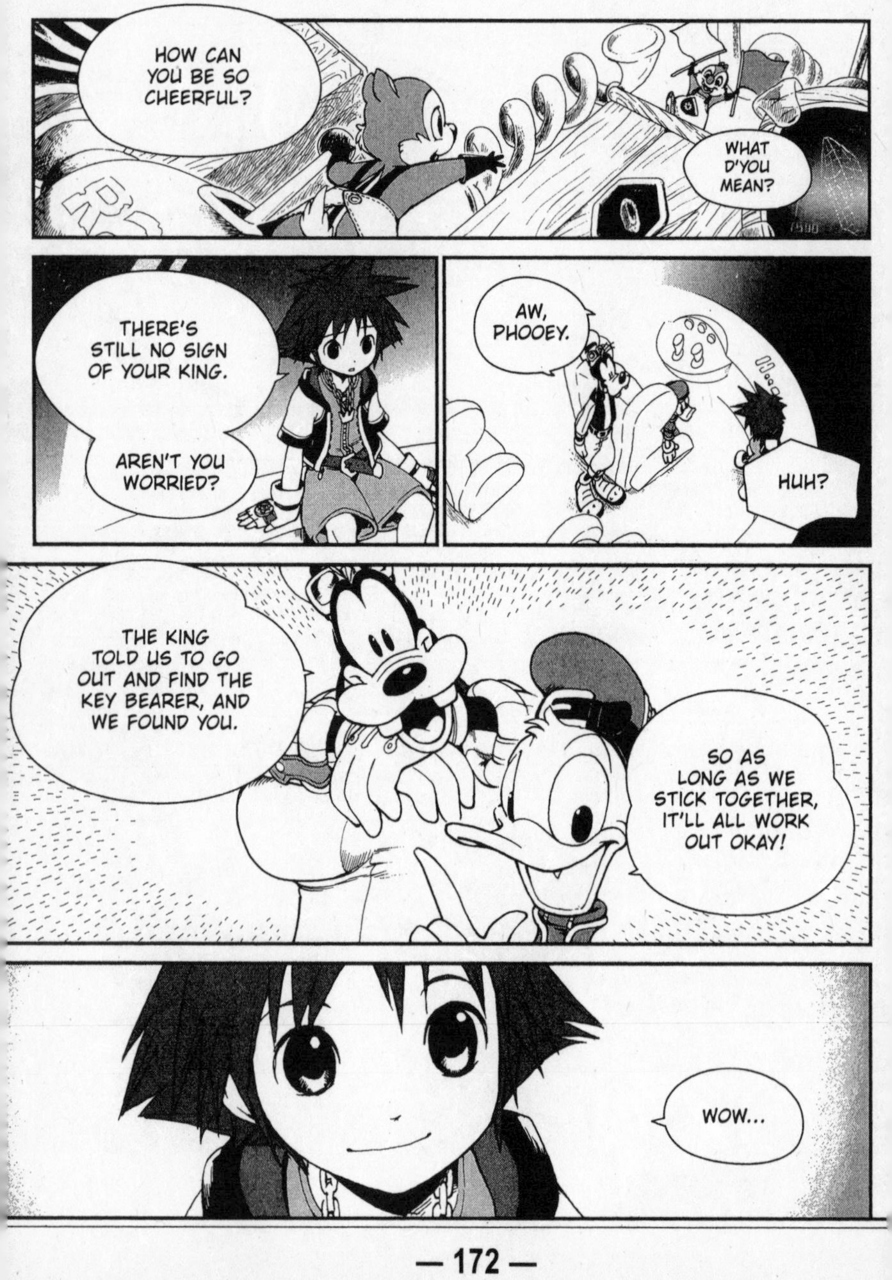
HOW CAN YOU BE SO CHEERFUL?
WHAT D'YOU MEAN?
THERE'S STILL NO SIGN OF YOUR KING.
AREN'T YOU WORRIED?
AW, PHOOEY.
HUH?
THE KING TOLD US TO GO OUT AND FIND THE KEY BEARER, AND WE FOUND YOU.
SO AS LONG AS WE STICK TOGETHER, IT'LL ALL WORK OUT OKAY!
WOW...

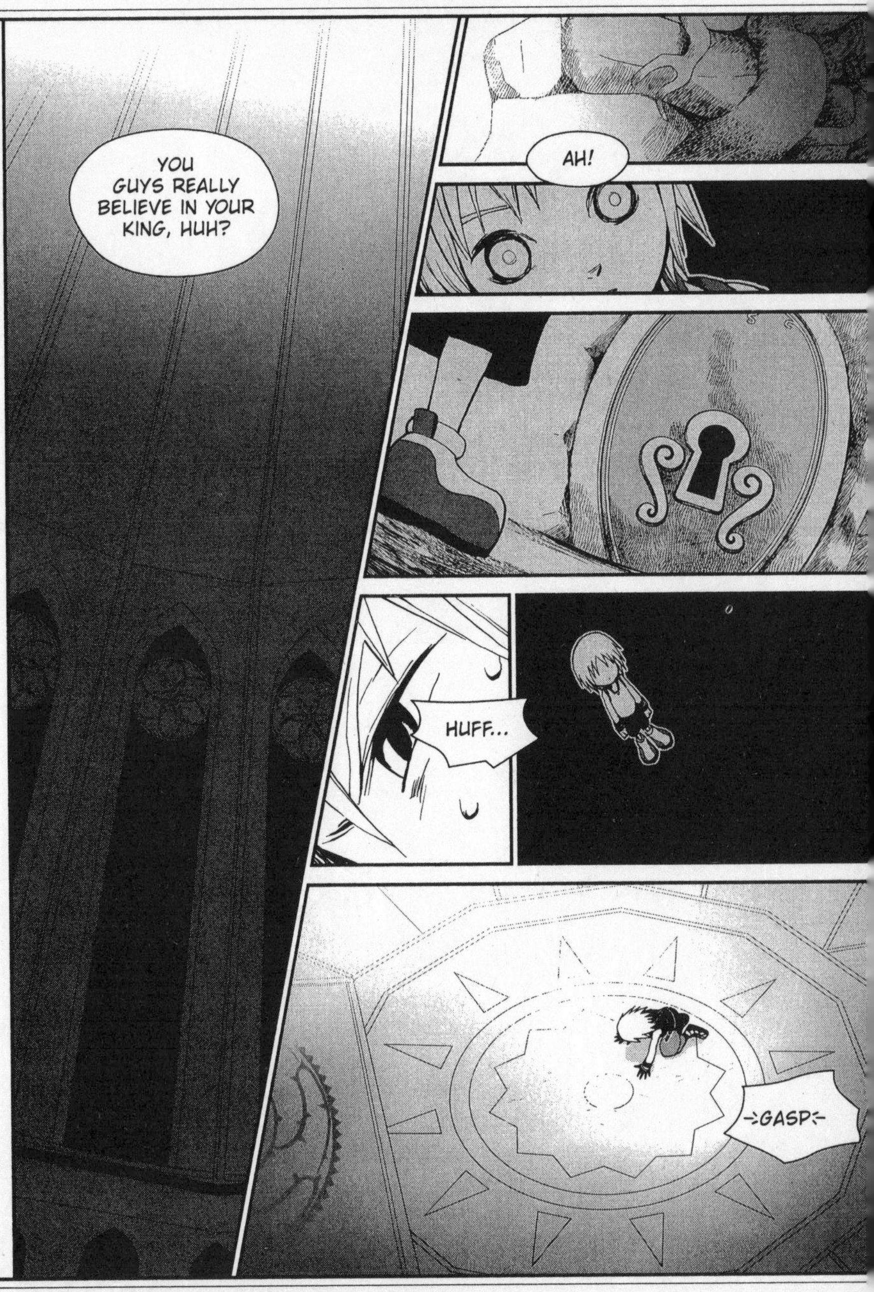
YOU GUYS REALLY BELIEVE IN YOUR KING, HUH?
AH!
HUFF...
-GASP-

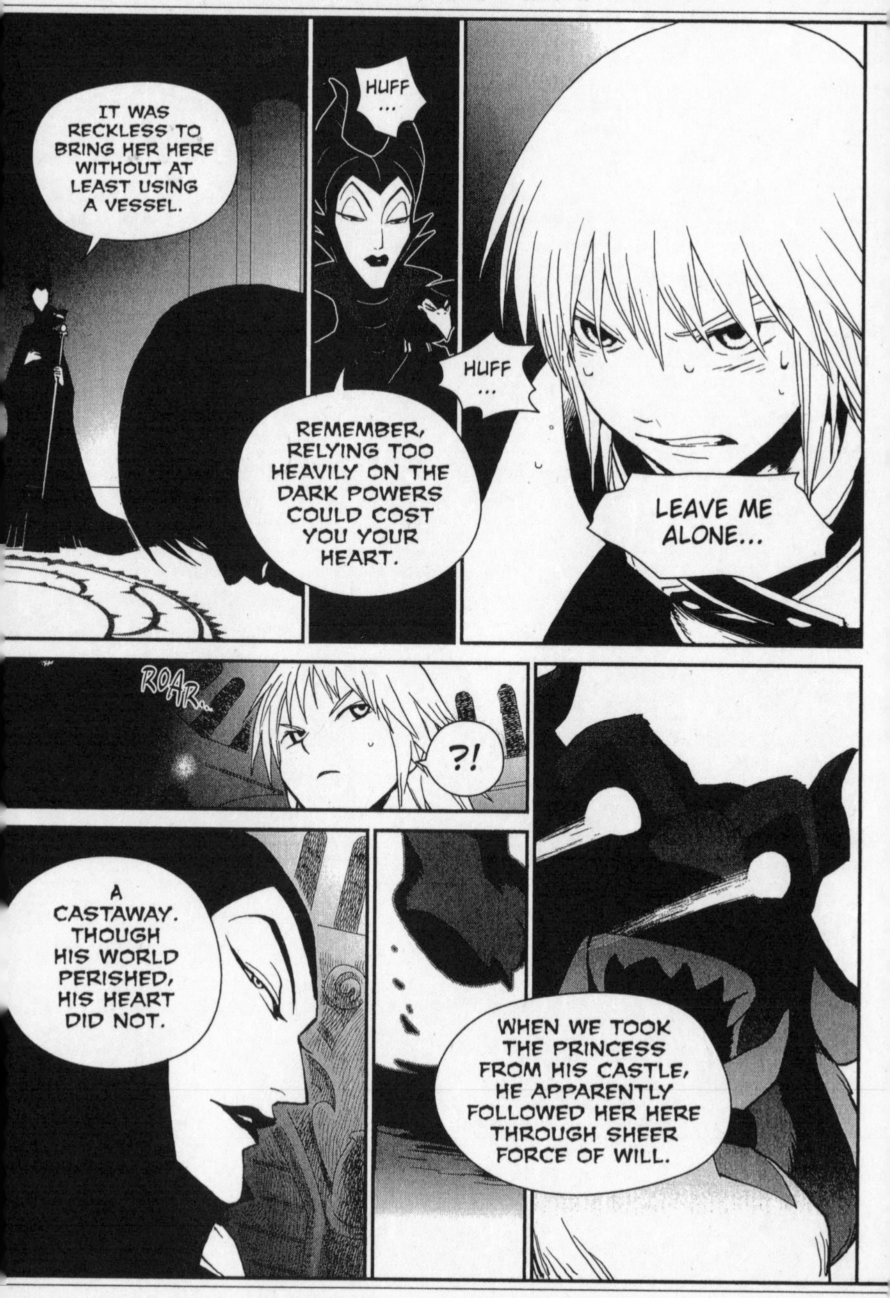
IT WAS RECKLESS TO BRING HER HERE WITHOUT AT LEAST USING A VESSEL.
HUFF ...
REMEMBER, RELYING TOO HEAVILY ON THE DARK POWERS COULD COST YOU YOUR HEART.
HUFF ...
LEAVE ME ALONE...
ROAR...
?!
A CASTAWAY. THOUGH HIS WORLD PERISHED, HIS HEART DID NOT.
WHEN WE TOOK THE PRINCESS FROM HIS CASTLE, HE APPARENTLY FOLLOWED HER HERE THROUGH SHEER FORCE OF WILL.

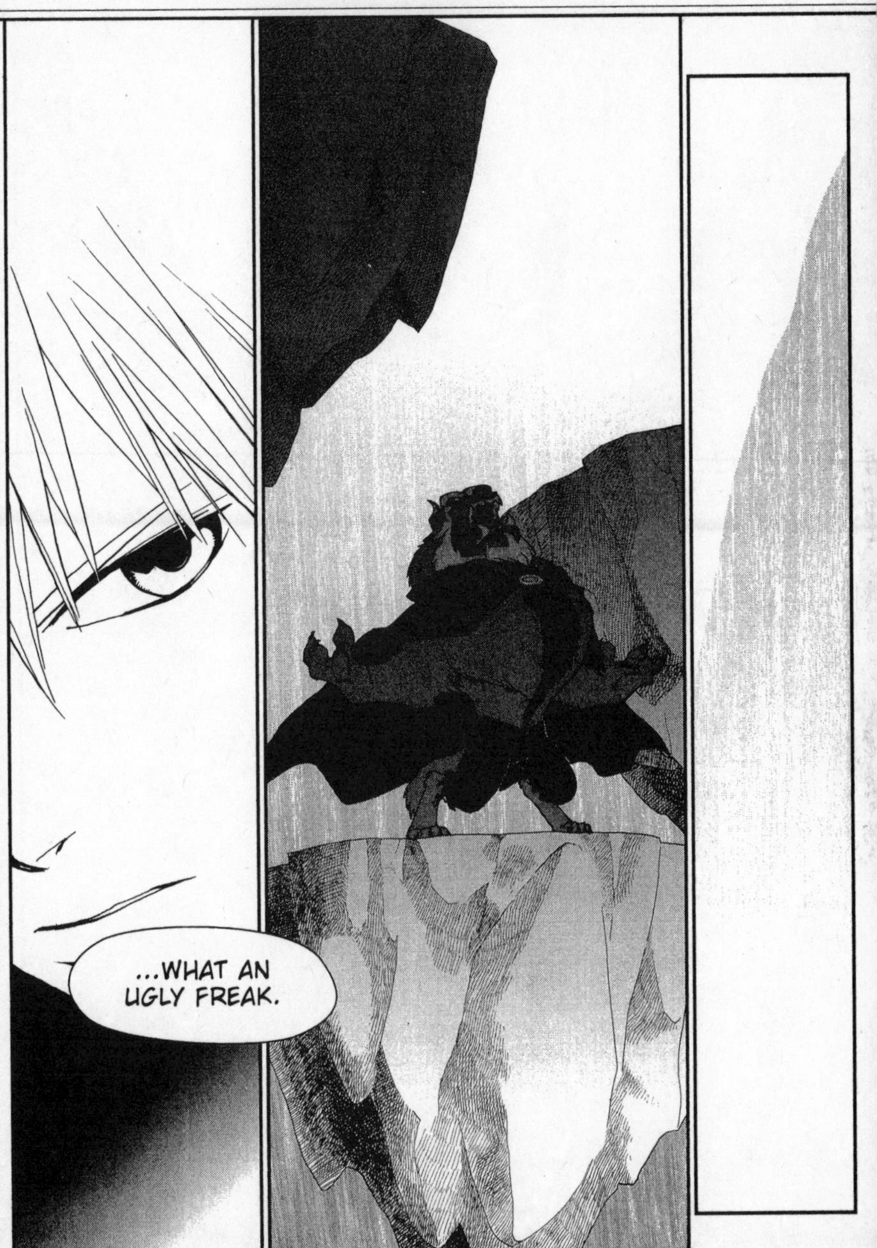
...WHAT AN
UGLY FREAK.

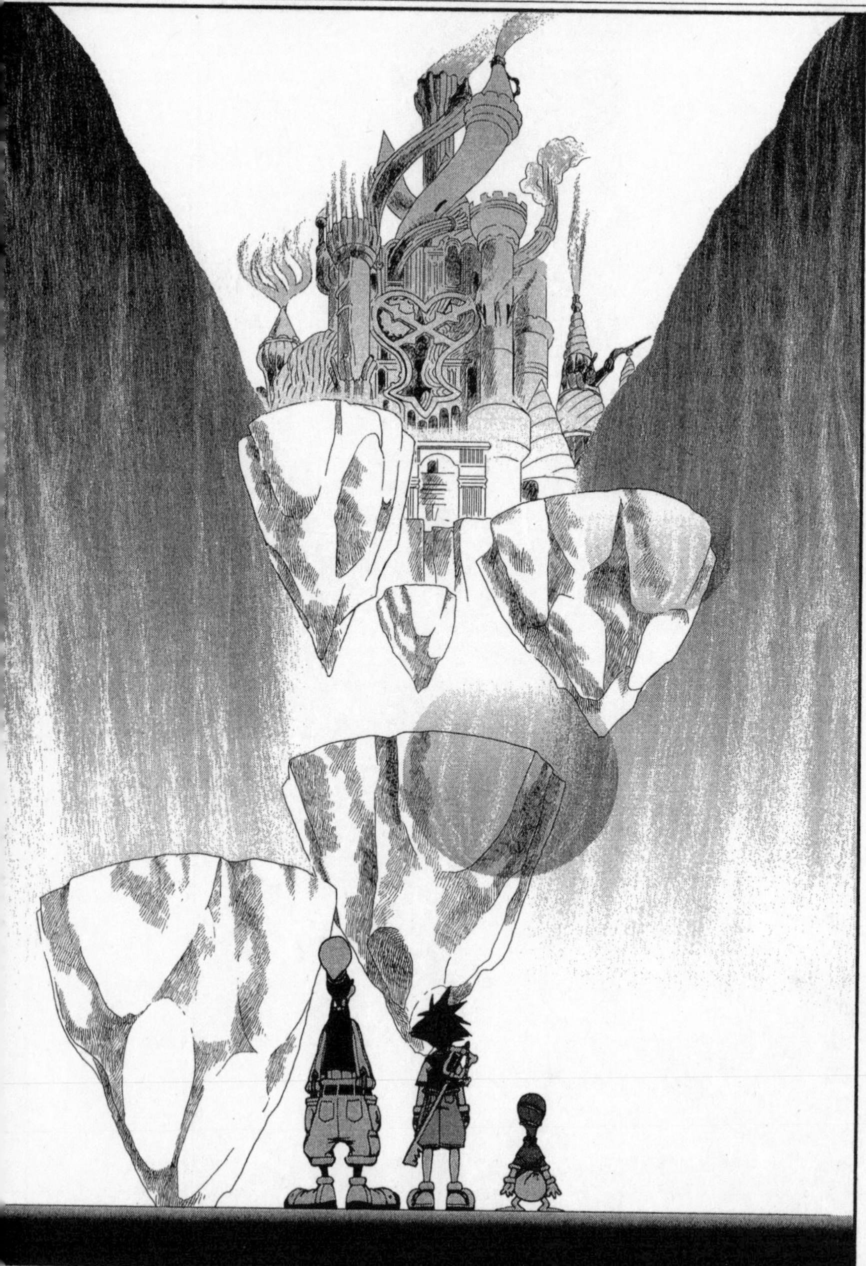

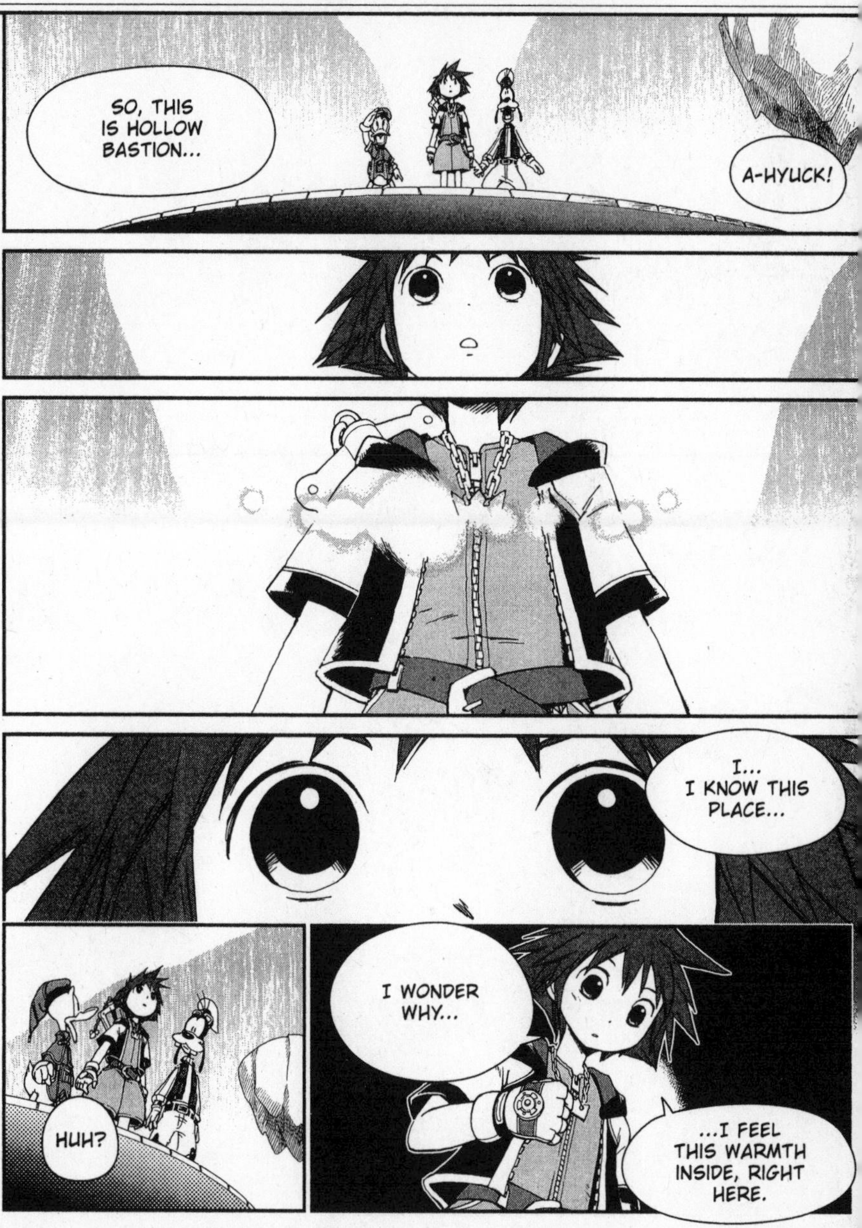
SO, THIS IS HOLLOW BASTION...
A-HYUCK!
I... I KNOW THIS PLACE...
HUH?
I WONDER WHY...
...I FEEL THIS WARMTH INSIDE, RIGHT HERE.

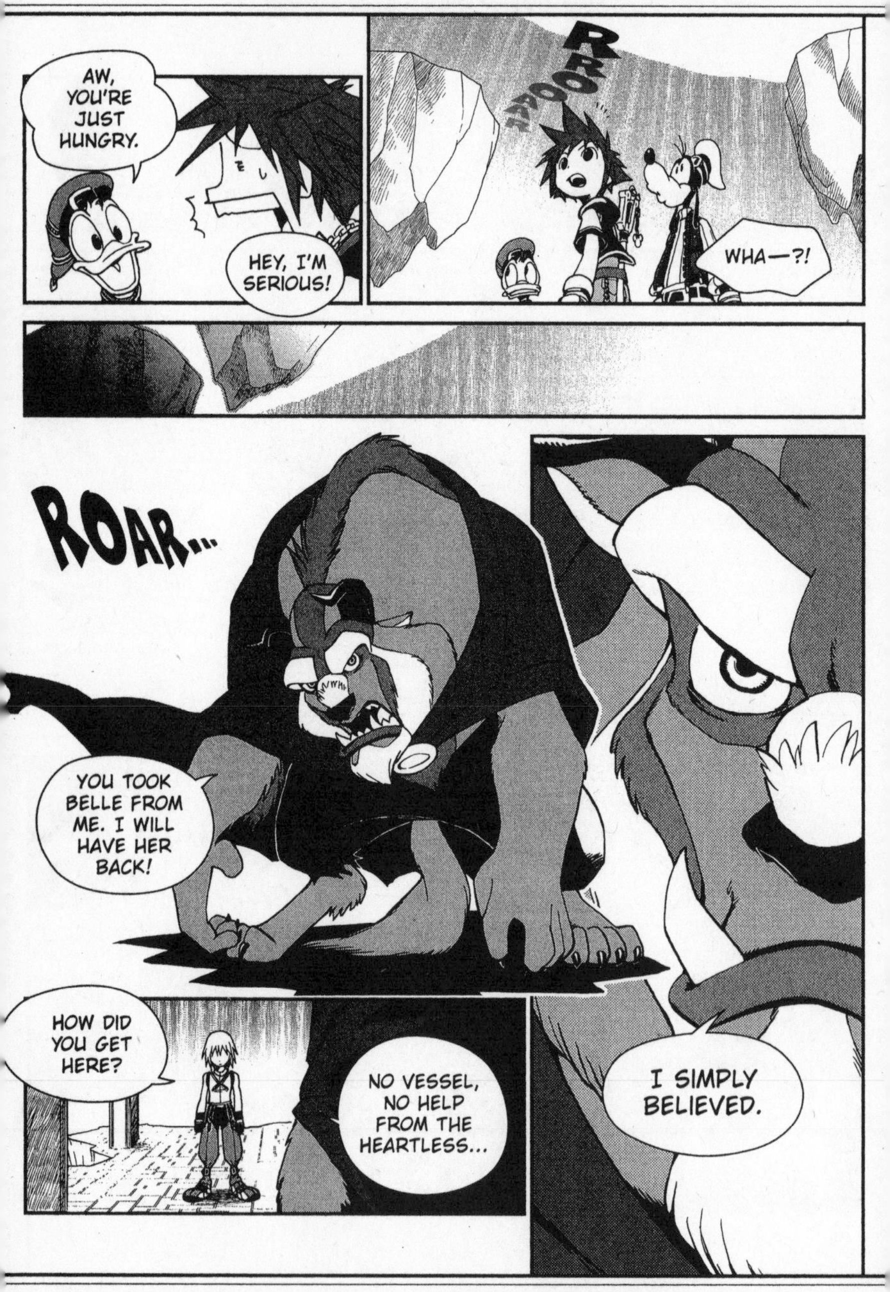
AW, YOU'RE JUST HUNGRY.
HEY, I'M SERIOUS!
RROAR
RROAR...
WHA—?!
ROAR...
YOU TOOK BELLE FROM ME. I WILL HAVE HER BACK!
HOW DID YOU GET HERE?
NO VESSEL, NO HELP FROM THE HEARTLESS...
I SIMPLY BELIEVED.

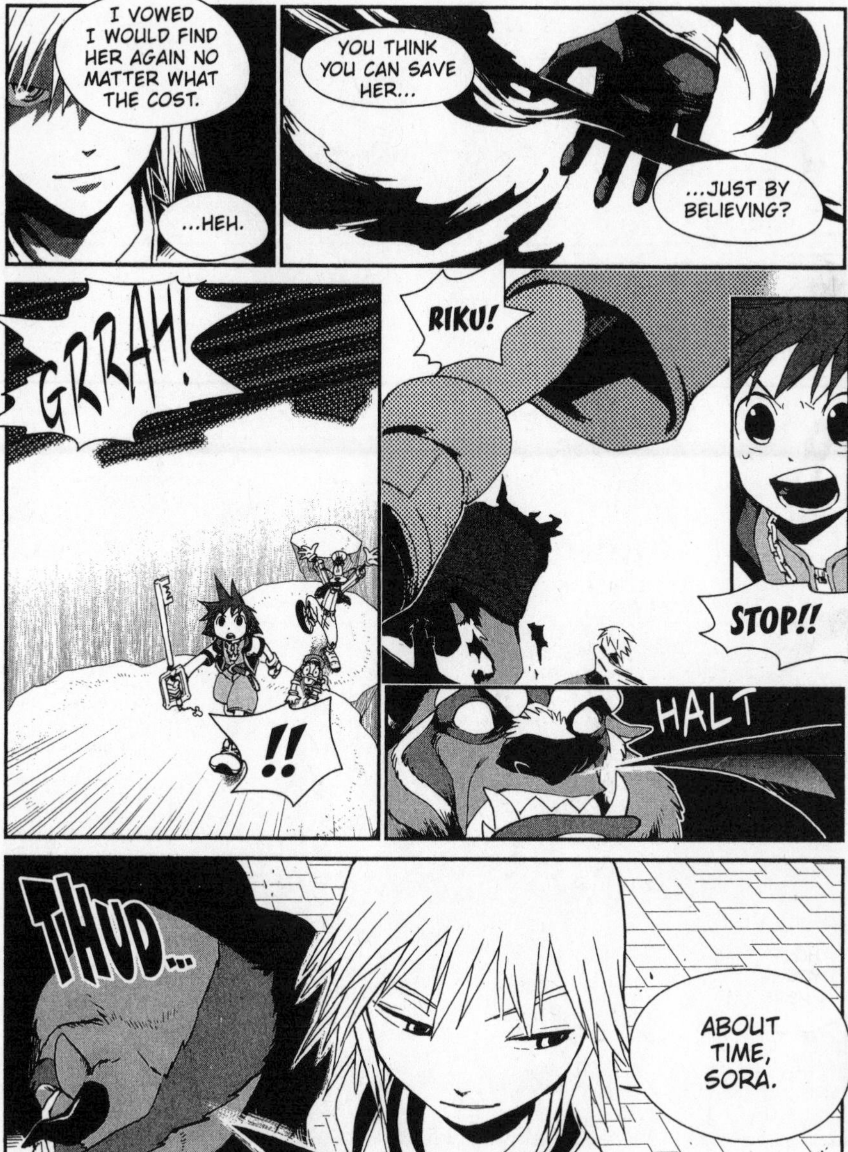
I VOWED I WOULD FIND HER AGAIN NO MATTER WHAT THE COST.
...HEH.
YOU THINK YOU CAN SAVE HER...
...JUST BY BELIEVING?
GRRAH!
!!
RIKU!
STOP!!
HALT
THUD...
ABOUT TIME, SORA.

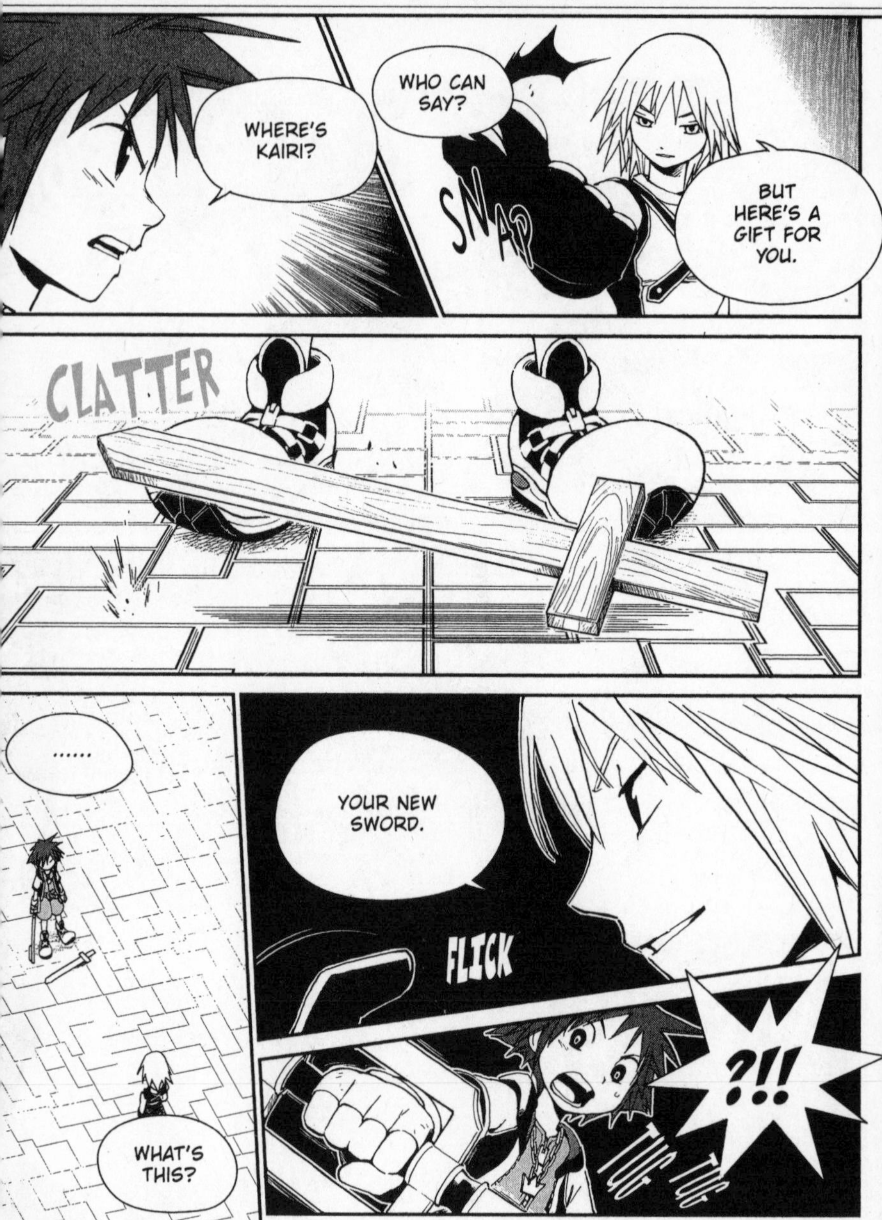
WHERE'S KAIRI?
WHO CAN SAY?
SNAP
BUT HERE'S A GIFT FOR YOU.
CLATTER
......
WHAT'S THIS?
YOUR NEW SWORD.
FLICK
?!!
TUG TUG

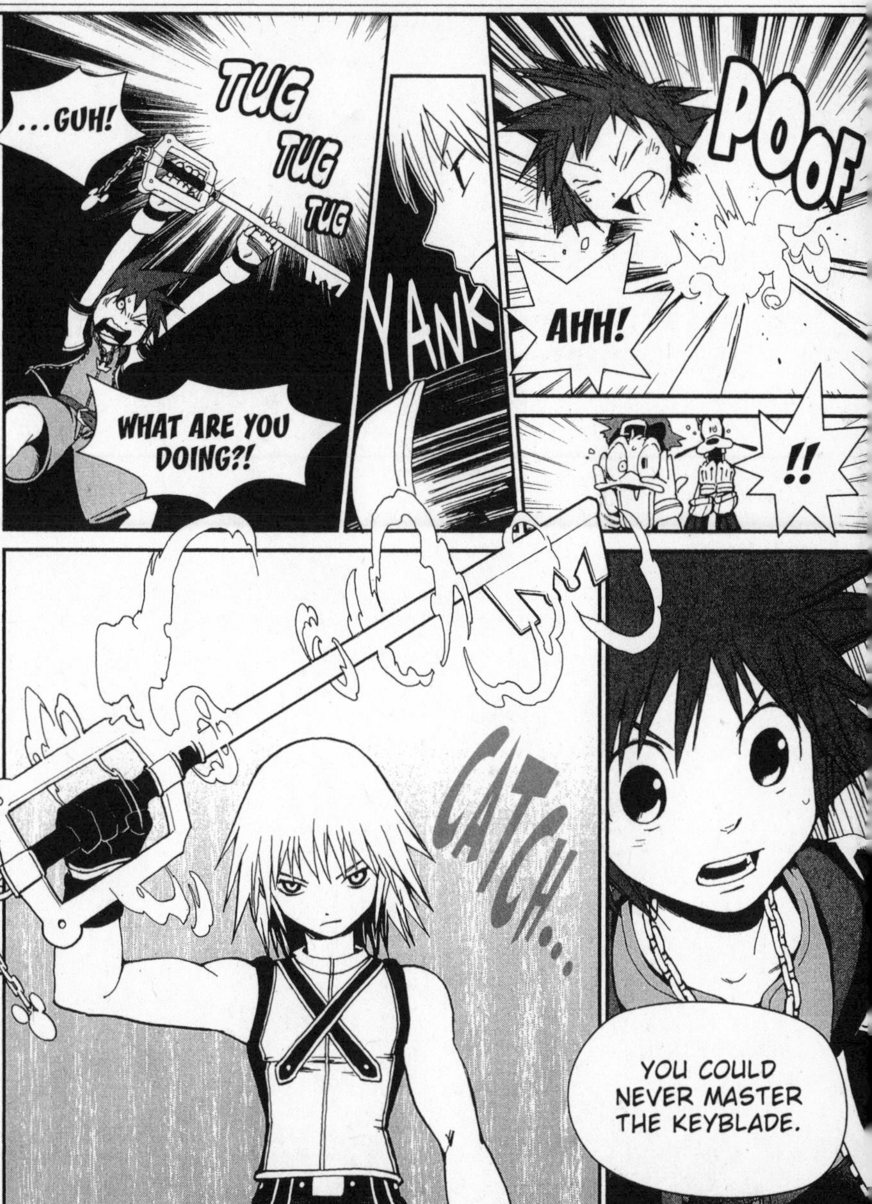
...GUH!
TUG
TUG
TUG
WHAT ARE YOU DOING?!
YANK
POOF
AHH!
!!
CATCH...
YOU COULD NEVER MASTER THE KEYBLADE.

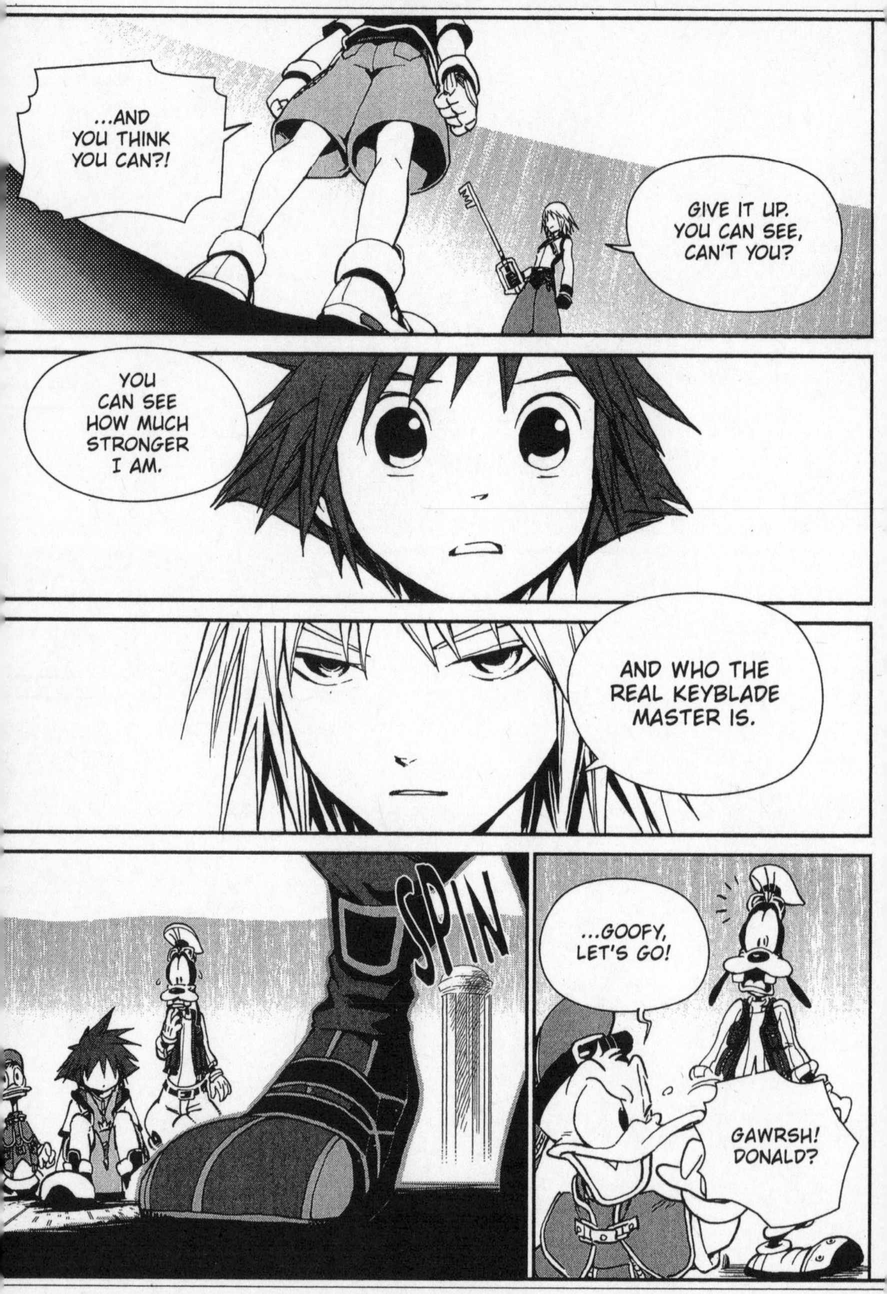
...AND YOU THINK YOU CAN?!
GIVE IT UP. YOU CAN SEE, CAN'T YOU?
YOU CAN SEE HOW MUCH STRONGER I AM.
AND WHO THE REAL KEYBLADE MASTER IS.
SPIN
...GOOFY, LET'S GO!
GAWRSH! DONALD?

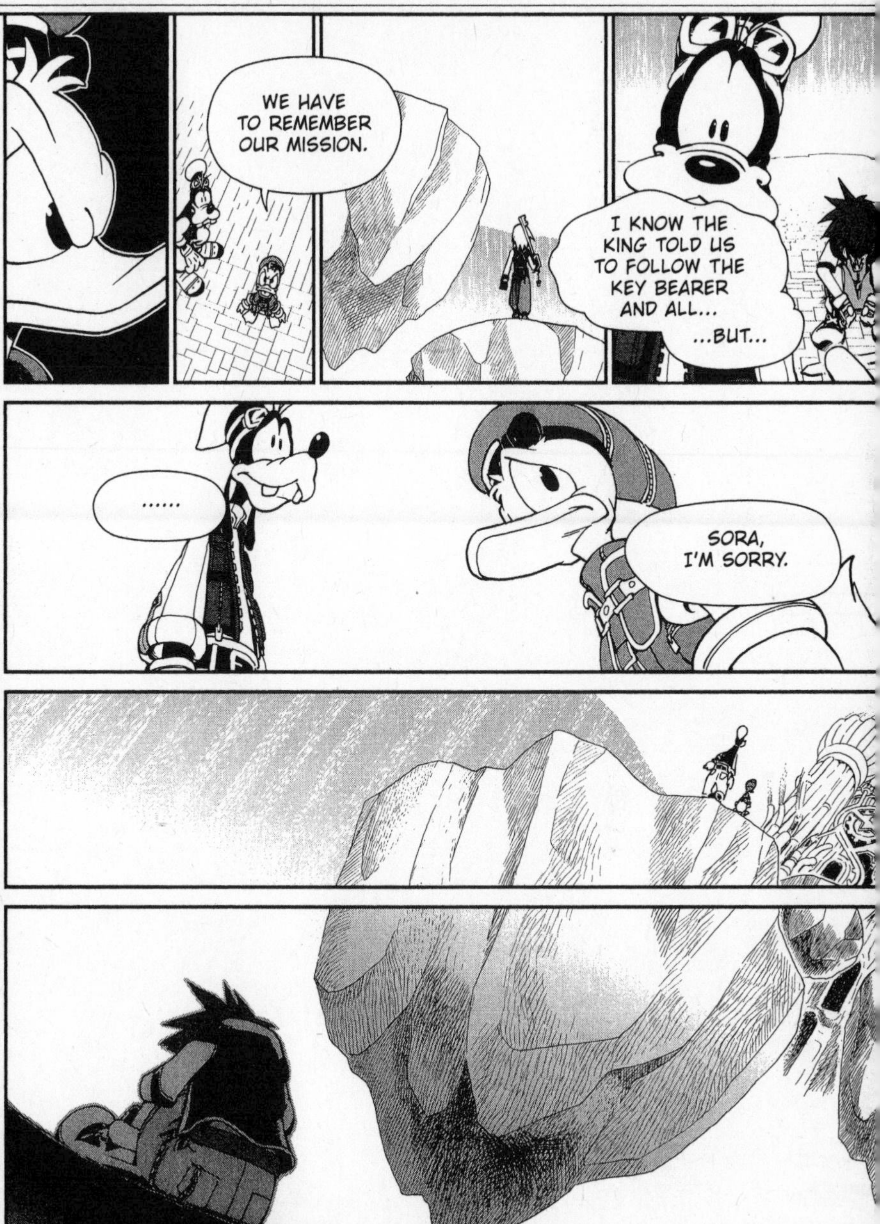
WE HAVE TO REMEMBER OUR MISSION.
I KNOW THE KING TOLD US TO FOLLOW THE KEY BEARER AND ALL...
...BUT...
......
SORA, I'M SORRY.

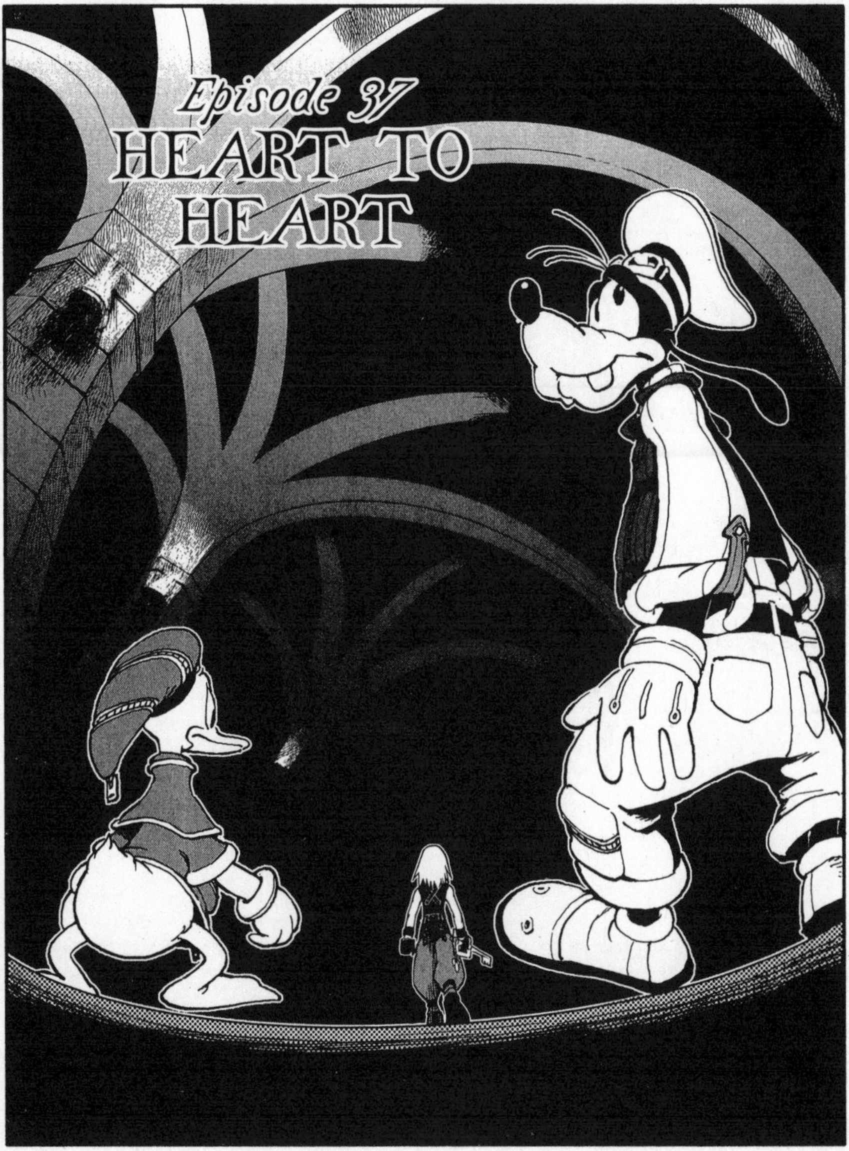
Episode 37
HEART TO HEART

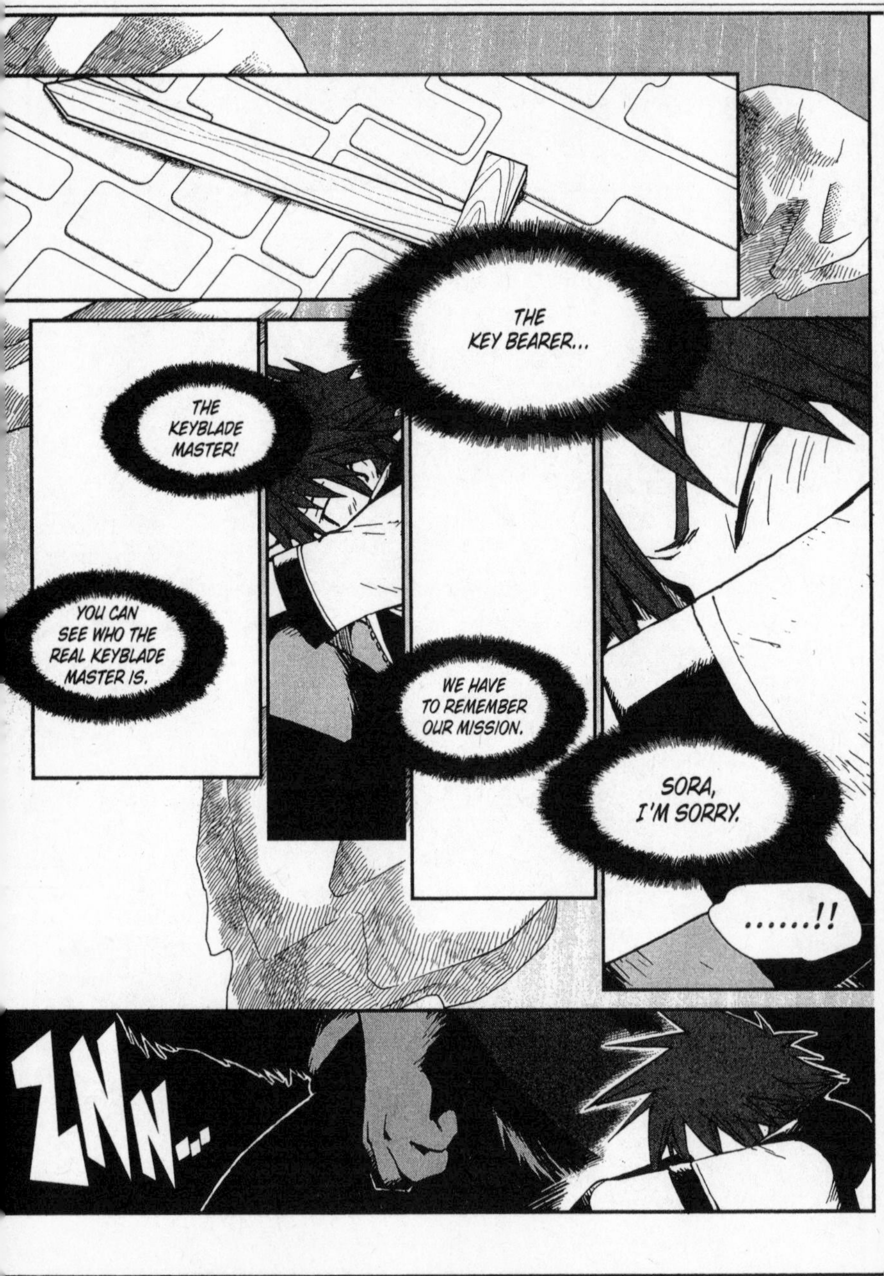
THE KEY BEARER...
THE KEYBLADE MASTER!
YOU CAN SEE WHO THE REAL KEYBLADE MASTER IS.
WE HAVE TO REMEMBER OUR MISSION.
SORA, I'M SORRY.
......!!
ZNN...

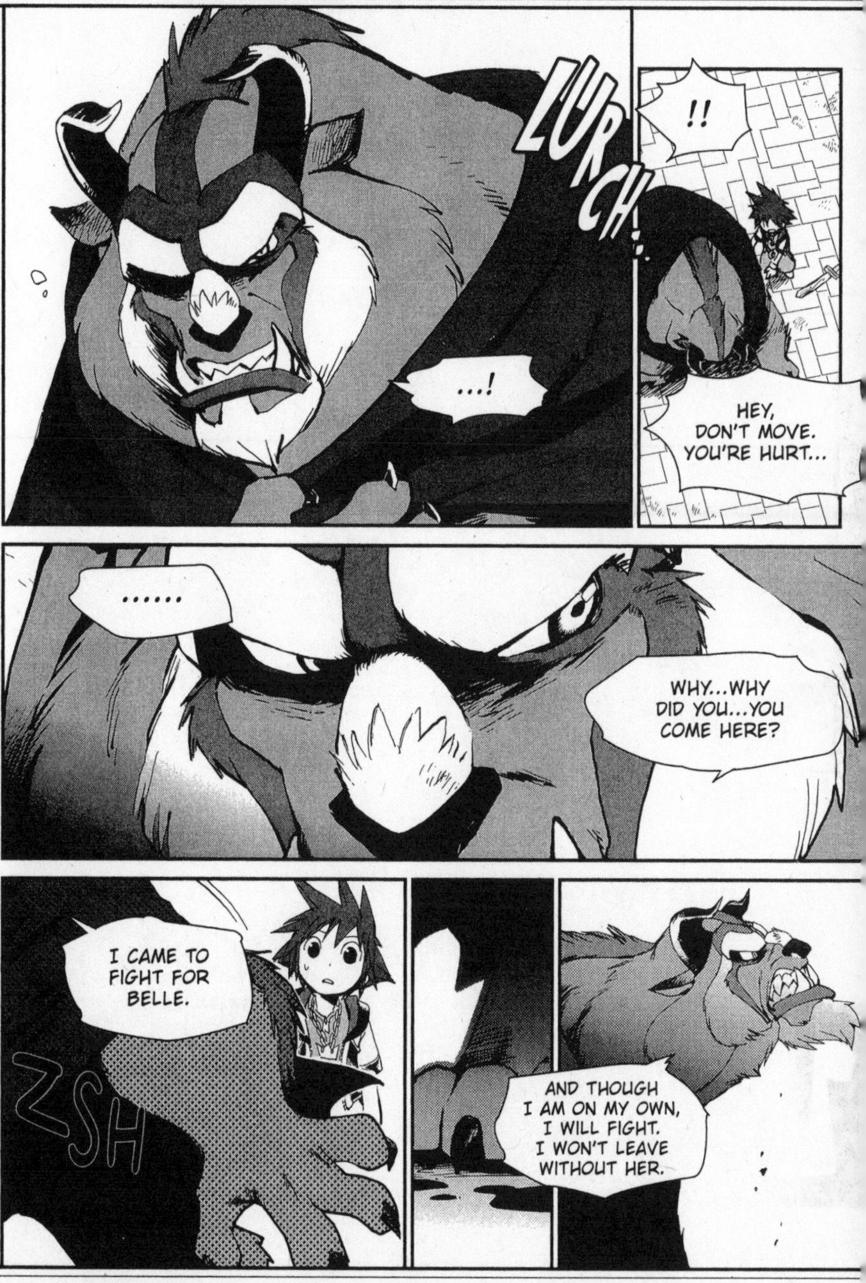
LURCH
...!
!!
HEY, DON'T MOVE. YOU'RE HURT...
......
WHY...WHY DID YOU...YOU COME HERE?
I CAME TO FIGHT FOR BELLE.
ZSH
AND THOUGH I AM ON MY OWN, I WILL FIGHT. I WON'T LEAVE WITHOUT HER.

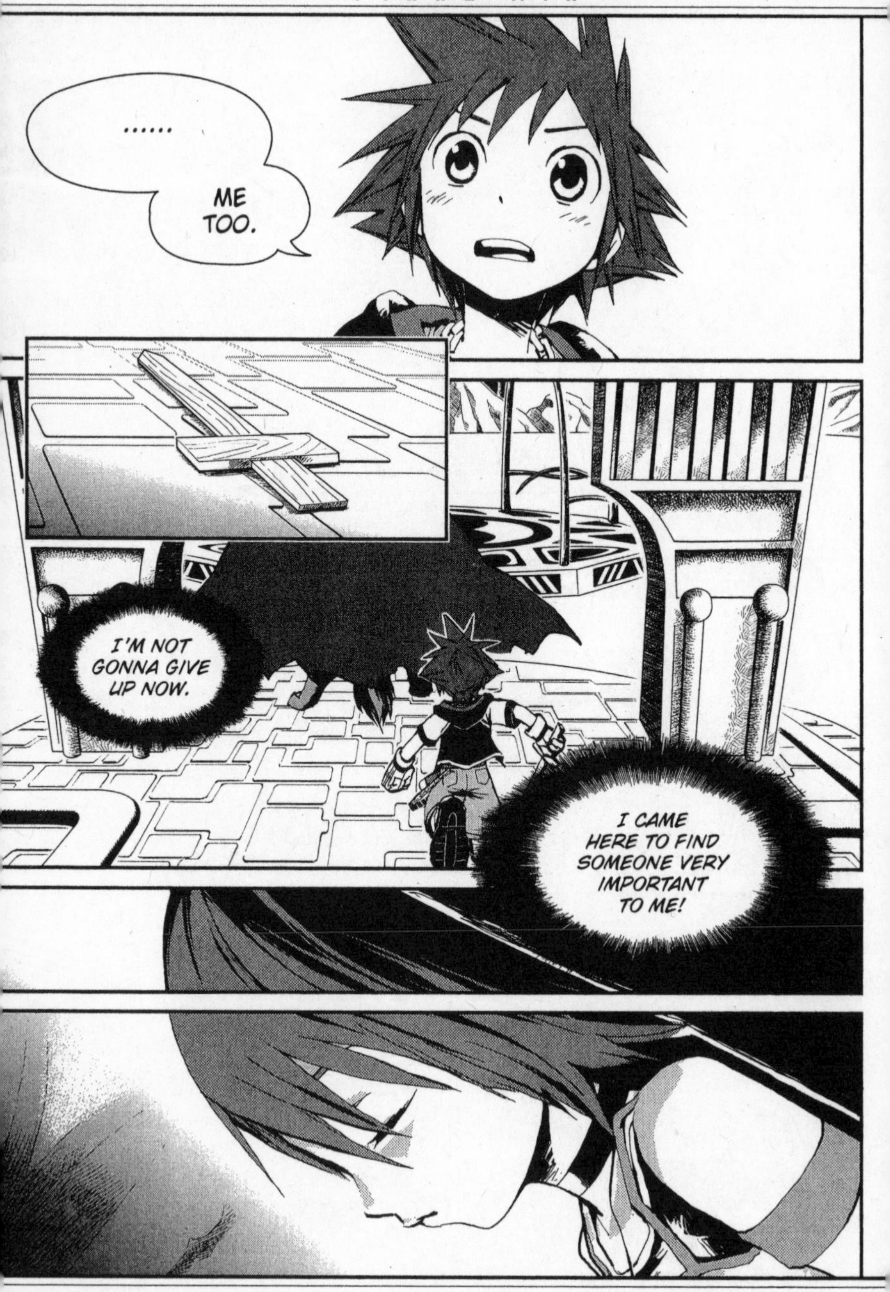
......
ME TOO.
I'M NOT GONNA GIVE UP NOW.
I CAME HERE TO FIND SOMEONE VERY IMPORTANT TO ME!

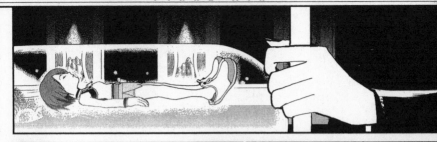

O PUREST OF HEARTS!

REVEAL TO ME THE KEYHOLE!

WAIT! I SAID, WAIT!

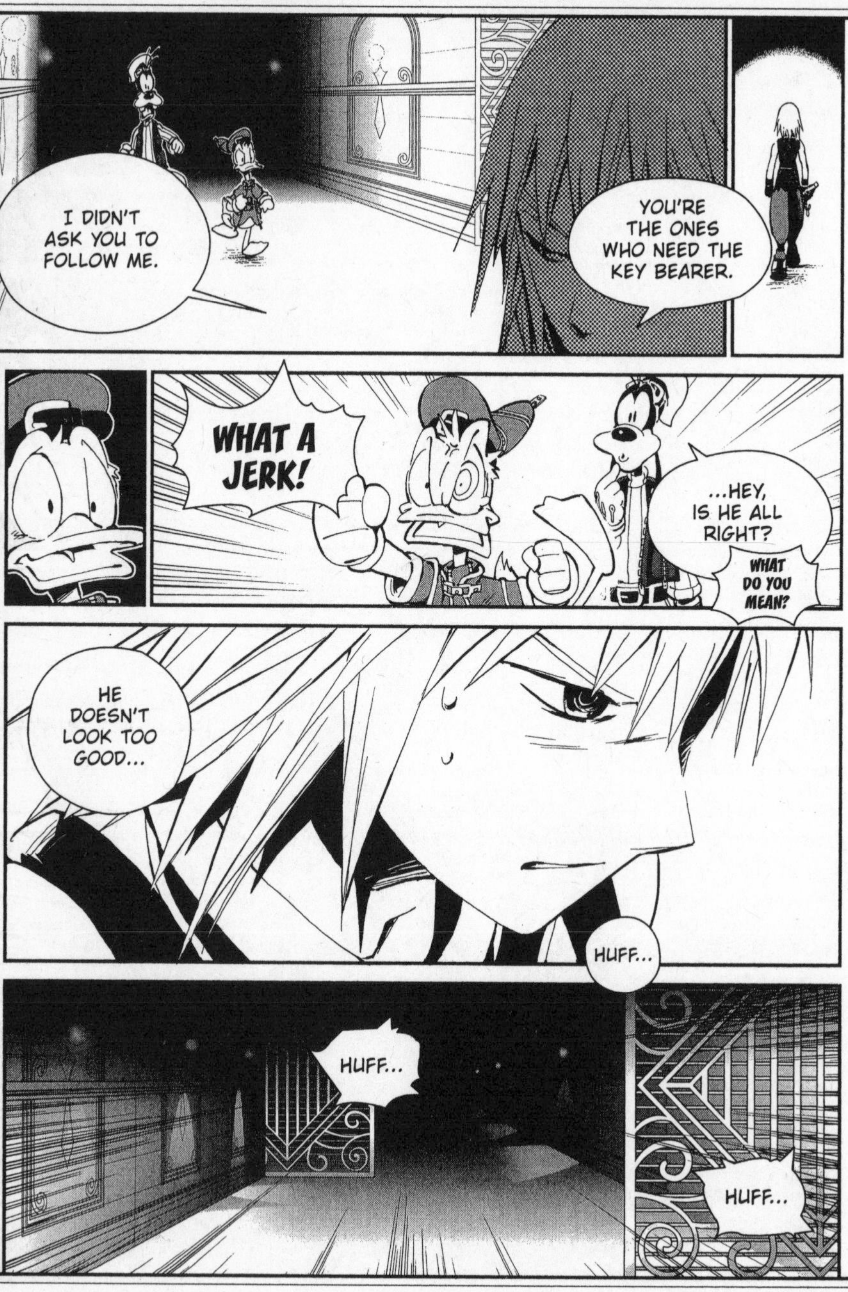
I DIDN'T ASK YOU TO FOLLOW ME.
YOU'RE THE ONES WHO NEED THE KEY BEARER.
WHAT A JERK!
...HEY, IS HE ALL RIGHT?
WHAT DO YOU MEAN?
HE DOESN'T LOOK TOO GOOD...
HUFF...
HUFF...
HUFF...

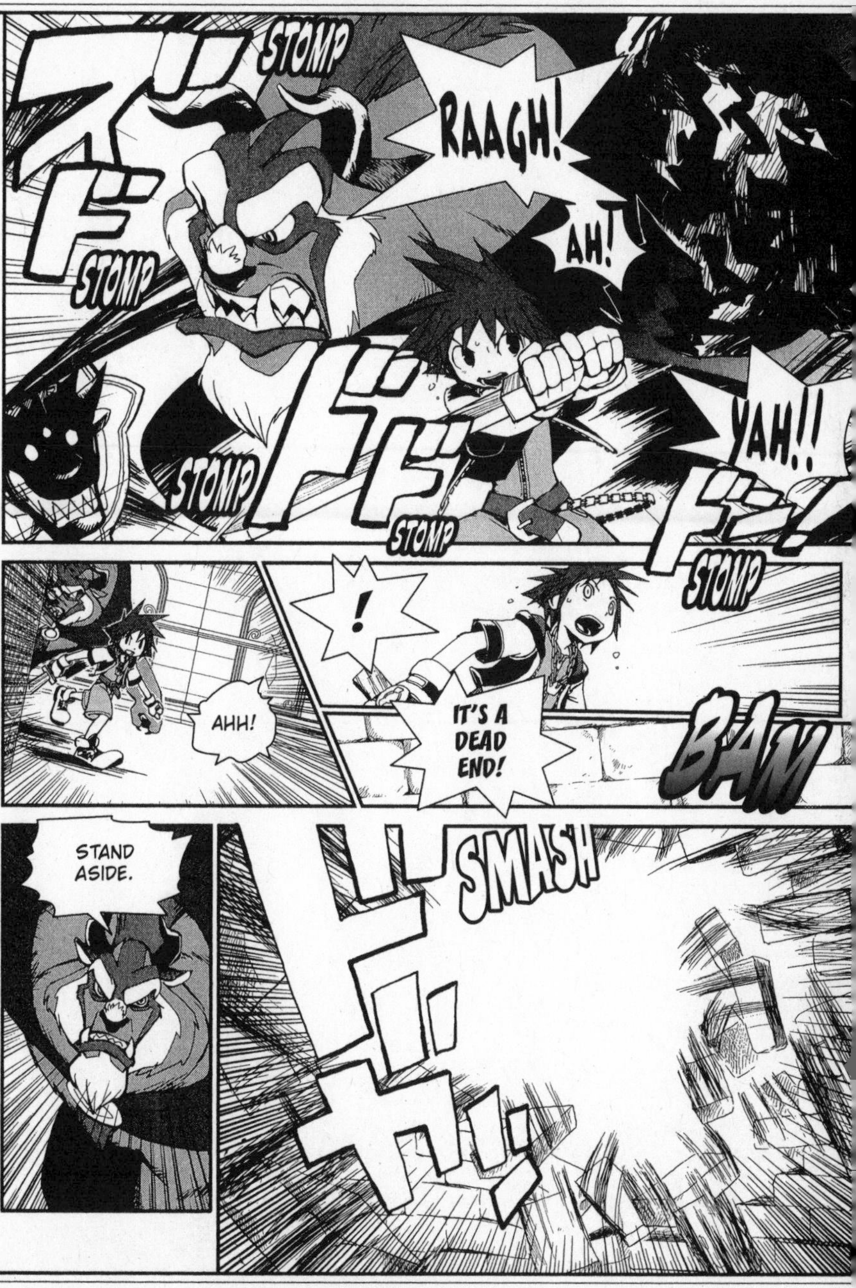
STOMP
RAAGH!
STOMP
AH!
STOMP
STOMP
YAH!!
STOMP
AHH!
!
IT'S A DEAD END!
BAM
STAND ASIDE.
SMASH

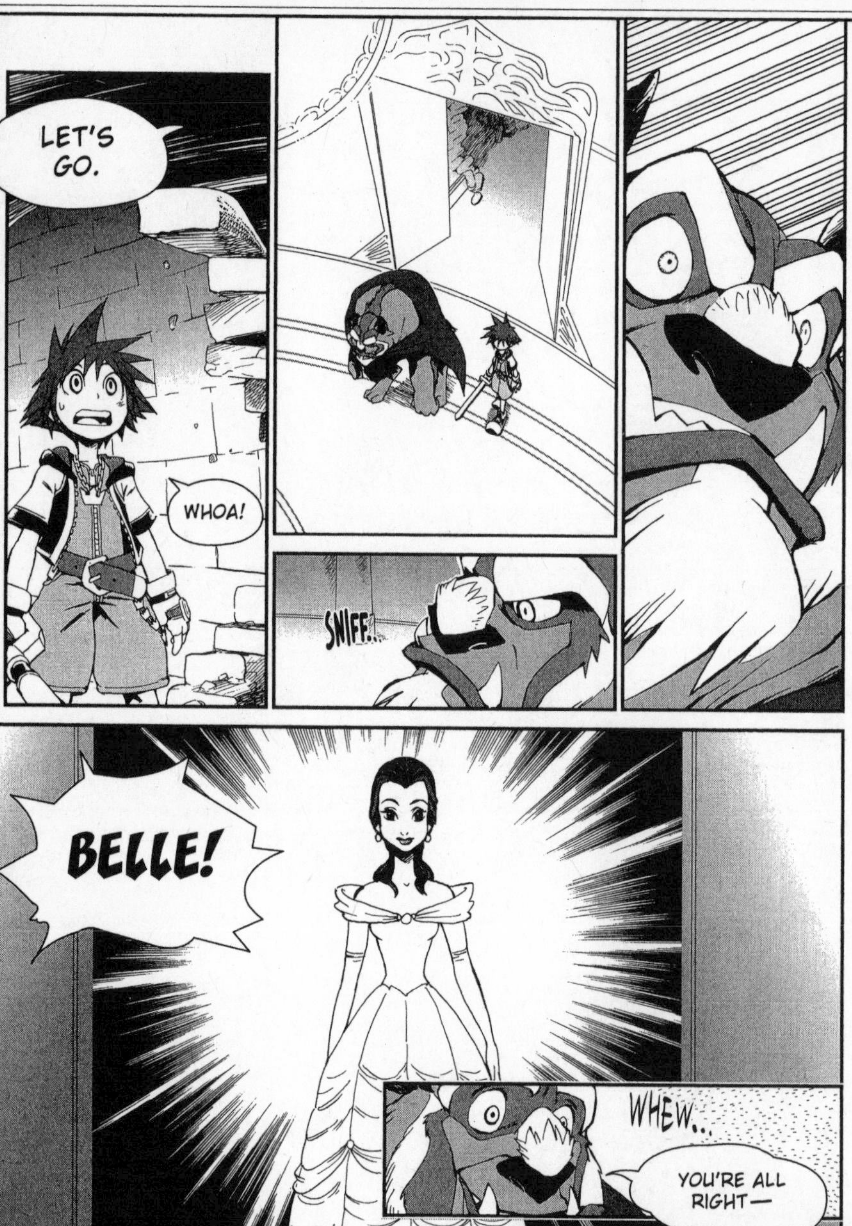
LET'S GO.
WHOA!
SNIFF...
BELLE!
WHEW...
YOU'RE ALL RIGHT—

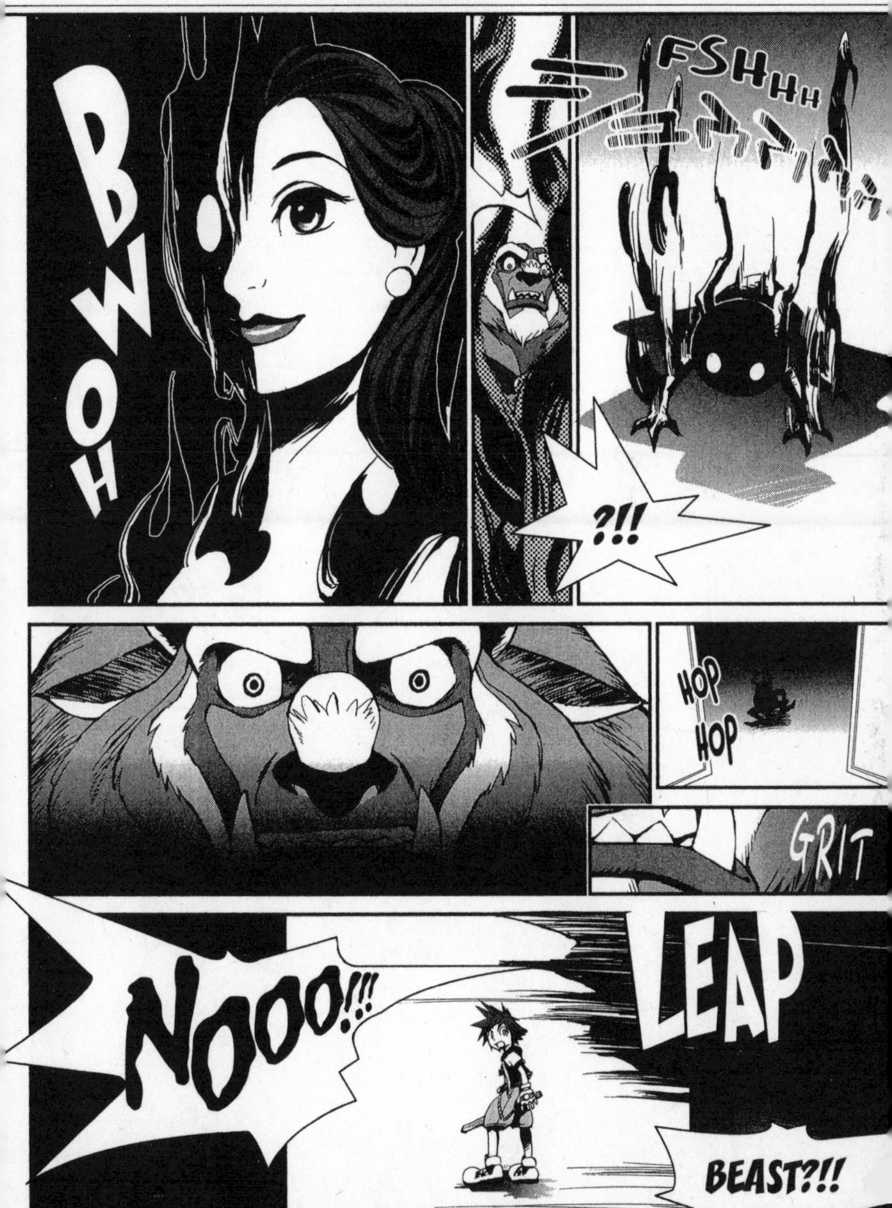
BWOOH
FSHHHH
?!!
HOP
HOP
GRIT
NOOO!!!
LEAP
BEAST?!!

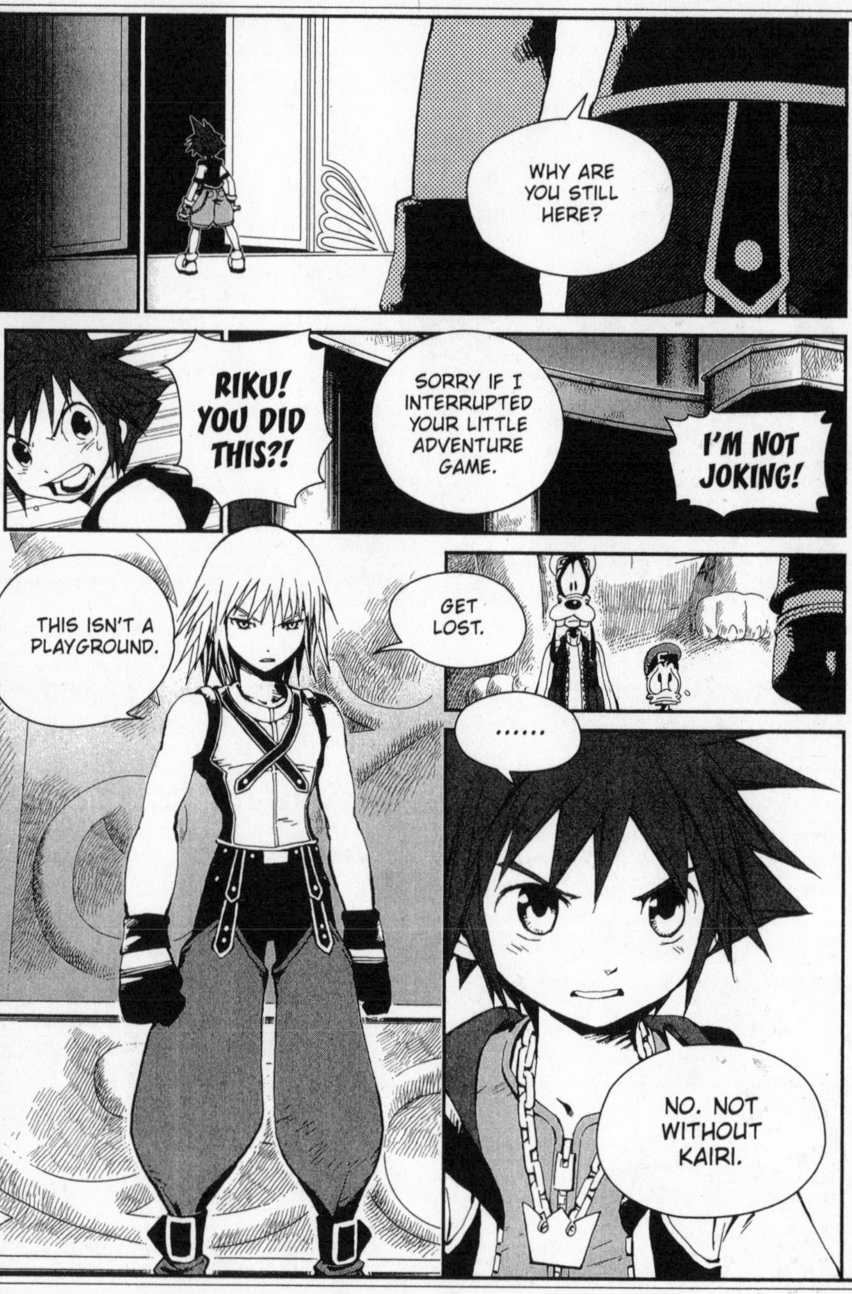
WHY ARE YOU STILL HERE?
RIKU! YOU DID THIS?!
SORRY IF I INTERRUPTED YOUR LITTLE ADVENTURE GAME.
I'M NOT JOKING!
THIS ISN'T A PLAYGROUND.
GET LOST.
......
NO. NOT WITHOUT KAIRI.

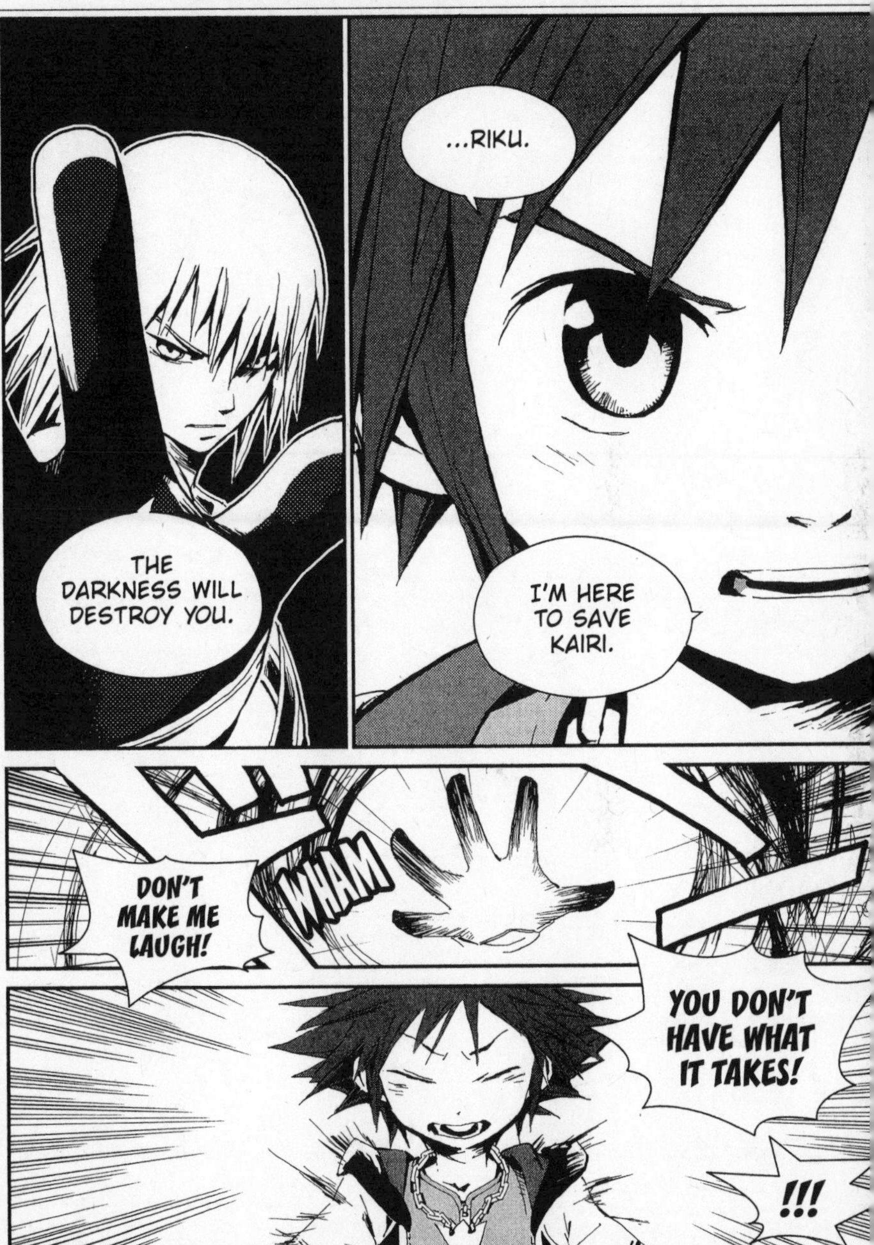
THE DARKNESS WILL DESTROY YOU.
...RIKU.
I'M HERE TO SAVE KAIRI.
DON'T MAKE ME LAUGH!
WHAM
YOU DON'T HAVE WHAT IT TAKES!
!!!

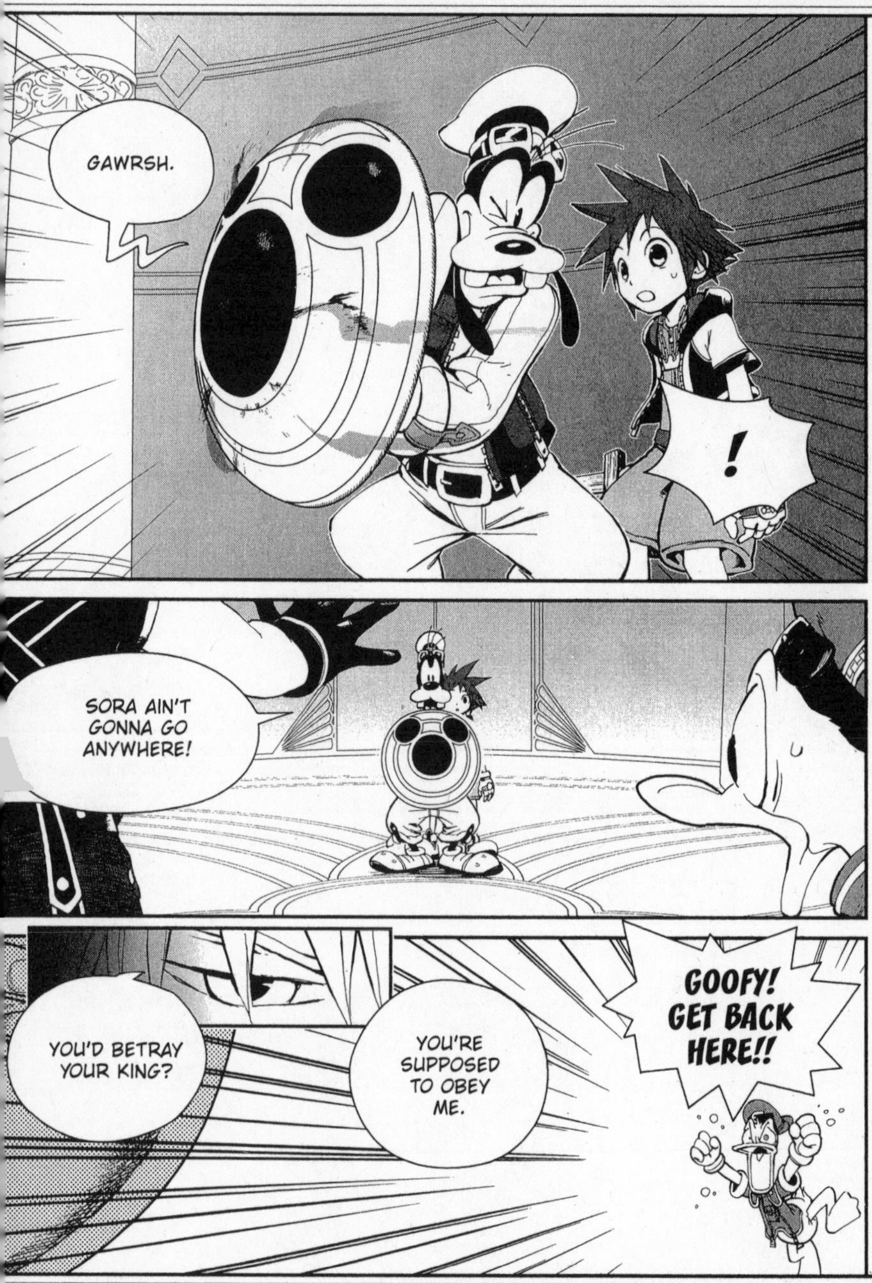
GAWRSH.
!
SORA AIN'T GONNA GO ANYWHERE!
YOU'D BETRAY YOUR KING?
YOU'RE SUPPOSED TO OBEY ME.
GOOFY! GET BACK HERE!!

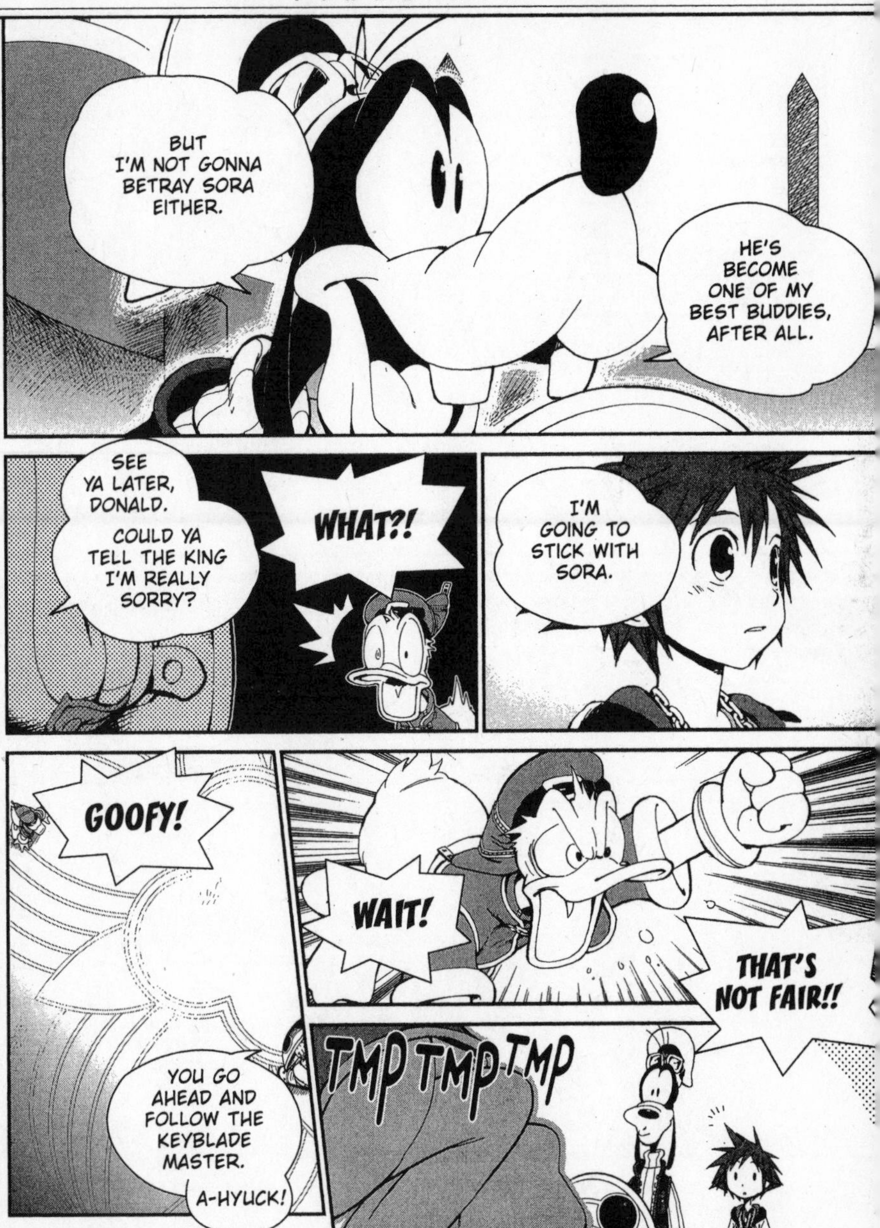
BUT I'M NOT GONNA BETRAY SORA EITHER.
HE'S BECOME ONE OF MY BEST BUDDIES, AFTER ALL.
SEE YA LATER, DONALD.
COULD YA TELL THE KING I'M REALLY SORRY?
WHAT?!
I'M GOING TO STICK WITH SORA.
GOOFY!
WAIT!
THAT'S NOT FAIR!!
TMP TMP TMP
YOU GO AHEAD AND FOLLOW THE KEYBLADE MASTER.
A-HYUCK!

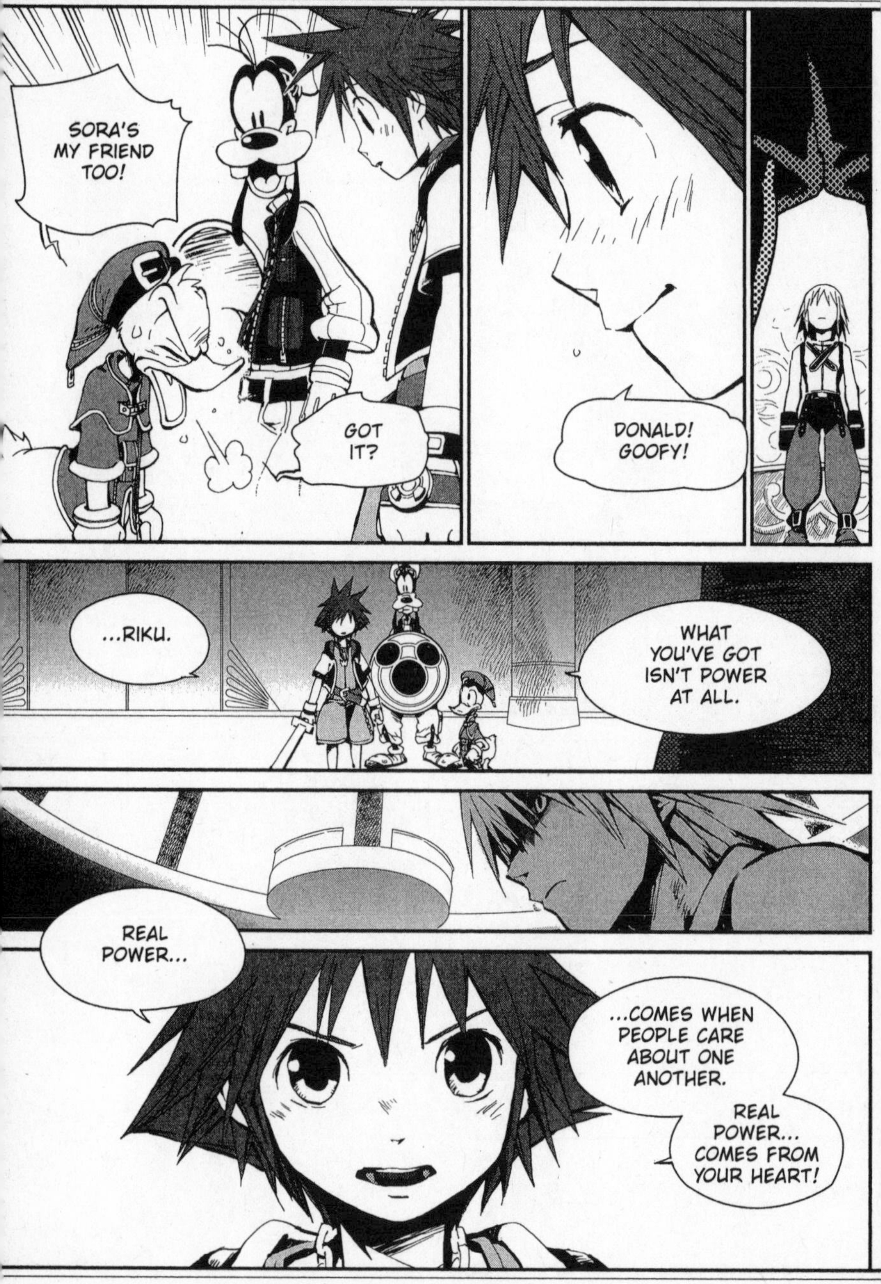
SORA'S MY FRIEND TOO!
GOT IT?
DONALD! GOOFY!
...RIKU.
WHAT YOU'VE GOT ISN'T POWER AT ALL.
REAL POWER...
...COMES WHEN PEOPLE CARE ABOUT ONE ANOTHER.
REAL POWER... COMES FROM YOUR HEART!

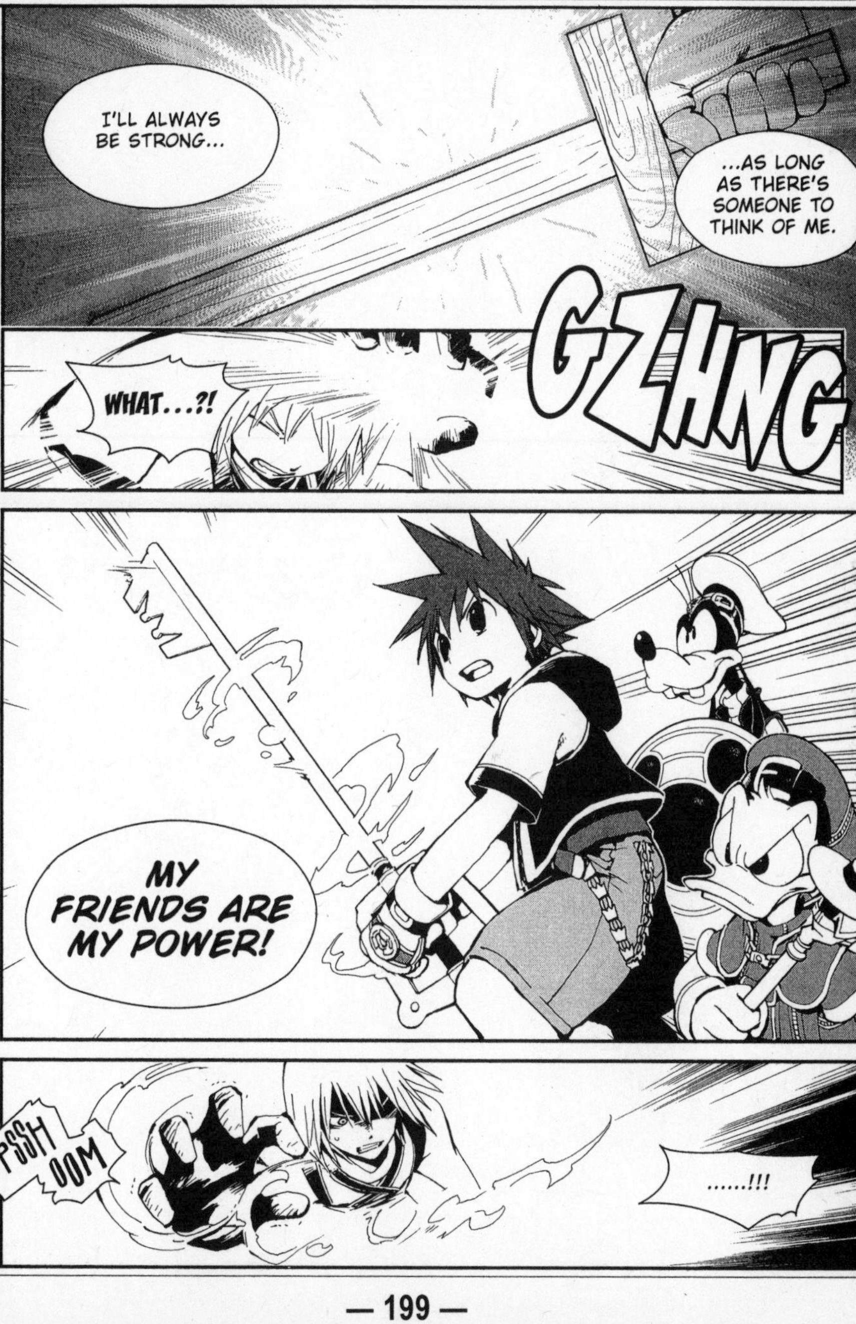
I'LL ALWAYS BE STRONG...
...AS LONG AS THERE'S SOMEONE TO THINK OF ME.
WHAT...?!
GZHNG
MY FRIENDS ARE MY POWER!
PSSH OOM
......!!!

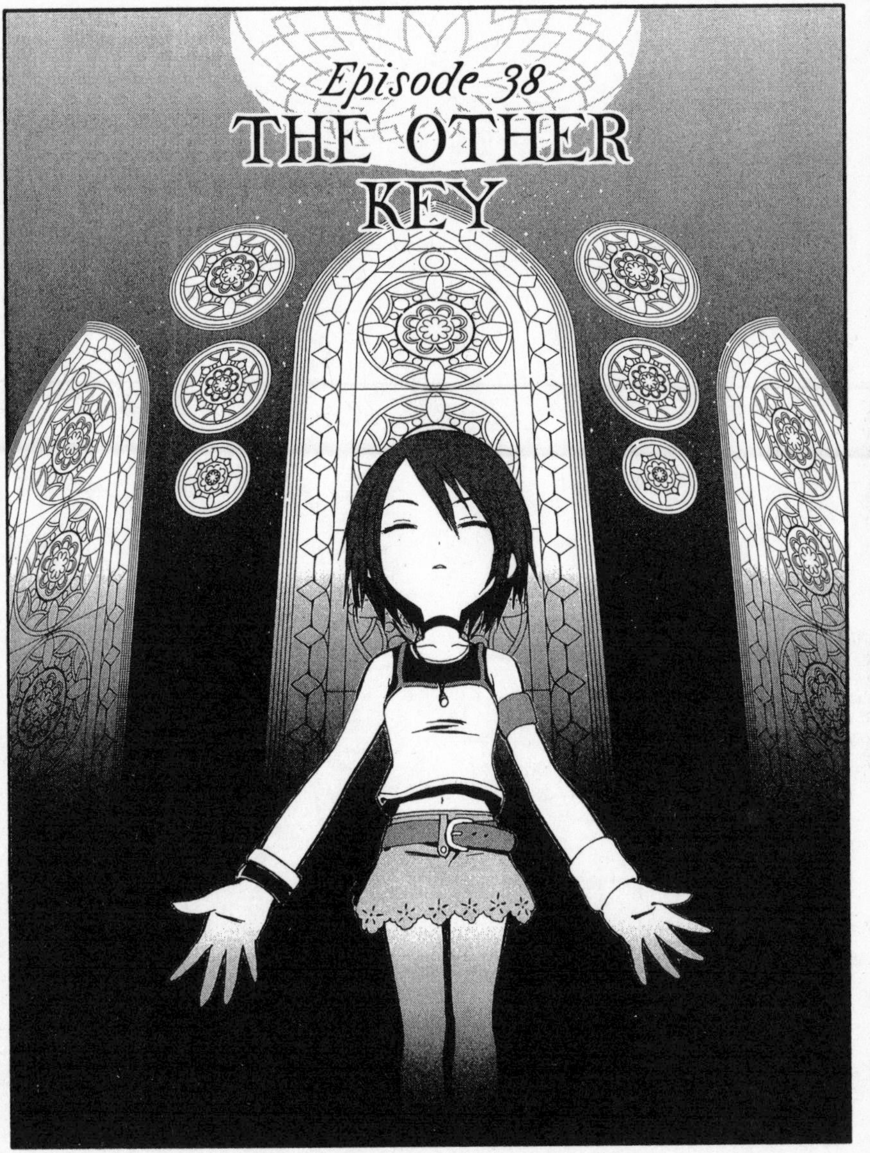
Episode 38
THE OTHER KEY

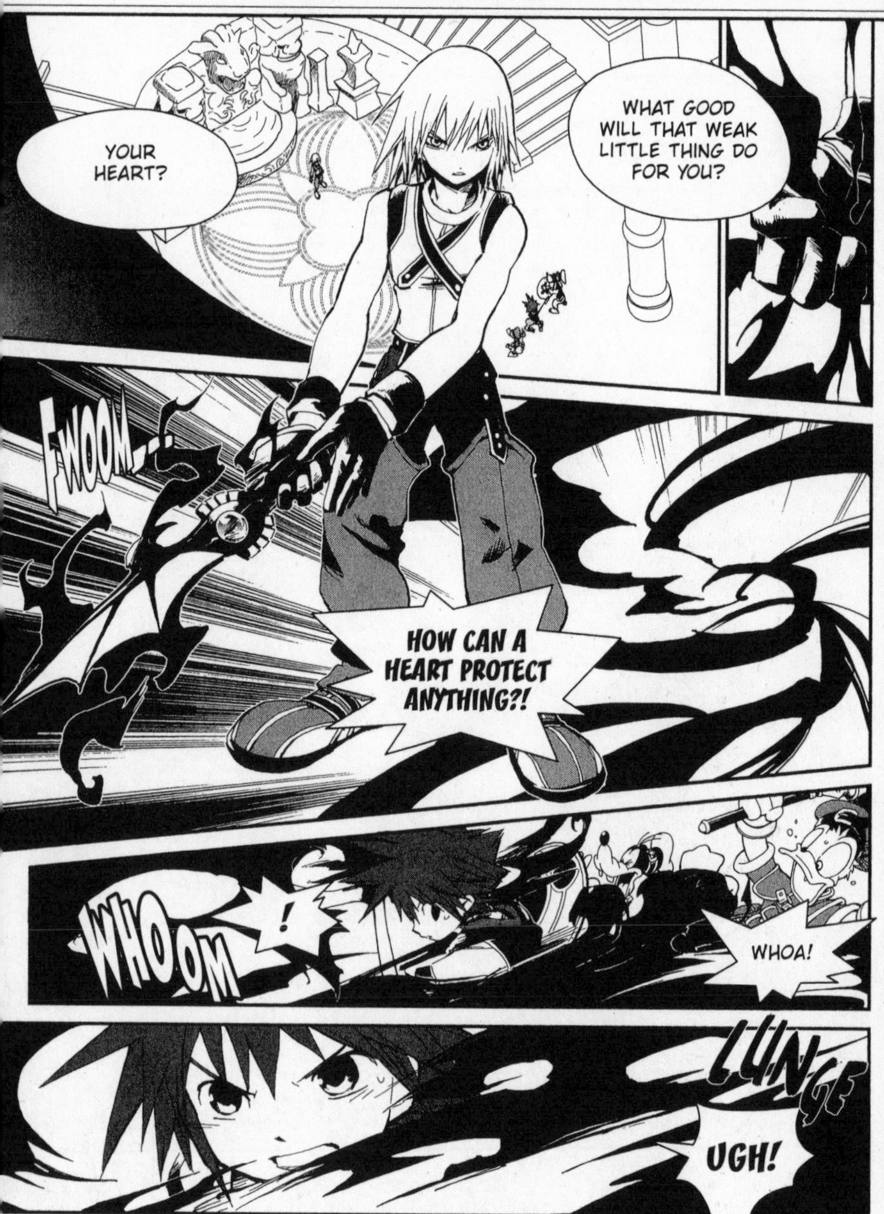
YOUR HEART?
WHAT GOOD WILL THAT WEAK LITTLE THING DO FOR YOU?
FWOOM...
HOW CAN A HEART PROTECT ANYTHING?!
WHOOM
!
WHOA!
LUNGE
UGH!

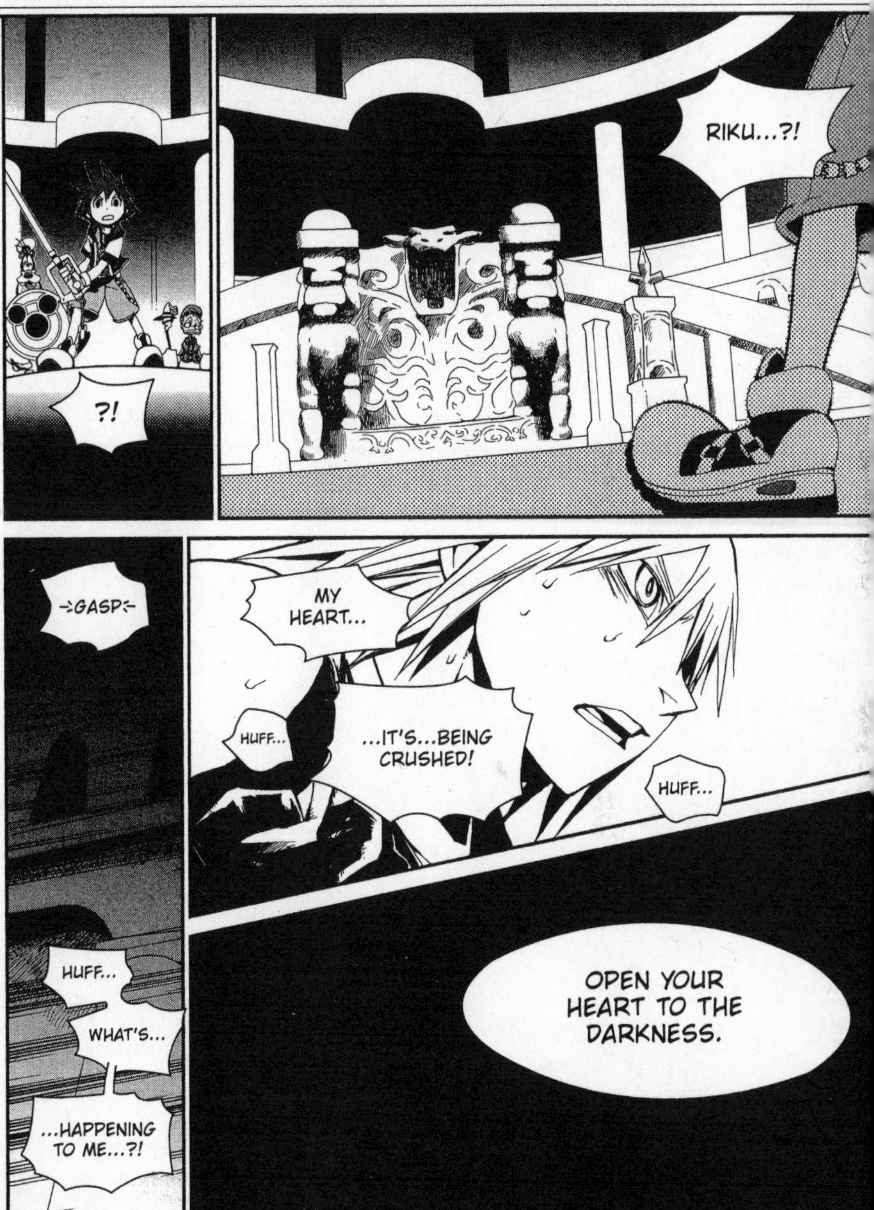
?!
RIKU...?!
-GASP-
HUFF...
WHAT'S...
...HAPPENING TO ME...?!
MY HEART...
HUFF...
...IT'S...BEING CRUSHED!
HUFF...
OPEN YOUR HEART TO THE DARKNESS.

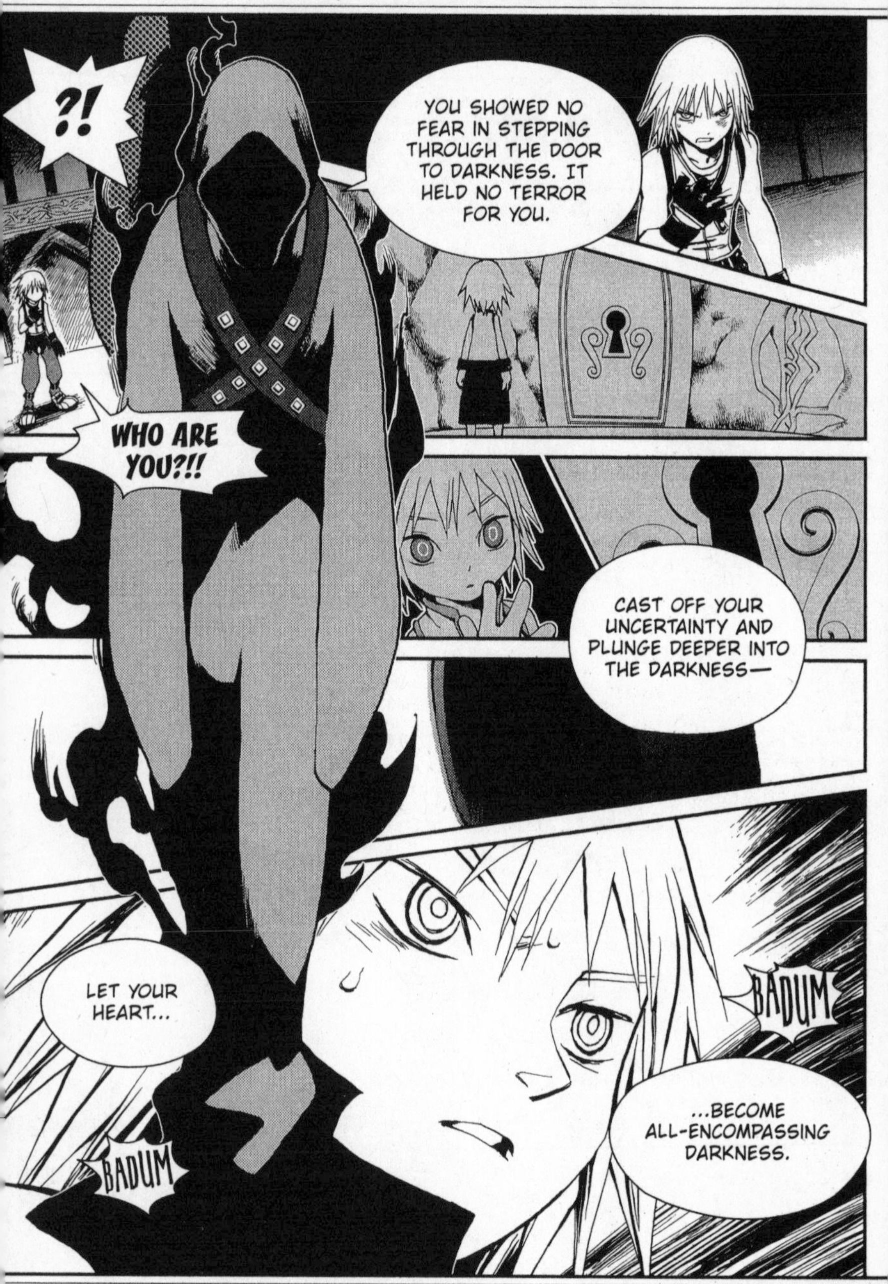
?!
WHO ARE YOU?!!
YOU SHOWED NO FEAR IN STEPPING THROUGH THE DOOR TO DARKNESS. IT HELD NO TERROR FOR YOU.
CAST OFF YOUR UNCERTAINTY AND PLUNGE DEEPER INTO THE DARKNESS—
LET YOUR HEART...
BADUM
BADUM
...BECOME ALL-ENCOMPASSING DARKNESS.

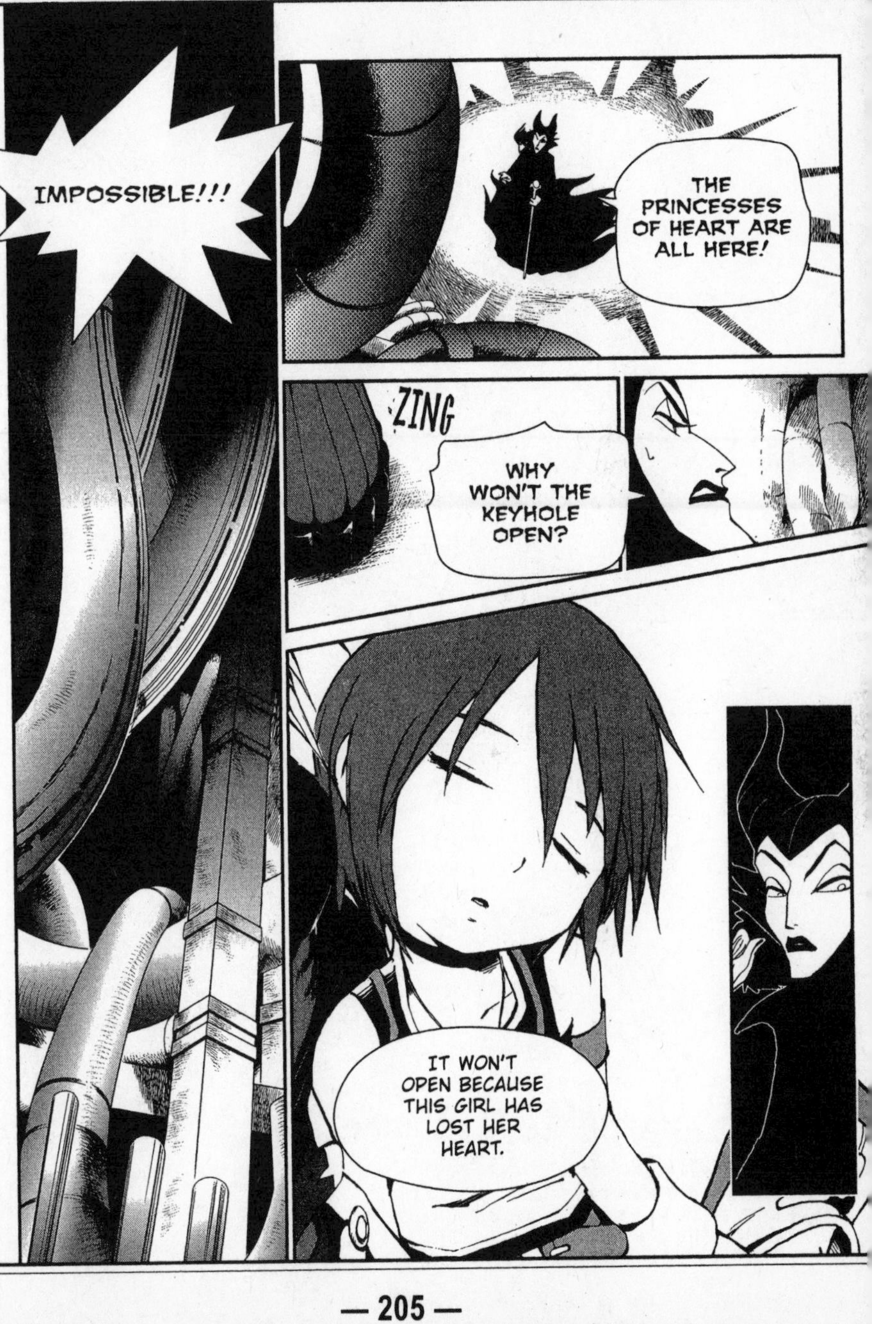
IMPOSSIBLE!!!
THE PRINCESSES OF HEART ARE ALL HERE!
ZING
WHY WON'T THE KEYHOLE OPEN?
IT WON'T OPEN BECAUSE THIS GIRL HAS LOST HER HEART.

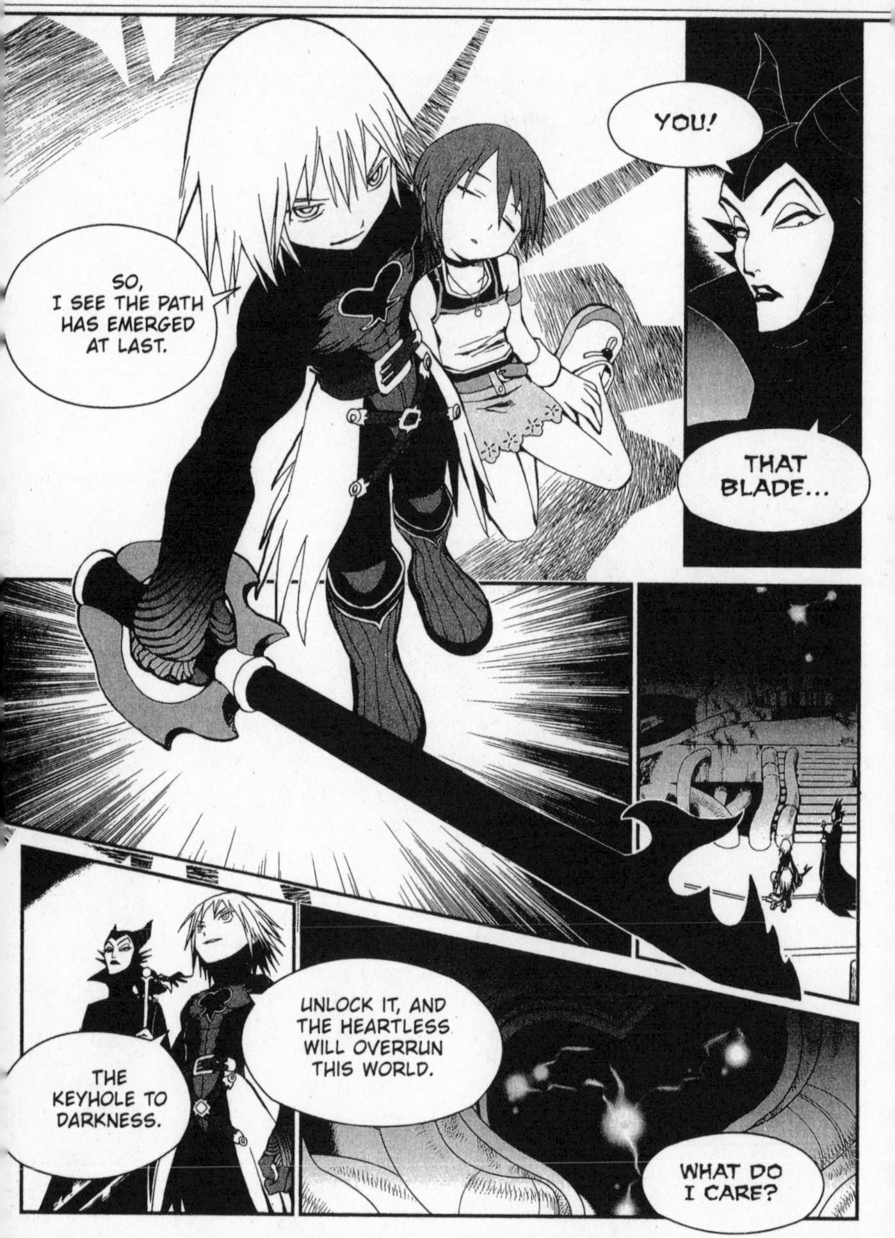
SO, I SEE THE PATH HAS EMERGED AT LAST.
YOU!
THAT BLADE...
THE KEYHOLE TO DARKNESS.
UNLOCK IT, AND THE HEARTLESS WILL OVERRUN THIS WORLD.
WHAT DO I CARE?

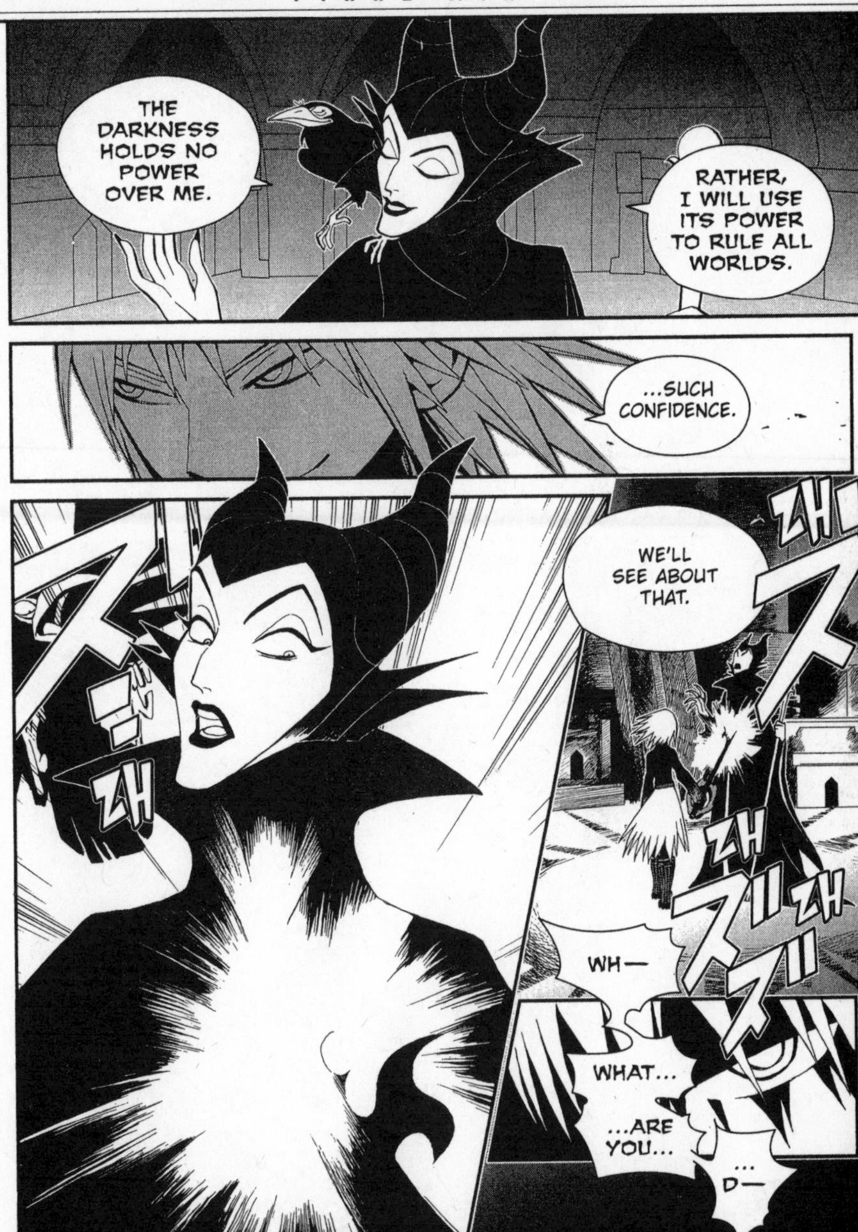
THE DARKNESS HOLDS NO POWER OVER ME.
RATHER, I WILL USE ITS POWER TO RULE ALL WORLDS.
...SUCH CONFIDENCE.
WE'LL SEE ABOUT THAT.
ZH
ZH
ZH
ZH
WH—
WHAT...
...ARE YOU...
...D—

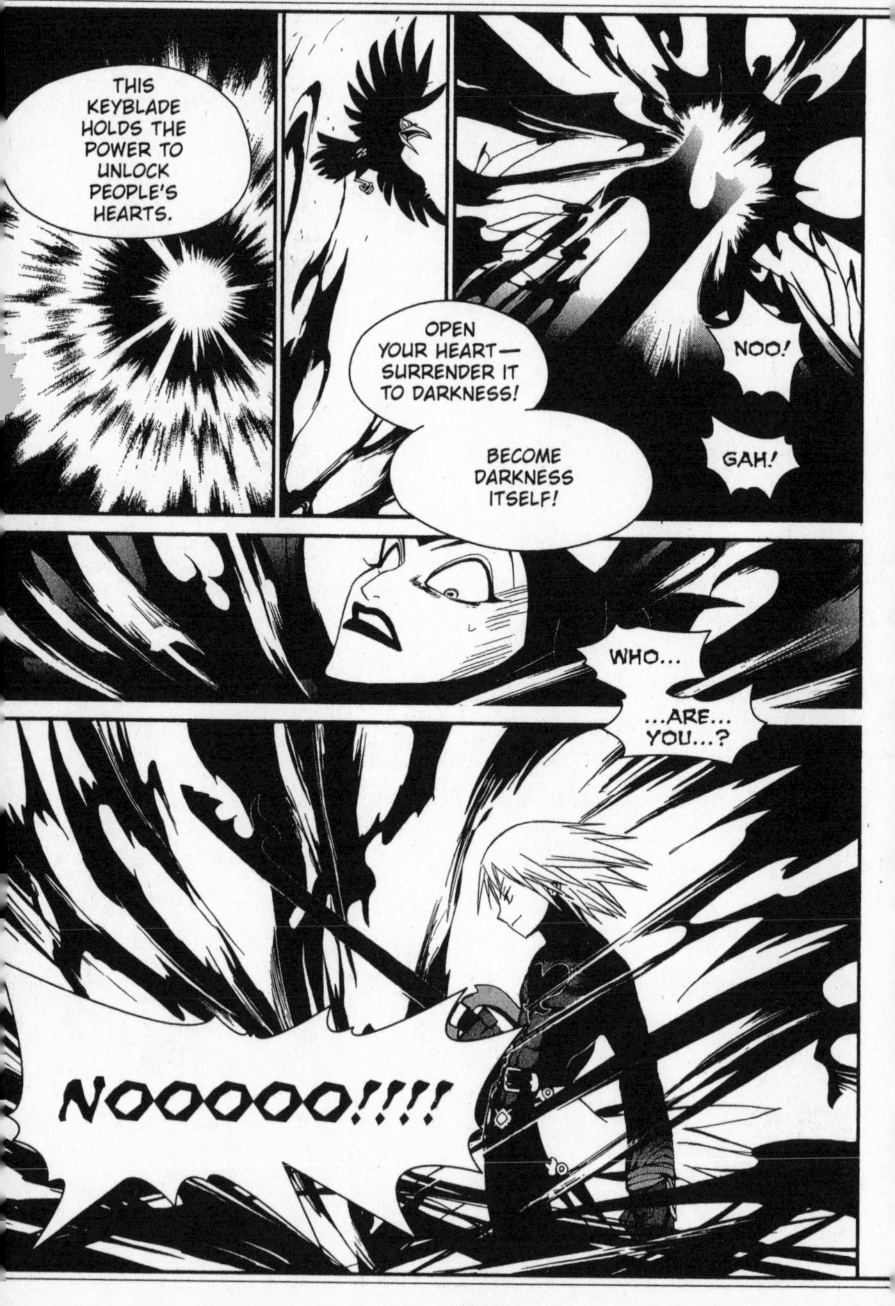
THIS KEYBLADE HOLDS THE POWER TO UNLOCK PEOPLE'S HEARTS.
OPEN YOUR HEART— SURRENDER IT TO DARKNESS!
BECOME DARKNESS ITSELF!
NOO!
GAH!
WHO...
...ARE... YOU...?
NOOOOO!!!!

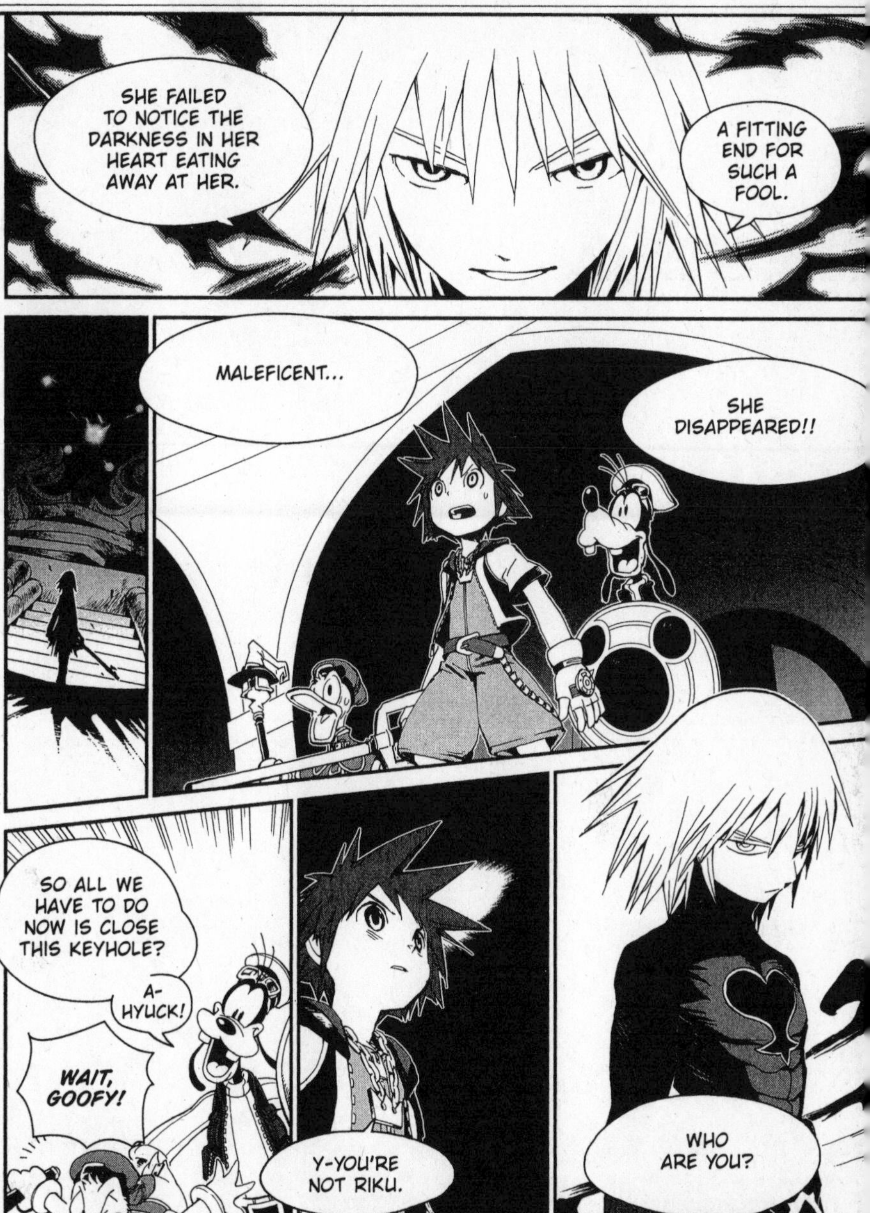
SHE FAILED TO NOTICE THE DARKNESS IN HER HEART EATING AWAY AT HER.
A FITTING END FOR SUCH A FOOL.
MALEFICENT...
SHE DISAPPEARED!!
SO ALL WE HAVE TO DO NOW IS CLOSE THIS KEYHOLE?
A-HYUCK!
WAIT, GOOFY!
Y-YOU'RE NOT RIKU.
WHO ARE YOU?

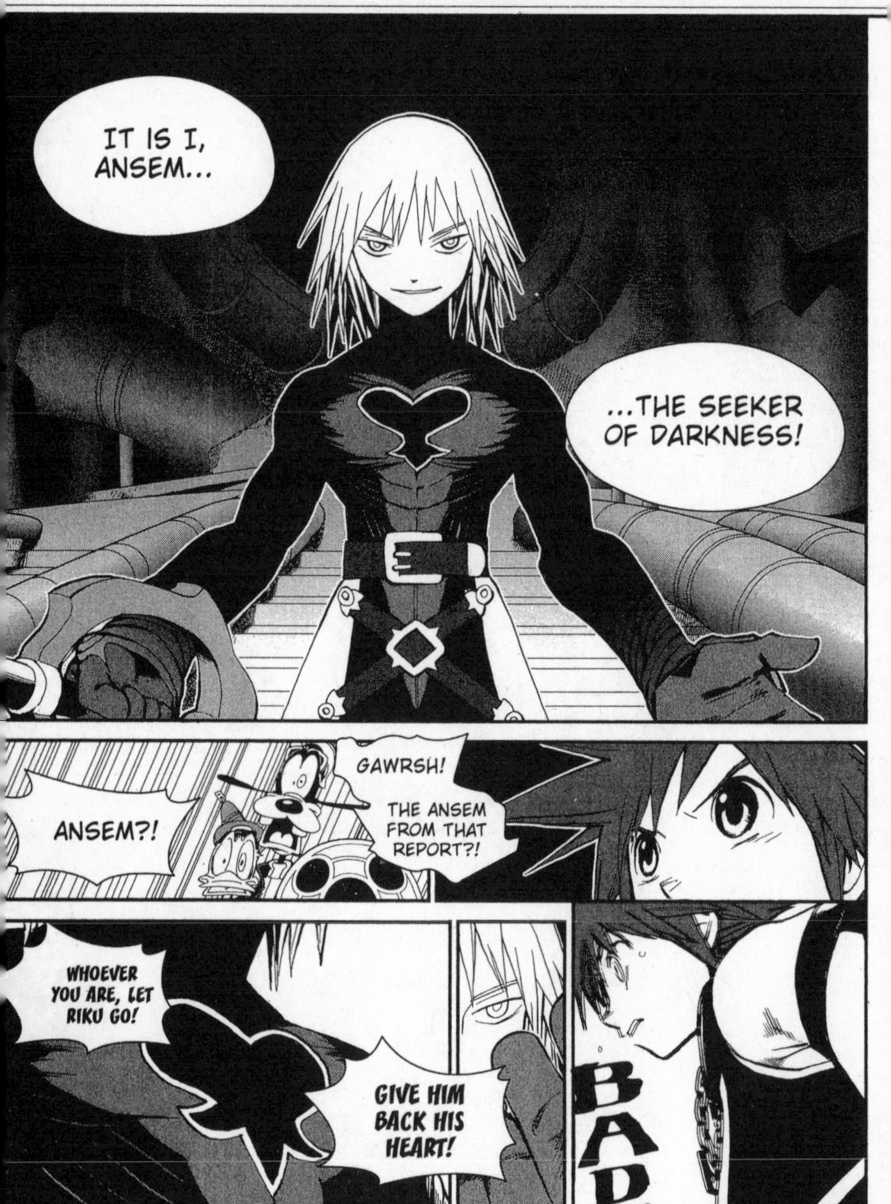
IT IS I, ANSEM...
...THE SEEKER OF DARKNESS!
ANSEM?!
GAWRSH!
THE ANSEM FROM THAT REPORT?!
WHOEVER YOU ARE, LET RIKU GO!
GIVE HIM BACK HIS HEART!
BADUM

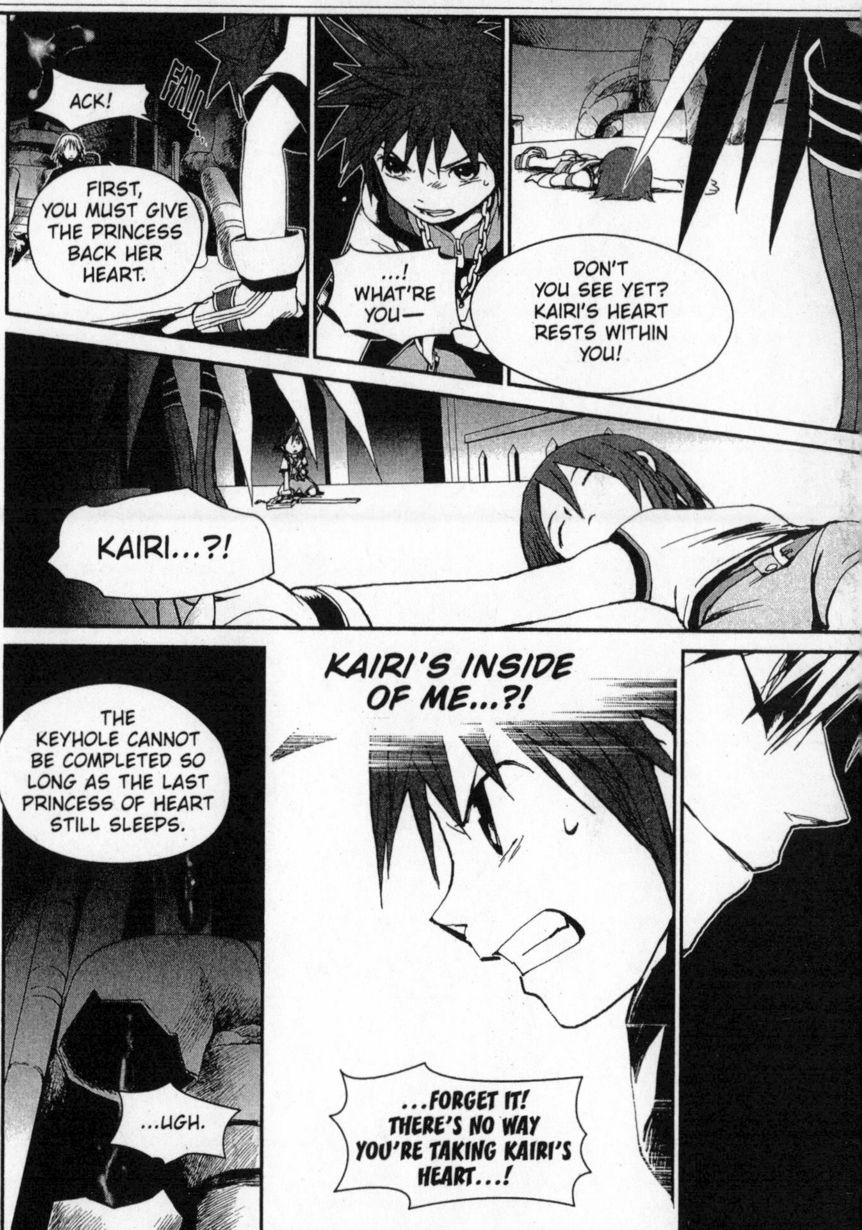
ACK!
FALL...
FIRST, YOU MUST GIVE THE PRINCESS BACK HER HEART.
...! WHAT'RE YOU—
DON'T YOU SEE YET? KAIRI'S HEART RESTS WITHIN YOU!
KAIRI...?!
THE KEYHOLE CANNOT BE COMPLETED SO LONG AS THE LAST PRINCESS OF HEART STILL SLEEPS.
...UGH.
KAIRI'S INSIDE OF ME...?!
...FORGET IT! THERE'S NO WAY YOU'RE TAKING KAIRI'S HEART...!

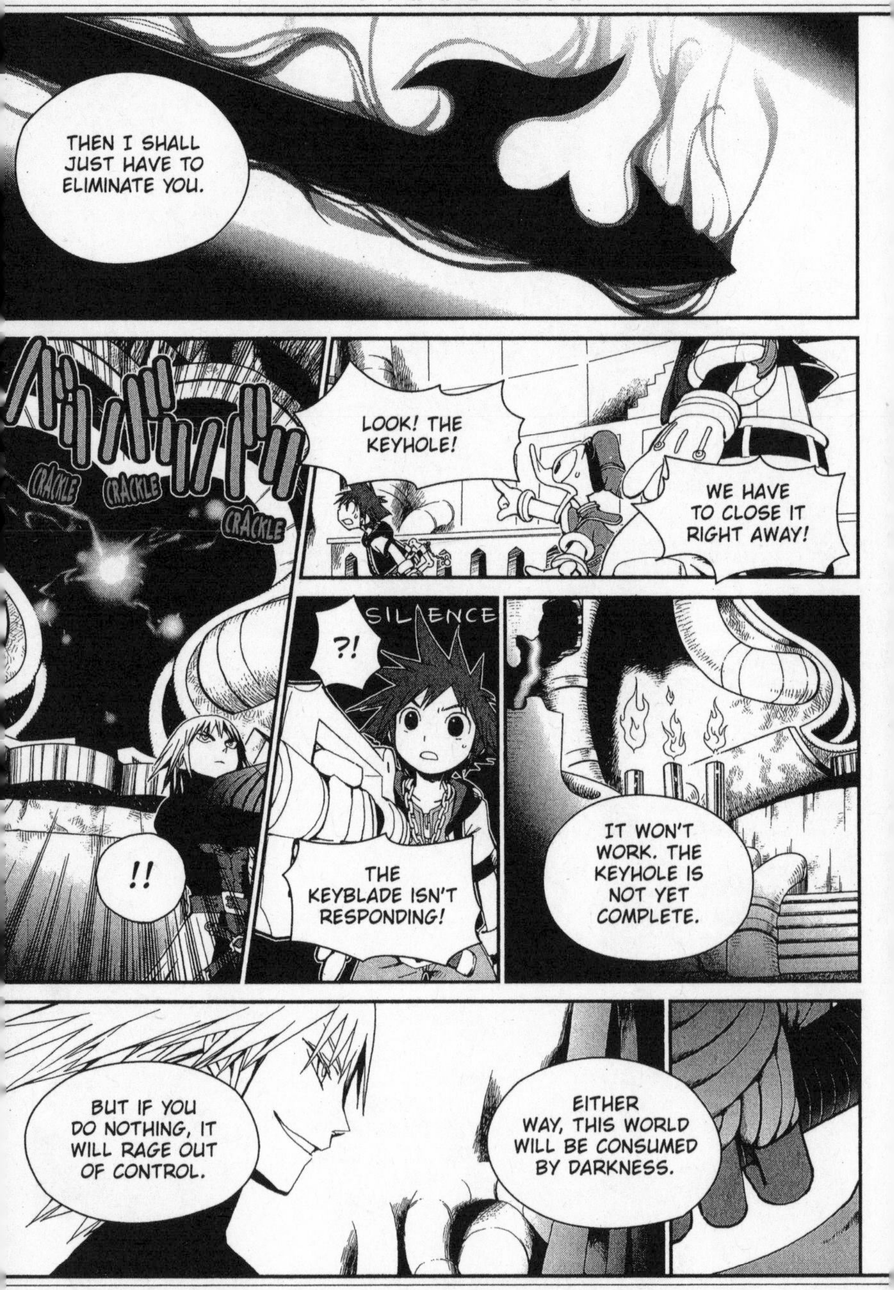
THEN I SHALL JUST HAVE TO ELIMINATE YOU.
CRACKLE
CRACKLE
CRACKLE
!!
LOOK! THE KEYHOLE!
WE HAVE TO CLOSE IT RIGHT AWAY!
SILENCE
?!
THE KEYBLADE ISN'T RESPONDING!
IT WON'T WORK. THE KEYHOLE IS NOT YET COMPLETE.
BUT IF YOU DO NOTHING, IT WILL RAGE OUT OF CONTROL.
EITHER WAY, THIS WORLD WILL BE CONSUMED BY DARKNESS.

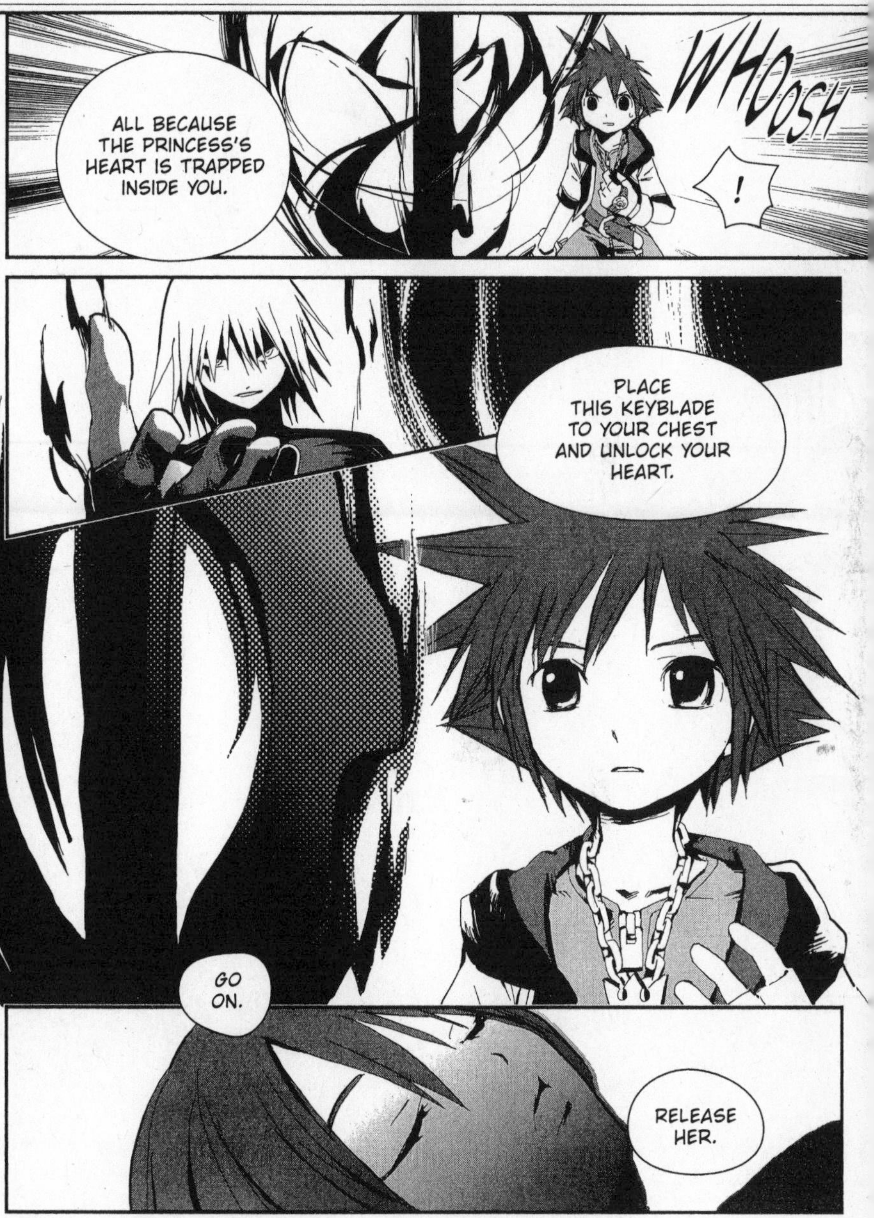
ALL BECAUSE THE PRINCESS'S HEART IS TRAPPED INSIDE YOU.
WHOOSH
!
PLACE THIS KEYBLADE TO YOUR CHEST AND UNLOCK YOUR HEART.
GO ON.
RELEASE HER.

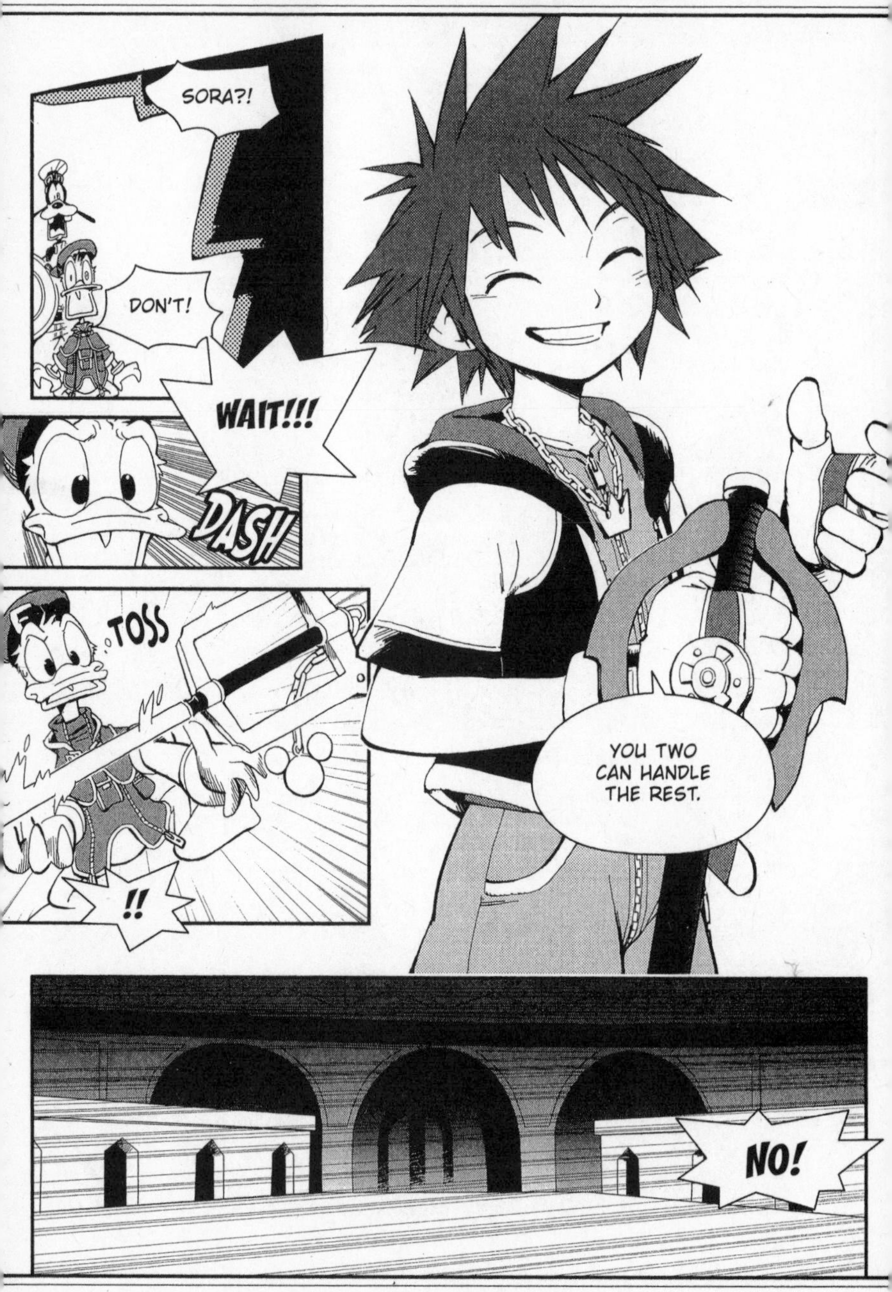
SORA?!
DON'T!
WAIT!!!
DASH
TOSS
!!
YOU TWO CAN HANDLE THE REST.
NO!

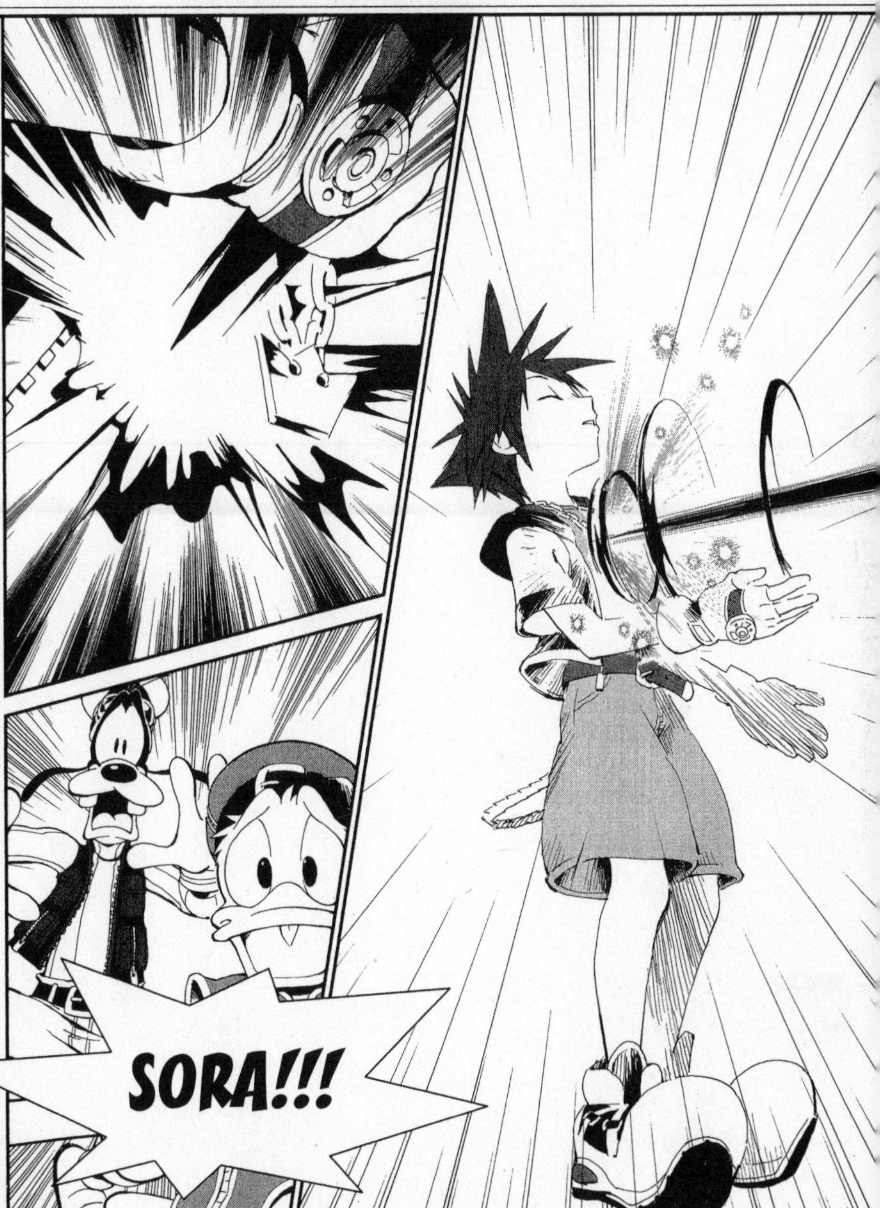
SORA!!!

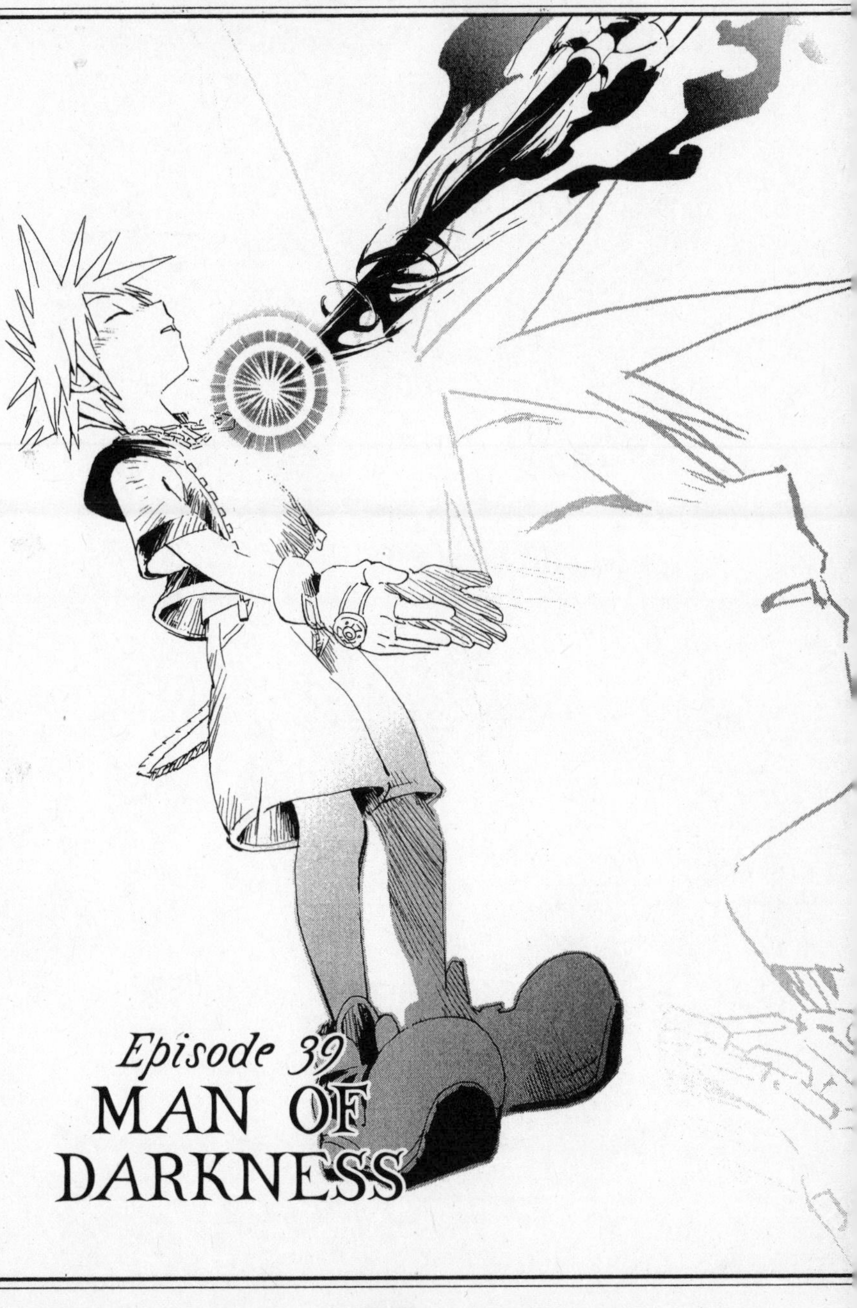

Episode 39
MAN OF DARKNESS

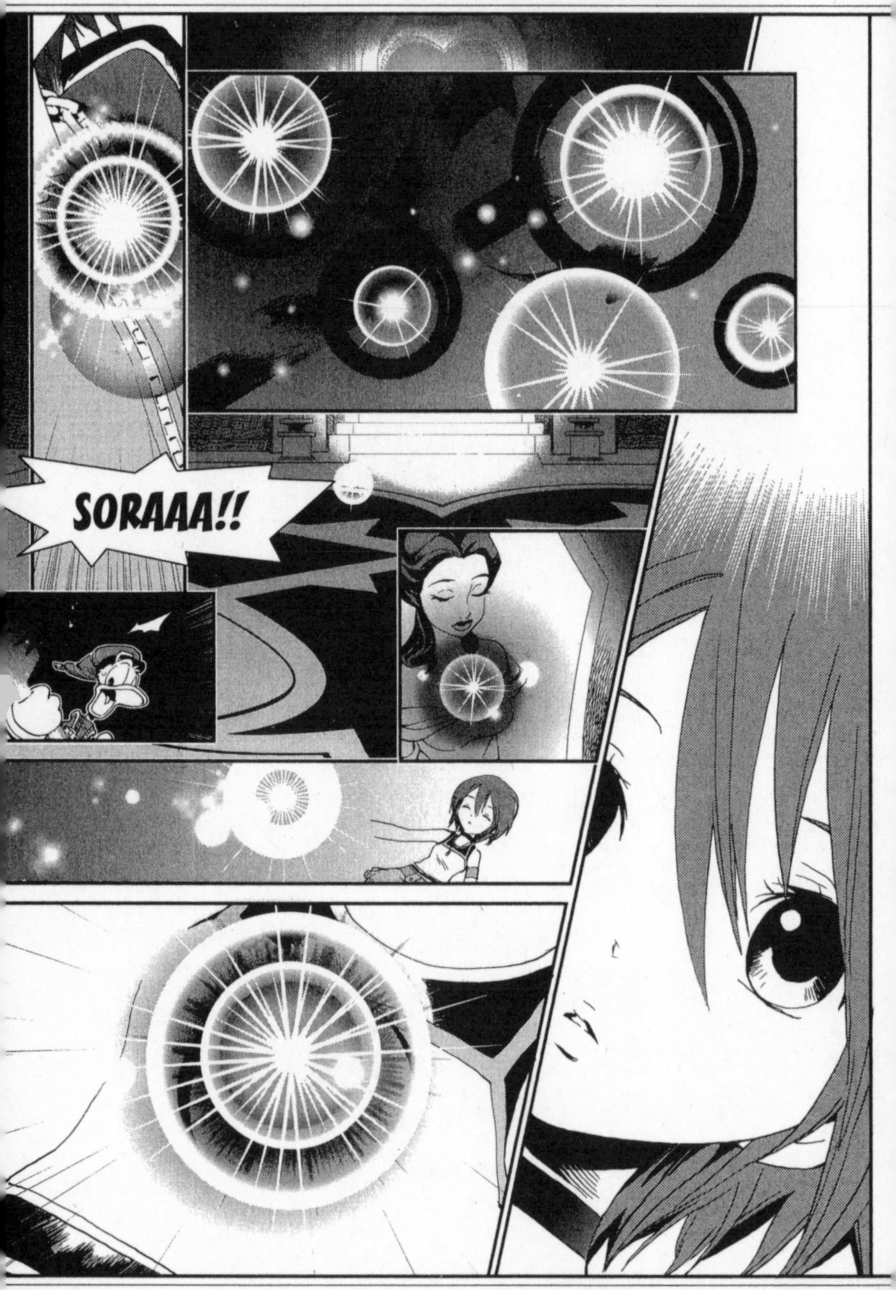
SORAAA!!

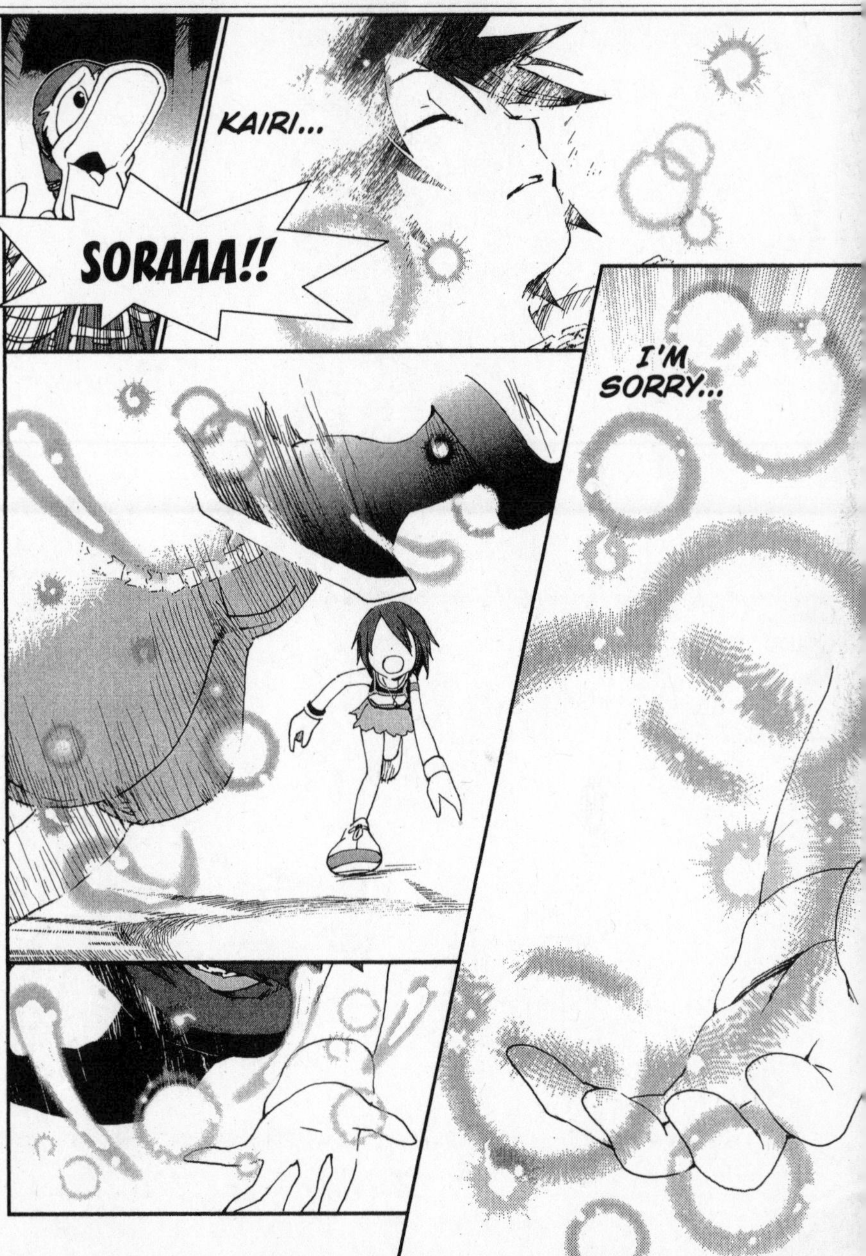
KAIRI...
SORAAA!!
I'M SORRY...

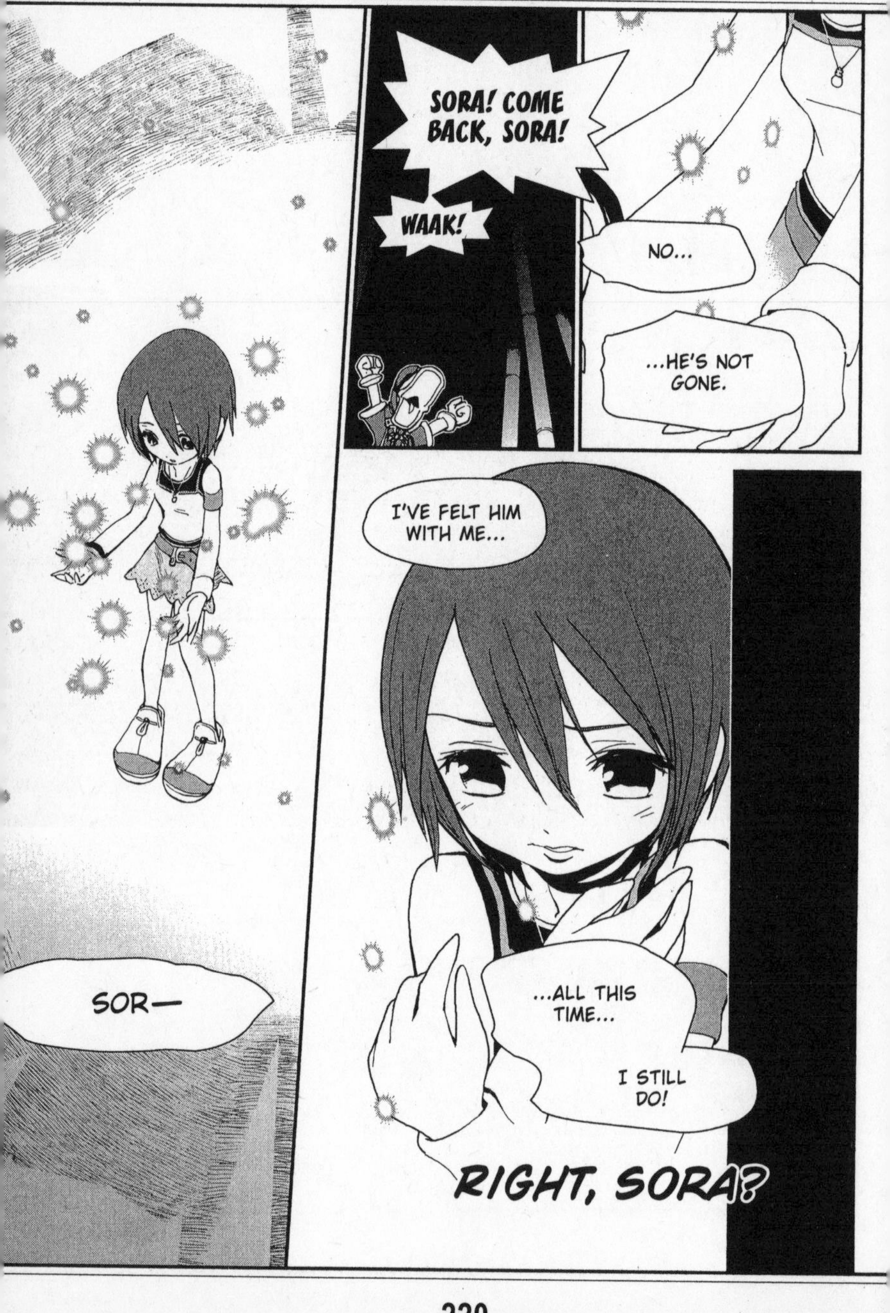
SOR—
SORA! COME BACK, SORA!
WAAK!
NO...
...HE'S NOT GONE.
I'VE FELT HIM WITH ME...
...ALL THIS TIME...
I STILL DO!
RIGHT, SORA?

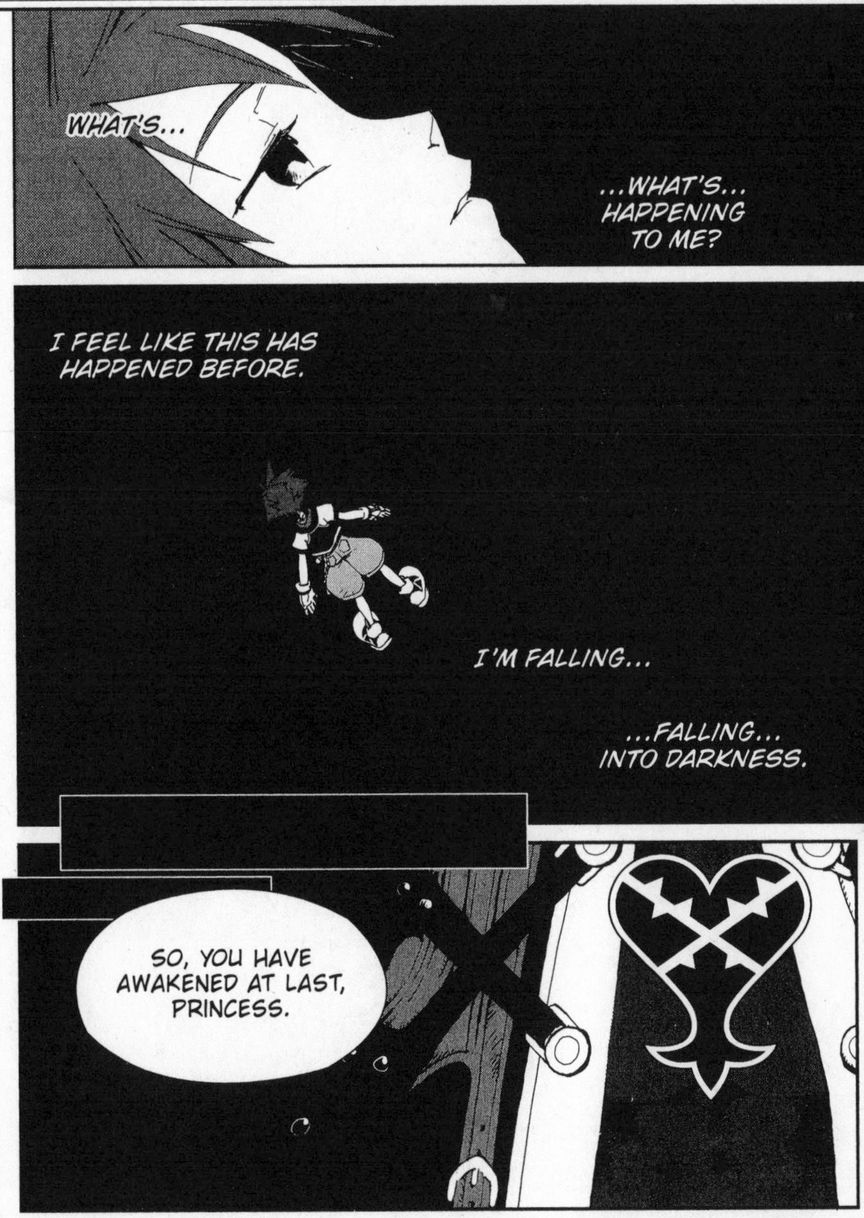
WHAT'S...
...WHAT'S... HAPPENING TO ME?
I FEEL LIKE THIS HAS HAPPENED BEFORE.
I'M FALLING...
...FALLING... INTO DARKNESS.
SO, YOU HAVE AWAKENED AT LAST, PRINCESS.

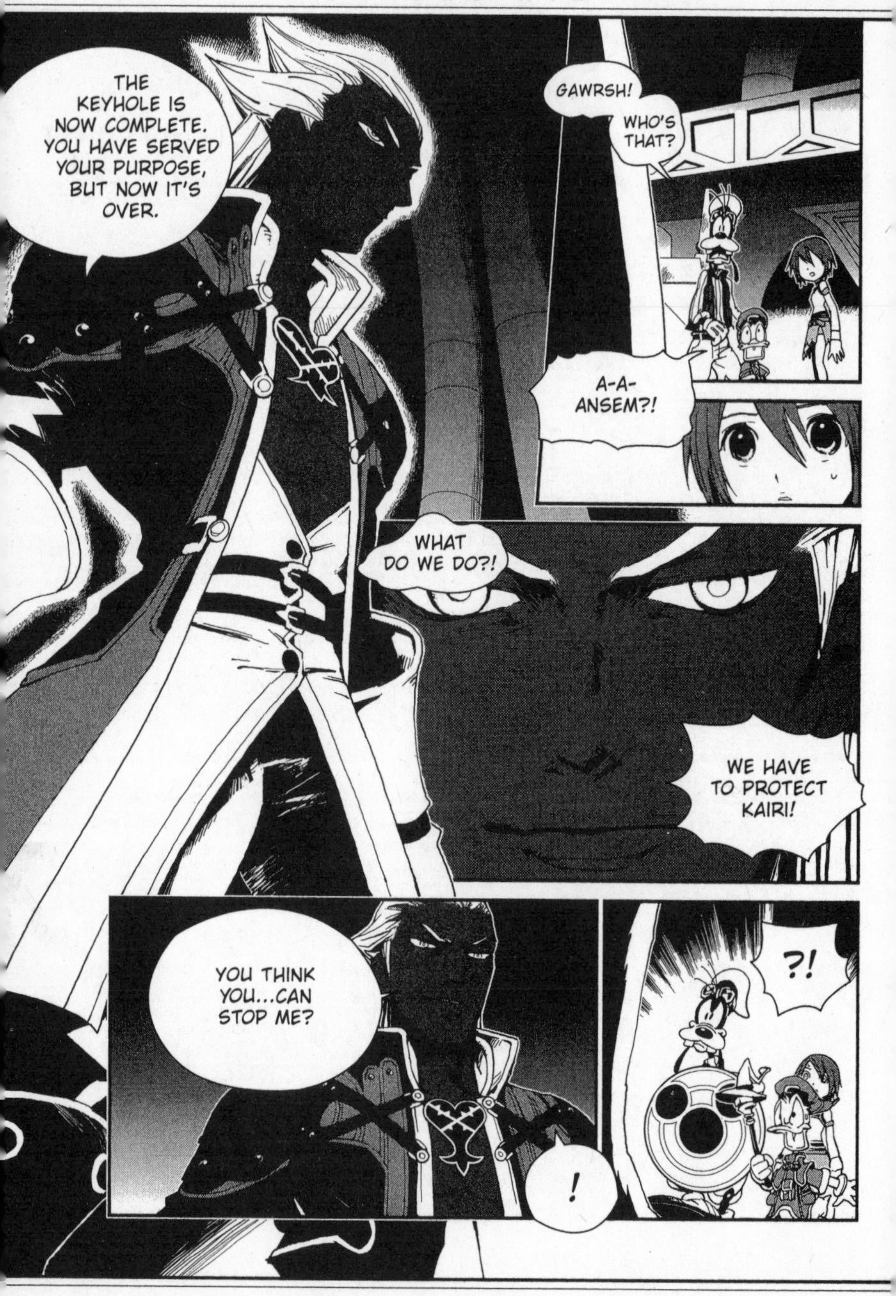
THE KEYHOLE IS NOW COMPLETE. YOU HAVE SERVED YOUR PURPOSE, BUT NOW IT'S OVER.
GAWRSH!
WHO'S THAT?
A-A-ANSEM?!
WHAT DO WE DO?!
WE HAVE TO PROTECT KAIRI!
YOU THINK YOU...CAN STOP ME?
!
?!

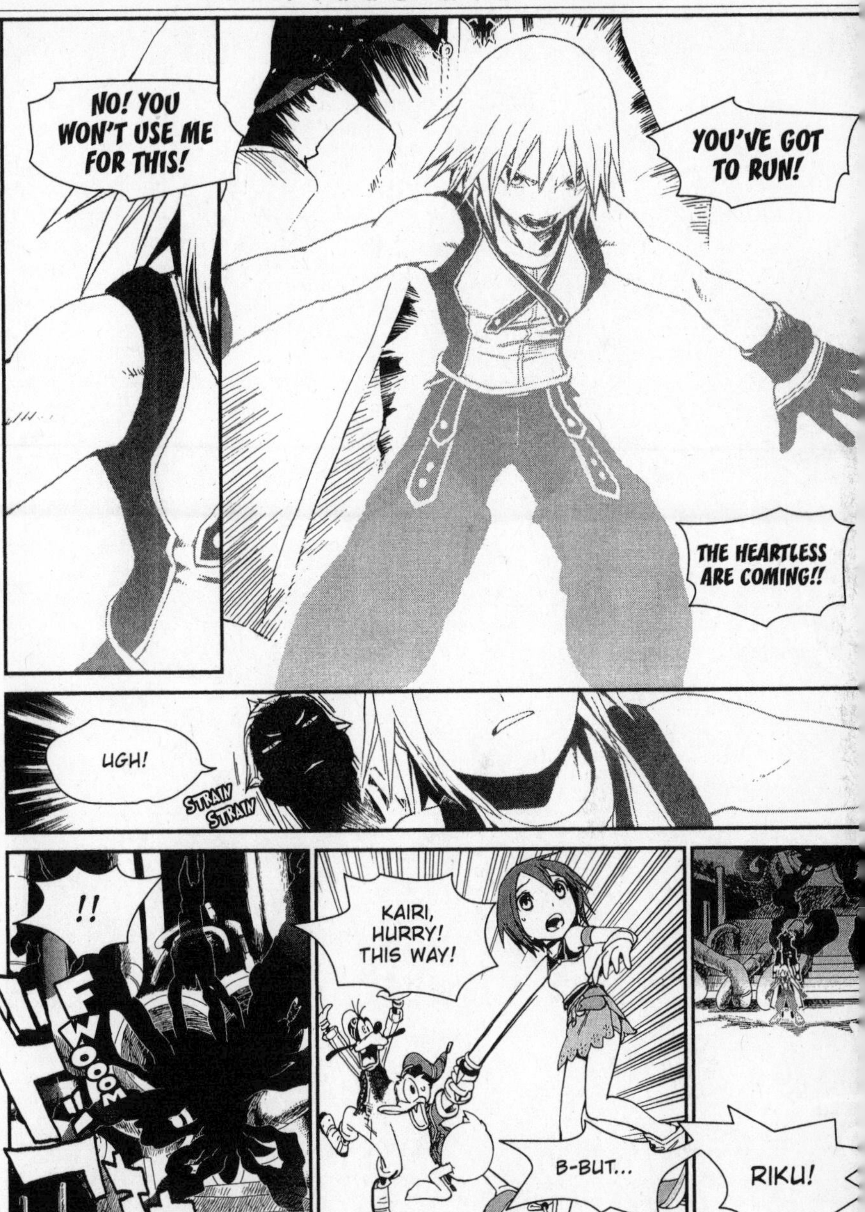
NO! YOU WON'T USE ME FOR THIS!
YOU'VE GOT TO RUN!
THE HEARTLESS ARE COMING!!
UGH!
STRAIN STRAIN
!!
FWOOOM
KAIRI, HURRY! THIS WAY!
B-BUT...
RIKU!

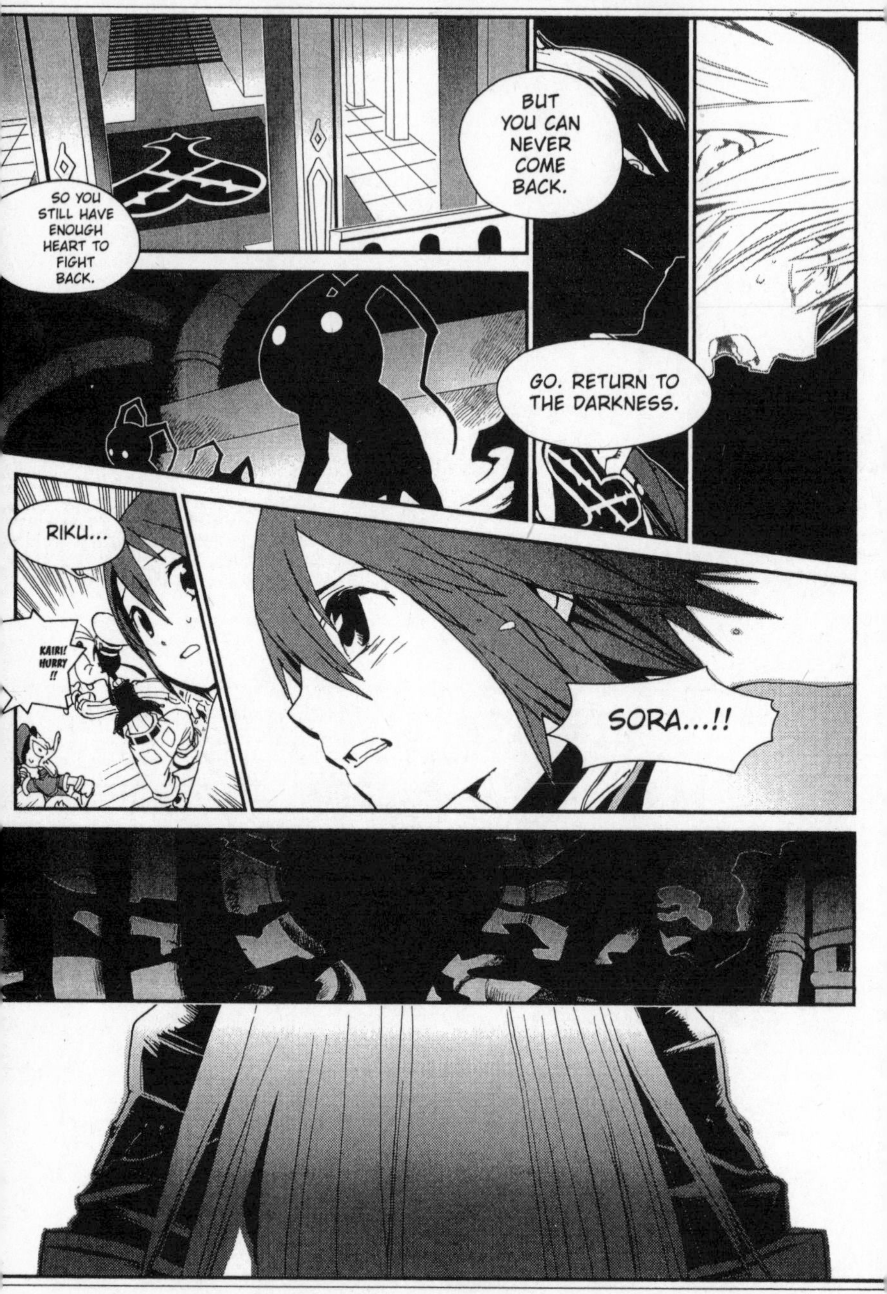
SO YOU STILL HAVE ENOUGH HEART TO FIGHT BACK.
BUT YOU CAN NEVER COME BACK.
GO. RETURN TO THE DARKNESS.
RIKU...
KAIRI! HURRY !!
SORA...!!

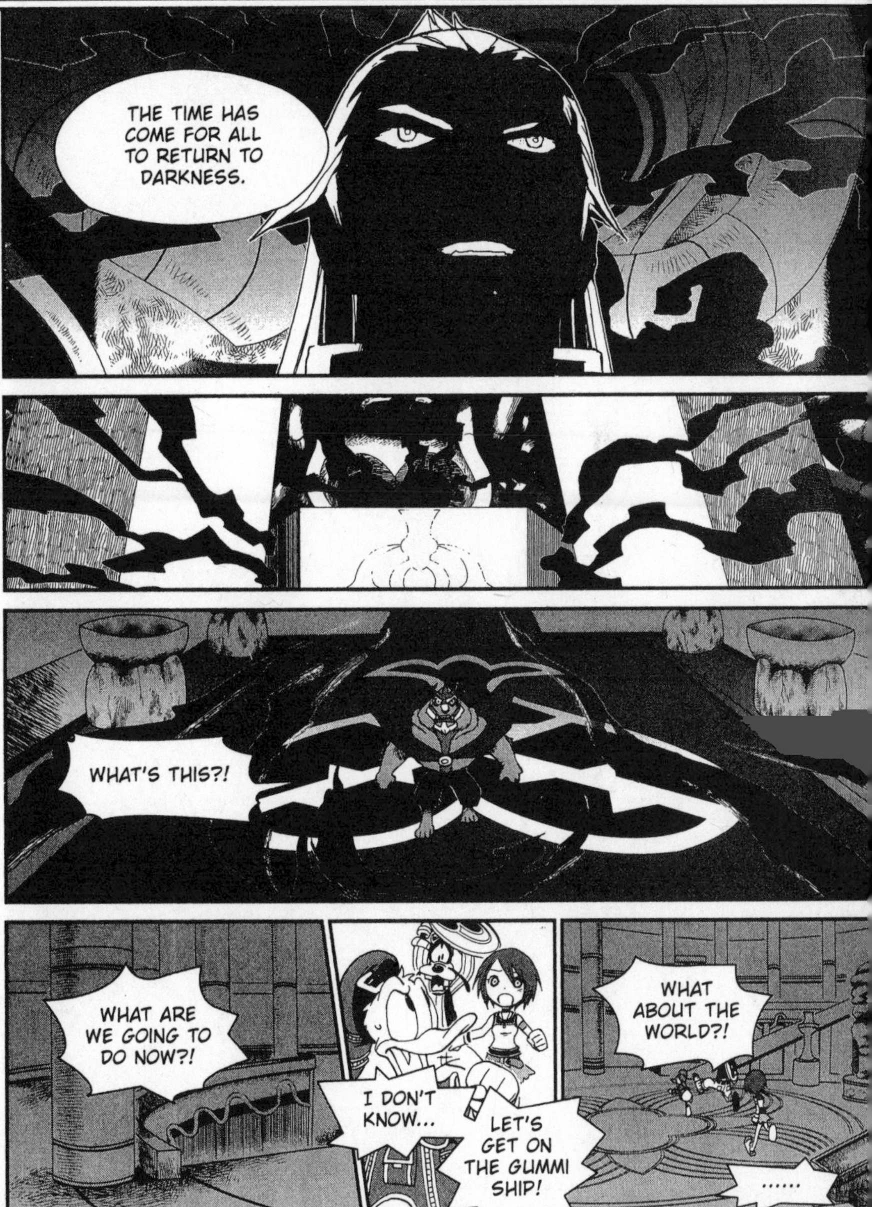
THE TIME HAS COME FOR ALL TO RETURN TO DARKNESS.
WHAT'S THIS?!
WHAT ARE WE GOING TO DO NOW?!
I DON'T KNOW...
LET'S GET ON THE GUMMI SHIP!
WHAT ABOUT THE WORLD?!
......

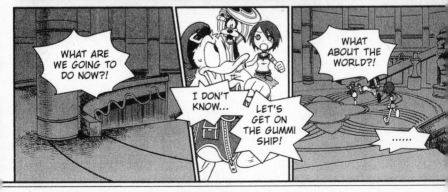

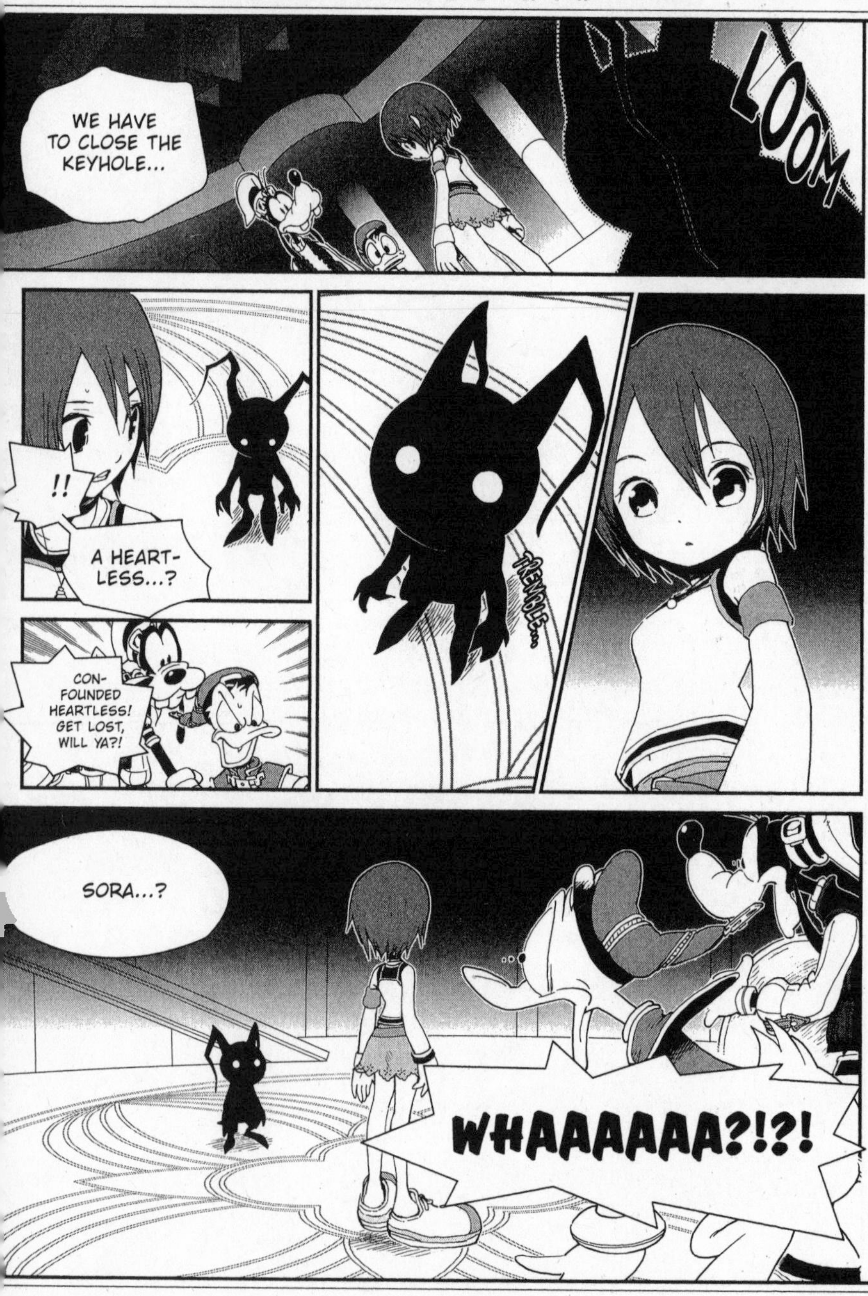
WE HAVE TO CLOSE THE KEYHOLE...
LOOM
!!
A HEART-LESS...?
CON-FOUNDED HEARTLESS! GET LOST, WILL YA?!
TREMBLE...
SORA...?
WHAAAAAA?!?!

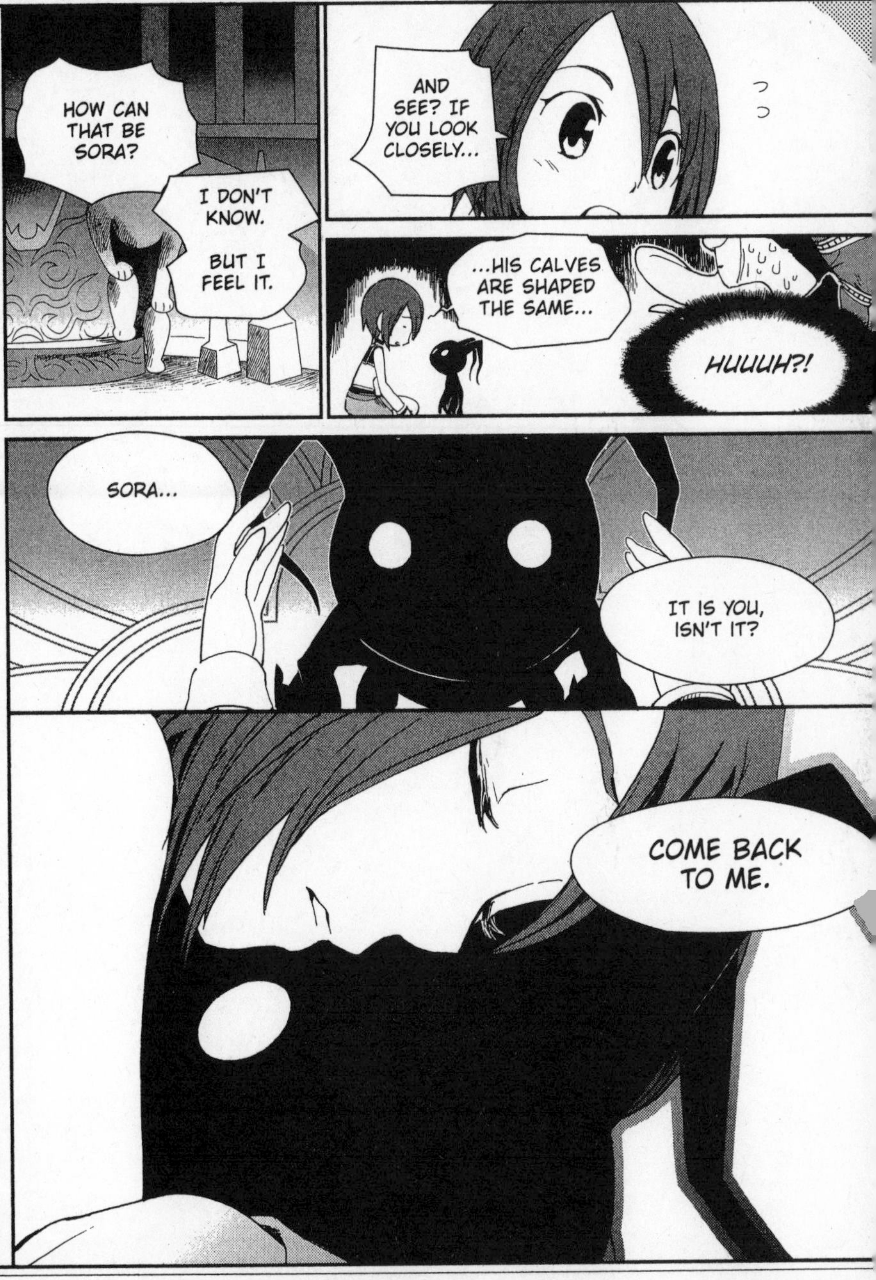
HOW CAN THAT BE SORA?
I DON'T KNOW.
BUT I FEEL IT.
AND SEE? IF YOU LOOK CLOSELY...
...HIS CALVES ARE SHAPED THE SAME...
HUUUH?!
SORA...
IT IS YOU, ISN'T IT?
COME BACK TO ME.

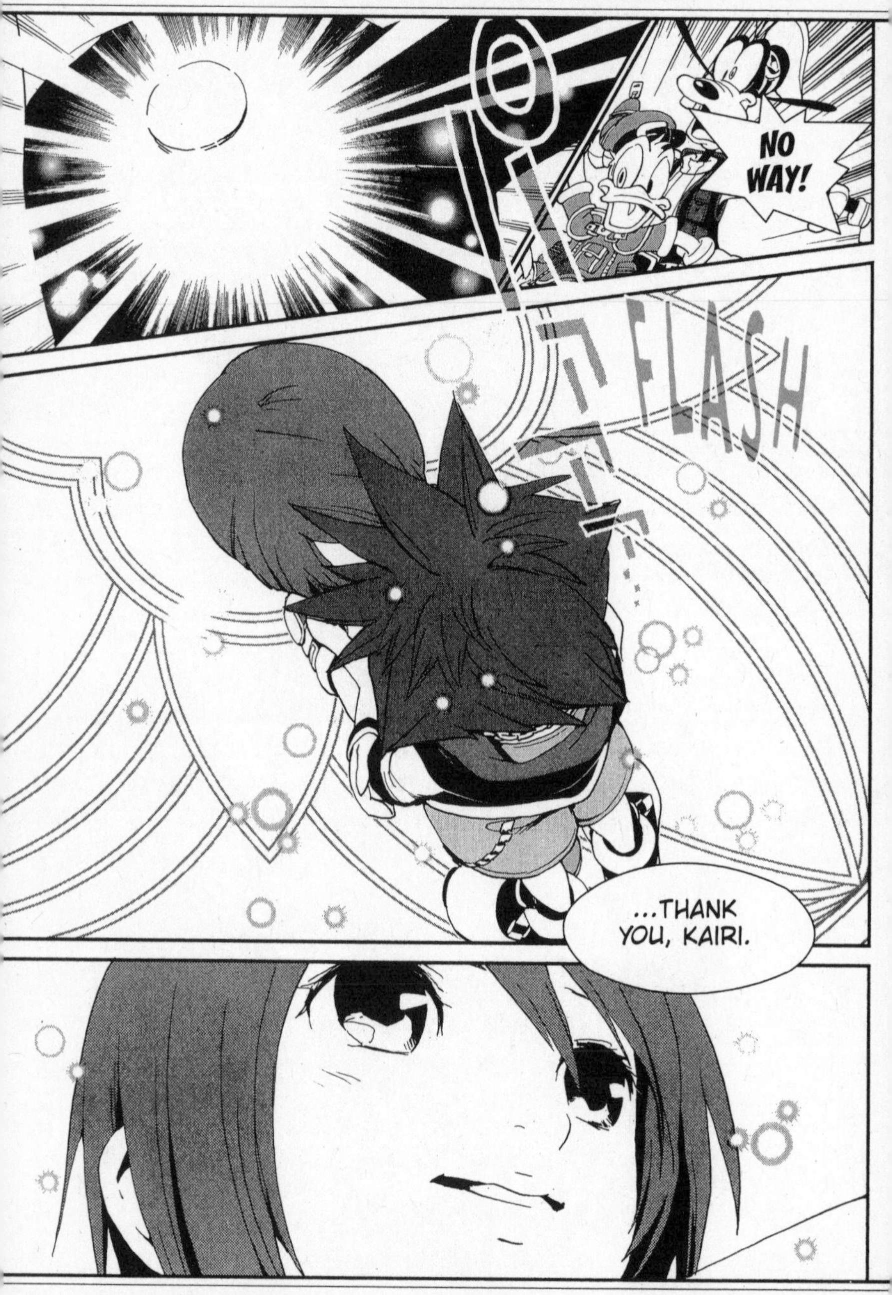
NO WAY!
FLASH
...THANK YOU, KAIRI.

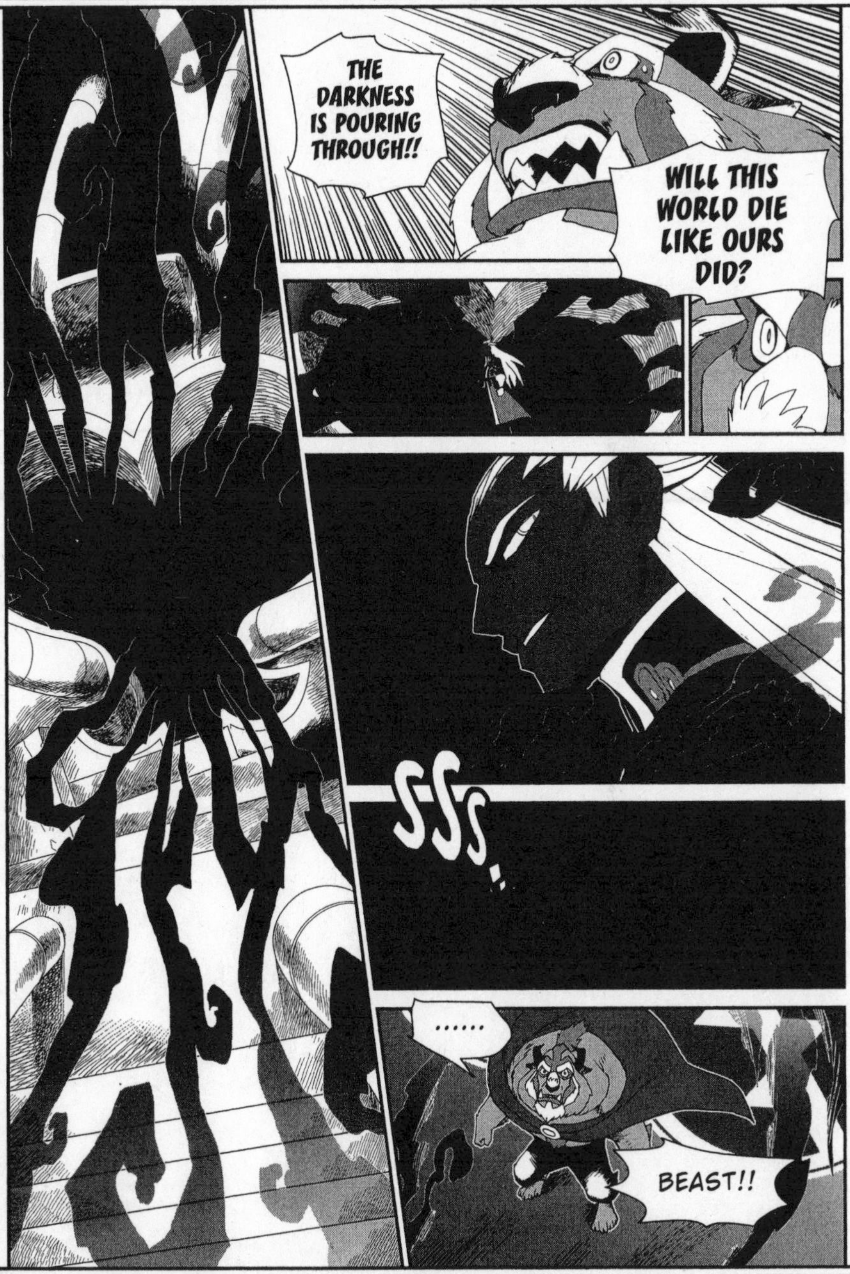
THE DARKNESS IS POURING THROUGH!!
WILL THIS WORLD DIE LIKE OURS DID?
SSS!!
......
BEAST!!

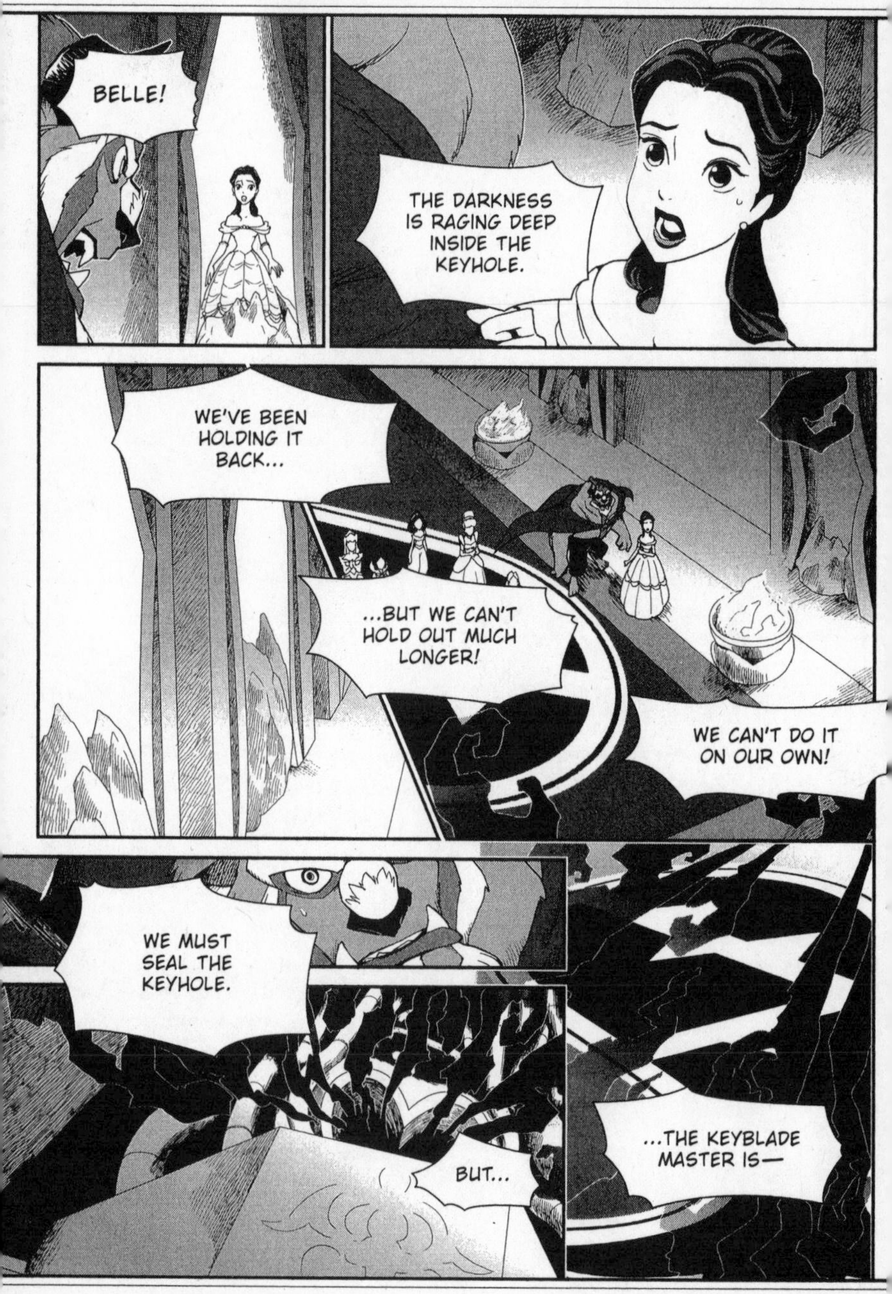
BELLE!
THE DARKNESS IS RAGING DEEP INSIDE THE KEYHOLE.
WE'VE BEEN HOLDING IT BACK...
...BUT WE CAN'T HOLD OUT MUCH LONGER!
WE CAN'T DO IT ON OUR OWN!
WE MUST SEAL THE KEYHOLE.
BUT...
...THE KEYBLADE MASTER IS—

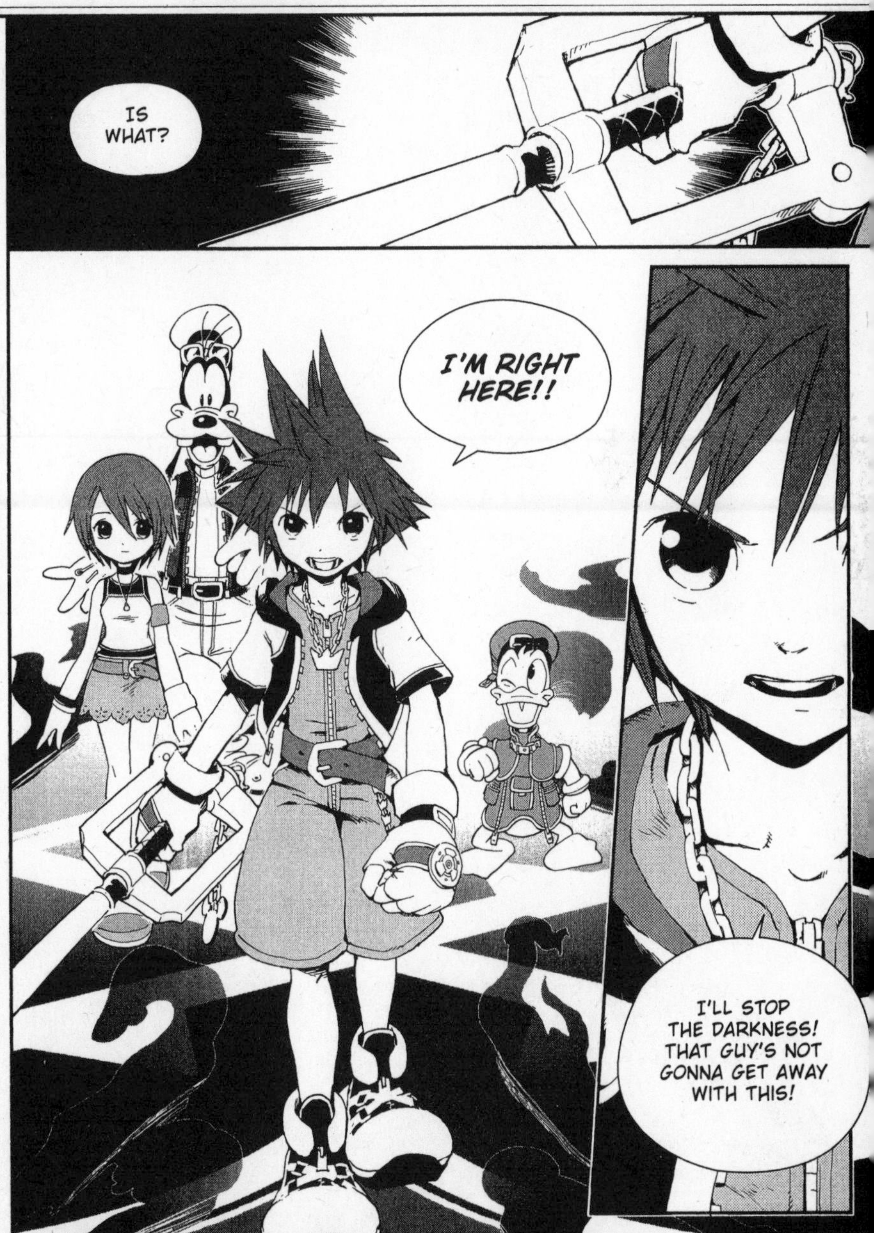
IS WHAT?
I'M RIGHT HERE!!
I'LL STOP THE DARKNESS! THAT GUY'S NOT GONNA GET AWAY WITH THIS!

Episode 40
I WON'T SAY GOOD-BYE

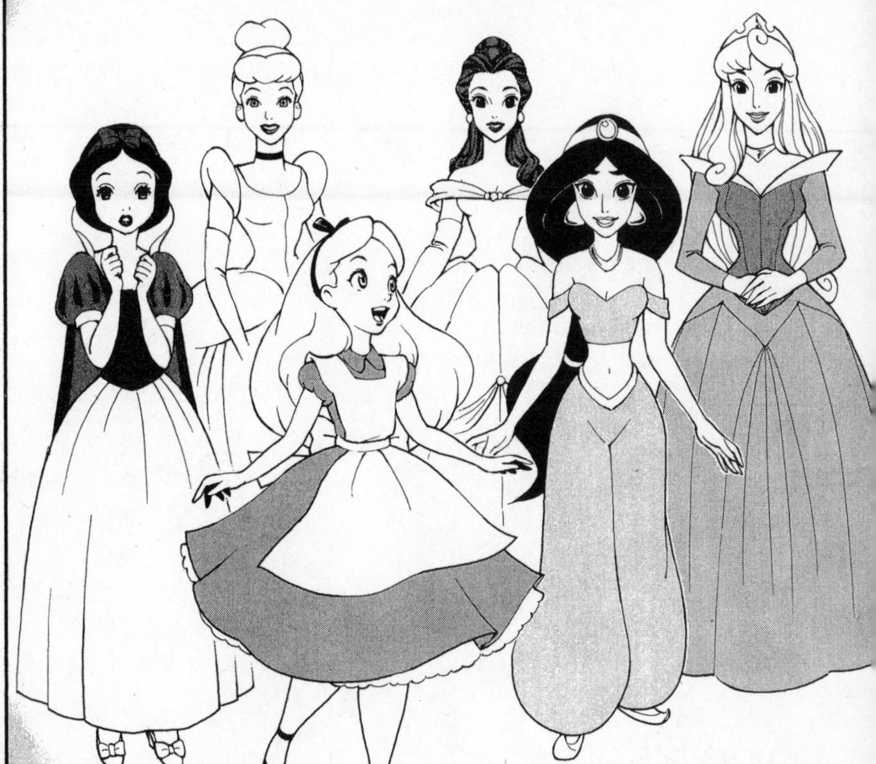

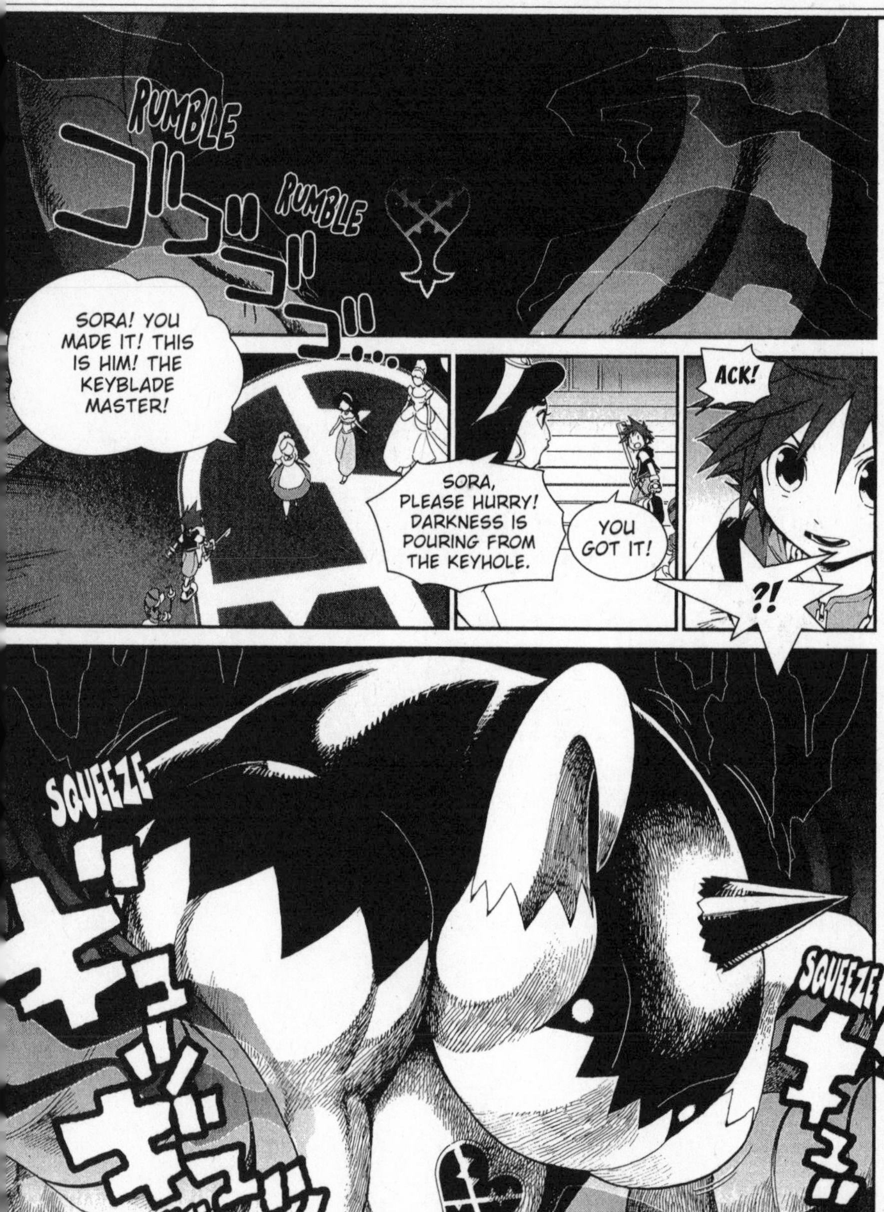
RUMBLE
RUMBLE
SORA! YOU MADE IT! THIS IS HIM! THE KEYBLADE MASTER!
SORA, PLEASE HURRY! DARKNESS IS POURING FROM THE KEYHOLE.
YOU GOT IT!
ACK!
?!
SQUEEZE
SQUEEZE
SQUEEZE

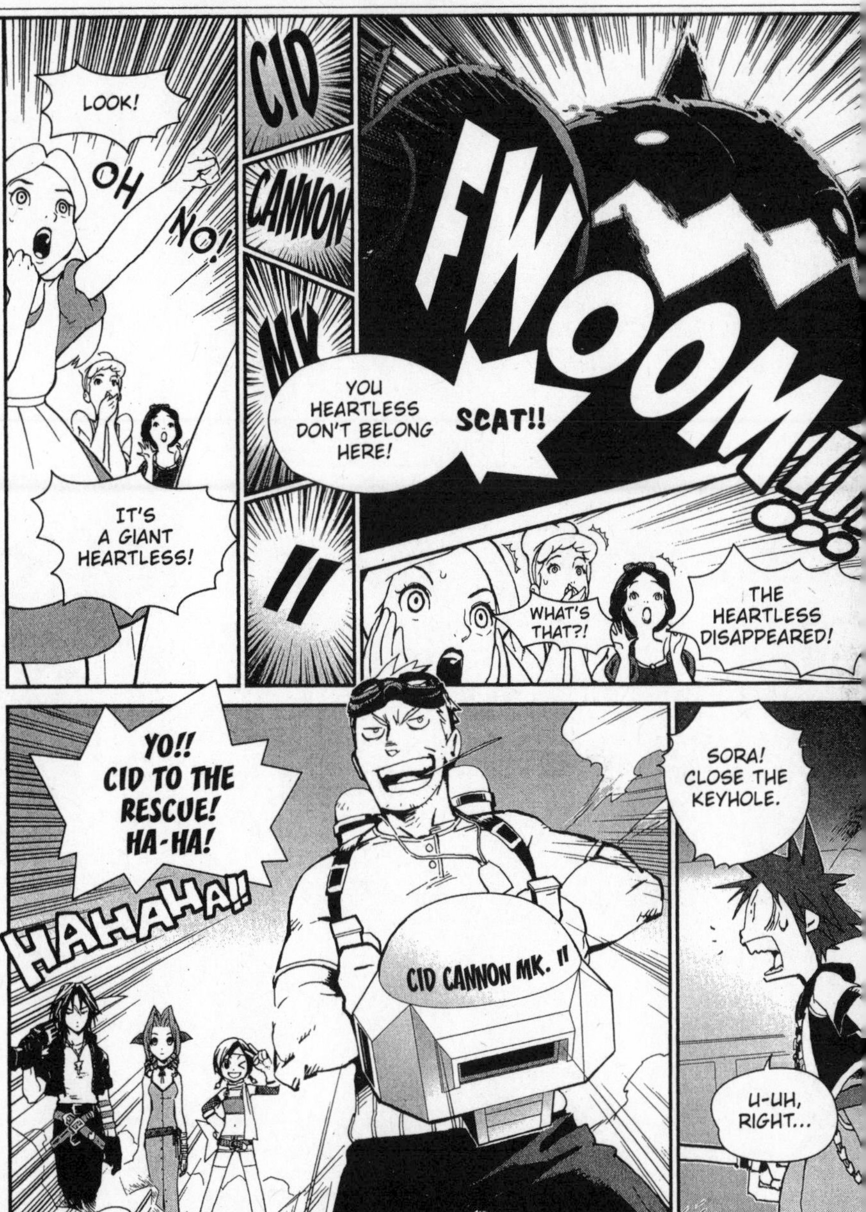
LOOK!
OH NO!
IT'S A GIANT HEARTLESS!
CID
CANNON
MK
II
FWOOM!!!
YOU HEARTLESS DON'T BELONG HERE!
SCAT!!
WHAT'S THAT?!
THE HEARTLESS DISAPPEARED!
YO!! CID TO THE RESCUE! HA-HA!
HAHAHA!!
CID CANNON MK. II
SORA! CLOSE THE KEYHOLE.
U-UH, RIGHT...

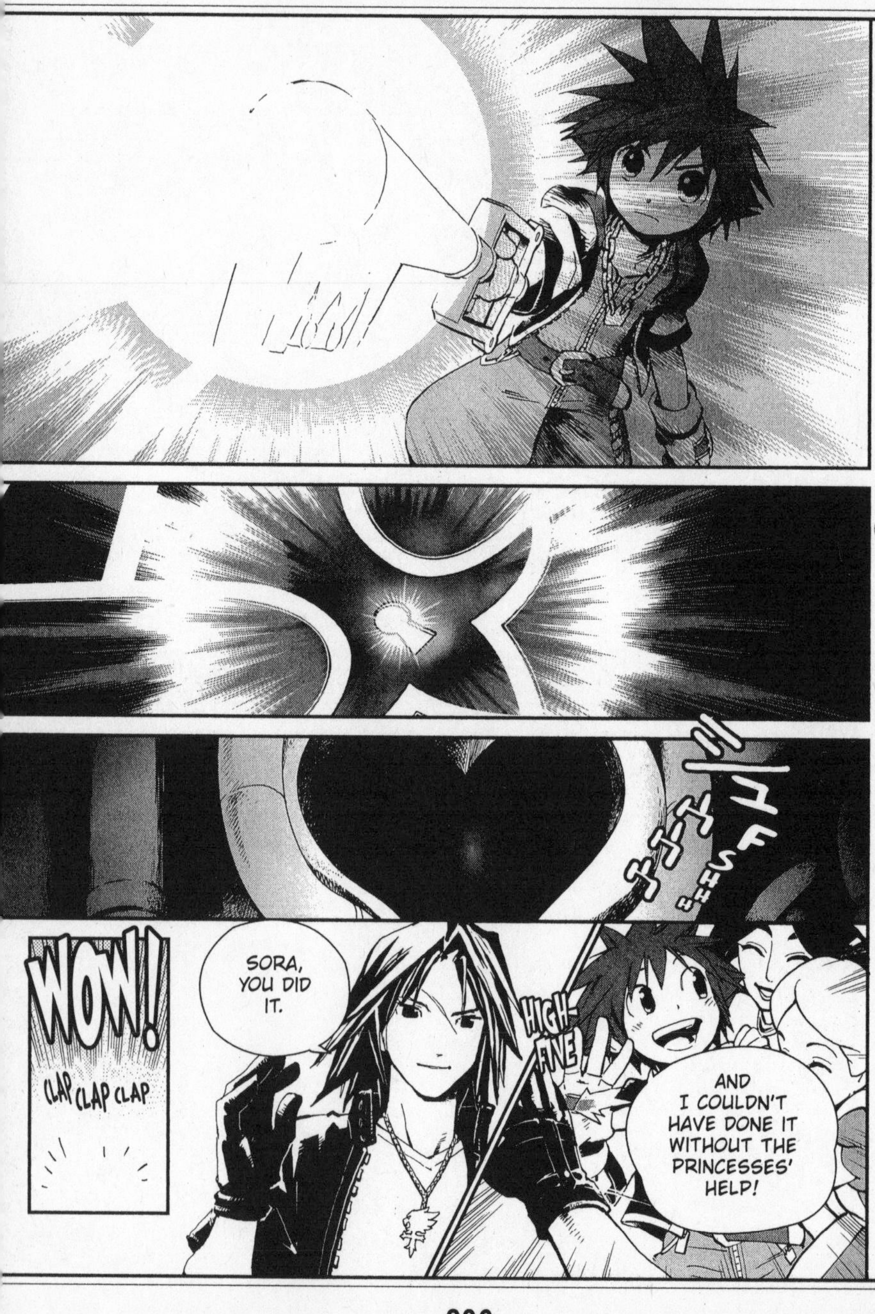
FSHHH
WOW!
CLAP CLAP CLAP
SORA, YOU DID IT.
HIGH-FIVE!
AND I COULDN'T HAVE DONE IT WITHOUT THE PRINCESSES' HELP!

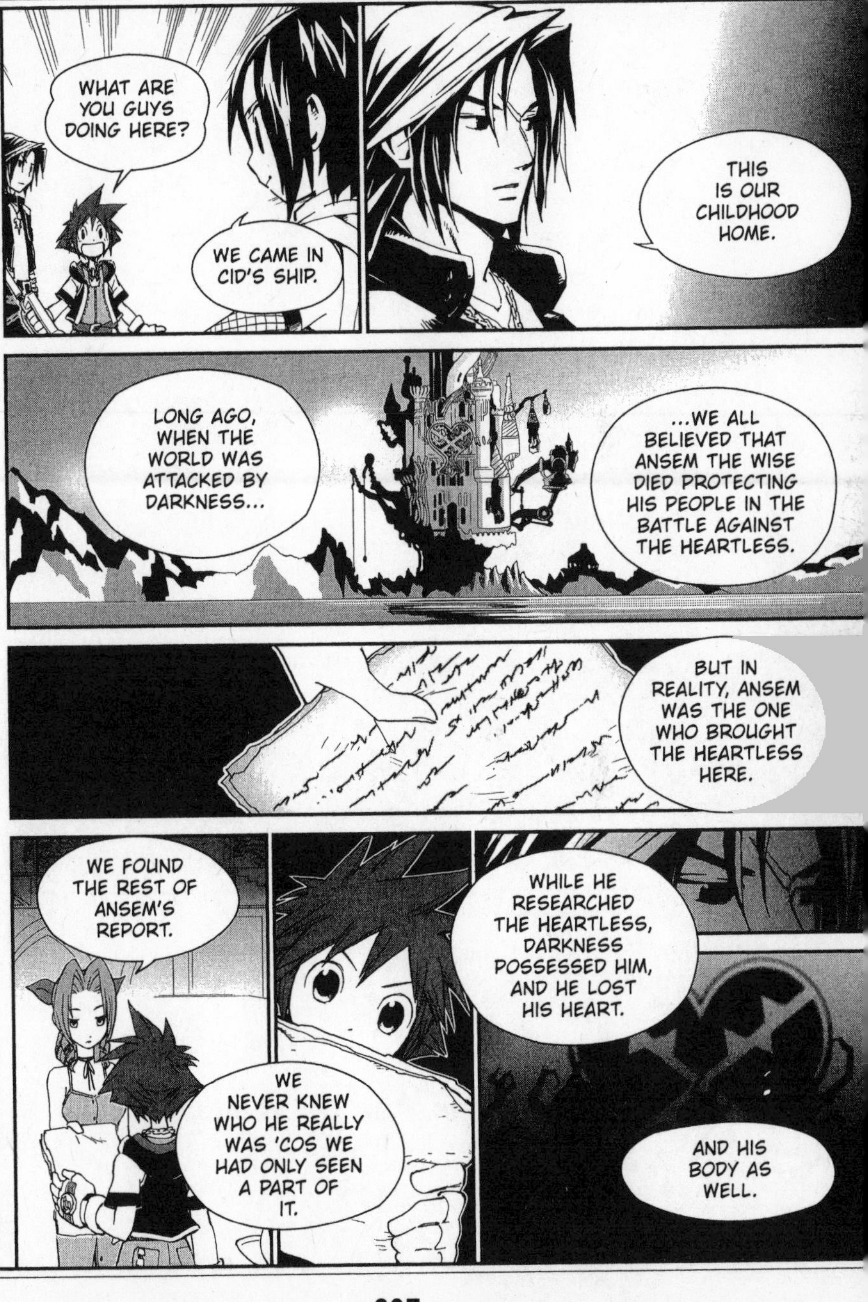
WHAT ARE YOU GUYS DOING HERE?
WE CAME IN CID'S SHIP.
THIS IS OUR CHILDHOOD HOME.
LONG AGO, WHEN THE WORLD WAS ATTACKED BY DARKNESS...
...WE ALL BELIEVED THAT ANSEM THE WISE DIED PROTECTING HIS PEOPLE IN THE BATTLE AGAINST THE HEARTLESS.
BUT IN REALITY, ANSEM WAS THE ONE WHO BROUGHT THE HEARTLESS HERE.
WE FOUND THE REST OF ANSEM'S REPORT.
WE NEVER KNEW WHO HE REALLY WAS 'COS WE HAD ONLY SEEN A PART OF IT.
WHILE HE RESEARCHED THE HEARTLESS, DARKNESS POSSESSED HIM, AND HE LOST HIS HEART.
AND HIS BODY AS WELL.

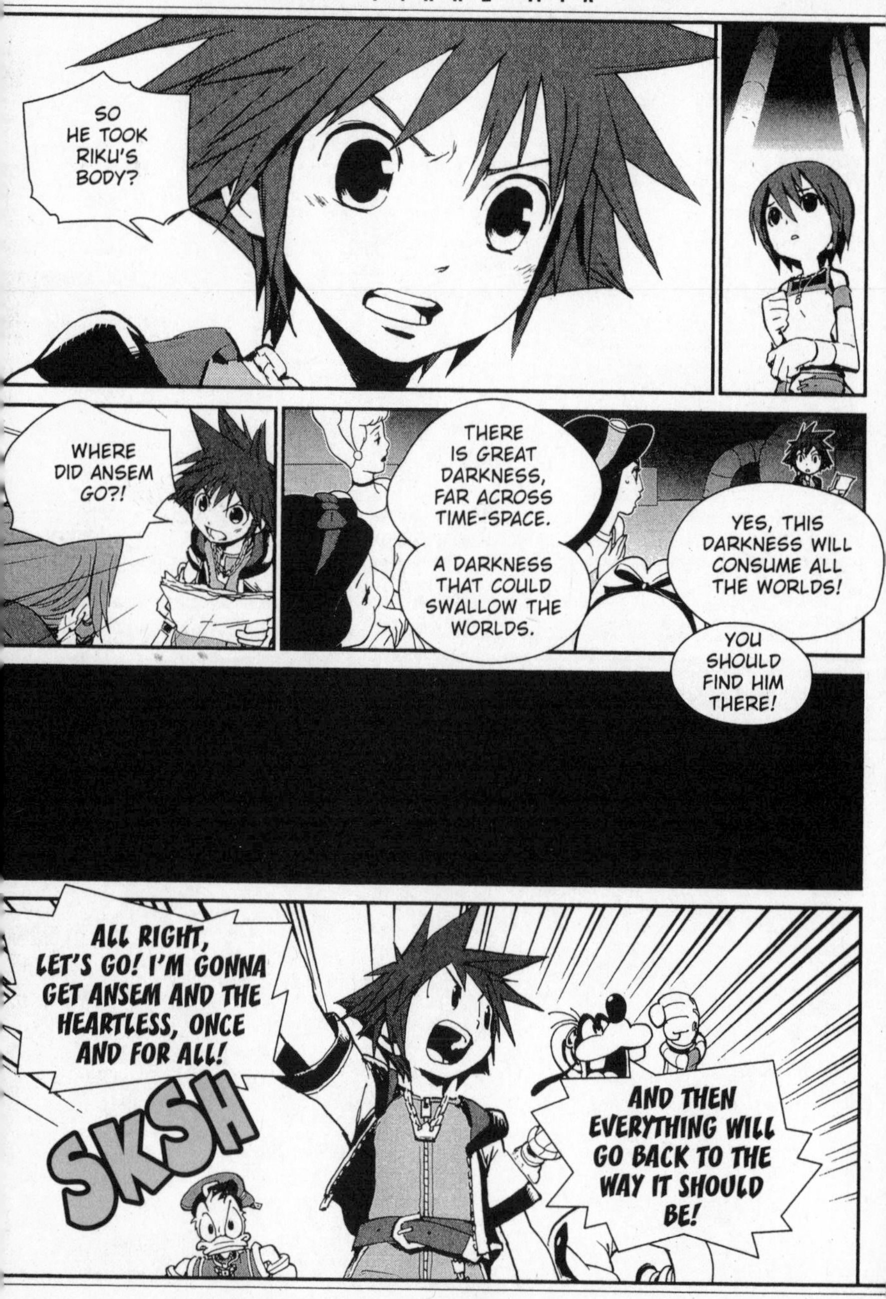
SO HE TOOK RIKU'S BODY?
WHERE DID ANSEM GO?!
THERE IS GREAT DARKNESS, FAR ACROSS TIME-SPACE.
A DARKNESS THAT COULD SWALLOW THE WORLDS.
YES, THIS DARKNESS WILL CONSUME ALL THE WORLDS!
YOU SHOULD FIND HIM THERE!
ALL RIGHT, LET'S GO! I'M GONNA GET ANSEM AND THE HEARTLESS, ONCE AND FOR ALL!
SKSH
AND THEN EVERYTHING WILL GO BACK TO THE WAY IT SHOULD BE!

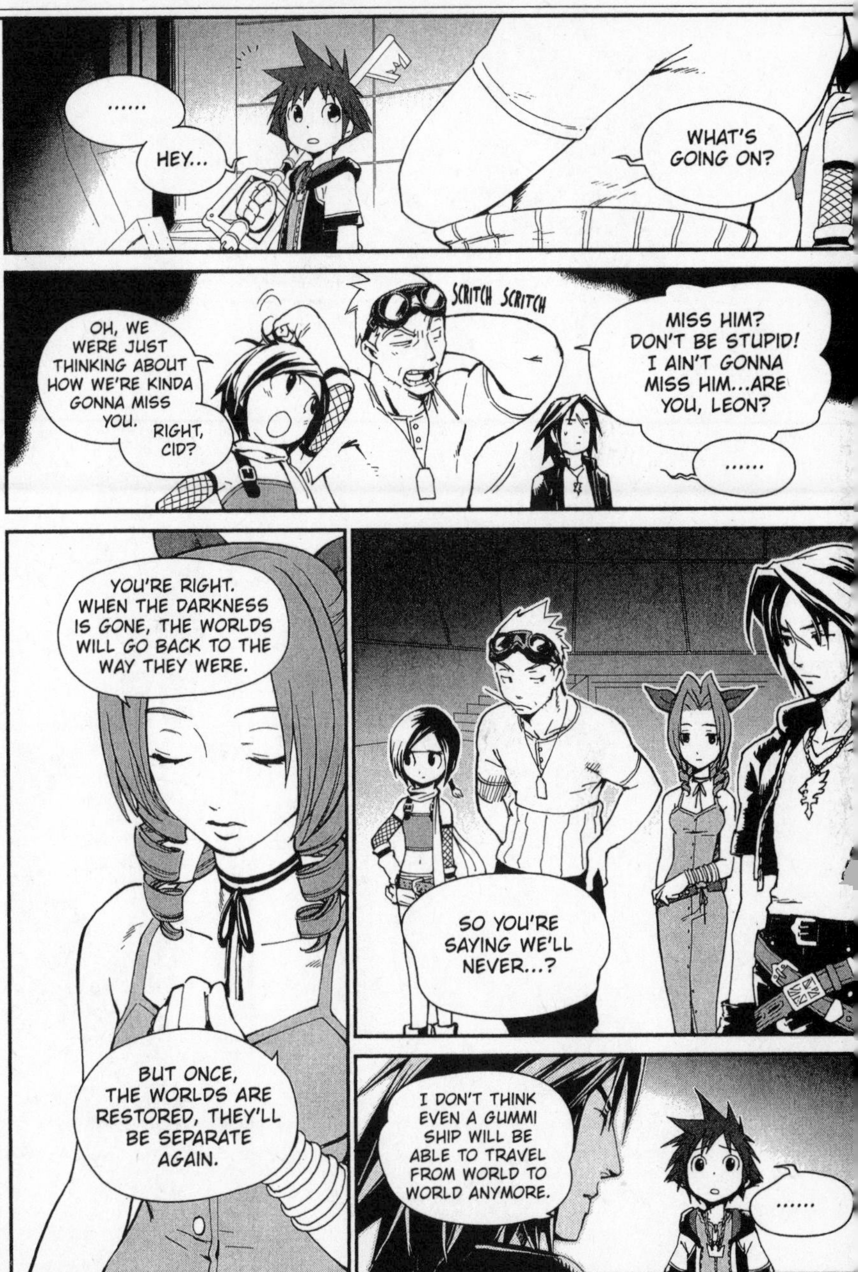
......
HEY...
WHAT'S GOING ON?
OH, WE WERE JUST THINKING ABOUT HOW WE'RE KINDA GONNA MISS YOU.
RIGHT, CID?
SCRITCH SCRITCH
MISS HIM? DON'T BE STUPID! I AIN'T GONNA MISS HIM...ARE YOU, LEON?
......
YOU'RE RIGHT. WHEN THE DARKNESS IS GONE, THE WORLDS WILL GO BACK TO THE WAY THEY WERE.
BUT ONCE, THE WORLDS ARE RESTORED, THEY'LL BE SEPARATE AGAIN.
SO YOU'RE SAYING WE'LL NEVER...?
I DON'T THINK EVEN A GUMMI SHIP WILL BE ABLE TO TRAVEL FROM WORLD TO WORLD ANYMORE.
......

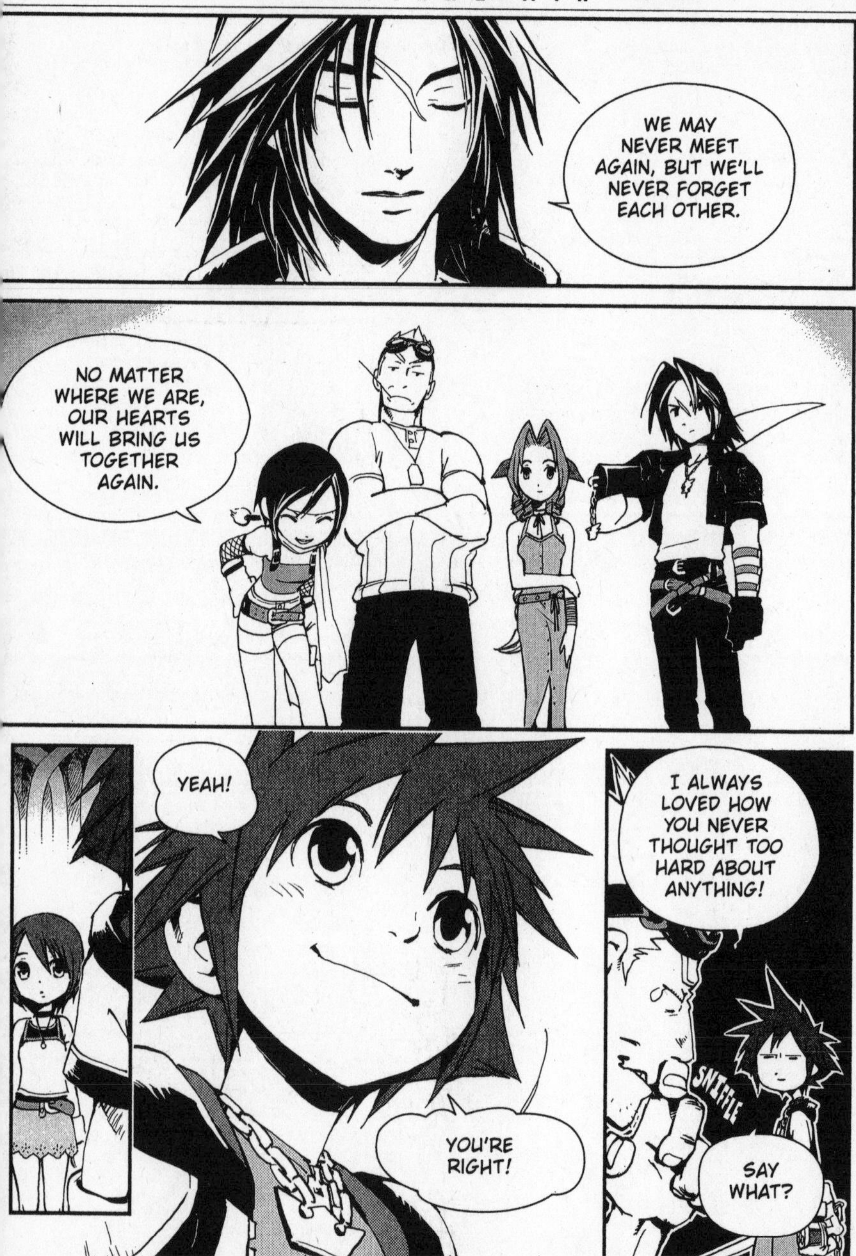
WE MAY NEVER MEET AGAIN, BUT WE'LL NEVER FORGET EACH OTHER.
NO MATTER WHERE WE ARE, OUR HEARTS WILL BRING US TOGETHER AGAIN.
YEAH!
YOU'RE RIGHT!
I ALWAYS LOVED HOW YOU NEVER THOUGHT TOO HARD ABOUT ANYTHING!
SNIFFLE
SAY WHAT?

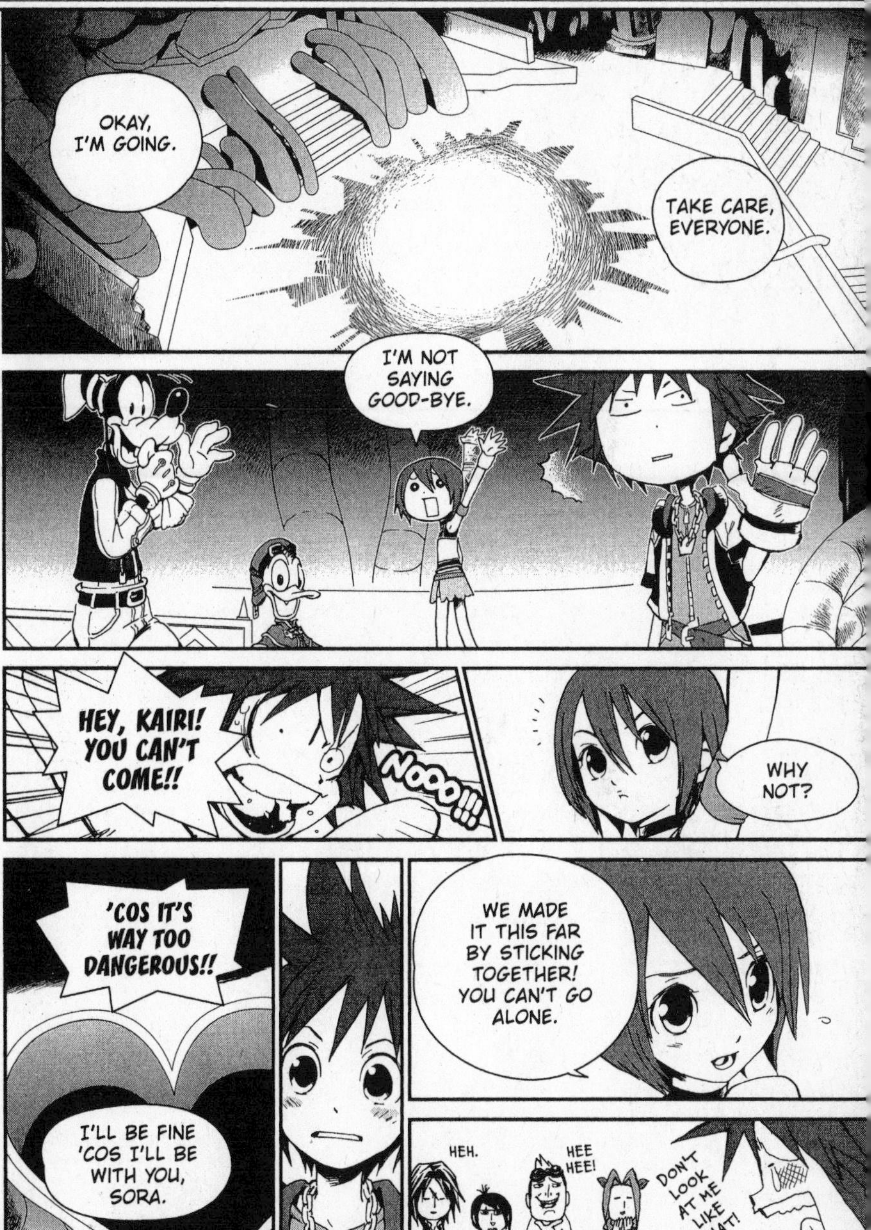
OKAY, I'M GOING.
TAKE CARE, EVERYONE.
I'M NOT SAYING GOOD-BYE.
HEY, KAIRI! YOU CAN'T COME!!
NOOO!!!
WHY NOT?
'COS IT'S WAY TOO DANGEROUS!!
I'LL BE FINE 'COS I'LL BE WITH YOU, SORA.
WE MADE IT THIS FAR BY STICKING TOGETHER! YOU CAN'T GO ALONE.
HEH.
HEE HEE!
DON'T LOOK AT ME LIKE THAT!

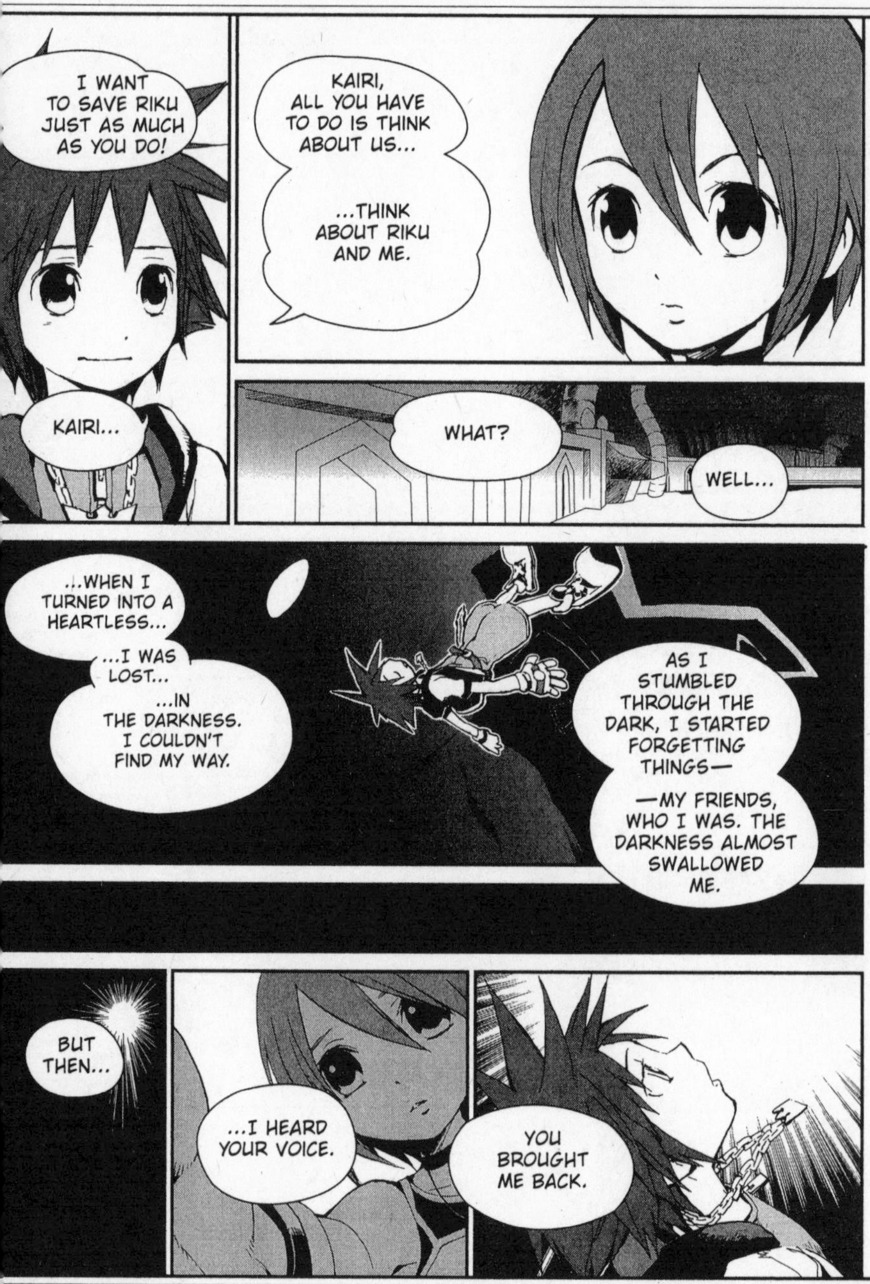
I WANT TO SAVE RIKU JUST AS MUCH AS YOU DO!
KAIRI...
KAIRI, ALL YOU HAVE TO DO IS THINK ABOUT US...
...THINK ABOUT RIKU AND ME.
WHAT?
WELL...
...WHEN I TURNED INTO A HEARTLESS...
...I WAS LOST...
...IN THE DARKNESS. I COULDN'T FIND MY WAY.
AS I STUMBLED THROUGH THE DARK, I STARTED FORGETTING THINGS—
—MY FRIENDS, WHO I WAS. THE DARKNESS ALMOST SWALLOWED ME.
BUT THEN...
...I HEARD YOUR VOICE.
YOU BROUGHT ME BACK.

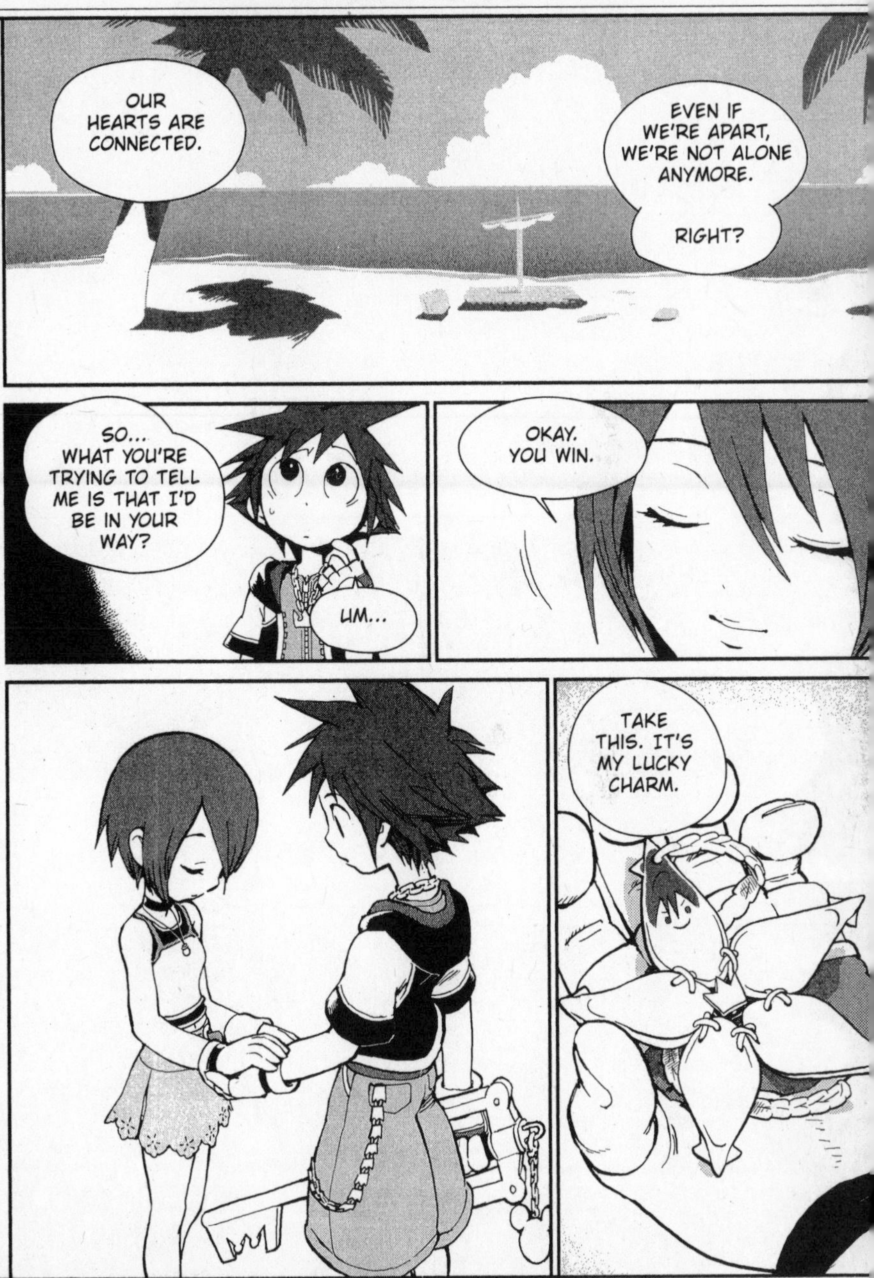
OUR HEARTS ARE CONNECTED.
EVEN IF WE'RE APART, WE'RE NOT ALONE ANYMORE.
RIGHT?
SO... WHAT YOU'RE TRYING TO TELL ME IS THAT I'D BE IN YOUR WAY?
UM...
OKAY. YOU WIN.
TAKE THIS. IT'S MY LUCKY CHARM.

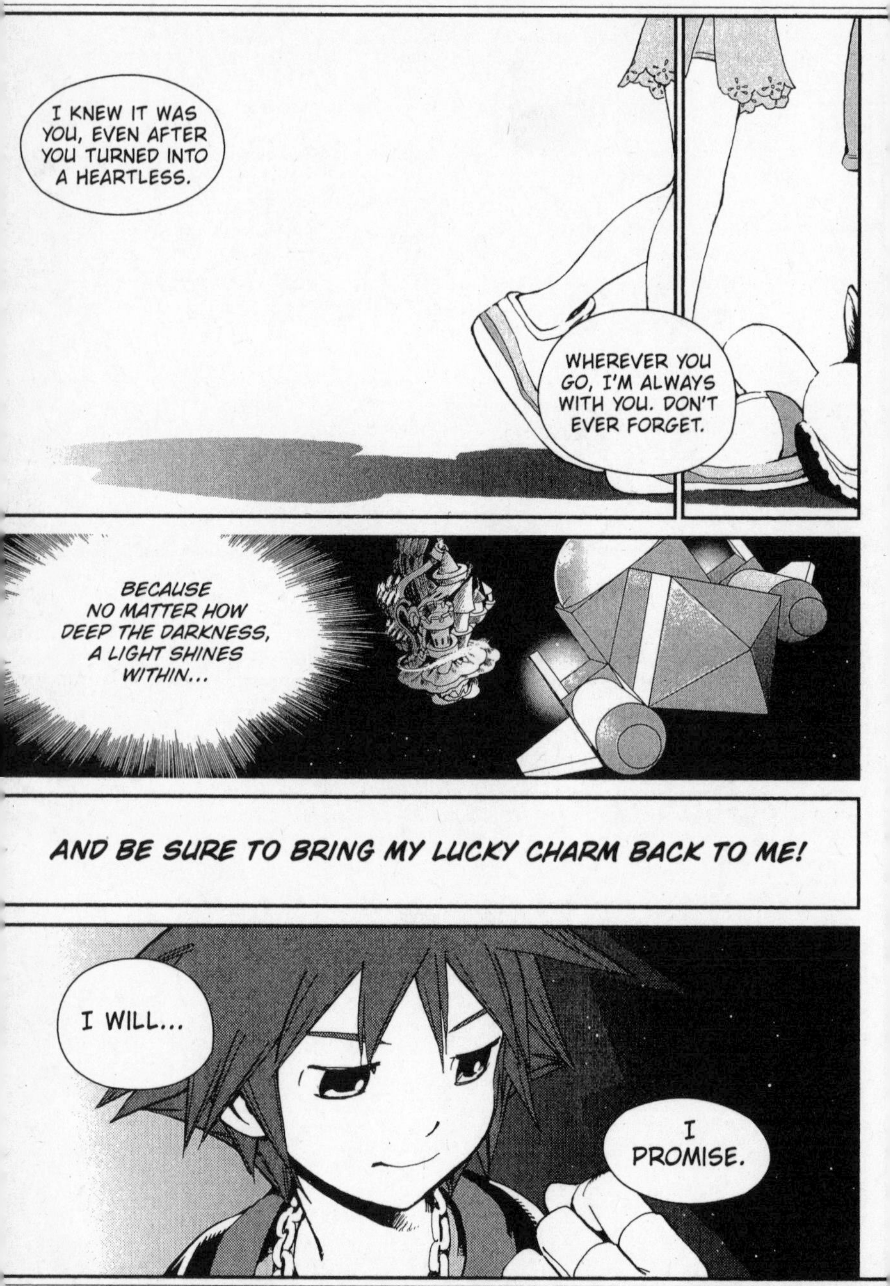
I KNEW IT WAS YOU, EVEN AFTER YOU TURNED INTO A HEARTLESS.
WHEREVER YOU GO, I'M ALWAYS WITH YOU. DON'T EVER FORGET.
BECAUSE NO MATTER HOW DEEP THE DARKNESS, A LIGHT SHINES WITHIN...
AND BE SURE TO BRING MY LUCKY CHARM BACK TO ME!
I WILL...
I PROMISE.

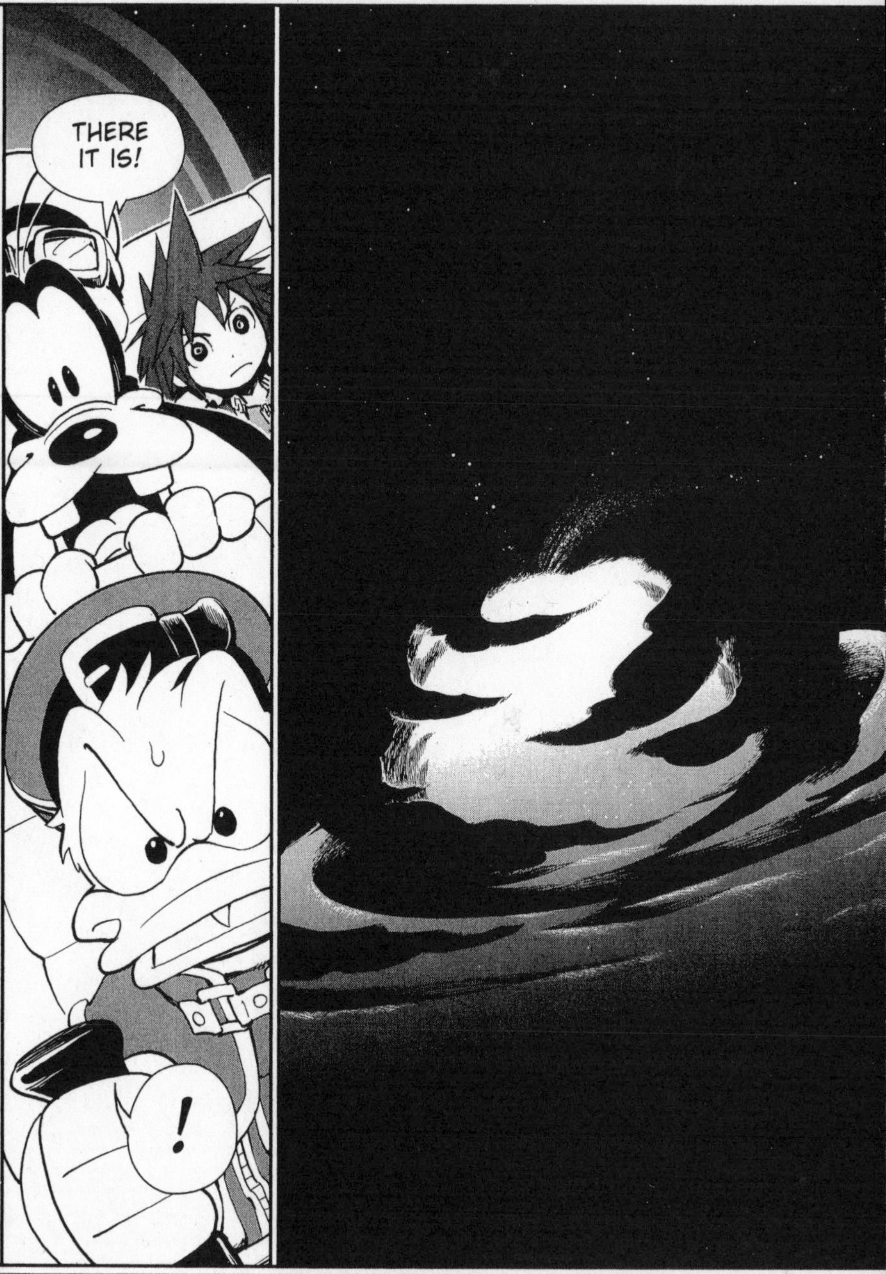
THERE IT IS!
!

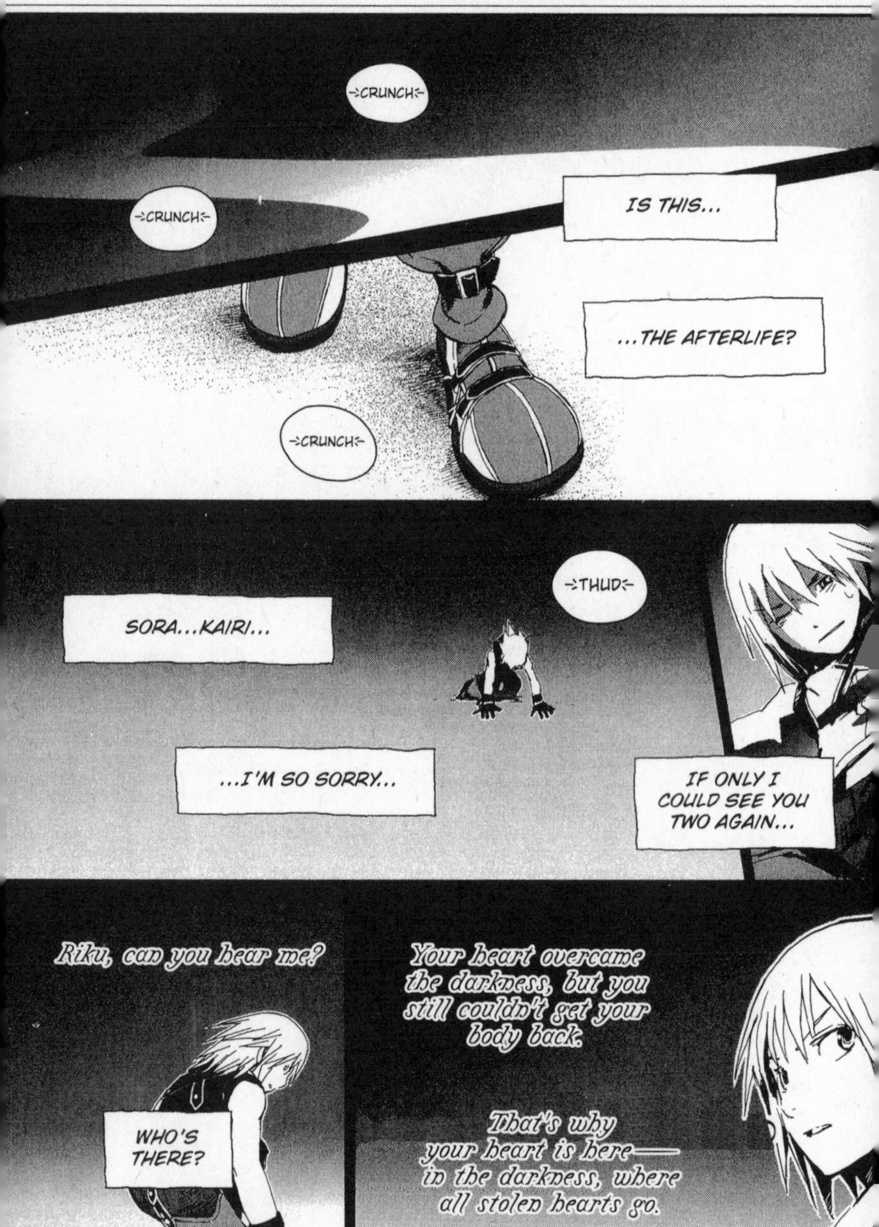
-CRUNCH-
-CRUNCH-
IS THIS...
...THE AFTERLIFE?
-CRUNCH-
-THUD-
SORA...KAIRI...
...I'M SO SORRY...
IF ONLY I COULD SEE YOU TWO AGAIN...
Riku, can you hear me?
WHO'S THERE?
Your heart overcame the darkness, but you still couldn't get your body back.
That's why your heart is here—in the darkness, where all stolen hearts go.

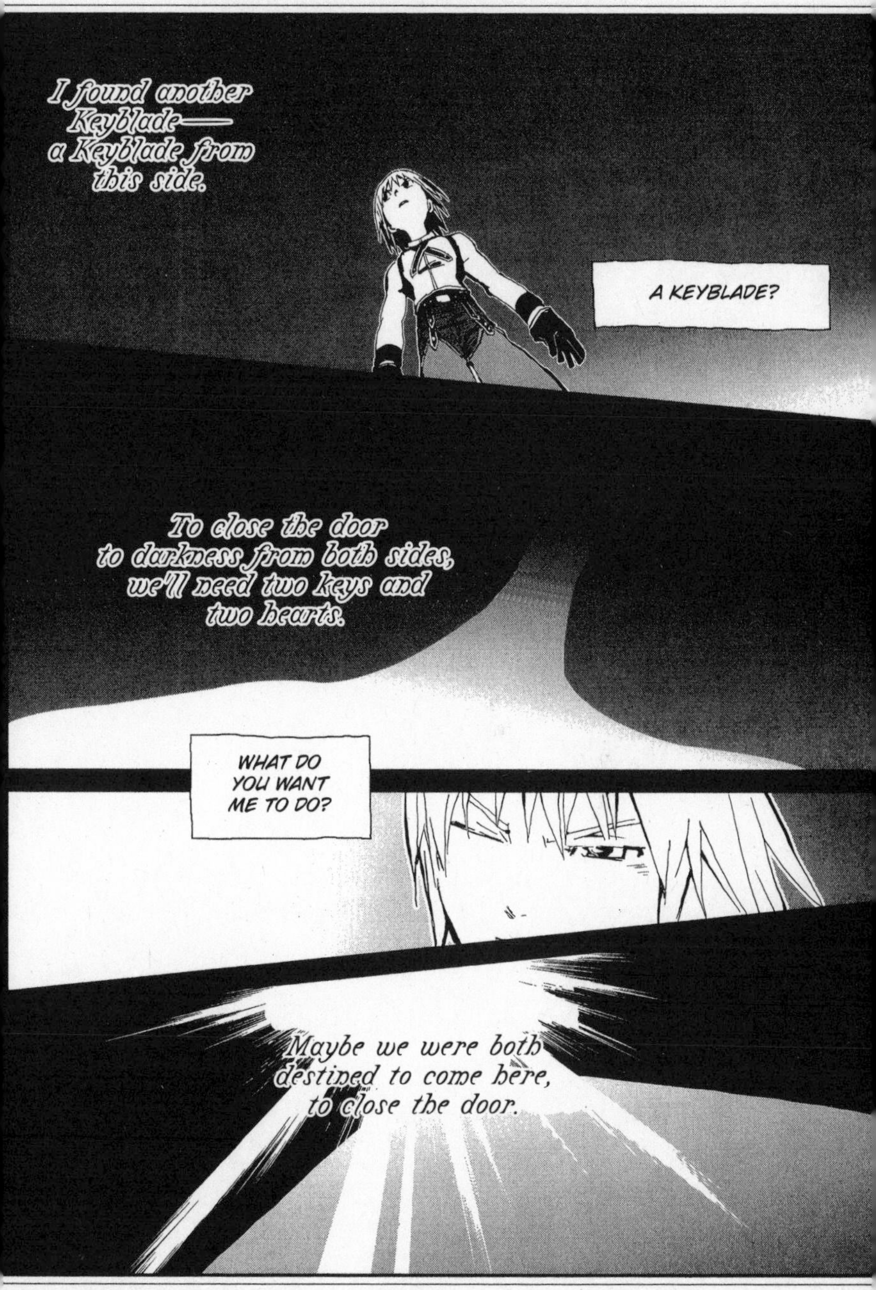
I found another Keyblade—a Keyblade from this side.
A KEYBLADE?
To close the door to darkness from both sides, we'll need two keys and two hearts.
WHAT DO YOU WANT ME TO DO?
Maybe we were both destined to come here, to close the door.

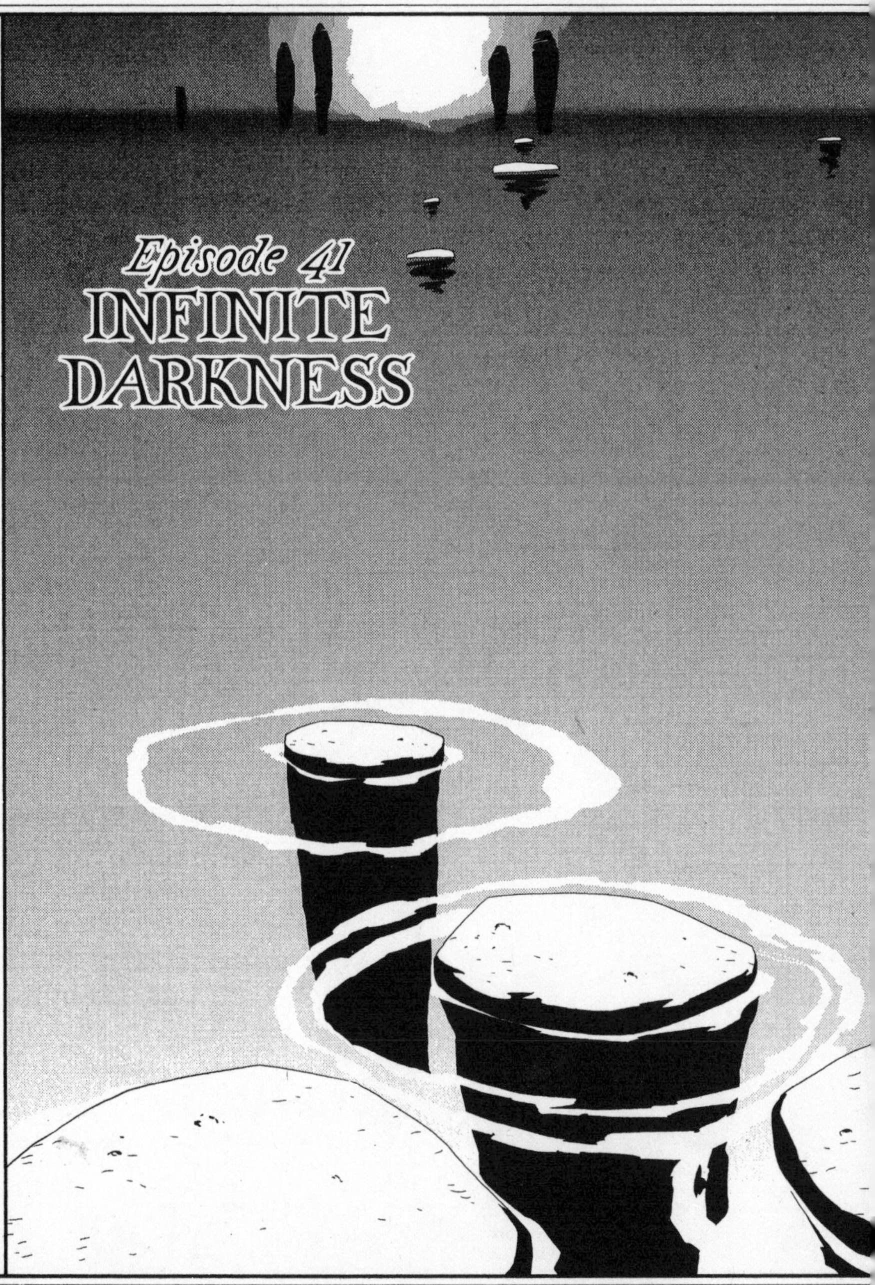
Episode 41
INFINITE DARKNESS

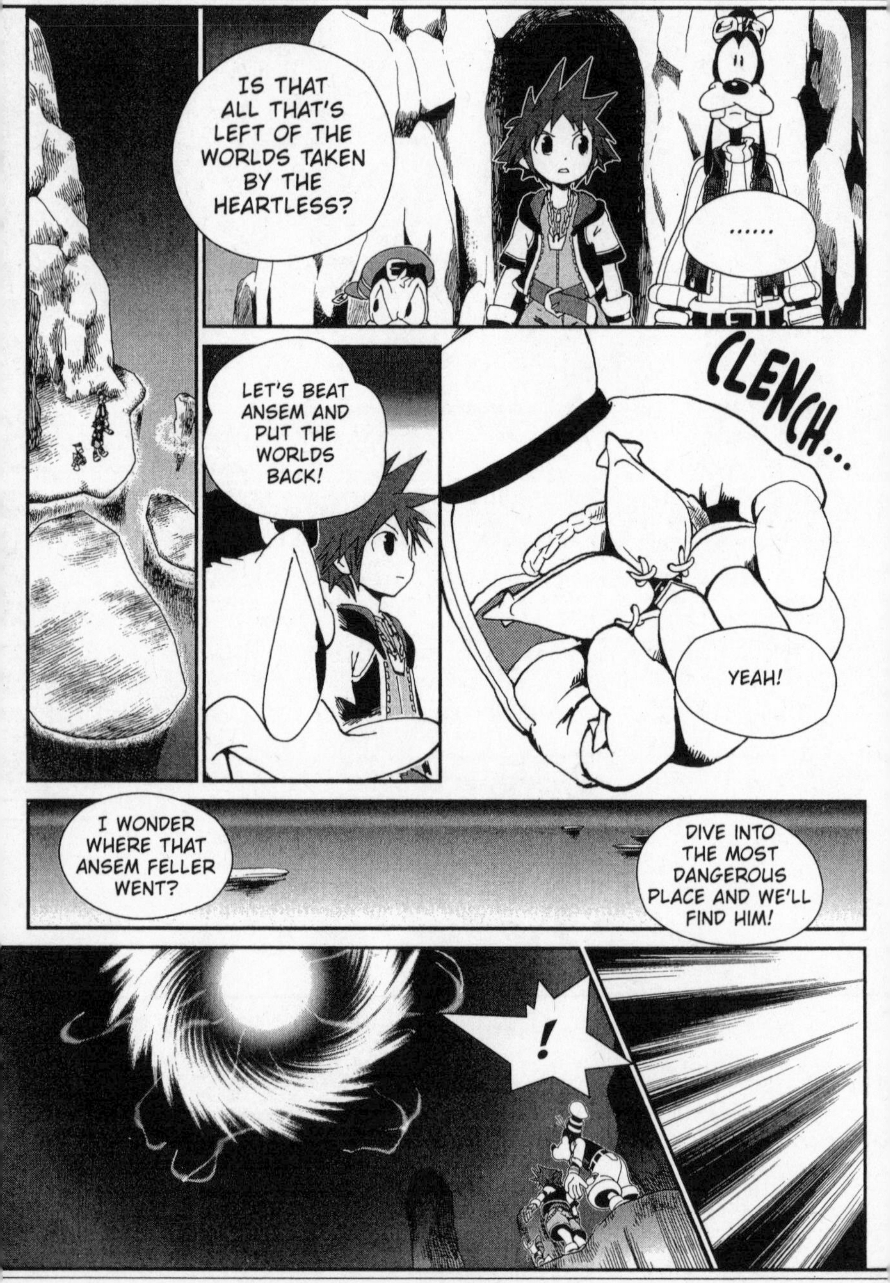
IS THAT ALL THAT'S LEFT OF THE WORLDS TAKEN BY THE HEARTLESS?
......
LET'S BEAT ANSEM AND PUT THE WORLDS BACK!
CLENCH...
YEAH!
I WONDER WHERE THAT ANSEM FELLER WENT?
DIVE INTO THE MOST DANGEROUS PLACE AND WE'LL FIND HIM!
!

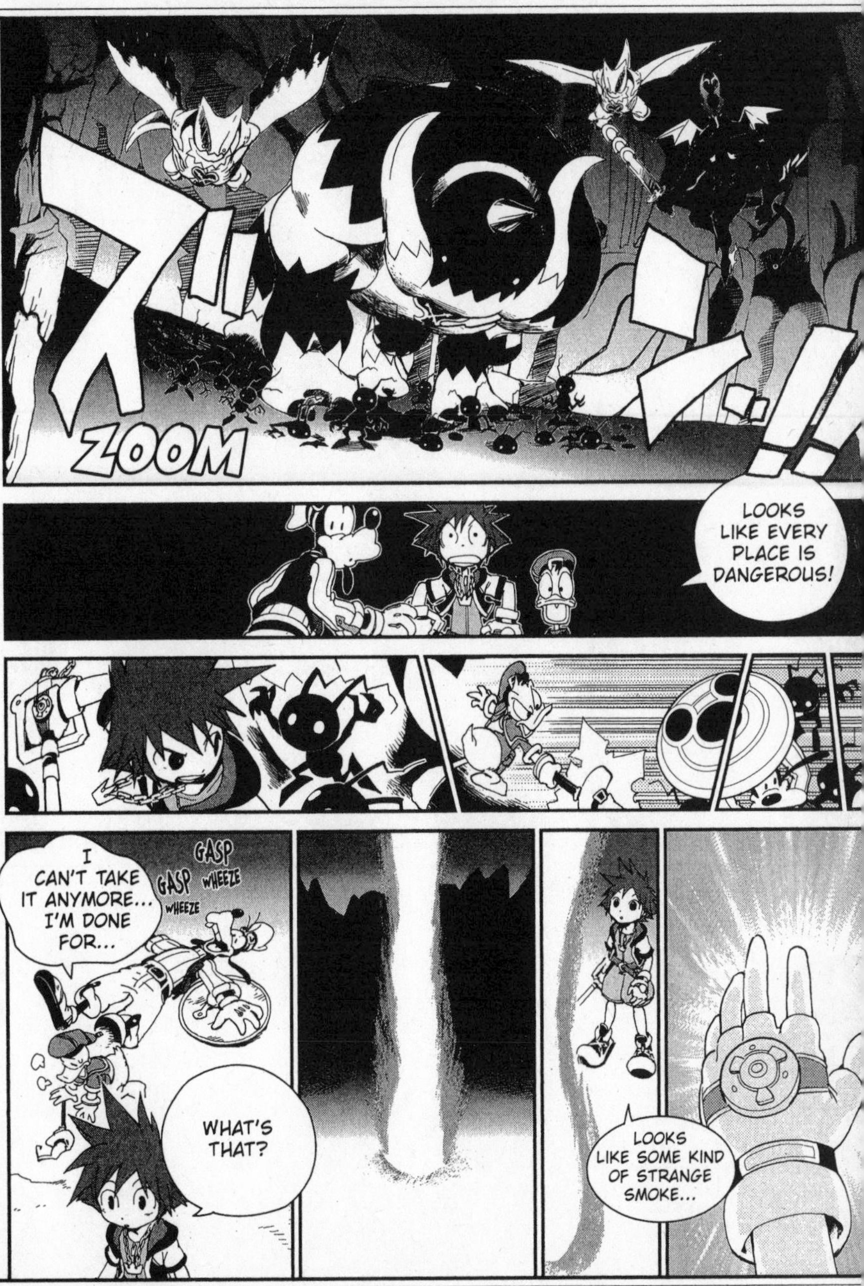
ZOOM
LOOKS LIKE EVERY PLACE IS DANGEROUS!
I CAN'T TAKE IT ANYMORE... I'M DONE FOR...
GASP GASP
WHEEZE WHEEZE
WHAT'S THAT?
LOOKS LIKE SOME KIND OF STRANGE SMOKE...

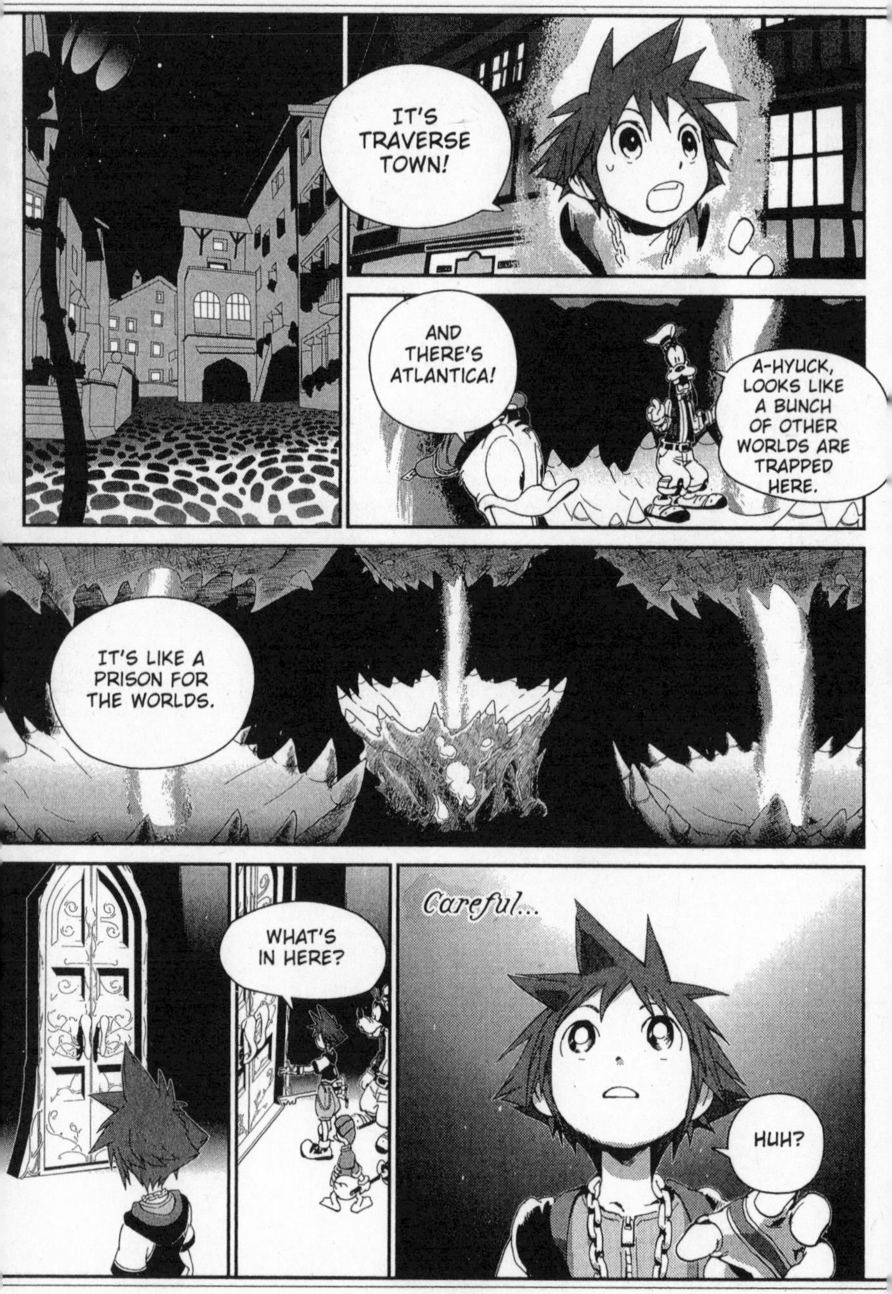
IT'S TRAVERSE TOWN!
AND THERE'S ATLANTICA!
A-HYUCK, LOOKS LIKE A BUNCH OF OTHER WORLDS ARE TRAPPED HERE.
IT'S LIKE A PRISON FOR THE WORLDS.
WHAT'S IN HERE?
Careful...
HUH?

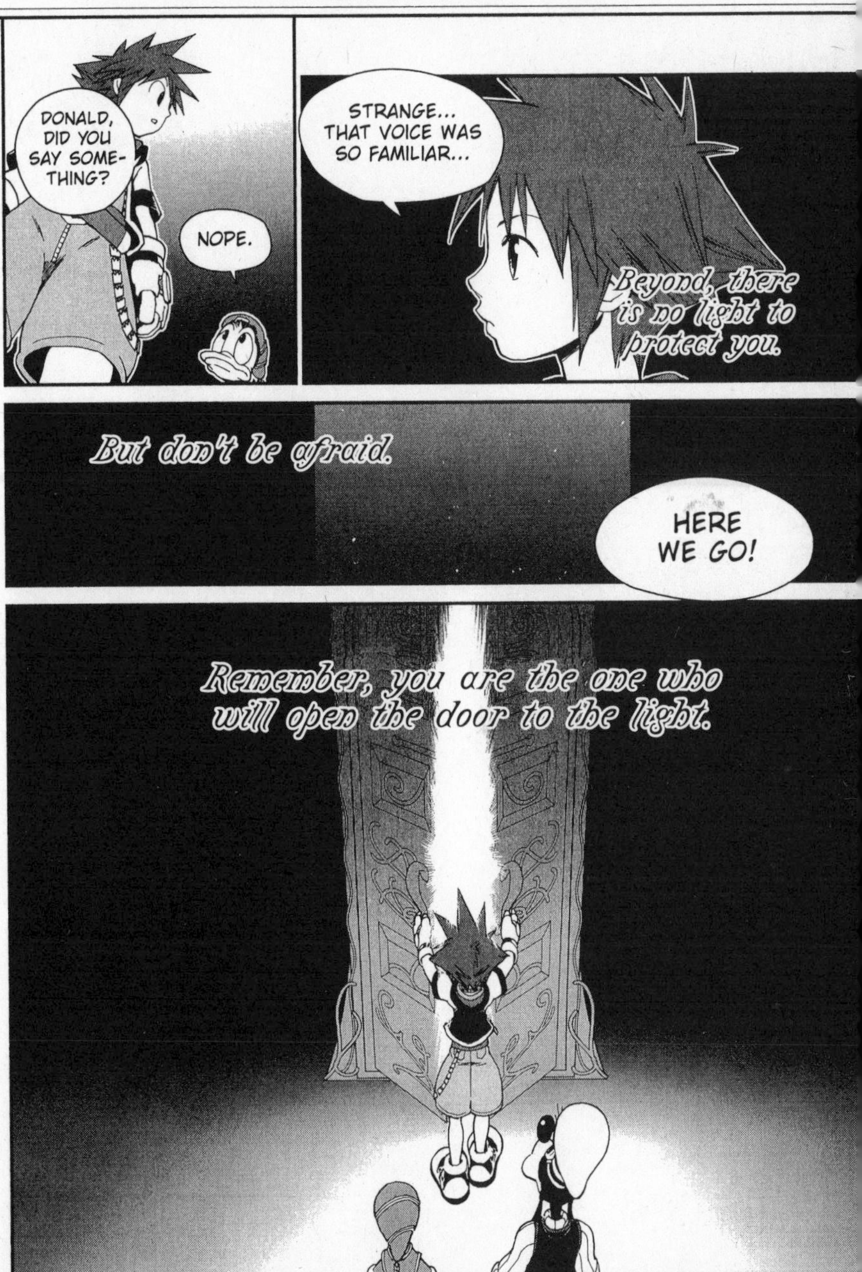
DONALD, DID YOU SAY SOME-THING?
NOPE.
STRANGE... THAT VOICE WAS SO FAMILIAR...
Beyond, there is no light to protect you.
But don't be afraid.
HERE WE GO!
Remember, you are the one who will open the door to the light.

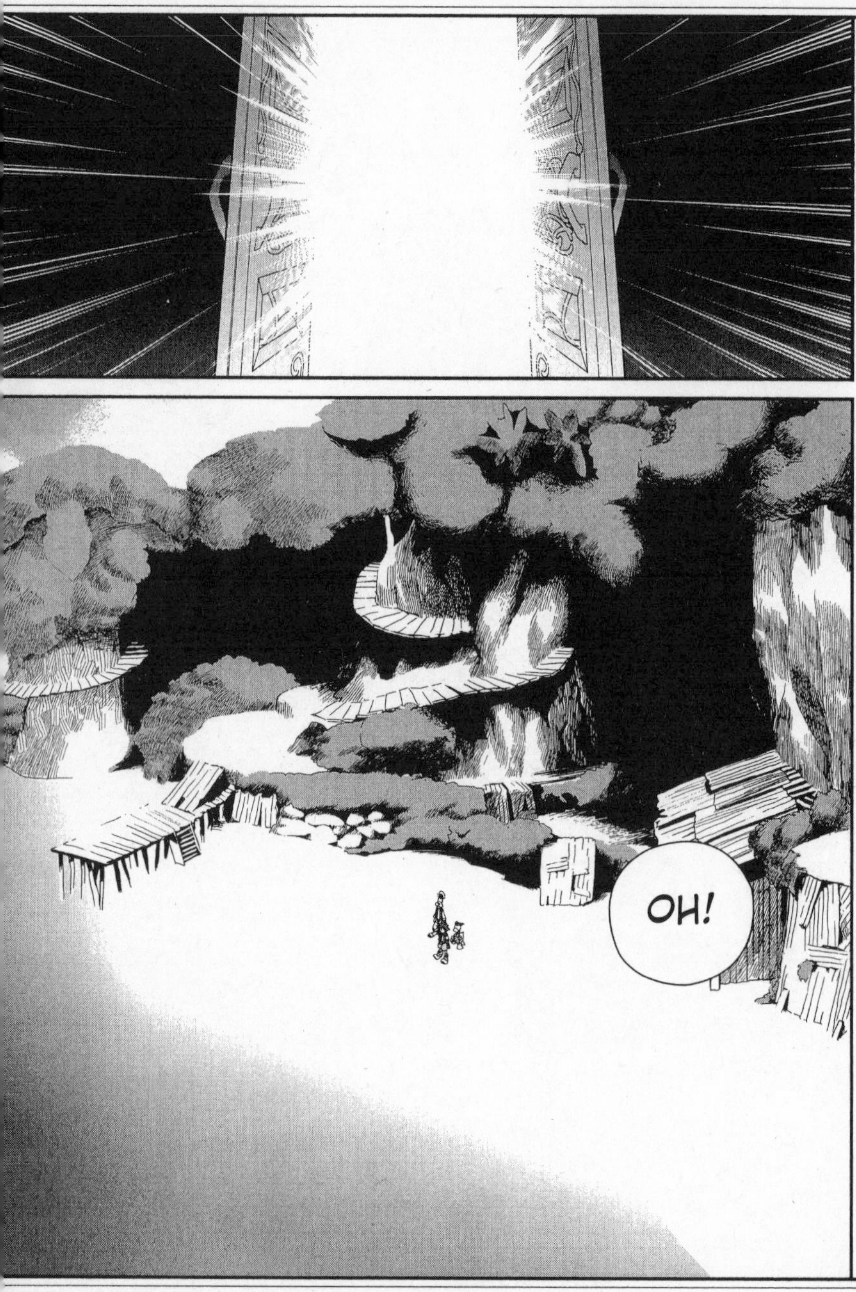
OH!

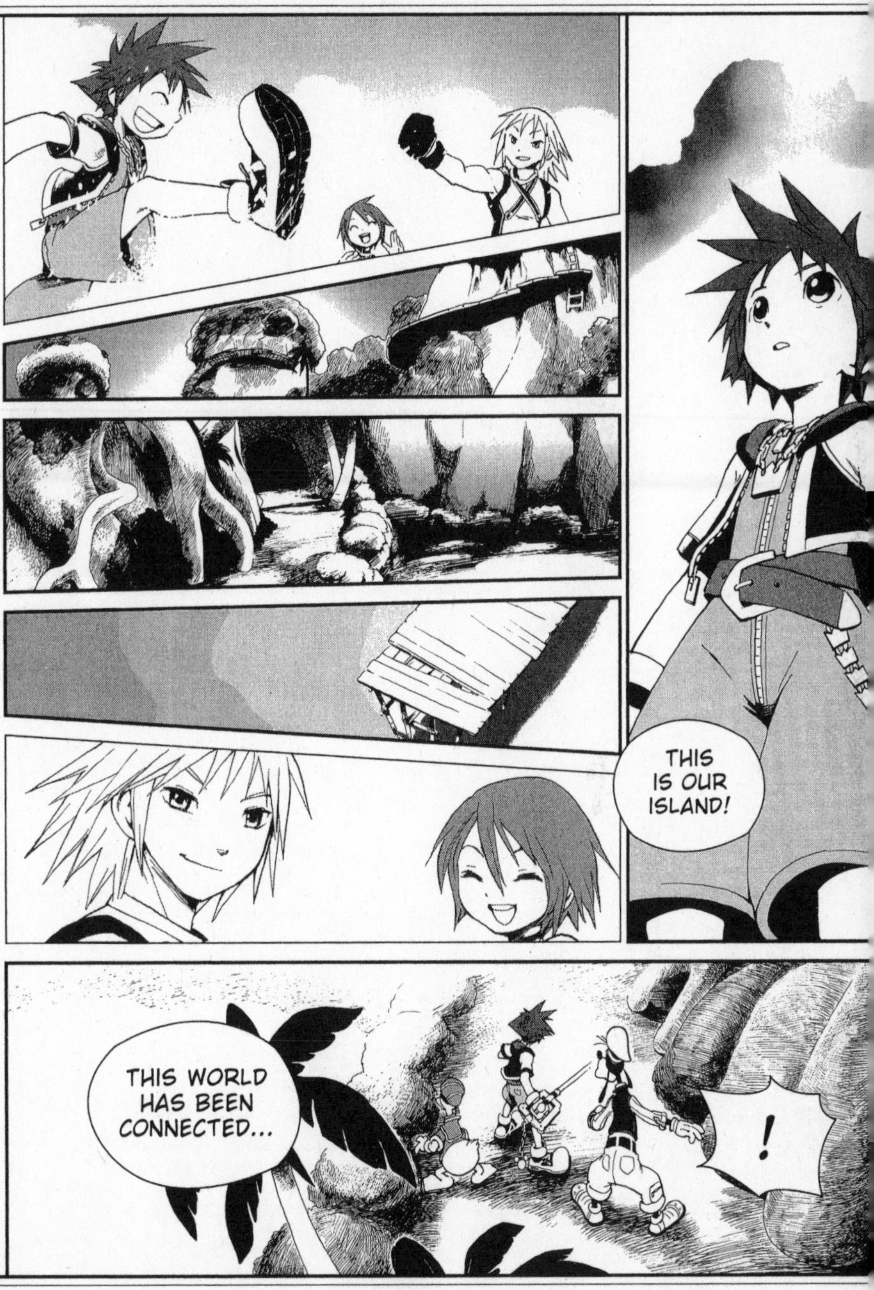
THIS IS OUR ISLAND!
THIS WORLD HAS BEEN CONNECTED...
!

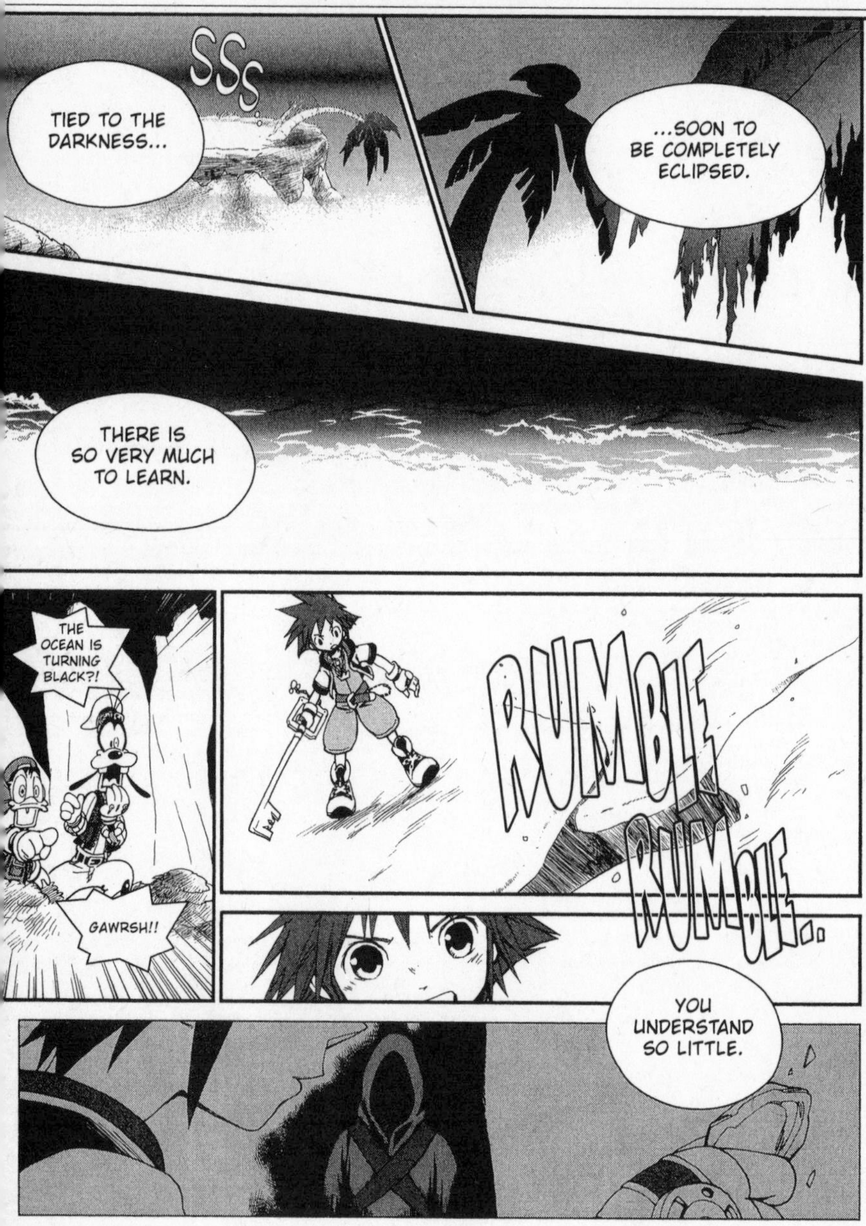
SSS
TIED TO THE DARKNESS...
...SOON TO BE COMPLETELY ECLIPSED.
THERE IS SO VERY MUCH TO LEARN.
THE OCEAN IS TURNING BLACK?!
GAWRSH!!
RUMBLE
RUMBLE..
YOU UNDERSTAND SO LITTLE.

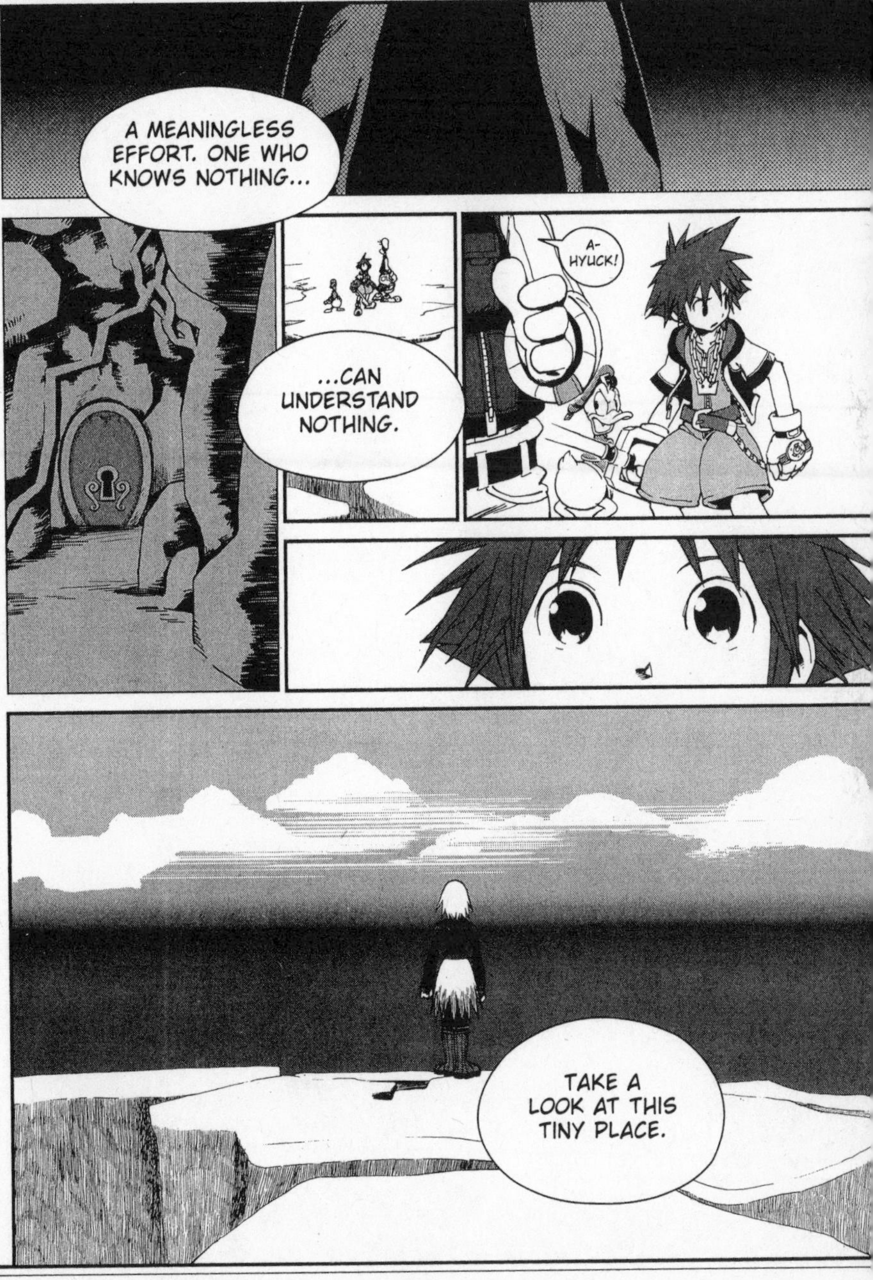
A MEANINGLESS EFFORT. ONE WHO KNOWS NOTHING...
...CAN UNDERSTAND NOTHING.
A-HYUCK!
TAKE A LOOK AT THIS TINY PLACE.

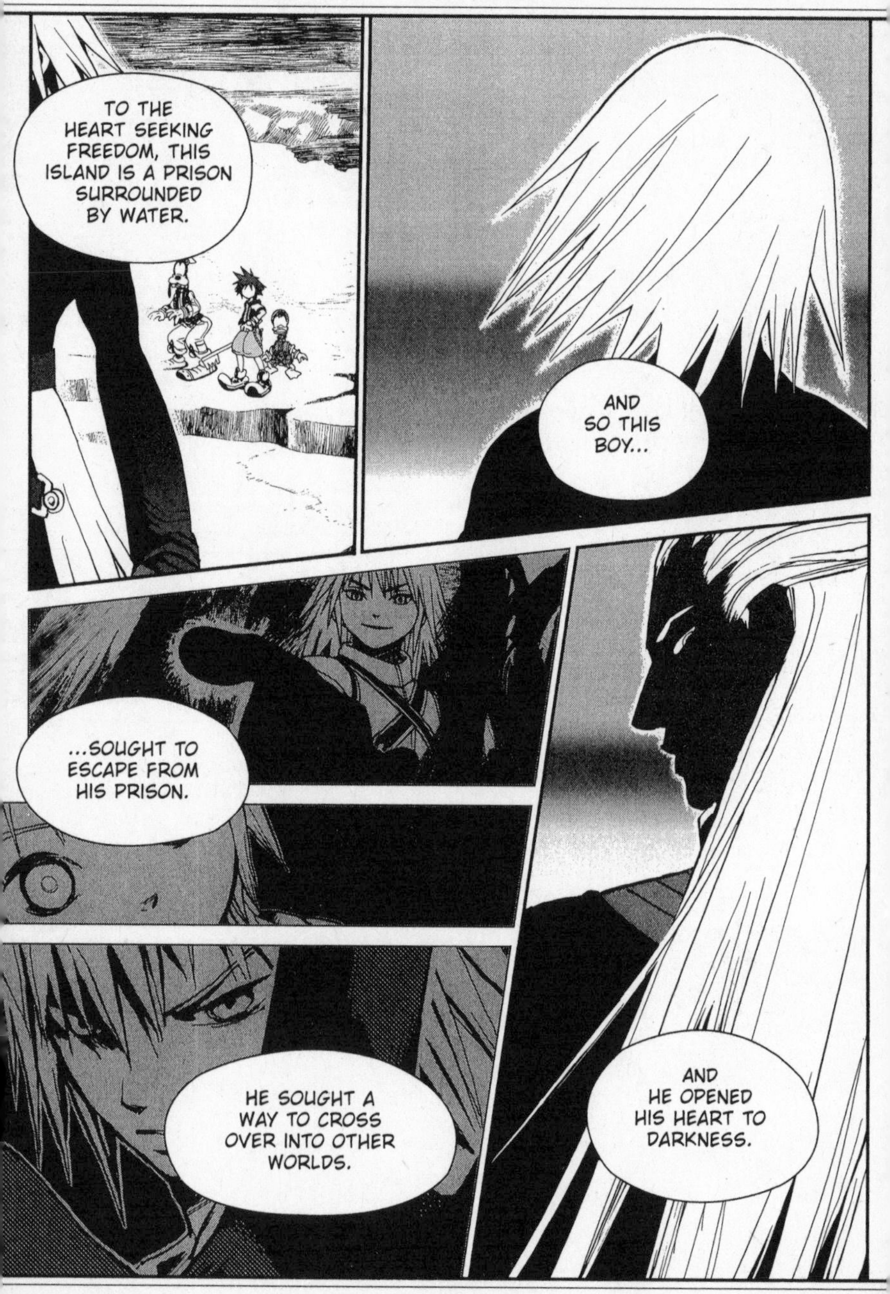
TO THE HEART SEEKING FREEDOM, THIS ISLAND IS A PRISON SURROUNDED BY WATER.
AND SO THIS BOY...
...SOUGHT TO ESCAPE FROM HIS PRISON.
HE SOUGHT A WAY TO CROSS OVER INTO OTHER WORLDS.
AND HE OPENED HIS HEART TO DARKNESS.

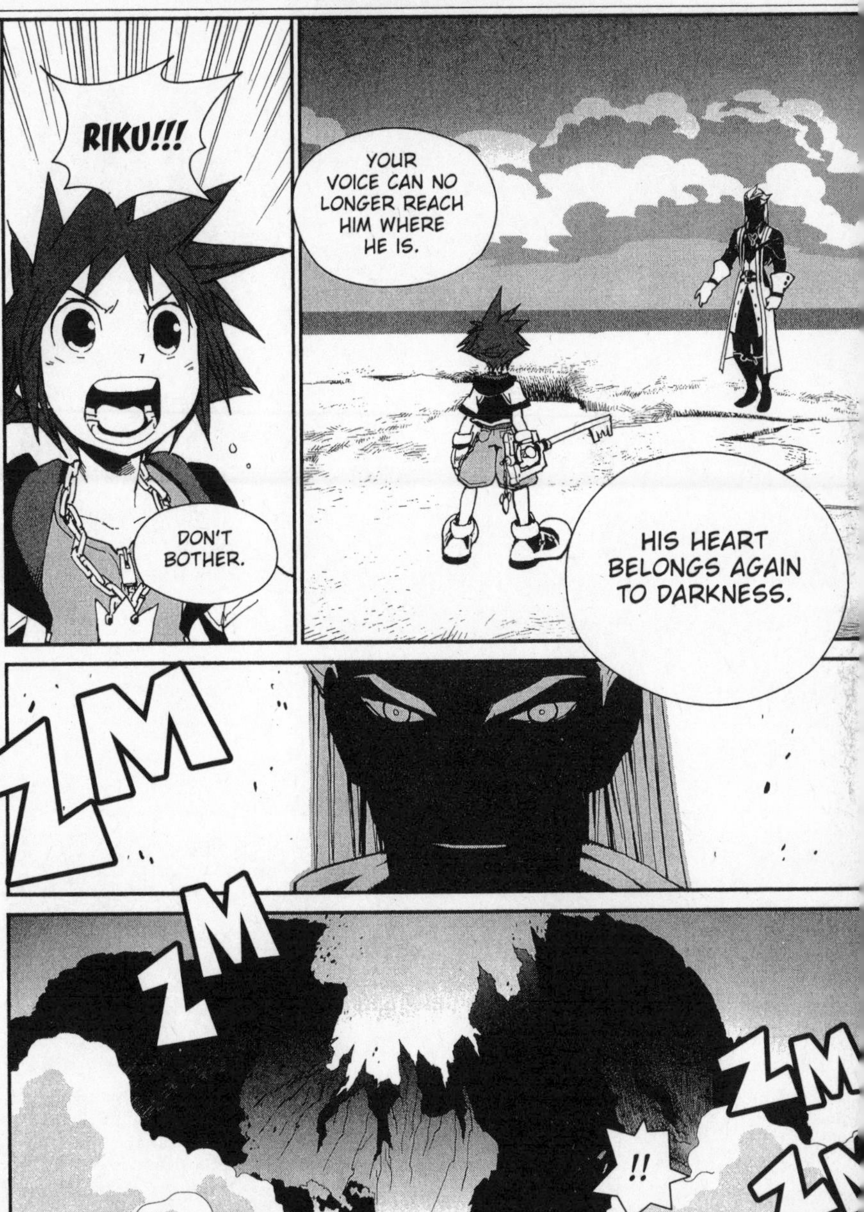
RIKU!!!
DON'T BOTHER.
YOUR VOICE CAN NO LONGER REACH HIM WHERE HE IS.
HIS HEART BELONGS AGAIN TO DARKNESS.
ZM
ZM
!!
ZM

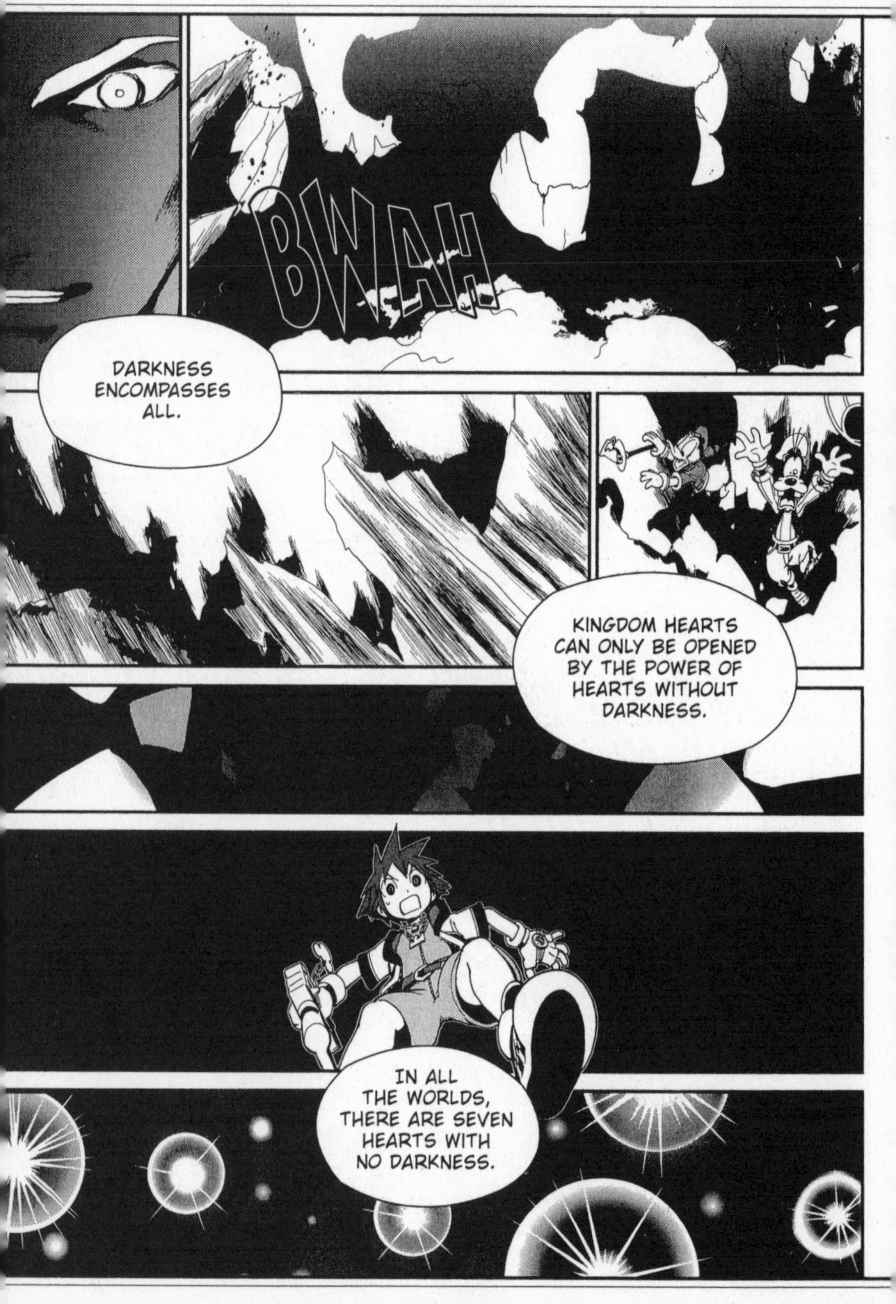
BWAH
DARKNESS ENCOMPASSES ALL.
KINGDOM HEARTS CAN ONLY BE OPENED BY THE POWER OF HEARTS WITHOUT DARKNESS.
IN ALL THE WORLDS, THERE ARE SEVEN HEARTS WITH NO DARKNESS.

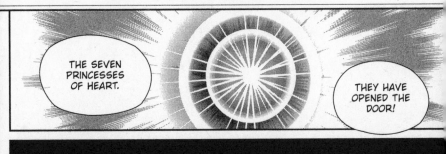

THE SEVEN PRINCESSES OF HEART.

THEY HAVE OPENED THE DOOR!

BEHOLD THE ENDLESS ABYSS!

WITHIN LIES THE HEART OF ALL WORLDS— KINGDOM HEARTS!

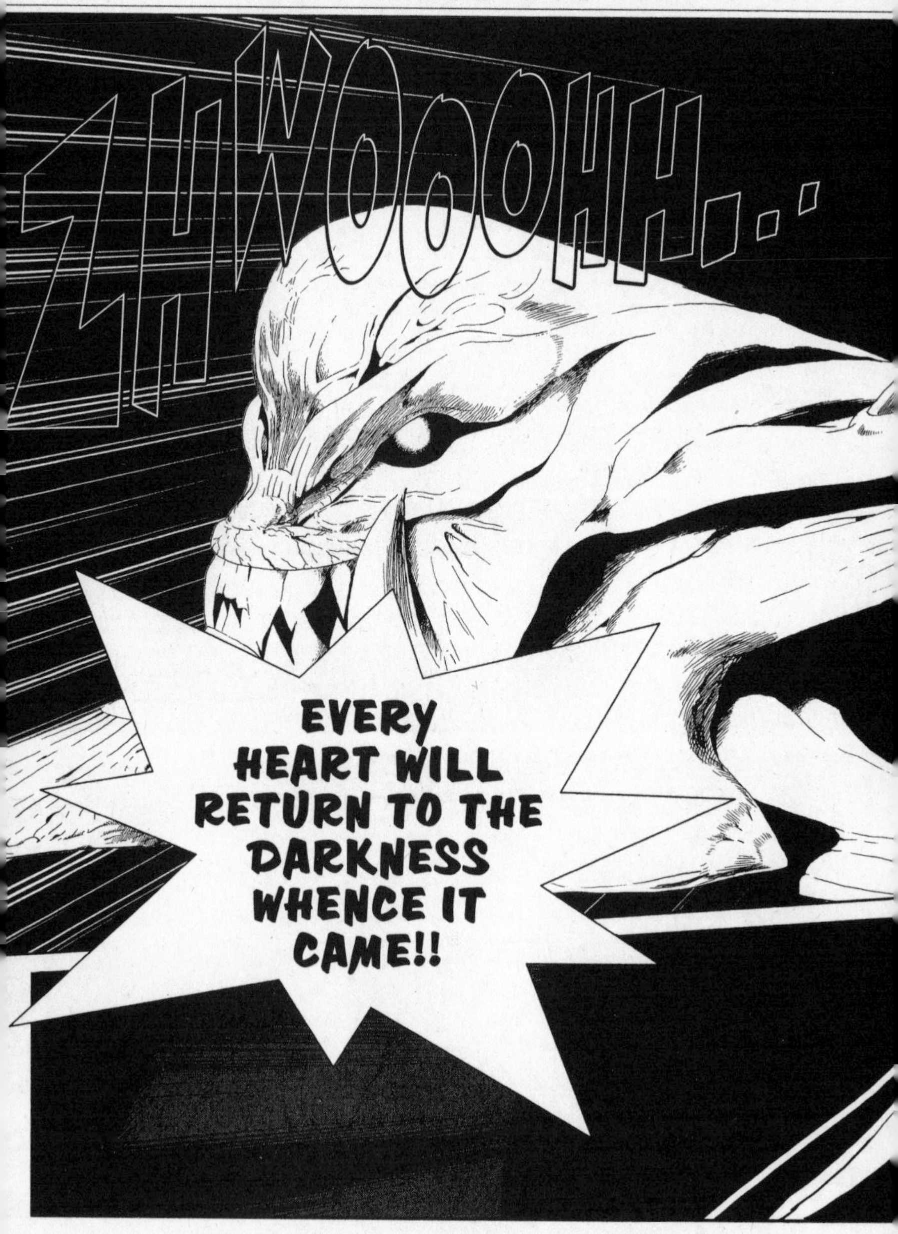
ZHWOOOHH...
EVERY HEART WILL RETURN TO THE DARKNESS WHENCE IT CAME!!

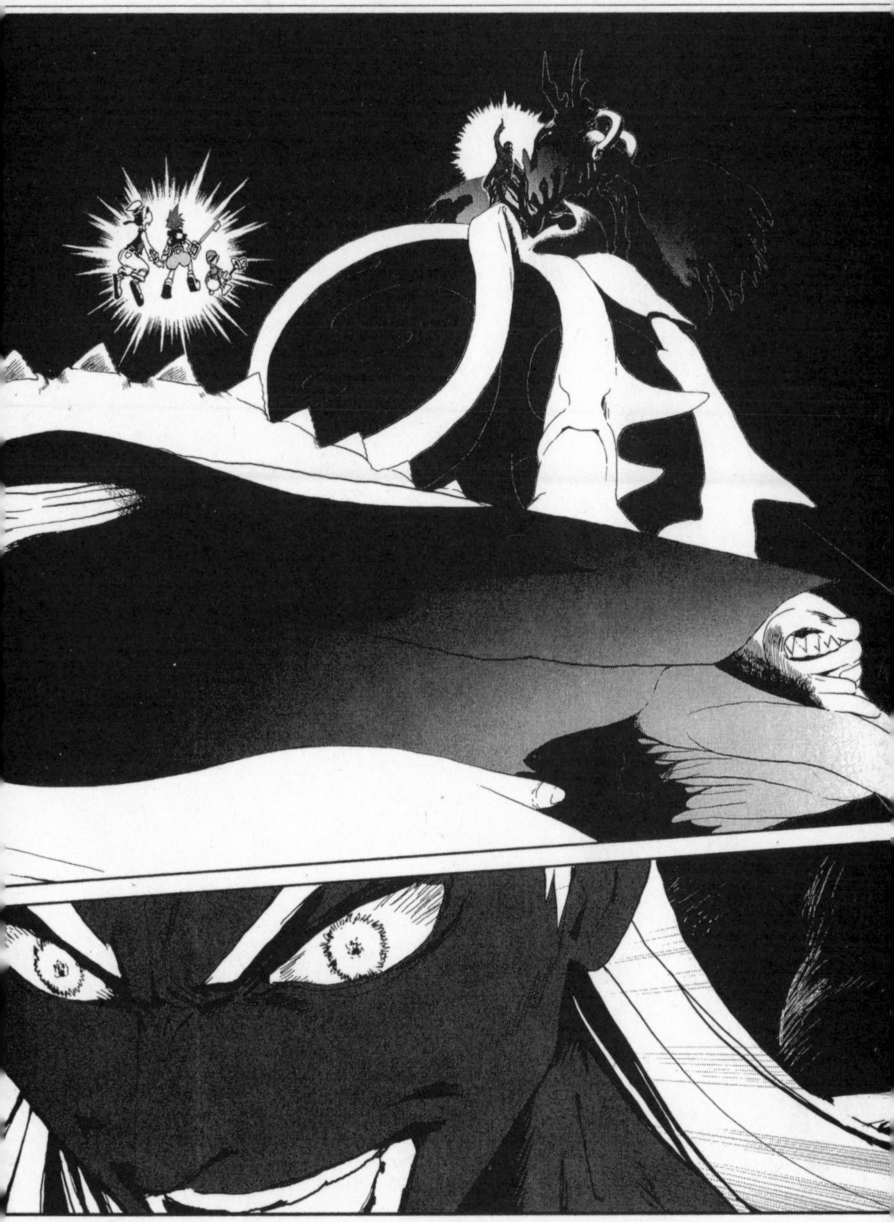

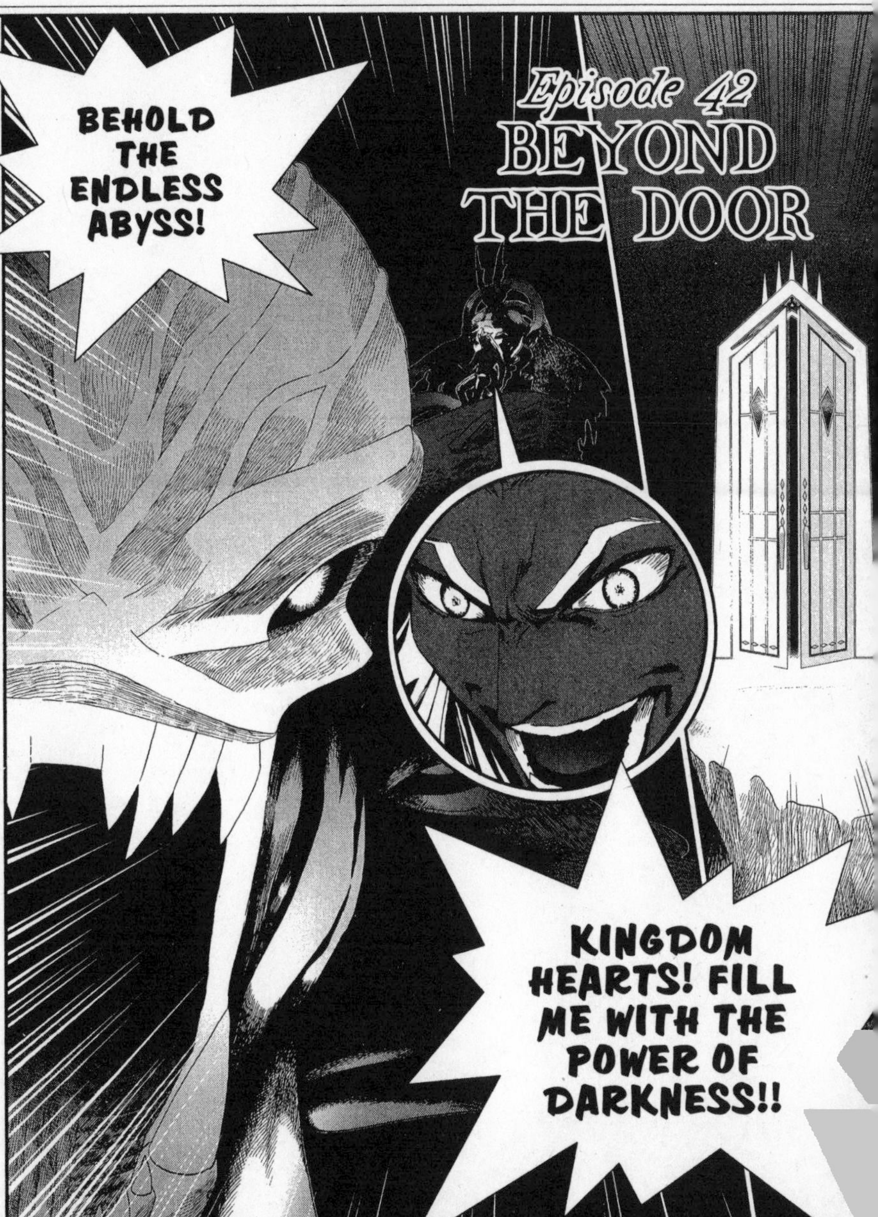
BEHOLD THE ENDLESS ABYSS!
Episode 42 BEYOND THE DOOR
KINGDOM HEARTS! FILL ME WITH THE POWER OF DARKNESS!!

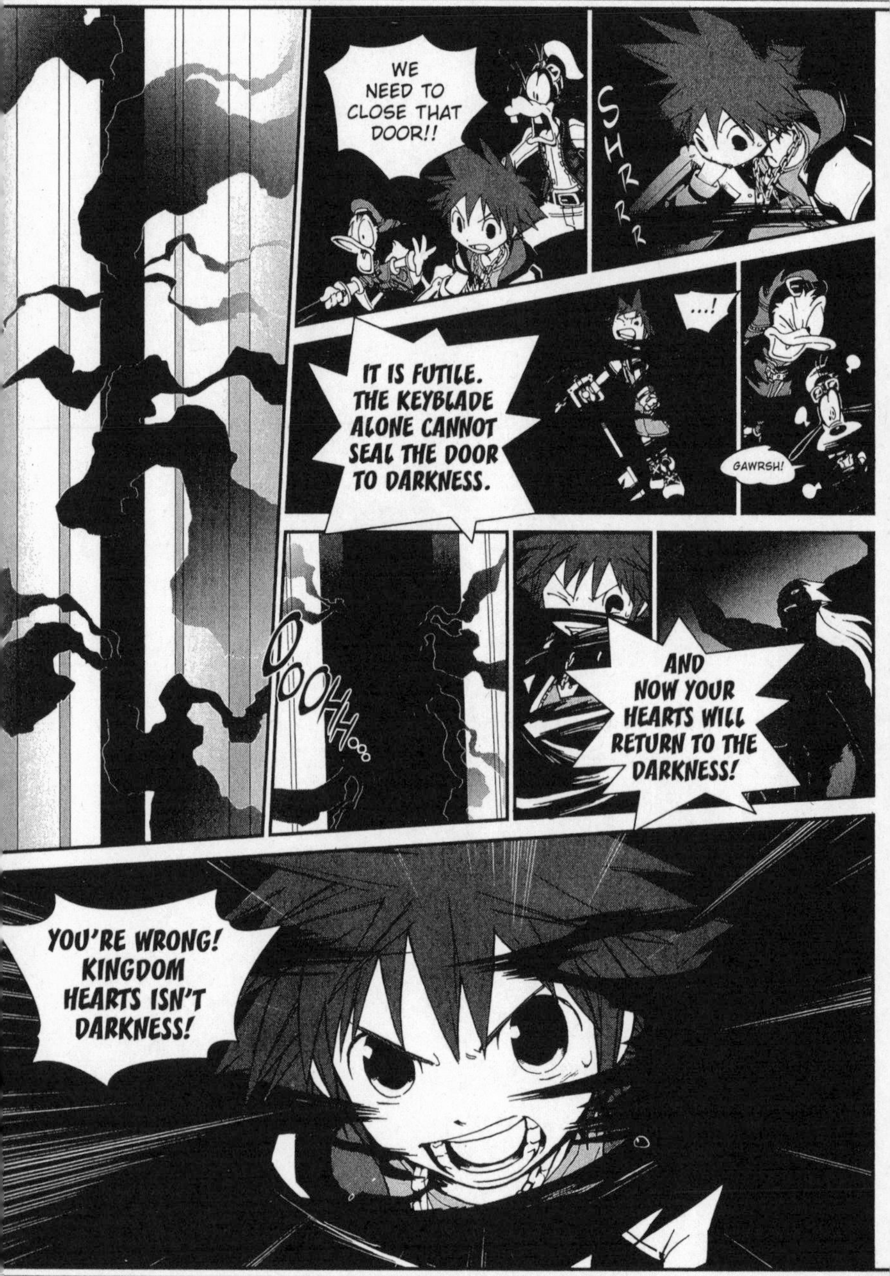
WE NEED TO CLOSE THAT DOOR!!
SHRRR
...!
IT IS FUTILE. THE KEYBLADE ALONE CANNOT SEAL THE DOOR TO DARKNESS.
GAWRSH!
OOOHH...
AND NOW YOUR HEARTS WILL RETURN TO THE DARKNESS!
YOU'RE WRONG! KINGDOM HEARTS ISN'T DARKNESS!

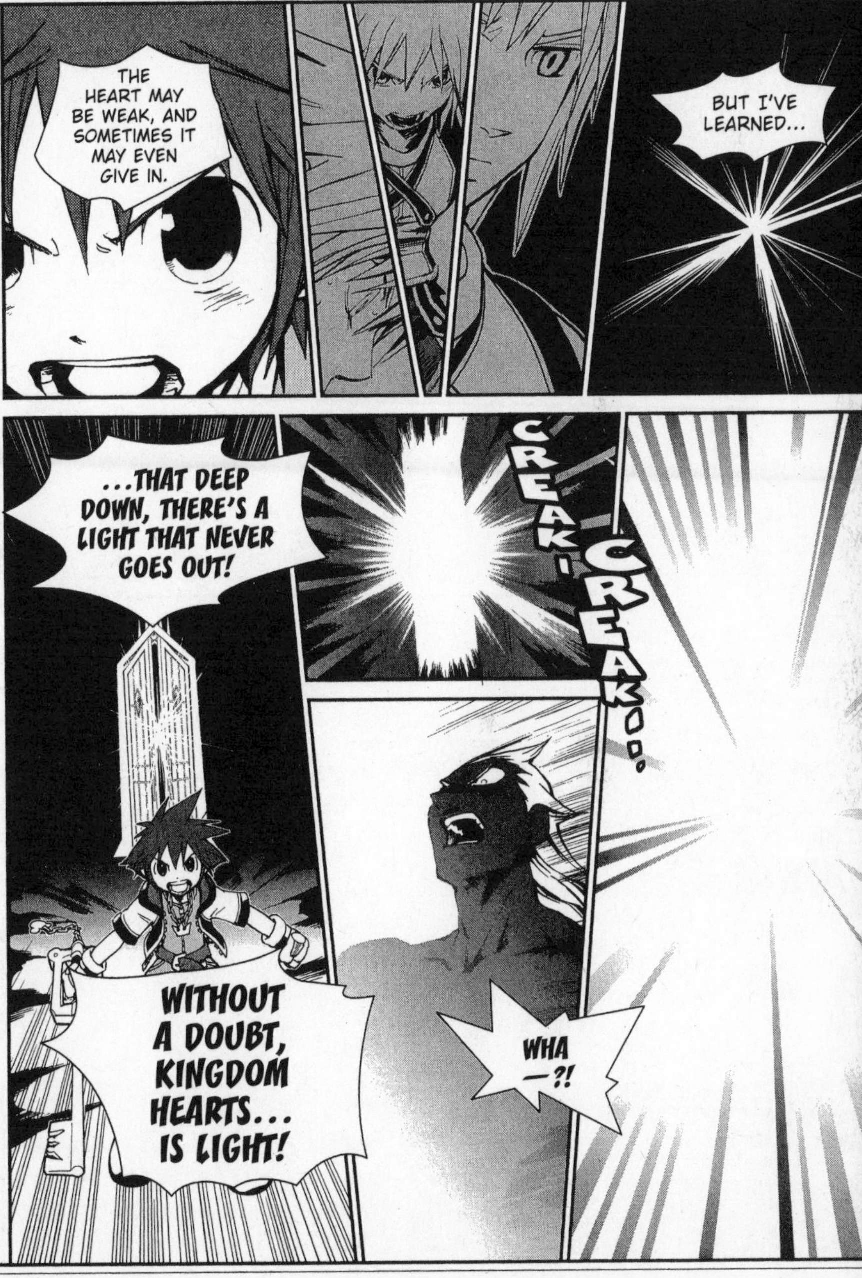
THE HEART MAY BE WEAK, AND SOMETIMES IT MAY EVEN GIVE IN.
BUT I'VE LEARNED...
...THAT DEEP DOWN, THERE'S A LIGHT THAT NEVER GOES OUT!
CREAK. CREAKOO..
WITHOUT A DOUBT, KINGDOM HEARTS... IS LIGHT!
WHA —?!

LIGHT?! BUT WHY ...?

SO WARM—!!!!!

THAT LIGHT CAME FROM THE HEARTS OF ALL MY FRIENDS.

I KNOW IT!

LET'S CLOSE THE DOOR!

ALL RIGHT!

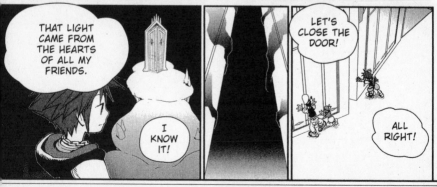

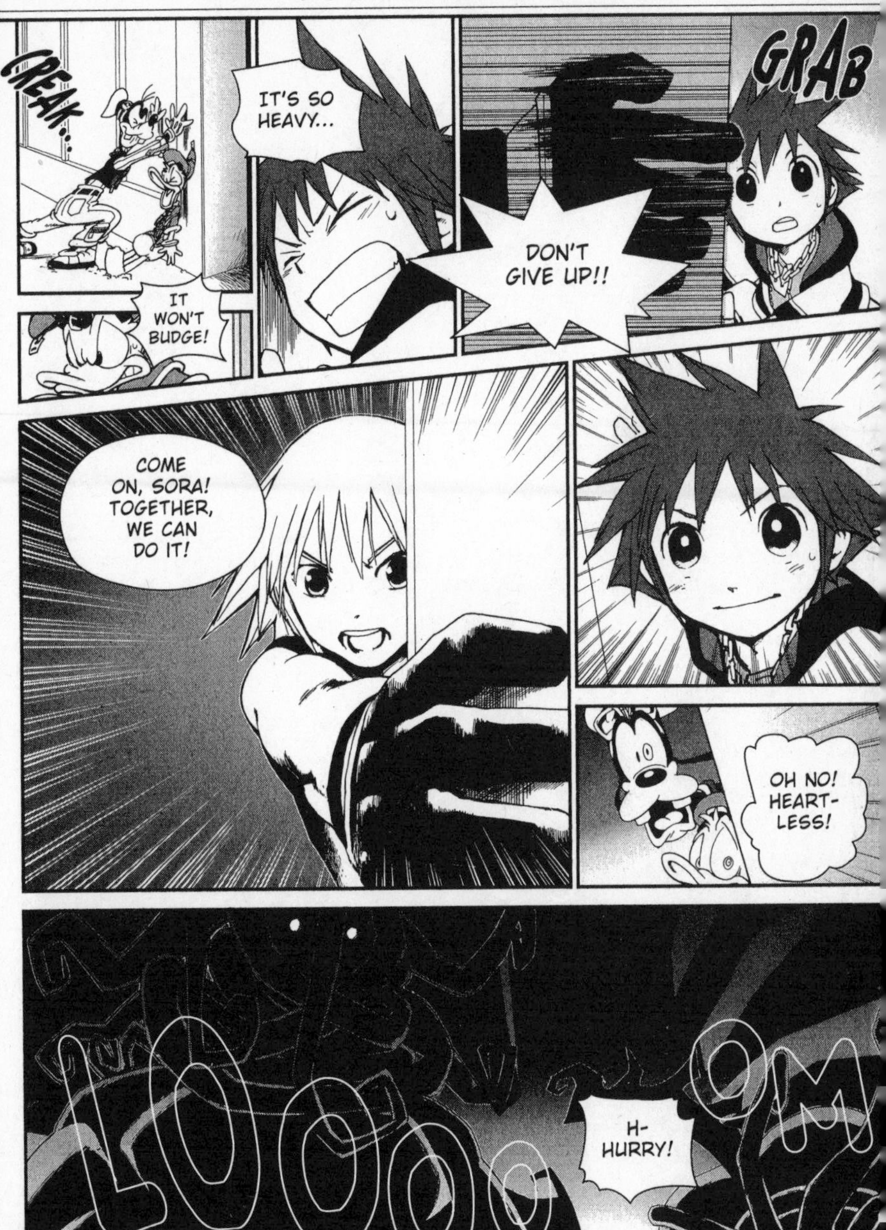
CREAK...
IT WON'T BUDGE!
IT'S SO HEAVY...
DON'T GIVE UP!!
GRAB
COME ON, SORA! TOGETHER, WE CAN DO IT!
OH NO! HEART-LESS!
LOOOOOOM
H-HURRY!

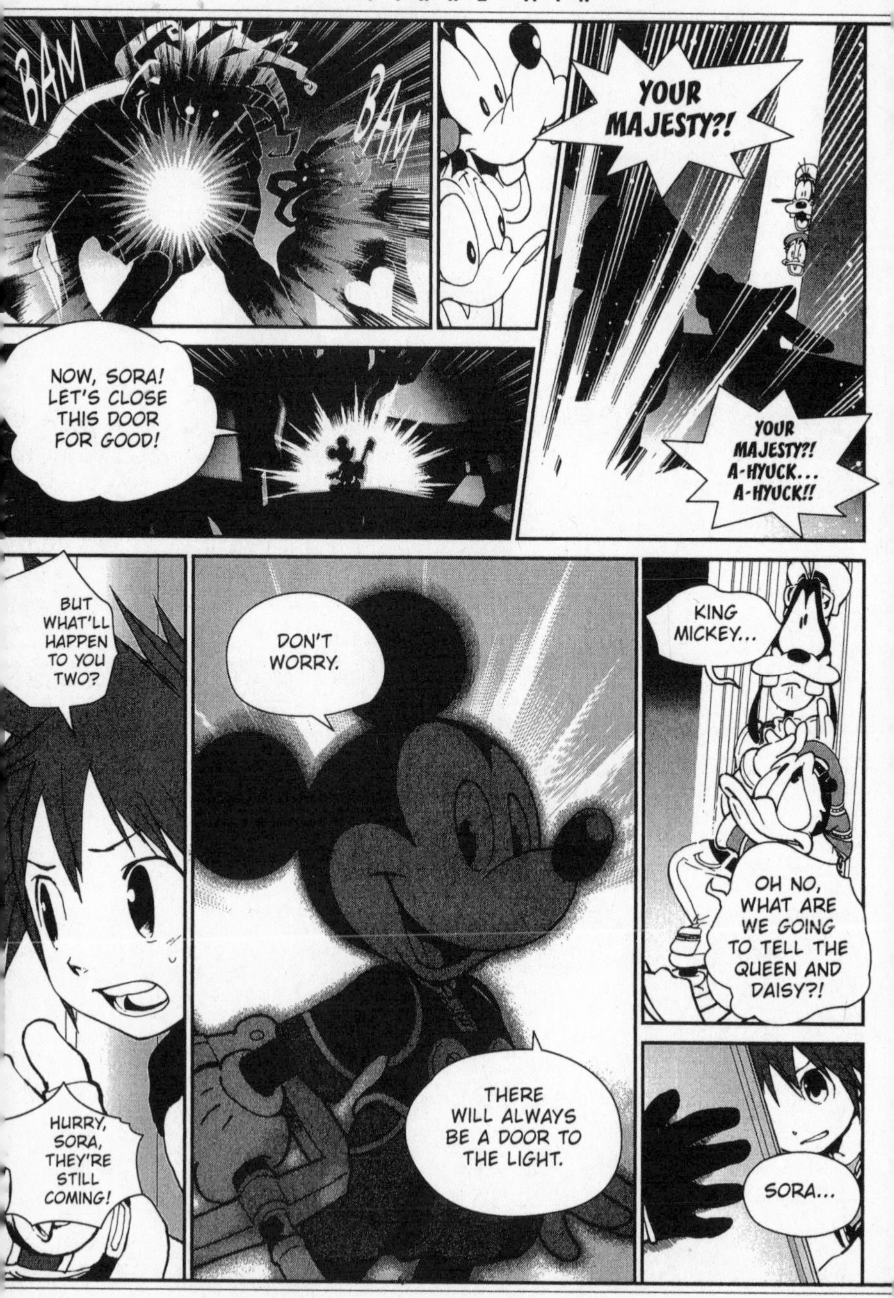
BAM
BAM
YOUR MAJESTY?!
NOW, SORA! LET'S CLOSE THIS DOOR FOR GOOD!
YOUR MAJESTY?! A-HYUCK... A-HYUCK!!
BUT WHAT'LL HAPPEN TO YOU TWO?
HURRY, SORA, THEY'RE STILL COMING!
DON'T WORRY.
THERE WILL ALWAYS BE A DOOR TO THE LIGHT.
KING MICKEY...
OH NO, WHAT ARE WE GOING TO TELL THE QUEEN AND DAISY?!
SORA...

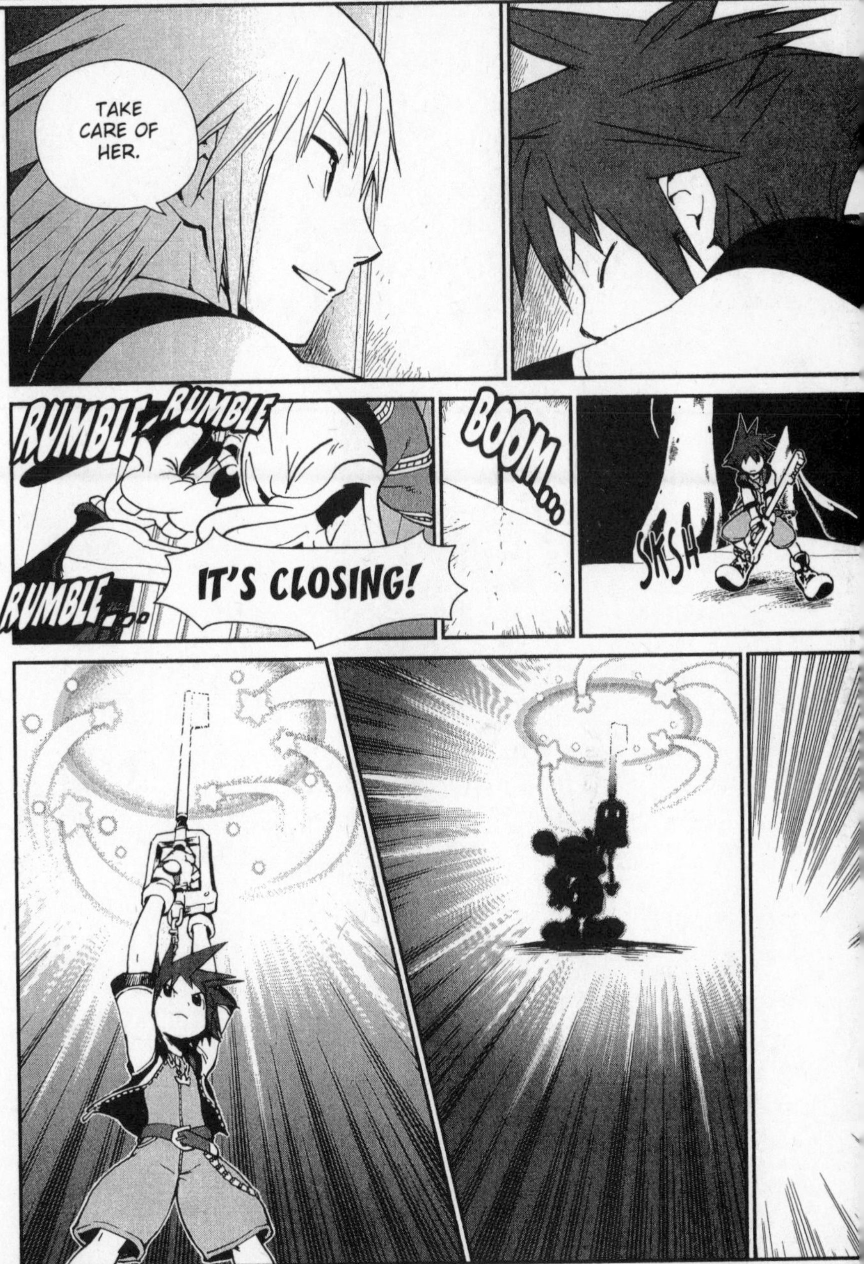
TAKE CARE OF HER.
RUMBLE RUMBLE
RUMBLE...
IT'S CLOSING!
BOOM...
SKSH

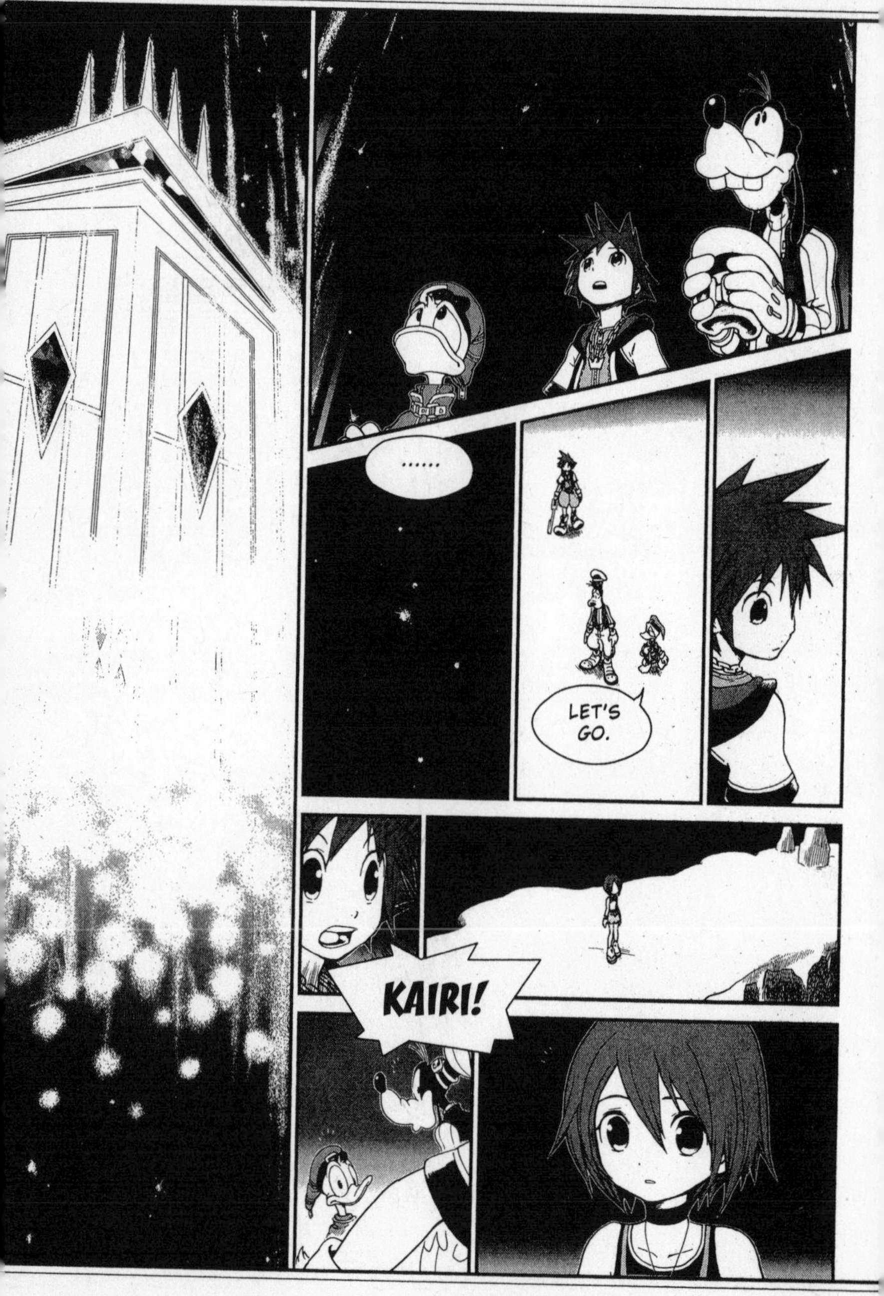
......
LET'S GO.
KAIRI!

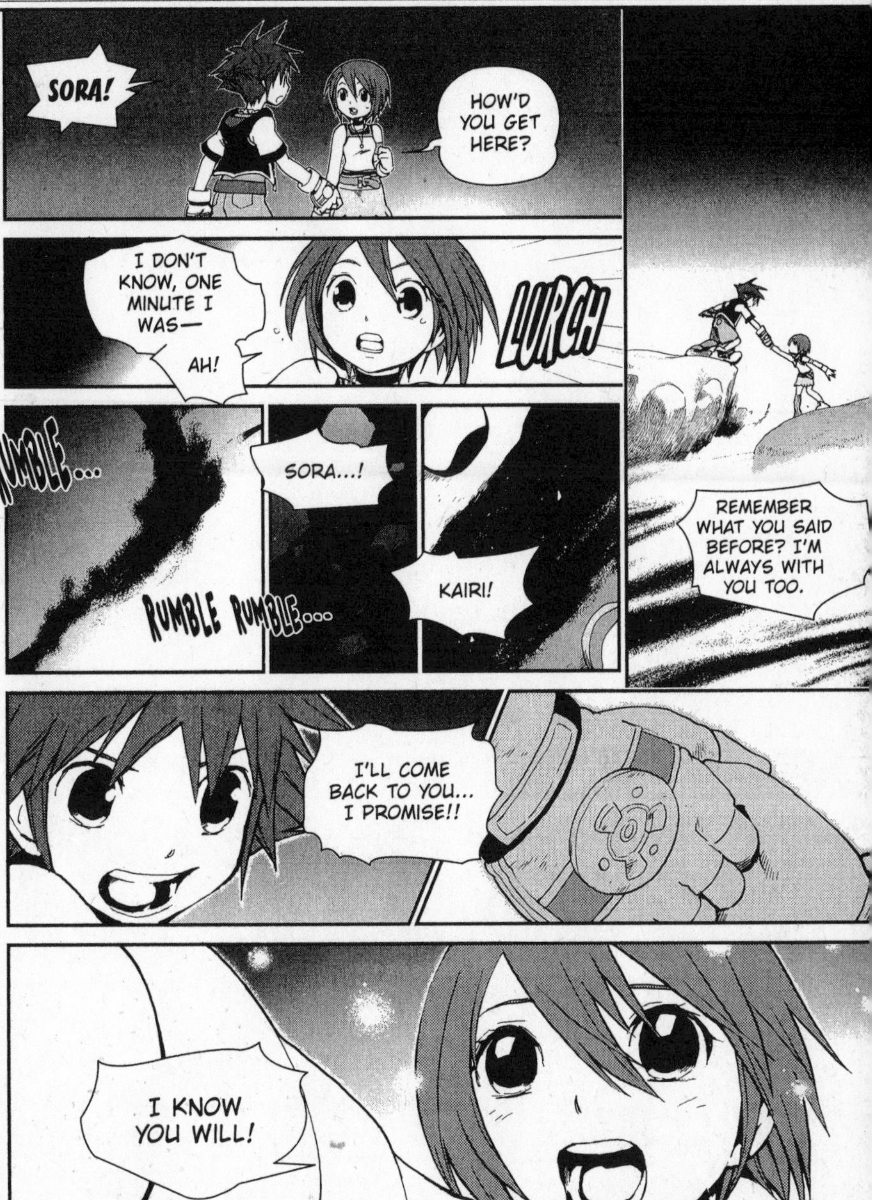
SORA!
HOW'D YOU GET HERE?
I DON'T KNOW, ONE MINUTE I WAS—
AH!
LURCH
RUMBLE...
RUMBLE RUMBLE...
SORA...!
KAIRI!
REMEMBER WHAT YOU SAID BEFORE? I'M ALWAYS WITH YOU TOO.
I'LL COME BACK TO YOU... I PROMISE!!
I KNOW YOU WILL!

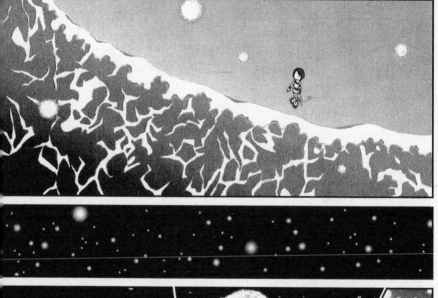

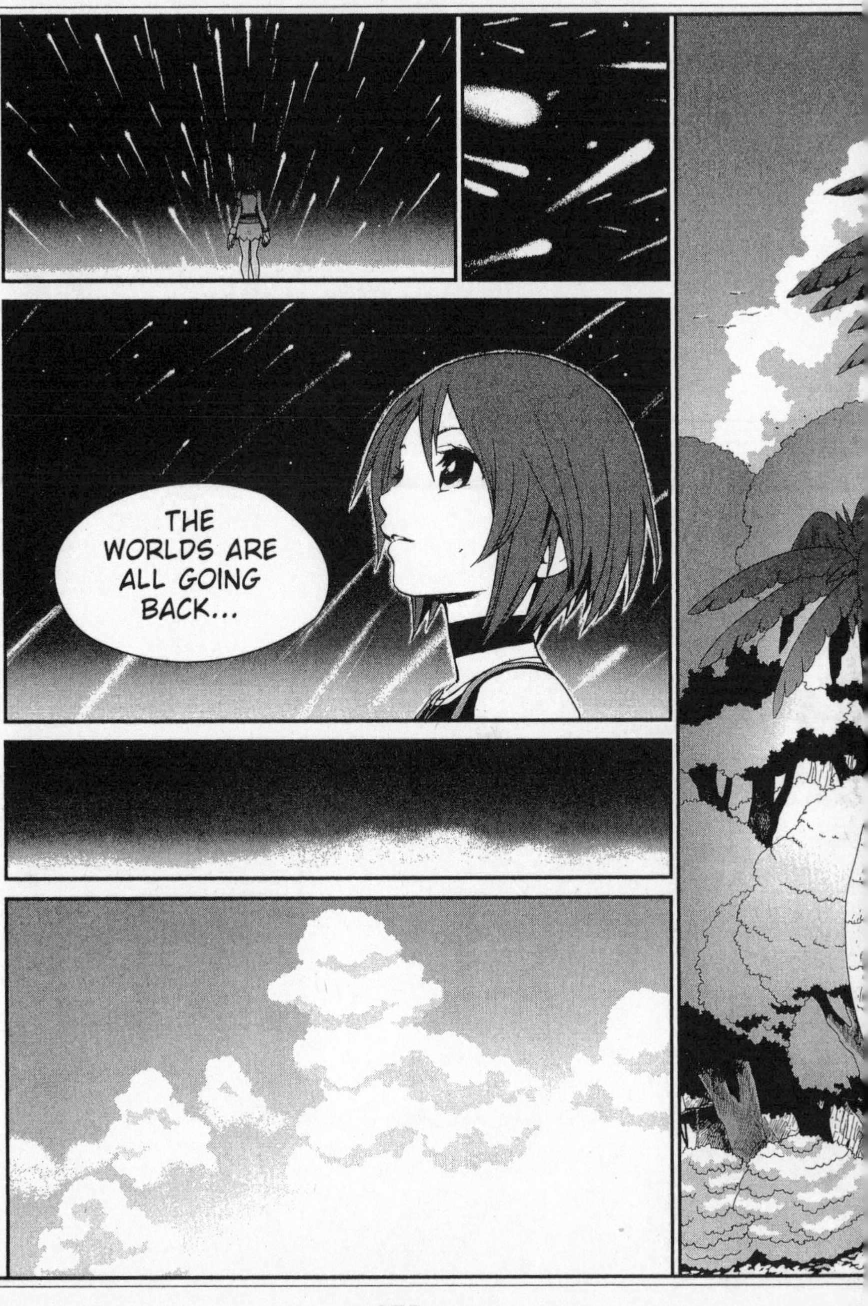
THE WORLDS ARE ALL GOING BACK...

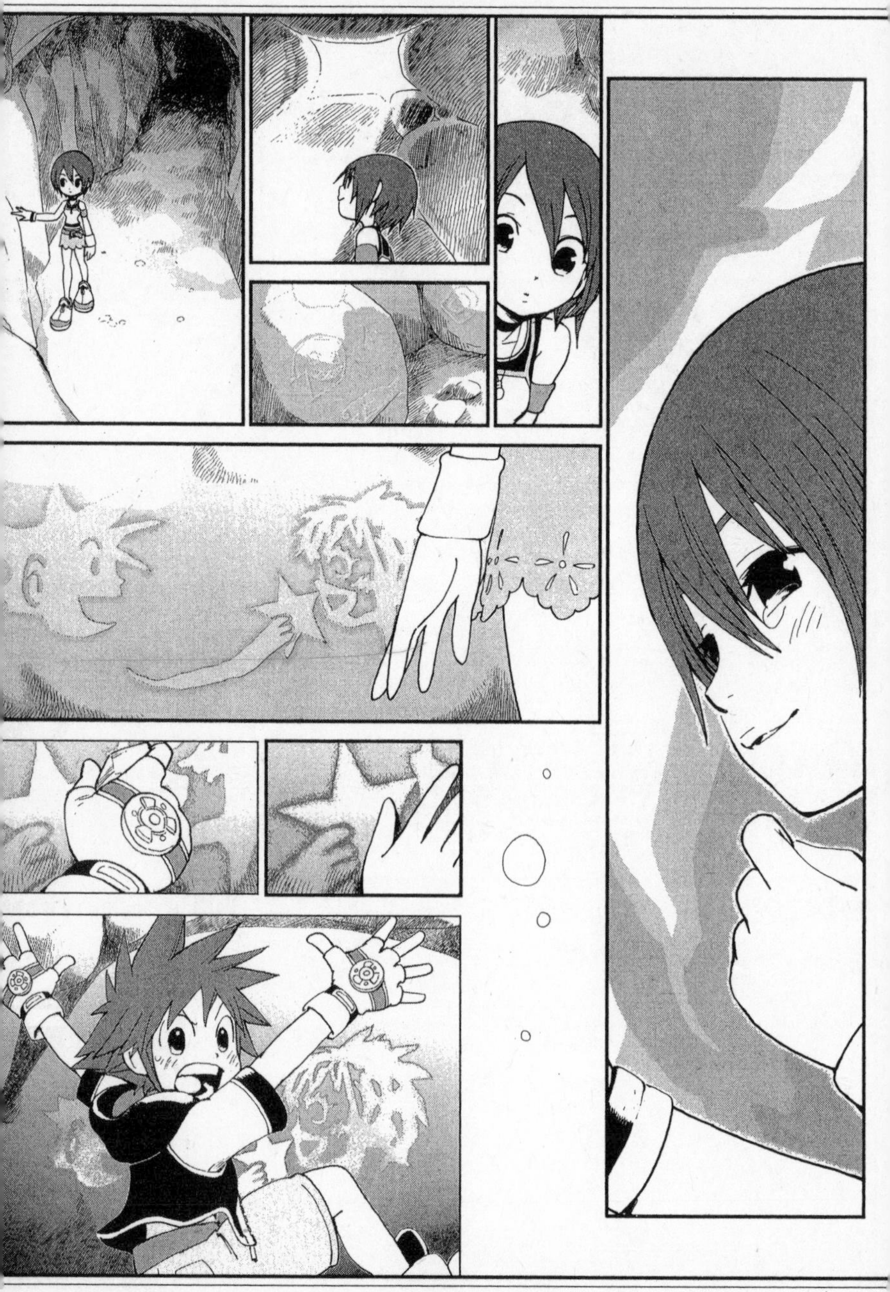

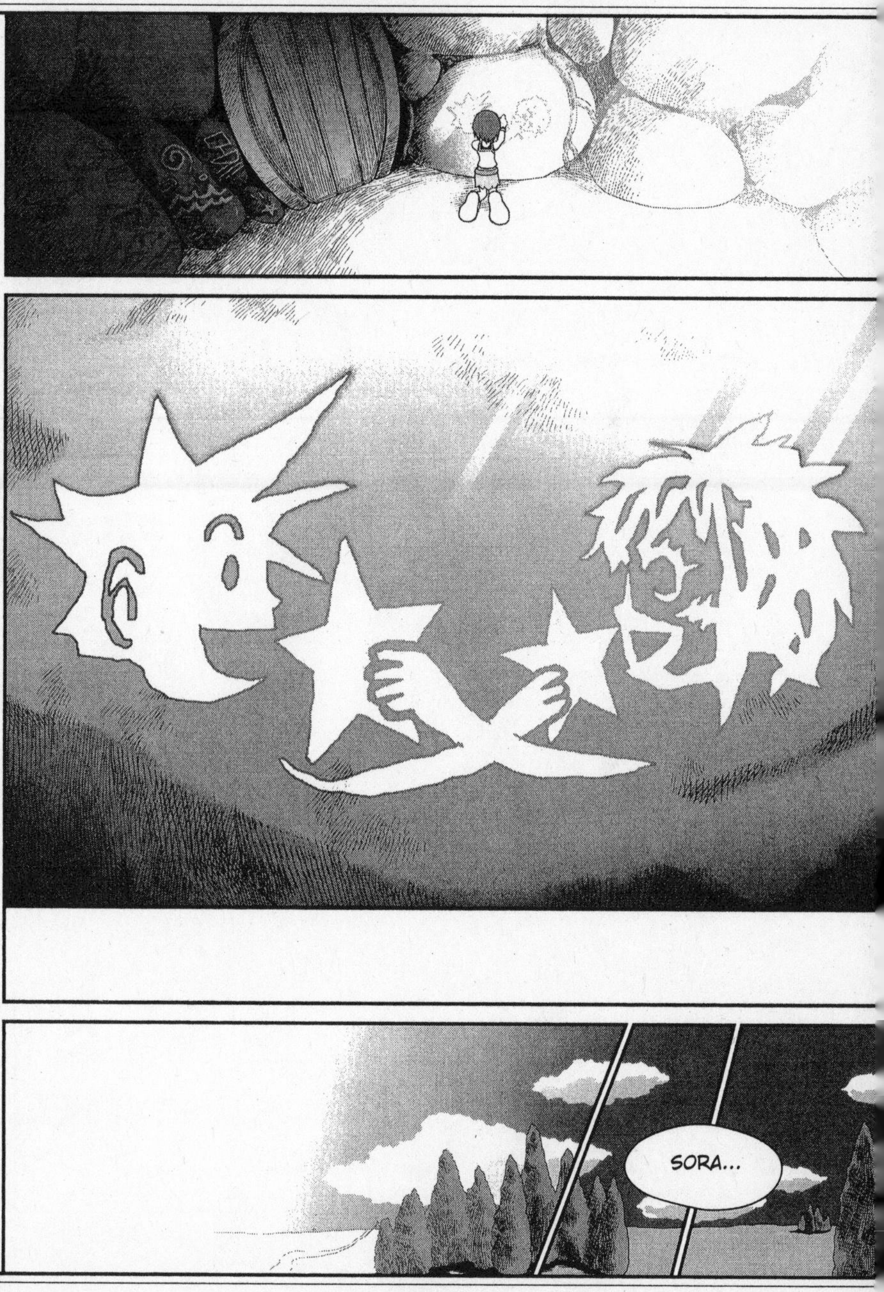
SORA...

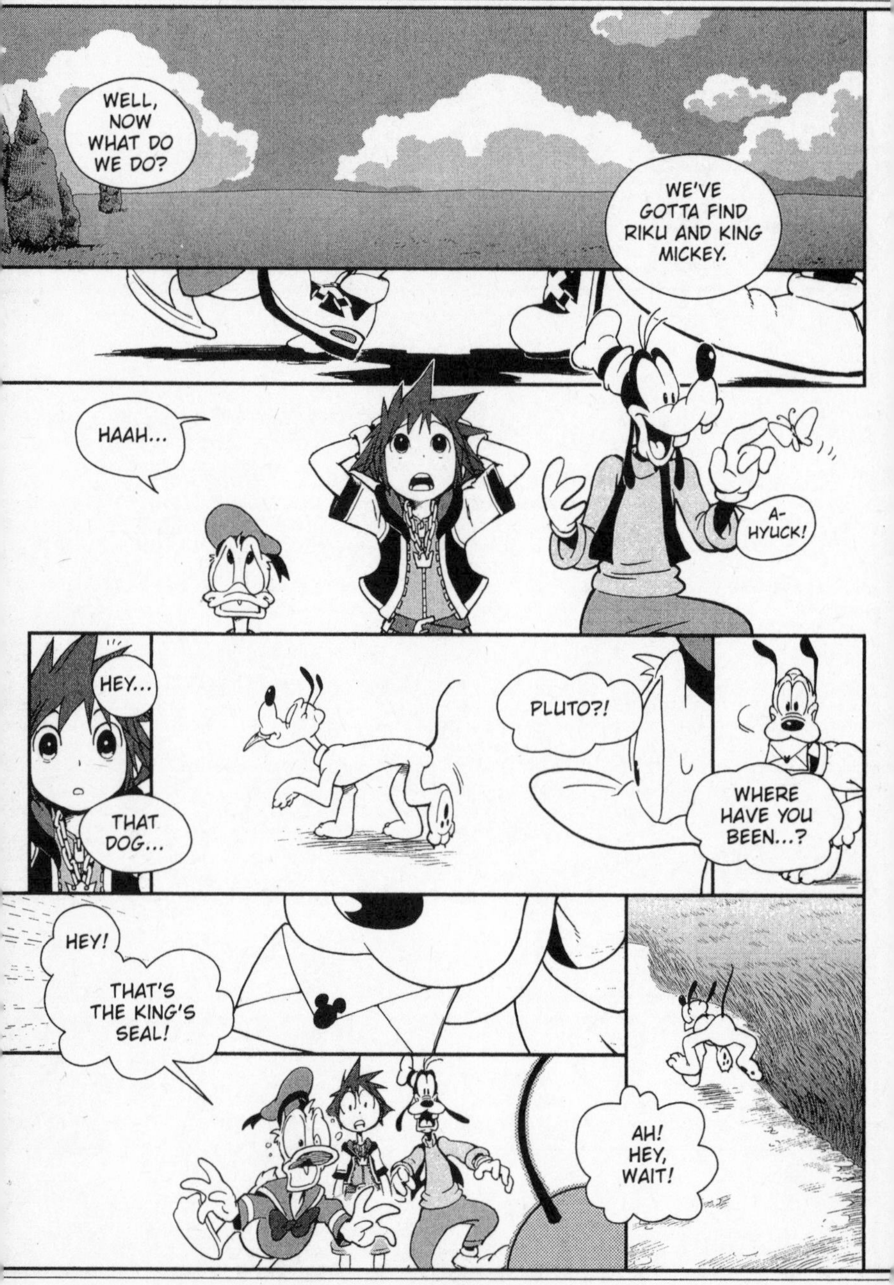
WELL, NOW WHAT DO WE DO?
WE'VE GOTTA FIND RIKU AND KING MICKEY.
HAAH...
A-HYUCK!
HEY...
THAT DOG...
PLUTO?!
WHERE HAVE YOU BEEN...?
HEY!
THAT'S THE KING'S SEAL!
AH! HEY, WAIT!

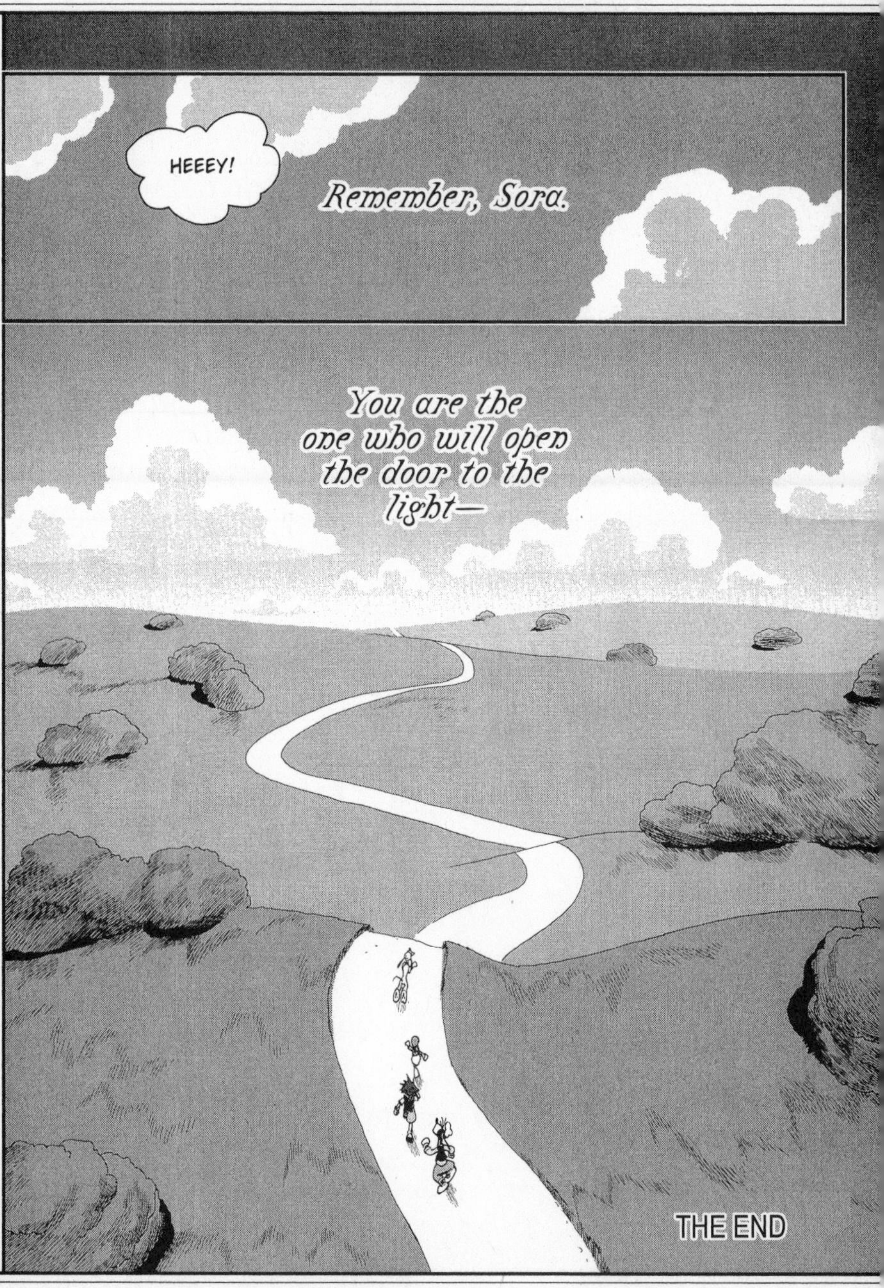
HEEEY!
Remember, Sora.
You are the one who will open the door to the light—
THE END

Special Short I: WINNIE THE POOH

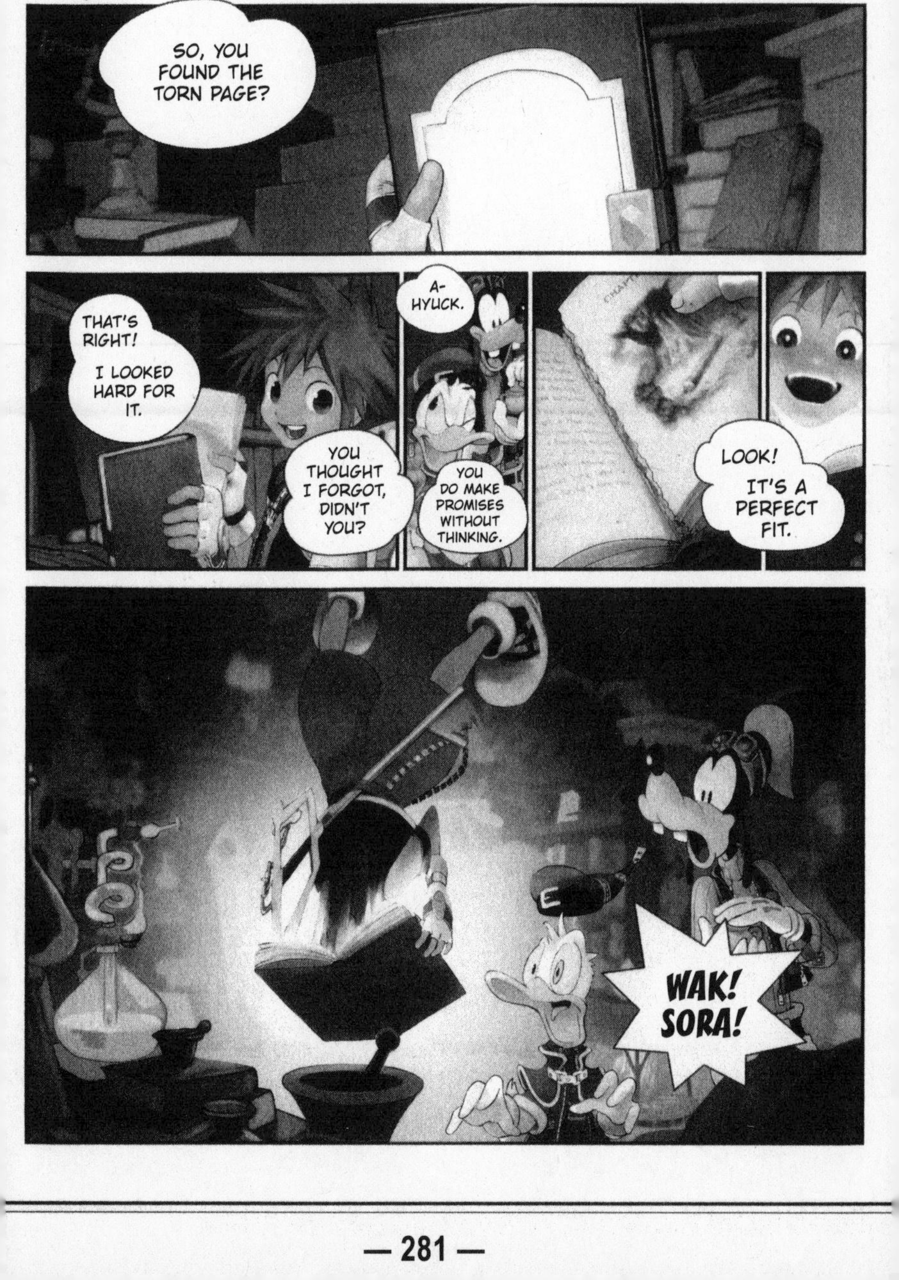
SO, YOU FOUND THE TORN PAGE?
THAT'S RIGHT!
I LOOKED HARD FOR IT.
YOU THOUGHT I FORGOT, DIDN'T YOU?
A-HYUCK.
YOU DO MAKE PROMISES WITHOUT THINKING.
LOOK!
IT'S A PERFECT FIT.
WAK! SORA!

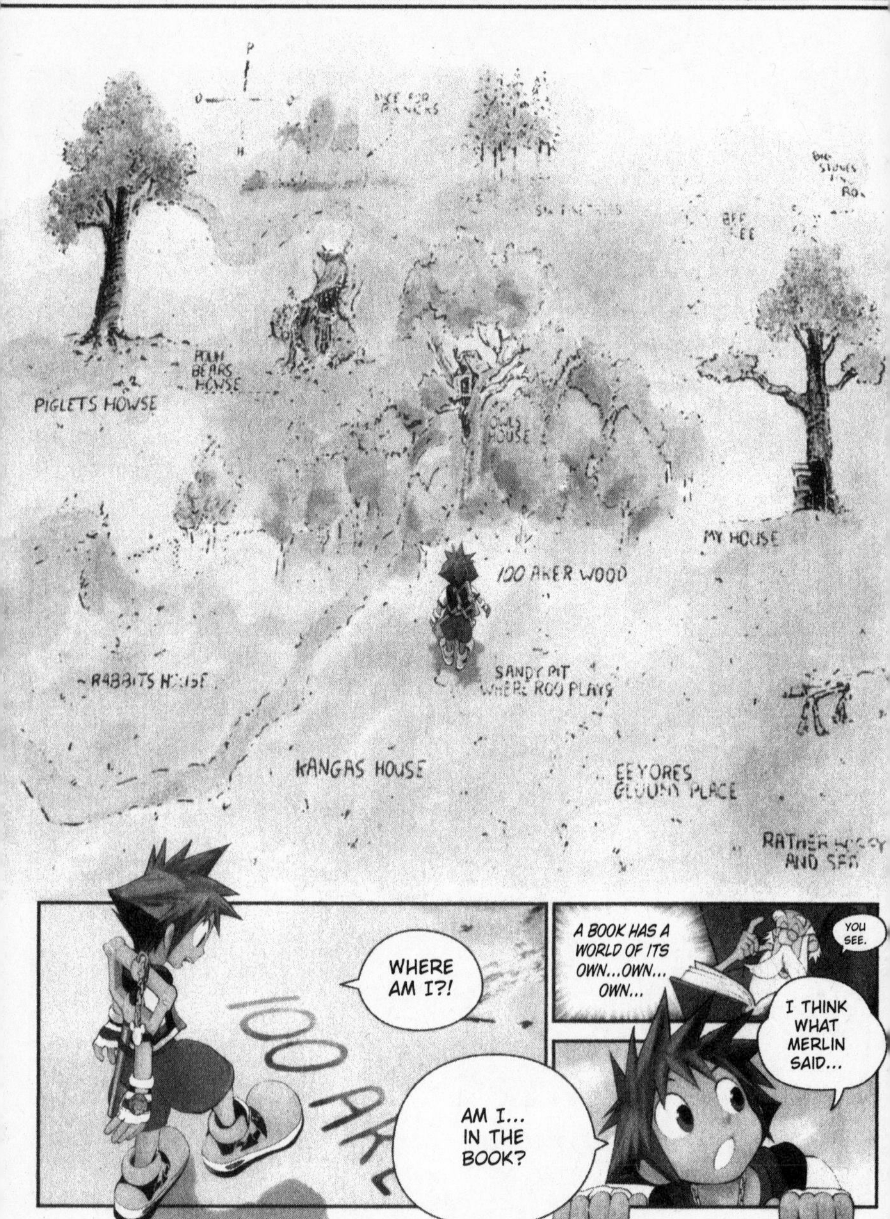
PIGLETS HOWSE
POOH BEARS HOWSE
OWLS HOUSE
MY HOUSE
100 AKER WOOD
RABBITS HOUSE
SANDY PIT WHERE ROO PLAYS
KANGAS HOUSE
EEYORES
WHERE AM I?!
100 AKE
A BOOK HAS A WORLD OF ITS OWN...OWN... OWN...
YOU SEE.
I THINK WHAT MERLIN SAID...
AM I... IN THE BOOK?

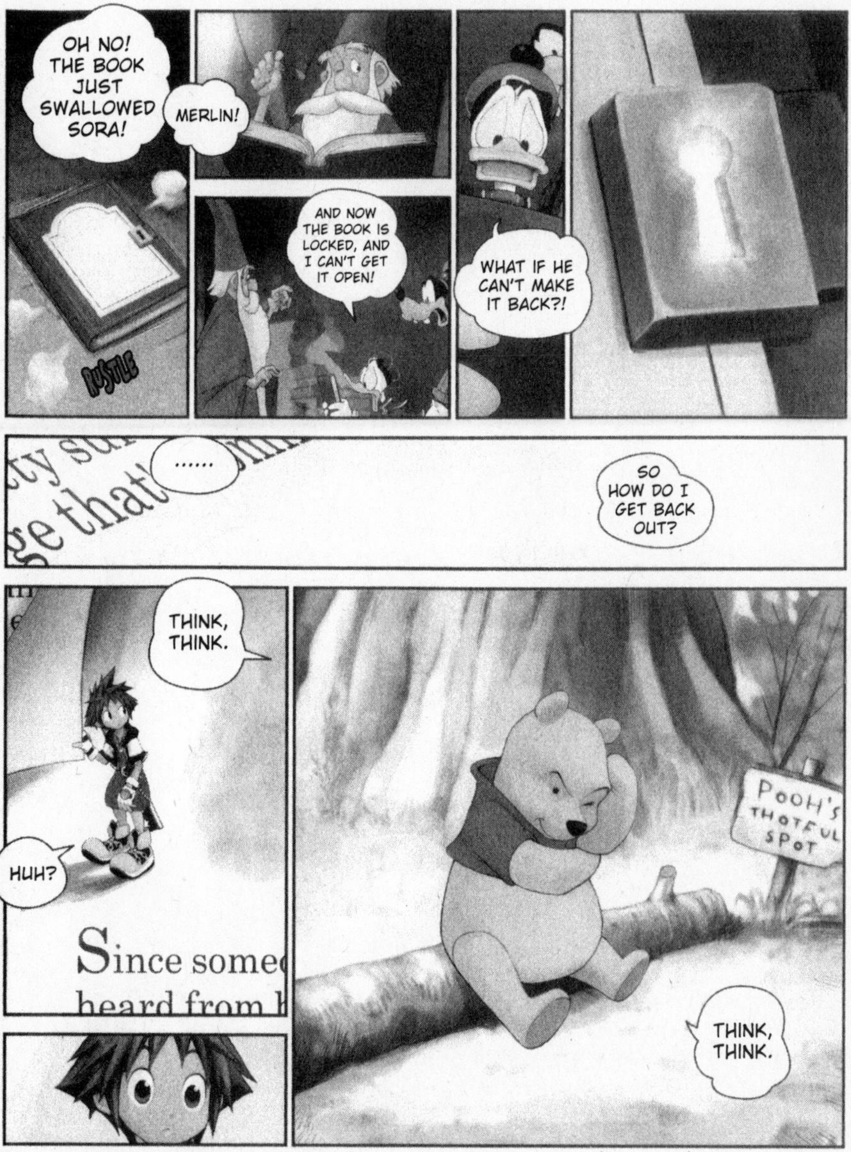
OH NO! THE BOOK JUST SWALLOWED SORA!
RUSTLE
MERLIN!
AND NOW THE BOOK IS LOCKED, AND I CAN'T GET IT OPEN!
WHAT IF HE CAN'T MAKE IT BACK?!
......
SO HOW DO I GET BACK OUT?
THINK, THINK.
HUH?
POOH'S THOTFUL SPOT
THINK, THINK.

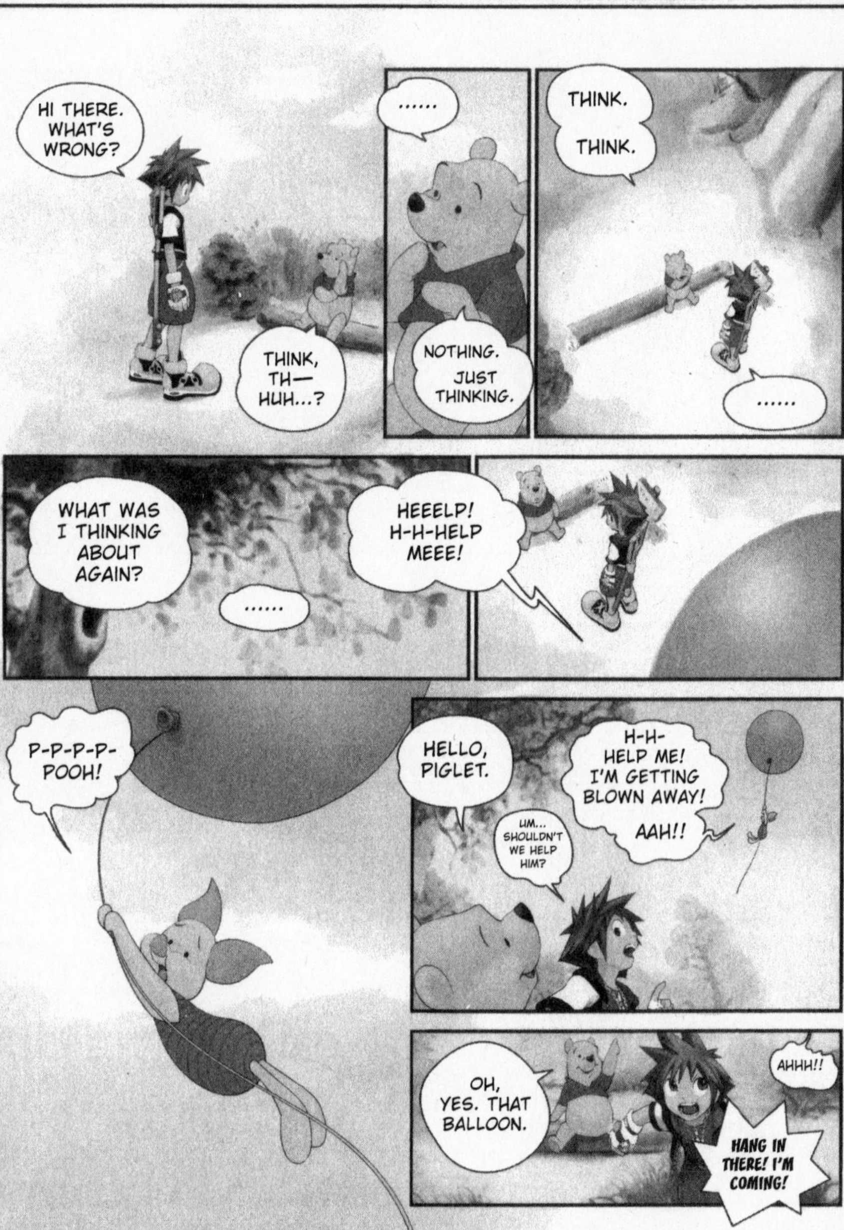
HI THERE. WHAT'S WRONG?
THINK, TH— HUH...?
......
NOTHING. JUST THINKING.
THINK. THINK.
......
WHAT WAS I THINKING ABOUT AGAIN?
......
HEEELP! H-H-HELP MEEE!
P-P-P-P-POOH!
HELLO, PIGLET.
H-H-HELP ME! I'M GETTING BLOWN AWAY!
AAH!!
UM... SHOULDN'T WE HELP HIM?
OH, YES. THAT BALLOON.
AHHH!!
HANG IN THERE! I'M COMING!

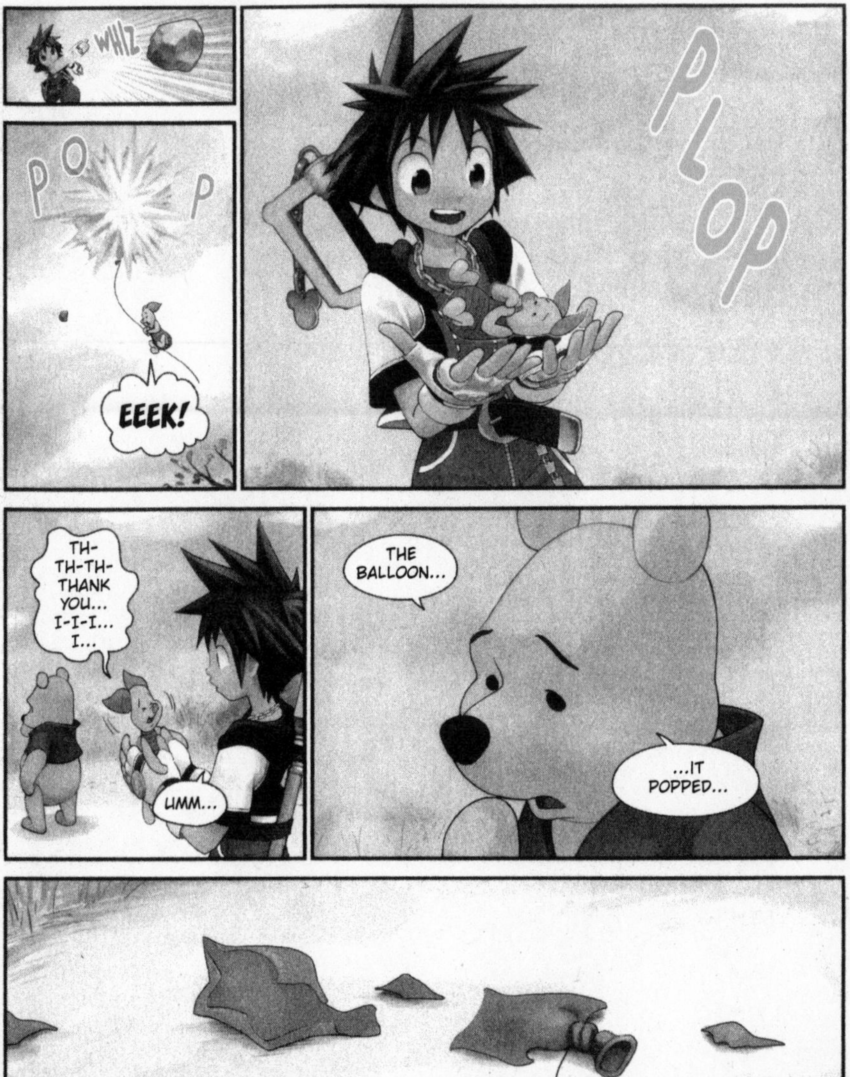
WHIZ
POP
EEEK!
PLOP
TH-TH-TH-THANK YOU... I-I-I... I...
UMM...
THE BALLOON...
...IT POPPED...

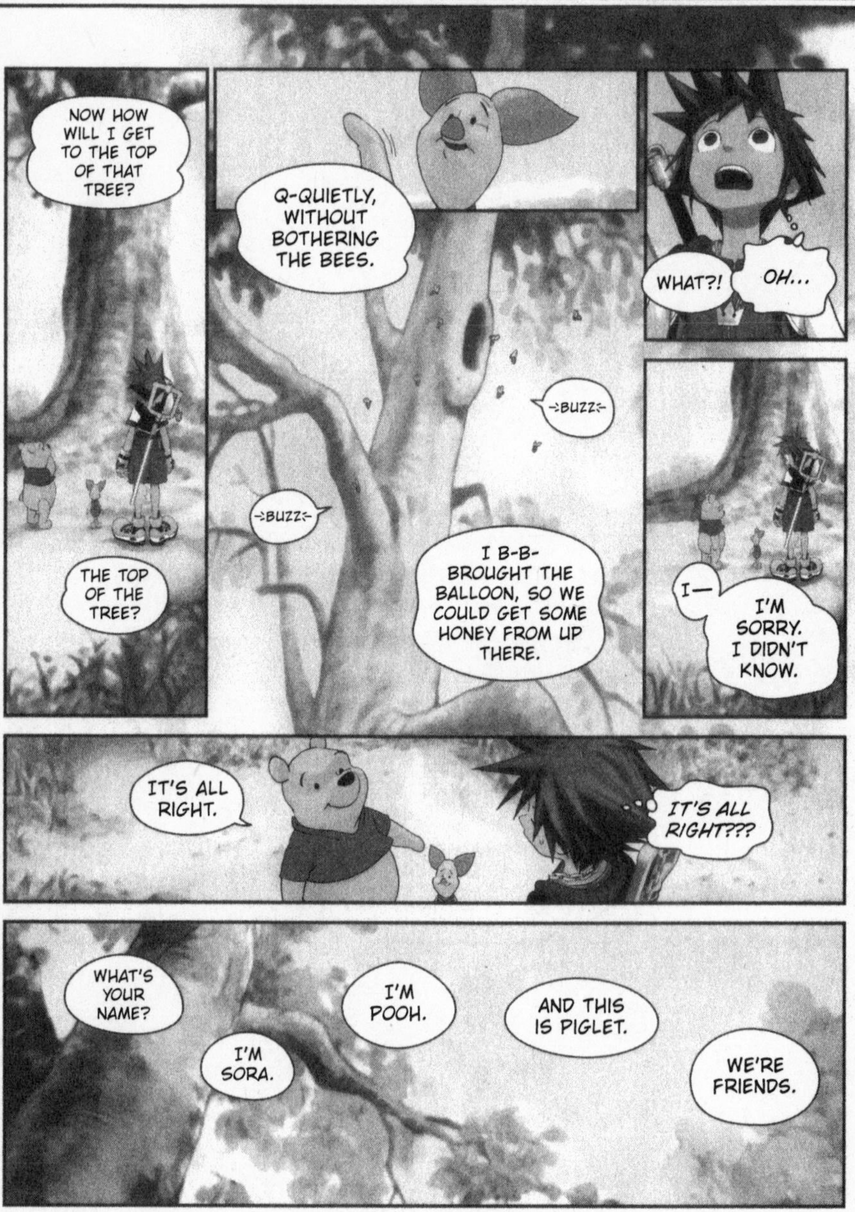
NOW HOW WILL I GET TO THE TOP OF THAT TREE?
THE TOP OF THE TREE?
Q-QUIETLY, WITHOUT BOTHERING THE BEES.
-BUZZ-
-BUZZ-
I B-B-BROUGHT THE BALLOON, SO WE COULD GET SOME HONEY FROM UP THERE.
WHAT?!
OH...
I—
I'M SORRY. I DIDN'T KNOW.
IT'S ALL RIGHT.
IT'S ALL RIGHT???
WHAT'S YOUR NAME?
I'M SORA.
I'M POOH.
AND THIS IS PIGLET.
WE'RE FRIENDS.

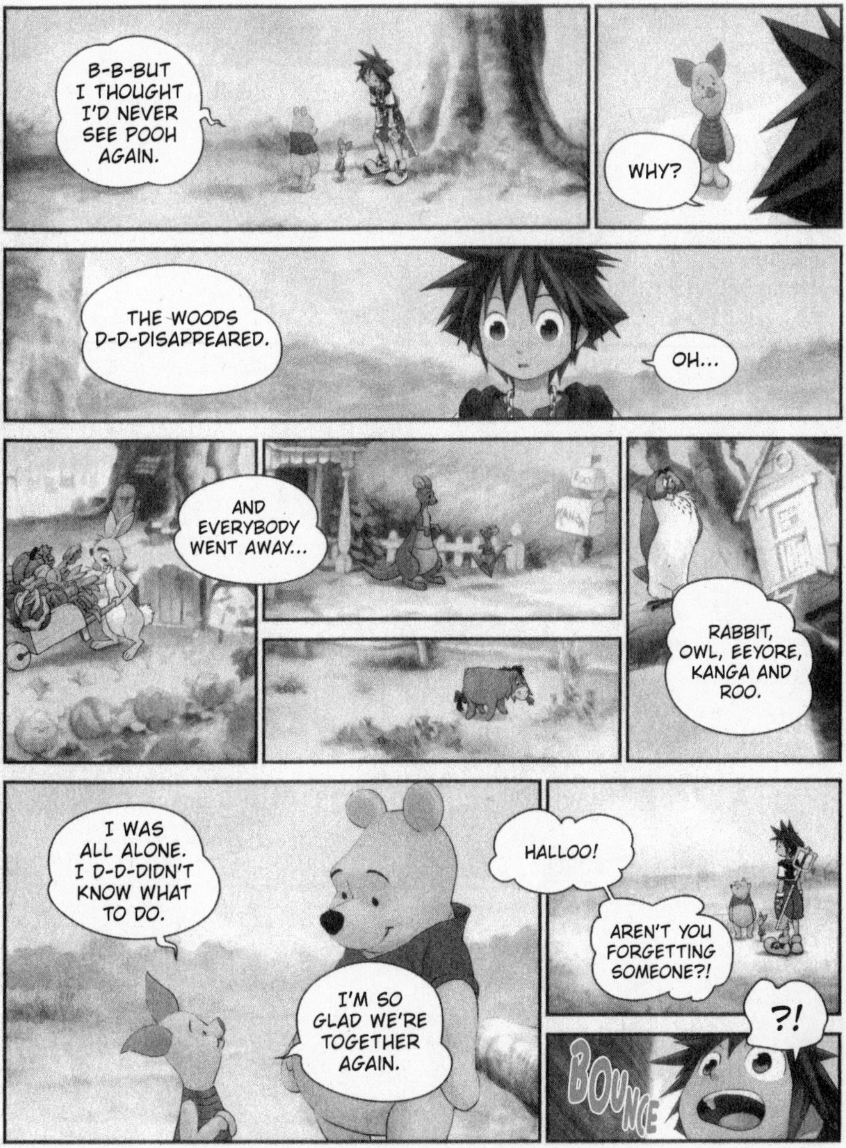
B-B-BUT I THOUGHT I'D NEVER SEE POOH AGAIN.
WHY?
THE WOODS D-D-DISAPPEARED.
OH...
AND EVERYBODY WENT AWAY...
RABBIT, OWL, EEYORE, KANGA AND ROO.
I WAS ALL ALONE. I D-D-DIDN'T KNOW WHAT TO DO.
I'M SO GLAD WE'RE TOGETHER AGAIN.
HALLOO!
AREN'T YOU FORGETTING SOMEONE?!
?!
BOUNCE

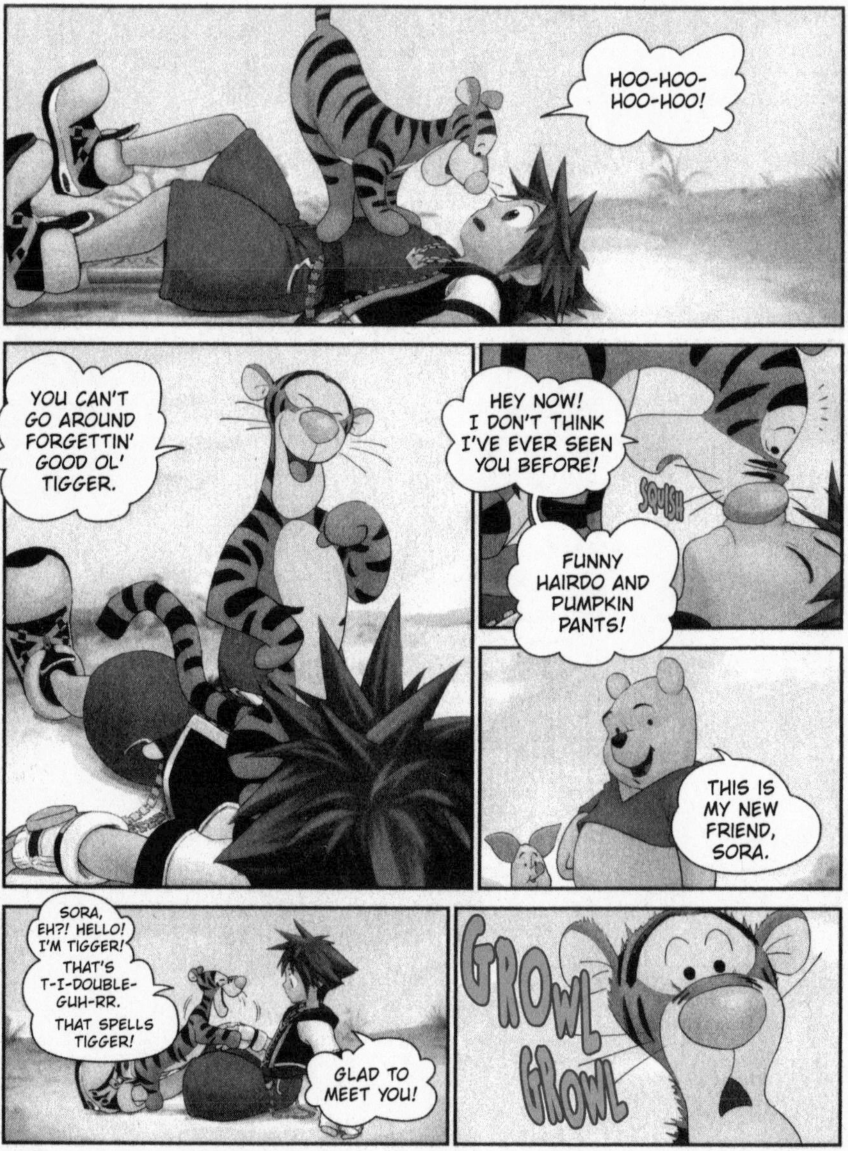
HOO-HOO-HOO-HOO!
YOU CAN'T GO AROUND FORGETTIN' GOOD OL' TIGGER.
HEY NOW! I DON'T THINK I'VE EVER SEEN YOU BEFORE!
SQUISH
FUNNY HAIRDO AND PUMPKIN PANTS!
THIS IS MY NEW FRIEND, SORA.
SORA, EH?! HELLO! I'M TIGGER!
THAT'S T-I-DOUBLE-GUH-RR.
THAT SPELLS TIGGER!
GLAD TO MEET YOU!
GROWL GROWL

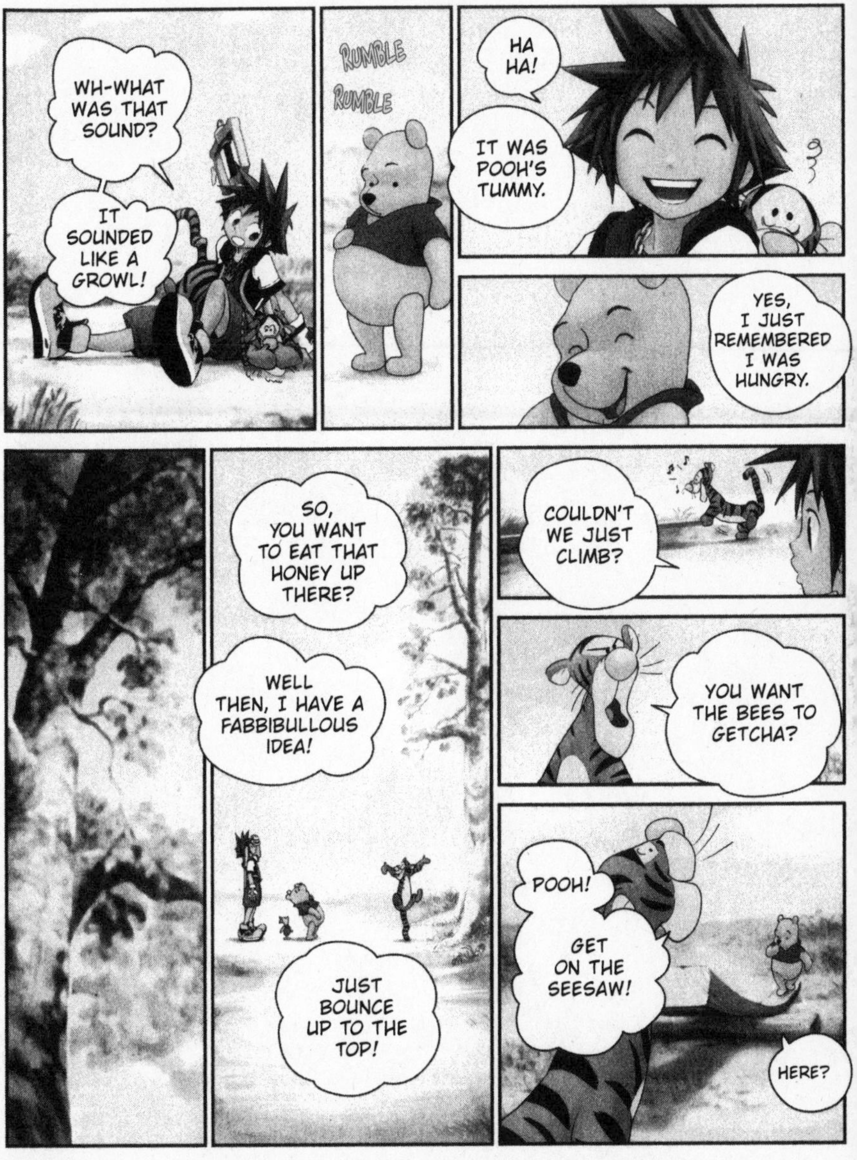
WH-WHAT WAS THAT SOUND?
IT SOUNDED LIKE A GROWL!
RUMBLE
RUMBLE
HA HA!
IT WAS POOH'S TUMMY.
YES, I JUST REMEMBERED I WAS HUNGRY.
SO, YOU WANT TO EAT THAT HONEY UP THERE?
WELL THEN, I HAVE A FABBIBULLOUS IDEA!
JUST BOUNCE UP TO THE TOP!
COULDN'T WE JUST CLIMB?
YOU WANT THE BEES TO GETCHA?
POOH!
GET ON THE SEESAW!
HERE?

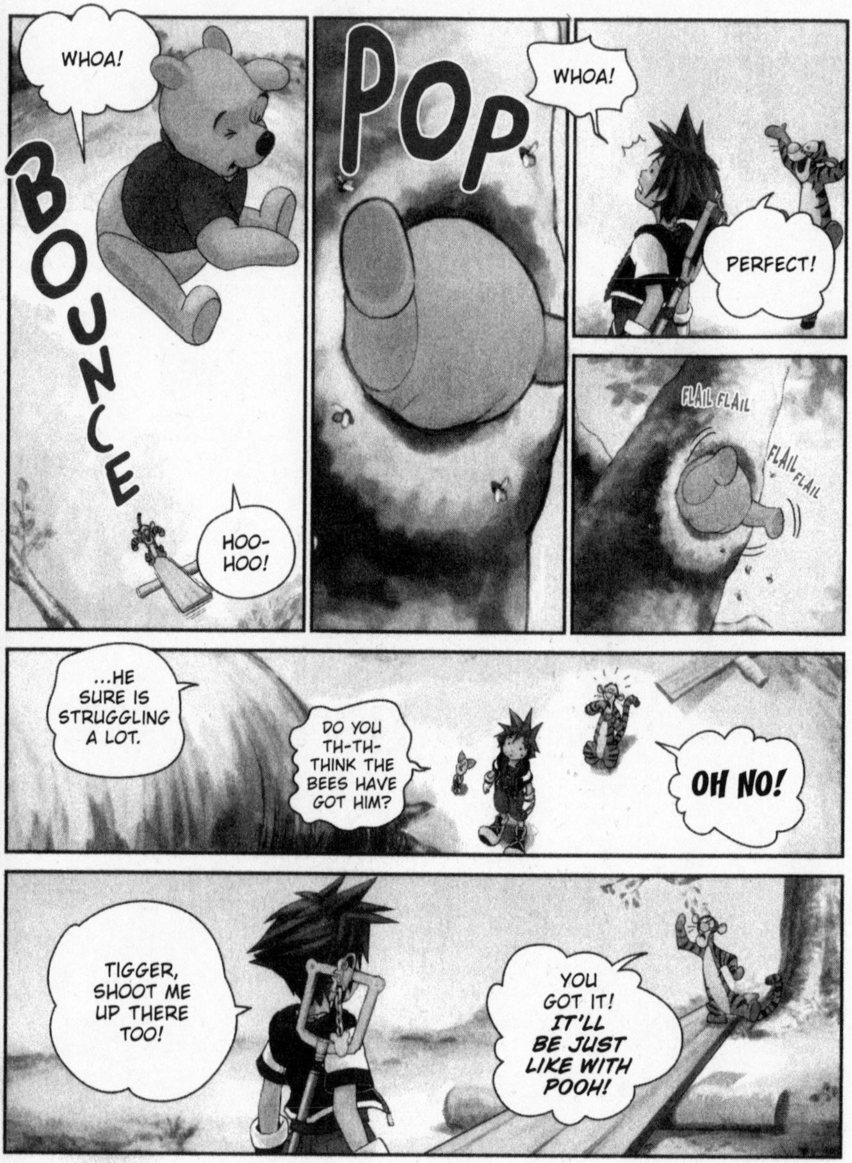
WHOA!
BOUNCE
HOO-HOO!
POP
WHOA!
PERFECT!
FLAIL FLAIL
FLAIL FLAIL
...HE SURE IS STRUGGLING A LOT.
DO YOU TH-TH-THINK THE BEES HAVE GOT HIM?
OH NO!
TIGGER, SHOOT ME UP THERE TOO!
YOU GOT IT! IT'LL BE JUST LIKE WITH POOH!

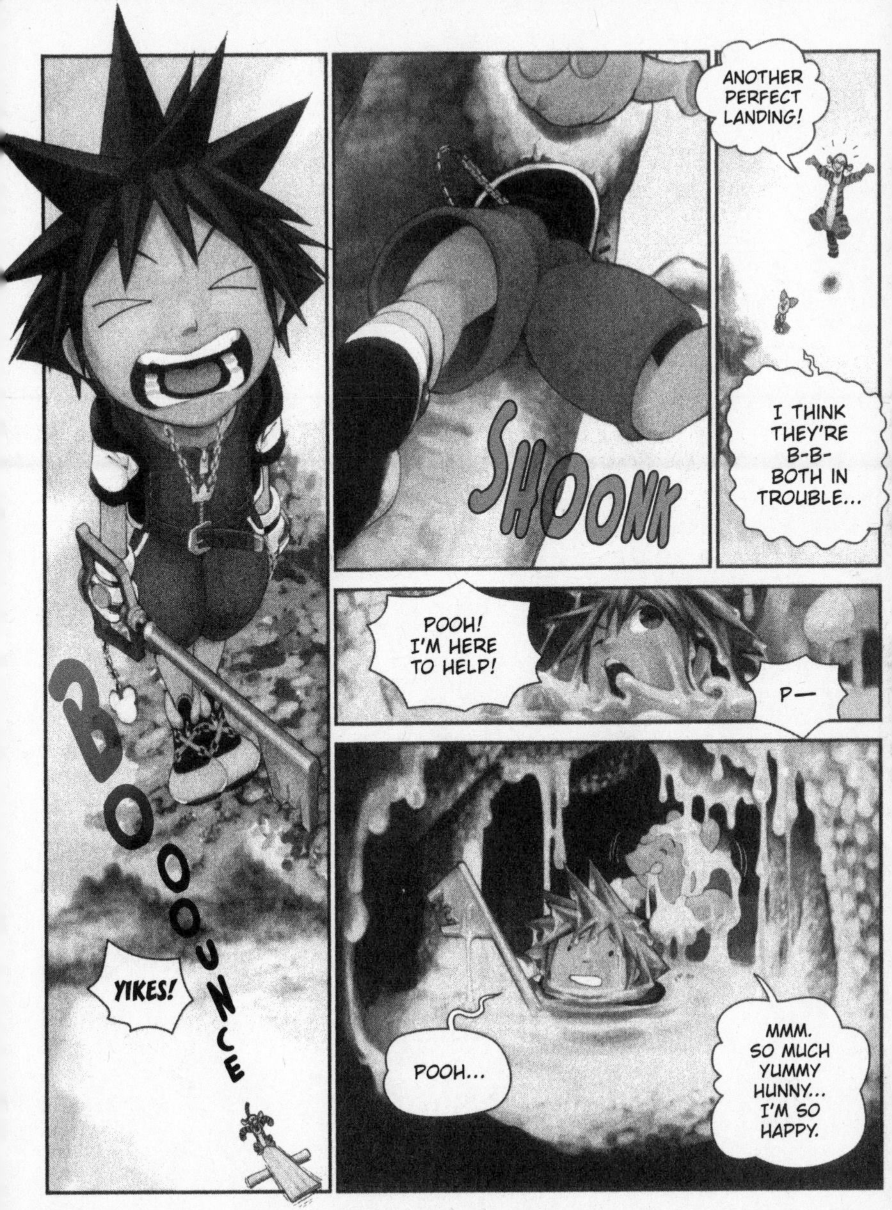
BOOOOUNCE
YIKES!
SHOONK
ANOTHER PERFECT LANDING!
I THINK THEY'RE B-B-BOTH IN TROUBLE...
POOH! I'M HERE TO HELP!
P—
POOH...
MMM. SO MUCH YUMMY HUNNY... I'M SO HAPPY.

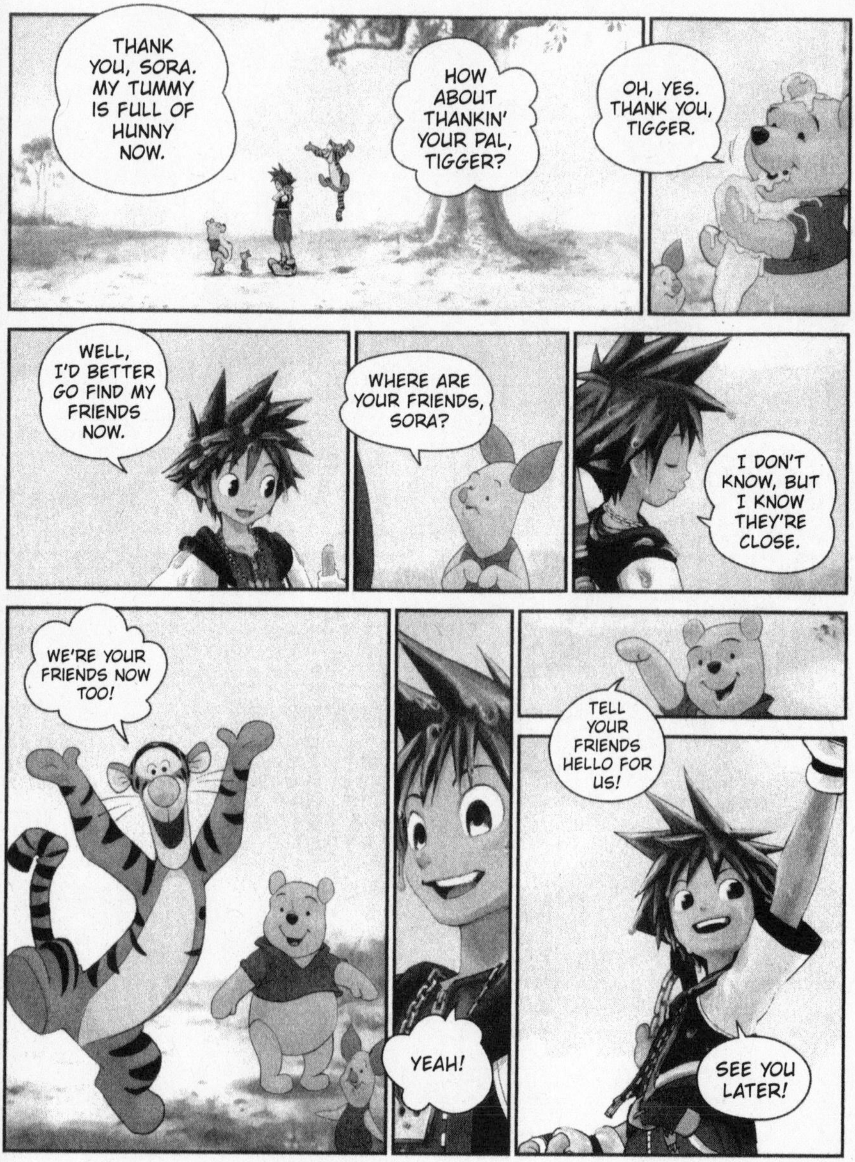
THANK YOU, SORA. MY TUMMY IS FULL OF HUNNY NOW.
HOW ABOUT THANKIN' YOUR PAL, TIGGER?
OH, YES. THANK YOU, TIGGER.
WELL, I'D BETTER GO FIND MY FRIENDS NOW.
WHERE ARE YOUR FRIENDS, SORA?
I DON'T KNOW, BUT I KNOW THEY'RE CLOSE.
WE'RE YOUR FRIENDS NOW TOO!
YEAH!
TELL YOUR FRIENDS HELLO FOR US!
SEE YOU LATER!

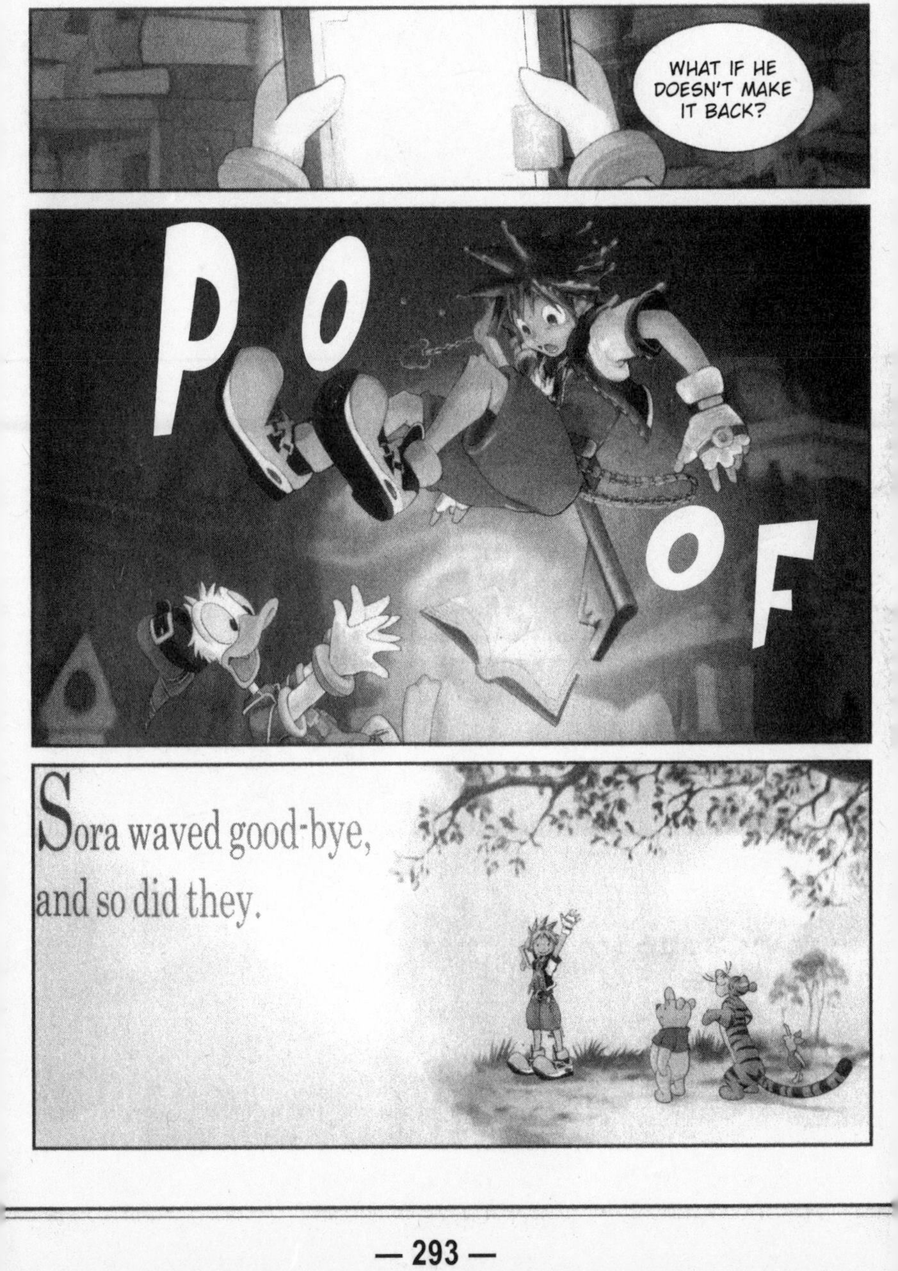
WHAT IF HE DOESN'T MAKE IT BACK?
POOF
Sora waved good-bye, and so did they.

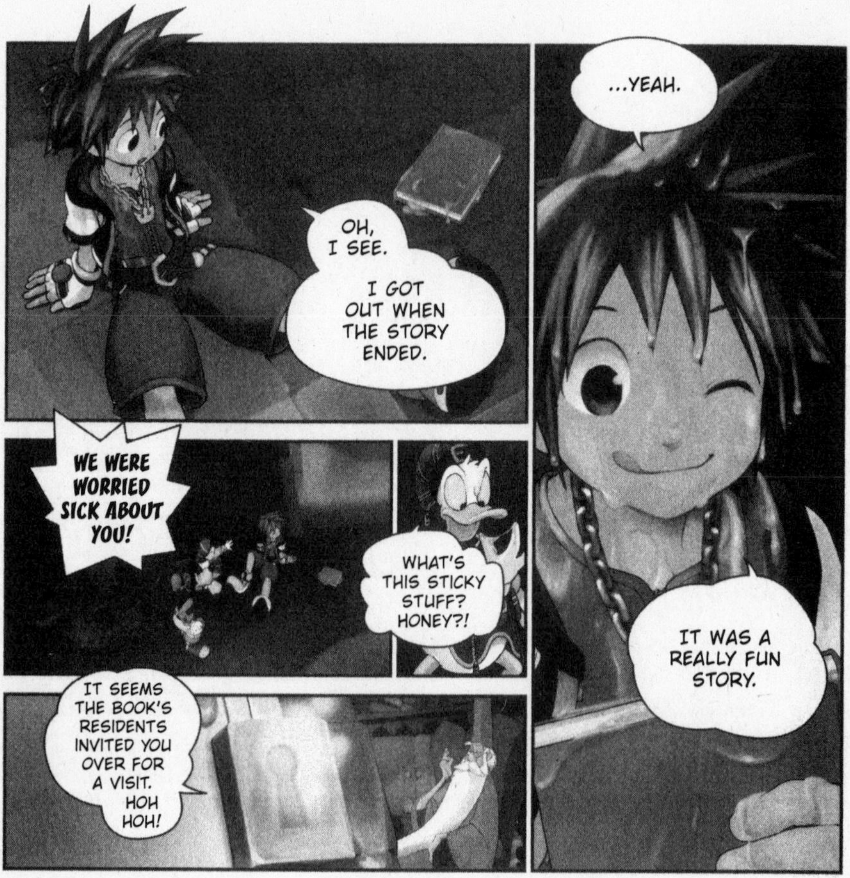
OH, I SEE.
I GOT OUT WHEN THE STORY ENDED.
...YEAH.
WE WERE WORRIED SICK ABOUT YOU!
WHAT'S THIS STICKY STUFF? HONEY?!
IT SEEMS THE BOOK'S RESIDENTS INVITED YOU OVER FOR A VISIT. HOH HOH!
IT WAS A REALLY FUN STORY.

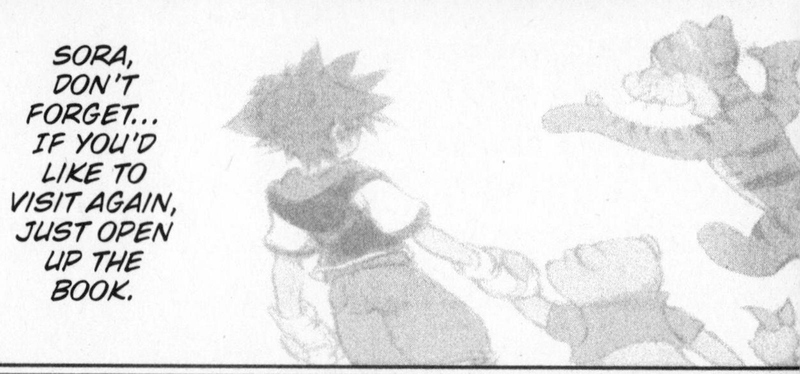
SORA, DON'T FORGET... IF YOU'D LIKE TO VISIT AGAIN, JUST OPEN UP THE BOOK.

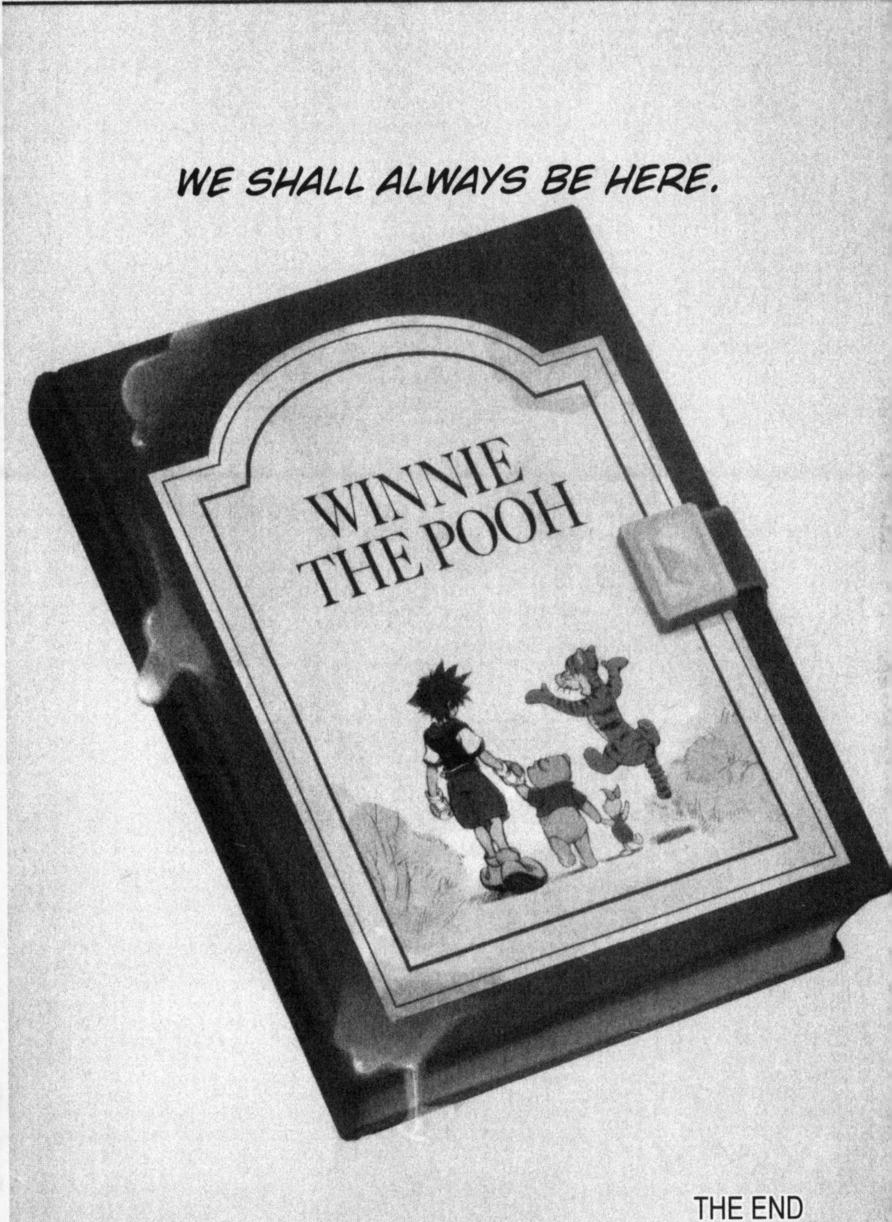
WE SHALL ALWAYS BE HERE.
WINNIE THE POOH
THE END

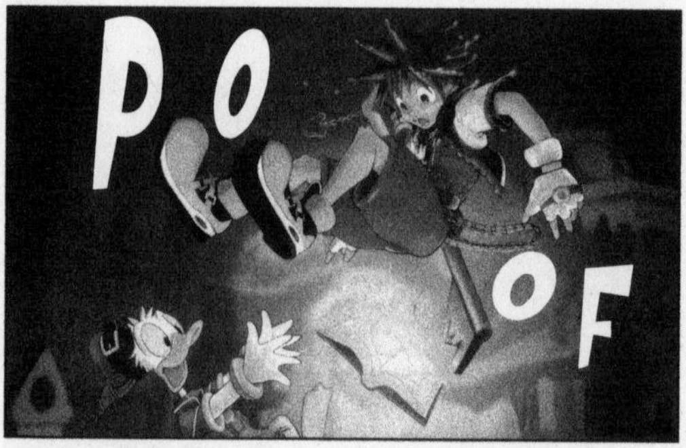
PO
OF

Special Short 2: UNKNOWN

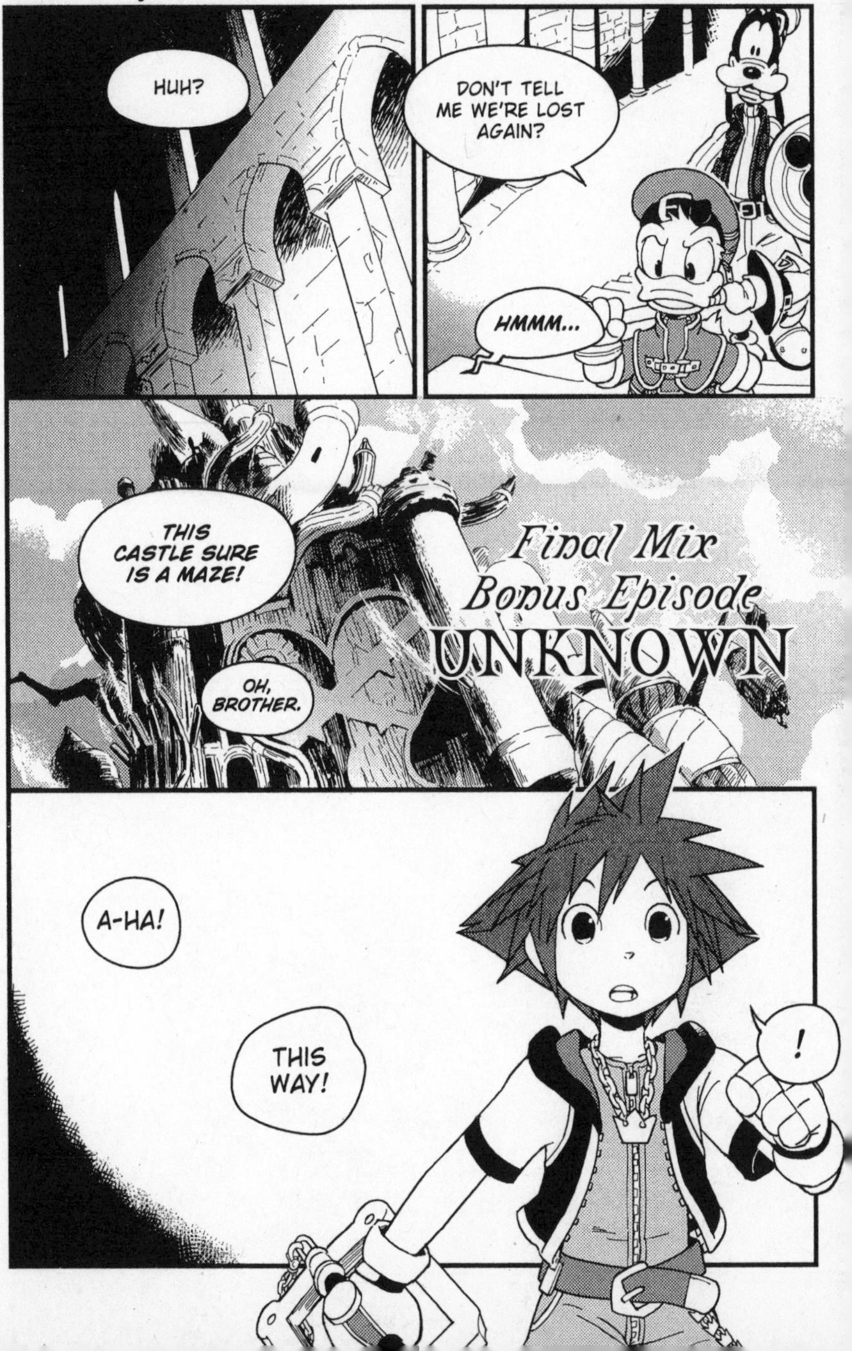
HUH?
DON'T TELL ME WE'RE LOST AGAIN?
HMMM...
THIS CASTLE SURE IS A MAZE!
OH, BROTHER.
Final Mix Bonus Episode UNKNOWN
A-HA!
THIS WAY!
!

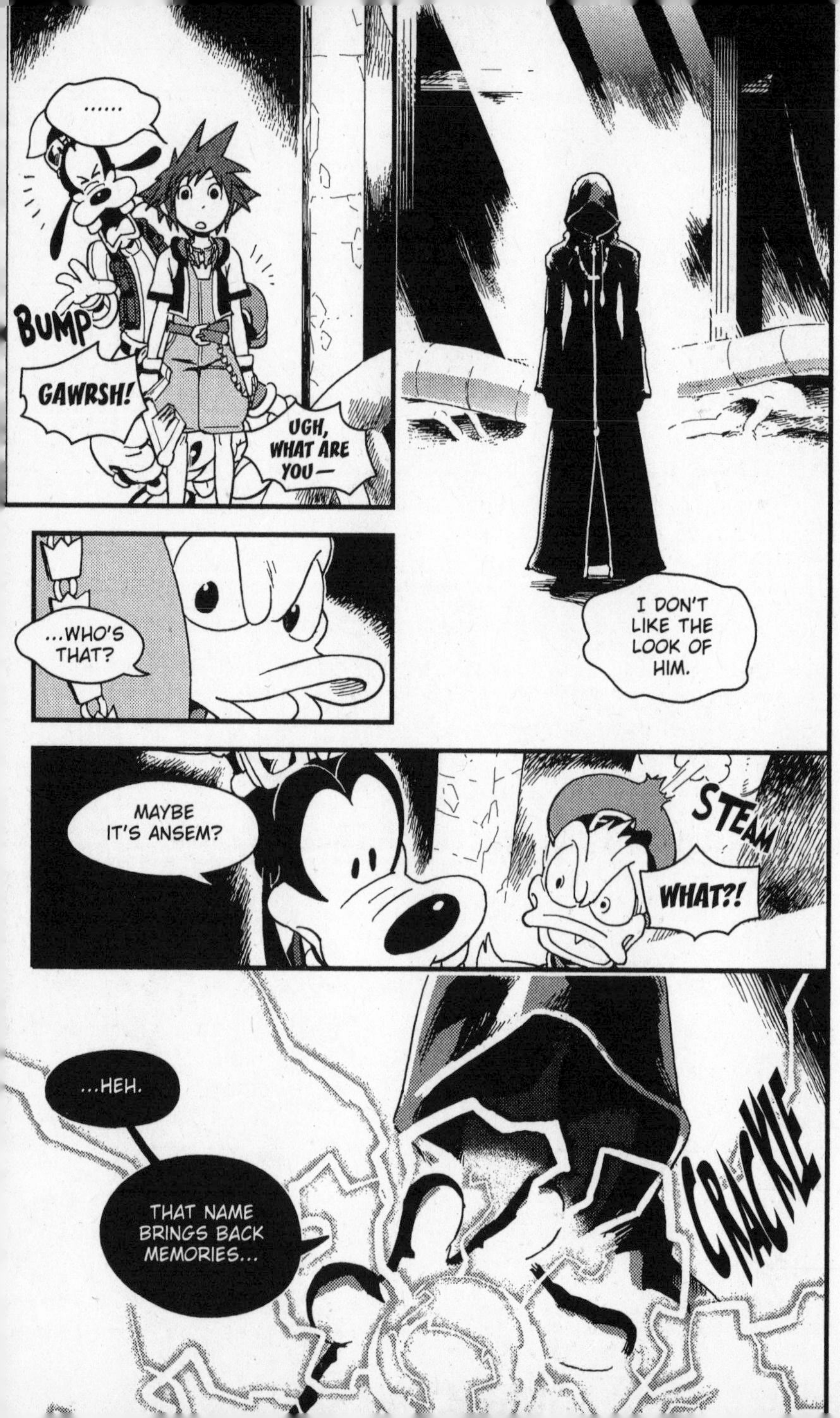
......
BUMP
GAWRSH!
UGH, WHAT ARE YOU—
...WHO'S THAT?
I DON'T LIKE THE LOOK OF HIM.
MAYBE IT'S ANSEM?
STEAM
WHAT?!
...HEH.
THAT NAME BRINGS BACK MEMORIES...
CRACKLE

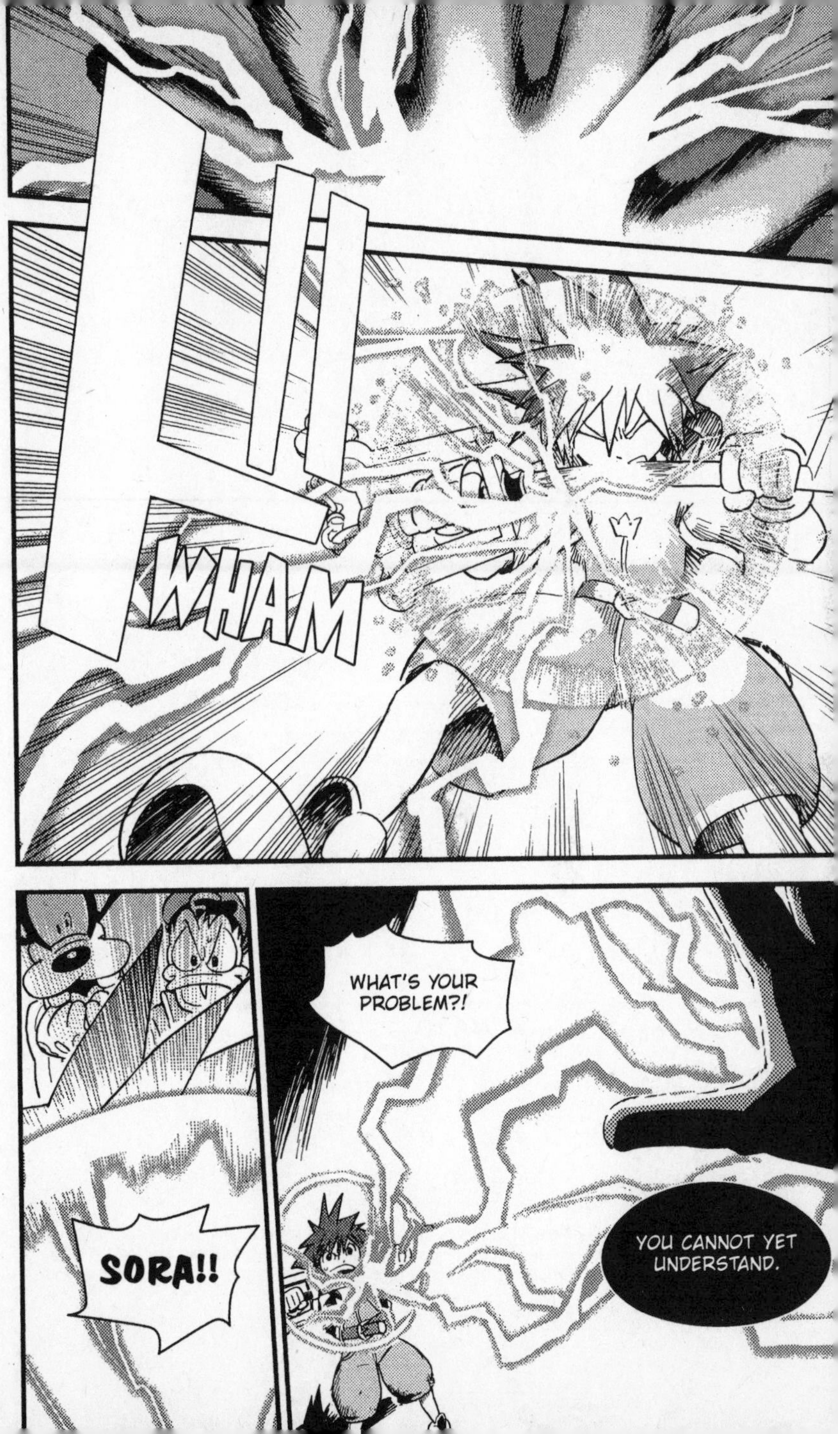
WHAM
WHAT'S YOUR PROBLEM?!
SORA!!
YOU CANNOT YET UNDERSTAND.

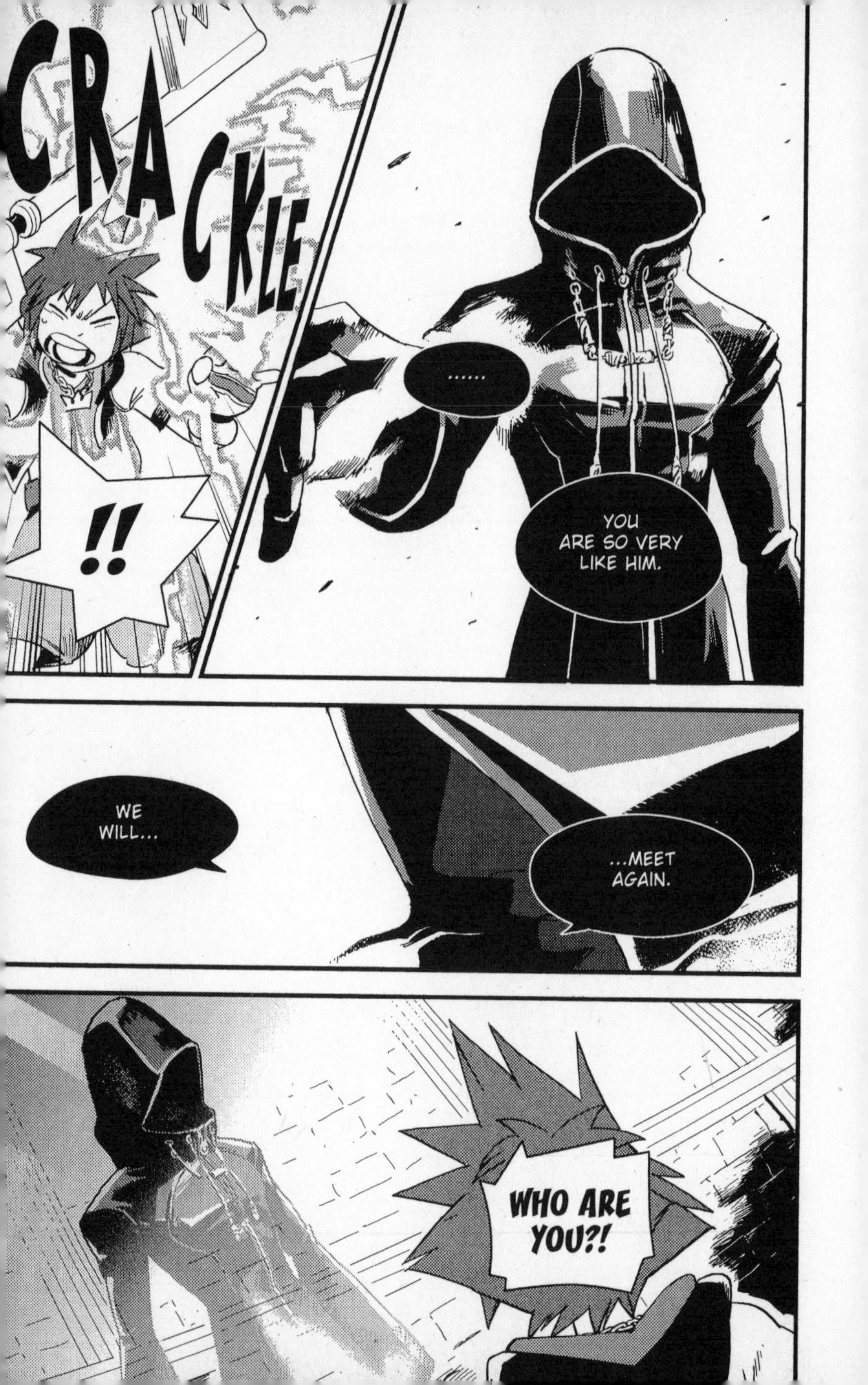
CRACKLE
!!
......
YOU ARE SO VERY LIKE HIM.
WE WILL...
...MEET AGAIN.
WHO ARE YOU?!

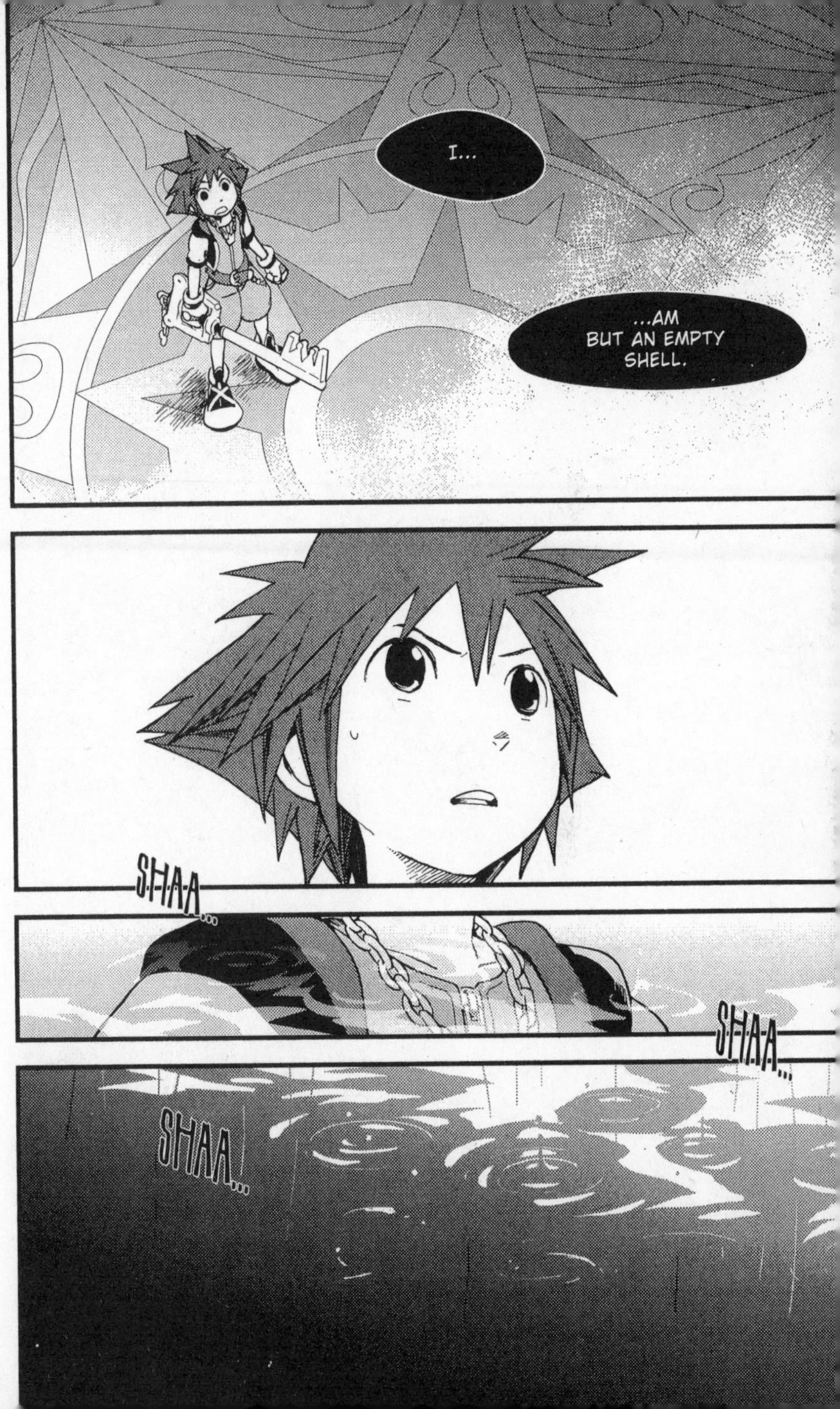
I...
...AM BUT AN EMPTY SHELL.
SHAA...
SHAA...
SHAA...

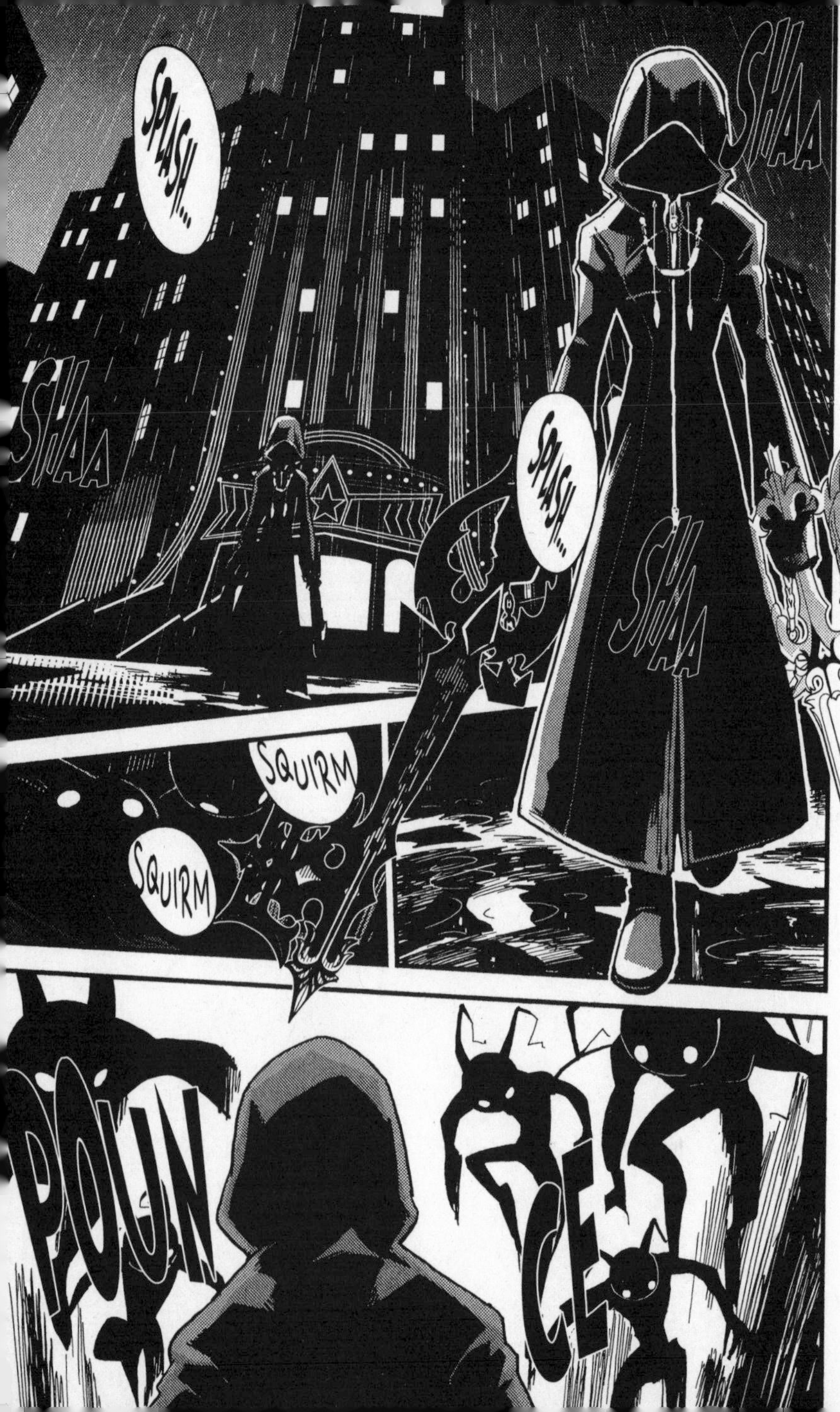
SPLASH...
SHAA
SHAA
SPLASH...
SHAA
SQUIRM
SQUIRM
POUN
CE